SCIENCE FICTION

Classic Stories from the Golden Age of Science Fiction

SCIENCE FICTION

CLASSIC STORIES FROM THE GOLDEN AGE OF SCIENCE FICTION

Compiled by Isaac Asimov
Charles G. Waugh ▸ Martin Greenberg

GALAHAD BOOKS
NEW YORK

First Galahad Books edition published in 1991.

Galahad Books
A division of BBS Publishing Corporation
386 Park Avenue South
New York, NY 10016

Galahad Books is a registered trademark of BBS Publishing Corporation.

Abridged from *The Mammoth Book of Golden Age Science Fiction.*

Published by arrangement with Carroll & Graf Publishers, Inc., and Robinson Publishing.

Library of Congress Control Number: 90-86021

ISBN: 1-57866-106-4

Printed in the United States of America.

CONTENTS

ISAAC ASIMOV, one of America's great resources, has by now written more than 330 books. No other writer in history has published so much on such a wide variety of subjects, which range from science fiction and murder novels to books on history, the physical sciences, and Shakespeare. Born in the Soviet Union and raised in Brooklyn, he lives in New York City with his wife, electric typewriter, and word processor.

MARTIN H. GREENBERG, who has been called 'the king of anthologists', now has some 130 collections to his credit. Greenberg is professor of regional analysis and political science at the University of Wisconsin, Green Bay, USA, where he also teaches a course in history of science fiction.

CHARLES G. WAUGH is professor of psychology and mass communications at the University of Maine at Augusta, USA. He is a leading authority on science fiction and fantasy and has collaborated on more than 80 anthologies and single-author collections with Isaac Asimov, Martin H. Greenberg, and assorted colleagues.

ACKNOWLEDGEMENTS

Ross Rocklynne—Copyright 1941 by Street & Smith Publications, Inc.; renewed © 1969. Reprinted by permission of the author's agent, Forrest J. Ackerman, 2495 Glendower Ave., Hollywood, CA 90027.

A. E. van Vogt—Copyright 1942 by Street & Smith Publications, Inc.; renewed © 1970 by A. E. van Vogt. Reprinted by permission of Richard Curtis Associates, Inc.

Lester del Rey—Copyright 1942 by Street & Smith Publications, Inc.; renewed © 1970 by Lester del Rey. Reprinted by permission of the Scott Meredith Literary Agency, Inc., 845 Third Avenue, New York, NY 10022.

Theodore Sturgeon—Copyright 1944 by Street & Smith Publications, Inc.; renewed © 1972 by Theodore Sturgeon. Reprinted by permission of Kirby McCauley, Ltd.

C. L. Moore—Copyright 1944 by Street & Smith Publications, Inc.; renewed © 1972 by Catherine Reggie. Reprinted by permission of Don Congdon Associates, Inc.

Isaac Asimov—Copyright 1944 by Street & Smith Publications, Inc.; renewed © 1972 by Isaac Asimov. Reprinted by permission of the author.

A. Bertram Chandler—Copyright 1945 by Street & Smith Publications, Inc.; renewed © 1973 by A. Bertram Chandler. Reprinted by permission of the agents for the author's Estate, the Scott Meredith Literary Agency, Inc., 845 Third Avenue, New York, NY 10022.

T. L. Sherred—Copyright 1947, renewed © 1975 by T. L. Sherred. Reprinted by permission of the author's Estate and the author's agent, Virginia Kidd.

Jack Williamson—Copyright 1947 by Street & Smith Publications, Inc.; renewed © 1975 by Jack Williamson. Reprinted by permission of the Spectrum Literary Agency.

SCIENCE FICTION

CLASSIC STORIES FROM THE
GOLDEN AGE OF SCIENCE FICTION

INTRODUCTION

'The Age of Campbell'

Isaac Asimov

In the first book of the series, which dealt with classic science fiction (s.f.) novellas of the 1930s, I said that the 1930s was the decade in which science fiction found its voice. Toward the end of that decade, the voice began to resemble, more and more, that of John Wood Campbell, Jr., and in the 1940s, J.W.C. dominated the field to the point where to many he seemed *all* of science fiction.

It was a phenomenon that had never happened before and can never be repeated. Before the 1940s, science fiction was so small a field that, in a way, there was nothing to dominate. Hugo Gernsback had been important in the 1920s, but he was alone. F. Orlin Tremaine had been important in the 1930s, but he did not drown out the other voices completely.

Campbell, however, towered. He had a charismatic personality that utterly dominated everyone he met. He overflowed with energy and he had his way with science fiction. He found it pulp and he turned into something that was his heart's desire. He then made it the heart's desire of the reader.

To put it another way, he found science fiction a side-issue written by eager fans with only the beginnings of ability, or by general pulp writers who substituted spaceships for horses, or disintegration rays for revolvers, and then wrote their usual stuff. Campbell put science fiction center stage and made it a field that could be written successfully only by *science fiction writers* who had learned their craft.

To put it still another way, he found science fiction a trifling thing that could only supply writers with occasional pin-money and he labored to make of it something at which science fiction writers could make a living. He could not, in the 1940s, drag the field upward to the point of making writers *rich*, but he laid the foundations for the coming of that time in later decades.

It is impossible for anyone ever to repeat the feat of John W. Campbell, Jr. For one thing you cannot lay the foundations for quality science fiction a second time. The foundation is there for all time and it was laid by Campbell. For another thing, the field has grown to such a pitch (thanks to Campbell) that it is too large ever to be dominated by one man. Even Campbell, larger than life though he was, if he were miraculously brought back into existence, could not dominate the field today.

So who was John Campbell? He was born in Newark, New Jersey on June 8, 1910. I have never found out much about his childhood, except that I received the impression that it was a very unhappy one. He attended M.I.T. between 1928 and 1931, but never finished his schooling there. The story I heard was that he couldn't pass German. He transferred to Duke University.

This double experience at college was reflected in his later work. At M.I.T. he picked up his interest in science. At Duke, where R.B. Rhine was conducting his dubious experiments on extra-sensory perception, he picked up his interest in the scientific fringe. In the 1940s, science dominated Campbell's mind, and in the 1950s the scientific fringe did. He went from M.I.T. to Duke in science fiction as well as in his college training. In this volume, however, we are concerned with his earlier phase.

He sold his first science fiction story while he was still a teenager (not unusual among the true devotees) but he was too inexperienced to keep a carbon and T. O'Conor Sloane of *Amazing Stories* lost the manuscript (which *was* unusual). It was Campbell's second sale, then, that marked his first actual appearance. This was 'When the Atoms Failed' in the January 1930, *Amazing*. He was still only nineteen at the time.

In those days, the greatest name among the science fiction writers was E.E. Smith, Ph.D., who had climbed to fame with his 'The Skylark of Space', a three-part serial that appeared in the August, September, and October 1928 issues of *Amazing*. 'The Skylark of Space' featured interstellar travel and dealt with megaforces and megadistances. It was an example of what came to be called 'super-science stories' and Smith made it his specialty. Naturally, others followed the trend, and Campbell did so from the start. He quickly became second only to Smith in the super-science field.

There was a difference, though Smith could not change. He remained super-science to the end. Campbell could change and did. He wanted to write science fiction less in scale and more in introspection, less with ravening forces and more with puzzling mind.

He even changed his name for the purpose, writing a series of stories as Don A. Stuart. (His first wife's maiden name was Dona Stuart.) The first Stuart story was 'Twilight' which appeared in the November 1934, *Astounding Stories*, a sad, haunting tale of the end of humanity. It proved an enormous hit, and instantly began the change of making science fiction smaller in scope and deeper in thought.

He wrote Stuart stories predominantly, thereafter, until he published his towering masterpiece 'Who Goes There?' which appeared in the August 1938, *Astounding*, and which was reprinted in the first book of this series.

By October 1937, however, he had been appointed to an editorial position at *Astounding* and, within a few months, he was in full charge. His first significant action was to change the name of the magazine, a change which reflected his thinking. He wanted to get rid of words like 'amazing', 'astounding', and 'wonder', which stressed the shock-value and superficiality of science fiction. He wanted to call the magazine simply *Science Fiction*, thus merely defining its scope but allowing him to fiddle with the details at will.

Unfortunately, he was too late. Columbia Publications had already registered that name, and a magazine so-named (not at all successful) eventually appeared in the spring of 1939. Campbell was therefore forced to make only a partial change. With its March 1938 issue *Astounding Stories* became *Astounding Science Fiction*.

As editor, Campbell was a phenomenon even greater than he had been as a writer. He held open house and anyone who might conceivably help him achieve his aims was welcome. When, on June 21, 1938, a frightened eighteen-year-old, named Isaac Asimov, appeared with his first story at Street & Smith Publications, Inc. (which published *Astounding*), he was invited into Campbell's office, and Campbell spoke to him for an hour and a half.

I say 'spoke to him' not 'spoke with him', for Campbell's idea of
a conversation was to launch into a long monolog. Oddly enough,
though, he was no bore. He was an inexhaustible fount of odd and
exciting viewpoints, novel thoughts, and endless story ideas.

He had an unfailing eye for potential. He rejected my first story
at once. He had said he would read it right off and had kept his
word (very unusual in an editor) so that it was mailed back to me the
very next day. However, he saw something in it, or in me, or both
(Heaven only knows what it could have been at that stage) and
encouraged me to continue writing. I could see him whenever I
came in and he was unfailingly courteous and encouraging, even as
he continued to reject my stories, until I had learned enough about
writing (from actual experience at it and from listening to him) to
begin selling.

I was not the only one. He talked to dozens of writers and slowly
taught them that science fiction was not about adventure primarily,
but about science. It was not about rescuing damsels in distress, but
it was about solving problems. It was not about mad scientists, but
about hard working thinkers. It was not by writers who had a facile
hand with a cliché, but it was by writers who understood science and
engineering and how those things worked and by whom they were
 onducted. In short, he found magazine science fiction childish,
and he made it adult.

The wonder is that he was successful in doing so. It is hard not
to view the world with cynical eyes and, to the cynic, improving
the quality of an object and reducing its sensationalism, is the
quickest road to bankruptcy one can imagine. Somehow, Campbell
managed. As *Astounding* improved in quality, it also improved in
general acceptance and in profitability.

The true test came in 1948. Pulp fiction had been fighting a losing
battle during the 1940s. World War II had created a paper shortage
and a combination of the draft and of war-work had reduced the
number of writers. (Campbell's other magazines, the wonderful
Unknown, succumbed to this.) In addition, comic magazines had
come into being, had proliferated unimaginably, and had begun to
draw off younger readers delaying and, sometimes, totally aborting
their eventual reading of pulp fiction.

In 1948, Street & Smith, which had been the most prominent
and successful of all the pulp fiction publishers gave up and put
an end to all their pulp magazines—all but one. *Astounding Science
Fiction*, and only *Astounding Science Fiction*, continued. It was John
Campbell who had made that possible. Had he not been there for

ten years, improving *Astounding* and making it the phenomenon it was, the magazine might have ceased publication at that time and magazine science fiction might have been dead.

Who were the authors with whom Campbell worked? Some had already published stories in the pre-Campbell era, and Campbell could work with them, either because they were already thinking along Campbellesque lines or because they could do so once they were shown what it was that Campbell wanted. Outstanding among these were Jack Williamson, Clifford D. Simak and L. Sprague de Camp.

For the most part, though, Campbell found new writers. The July 1939, issue was the first issue that was truly marked by Campbell's thinking and Campbell's new authors, and it is usually considered as the first issue of 'the Golden Age of science fiction'.

As its lead novelette, the issue had 'Black Destroyer', the first science fiction story written by A.E. van Vogt. It also contained 'Trends' by Isaac Asimov, 'Greater Than Gods' by C.L. Moore, and 'The Moth' by Ross Rocklynne. All four of these authors have novellas in this collection. Van Vogt and Asimov are perfect examples of what are still referred to as 'Campbell authors'. Moore and Rocklynne had published before, but Rocklynne became a Campbell author too.

In the very next issue, August 1939, there was a first story, 'Life-Line', by a new Campbell author named Robert A. Heinlein. He and van Vogt were the mainstays of *Astounding* for several years and were the science fiction 'superstars' of the time. Indeed, Heinlein remained a superstar and the pre-eminent science fiction writer until his death a half-century later in 1988. We would certainly have included any of several Heinlein novellas in this book were it not for difficulties over permissions.

Another particularly great Campbell author who does not appear in this collection is Arthur C. Clarke, whose first science fiction story was 'Loophole' which appeared in the April 1946, *Astounding*. Unfortunately, his 1940s output was almost entirely in the short story length.

In the September 1939, issue came 'Ether Breather', the first science fiction story of a new Campbell author named Theodore Sturgeon.

Among the earliest of the Campbell authors was Lester del Rey, whose first story, 'The Faithful' appeared in the April 1938 *Astounding*. T.L. Sherred and A. Bertram Chandler were Campbell authors who first appeared later in the 1940s.

It is only fair to remember that not all great science fiction writers could write for Campbell. Some simply did not have, or did not want, the Campbell touch, and went their own way. Fredric Brown was one of these. Another--and perhaps the greatest of all science fiction writers who couldn't or wouldn't be a Campbell author—was Ray Bradbury.

In this collections of stories you will find yourself once again in the Golden Age of science fiction and the great days of John W. Campbell, Jr.

TIME WANTS A SKELETON

Ross Rocklynne

Asteroid No. 1007 came spinning relentlessly up.

Lieutenant Tony Crow's eyes bulged. He released the choked U-bar frantically, and pounded on the auxiliary underjet controls. Up went the nose of the ship, and stars, weirdly splashed across the heavens, showed briefly.

Then the ship fell, hurling itself against the base of the mountain. Tony was thrown from the control chair. He smacked against the wall, grinning twistedly. He pushed against it with a heavily shod foot as the ship teetered over, rolled a bit, and then was still—still, save for the hiss of escaping air.

He dived for a locker, broke out a pressure suit, perspiration pearling his forehead. He was into the suit, buckling the helmet down, before the last of the air escaped. He stood there, pained dismay in his eyes. His roving glance rested on the wall calendar.

"Happy December!" he snarled.

Then he remembered. Johnny Braker was out there, with his two fellow outlaws. By now, they'd be running this way. All the more reason why Tony should capture them now. He'd need their ship.

He acted quickly, buckling on his helmet, working over the air lock. He expelled his breath in relief as it opened. Nerves humming, he went through, came to his feet, enclosed by the bleak soundlessness of a twenty-mile planetoid more than a hundred million miles removed from Earth.

To his left the mountain rose sharply. Good. Tony had wanted to put the ship down there anyway. He took one reluctant look at

7

the ship. His face fell mournfully. The stern section was caved in and twisted so much it looked ridiculous. Well, that was *that*.

He quickly drew his Hampton and moved soundlessly around the mountain's shoulder. He fell into a crouch as he saw the gleam of the outlaw ship, three hundred yards distant across a plain, hovering in the shadow thrown by an over-hanging ledge.

Then he saw the three figures leaping towards him across the plain. His Hampton came viciously up. There was a puff of rock to the front left of the little group. They froze.

Tony left his place of concealment, snapping his headset on.

"Stay where you are!" he bawled.

The reaction was unexpected. Braker's voice came blasting back. "The hell you say!"

A tiny crater came miraculously into being to Tony's left. He swore, jumped behind his protection, came out a second later to send another projectile winging its way. One of the figures pitched forward, to move no more, the balloon rotundity of its suit suddenly lost. The other two turned tail, only to halt and hole up behind a boulder gracing the middle of the plain. They proceeded to pepper Tony's retreat.

Tony shrank back against the mountainside, exasperated beyond measure. His glance, roving around, came to rest on a cave, a fault in the mountain that tapered out a hundred feet up.

He stared at the floor of the cave unbelievingly.

"I'll be double-damned," he muttered.

What he saw was a human skeleton.

He paled. His stomach suddenly heaved. Outrageous, haunting thoughts flicked through his consciousness. The skeleton was—— horror!

And it had existed in the dim, unutterably distant past, before the asteroids, before the human race had come into existence!

The thoughts were gone, abruptly. Consciousness shuddered back. For a while, his face pasty white, his fingers trembling, he thought he was going to be sick. But he wasn't. He stood there, staring. Memories! If he knew where they came from— His very mind revolted suddenly from probing deeper into a mystery that tore at the very roots of his sanity!

"It existed before the human race," he whispered. "Then where did the skeleton come from?"

His lips curled. Illusion! Conquering his maddening revulsion, he approached the skeleton, knelt near it. It lay inside the cave.

Colorless starlight did not allow him to see it as well as he might. Yet, he saw the gleam of gold on the long, tapering finger. Old yellow gold, untarnished by atmosphere; and inset with an emerald, with a flaw, a distinctive, ovular air bubble, showing through its murky transparency.

He moved backward, away from it, face set stubbornly. "Illusion," he repeated

Chips of rock, flaked off the mountainside by the exploding bullets of a Hampton, completed the transformation. He risked stepping out, fired.

The shot struck the boulder, split it down the middle. The two halves parted. The outlaws ran, firing back to cover their hasty retreat. Tony waited until the fire lessened, then stepped out and sent a shot over their heads.

Sudden dismay showed in his eyes. The ledge overhanging the outlaw ship cracked—where the bullet had struck it.

"What the hell—" came Braker's gasp. The two outlaws stopped stock-still.

The ledge came down, its ponderousness doubled by the absence of sound. Tony stumbled panting across the plain as the scene turned into a churning hell. The ship crumbled like clay. Another section of the ledge descended to bury the ship inextricably under a small mountain.

Tony Crow swore blisteringly. But ship or no ship, he still had a job to do. When the outlaws finally turned, they were looking into the menacing barrel of his Hampton.

"Get'em up," he said impassively.

With studied insolence, Harry Jawbone Yates, the smaller of the two, raised his hands. A contemptuous sneer merely played over Braker's unshaved face and went upward to his smoky eyes.

"Why should I put my hands up? We're all pals, now—theoretically." His natural hate for any form of the law showed in his eyes. "You sure pulled a prize play, copper. Chase us clear across space, and end up getting us in a jam it's a hundred-to-one shot we'll get out of."

Tony held them transfixed with the Hampton, knowing what Braker meant. No ship would have reason to stop off on the twenty-mile mote in the sky that was Asteroid 1007.

He sighed, made a gesture. "Hamptons over here, boys. And be careful." The weapons arced groundward. "Sorry. I was intending to use your ship to take us back. I won't make another error like that one, though. Giving up this early in the game, for instance. Come here, Jawbone."

Yates shrugged. He was blond, had pale, wide-set eyes. By nature, he was conscienceless. A broken jawbone, protruding at a sharp angle from his jawline, gave him his nickname.

He held out his wrists. "Put 'em on." His voice was an effortless affair which did not go as low as it could; rather womanish, therefore. Braker was different. Strength, nerve, and audacity showed in every line of his heavy, compact body. If there was one thing that characterized him it was his violent desire to live. These were men with elastic codes of ethics. A few of their more unscrupulous activities had caught up with them.

Tony put cuffs over Yates' wrist.

"Now you, Braker."

"Damned if I do," said Braker.

"Damned if you don't," said Tony. He waggled the Hampton, his normally genial eyes hardening slightly. "I mean it, Braker," he said slowly.

Braker sneered and tossed his head. Then, as if resistance was below his present mood, he submitted.

He watched the cuffs click silently. "There isn't a hundred-to-one chance, anyway," he growled.

Tony jerked slightly, his eyes turned skyward. He chuckled.

"Well, what's so funny?" Braker demanded.

"What you just said." Tony pointed. "The hundred-to-one shot—there she is!"

Braker turned.

"Yeah," he said. "Yeah. Damnation!"

A ship, glowing faintly in the starlight, hung above an escarpment that dropped to the valley floor. It had no visible support, and, indeed, there was no trace of the usual jets.

"Well, that's an item!" Yates muttered.

"It is at that," Tony agreed.

The ship moved. Rather, it simply disappeared, and next showed up a hundred feet away on the valley floor. A valve in the side of the cylindrical affair opened and a figure dropped out, stood looking at them.

A metallic voice said, "Are you the inhabitants or just people?"

The voice was agreeably flippant, and more agreeably feminine. Tony's senses quickened.

"We're people," he explained. "See?" He flapped his arms like wings. He grinned. "However, before you showed up, we had made up our minds to be—inhabitants."

"Oh. Stranded." The voice was slightly chilly. "Well, that's too bad. Come on inside. We'll talk the whole thing over. Say, are those handcuffs?"

"Right."

"Hm-m-m. Two outlaws—and a copper. Well, come on inside and meet the rest of us."

An hour later, Tony, agreeably relaxed in a small lounge, was smoking his third cigarette, pressure suit off. Across the room was Braker and Yates. The girl, whose name, it developed, was Laurette, leaned against the door jamb, clad in jodhpurs and white silk blouse. She was blond and had clear deep-blue eyes. Her lips were pursed a little and she looked angry. Tony couldn't keep his eyes off her.

Another man stood beside her. He was dark in complexion and looked as if he had a short temper. He was snapping the fingernails of two hands in a manner that showed characteristic impatience and nervousness. His name was Erle Masters.

An older man came into the room, fitting glasses over his eyes. He took a quick look around the room. Tony came to his feet.

Laurette said tonelessly, "Lieutenant, this is my father. Daddy, Lieutenant Tony Crow of the IPF. Those two are the outlaws I was telling you about."

"Outlaws, eh? said Professor Overland. His voice seemed deep enough to count the separate vibrations. He rubbed at a stubbled jaw. "Well, that's too bad. Just when we had the DeTosque strata 1007 fitting onto 70. And there were ample signs to show a definite dovetailing of apex 1007 into Morrell's fourth crater on Ceres, which would have put 1007 near the surface, if not on it. If we could have followed those up without an interruption—"

"Don't let this interrupt you," Masters broke in. His nails clicked. "We'll let these three sleep in the lounge. We can finish up the set of indications we're working on now, and then get rid of them."

Overland shook his graying head doubtfully. "It would be unthinkable to subject those two to cuffs for a full month."

Masters said irritably, "We'll give them a parole. Give them their temporary freedom if they agree to submit to handcuffs again when we land on Mars."

Tony laughed softly. "Sorry. You can't trust those two for five minutes, let alone a month." He paused. "Under the circumstances, professor, I guess you realize I've got full power to enforce my request that you take us back to Mars. The primary concern of the government in a case like this would be placing these two in custody. I suggest if we get under way now, you can devote more time to your project."

Overland said helplessly, "Of course. But it cuts off my chances of getting to the Christmas banquet at the university." Disappointment showed in his weak eyes. "There's a good chance they'll give me Amos, I guess, but it's already December third. Well, anyway, we'll miss the snow."

Laurette Overland said bitterly, "I wish we hadn't landed on 1007. You'd have got along without us then, all right."

Tony held her eyes gravely. "Perfectly, Miss Overland. Except that we would have been inhabitants. And, shortly, very, very dead ones."

"So?" She glared.

Erle Masters grabbed the girl's arm with a muttered word and led her out of the room.

Overland grasped Tony's arm in a friendly squeeze, eyes twinkling. "Don't mind them, son. If you or your charges need anything, you can use my cabin. But we'll make Mars in forty-eight hours, seven or eight of it skimming through the Belt."

Tony shook his head dazedly. "Forty-eight hours?"

Overland grinned. His teeth were slightly tobacco-stained. "That's it. This is one of the new ships—the H-H drive. They zip along."

"Oh! The Fitz-Gerald Contraction?"

Overland nodded absently and left. Tony stared after him. He was remembering something now—the skeleton.

Braker said indulgently, "What a laugh."

Tony turned.

"What," he asked patiently, "is a laugh?"

Braker thrust out long, heavy legs. He was playing idly with a gold ring on the third finger of his right hand.

"Oh," he said carelessly, "a theory goes the rounds the asteroids used to be a planet. They're not sure the theory is right, so they send a few bearded long faces out to trace down faults and strata and striations on one asteroid and link them up with others. The girl's old man was just about to nail down 1007 and 70 and Ceres. Good for him. But what the hell! They prove the theory and the asteroids still play ring around the rosy and what have they got for their money?"

He absently played with his ring.

Tony as absently watched him turning it round and round on his finger. Something peculiar about— He jumped. His eyes bulged.

That ring! He leaped to his feet, away from it.

Braker and Yates looked at him strangely.

Braker came to his feet, brows contracting. "Say, copper, what ails you? You gone crazy? You look like a ghost."

Tony's heart began a fast, insistent pounding. Blood drummed against his temple. So he looked like a ghost? He laughed hoarsely. Was it imagination that suddenly stripped the flesh from Braker's head and left nothing but—a skull?

"I'm not a ghost." He chattered senselessly, still staring at the ring.

He closed his eyes tight, clenched his fists.

"He's gone bats!" said Yates, incredulously.

"Bats! Absolutely bats!"

Tony opened his eyes, looked carefully at Braker, at Yates, at the tapestried walls of the lounge. Slowly, the tensity left him. Now, no matter what developed he would have to keep a hold on himself.

"I'm all right, Braker. Let me see that ring." His voice was low, controlled, ominous.

"You take a fit?" Braker snapped suspiciously.

"I'm all right." Tony deliberately took Braker's cuffed hands into his own, looked at the gold band inset with the flawed emerald. Revulsion crawled in his stomach, yet he kept his eyes on the ring.

"Where'd you get the ring, Braker?" He kept his glance down.

"Why—'29, I think it was; or '28." Braker's tone was suddenly angry, resentful. He drew away. "What is this, anyway? I got it legal, and so what?"

"What I really wanted to know," said Tony, "was if there was another ring like this one—ever. I hope not . . . I don't know if I do. Damn it!"

"And I don't know what you're talking about," snarled Braker. "I still think you're bats. Hell, flawed emeralds are like fingerprints, never two alike. You know that yourself."

Tony slowly nodded and stepped back. Then he lighted a cigarette, and let the smoke inclose him.

"You fellows stay here," he said, and backed out and bolted the door behind him. He went heavily down the corridor, down a short flight of stairs, then down another short corridor.

He chose one of two doors, jerked it open. A half dozen packages slid from the shelves of what was evidently a closet. Then the other door opened. Tony staggered backward, losing his balance under the flood of packages. He bumped into Laurette Overland. She gasped and started to fall. Tony managed to twist around in time to grab her. They both fell anyway. Tony drew her to him on impulse and kissed her.

She twisted away from him, her face scarlet. Her palm came around, smashed into his face with all her considerable strength. She jumped to her feet, then the fury in her eyes died. Tony came erect, smarting under the blow.

"Sportsmanlike," he snapped angrily.

"You've got a lot of nerve," she said unsteadily. Her eyes went past him. "You clumsy fool. Help me get these packages back on the shelves before daddy or Erle come along. They're Christmas presents, and if you broke any of the wrappings— Come on, can't you help?"

Tony slowly hoisted a large carton labeled with a 'Do Not Open Before Christmas' sticker, and shoved it onto the lower rickety shelf, where it stuck out, practically ready to fall again. She put the smaller packages on top to balance it.

She turned, seeming to meet his eyes with difficulty.

Finally she got out, "I'm sorry I hit you like that, lieutenant. I guess it was natural—your kissing me I mean." She smiled faintly at Tony, who was ruefully rubbing his cheek. Then her composure abruptly returned. She straightened.

"If you're looking for the door to the control room, that's it."

"I wanted to see your father," Tony explained.

"You can't see him now. He's plotting our course. In fifteen minutes—" She let the sentence dangle. "Erle Masters can help you in a few minutes. He's edging the ship out of the way of a polyhedron."

"Polyhedron?"

"Many-sided asteroid. That's the way we designate them." She was being patronizing now.

"Well, of course. But I stick to plain triangles and spheres and cubes. A polyhedron is a sphere to me. I didn't know we were on the way. Since when? I didn't feel the acceleration."

"Since ten minutes ago. And naturally there wouldn't be any acceleration with an H-H drive. Well, if you want anything, you can talk to Erle." She edged past him, went swinging up the corridor. Tony caught up with her.

"You can help me," he said, voice edged. "Will you answer a few questions?"

She stopped, her penciled brows drawn together. She shrugged. "Fire away, lieutenant."

She leaned against the wall, tapping it patiently with one manicured fingernail.

Tony said, "All I know about the Hoderay-Hammond drive, Miss Overland, is that it reverses the Fitz-Gerald Contraction principle. It makes use of a new type of mechanical advantage. A moving object contrasts in the direction of motion. Therefore a stationary object, such as a ship, can be made to move if you contract it in the direction you want it to move. How that's accomplished, though, I don't know."

"By gravitons— Where have you been all your life?"

"Learning," said Tony, "good manners."

She flushed. Her fingers stopped drumming. "If you realized you were interrupting important work, you'd know why I forget my manners. We trying to finish this up so daddy could get back to his farewell dinner at the university. I guess the professors guessed right when they sent his— Well, why should I explain that to you?"

"I'm sure," said Tony, "I don't know."

"Well, go on," she said coldly.

Tony lighted a cigarette, offered her one with an apology. She shook her head impatiently.

Tony eyed her through the haze of smoke. "Back there on 1007 I saw a skeleton with a ring on its finger."

She seemed nonplused. "Well. Was it a pretty ring?"

Tony said grimly, "The point is, Braker never got near that skeleton after I saw it, but that same ring is now on his finger."

Startlement showed in her eyes. "That doesn't sound very plausible, lieutenant!"

"No, of course it doesn't. Because then the same ring is in two different places at the same time"

"And of course," she nodded, "that would be impossible. Go on. I don't know what you're getting at, but it certainly is interesting."

"Impossible?" said Tony. "Except that it happens to be the truth. I'm not explaining it away, Miss Overland, if that's your idea. Here's something else. The skeleton is a human skeleton, but it existed before the human race existed."

She shoved herself away from her indolent position. "You must be crazy."

Tony said nothing.

"How did you know?" she said sharply.

"I *know*. Now *you* explain the H-H drive, if you will."

"I will!" She said: "Gravitons are the ultimate particle of matter. There are 1846 in a proton, one in an electron, which is the reason why a proton is 1846 times as heavy as an electron.

"Now you can give me a cigarette, lieutenant. I'm curious about this thing, and if I can't get to the bottom of it, my father certainly will."

After a while, she blew out smoke nervously.

She continued, speaking rapidly: "A Wittenberg disrupter tears atoms apart. The free electrons are shunted off into accumulators, where we get power for lighting, cooking, heating and so forth. The protons go into the proton analyzer, where the gravitons are ripped out of them and stored in a special type of spherical field. When we want to move the ship, the gravitons are released. They spread through the ship and everything in the ship.

"The natural place for a graviton is in a proton. The gravitons rush for the protons—which are already saturated with 1846 gravitons. Gravitons are unable to remain free in three-dimensional space. They escape along the time line, into the past. The reaction contracts the atoms of the ship and everything in the ship, and shoves it forward along the opposite space-time line—forward into the future and forward in space. In the apparent space of a second, therefore, the ship can travel thousands of miles, with no acceleration effects.

"Now, there you have it, lieutenant. Do what you can with it."

Tony said, "What would happen if the gravitons were forced into the future rather than the past?"

"Lieutenant, I would have been surprised if you hadn't said that! Theoretically, it's an impossibility. Anybody who knows gravitons would say so. But if Braker is wearing a ring that a skeleton older than the human race is also wearing—*Ugh!*"

She put her hands to her temples in genuine distaste. "We'll have to see my father," she said wearily. "He'll be the one to find out whether or not you make this up as you go along."

Erle Masters looked from Tony to Laurette.

"You believe this bilge he's been handing you?"

"I'm not interested in what you think, Erle. But I am in what you do, Daddy."

Overland looked uneasy, his stubbled jaws barely moving over a wad of rough-cut.

"It does sound like . . . er . . . bilge," he muttered. "If you weren't an IPF man, I'd think you were slightly off-center. But—one thing, young man. How did you know the skeleton was older than the human race?"

"I said it existed *before* the human race."

"Is there any difference?"

"I think there is—somehow."

"Well," said Overland patiently, "how do you know it?"

Tony hesitated. "I don't really know. I was standing at the mouth of the cave, and something—or someone—told me."

"*Someone!*" Masters blasted the word out incredulously.

"I don't know!" said Tony. "All I know is what I'm telling you. It couldn't have been supernatural—could it?"

Overland said quickly, "Don't let it upset you, son. Of course it wasn't supernatural. There's a rational explanation somewhere, I guess. But it's going to be hard to come by."

He nodded his head abstractedly, and kept on nodding it like a marionette. Then he smiled peculiarly.

"I'm old now, son—you know? And I've seen a lot. I don't disbelieve anything. There's only one logical step for a scientist to take now, and that's to go back and take a look at that skeleton."

Masters' breath sounded. "You can't do that!"

"But we're going to. And remember that I employ *you*, because Laurette asked me to. Now turn this ship back to 1007. This might be more important than patching up a torn-up world at that." He chuckled.

Laurette shook her blond head. "You know," she said musingly, "this might be the very thing we *shouldn't* do, going back like this. On the other hand, if we went on our way, *that* might be the thing we shouldn't do."

Masters muttered, "You're talking nonsense, Laurette."

He ostentatiously grabbed her bare arm, and led her from the room after her father, throwing Tony a significant glance as he passed.

Tony expelled a long breath. Then, smiling twistedly, he went back to the lounge, to wait—for what? His stomach contracted again with revulsion—or was it a premonition?

Braker came sharply to his feet. "What's up, Crow?"

"Let me see that ring again," Tony said. After a minute he raised his eyes absently. "It's the same ring," he muttered.

"I wish to hell," Braker exploded, "I knew what you were talking about!"

Tony looked at him obliquely, and said under his breath, "Maybe it's better you don't."

He sat down and lighted a cigarette. Braker swore, and finally wandered to the window. Tony knew what he was thinking: of Earth; of the cities that teemed; of the vast stretches of open space between the planets. Such would be his thoughts. Braker, who loved life and freedom.

Braker, who wore a ring—

Then the constellations showing through the port abruptly changed pattern.

Braker leaped back, eyes bulging. "What the—"

Yates, sitting sullenly in the corner, came alertly to his feet. Braker mutely pointed at the stars.

"I could have sworn," he said thickly.

Tony came to his feet. He had seen the change. But his thoughts flowed evenly, coldly, a smile frozen on his lips.

"You saw right, Braker," he said coldly, then managed to grab the guide rail as the ship bucked. Braker and Yates sailed across the room, faces ludicrous with surprise. The ship turned the other way. The heavens spun, the stars blurring. Something else Tony saw besides blurred stars: a dull-gray, monstrous landscape, a horizon cut with mountains, a bright, small sun fringing tumbled clouds with reddish, ominous silver. Then stars again, rushing past the port, simmering through an atmosphere—

Blackness crushed its way through Tony Crow's consciousness, occluding it until, finally, his last coherent thought had gone. Yet he seemed to know what had happened. There was a skeleton in a cave on an asteroid—millions of years from now. And the ship had struck.

Tony moved, opened his eyes. The lights were out, but a pale shaft of radiance was streaming through the still-intact port. Sounds insinuated themselves into his consciousness. The wet drip of rain, the low murmur of spasmodic wind, a guttural *kutakikchkut* that drifted eerily, insistently, down the wind.

Tony slowly levered himself to his feet. He was lying atop Braker. The man was breathing heavily, a shallow gash on his forehead. Involuntarily, Tony's eyes dropped to the ring. It gleamed—a wicked eye staring up at him. He wrenched his eyes away.

Yates was stirring, mumbling to himself. His eyes snapped open, stared at Tony.

"What happened?" he said thickly. He reeled to his feet. *"Phew!"*

Tony smiled through the gloom. "Take care of Braker," he said, and turned to the door, which was warped off its hinges. He loped down the corridor to the control room, slowing down on the lightless lower deck ramp. He felt his way into the control room. He stumbled around until his foot touched a body. He stooped, felt a soft, bare arm. In sudden, stifling panic, he scooped Laurette's feebly breathing body into his arms. She might have been lead, as his feet seemed made of lead. He forced himself up to the upper corridor, kicked open the door of her father's room, placed her gently on the bed. There was light here, probably that of a moon. He scanned her pale face anxiously, rubbing her arms toward the heart. Blood came to her cheeks. She gasped, rolled over. Her eyes opened.

"Lieutenant," she muttered.

"You all right?"

Tony helped her to her feet.

"Thanks, lieutenant. I'll do." She tensed. "What about my father?"

"I'll bring him up," said Tony.

Five minutes later, Overland was stretched on the bed, pain in his open eyes. Three ribs were broken. Erle Masters hovered at the foot of the bed, dabbing at one side of his face with a reddened handkerchief, a dazed, scared look in his eyes. Tony knew what he was scared of, but even Tony wasn't playing with that thought now.

He found a large roll of adhesive in the ship's medicine closet. He taped Overland's chest. The breaks were simple fractures. In time, they would do a fair job of knitting. But Overland would have to stay on his back.

Masters met Tony's eyes reluctantly.

"We'll have to get pressure suits and take a look outside."

Tony shrugged. "We won't need pressure suits. We're already breathing outside air, and living under this planet's atmospheric pressure. The bulkheads must be stowed in some place."

Overland's deep voice sounded, slowly. "I think we've got an idea where we are, Erle. You can feel the drag of this planet—a full-size planet, too. Maybe one and a half gravities. I can feel it pulling on my ribs." A bleak expression settled on his stubbled face. He looked at Tony humorlessly. "Maybe I'm that skeleton, son."

Tony caught his breath. "Nonsense. Johnny Braker's wearing the ring. If anybody's that skeleton, he is. *Not* that I wish him any bad luck, of course." He nodded once, significantly, then turned toward the door with a gesture at Masters. Masters, plainly resenting the soundless command, hesitated, until Laurette made an impatient motion at him.

They prowled through the gloomy corridor toward the small engine room, pushed the door open. The overpowering odor of ozone and burning rubber flung itself at them.

Masters uttered an expressive curse as Tony played a beam over what was left of the reversed Fitz-Gerald Contraction machinery. His nails clicked startlingly loud in the heavy silence.

"Well, that's that," he muttered.

"What d'you mean—that's that?" Tony's eyes bored at him through the darkness.

"I mean that we're stuck here, millions of years ago." He laughed harshly, unsteadily.

Tony said without emotion, "Cut it out. Hasn't this ship got auxiliary rocket blasts?"

"Naturally. But this is a one and a half gravity planet. Anyway, the auxiliary jets won't be in such good condition after a fifty-foot drop."

"Then we'll fix 'em," said Tony sharply. He added, "What makes you so sure it's millions of years ago, Masters?"

Masters leaned back against the door jamb, face as cold and hard as stone.

"Don't make me bow to you any more than I have to, lieutenant," he said ominously. "I didn't believe your story before, but I do now. You predicted this crack-up—it had to happen. So I'm ready to concede it's millions of years ago; mainly because there wasn't any one and a half gravity planet within hundreds of millions of miles of the asteroid belt. But there *used* to be one."

Tony said, lips barely moving, "Yes?"

"There used to be one—*before the asteroids.*"

Tony smiled twistedly. "I'm glad you realize that."

He turned and went for the air lock, but, since the entire system of electric transmission had gone wrong somewhere, he abandoned it and followed a draft of wet air. He jerked open the door of a small storage bin, and crawled through. There was a hole here, that had thrust boxes of canned goods haphazardly to one side. Beyond was the open night.

Tony crawled out, stood in the lee of the ship, occasional stinging drops of rain lashing at their faces. Wind soughed across a rocky plain. A low roar heralded a nearby, swollen stream. A low *kutakikchkut* monotonously beat against the night, night-brooding bird, Tony guessed, nested in the heavy growth flanking a cliff that cut a triangular section from a heavily clouded sky. Light from a probably moon broke dimly through clouds on the leftward horizon.

Masters' teeth chattered in the cold.

Tony edged his way around the ship, looking the damage over. He was gratified to discover that although the auxiliary rocket jets were twisted and broken, the only hole was in the storage bin bulkheads. That could be repaired, and so, in time, could the jets.

They started to enter the ship when Masters grasped his arm. He pointed up into the sky, where a rift in the clouds showed.

Tony nodded slowly. Offsetting murkily twinkling stars, there was another celestial body, visible as a tiny crescent.

"A planet?" muttered Tony.

"Must be." Masters' voice was low.

They stared at it for a moment, caught up in the ominous, baleful glow. Then Tony shook himself out of it, went for the storage bin.

Walking down the corridor with Masters, Tony came upon Braker and Yates.

Braker grinned at him, but his eyes were ominous.

"What's this I hear about about a skeleton?"

Tony bit his lip. "Where'd you hear it?"

"From the girl and her old man. We stopped outside their room a bit. Well, it didn't make sense, the things they were saying. Something about an emerald ring and a skeleton and a cave." He took one step forward, an ugly light in his smoky eyes. "Come clean, Crow. How does this ring I've got on my finger tie with a skeleton?"

Tony said coldly, "You're out of your head. Get back to the lounge."

Braker sneered. "Why? You can't make us stay there with the door broken down."

Masters made an impatient sound. "Oh, let them go, lieutenant. We can't bother ourselves about something as unimportant as this. Anyway, we're going to need these men for fixing up the ship."

Tony said to Yates, "You know anything about electricity? Seems to me you had an E.E. once."

Yates' thin face lighted, before he remembered his sullen pose. "O.K., you're right,' he muttered. He looked at Braker interrogatively.

Braker said "Sorry. We're not obligated to work for you. As prisoners, you're responsible for us and our welfare. We'll help you or whoever's bossing the job *if* we're not prisoners."

Tony nodded. "Fair enough. But tonight, you stay prisoners. Tomorrow, maybe not," and he herded them back into the lounge. He cuffed them to the guide rail and so left them, frowning a little. Braker had been too acquiescent

The reason for that struck Tony hard. Walking back along the corridor, he saw something gleaming on the floor. He froze. Revulsion gripping him, he slowly picked up the ring.

Masters turned, said sharply, 'What's up?"

Tony smiled lopsidedly, threw the ring into the air twice, speculatively, catching it in his palm. He extended it to Masters.

"Want a ring?"

Masters' face went white as death. He jumped back.

"Damn you!" he said violently. "Take that thing away!"

"Braker slipped it off his finger," said Tony, his voice edging into the aching silence. Then he turned on his heel, and walked back to the lounge. He caught Braker's attention.

He held the ring out.

"You must have dropped it," he said.

Braker's lips opened in a mirthful, raucous laugh.

"You can have it, copper," he gasped. "*I* don't want to be any damned skeleton!"

Tony slipped the ring into his pocket and walked back down to the corridor with a reckless swing to his body.

He knocked on the door to Overland's room, opened it when Laurette's voice sounded.

Masters and Laurette looked at him strangely.

Overland looked up from the bed.

"Lieutenant," he said, an almost ashamed look on his face, "sometimes I wonder about the human mind. Masters seems to think that now *you've* got the ring, *you're* going to be the skeleton."

Masters' nails clicked. "It's true, isn't it? The outlaws know about the ring. We know about it. But Crow *has* the ring, and it's certain none of us is going to take it."

Overland made an exasperated clicking sound.

"It's infantile," he snapped. "Masters, you're acting like a child, not like a scientist. There's only one certainty, that one of us is going to be the skeleton. But there's no certainty which one. And there's even a possibility that all of us will die." His face clouded angrily. "And the most infantile viewpoint possible seems to be shared by all of you. You've grown superstitious about the ring. Now it's—a ring of death! Death to him who wears the ring! *Pah!*"

He stretched forth an imperative hand.

"Give it to me, lieutenant! I'll tell you right now that no subterfuge in the universe will change the fact of my being a skeleton if I *am* the skeleton; and vice versa."

Tony shook his head. "I'll be keeping it—for a while. And you might as well know that no scientific argument will convince anybody the ring is not a ring of death. For, you see, it is."

Overland sank back, lips pursed. "What are you going to do with it?" he charged. When Tony didn't answer, he said pettishly, "Oh, what's the use! On the face of it, the whole situation's impossible." Then his face lighted. "What did you find out?"

Tony briefly sketched his conclusions. It would be two or three weeks before they could repair the rocket jets, get the electric transmission system working properly.

Overland nodded absently. "Strange, isn't it!" he mused. "All that work DeTosque, Bodley, Morrell, Haley, the Farr brothers and myself have done goes for nothing. Our being here proves the theory they were working on."

Laurette smiled lopsidedly at Tony.

"Lieutenant," she said, "maybe the skeleton was a woman."

"A woman!" Masters' head snapped around, horror on his face. "Not you, Laurette!"

"Why not? Women have skeletons, too—or didn't you know?" She kept her eyes on Tony. "Well, lieutenant? I put a question up to you."

Tony kept his face impassive. "The skeleton," he said, without a tremor, "was that of a man."

"Then," said Laurette Overland, stretching out her palm, cup-shaped, "give me the ring."

Tony froze, staring. That his lie should have this repercussion was unbelievable. Out of the corner of his eye he saw Overland's slowly blanching face. On Masters, Laurette's statement had the most effect.

"Damn you, Crow!" he said thickly. "This is just a scheme of yours to get rid of the ring!" He lunged forward.

The action was unexpected. Tony fell backward under the impact of the man's fist. He sprawled on his back. Masters threw himself at him.

"Erle, you utter fool!" That was Laurette's wail.

Disgust settled on Tony's face. He heaved, by sheer muscular effort, and threw Masters over his back. His fist came down with a brief but pungent *crack*. Masters slumped, abruptly lifeless.

Tony drew himself to his feet, panting. Laurette was on her knees beside Masters, but her dismayed eyes were turned upward to Tony.

"I'm sorry, lieutenant!" she blurted.

"What have you got to be sorry about?" he snapped. "Except for being in love with a fool like that one."

He was sorry for it the second he said it. He didn't try to read Laurette's expression, but turned sullen eyes to Overland.

"It's night," he said abruptly, "and it's raining. Tomorrow, when the sun comes up, it'll probably be different. We can figure out the situation then, and start our plans for—" He let the sentence dangle. Plans for what? He concluded, "I suggest we all get some sleep," and left.

He arranged some blankets on the floor of the control room, and instantly went to sleep, though there were times when he stirred violently. The skeleton was in his dreams—

There were five of them at the breakfast table. Laurette serving; Masters beside her, keeping his eyes sullenly on the food; Braker, eating as heartily as his cuffed hands would allow; Yates, picking at his food with disinterest.

Tony finished his second cup of coffee, and scraped his chair back.

"I'll be taking a look around," he told Laurette in explanation. He turned to the door.

Braker leaned back in his chair until it was balanced on two legs, and grinned widely.

"Where you going, Mr. Skeleton?"

Tony froze.

"After a while, Braker," he said, eyes frigid, "the ring will be taken care of."

Yates' fork came down. "If you mean you're going to try to get rid of it, you know you can't do it. It'll come back." His eyes were challenging.

Masters looked up, a strange milling series of thoughts in his sullen eyes. Then he returned to his food.

Tony, wondering what that expression had meant, shrugged and left the room; and shortly the ship, by way of the cavity in the storage bin.

He wandered away from the ship, walking slowly, abstractedly, allowing impressions to slip his mind without conscious resistance. There was a haunting familiarity in this tumbled plain, though life had no place in the remembrance. There was some animal life, creatures stirring in the dank humus, in long, thick grass, in gnarled tree tops. This was mountain country and off there was a tumbling mountain stream.

He impelled himself toward it, the tiny, yet phenomenally bright sun throwing a shadow that was only a few inches long. It was high "noon."

He stood on the brink of the rocky gorge, spray prismatically alive with color, dashing up into his face. His eyes followed the stream up to the mountain fault where water poured downward to crush at the rocks with the steady, pummeling blow of a giant. He stood there, lost in abstraction, other sounds drowned out.

All except the grate of a shoe behind him. He tried to whirl; too late! Hands pushed against his back—in the next second, he had tumbled off the brink of the chasm, clutching wildly, vainly, at thick spray. Then, an awful moment of freezing cold, and the waters had enclosed him. He was borne away, choking for air, frantically flailing with his arms.

He was swept to the surface, caught a chaotic glimpse of sun and clouded sky and rock, and then went under again, with a half lungful of air. He tensed, striving to sweep away engulfing panic. A measure of reason came back. Hands and feet began to work in purposeful unison. The surface broke around him. He stayed on top. But that was only because the stream was flowing darkly, swiftly, evenly. He was powerless to force himself against this current.

He twisted, savagely looking for some sign of release. A scaly, oily tree limb came at him with a rush. One wild grab, and the limb was bending downstream, straining against the pressure his body was exerting. He dashed hair from his eyes with one trembling hand, winced as he saw the needle-bed of rapids a hundred feet downstream. If that limb hadn't been there— His mind shuddered away from the thought.

Weakly, he drew himself hand over hand upward, until the tree trunk was solidly below him. He dropped to the ground, and lay there, panting. Then he remembered the hands on his back. With a vicious motion, he jerked out his key ring. That was the answer—the key to the cuffs was gone, taken during the night, of course! Erle Masters, then, had pulled this prize play, or perhaps one of the outlaws, after Masters released him.

After a while, he came to his feet, took stock of his surroundings. Off to his left, a cliff side, and scarcely a half-mile distant, the pathetically awry hulk of the ship, on the top of the slope that stretched away.

The cliff side came into his vision again. A fault in the escarpment touched a hidden spot in his memory. He involuntarily started toward it. But he slowed up before he got to the fault—which was really a cave that tapered out to nothingness as its sides rose.

The cave!

And this sloping plain, these mountains, composed the surface of Asteroid 1007, millions of years from now.

Tony dropped emotionlessly to his knees at the mouth of the cave. Not so long ago, he had done the same thing. Then there had been a complete, undisjointed skeleton lying there. Somehow, then, he had known the skeleton existed before the human race—as if it were someone—the skeleton?—that had spoken to him across the unutterable years. The skeleton? That could not be! Yet, whence had come the memory?

He took the ring from his pocket and put it on his finger. It gleamed.

He knelt there for minutes, like a man who worships at his own grave, and he was not dead. Not dead! He took the ring from his finger, then, a cold, bleak smile growing on his face.

He came to his feet, a rising wind whipping at his hair. He took a half dozen running steps toward the river, brought his arm over his shoulder in a throwing gesture.

Somehow the ring slipped from his fingers and fell.

He stooped, picked it up. This time, he made it leave his hand. It spun away, twinkling in the faint sunlight. But the gravity had hold of it, and it fell on the brink of the river, plainly visible.

A dry, all-gone feeling rose in Tony's throat. Grimly, he went forward, picked it up again. Keeping his eyes on it, he advanced to the brink of the river gorge. He held the ring over the darkly swirling waters, slowly released it.

It struck the river like a plummet. The waters enclosed it and it was gone. He looked at the spot where it had disappeared, half expecting it to spring back up into his hand. But it was gone. Gone for good!

He started dazedly back to the ship, moving in an unreal dream. Paradoxical that he had been able to get rid of it. It had dropped from his hand once, fallen short of the river once. The third time it had given up trying!

When he came up to the ship, Masters was standing at the stern, looking at the broken rocket jets. He turned, and saw Tony, water still dripping from his uniform. He fell back a step, face turned pallid.

Tony's lips curled. 'Who did it?"

"D-did what?"

"You know what I mean," Tony bit out. He took three quick steps forward.

Masters saw that, and went reckless. Tony side-stepped him, brought his left arm around in a short arc. Masters went down cursing. Tony knelt, holding Masters down by the throat. He felt through his pockets, unearthed the key to the cuffs. Then he hauled Masters to his feet and shook him. Masters' teeth clicked.

"Murderer!" Tony snapped, white with rage.

Masters broke loose. "I'd do it again," he said wildly, and swung. He missed. Tony lashed out with the full power of his open palm, caught Masters on the side of the head. Masters went reeling back, slammed against the side of the ship. Tony glared at him, and then turned on his heel.

He met Laurette Overland coming down the stairs to the upper corridor.

"Lieutenant!" Her eyes danced with excitement. "I've been looking for you. Where in the world have you been?"

"Ask Masters." He urged himself down the corridor, jaw set. She fell into step beside him, running to keep up with his long strides.

"You're all wet!" she exclaimed. "Can't you tell me what happened? Did you go swimming?"

"Involuntarily." He kept on walking.

She grabbed his arm, and slowed him to a stop. An ominous glint replaced her excitement.

"What," she said, "did you mean when you said I should ask Erle about it? Did he push you in? If he did, I'll—" She was unable to speak.

Tony laughed humorlessly. "He admitted it. He stole my key to the handcuffs with the idea that it would be easier to free Braker and Yates that way after I was . . uh . . . properly prepared to be a skeleton."

Her head moved back and forth. "That's horrible," she said lowly. "Horrible."

He held her eyes. "Perhaps I shouldn't have told you about it," he said, voice faintly acid. "He's your fiancé, isn't he?"

She nodded, imperceptibly, studying him through the half gloom. "Yes. But maybe I'll change my mind, lieutenant. Maybe I will. But in the meantime, come along with me. Daddy's discovered something wonderful."

Professor Overland's head was propped up. He had a pencil and paper on his pyramided legs.

"Oh. Lieutenant! Come in." His face lighted. "Look here! Gravitons *can* thrust their way through to the future, giving the ship a thrust into the past. But only if it happened to enter the spherical type of etheric vacuum. This vacuum would be minus everything—electrons, photons, cosmic rays and so forth, except under unusual circumstances. At some one time, in either the past or future, there might be a stream of photons bridging the vacuum. Now, when gravitons are ejected into the past, they grab hold of light photons, and become ordinary negative electrons. Now say the photons are farther away in the past than they are in the future. The gravitons therefore follow the line of least resistance and hook up with photons of the future. The photons in this case were perhaps hundreds of millions of years away in the vacuum. In traveling that time-distance, the gravitons kicked the ship back for a proportionate number of years, burned up our machinery, and wrecked us on this suddenly appearing before-the-asteroid world."

Laurette said brightly, "But that isn't the important part, daddy.'

"I can find another of those etheric vacuums," Overland went on, preoccupiedly, pointing out a series of equations. "Same type, same structure. But we have to go to the planet Earth in order to rebuild the reversed contraction machinery. We'll find the materials we need there.'' He glanced up. "But we have to get off this world before it cracks up, lieutenant."

Tony started. "Before this world cracks up?"

"Certainly. Naturally. You can—" His heavy brows came down abruptly. "You didn't know about that, did you? Hm-m-m." He stroked his jaw, frowning. "You recall the crescent planet you and Masters saw? Well, he took some readings on that. It's wonderful, son!" His eyes lighted. "It's an ill wind that blows nobody good. Not only do we know now that the asteroid evolved from a broken-up planet, but we also know the manner in which that planet broke up. Collision with a heavy, smaller body."

Tony paled. "You mean—" he said huskily. "Good heavens!" Sweat stood out on his forehead. "How soon will that happen?" he said ominously.

"Well, Erle has the figures. Something over eighteen or nineteen days. It'll be a crack-up that'll shake the sun. And we'll be here to witness it." He smiled wryly. "I'm more scientist than man, I guess. I never stop to think we might die in the crack-up, and furnish six skeletons instead of one."

"There'll be no skeletons," Tony said, eyes narrowed. "For one thing, we can repair the ship, though we'll have to work like mad. For another—I threw the ring into the river. It's gone."

Laurette seemed to pale. "I . . . I don't see how that could be done," she stammered. "You couldn't get rid of it, not really—could you?"

"It's gone," Tony said stubbornly. "For good. And don't forget it. There'll be no skeleton. And you might try to impress that on Masters, so he doesn't try to produce one," he added significantly.

He left the room with a nod, a few seconds later stepped into the lounge. Braker and Yates turned around. Both were cuffed.

Tony took the key from his pocket and the cuffs fell away. In brief, pungent tones, then, he explained the situation, the main theme being that the ship had to be well away from the planet before the crack-up. Yates would go over the wiring system. Braker, Masters and Tony would work with oxyacetylene torches and hammers over the hole in the hull and the rocket jets.

Then he explained about the ring.

Yates ran a thin hand through his yellow hair.

"You don't do it that easy," he said in his soft, effortless voice. "There's a skeleton up there, and it's got Braker's ring on its finger. It's got to be accounted for, don't it? It's either me or you or Braker or the girl or her old man or Masters. There ain't any use trying to avoid it, either." His voice turned sullen. He looked at Braker, then at Tony. "Anyway, I'm keeping my back turned the right way so there won't be any dirty work."

Braker's breath sounded. "Why, you dirty rat," he stated. He took a step toward Yates. "You would think of that. And probably you'd try it on somebody else, too. Well, don't go pulling it on me, understand." He scowled. "And you better watch him, too, Crow. He's pure poison—in case you got the idea we were friends."

"Oh, cut it out," Tony said wearily. He added, "If we get the ship in working order, there's no reason why all six of us shouldn't get off—alive." He turned to the door, waved Braker and Yates after him. Yet he was sickeningly aware that *his* back was turned to men who admittedly had no conscience to speak of.

A week passed. The plain rang with sledgehammer strokes directed against the twisted tubes. Three were irreplaceable.

Tony, haggard, tired, unbelievably grimed from his last trip up the twisted, hopeless-looking main blast tube, was suddenly shocked into alertness by sounds of men's voices raised in fury outside the ship. He ran for the open air lock, and urged himself toward the ship's stern. Braker and Yates were tangling it.

"I'll kill him!" Braker raged. He had a rock the size of his fist in his hand. He was attempting, apparently, to knock Jawbone Yates' brains out. Erle Masters stood near, chewing nervously at his upper lip.

With an oath, Tony wrenched the rock from Braker's hand, and hauled the man to his feet. Yates scrambled erect, whimpering, mouth bleeding.

Braker surged wildly toward him. "The dirty—!" he snarled. "Comes up behind me with an oxy torch!"

Yates shrilled, backing up, "That's a lie!" He pointed a trembling hand at Braker. "It was *him* that was going to use the torch on *me!*"

"Shut up!" Tony bawled. He whirled on Masters. "You've got a nerve to stand there," he snarled. "But then you *want* a skeleton! Damned if you're going to get one! Which one did it?"

Masters stammered, "I didn't see it! I . . . I was just—"

"The hell you say!" Tony whirled on the other two, transfixing them with cold eyes.

"Cut it out," he said, lips barely moving. "Either you're letting your nerves override you, or either one or both of you is blaming the other for a move he made himself. You might as well know the skeleton I saw was intact. What do you think a blow torch would do to a skeleton?" His lips curled.

Braker slowly picked up his torch with a poisonous glance at Yates. Yates as slowly picked his sledgehammer. He turned on Tony.

"You said the skeleton was intact?" Eagerness, not evident from his carefully sullen voice, was alive in his eyes.

Tony's glance passed over the man's broken, protruding jaw.

"The head," he replied, "was in shadow."

He winced. The passing of hope was a hard thing to watch, even in a man like Jawbone Yates.

He turned, releasing his breath in a long, tired sigh. What a man-sized job this was. Outwitting fate—negating what *had* happened!

Tony worked longer than he expected that day, tracing down the web of asbestos-covered rocket fuel conduits, marking breaks down on the chart. The sun sank slowly. Darkness swept over the plain, along with a rising wind. He turned on the lights, worked steadily on, haggard, nerves worn. Too much work to allow a slowing up. The invading planet rose each night a degree or more larger. Increasing tidal winds and rainstorms attested to a growing gravitational attraction.

He put an x-mark on the check—and then froze. A scream had gone blasting through the night.

Tony dropped pencil and chart, went flying up the ramp to the upper corridor. He received the full impact of Masters' second scream. Masters had left his room, was running up the corridor, clad in pajamas. There was a knife sticking out of his shoulder.

Tony, gripped with horror, impelled himself after the man, caught up with him as he plunged face downward. He dropped to one knee, staring at a heavy meat knife that had been plunged clear through the neck muscles on Masters' left shoulder, clearly a bid for a heart stroke.

Masters turned on his side. He babbled, face alive with horror. Tony rose, went with the full power of his legs toward the lounge.

A figure showed, running ahead of him. He caught up with it, whipped his arm around the man's neck.

"You!"

Yates squirmed tigerishly. He turned, broke loose, face alive with fury. Tony's open palm lashed out, caught Yates full on the face. Yates staggered and fell. He raised himself to one elbow.

"Why'd you do it?" Tony rasped, standing over him.

Yates' face was livid. "Because I'd rather live than anything else I can think of!" His booted foot lashed out. Tony leaped back. Yates rose. Tony brought his bunched fist up from his knees with all the ferocity he felt. Yates literally rose an inch off the floor, sagged, and sopped to the floor.

Tony picked him up in one arm, and flung him bodily into the lounge.

Braker rose from his sleeping position on a cushioned bench, blinking.

Tony said cuttingly, "Your pal ran a knife through Masters shoulder."

"Huh?" Braker was on his feet. "Kill him?" In the half-light his eyes glowed.

"You'd be glad if he did!"

Braker looked at Yates. Then, slowly, "Listen, copper. Don't make the mistake of putting me in the same class with a rat like

Yates. I don't knife people in the back. But if Masters was dead, I'd be glad of it. It might solve a problem that's bothering the rest of us. What you going to do with him?"

"I already did it. But tell Yates he better watch out for Masters, now."

Braker grunted scornfully. "Huh. Masters'll crack up and down his yellow back."

Tony left.

Laurette and Overland were taking care of Masters in his room. The wound was clean, hardly bleeding.

Overland, somewhat pale, was hanging onto the door. "It's not serious, honey," he said, as her fingers nimbly wound bandages.

"Not serious?" She turned stricken eyes up to Tony. "Look at him. And Daddy says it's not serious!"

Tony winced. Masters lay face down on the bed, babbling hysterically to himself, his eyes preternaturally wide. His skin was a pasty white, and horror had etched flabby lines around his lips.

"Knifed me," he gasped. "Kniffed me. I was sleeping, that was the trouble. But I heard him—" He heaved convulsively, and buried his face in his pillow.

Laurette finished her job, face pale.

"I'll stay here the rest of the night," Tony told her.

Overland gnawed painfully at his lower lip.

"Who did it?"

Tony told him.

"What?" Tony laughed scornfully. "Masters had the same trick pulled on him that he pulled on me. He isn't any angel himself."

Overland nodded wearily. His daughter helped him out of the room.

During the night, Masters tossed and babbled. Finally he fell into a deep sleep. Tony leaned back in a chair, moodily listening to the sough of the wind, later on watching the sun come up, staining the massed clouds with running, changing streaks of color.

Masters awoke. He rolled over. He saw Tony, and went rigid. He came to his feet, and huddled back against the wall.

"Get out," he gasped, making a violent motion with his hand.

"You're out of your head," said Tony angrily. "It was Yates."

Masters panted, "I know it was. What difference does it make? You're all in the same class. I'm going to watch myself after this. I'm going to keep my back turned the right way. I'm going to be sure that none of you—"

Tony put his hands on his hips, eyes narrowed.

"If you've got any sense, you'll try to forget this and act like a human being. Better to be dead than the kind of man you'll turn into."

"Get out. Get out!" Masters waved his hand again, shuddering.

Tony left, shaking his head slowly.

Tony stood outside the ship, smoking a cigarette. It was night. He heard a footstep behind him. He fell back a step, whirling.

"Nerves getting you, too?" Laurette Overland laughed shakily, a wool scarf blowing back in the heavy, unnatural wind.

Tony relaxed. "After two weeks of watching everybody watching everybody else, I guess so."

She shivered. He sensed it was not from the bite of the wind. "I suppose you mean Erle."

"Partly. Your father's up and around today, isn't he? He shouldn't have gotten up that night."

"He can get around all right."

"Maybe he better lock himself in his room." He smiled with little amusement. "The others are certain the ring will come back."

She was silent. Through the ominous gloom, lit now by a crescent planet that was visible as a small moon, and growing steadily larger, he saw a rueful, lopsided smile form on her face. Then it was gone.

She said, "Erle was telling me the jets are in bad condition. A trial blast blew out three more."

"That's what happened."

She went on: "He also told me there was a definite maximum weight the jets could lift in order to get us free of the gravity. We'll have to throw out everything we don't need. Books, rugs, clothing, beds." She drew a deep breath. "And in the end, maybe a human being."

Tony's smile was frozen. "Then the prophecy would come true."

"Yes. It is a prophecy, isn't it?" She seemed childishly puzzled. She added, "And it looks like it has to come true. Because— Excuse me, lieutenant," she said hurriedly, and vanished toward the air lock.

Tony stared after her, his mind crawling with unpleasant thoughts. It was unbelievable, fantastic. So you couldn't outwit fate. The ship would have to be lightened. Guesswork might easily turn into conviction. There might be one human being too many—

Professor Overland came slowly from the air lock, wincing from the cold after his two weeks of confinement. His haggard eyes turned on Tony. He came forward, looking up at the growing planet of destruction.

"Erle has calculated three days, eight hours and a few minutes. But it's ample time, isn't it, lieutenant?"

"One jet will straighten out with some man-size labor. Then we can start unloading extra tonnage. Lots of it."

"Yes. Yes. I know." He cleared his throat. His eyes turned on Tony, filled with a peculiar kind of desperation. "Lieutenant," he said huskily, "there's something I have to tell you. The ring came back."

Tony's head jerked. "It came back?" he blurted.

"In a fish."

"*Fish?*"

Overland ran a trembling hand across his brow. "Yesterday a week ago, Laurette served fried fish. She used an old dress for a net, I found the ring in what she brought to my room. Well, I'm not superstitious about the ring. One of us *is* the skeleton—up there. We can't avoid it. I put the ring on— more bravado than anything else. But this morning"—his voice sank to a whisper—"the ring was gone. Now I'm becoming superstitious, unscientifically so. Laurette is the only one who could—or would—have taken it. The others would have been glad it was on my finger rather than theirs. Even Erle."

Tony stared through him. He was remembering Laurette's peculiar smile. Abruptly, he strode toward the ship, calling back hurriedly:

"Better go inside, sir."

In the ship, he knocked sharply on Laurette's door.

She answered nervously, "Yes."

"May I come in?"

"No. No. Do you have to?"

He thought a moment, then opened the door and stepped inside. She was standing near her bed, her eyes haunted.

Tony extended a hand imperatively. "Give me the ring."

She said, her voice low, controlled, "Lieutenant, I'll keep the ring. You tell that to the others. Then there won't be any of this nervous tension and this murder plotting."

He said ominously, "You may wind up a skeleton."

"You said the skeleton was not a woman."

"I was lying."

"You mean," she said, "it *was* a woman?"

Tony said patiently, "I mean that I don't know. I couldn't tell. Do I get the ring, or don't I?"

She drew a deep breath. "Not in the slightest can it decide who will eventually die."

Tony advanced a step. "Even your father doesn't believe that now," he grated.

She winced. "I'll keep the ring and stay in my room except when I cook. You can keep everybody out of the ship. Then there won't be anybody to harm me."

Footsteps sounded in the corridor. Masters entered the room. Tension had drawn hollow circles under eyes that refused to stay still.

"You," he said to Laurette, his voice thin, wavering. He stood with his back to the wall. He wet his lips. "I was talking with your father."

"All right, all right," she said irritably. "I've got the ring, and I'm keeping it."

"No, you can't, Laurette. We're going to get rid of it, this time. The six of us are going to watch."

"You can't get rid of it!" Then, abruptly, she snatched it off her finger. "Here!"

Imperceptibly, he shrank back against the wall.

"There's no use transferring it now. You've got it, you might as well carry it." His eyes swiveled, lighted with a sudden burst of inspiration. "Better yet, let Crow carry it. He represents the law. That would make it proper."

She seemed speechless.

"Can you imagine it? Can you imagine a sniveling creature like him— I'll keep the ring. First my father gets weak in the knees, and then—" She cast a disdainful look at Masters. "I wish you'd both leave me alone, please."

Tony shrugged, left the room, Masters edging out after him.

Tony stopped him.

"How much time have we got left?"

Masters said jerkily, "We've been here fourteen days. It happens on the twenty-fifth. That's eleven days from now, a few hours either way."

"How reliable are your figures?"

Masters muttered, "Reliable enough. We'll have to throw out practically everything. Doors, furniture, clothes. And then—"

"Yes?"

"I don't know," Masters muttered, and slunk away.

It was the twenty-fourth of December.

Tidal winds increased in savagery in direct proportion to the growing angular diameter of the invading planet. Heavy, dully colored birds fought their way overhead. On the flanks of abruptly rising cliff edges, gnarled trees lashed. Rain fell spasmodically. Clouds moved in thoroughly indiscriminate directions. Tentacular leaves whirlpooled. Spray, under the wind's impact, cleared the river gorge. The waterfall was muted.

Rushing voluminous air columns caught at the growing pile emerging from the ship's interior, whisked away clothing, magazines, once a mattress. It did not matter. Two worlds were to crash in that momentous, before-history forming of the asteroids. There was but one certainty. This plain, these mountains—and a cave—were to stay intact through the millions of years.

Inside the air lock, Masters stood beside a heavy weight scale. Light bulbs, dishes, silverware, crashed into baskets indiscriminately, the results weighed, noted, discarded. Doors were torn off their hinges, floors ripped up. Food they would keep, and water, for though they eventually reached Earth, they could not know whether it yet supported life.

The ship, devoid of furnishings, had been a standard eleven tons for an H-H drive. Furnishing, food, et cetera, brought her to over thirteen tons. Under a one and a half gravity, it was twenty tons. Masters' figures, using the firing area the ship now had, with more than half the jets beyond use, were exact enough. The maximum lift the jets would or could afford was plus or minus a hundred pounds of ten and three quarter tons.

Masters looked up from his last notation, eyes red-rimmed, lips twitching. Braker and Yates and Tony were standing in the air lock, watching him.

Fear flurried in Masters' eyes. "What are you looking at me like that for?" he snarled. Involuntarily, he fell back a step.

Yates giggled.

"You sure do take the fits. We was just waiting to see how near we was to the mark. There ain't anything else to bring out."

"Oh, there isn't?" Masters glared. "We're still eight hundred pounds on the plus side. How about the contraction machinery?"

Tony said: "It's our only hope of getting back to the present. Overland needs it to rebuild the drive."

"Pressure suits!"

"We're keeping six of them, in case the ship leaks."

"Doors!" said Masters wildly. "Rugs!"

"All," said Tony, "gone."

Masters' nails clicked. "Eight hundred pounds more," he said hoarsely. He looked at his watch, said, "Eleven hours plus or minus," took off his watch and threw it out. He made a notation on his pad, grinning crookedly. "Another ounce gone."

"I'll get Overland," Tony decided.

"Wait!" Masters thrust up a pointing finger. "Don't leave me alone with those two wolves. They're waiting to pounce on us. Four times one hundred and fifty is six hundred."

"You're bats," said Braker coldly.

"Besides," said Yates, "where would we get the other two hundred pounds?"

Masters panted at Tony, "You hear that? He wants to know where they'd get the other two hundred pounds!"

"I was joking," said Yates.

"Joking! *Joking!* When he tried to knife me once!"

"Because," concluded Yates, "the cards call for only one skeleton. *I'll* get him."

He came back shortly with Laurette and her father.

Overland fitted his glasses over his weak eyes while he listened, glancing from face to face.

"It would be suicidal to get rid of the machinery, what's left of it. I have another suggestion. We'll take out all the direct-vision ports. They might add up to eight hundred pounds."

"Not a bad idea," said Braker slowly. "We can wear pressure suits. The ship might leak anyway."

Masters waved a hand. "Then get at it! Laurette, come here. You've got the ring. *You* don't want to be the skeleton, do you? Put your back to this wall with me."

"Oh, Erle," she said in disgust, and followed her father out.

Tony brought three hack saws from the pile of discarded tools. Working individual rooms, the three of them went through the ship, sawing the ports off at the hinges, pulling out the port packing material. The ship was now a truly denuded spectacle, the floors a mere grating of steel.

The ports and packing were placed on the scale.

"Five hundred—five twenty-five—five sixty-one. That's all!" Masters sounded as if he were going to pieces.

Tony shoved him aside. "Five sixty-one it is. There may be a margin of error, though," he added casually. "Braker, Yates—out with this scale."

The two stooped, heaved. The scale, its computed weight already noted, went out—

Tony said, "Come on, Masters."

Masters trotted behind, doglike, as if he had lost the power of thought. Tony got the six pressure suits out of the corner of the control room, and gestured toward them. Everybody got into the suits.

Tony buckled his helmet down. "Now give her the gun."

Masters stood at the auxiliary rocket control board, face pale, eyes unnaturally wide.

He made numerous minor adjustments. He slowly depressed a plunger. A heavy, vibrating roar split the night. The ship leaped. There was a sensation of teetering motion. In the vision plates, the plain moved one step nearer, as if a new slide had been inserted in a projector. The roar swept against them voluminously. The picture remained the same.

Masters wrenched up the plunger, whirled.

"You see?" he panted. "I could have told you!"

Professor Overland silenced him with a wave of the hand, pain showing in his eyes.

"I make this admission almost at the expense of my sanity," he said slowly. "Events have shaped themselves—incredibly. Backward. In the future, far away, in a time none of us may ever see again, lies a skeleton with a ring on its finger.

"Now which causes which—the result or its cause?"

He took off his glasses, blinked, fitted them back on.

"You see," he said carefully, "some of the things that have happened to us are a little bit incredible. There is Lieutenant Crow's—*memory* of these events. He saw the skeleton and it brought back memories. From where? From the vast storehouse of the past? That does not seem possible. Thus far it is the major mystery, how he *knew* that the skeleton existed before the human race.

"Other things are perhaps more incredible. Three shipwrecks! Incredible coincidence! Then there is the incident of the ring. It is—a ring of death. I say it who thought I would never say it. Lieutenant Crow even had some difficulty throwing it into the river. A fish swallowed it and it came back to me. Then my daughter stole it from me. And she refused to give it up, or let us know what her plans for disposition of it are.

"I do not know whether we are shaping a future that is, or whether a future that is is shaping us.

"And finally we come to the most momentous occurrence of this

whole madness. An utterly ridiculous thing like two hundred or two
hundred and fifty pounds.

"So we must provide a skeleton. The future that *is* says so."

Silence held. The roar of the river, and the growing violence of
the tidal wind rushed in at them. Braker's breath broke loose.

"He's right. Somebody has to get off—and stay off! And it isn't
going to be the old man, him being the only one knows how to
get us back."

"That's right," said Yates. "It ain't going to be the old man."

Masters shrank back. "Well, don't look at me!" he snarled.

"I wasn't looking at you," Yates said mildly.

Tony's stomach turned rigid. This was what you had to go
through to choose a skeleton to die on an asteroid, its skin and
flesh to wear and evaporate away and finally wind up millions of
years later as a skeleton in a cave with a ring on its finger. These
were some of the things you had to go through before you became
that skeleton yourself—

"Laurette," he said, "isn't in this lottery."

Braker turned on him. "The hell she isn't!"

Laurette said, voice edged, "I'm in. I might be the straw that
broke the camel's back."

Overland said painfully, "Minus a hundred and five might take
us over the escarpment. Gentlemen, I'll arrange this lottery, being
the only nonparticipant."

Masters snarled, eyes glittering, "You're prejudiced in favor of
your daughter!"

Overland looked at him mildly, curiously, as he would some
insect. He made a clicking sound with his lips.

Masters pursued his accusation.

"We'll cut for high man, low card to take the rap!"

"Yah!" jeered Yates. "With your deck, I suppose."

"Anybody's deck!" said Masters.

"All the cards were thrown out. Why weren't yours?"

"Because he knew it would come to this."

"Gentlemen," said Overland wearily. "It won't be a deck.
Laurette, the ring."

She started, paled. She said, "I haven't got it."

"Then," said her father, without surprise, "we'll wait around until
it shows up."

Braker whirled on him. "You're crazy! We'll draw lots anyway.
Better still, we'll find where she put the ring."

"I buried it," said the girl, and her eyes fluttered faintly. "You better leave it buried. You're just proving—"

"Buried it!" blasted Masters. "When she could have used a hammer on it. When she could have melted it in an oxyacetylene torch. When she could—"

"When she could have thrown it in the river and have a fish bring it back! Shut up, Masters." Braker's jawline turned ominous. "Where's the ring? The skeleton's got to have a ring and it's going to have one."

"I'm not going to tell you." She made a violent motion with her hand. "This whole thing is driving me crazy. We don't need the ring for the lottery. Leave it there, can't you?" Her eyes were suddenly pleading. "If you dig it up again, you'll just complete a chain of coincidence that couldn't possibly—"

Overland said, "We won't use the ring in the lottery. It'll turn up later and the skeleton will wear it. We don't have to worry about it, Braker."

Yates said, "Now we're *worrying* about it!"

"Well, it has to be there, doesn't it?" Braker charged.

Tony interrupted by striking a match. He applied flame to a cigarette, sucked in the nerve-soothing smoke.

His eyes were hard, watchful. "Ten hours to get out of range of the collision," his lips said.

"Then we'll hold the lottery now," said Overland. He turned and left the room. Tony heard his heavy steps dragging up the ramp.

The five stood statuesque until he came back. He had a book in one hand. Five straws stuck out from between the pages, their ends making an even line parallel with the book.

Overland's extended hand trembled slightly.

"Draw," he said. "My daughter may draw last, so you may be sure I am not tricking anybody. Lieutenant? Braker? Anybody. And the short straw loses."

Tony pulled a straw.

"Put it down on the floor at your feet," said Overland, "since someone may have previously concealed a straw."

Tony put it down, face stony.

The straw was as long as the book was wide.

Braker said, in an ugly tone, "Well, I'll be damned!"

Braker drew a shorter one. He put it down.

Yates drew a still shorter one. His smile of bravado vanished. Sweat stood suddenly on his pale forehead.

"Go ahead, Masters!" he grated. "The law of averages says you'll draw a long one."

"I don't believe in the law of averages," said Masters sulkily. "Not on this planet, anyway— I'll relinquish the chance to Laurette."

"That," said Laurette, "is sweet of you."

She took a straw without hesitation.

Masters said nervously, "It's short, isn't it?"

"Shorter than mine." Yates, breath came out in a long sigh. "Go ahead, Masters. Only one straw left, so you don't have to make a decision."

Masters jerked it out.

He put it on the floor. It was long.

A cry burst from Overland's lips. "Laurette!"

She faced their silent stares with curled lips.

"That's that. I hope my hundred and five helps."

Tony dropped his cigarette. "It won't," he snapped. "We were fools for including you."

Suddenly he was watching Braker out of the corner of his eye, his nerves tense.

Overland said in a whisper, "How could I suggest leaving my daughter out? I said a hundred pounds *might* be the margin. If I'd have suggested leaving her out, you'd have accused me of favoritism."

Braker said casually, "There's only going to be one lottery held here."

Yates looked dumfounded. "Why, you blasted fool," he said. "What if we're stuck back here before the human race and there ain't any women?"

"That's what I mean. I thought we'd include the girl. If she was drawn, then we could ask some gentleman to volunteer in her place."

He made a sudden motion. Tony made a faster one. His Hampton came out and up.

"Drop it!" he rasped. "I said—*drop it!*"

Braker's eyes bulged. He looked at the Hampton as if he were unable to comprehend it. He cursed rackingly and dropped the automatic as if it were infested with a radioactive element. It clattered on the metal grating of the denuded floor.

A smile froze on Tony's lips. "Now you can explain where you got that automatic."

Braker, eyes fuming like those of a trapped animal, involuntarily shot a glance at Masters.

Tony turned his head slightly toward Masters. "It would be you," he said bitterly.

He whirled—too late. Yates hurtled toward him, struck him in a flying tackle. Tony fell audibly. He tangled furiously with Yates. No good! Braker, face contorted with glee, leaped on top of him, struggled mightily, and then with the main force of his two gloved hands wrenched the Hampton away, rolled from Tony's reach, then snapped himself to his feet, panting.

"Thanks, Yates!" he exclaimed. "Now get up, Crow. Get up. What a man. What a big hulking man. Weighs two hundred if he weighs an ounce." His lips curled vengefully. "Now get up and get out!"

Overland made a step forward, falteringly.

Braker waved the weapon all-inclusively.

"Back, you," he snarled. "This is my party, and it's a bad-taste party, too. Yates, corner the girl. Masters, stand still—you're my friend if you want to be. All right, lieutenant, get going—and dig! For the ring!" His face screwed up sadistically. "Can't disappoint that skeleton, can we?"

Tony came to his feet slowly, heart pounding with what seemed like long-spaced blows against his ribs. Painfully, his eyes ran from face to face, finally centered on Laurette's.

She surged forward against Yates' retaining grip.

"Don't let them do it, lieutenant," she cried. "It's a dirty trick. You're the one person out of the four who doesn't deserve it. I'll—" She slumped back, her voice fading, her eyes burning. She laughed jerkily. "I was just remembering what you did when all the Christmas packages came tumbling down on us. You kissed me, and I slapped you, but I really wanted you to kiss me again."

Yates laughed nastily. "Well, would you listen to that. Masters, you going to stand there and watch them two making love?"

Masters shuddered, his face graying. He whispered, "It's all right. I wish—"

"Cut out the talk!" Braker broke in irritably.

Tony said, as if the other conversation had not intervened, I wanted to kiss you again, too." He held her wide, unbelieving eyes for along moment, then dropped his and bit at his shuddering lower lip. It seemed impossible to stand here and realize that this was defeat and that there was no defense against it! He shivered with an unnatural jerk of the shoulders.

"All right," Braker said caustically, "get going."

Tony stood where he was. Braker and everybody else except Laurette Overland faded. Her face came out of the mist, wild, tense, lovely and lovable. Tears were coming from her eyes, and her racking sobs were muted. For a long moment, he hungrily drank in that last glimpse of her.

"Lieutenant!"

He said dully, his eyes adding what his lips did not, "Good-bye, Laurette."

He turned, went toward the air lock with dragging feet, like a man who leaves the death house only to walk toward a worse fate. He stopped at the air lock. Braker's gun prodded him.

He stood faintly in the air lock until Braker said, "Out, copper! Get moving."

And then he stepped through, the night and the wild wind enclosing him, the baleful light of the invading planet washing at him.

Faintly he heard Braker's jeering voice, "So long, copper." Then, with grim, ponderous finality, came the wheeze of the closing air lock.

He wandered into the night for a hundred feet, somehow toward the vast pile that had been extracted from the ship's interior. He seemed lost in unreality. This was the pain that went beyond all pains, and therefore numbed.

He turned. A blast of livid flame burst from the ship's main tube. Smaller parallels of fire suddenly ringed it. The ship moved. It slid along the plain on its runners, hugged the ground for two hundred feet, plummeting down the slope. Tony found himself tense, praying staccato curses. Another hundred feet. The escarpment loomed.

He thrust his arms forcefully upward.

"Lift!" he screamed. *"Lift!"*

The ship's nose turned up, as her short wings caught the force of the wind. Then it roared up from the plain, cleared the escarpment by a scant dozen feet. The echoes of the blast muted the very howl of the wind. The echoes died. Then there was nothing but a bright jewel of light receding. Then there was—nothing.

Tony looked after it, conscious that the skin was stretched dry and tight across his cheekbones. His upflung arms dropped. A little laugh escaped his lips. He turned on his heels. The wind was so furious he could lean against it. It was night, and though the small moon this before-the-asteroids world boasted was invisible, the heavens overflowed with the baleful, pale-white glow of the invading planet.

It was still crescent. He could clearly see the ponderous immensity the lighted horns embraced. The leftward sky was occluded a full two-fifths by the falling monster, and down in the seas the shores would be overborne by tidal waves.

He stood motionless. He was at a loss in which direction to turn. An infinity of directions, and there could be no purpose in any. What type of mind could choose a direction?

That thought was lost. He moved toward the last link he had with humanity—with Laurette. He stood near the trembling pile. There was a cardboard carton, addressed to Professor Henry Overland, a short chain of canceled stamps staring up at him, pointing to the nonexistence of everything that would be. America and Christmas and the post office.

He grinned lopsidedly. The grin was lost. It was even hard to know what to do with one's face. He was the last man on a lost world. And even though he was doomed to death in this unimaginably furious crack-up, he should have some goal, something to live for up to the very moment of death!

He uttered a soft, trapped cry, dashed his gloves to his helmeted face. Then a thought simmered. Of course! The ring! He had to find that ring, and he would. The ring went with the skeleton. And the skeleton went with the ring. Lieutenant Tony Crow—and there could be no doubt of this whatsoever—was to be that skeleton which had grinned up at him so many years ago—no, not ago, acome.

A useless task, of course. The hours went past, and he wandered across the tumbled, howling plain, traversing each square foot, hunting for a telltale, freshly turned mound of earth. He went to the very brink of the river gorge, was immersed in leaping spumes of water. Of the ring that he must have there was no trace.

Where would she have buried it? How would her mind work? Surely, she could not have heartlessly buried the ring, hiding it forever, when Tony Crow needed it for the skeleton he was to turn into!

He knew the hours were flying. Yet, better to go mad with this tangible, positive purpose, than with the intangible, negative one of waiting spinelessly for death from the lowering monster who now owned the heavens.

How convenient this was. One time-traveled. One witness to the origin of the asteroids. Similarly, one might time-travel and understand at last the unimaginable, utterly baffling process by which the solar system came into being. Nothing as simple as a collision. Or a binary sweeping past a single. Or a whirling nebula. It would be connected with the expanding universe, in some outrageously simple manner. But everything was simple once one knew the answer. For instance—

The ring! Yes, it was as simple as that. Even Laurette Overland would be forced to yield to the result that was influencing its own cause!

Tenseness gave way to relief. One could not baffle the future. Naturally, she'd burried the ring in the cave. Unless she wanted to be perverse. But she would *not* be perverse in a matter like this. Future and present demanded co-operation, if there was to be a logical future!

Forcing himself against a wind that blew indiscriminately, he reached the funnel in the mountainside. The skeleton was not here, naturally. But it would be—with the necessary ring on its finger. Unbelievable how the future shapes its own past! It was as if his own skeleton, which existed millions of years *acome*, on which his own healthy flesh rode *now*, were plainly telling him what he should do.

He dug with a cold methodicity, starting from the rear of the cave. No sign of the ring, and no sign of recently turned earth. He discarded his gloves, placed them carefully to one side, and dug with a sharp rock.

No sign of the ring! The hours passed. What was he to do? His thoughts sharpened with desperation. An hour, little more, remained. Then would come the smash—and death.

He was in the cave! He, the skeleton!

He lay on his back, head propped up in locked hands. Trees and limbs and leaves hurtled by in a tempestuous wind. Soon, out in the sky, would float the remnants of this very substantial world. The millions of years would pass. A Lieutenant Tony Crow, on the trail of three criminals, would land here, look into this cave, and see his own skeleton—only he would not know it.

He lay there, tense, waiting. The wind would dig up the ring, whip it through the air. He would hear a tinkling sound. That would be the ring, striking against the wall of the cave. He would pick it up and put it on his finger. In a few moments after that would come the sound—the heavy vibration—the ear-splitting concussion—the cosmic clash—the . . . the . . . *bang* of a world breaking up. *Bang!*

He listened, waiting for the ring.

He listened, and heard a voice, screaming down the wind.

He impelled himself to his feet, in one surge of motion. He stood there, blood pounding against his temples, his lips parted and trembling. There could be no sound like that. Not when he was the last human being on this world. Not when the scream could be that of Laurette Overland, calling to him.

Of course, it was not she. Of course, it could not be. This was merely one of those things previewing the preparation of a skeleton with a ring in a— *Stop!*

He moved from the cave, out into the wind, and stood there. He heard nothing—did he? A pound of feet—such as death running might make.

A scream!

He ran around the shoulder of the mountain, stood there, panting, clasping his helmeted head between his trembling, cold hands.

"Lieutenant!"

A voice, whipped into his imagination by the ungodly wind!

He would not believe it.

A form, stumbling out of the pale night! Running toward him, its lips moving, saying words that the wind took away. And it was Laurette Overland, forming in his imagination now that he had gone completely mad.

He waited there, in cold amusement. There was small use in allowing himself to be fooled. And yet—and yet—the ring had to come back; to him. This was Laurette Overland, and she was bringing it—for him to wear. That was selfish of her. If *she* had the ring, if *she* had dug it up, why didn't *she* wear it?

Then she would be the skeleton.

Then there would be two skeletons!

His mind froze, then surged forward into life and sanity. A cold cry of agony escaped him. He stumbled forward and caught the girl up in his arms. He could feel the supple firmness of her body even through the folds of her undistended pressure suit.

Laurette's lips, red and full against the ghastly induced paleness of her face, parted and words came out. Yet he could make no sense of it, for the unimaginable wind, and the cold horror lancing through his mind occluded words and sentences.

"—had to . . . out. A hundred pounds." He felt her hysterical laugh. So the ship had started to fall. She had bailed out, had swept to solid ground on streams of flame shooting from the rocket jets in the shoulders of her suit. This much he knew. Hours and hours she had fought her way—toward the plain. Because she remembered something. The ship was gone. Safe. She remembered something that was important and it had to do with the skeleton and the ring. She had to get out. It was her part in the ghastly across-the-millions-of-years stage play. She had to dig up the ring.

He held her out at arm's length and looked down at her gloved hands. Yes, there was mud on them. So the ring had not been in the cave.

His eyes shuddered upward to hers.

"Give me the ring." His lips formed the words slowly.

"No, no, lieutenant," she blurted out. "It's not going to be *that* way. Don't you see? It's Amos! Amos!"

"You must be crazy to have come back!" he panted. He shook in sudden overwhelming, maddening fury. "You're crazy anyway!"

He suddenly wrenched at her hands, forced them open. But there was no ring. He shook her madly.

"Where's the ring? Give it to me, you damned little fool! If you're wearing it—if you think for one moment—you can't do this—"

The wind whipped the words away from her, she knew, even as that which she was saying was lost to him.

He stopped talking, and with a cold ferocity wrapped one arm around her, and with the other started to unbuckle her gloves with his own bare hands. She struggled suddenly, tigerishly. She wrenched herself away from him. She ran backward three steps. She looked up into the sky for one brief second, at the growing monster. He could see the cold, frantic horror settling on her face. Collision! And it was a matter of moments! And he, the true skeleton, did not have the ring!

He moved toward her, one slow step at a time, his eyes wild, his jaw set with purpose.

She darted past him. He whirled, panting, went frantically after her. And every step he took grew more leaden, for the moment was here. The collision was about to occur. And the girl was running toward the cave.

Laurette vanished around the shoulder of the mountain. The cave swallowed her. His steps slowed down. He stood there, drew a deep, tremulous breath. Then he entered the cave, and stood facing her, the wind's howl diminishing.

She said, coldly, "We haven't much time to talk or fight, lieutenant. You're acting like a madman. Here." She stooped and picked up his gloves. She held them out. "Put these on."

He said, "Give me the ring."

She stared at him through the gloom, at his preternaturally wide eyes.

"All right," she said. She unbuckled the glove of her right hand. She moved close to him, holding his eyes with her own. "If you want to be the skeleton, you may."

He felt her fingers touch his right hand. He felt something cold traveling up his fingers. He felt the ring enclosing his finger. Yes, the ring was on there, where it should be. He felt it—coldly. It could not very well be his imagination—could it? Of course not. She would not try to fool him. Yet her eyes were hypnotic, and he was in a daze. Feebly, he knew he should resist. But she forced his glove over his right hand, and he heard the buckles click. Then the left hand glove went on, and was buckled.

Her arms crept up around his neck. Tears glinted unashamedly in her eyes.

"Hold me tight, lieutenant," she whispered huskily. "You know . . . you know, there may be a chance."

"No, there isn't, Laurette. There can't be. I've got the ring on my finger."

He could feel her drawing a deep breath. "Of course—you've got the ring on your finger! I think it can't be very far away, lieutenant. Hold me." Her voice was a whimper. "Maybe we'll live."

"Not I. Perhaps you."

"This cave, this very mountain, lived through the holocaust. And perhaps we will, too. Both of us."

She was being illogical, he knew. But he had sunk into a dull, apathetic state of mind. Let her try to believe what was impossible. He had the ring on his finger. He *did*.

Did he?

He jerked. He had felt the cold of its metal encircling his finger. He had *thought* he had felt it! His fingers moved. A dull, sickening sense of utter defeat engulfed him. This was defeat. *She* had the ring! *She* was the skeleton!

And there was no time to change it. There would be no time. The blood rushed in his head, giddily. He caught her eyes, and held them, and tried to let her know in that last moment that

he knew what she had done. She bit her lip and smiled. Then—
her face clouded. Clouded as his thoughts clouded. It was like
that.

He heard no monstrous sound, for here was sound that was no
sound. It was simply the ponderous headlong meeting of two planets. They had struck. They were flattening out against each other,
in the immeasurable second when consciousness was whipped away,
and fragments of rock, some large, some small, were dribbling out
in a fine frothy motion from underneath the circle of collision. The
planet was yawning mightily. A jigsaw of pieces, a Humpty Dumpty
that all the king's horses and all the king's men could never put
together again. This was the mighty prelude to the forming of an
asteroid belt, and of a girl skeleton on Asteroid No. 1007.

He was alive.

Alive and thinking.

It did not seem possible.

He was wedged into the back of the cave. A boulder shut off
light, and a projecting spur of it reached out and pinioned him with
gentle touch against the wall at his back. He was breathing. His suit
was inflated with ten pounds of pressure. Electric coils were keeping
his body warm. He was alive and the thoughts were beginning in
his brain. Slow, senseless thought. Thoughts that were illogical.
He could not even bring himself to feel emotion. He was pinioned
here in the darkness, and out there was an asteroid of no air, small
gravity, and a twenty-mile altitude.

Laurette Overland would be dead, and she would be wearing the
ring. Tears, unashamed, burned at his eyes.

How long had he been here, wedged in like this: minutes, hours,
days? Where were Overland, Masters, Braker and Yates? Would
they land and move this boulder away?

Something suddenly seemed to shake the mountain. He felt
the vibration rolling through his body. What had caused that?
Some internal explosion, an aftermath of the collision? That did
not seem likely, for the vibration had been brief, barely perceptible.

He stood there, wedged, his thoughts refusing to work except
with a monotonous regularity. Mostly he thought of the skeleton;
so that skeleton *had* existed before the human race!

After a while, it might have been five minutes or an hour or
more, he became aware of arms and legs and a sluggishly beating
heart. He raised his arms slowly, like an automaton that has come

to life after ages of motionlessness, and pushed against the boulder that hemmed him in. It seemed to move away from him easily. He stepped to one side and imparted a ponderous, rocking motion to the boulder. It fell forward and stopped. Light, palely emanating from the starry, black night that overhung Asteroid No. 1007, burst through over the top of the boulder. Good. There was plenty of room to crawl through—after a while. He leaned against the boulder, blood surging weakly in his veins.

He felt a vibration so small that it might have been imagination. Then again, it might have been the ship, landing on the asteroid. At least, there was enough likelihood of that to warrant turning his headset receiver on.

He listened, and heard the dull undertone of a carrier wave; or was that the dull throb of blood against his temples? No, it couldn't be. He strained to listen, coherent thoughts at last making headway in his mind.

Then:

"Go on, professor— Masters." That was Braker's voice! "We'll all go crazy if we don't find out who the skeleton is."

Then Braker had landed the ship, after escaping the holocaust that had shattered that before-the-asteroids world! Tony almost let loose a hoarse breath, then withheld it, savagely. If Braker heard that, he might suspect something. Whatever other purpose Tony had in life now, the first and most important was to get the Hampton away from Braker.

Overland muttered, his voice lifeless, "If it's my daughter, I'd rather you'd go first, Braker."

Masters spoke. "I'll go ahead, professor. I'd do anything to—" His voice broke.

Overland muttered, "Don't take it so hard, son. We all have our bad moments. It couldn't be a skeleton, anyway."

"Why not?" That was Yates. Then, "Oh, hell, yes! It couldn't be, could it, professor? You know, this is just about the flukiest thing that has ever happened I guess. Sometimes it makes me laugh! On again, off again!"

"Finnegan," finished Braker absently. "Say, I don't get it. This time business. You say the gravity of that planet was holding us back in time like a rubber band stretched tight. When the planet went, the rubber band broke—there wasn't that gravity any more. And then we snapped back to our real time. But what if Crow and your daughter weren't released like that? Then we ought to find the skeleton—maybe two of 'em."

"The gravity of the asteroid would not be enough to hold them back," Overland said wearily.

"Then I don't get it," Braker snapped with exasperation. "This is the present, our real present. Back there is the ledge that cracked our ship up, so it has to be the present. Then how come Crow said he saw a skeleton? Say," he added, in a burst of anger, "do you think that copper was pulling the wool over our eyes? Well, I'll be—"

Yates said, "Grow up! Crow was telling the truth."

Overland said, "The skeleton will be there. The lieutenant saw it."

Masters: "Maybe he saw his own skeleton."

Yates: "Say, that's right!"

Braker: "Well, why not? The same ring was in two different places at the same time, so I guess the same skeleton could be in Crow at the same time as in the cave. It's a fact, and you don't talk yourself out of it."

Tony's head was whirling. What in heaven were they talking about? Were they intimating that the release of gravity, when the planet broke up, released everything back to the real present, as if some sort of bond had been broken? His hands started to tremble. Of course. It was possible. The escapage of gravitons had thrust them back into the past. Gravitons, the very stuff of gravity, had helped them there. And when that one and a half gravity had dispersed, when the gravitons were so far distant that they no longer exerted that tension, everything had snapped back—to the present!

Everything! His thoughts turned cold. Somewhere, somehow, something was terribly wrong. His head ached. He clenched his hands, and listened again. For a full minute, there was no voice. Tony could envision them walking along, Masters and Overland in front, Braker and Yates behind, making their slow way to the cave, Overland dreading what he was to find there.

Then: "Hurry it up, professor. Should be right around here."

Overland whispered, throatily, "There it is, Braker. My God!" He sounded as if he were going all to pieces.

"The skeleton!" Yates blurted out, burrs in his voice. "Ye gods, professor, d'you suppose— Why sure—they just weren't snapped back."

Shaking, pasty white of face, Tony clawed his way halfway up the boulder. He hung there, just able to look outside. The whole floor of the cave was visible. And the skeleton lay there, gleaming white, and the ring shone on its tapering finger!

Laurette.

He lifted his head, conscious that his eyes were smarting painfully. Through a blur, he saw Braker, Yates, Masters and Overland, standing about thirty feet distant from the cave, silent, speechless, staring at the skeleton.

Braker said, his voice unsteady, "It's damned strange, isn't it? We knew it was going to be there, and there it is, and it robs you of your breath."

Yates cleared his throat, and said firmly, "Yeah, but who is it? Crow or the girl?"

Overland took a step forward, his weak eyes straining.

"It's not a very long skeleton, is it?" he whispered.

Braker said, harshly, "Now don't try talking yourself into anything, professor. You can't see the skeleton well enough from here to tell who it is. Masters, stop shaking." His words were implicit with scorn. "Move over there and don't try any funny stuff like you did on the ship a while ago. I should have blasted you then. I'm going to take a look at that skeleton."

He went forward sideways, hand on his right hip where the Hampton was holstered.

He came up to the mouth of the cave, stood looking down on the skeleton, frowning. Then he knelt. Tony could see his face working with revulsion, but still he knelt there, as if fascinated.

Tony's lips stretched back from his teeth. Here's where Braker got his! He worked his way up to the top of the boulder, tensed, slid over to the other side on his feet. He took one step forward and bent his knees.

Braker raised his head.

His face contorted into a sudden mask of horror.

"*You!*" he screamed. His eyes bulged.

Tony leaped.

Braker fell backward, face deathly pale, clawing at the Hampton. Tony was on top of him before he could use it. He pinned Braker down, going for the Hampton with hands, feet, and blistering curses. His helmet was a sudden madhouse of consternated voices. Overland, Masters, and Yates swept across his vision. And Yates was coming forward.

He caught hold of the weapon, strained at it mightily, the muscles of his stomach going rigid under the exertion.

Braker kicked at Tony's midriff with heavy boots, striving to puncture the pressure suit. Tony was forced over on his back, saw Braker's sweating face grinning mirthlessly into his.

Stars were suddenly occluded by Yates' body. The man fell to his knees, pinned Tony down, and with Braker's help broke Tony's hold on the Hampton.

"Give it to me!" That was Masters' voice, blasting out shrilly. By sheer surprise, he wrenched the weapon from Yates. Tony flung himself to his feet as the outlaw hurled himself at Masters with a snarl, made a grab for Yates' foot. Yates tried to shake him off, hopped futilely, then stumbled forward, falling. But he struck against Masters. Masters' hold on the weapon was weak. It went sailing away in an arc, fell at the mouth of the cave.

"Get it!" Braker's voice blasted out as he struggled to his feet. Masters was ahead of him. Wildly, he thrust Braker aside. Yates reached out, tripped Masters. Braker went forward toward the Hampton, and then stopped, stock-still.

A figure stepped from the cave, picked up the weapon, and said, in cold, unmistakable tones, "Up with them. You, Braker. Yates!"

Braker's breath released in a long shuddering sigh, and he dropped weakly, helplessly to his knees.

His voice was horrible. "I'm crazy," he said simply, and continued to kneel there and continued to look up at the figure as if it were a dead figure come to life at which he stared.

The blood drummed upward in Tony's temples, until it was a wild, crazy, diapason. His shuddering hands raised to clasp his helmet.

Then:

"Laurette," he whispered brokenly. *"Laurette!"*

There were six human beings here.

And *one skeleton on the floor of the cave.*

How long that tableau held, Tony had no way of knowing. Professor Overland, standing off to Tony's left, arms half raised, a tortured, uncomprehending look on his face. Masters, full length on his stomach, pushing at the ground with his clawed hands to raise his head upward. Yates, in nearly the same position, turned to stone. Braker, his breath beginning to sound out in little, bottled-up rasps.

And the girl, Laurette, she who should have been the skeleton, standing there at the mouth of the cave, her face indescribably pale, as she centered the Hampton on Braker and Yates.

Her voice edged into the aching silence.

"It's Amos," she said. She was silent, looking at her father's haggard face, smiling twistedly.

"Amos," said Overland hoarsely, saying nothing else, but in that one word showing his utter, dismaying comprehension. He stumbled forward three steps. "We thought— We thought—" He seemed unable to go on. Tears sounded in his voice. He said humbly, "We thought you were the— But no. It's Amos!" His voice went upward hysterically.

"Stop it!" Laurette's voice lashed out. She added softly, tenderly, "No, I'm not the skeleton. Far from it, Daddy. Amos is the skeleton. He was the skeleton all along. I didn't realize it might be that way until the ship lifted. Then it seemed that the ship was going to fall and I thought my hundred and five might help after all and anyway, I decided that the lieutenant was all alone down there. And that somehow made me think of the time all the Christmas packages tumbled down on him and how I slapped him." She laughed unsteadily. "That made me remember that the university sent your present with a 'Do Not Open Before Christmas' sticker on it. I remembered you were leaving the university and they were giving you a combination farewell gift and Christmas present. You didn't know, but I did, that the professors decided you couldn't possibly be back before Christmas and so they sent it to the ship. You had always told them you admired— Amos. He hung on the biology classroom wall. It seemed I suddenly knew how things *had* to be. I put two and two together and I took a chance on it."

She fell silent, and the silence held for another full, shocking minute. She went on, as if with an effort.

"We threw everything out of the ship, remember? The Christmas presents, too. When I dropped from the ship later, I reached the plain and I broke open the carton with the 'Do Not Open' sticker on it, and there was Amos, as peaceful as you please. I put the ring on his finger and left him there, because I knew that some way the wind or crack-up or *something* would drop him in the cave. He *had* to turn up in the cave."

"Anyway," she added, her lips quirking roguishly, "by our time, back there, it was December 25th."

Masters clawed his way to his knees, his lips parted unnaturally.

"A Christmas present!" he croaked. "A Christmas present!" His face went white.

The girl said unsteadily, "Cut it out, Erle!"

She leaned weakly against the wall of the cave. "Now come up here, lieutenant, and take this gun out of my hands and don't stare at me as if you've lost your senses."

Tony forced himself to his feet, and like an automaton skirted around Braker and Yates and took the suddenly shaking weapon from her.

She uttered a weary sigh, smiled at him faintly, bemusedly, and whispered, "Merry Christmas, lieutenant!" She slumped slowly to the ground.

Tony gestured soundlessly at Masters. Masters, face abject and ashamed, picked her up in tender arms.

"Come up here, professor," Tony said dully. He felt as if all the life had been pumped from his bones.

Overland came forward, shaking his head with emotion. "Amos!" he whispered. He broke in a half-hysterical chuckle, stopped himself. He hovered around Laurette, watching her tired face. "At least my girl lives," he whispered brokenly.

"Get up, Braker," said Tony. "You, too, Yates."

Yates rose, vaguely brushing dust from his pressure suit, his lips working over words that refused to emerge.

Braker's voice was a hoarse, unbelieving whisper. His eyes were abnormally wide and fixed hypnotically on the skeleton.

"So that's what we went through—for a damned classroom skeleton." He repeated it. "For a damned classroom skeleton!"

He came to his feet, fighting to mold his strained face back to normal. "Just about back where we started, eh? Well," he added in a shaking, bitter tone, "Merry Christmas." He forced his lips into half-hearted cynicism.

Tony's face relaxed. He drew in a full, much-needed breath of air. "Sure. Sure— Merry Christmas. Everybody. Including Amos—whoever he used to be."

Nobody seemed to have anything to say. Or perhaps their thoughts were going back for the moment to a pre-asteroid world. Remembering. At least Masters was remembering, if the suffering, remorseful look on his face meant anything.

Tony broke it. "That's that, isn't it? Now we can go back to the ship. From there to Earth. Professor— Masters—start off." He made a tired gesture.

Masters went ahead, without a backward look, carrying the gently breathing, but still unconscious girl. Overland stole a last look at the skeleton, at Amos, where he lay unknowing of the chaos the mere fact of his being there, white and perfect and wired together, and with a ring on his perfect tapering finger, had caused.

Overland walked away hurriedly after Masters. Amos would stay where he was.

Tony smiled grimly at Braker. He pointed with his free hand.

"Want your ring back, Braker?"

Braker's head jerked minutely. He stared at the ring, then back at Tony. His fists clenched at his sides. *"No!"*

Tony grinned—for the first time in three weeks.

"Then let's get going."

He made a gesture. Braker and Yates, walking side by side, went slowly for the ship, Tony following behind. He turned only once, and that was to look at his wrecked patrol ship, where it lay against the base of the mountain. A shudder passed down his spine. There was but one mystery that remained now. And its solution was coming to Tony Crow, in spite of his effort to shove its sheerly maddening implications into the back of his mind—

Professor Overland and Masters took Laurette to her room. Tony took the two outlaws to the lounge, wondering how he was going to secure them. Masters solved his problem by entering with a length of insulated electric wire. He said nothing, but wordlessly went to work securing Braker and Yates to the guide rail while Tony held the Hampton on them. After he had finished, Tony bluntly inspected the job. Masters winced, but he said nothing.

After they were out in the hall, going toward Laurette's room, Masters stopped him. His face was white, strained in the half-darkness.

"I don't know how to say this," he began huskily.

"Say what?"

Masters' eyes shifted, then, as if by a deliberate effort of will, came back.

"That I'm sorry."

Tony studied him, noted the lines of suffering around his mouth, the shuddering pain in his eyes.

"Yeah, I know how you feel," he muttered. "But I guess you made up for it when you tackled Braker and Yates. They might have been using electric wire on us by now." He grinned lopsidedly, and clapped Masters on the arm. "Forget it, Masters. I'm with you all the way."

Masters managed a smile, and let loose a long breath. He fell into step beside Tony's hurrying stride. "Laurette's O.K."

"Well, lieutenant," said Laurette, stretching lazily, and smiling up at him, "I guess I got weak in the knees at the last minute."

"Didn't we all!" He smiled ruefully. He dropped to his knees. She was still in her pressure suit and lying on the floor. He helped her to a sitting position, and then to her feet.

Overland chuckled, though there was a note of uneasy reminiscence in his tone. "Wait till I tell the boys at Lipton U. about this."

"You'd better not," Laurette warned. She added, "You broke down and admitted the ring was an omen. When a scientist gets superstitious—"

Tony broke in. "Weren't we all?"

Masters said, dropping his eyes, "I guess we had good enough reason to be superstitious about it." His hand went absently upward to his shoulder.

Overland frowned, and, hands behind his back, walked to the empty porthole. "All that work DeTosque, the Farr brothers, Morrell, and myself put in. There's no reason to patch up the asteroids and try to prove they were all one world. But at the same time, there's no proof—no absolute proof—" He clicked his tongue. Then he swung on Tony, biting speculatively at his lower lip, his eyes sharpening.

"There's one thing that needs explaining which probably never will be explained, I guess. It's too bad. Memory? Bah! That's not the answer, lieutenant. You stood in the cave there, and you saw the skeleton, and somehow you *knew* it had existed before the human race, but was not *older* than the human race. It's something else. You didn't pick up the memory from the past—not over a hundred million years. What then?" He turned away, shaking his head, came back abruptly as Tony spoke, eyes sharpening.

"I'll tell you why," Tony said evenly.

His head moved up and down slowly, and his half-lidded eyes looked lingeringly out the porthole toward the mountain where his wrecked patrol ship lay. "Yes, I'll tell you why."

Laurette, Masters and Overland were caught up in tense silence by the strangeness of his tone.

He said faintly: "Laurette and I were trapped alive in the back of the cave when the two worlds crashed. We lived through it. I didn't know she was back there, or course; she recovered consciousness later—at the right time, I'd say!" He grinned at her obliquely, then sobered again. "I saw the skeleton and somehow I was too dazed to realize it couldn't be Laurette. Because when the gravity was dispersed, the tension holding everything back in time was released, and everything went back to the present—just a little less than the present. I'll explain that later."

He drew a long breath.

"This is hard to say. I was in the back of the cave. I felt something strike the mountainside.

"That was my patrol ship—with me in it."

His glance roved around. Overland's breath sucked in audibly.

"Careful now, boy," he rumbled warningly, alarm in his eyes.

Tony's lips twisted. "It happens to be the truth. After my ship crashed I got out. A few minutes later I stood at the mouth of the cave, looking at the skeleton. For a minute, I—remembered. Fragmentary things. The skeleton was—horror.

"And why not? I was also in the back of the cave, thinking that Laurette was dead and that she was the skeleton. The Tony Crow at the mouth of the cave and the Tony Crow trapped in the rear of the cave were *en rapport* to an infinite degree. They were the same person, in two different places at the same time, and their brains were the same."

He stopped.

Masters whispered through his clenched teeth, "Two Tony Crows. It couldn't be."

Tony leaned back against the wall. "There were two rings, at the same time. There were two skeletons, at the same time. Braker had the skeleton's ring on his finger. Amos was wrapped up in a carton with a Christmas sticker on it. They were both some place else. You all know that and admit it. Well, there were two Tony Crows, and if I think about it much longer, it'll drive me—"

"Hold it, boy!" Overland's tone was sharp. Then he said mildly, "It's nothing to get excited about. The mere fact of time-travel presupposes duplicity of existence. Our ship and everything in it was made of electrons that existed somewhere else at the same time—a hundred million years ago, on the pre-asteroid world. You can't get away from it. And you don't have to get scared just because two Tony Crows were a few feet distant from each other. Remember that all the rest of us were duplicated, too. Ship A was thrust *back* into time just an hour or so before Ship B landed here after being thrust *forward*. You see?"

Laurette shuddered. "It's clear, but it's—" She made a confused motion.

Overland's tired, haggard eyes twinkled. "Anyway, there's no danger of us running across ourselves again. The past is done for. That's the main thing."

Neither Laurette nor Tony said anything. They were studying each other, and a smile was beginning at the corner of Laurette's lips. Erle Masters squirmed uncomfortably.

Overland continued, speculatively: "There was an energy loss some place. We weren't snapped back to the real present at all. We should have come back to the present that we left, *plus* the three weeks we stayed back in time. Back there it was Christmas—and Laurette was quite correct when she broke open my package." He grinned crookedly. "But it's still more than three weeks to Christmas here. It was a simple energy loss, I guess. If I had a penc—"

Erle Masters broke in on him, coughing uncomfortably and grinning wryly at the same time. "We'd better get down to the control room and plot out our course, professor."

"What?" Overland's eyes widened. He looked around at the man and girl. "Oh." He studied them, then turned, and clapped Masters on the back. "You're dead right, son. Let's get out!"

"I'm glad you weren't Amos," Tony told the girl.

"I couldn't very well have been, lieutenant."

He grinned, coloring slightly.

Then he took her hands in his, and put his head as close to hers as the helmets would allow.

He said, "When we get back to Earth, I'm going to put a r—" He stopped, biting at his lip. Remembrances of another time, on a pre-asteroid world, flooded back with the thought.

She started, paled. Involuntarily, her eyes turned to the open port, beyond which was a mountain, a cave, a skeleton, a ring.

She nodded, slowly, faintly. "It's a good idea," she murmured. She managed a smile. "But not—an emerald."

THE WEAPONS SHOP

A.E. van Vogt

The village at night made a curiously timeless picture. Fara walked contentedly beside his wife along the street. The air was like wine; and he was thinking dimly of the artist who had come up from Imperial City and made what the telestats called—he remembered the phrase vividly—"a symbolic painting reminiscent of a scene in the electrical age of seven thousand years ago."

Fara believed that utterly. The street before him with its weed-less, automatically tended gardens, its shops set well back among the flowers, its perpetual hard, grassy sidewalks and its street lamps that glowed from every pore of their structure—this was a restful paradise where time had stood still.

And it was like being a part of life that the great artist's picture of this quiet, peaceful scene before him was now in the collection of the empress herself. She had praised it, and naturally the thrice-blest artist had immediately and humbly begged her to accept it.

What a joy it must be to be able to offer personal homage to the glorious, the divine, the serenely gracious and lovely Innelda Isher, one thousand one hundred eightieth of her line.

As they walked, Fara half turned to his wife. In the dim light of the nearest street lamp, her kindly, still youthful face was almost lost in shadow. He murmured softly, instinctively muting his voice to harmonize with the pastel shades of night:

"She said—our empress said—that our little village of Glay seemed to her to have in it all the wholesomeness, the gentleness, that constitutes the finest qualities of her people. Wasn't that a

60

wonderful thought, Creel? She must be a marvelously understanding woman. I—"

He stopped. They had come to a side street, and there was something about a hundred and fifty feet along in that—

"Look!" Fara said hoarsely.

He pointed with rigid arm and finger at a sign that glowed in the night, a sign that read:

FINE WEAPONS
THE RIGHT TO BUY WEAPONS IS THE RIGHT
TO BE FREE

Fara had a strange, empty feeling as he stared at the blazing sign. He saw that other villagers were gathering. He said finally, huskily, "I've heard of these shops. They're places of infamy, against which the government of the empress will act one of these days. They're built in hidden factories, and then transported whole to towns like ours and set up in gross defiance of property rights. That one wasn't there an hour ago."

Fara's face hardened. His voice had a harsh edge in it, as he said, "Creel, go home."

Fara was surprised when Creel did not move off at once. All their married life she had had a pleasing habit of obedience that had made cohabitation a wonderful thing. He saw that she was looking at him wide-eyed, and that it was a timid alarm that held her there. She said, "Fara, what do you intend to do? You're not thinking of—"

"Go home!" Her fear brought out all the grim determination in his nature. "We're not going to let such a monstrous thing desecrate our village. Think of it"—his voice shivered before the appalling thought—"this fine, old-fashioned community, which we had resolved always to keep exactly as the empress has it in her picture gallery, debauched now, ruined by this . . . this thing— But we won't have it; that's all there is to it."

Creel's voice came softly out of the half-darkness of the street corner, the timidity gone from it: "Don't do anything rash, Fara. Remember it is not the first new building to come into Glay—since the picture was painted."

Fara was silent. This was a quality of his wife of which he did not approve, this reminding him unnecessarily of unpleasant facts. He knew exactly what she meant. The gigantic, multitentacled corporation, Automatic Atomic Motor Repair Shops, Inc., had come in

under the laws of the state with their flashy building, against the
wishes of the village council—and had already taken half of Fara's
repair business.

"That's different!" Fara growled finally. "In the first place people
will discover in good time that these new automatic repairers do a
poor job. In the second place it's fair competition. But this weapon
shop is a defiance of all the decencies that make life under the House
of Isher such a joy. Look at the hypocritical sign: 'The right to buy
weapons— ' Aaaaahh!"

He broke off with: "Go home, Creel. We'll see to it that they sell
no weapons in this town."

He watched the slender woman-shape move off into the shadows.
She was halfway across the street when a thought occurred to Fara.
He called, "And if you see that son of ours hanging around some
street corner, take him home. He's got to learn to stop staying out
so late at night."

The shadowed figure of his wife did not turn; and after watching
her for a moment moving along against the dim background of softly
glowing street lights, Fara twisted on his heel, and walked swiftly
toward the shop. The crowd was growing larger every minute and
the night pulsed with excited voices.

Beyond doubt, here was the biggest thing that had ever happened
to the village of Glay.

The sign of the weapon shop was, a normal-illusion affair. No
matter what his angle of view, he was always looking straight at it.
When he paused finally in front of the great display window, the
words had pressed back against the store front, and were staring
unwinkingly down at him.

Fara sniffed once more at the meaning of the slogan, then
forgot the simple thing. There was another sign in the window,
which read:

THE FINEST ENERGY WEAPONS IN THE KNOWN UNIVERSE

A spark of interest struck fire inside Fara. He gazed at that
brilliant display of guns, fascinated in spite of himself. The
weapons were of every size, ranging from tiny little finger pistols
to express rifles. They were made of every one of the light, hard,
ornamental substances: glittering glassein, the colorful but opaque
Ordine plastic, viridescent magnesitic beryllium. And others.

It was the very deadly extent of the destructive display that brought a chill to Fara. So many weapons for the little village of Glay, where not more that two people to his knowledge had guns, and those only for hunting. Why, the thing was absurd, fantastically mischievous, utterly threatening.

Somewhere behind Fara, a man said: "It's right on Lan Harris' lot. Good joke on that old scoundrel. Will he raise a row!"

There was a faint titter from several men, that made an odd patch of sound on the warm, fresh air. And Fara saw that the man had spoken the truth. The weapon shop had a forty-foot frontage. And it occupied the very center of the green, gardenlike lot of tight-fisted old Harris.

Fara frowned. The clever devils, the weapon shop people, selecting the property of the most disliked man in town, coolly taking it over and giving everybody an agreeable titillation. But the very cunning of it made it vital that the trick shouldn't succeed.

He was still scowling anxiously when he saw the plump figure of Mel Dale, the mayor. Fara edged toward him hurriedly, touched his hat respectfully, and said, "Where's Jor?"

"Here." The village constable elbowed his way through a little bundle of men. "Any plans?" he said.

"There's only one plan," said Fara boldly. "Go in and arrest them."

To Fara's amazement, the two men looked at each other, then at the ground. It was the big constable who answered shortly, "Door's locked. And nobody answers our pounding. I was just going to suggest we let the matter ride until morning."

"Nonsense!" His very astonishment made Fara impatient. "Get an ax and we'll break the door down. Delay will only encourage such riffraff to resist. We don't want their kind in our village for so much as a single night. Isn't that so?"

There was a hasty nod of agreement from everybody in his immediate vicinity. Too hasty. Fara looked around puzzled at eyes that lowered before his level gaze. He thought: "They are all scared. And unwilling." Before he could speak, Constable Jor said, "I guess you haven't heard about those doors or these shops. From all accounts, you can't break into them."

It struck Fara with a sudden pang that it was he who would have to act here. He said, "I'll get my atomic cutting machine from my shop. That'll fix them. Have I your permission to do that, Mr. Mayor?"

In the glow of the weapon shop window, the plump man was
sweating visibly. He pulled out a handkerchief and wiped his
forehead. He said, "Maybe I'd better call the commander of the
Imperial garrison at Ferd, and ask them."

"No!" Fara recognized evasion when he saw it. He felt himself
steel; the conviction came that all the strength in this village was
in him. "We must act ourselves. Other communities have let these
people get in because they took no decisive action. We've got to
resist to the limit. Beginning now. This minute. Well?"

The mayor's "All right!" was scarcely more than a sigh of sound.
But it was all Fara needed.

He called out his intention to the crowd; and then, as he pushed
his way out of the mob, he saw his son standing with some other
young men staring at the window display.

Fara called, "Cayle, come and help me with the machine."

Cayle did not even turn; and Fara hurried on, seething. That
wretched boy! One of these days he, Fara, would have to take a
firm action there. Or he'd have a no-good on his hands.

The energy was soundless—and smooth. There was no sputter,
no fireworks. It glowed with a soft, pure white light, almost
caressing the metal panels of the door—but not even beginning
to sear them.

Minute after minute, the dogged Fara refused to believe the
incredible failure, and played the boundlessly potent energy on
that resisting wall. When he finally shut off his machine, he was
perspiring freely.

"I don't understand it," he gasped. "Why—no metal is supposed
to stand up against a steady flood of atomic force. Even the hard
metal plates used inside the blast chamber of a motor take the
explosions in what is called infinite series, so that each one has
unlimited rest. That's the theory, but actually steady running
crystallizes the whole plate after a few months."

"It's as Jor told you," said the mayor. "These weapons shops
are—big. They spread right through the empire, *and* they *don't
recognize the empress*."

Fara shifted his feet on the hard grass, disturbed. He didn't
like this kind of talk. It sounded—sacrilegious. And besides it was
nonsense. It must be. Before he could speak, a man said somewhere
behind him, "I've heard it said that that door will open only to those
who cannot harm the people inside."

The words shocked Fara out of his daze. With a start, and for the first time, he saw that his failure had had a bad psychological effect. He said sharply, "That's ridiculous! If there were doors like that, we'd all have them. We—"

The thought that stopped his words was the sudden realization that *he* had not seen anybody try to open the door; and with all this reluctance around him it was quite possible that—

He stepped forward, grasped at the doorknob and pulled. The door opened with an unnatural weightlessness that gave him the fleeting impression that the knob had come loose in his hand. With a gasp, Fara jerked the door wide open.

"Jor!" he yelled. "Get in!"

The constable made a distorted movement—distorted by what must have been a will to caution, followed by the instant realization that he could not hold back before so many. He leaped awkwardly toward the open door—and it closed in his face.

Fara stared stupidly at his hand, which was still clenched. And then, slowly, a hideous thrill coursed along his nerves. The knob had—withdrawn. It had twisted, become viscous and slipped amorphously from his straining fingers. Even the memory of that brief sensation gave him a feeling of abnormal things.

He grew aware that the crowd was watching with a silent intentness. Fara reached again for the knob, not quite so eagerly this time; and it was only a sudden realization of his reluctance that mad him angry when the handle neither turned nor yielded in any way.

Determination returned in full force, and with it came a thought. He motioned to the constable. "Go back, Jor, while I pull."

The man retreated, but it did no good. And tugging did not help. The door would not open. Somewhere in the crowd, a man said darkly, "It decided to let you in, then it changed its mind."

"What foolishness are you talking!" Fara spoke violently. "*It* changed its mind. Are you crazy? A door has no sense."

But a surge of fear put a half-quaver into his voice. It was the sudden alarm that made him bold beyond all his normal caution. With a jerk of his body, Fara faced the shop.

The building loomed there under the night sky, in itself bright as day, huge in width and length, and alien, menacing, no longer easily conquerable. The dim queasy wonder came as to what the soldiers of the empress would do if they were invited to act. And suddenly—a bare, flashing glimpse of a grim possibility—the feeling grew that even they would be able to do nothing.

Abruptly, Fara was conscious of horror that such an idea could enter his mind. He shut his brain tight, said wildly, "The door opened for me once. It will open again."

It did. Quite simply it did. Gently, without resistance, with that same sensation of weightlessness, the strange, sensitive door followed the tug of his fingers. Beyond the threshold was dimness, a wide, darkened alcove. He heard the voice of Mel Dale behind him, the mayor saying, "Fara, don't be a fool. What will you do inside?"

Fara was vaguely amazed to realize that he had stepped across the threshold. He turned, startled, and stared at the blur of faces. "Why—" he began blankly; then he brightened; he said, "Why, I'll buy a gun, of course."

The brilliance of his reply, the cunning implicit in it, dazzled Fara for half a minute longer. The mood yielded slowly, as he found himself in the dimly lighted interior of the weapons shop.

It was preternaturally quiet inside. Not a sound penetrated from the night from which he had come, and the startled thought came that the people of the shop might actually be unaware that there was a crowd outside.

Fara walked forward gingerly on a rugged floor that muffled his footsteps utterly. After a moment, his eyes accustomed themselves to the soft lighting, which came like a reflection from the walls and ceilings. In a vague way, he had expected ultranormality; and the ordinariness of the atomic lighting acted like a tonic to his tensed nerves.

He shook himself angrily. Why should there be anything really superior? He was getting as bad as those credulous idiots out in the street.

He glanced around with gathering confidence. The place looked quite common. It was a shop, almost scantily furnished. There were showcases, on the walls and on the floor, glitteringly lovely things, but nothing unusual, and not many of them—a few dozens. There was in addition, a double, ornate door leading to a back room—

Fara tried to keep one eye on that door, as he examined several showcases, each with three or four weapons either mounted or arranged in boxes or holsters.

Abruptly, the weapons began to excite him. He forgot to watch the door, as the wild thought struck that he ought to grab one of those guns from a case, and then the moment someone came, force him outside where Jor would perform the arrest and—

Behind him, a man said quietly, "You wish to buy a gun?"

Fara turned with a jump. Brief rage flooded him at the way his plan had been wrecked by the arrival of the clerk.

The anger died as he saw that the intruder was a fine-looking, silver-haired man, older than himself. That was immeasurably disconcerting. Fara had an immense and almost automatic respect for age, and for a long second he could only stand there gaping. He said at last, lamely, "Yes, yes, a gun."

"For what purpose?" said the man in his quiet voice.

Fara could only look at him blankly. It was too fast. He wanted to get mad. He wanted to tell these people what he thought of them. But the age of this representative locked his tongue, tangled his emotions. He managed speech only by an effort of will:

"For hunting." The plausible word stiffened his mind. "Yes, definitely for hunting. There is a lake to the north of here," he went on more fulsomely, glibly, "and—"

He stopped, scowling, startled at the extent of his dishonesty. He was not prepared to go so deeply into prevarication. He said curtly, "For hunting."

Fara was himself again. Abruptly, he hated the man for having put him so completely at a disadvantage. With smoldering eyes he watched the old fellow click open a showcase, and take out a green-shining rifle.

As the man faced him, weapon in hand, Fara was thinking grimly, "Pretty clever, having an old man as a front." It was the same kind of cunning that had made them choose the property of Miser Harris. Icily furious, taut with his purpose, Fara reached for the gun; but the man held it out of his reach, saying, "Before I can even let you test this, I am compelled by the by-laws of the weapons shops to inform you under what circumstances you may purchase a gun."

So they had private regulations. What a system of psychology tricks to impress gullible fools! Well, let the old scoundrel talk. As soon as he, Fara, got hold of the rifle, he'd put an end to hypocrisy.

"We weapons makers," the clerk was saying mildly, "have evolved guns that can, in their particular ranges, destroy any machine or object made of what is called matter. Thus whoever possesses one of our weapons is the equal and more of any soldier of the empress. I say more because each gun is the center of a field of force which acts as a perfect screen against immaterial destructive forces. That screen offers no resistance to clubs or spears or bullets, or other material substances, but it would require a small atomic cannon to penetrate the superb barrier it creates around its owner.

"You will readily comprehend," the man went on, "that such a potent weapon could not be allowed to fall, unmodified, into irresponsible hands. Accordingly, no gun purchased from us may be used for aggression or murder. In the case of hunting rifle, only such specified game birds and animals as we may from time to time list in our display windows may be shot. Finally, no weapon can be resold without our approval. Is that clear?"

Fara nodded dumbly. For the moment, speech was impossible to him. The incredible, fantastically stupid words were still going round and round in his head. He wondered if he ought to laugh out loud, or curse the man for daring to insult his intelligence so tremendously.

So the gun mustn't be used for murder or robbery. So only certain birds and animals could be shot. And as for reselling it, suppose—suppose he bought this thing, took a trip of a thousand miles, and offered it to some wealthy stranger for two credits—who would ever know?

Or suppose he held up the stranger. Or shot him. How could the weapons shop ever find out? The thing was so ridiculous that—

He grew aware that the gun was being held out to him stock first. He took it eagerly, and had to fight the impulse to turn the muzzle directly on the old man. Mustn't rush this, he thought tautly. He said, "How does it work?"

"You simply aim it, and pull the trigger. Perhaps you would like to try it on a target we have."

Fara swung the gun up. "Yes," he said triumphantly, "and you're it. Now, just get over there to the front door, and then outside."

He raised his voice: "And if anybody's thinking of coming through the back door, I've got that covered too."

He motioned jerkily at the clerk. "Quick now, move! I'll shoot! I swear I will."

The man was cool, unflustered. "I have no doubt you would. When we decided to attune the door so that you could enter despite your hostility, we assumed the capacity for homicide. However, this is our party. You had better adjust yourself accordingly, and look behind you—"

There was silence. Finger on trigger, Fara stood motionless. Dim thoughts came of all the *half-things* he had heard in his days about the weapons shops: that they had secret supporters in every district, that they had a private and ruthlesss hidden government, and that once you got into their clutches, the only way out was death and—

But what finally came clear was a mind picture of himself, Fara Clark, family man, faithful subject of the empress, standing here in this dimly lighted store, deliberately fighting an organization so vast and menacing that— He must have been mad.

Only—here he was. He forced courage into his sagging muscles. He said, "You can't fool me with pretending there's someone behind me. Now, get to that door. And *fast!*"

The firm eyes of the old man were looking past him. The man said quietly, "Well, Rad, have you all the data?"

"Enough for a primary," said a young man's baritone voice behind Fara. "Type A-7 conservative. Good average intelligence, but a Monaric development peculiar to small towns. One-sided outlook fostered by the Imperial schools present in exaggerated form. Extremely honest. Reason would be useless. Emotional approach would require extended treatment. I see no reason why we should bother. Let him live his life as it suits him."

"If you think," Fara said shakily, "that that trick voice is going to make me turn, you're crazy. That's the left wall of the building. I know there's no one there."

"I'm all in favor, Rad," said the old man, "of letting him live his life. But he was the prime mover of the crowd outside. I think he should be discouraged."

"We'll advertise his presence," said Rad. "He'll spend the rest of his life denying the charge."

Fara's confidence in the gun had faded so far that, as he listened in puzzled uneasiness to the incomprehensible conversation, he forgot it completely. He parted his lips, but before he could speak, the old man cut in, persistently, "I think a little emotion might have a long-run effect. Show him the palace."

Palace! The startling word tore Fara out of his brief paralysis. "See here," he began, "I can see now that you lied to me. This gun isn't loaded at all. It's—"

His voice failed him. Every muscle in his body went rigid. He stared like a madman. *There was no gun in his hands.*

"Why, you—" he began wildly. And stopped again. His mind heaved with imbalance. With a terrible effort he fought off the spinning sensation, thought finally, tremblingly: Somebody must have sneaked the gun from him. That meant—there was someone behind him. The voice was no mechanical thing. Somehow, they had—

He started to turn—and couldn't. What in the name of— He struggled, pushing with his muscles. And couldn't move, couldn't budge, couldn't even—

The room was growing curiously dark. He had difficulty seeing the old man and— He would have shrieked then if he could. Because the weapons shop was gone. He was—

He was standing in the sky above an immense city.

In the sky, and nothing beneath him, nothing around him but air, and blue summer heaven, and the city a mile, two miles below.

Nothing, nothing— He would have shrieked, but his breath seemed solidly embedded in his lungs. Sanity came back as the remote awareness impinged upon his terrified mind that he was actually standing on a hard floor, and that the city must be a picture somehow focused directly into his eyes.

For the first time, with a start, Fara recognized the metropolis below. It was the city of dreams', Imperial City, capital of the glorious Empress Isher— From his great height, he could see the gardens, the gorgeous grounds of the silver palace, the official Imperial residence itself—

The last tendrils of his fear were fading now before a gathering fascination and wonder; they vanished utterly as he recognized with a ghastly thrill of uncertain expectancy that the palace was drawing nearer at great speed.

"Show him the palace," they had said. Did that mean, could it mean—

That spray of tense thoughts splattered into nonexistence, as the glittering roof flashed straight at his face. He gulped, as the solid metal of it passed through him, and then other walls and ceilings.

His first sense of imminent and mind-shaking desecration came as the picture paused in a great room where a score of men sat around a table at the head of which sat—a young woman.

The inexorable, sacrilegious, limitlessly powered cameras that were taking the picture swung across the table, and caught the woman full face.

It was a handsome face, but there was passion and fury twisting it now, and a very blaze of fire in her eyes, as she leaned forward, and said in a voice at once familiar—how often Fara had heard its calm, measured tones on the telestats—and distorted. Utterly distorted by anger and an insolent certainty of command. That caricature of a beloved voice slashed across the silence as clearly as if he, Fara, was there in that room: "I want that skunk killed, do you understand? I don't care how you do it, but I want to hear by tomorrow night that he's dead."

The picture snapped off and instantly—it was as swift as that—Fara was back in the weapon shop. He stood for a moment, swaying, fighting to accustom his eyes to the dimness; and then—

His first emotion was contempt at the simpleness of the trickery—a motion picture. What kind of a fool did they think he was, to swallow something as transparently unreal as that? He'd—

Abruptly, the appalling lechery of the scheme, the indescribable wickedness of what was being attempted here brought red rage.

"Why, you scum!" he flared. "So you've got somebody to act the part of the empress, trying to pretend that— Why, you—"

"That will do," said the voice of Rad; and Fara shook as a big young man walked into his line of vision. The alarmed thought came that people who would besmirch so vilely the character of her imperial majesty would not hesitate to do physical damage to Fara Clark. The young man went on in a steely tone, "We do not pretend that what you saw was taking place this instant in the palace. That would be too much of a coincidence. But it was taken two weeks ago; the woman *is* the empress. The man whose death she ordered is one of her many former lovers. He was found murdered two weeks ago; his name, if you care to look it up in the new files, is Banton McCreddie. However, let that pass. We're finished with you now and—"

"But I'm not finished," Fara said in a thick voice. "I've never heard or seen so much infamy in all my life. If you think this town is through with you, you're crazy. We'll have a guard on this place day and night, and nobody will get in or out. We'll—"

"That will do." It was the silver-haired man; and Fara stopped out of respect for age, before he thought. The old man went on: "The examination has been most interesting. As an honest man, you may call on us if you are ever in trouble. That is all. Leave through the side door."

It was all. Impalpable forces grabbed him, and he was shoved at a door that appeared miraculously in the wall, where seconds before the palace had been.

He found himself standing dazedly in a flower bed, and there was a swarm of men to his left. He recognized his fellow townsmen and that he was—outside.

The incredible nightmare was over.

"Where's the gun?" said Creel, as he entered the house half an hour later.

"The gun?" Fara stared at his wife.

"It said over the radio a few minutes ago that you were the first customer of the new weapon shop. I thought it was queer, but—"

He was eerily conscious of her voice going on for several words longer, but it was the purest jumble. The shock was so great that he had the horrible sensation of being on the edge of an abyss.

So that was what the young man had meant: "Advertise! We'll advertise his presence and—"

Fara thought: His reputation! Not that his was a great name, but he had long believed with a quiet pride that Fara Clark's motor repair shop was widely known in the community and countryside.

First, his private humiliation inside the shop. And now this—lying—to people who didn't know why he had gone into the store. Diabolical.

His paralysis ended, as a frantic determination to rectify the base charge drove him to the telestat. After a moment, the plump, sleepy face of Mayor Mel Dale appeared on the plate. Fara's voice made a barrage of sound, but his hopes dashed, as the man said, "I'm sorry, Fara. I don't see how you can have free time on the telestat. You'll have to pay for it. They did."

"They did!" Fara wondered vaguely if he sounded as empty as he felt.

"And they've just paid Lan Harris for his lot. The old man asked top price, and got it. He just phoned me to transfer the title."

"Oh!" The world was shattering. "You mean nobody's going to do anything. What about the Imperial garrison at Ferd?"

Dimly, Fara was aware of the mayor mumbling something about the empress' soldiers refusing to interfere in civilian matters.

"Civilian matters!" Fara exploded. "You mean these people are just going to be allowed to come here whether we want them or not, illegally forcing the sale of lots by first taking possession of them?"

A sudden thought struck him breathless. "Look, you haven't changed your mind about having Jor keep guard in front of the shop?"

With a start, he saw that the plump face in the telestat plate had grown impatient. "Now, see here, Fara," came the pompous words, "let the constituted authorities handle this matter."

"But you're going to keep Jor there," Fara said doggedly.

The mayor looked annoyed, said finally peevishly: "I promised, didn't I? So he'll be there. And now—do you want to buy time on the telestat? It's fifteen credits for one minute. Mind you, as a friend, I think you're wasting your money. No one has ever caught up with a false statement."

Fara said grimly, "Put two on, one in the morning, one in the evening."

"All right. We'll deny it completely. Good night."

The telestat went blank; and Fara sat there. A new thought hardened his face. "That boy of ours—there's going to be a showdown. He either works in my shop, or he gets no more allowance."

Creel said: "You've handled him wrong. He's twenty-three and you treat him like a child. Remember, at twenty-three you were a married man."

"That was different," said Fara. "I had a sense of responsibility. Do you know what he did tonight?"

He didn't quite catch her answer. For the moment, he thought she said, "No; in what way did you humiliate him first?"

Fara felt too impatient to verify the impossible words. He rushed on: "He refused in front of the whole village to give me help. He's a bad one, all bad."

"Yes," said Creel in a bitter tone, "he is all bad. I'm sure you don't realize how bad. He's as cold as steel, but without steel's strength or integrity. He took a long time, but he hates even me now, because I stood up for your side so long, knowing you were wrong."

"What's that?" said Fara, startled; then gruffly: "Come, come my dear, we're both upset. Let's go to bed."

He slept poorly.

There were days then when the conviction that this was a personal fight between himself and the weapons shop lay heavily on Fara. Grimly, though it was out of his way, he made a point of walking past the weapon shop, always pausing to speak to Constable Jor and—

On the fourth day, the policeman wasn't there.

Fara waited patiently at first, then angrily: then he walked hastily to his shop, and called Jor's house. No, Jor wasn't home. He was guarding the weapon store.

Fara hesitated. His own shop was piled with work, and he had a guilty sense of having neglected his customers for the first time

in his life. It would be simple to call up the mayor and report Jor's
dereliction. And yet—

He didn't want to get the man into trouble—

Out in the street, he saw that a large crowd was gathering in
front of the weapon shop. Fara hurried. A man he knew greeted
him excitedly: "Jor's been murdered, Fara!"

"Murdered!" Fara stood stock-still, and at first he was not clearly
conscious of the grisly thought that was in his mind: Satisfaction!
A flaming satisfaction. Now, he thought, even the soldiers would
have to act. They—

With a gasp, he realized the ghastly tenor of his thoughts. He
shivered, but finally pushed the sense of shame out of his mind.
He said slowly, "Where's the body?"

"Inside."

"You mean, those . . . scum—" In spite of himself, he hesitated
over the epithet; even now, it was difficult to think of the fine-faced,
silver-haired old man in such terms. Abruptly, his mind hardened;
he flared: "You mean those scum actually killed him, then pulled
his body inside?"

"Nobody saw the killing," said a second man beside Fara, "but
he's gone, hasn't been seen for three hours. The mayor got the
weapons shop on the telestat, but they claim they don't know
anything. They've done away with him, that's what, and now they
are pretending innocence. Well, they won't get out of it as easy as
that. Mayor's gone to phone the soldiers at Ferd to bring up some
big guns and—"

Something of the intense excitement that was in the crowd
surged through Fara, the feeling of big things brewing. It was the
most delicious sensation that had ever tingled along his nerves, and
it was all mixed with a strange pride that he had been so right about
this, that he at least had never doubted that here was evil.

He did not recognize the emotion as the full-flowering joy that
comes to a member of a mob. But his voice shook, as he said,
"Guns? Yes, that will be the answer, and the soldiers will have to
come, of course."

Fara nodded to himself in the immensity of his certainty that
the Imperial soldiers would now have no excuse for not acting. He
started to say something dark about what the empress would do if
she found out that a man had lost his life because the soldiers had
shirked their duty, but the words were drowned in a shout:

"Here comes the mayor! Hey, Mr. Mayor, when are the atomic
cannons due?"

There was more of the same general meaning, as the maʸor's sleek, all-purpose car landed lightly. Some of the questions must have reached his honor, for he stood up in the open two-seater and held up his hand for silence.

To Fara's astonishment, the plump-faced man looked at him with accusing eyes. The thing seemed so impossible that, quite instinctively, Fara looked behind him. But he was almost alone; everybody else had crowded forward.

Fara shook his head, puzzled by that glare; and then, astoundingly, Mayor Dale pointed a finger at him, and said in a voice that trembled, "There's the man who's responsible for the trouble that's come upon us. Stand forward, Fara Clark, and show yourself. You've cost this town seven hundred credits that we could ill afford to spend."

Fara couldn't have moved or spoken to save his life. He just stood there in a maze of dumb bewilderment. Before he could even think, the mayor went on, and there was quivering self-pity in his tone, "We've all known that it wasn't wise to interfere with these weapons shops. So long as the Imperial government leaves them alone, what right have we to set up guards, or act against them? That's what I've thought from the beginning, but this man . . . this . . . this Fara Clark kept after all of us, forcing us to move against our wills, and so now we've got a seven-hundred-credit bill to meet and—"

He broke off with, "I might as well make it brief. When I called the garrison, the commander just laughed and said that Jor would turn up. And I had barely disconnected when there was a money call from Jor. He's on Mars."

He waited for the shouts of amazement to die down. "It'll take three weeks for him to come back by ship, and we've got to pay for it, and Fara Clark is responsible. He—"

The shock was over. Fara stood cold, his mind hard. He said finally, scathingly, "So you're giving up and trying to blame me all in one breath. I say you're all fools."

As he turned away, he heard Mayor Dale saying something about the situation not being completely lost, as he had learned that the weapons shop had been set up in Glay because the village was equidistant from four cities, and that it was the city business the shop was after. This would mean tourists, and accessary trade for the village stores and—

Fara heard no more. Head high, he walked back toward his shop. There were one or two catcalls from the mob, but he ignored them.

He had no sense of approaching disaster, simply a gathering fury
against the weapons shop, which had brought him to this miserable
status among his neighbors.

The worst of it, as the days passed, was the realization that the
people of the weapon shop had no personal interest in him. They
were remote, superior, undefeatable. That unconquerableness was
a dim, suppressed awareness inside Fara.

When he thought of it, he felt a vague fear at the way they had
transferred Jor to Mars in a period of less than three hours, when
all the world knew that the trip by fastest spaceship required nearly
three weeks.

Fara did not go to the express station to see Jor arrive home.
He had heard that the council had decided to charge Jor with
half of the expense of the trip, on the threat of losing his job if
he made a fuss.

On the second night after Jor's return, Fara slipped down
to the constable's house, and handed the officer one hundred
seventy-five credits. It wasn't that he was responsible, he told
Jor, but—

The man was only too eager to grant the disclaimer, provided
the money went with it. Fara returned home with a clearer conscience.

It was on the third day after that the door of his shop banged open
and a man came in. Fara frowned as he saw who it was: Castler, a
village hanger-on. The man was grinning.

"Thought you might be interested, Fara. Somebody came out of
the weapon shop today."

Fara strained deliberately at the connecting bolt of a hard plate
of the atomic motor he was fixing. He waited with a gathering
annoyance that the man did not volunteer further information.
Asking questions would be a form of recognition of the worthless
fellow. A developing curiosity made him say finally, grudgingly, "I
suppose the constable promptly picked him up."

He supposed nothing of the kind, but it was an opening.

"It wasn't a man. It was a girl."

Fara knitted his brows. He didn't like the idea of making trouble
for women. But—the cunning devils! Using a girl, just as they had
used an old man as a clerk. It was a trick that deserved to fail, the
girl probably a tough one who needed rough treatment. Fara said
harshly, "Well, what's happened?"

"She's still out, bold as you please. Pretty thing, too."

The bolt off, Fara took the hard plate over to the polisher, and began patiently the long, careful task of smoothing away the crystals that heat had seared on the once shining metal. The soft throb of the polisher made the background to his next words:

"Has anything been done?"

"Nope. The constable's been told, but he says he doesn't fancy being away from his family for another three weeks, and paying the cost into the bargain."

Fara contemplated that darkly for a minute, as the polisher throbbed on. His voice shook with suppressed fury, when he said finally, "So they're letting them get away with it. It's all been as clever as hell. Can't they see that they mustn't give an inch before these . . . these transgressors. It's like giving countenance to sin."

From the corner of his eye, he noticed that there was a curious grin on the face of the other. It struck Fara suddenly that the man was enjoying his anger. And there was something else in that grin; something—a secret knowledge.

Fara pulled the engine plate away from the polisher. He faced the ne'er-do-well, scathed at him, "Naturally, that sin part wouldn't worry you much."

"Oh," said the man nonchalantly, "the hard knocks of life make people tolerant. For instance, after you know the girl better, you yourself will probably come to realize that there's good in all of us."

It was not so much the words, as the curious I've-got-secret-information tone that made Fara snap: "What do you mean—if I get to know the girl better! I wont't even speak to the brazen creature."

"One can't always choose," the other said with enormous casualness. "Suppose he brings her home."

"Suppose who brings who home?" Fara spoke irritably. "Castler, you—"

He stopped; a dead weight of dismay plumped into his stomach; his whole being sagged. "You mean—" he said.

"I mean," replied Castler with a triumphant leer, "that the boys aren't letting a beauty like her be lonesome. And, naturally, your son was the first to speak to her."

He finished: "They're walkin' together now on Second Avenue, comin' this way, so—"

"Get out of here!" Fara roared. "And stay away from me with your gloating. Get out!"

The man hadn't expected such an ignominious ending. He flushed scarlet, then went out, slamming the door.

Fara stood for a moment, every muscle stiff; then, with an abrupt, jerky movement, he shut off his power, and went out into the street.

The time to put a stop to that kind of thing was—now!

He had no clear plan, just that violent determination to put an immediate end to an impossible situation. And it was all mixed up with his anger against Cayle. How could he have had such a worthless son, he who paid his debts and worked hard, and tried to be decent and to live up to the highest standards of the empress?

A brief, dark thought came to Fara that maybe there was some bad blood on Creel's side. Not from her mother, of course—Fara added the mental thought hastily. *There* was a fine, hard-working woman, who hung on to her money, and who would leave Creel a tidy sum one of these days.

But Creel's father had disappeared when Creel was only a child, and there had been some vague scandal about his having taken up with a telestat actress.

And now Cayle with this weapon shop girl. A girl who had let herself be picked up—

He saw them, as he turned the corner onto Second Avenue. They were walking a hundred feet distant, and heading away from Fara. The girl was tall and slender, almost as big as Cayle, and, as Fara came up, she was saying, "You have the wrong idea about us. A person like you can't get a job in our organization. You belong in the Imperial Service, where they can use young men of good education, good appearance and no scruples. I—"

Fara grasped only dimly that Cayle must have been trying to get a job with these people. It was not clear; and his own mind was too intent on his purpose for it to mean anything at the moment. He said harshly, "Cayle!"

The couple turned, Cayle with the measured unhurriedness of a young man who has gone a long way on the road to steellike nerves; the girl was quicker, but withal dignified.

Fara had a vague, terrified feeling that his anger was too great, self-destroying, but the very violence of his emotions ended that thought even as it came. He said thickly, "Cayle, get home—at once."

Fara was aware of the girl looking at him curiously from strange, gray-green eyes. No shame, he thought, and his rage mounted several degrees, driving away the alarm that came at the sight of the flush that crept into Cayle's cheeks.

The flush faded into a pale, tight-lipped anger, Cayle half-turned to the girl, said, "This is the childish old fool I've got to put up with. Fortunately, we seldom see each other; we don't even eat together. What do you think of him?"

The girl smiled impersonally. "Oh, we know Fara Clark; he's the backbone of the empress in Glay."

"Yes," the boy sneered. "You ought to hear him. He thinks we're living in heaven; and the empress is the divine power. The worst part of it is that there's no chance of his ever getting that stuffy look wiped off his face."

They walked off; and Fara stood there. The very extent of what had happened had drained anger from him as if it had never been. There was the realization that he had made a mistake so great that—

He couldn't grasp it. For long, long now, since Cayle had refused to work in his shop, he had felt this building up to a climax. Suddenly, his own uncontrollable ferocity stood revealed as a partial product of that—deeper—problem.

Only, now that the smash was here, he didn't want to face it—

All through the day in his shop, he kept pushing it out of his mind, kept thinking, would this go on now, as before, Cayle and he living in the same house, not even looking at each other when they met, going to bed at different times, getting up, Fara at 6:30, Cayle at noon? Would *that* go on through all the days and years to come?

When he arrived home, Creel was waiting for him. She said, "Fara, he wants you to loan him five hundred credits, so that he can go to Imperial City."

Fara nodded wordlessly. He brought the money back to the house the next morning, and gave it to Creel, who took it into the bedroom.

She came out a minute later. "He says to tell you goodbye."

When Fara came home that evening, Cayle was gone. He wondered whether he ought to feel relieved or—what?

The days passed. Fara worked. He had nothing else to do, and the gray thought was often in his mind that now he would be doing it till the day he died. Except—

Fool that he was—he told himself a thousand times how big a fool—he kept hoping that Cayle would walk into the shop and say, "Father, I've learned my lesson. If you can ever forgive me, teach me the business, and then you retire to a well-earned rest."

It was exactly a month to a day after Cayle's departure that the telestat clicked on just after Fara had finished lunch. "Money call," it sighed, "money call."

Fara and Creel looked at each other. "Eh," said Fara finally, "money call for us."

He could see from the gray look in Creel's face the thought that was in her mind. He said under his breath: "Damn that boy!"

But he felt relieved. Amazingly relieved! Cayle was beginning to appreciate the value of parents and—

He switched on the viewer. "Come and collect," he said.

The face that came on the screen was heavy-jowled, beetle-browed—and strange. The man said, "This is Clerk Pearton of the Fifth Bank of Ferd. We have received a sight draft on you for ten thousand credits. With carrying charges and government tax, the sum required will be twelve thousand one hundred credits. Will you pay it now or will you come in this afternoon and pay it?"

"B-but . . . b-but—" said Fara. "W-who—"

He stopped, conscious of the stupidity of the question, dimly conscious of the heavy-faced man saying something about the money having been paid out to one Cayle Clark that morning in Imperial City. At last, Fara found his voice:

"But the bank had no right," he expostulated, "to pay out the money without my authority. I—"

The voice cut him off coldly: "Are we then to inform our central that the money was obtained under false pretenses? Naturally, an order will be issued immediately for the arrest of your son."

"Wait . . . wait—" Fara spoke blindly. He was aware of Creel beside him, shaking her head at him. She was as white as a sheet, and her voice was a sick, stricken thing, as she said, "Fara, let him go. He's through with us. We must be as hard—let him go."

The words rang senselessly in Fara's ears. They didn't fit into any normal pattern. He was saying:

"I . . . I haven't got— How about my paying . . . installments? I—"

"If you wish a loan," said Clerk Pearton, "naturally we will be happy to go into the matter. I might say that when the draft arrived, we checked up on your status, and we are prepared to loan you eleven thousand credits on indefinite call with your shop as security. I have the form here, and if you are agreeable, we will switch this call through the registered circuit, and you can sign at once."

"Fara, no."

The clerk went on: "The other eleven hundred credits will have to be paid in cash. Is that agreeable?"

"Yes, yes, of course, I've got twenty-five hund—" He stopped his chattering tongue with a gulp; then: "Yes, that's satisfactory."

The deal completed, Fara whirled on his wife. Out of the depths of his hurt and bewilderment, he raged: "What do you mean, standing there and talking about not paying it? You said several times that I was responsible for his being what he is. Besides, we don't know why he needed the money. He—"

Creel said in a low, dead tone: "In one hour, he's stripped us of our life work. He did it deliberately, thinking of us as two old fools, who wouldn't know any better than to pay it."

Before he could speak, she went on, "Oh, I know I blamed you, but in the final issue, I knew it was he. He was always cold and calculating, but I was weak, and I was sure that if you handled him in a different . . . and besides I didn't want to see his faults for a long time. He—"

"All I see," Fara interrupted doggedly, "is that I have saved our name from disgrace."

His high sense of duty rightly done lasted until midafternoon, when the bailiff from Ferd came to take over the shop.

"But what—" Fara began.

The bailiff said, "The Automatic Atomic Repair Shops, Limited, took over your loan from the bank, and are foreclosing. Have you anything to say?"

"It's unfair," said Fara. "I'll take it to court. I'll—"

He was thinking dazedly: *If the empress ever learned of this, she'd . . . she'd—*

The courthouse was a big, gray building; and Fara felt emptier and colder every second, as he walked along the gray corridors. In Glay, his decision not to give himself into the hands of a bloodsucker of a lawyer had seemed a wise act. Here, in these enormous halls and palatial rooms, it seemed the sheerest folly.

He managed, nevertheless, to give an articulate acount of the criminal act of the bank in first giving Cayle the money, then turning over the note to his chief competitor, apparently within minutes of his signing it. He finished with: "I'm sure, sir, the empress would not approve of such goings-on against honest citizens. I—"

"How dare you," said the cold-voiced creature on the bench, "use the name of her holy majesty in support of your own gross self-interest?"

Fara shivered. The sense of being intimately a member of the empress' great human family yielded to a sudden chill and a vast mind-picture of the ten million icy courts like this, and the myriad malevolent and heartless men—*like this*—who stood between the empress and her loyal subject, Fara.

He thought passionately: If the empress knew what was happening here, how unjustly he was being treated, she would—

Or would she?

He pushed the crowding, terrible doubt out of his mind—came out of his hard reverie with a start, to hear the Cadi saying, "Plaintiff's appeal dismissed, with costs assessed at seven hundred credits, to be divided between the court and the defense solicitor in the ratio of five to two. See to it that the appellant does not leave till the costs are paid. Next case—"

Fara went alone the next day to see Creel's mother. He called first at "Farmer's Restaurant" at the outskirts of the village. The place was, he noted with satisfaction in the thought of the steady stream of money flowing in, half full, though it was only midmorning. But madame wasn't there. Try the feed store.

He found her in the back of the feed store, overseeing the weighing out of grain into cloth measures. The hard-faced old woman heard his story without a word. She said finally, curtly, "Nothing doing, Fara. I'm one who has to make loans often from the bank to swing deals. If I tried to set you up in business, I'd find the Automatic Atomic Repair people getting after me. Besides, I'd be a fool to turn money over to a man who lets a bad son squeeze a fortune out of him. Such a man has no sense about worldly things.

"And I won't give you a job because I don't hire relatives in my business." She finished: "Tell Creel to come and live at my house. I won't support a man, though. That's all."

He watched her disconsolately for a while, as she went on calmly superintending the clerks who were manipulating the old, no longer accurate measuring machines. Twice her voice echoed through the dust-filled interior, each time with a sharp: "That's overweight, a gram at least. Watch your machine."

Though her back was turned. Fara knew by her posture that she was still, aware of his presence. She turned at last with an abrupt movement and said, "Why don't you go to the weapons shop? You haven't anything to lose and you can't go on like this."

Fara went out, then, a little blindly. At first the suggestion that he buy a gun and commit suicide had no real personal application. But he felt immeasurably hurt that his mother-in-law should have made it.

Kill himself? Why, it was ridiculous. He was still only a young man, going on fifty. Given the proper chance, with his skilled hands, he could wrest a good living even in a world where automatic machines were encroaching everywhere. There was always room for a man who did a good job. His whole life had been based on that credo.

Kill himself—

He went home to find Creel packing. "It's the common sense thing to do," she said. "We'll rent the house and move into rooms."

He told her about her mother's offer to take her in, watching her face as he spoke. Creel shrugged.

"I told her 'No' yesterday," she said thoughtfully. "I wonder why she mentioned it to you."

Fara walked swiftly over to the great front window overlooking the garden, with its flowers, its pool, its rockery. He tried to think of Creel away from this garden of hers, this home of two thirds a lifetime, Creel living in rooms—and knew what her mother had meant. There was one more hope—

He waited till Creel went upstairs, then called Mel Dale on the telestat. The mayor's plump face took on an uneasy expression as he saw who it was.

But he listened pontifically, said finally, "Sorry, the council does not loan money; and I might as well tell you, Fara—I have nothing to do with this, mind you—but you can't get a license for a shop any more."

"W-what?"

"I'm sorry!" The mayor lowered his voice. "Listen, Fara, take my advice, and go to the weapon shop. These places have their uses."

There was a click, and Fara sat staring at the blank face of the viewing screen.

So it was to be—death!

He waited until the street was empty of human beings, then slipped across the boulevard, past a design of flower gardens, and so to the door of the shop. The brief fear came that the door wouldn't open, but it did, effortlessly.

As he emerged from the dimness of the alcove into the shop proper, he saw the silver-haired old man sitting in a corner chair, reading under a softly bright light. The old man looked up, put aside his book, then rose to his feet.

"It's Mr. Clark," he said quietly. "What can we do for you?"

A faint flush crept into Fara's cheeks. In a dim fashion, he had hoped that he would not suffer the humiliation of being recognized; but now that his fear was realized, he stood his ground stubbornly. The important thing about killing himself was that there be no body for Creel to bury at great expense. Neither knife nor poison would satisfy that basic requirement.

"I want a gun," said Fara, "that can be adjusted to disintegrate a body six feet in diameter in a single shot. Have you that kind?"

Without a word, the old man turned to a showcase, and brought forth a sturdy gem of a revolver that glinted with all the soft colors of the inimitable Ordine plastic. The old man said in a precise voice. "Notice the flanges on this barrel are little more than bulges. This makes the model ideal for carrying in a shoulder holster under the coat; it can be drawn very swiftly because, when properly attuned, it will leap toward the reaching hand of its owner. At the moment it is attuned to me. Watch while I replace it in its holster and—"

The speed of the draw was absolutely amazing. The old man's fingers moved; and the gun, four feet away, was in them. There was no blur of movement. It was like the door the night that it had slipped from Fara's grasp, and slammed noiselessly in Constable Jor's face. *Instantaneous!*

Fara, who had parted his lips as the old man was explaining, to protest the utter needlessness of illustrating any quality of the weapon except what he had asked for, closed them again. He stared in a brief, dazed fascination; and something of the wonder that was here held his mind and his body.

He had seen and handled the guns of soldiers, and they were simply ordinary metal or plastic things that one used clumsily like any other material substance, not like this at all, not possessed of a dazzling life of their own, leaping with an intimate eagerness to assist with all their superb power the will of their master. They—

With a start, Fara remembered his purpose. He smiled wryly, and said, "All this is very interesting. But what about the beam that can fan out?"

The old man said calmly, "At pencil thickness, this beam will pierce any body except certain alloys of lead up to four hundred yards. With proper adjustment of the firing nozzle, you can disintegrate a six-foot object at fifty yards or less. This screw is the adjustor."

He indicated a tiny device in the muzzle itself. "Turn it to the left to spread the beam, to the right to close it."

Fara said, "I'll take the gun. How much is it?"

He saw that the old man was looking at him thoughtfully; the oldster said finally, slowly, "I have previously explained our regulations to you, Mr. Clark. You recall them, of course?"

"Eh!" said Fara, and stopped, wide-eyed. It wasn't that he didn't remember them. It was simply—

"You mean," he gasped, "those things actually apply. They're not—"

With a terrible effort, he caught his spinning brain and blurring voice. Tense and cold, he said, "All I want is a gun that will shoot in self-defense, but which I can turn on myself if I have to or—want to."

"Oh, suicide!" said the old man. He looked as if a great understanding had suddenly dawned on him. "My dear sir, we have no objection to your killing yourself at any time. That is your personal privilege in a world where privileges grow scanter every year. As for the price of this revolver, it's four credits."

"Four cre . . . only four credits!" said Fara.

He stood, absolutely astounded, his whole mind snatched from its dark purpose. Why, the plastic alone was—and the whole gun with its fine, intricate workmanship—twenty-five credits would have been dirt cheap.

He felt a brief thrill of utter interest; the mystery of the weapon shops suddenly loomed as vast and important as his own black destiny. But the old man was speaking again:

"And now, if you will remove your coat, we can put on the holster—"

Quite automatically, Fara complied. It was vaguely startling to realize that, in a few seconds, he would be walking out of here, equipped for self-murder, and that there was now not a single obstacle to his death.

Curiously, he was disappointed. He couldn't explain it, but somehow there had been in the back of his mind a hope that these shops might, just might—what?

What indeed? Fara sighed wearily—and grew aware again of the old man's voice, saying:

"Perhaps you would prefer to step out of our side door. It is less conspicuous than the front."

There was no resistance in Fara. He was dimly conscious of the man's fingers on his arm, half guiding him; and then the old man pressed one of several buttons on the wall—so that's how it was done—and there was the door.

He could see flowers beyond the opening; without a word he walked toward them. He was outside before he realized it.

Fara stood for a moment in the neat little pathway, striving to grasp the finality of his situation. But nothing would come except a curious awareness of many men around him; for a long second, his brain was like a fog drifting along a stream at night.

Through that darkness grew consciousness of something wrong; the wrongness was there in the back of his mind, as he turned leftward to go to the front of the weapon store.

Vagueness transformed to a shocked, startled sound. For—he was not in Glay, and the weapon shop *wasn't* where it had been. In its place—

A dozen men brushed past Fara to join a long line of men farther along. But Fara was immune to their presence, their strangeness. His whole mind, his whole vision, his very being was concentrating on the section of machine that stood where the weapon shop had been.

A machine, oh, a machine—

His brain lifted, up in his effort to grasp the tremendousness of the dull-metaled immensity of what was spread here under a summer sun beneath a sky as blue as a remote southern sea.

The machine towered into the heavens, five great tiers of metal, each a hundred feet high; and the superbly streamlined five hundred feet ended in a peak of light, a gorgeous spire that tilted straight up a sheer two hundred feet farther, and matched the very sun for brightness.

And it *was* a machine, not a building, because the whole lower tier was alive with shimmering lights, mostly green, but sprinkled colorfully with red and occasionally a blue and yellow. Twice, as Fara watched, green lights directly in front of him flashed unscintillatingly into red.

The second tier was alive with white and red lights, although there were only a fraction as many lights as on the lowest tier. The third section had on its dull-metal surface only blue and yellow lights; they twinkled softly here and there over the vast area.

The fourth tier was a series of signs that brought the beginning of comprehension. The whole sign was:

WHITE   —   BIRTHS
RED   —   DEATHS
GREEN   —   LIVING
BLUE   —   IMMIGRATION TO EARTH
YELLOW   —   EMIGRATION

The fifth tier was also all sign, finally explaining:

POPULATIONS

SOLAR SYSTEM	19,174,463,747
EARTH	11,193,247,361
MARS	1,097,298,604
VENUS	5,141,053,811
MOONS	1,742,863,971

The numbers changed, even as he looked at them, leaping up and down, shifting below and above what they had first been. People were dying, being born, moving to Mars, to Venus, to the moons of Jupiter, to Earth's moon, and others coming back again, landing minute by minute in the thousands of spaceports. Life went on in its gigantic fashion—and here was the stupendous record. Here was—

"Better get in line," said a friendly voice beside Fara. "It takes quite a while to put through an individual case, I understand."

Fara stared at the man. He had the distinct impression of having had senseless words flung at him. "In line?" he started—and stopped himself with a jerk that hurt his throat.

He was moving forward, blindly, ahead of the younger man, thinking a curious jumble that this must have been how Constable Jor was transported to Mars—when another of the man's words penetrated.

"Case?" said Fara violently. "Individual case!"

The man, a heavy-faced, blue-eyed young chap of around thirty-five, looked at him curiously: "You must know why you're here," he said. "Surely, you wouldn't have been sent through here unless you had a problem of some kind that the weapons shop courts will solve for you; there's no other reason for coming to Information Center."

Fara walked on because he was in the line now, a fast-moving line that curved him inexorably around the machine; and seemed to be heading him toward a door that led into the interior of the great metal structure.

So it was a building as well as a machine.

A problem, he was thinking, why, of course, he had a problem, a hopeless, insoluble, completely tangled problem so deeply rooted in the basic structure of Imperial civilization that the whole world would have to be overturned to make it right.

With a start, he saw that he was at the entrance. And the awed thought came: In seconds he would be committed irrevocably to—what?

Inside was a long, shining corridor, with scores of completely transparent hallways leading off the main corridor. Behind Fara, the young man's voice said, "There's one, practically empty. Let's go."

Fara walked ahead; and suddenly he was trembling. He had already noticed that at the end of each side hallway were dozen young women sitting at desks, interviewing men and . . . and, good heavens, was it possible that all this meant—

He grew aware that he had stopped in front of one of the girls.

She was older than she had looked from a distance, over thirty, but good-looking, alert. She smiled pleasantly, but impersonally, and said, "Your name, please?"

He gave it before he thought and added a mumble about being from the village of Glay. The woman said, "Thank you. It will take a few minutes to get your file. Won't you sit down?"

He hadn't noticed the chair. He sank into it; and his heart beating so wildly that he felt chocked. The strange thing was that there was scarcely a thought in his head, nor a real hope; only an intense, almost mind-wrecking excitement.

With a jerk, he realized that the girl was speaking again, but only snatches of her voice came through that screen of tension in his mind:

"—Information Center is . . . in effect . . . a bureau of statistics. Every person born . . . registered here . . . their education, change of address . . . occupation . . . and the highlights of their life. The whole is maintained by . . . combination of . . . unauthorized and unsuspected liaison with Imperial Chamber of Statistics and . . . through medium of agents . . . in every community—"

It seemed to Fara that he was missing vital information, and that if he could only force his attention and hear more— He strained, but it was no use; his nerves were jumping madly and—

Before he could speak, there was a click, and a thin, dark plate slid onto the woman's desk. She took it up and examined it. After a moment, she said something into a mouthpiece, and in a short time two more plates precipitated out of the empty air onto her desk. She studied them passively, looked up finally.

"You will be interested to know," she said, "that your son, Cayle, bribed himself into a commission in the Imperial army with five thousand credits."

"Eh?" said Fara. He half rose from his chair, but before he could say anything, the young woman was speaking again, firmly, "I must inform you that the weapon shops take no action against individuals. Your son can have his job, the money he stole; we are not concerned with moral correction. That must come naturally from the individual, and from the people as a whole—and now if you will give me a brief account of your problem for the record and the court."

Sweating, Fara sank back into his seat; his mind was heaving; most desperately, he wanted more information about Cayle. He began: "But . . . but what . . . how—" He caught himself; and in a low voice described what had happened. When he finished, the girl said, "You will proceed now to the Name Room; watch for your name, and when it appears go straight to Room 474. Remember, 474—and now, the line is waiting, if you please—"

She smiled politely, and Fara was moving off almost before he realized it. He half turned to ask another question, but an old man was sinking into his chair. Fara hurried on, along a great corridor, conscious of curious blasts of sound coming from ahead.

Eagerly, he opened the door; and the sound crashed at him with all the impact of a sledgehammer blow.

It was such a colossal, incredible sound that he stopped short, just inside the door, shrinking back. He stood then trying to blink sense into a visual confusion that rivaled in magnitude that incredible tornado of noise.

Men, men, men everywhere; men by the thousands in a long, broad auditorium, packed into rows of seats, pacing with an abandon of restlessness up and down aisles, and all of them staring with a frantic interest at a long board marked off into squares, each square lettered from the alphabet, from A, B, C, and so on to Z. The tremendous board with its lists of names ran the full length of the immense room.

The Name Room, Fara was thinking shakily, as he sank into a seat—and his name would come up in the C's, and then—

It was like sitting in at a no-limit poker game, watching the jewel-precious cards turn up. It was like playing the exchange with all the world at stake during a stock crash. It was nerve-racking, dazzling, exhausting, fascinating, terrible, mind-destroying, stupendous. It was—

It was like nothing else on the face of the earth.

New names kept flashing on to the twenty-six squares; and men would shout like insane beings and some fainted, and the uproar was absolutely shattering; the pandemonium raged on, one continuous, unbelievable sound.

And every few minutes a great sign would flash along the board, telling everyone:

"WATCH YOUR OWN INITIALS."

Fara watched, trembling in every limb. Each second it seemed to him that he couldn't stand it an instant longer. He wanted to scream at the room to be silent; he wanted to jump up to pace the floor, but others who did that were yelled at hysterically, threatened wildly, hated with a mad, murderous ferocity.

Abruptly, the blind savagery of it scared Fara. He thought unsteadily: "I'm not going to make a fool of myself. I—"

"Clark, Fara—" winked the board. "Clark, Fara—"

With a shout that nearly tore off the top of his head, Fara leaped to his feet. "That's me!" he shrieked. "Me!"

No one turned; no one paid the slightest attention. Shamed, he slunk across the room where an endless line of men kept crowding into a corridor beyond.

The silence in the long corridor was almost as shattering as the mind-destroying noise it replaced. It was hard to concentrate on the idea of a number—474.

It was completely impossible to imagine what could lie beyond—474.

The room was small. It was furnished with a small, business-type table and two chairs. On the table were seven neat piles of folders, each file a different color. The piles were arranged in a row in front of a large, milky-white globe, that began to glow with a soft light. Out of its depths, a man's baritone voice said, "Fara Clark?"

"Yes," said Fara.

"Before the verdict is rendered in your case," the voice went on quietly, "I want you to take a folder from the blue pile. The list will show the Fifth Interplanetary Bank in its proper relation to yourself and the world, and it will be explained to you in due course."

The list, Fara saw, was simply that, a list of names of companies. The names ran from A to Z, and there were about five hundred of them. The folder carried no explanation; and Fara slipped it automatically into his side pocket, as the voice came again from the shining globe: "It has been established," the words came precisely, "that the Fifth Interplanetary Bank perpetrated upon you a gross swindle, and that it is further guilty of practicing scavengery, deception, blackmail and was accessory in a criminal conspiracy.

"The bank made contact with your son, Cayle, through what is quite properly known as a scavenger, that is, an employee who exists by finding young men and women who are normally capable of drawing drafts on their parents or other victims. The scavenger obtains for this service a commission of eight percent, which is always paid by the person making the loan, in this case your son.

"The bank practiced deception in that its authorized agents deceived you in the most culpable fashion by pretending that it had already paid out the ten thousand credits to your son, whereas the money was not paid until your signature had been obtained.

"The blackmail guilt arises out of a threat to have your son arrested for falsely obtaining a loan, a threat made at a time when no money had exchanged hands. The conspiracy consists of the action whereby your note was promptly turned over to your competitor.

"The bank is accordingly triple-fined, thirty-six thousand three hundred credits. It is not in our interest, Fara Clark, for you to know how this money is obtained. Suffice to know that the bank pays it, and that of the fine the weapon shops allocate to their own treasury a total of one half. The other half—"

There was a *plop*; a neatly packaged pile of bills fell onto the table. "For you," said the voice; and Fara, with trembling fingers, slipped the package into his coat pocket. It required the purest mental and physical effort for him to concentrate on the next words that came:

"You must not assume that your troubles are over. The re-establishment of your motor repair shop in Glay will require force and courage. Be discreet, brave and determined, and you cannot fail. Do not hesitate to use the gun you have purchased in defense of your rights. The plan will be explained to you. And now, proceed through the door facing you—"

Fara braced himself with an effort, opened the door and walked through.

It was a dim, familiar room that he stepped into, and there was a silver-haired, fine-faced man who rose from a reading chair, and came forward in the dimness, smiling gravely.

The stupendous, fantastic, exhilarating adventure was over; and he was back in the weapon shop of Glay.

He couldn't get over the wonder of it—this great and fascinating organization established here in the very heart of a ruthless civilization, a civilization that had in a few brief weeks stripped him of everything he possessed.

With a deliberate will, he stopped that glowing flow of thought. A dark frown wrinkled his solidly built face; he said, "The . . . judge—" Fara hesitated over the name, frowned again, annoyed at himself, then went on: "The judge said that, to reestablish myself I would have to—"

"Before we go into that," said the old man quietly, " I want you to examine the blue folder you brought with you."

"Folder?" Fara echoed blankly. It took a long moment to remember that he had picked up a folder from the table in Room 474.

He studied the list of company names with a gathering puzzlement, noting that the name of Automatic Atomic Motor Repair Shops was well down among the A's, and the fifth Interplanetary Bank only one of several great banks included. Fara looked up finally:

"I don't understand," he said: "are these the the companies you have had to act against?"

The silver-haired man smiled grimly, shook his head. "That is not what I meant. These firms constitute only a fraction of the eight hundred thousand companies that are constantly in our books."

He smiled again, humorlessly: "These companies all know that, because of us, their profits on paper bear no relation to their assets. What they don't know is how great the difference really is; and, as we want a general improvement in business morals, not merely more skillful scheming to outwit us, we prefer them to remain in ignorance."

He paused, and this time he gave Fara a searching glance, said at last: "The unique feature of the companies on this particular list is that they are every one wholly owned by Empress Isher."

He finished swiftly: "In view of your past opinions on that subject, I do not expect you to believe me."

Fara stood as still as death, for—he did believe with unquestioning conviction, completely, finally. The amazing, the unforgivable thing was that all his life he had watched the march of ruined men into the oblivion of poverty and disgrace—and blamed *them*.

Fara groaned. "I've been like a madman," he said. "Everything the empress and her officials did was right. No friendship, no personal relationship could survive with me that did not include belief in things as they were. I suppose if I started to talk against the empress I would receive equally short shrift."

"Under no circumstances," said the old man grimly, "must you say anything against her majesty. The weapons shops will not countenance any such words, and will give no further aid to anyone who is so indiscreet. The reason is that, for the moment, we have reached an uneasy state of peace with the Imperial government. We wish to keep it that way; beyond that I will not enlarge on our policy.

"I am permitted to say that the last great attempt to destroy the weapon shops was made seven years ago, when the glorious Innelda Isher was twenty-five years old. That was a secret attempt, based on a new invention; and failed by purest accident because of our sacrifice of a man from seven thousand years in the past. That may sound mysterious to you, but I will not explain.

"The worst period was reached some forty years ago when every person who was discovered receiving aid from us was murdered in some fashion. You may be surprised to know that your father-in-law was among those assassinated at that time."

"Creel's father!" Fara gasped. "But—"

He stopped. His brain was reeling; there was such a rush of blood to his head that for an instant he could hardly see.

"But," he managed at last, "it was reported that he ran away with another woman."

"They always spread a vicious story of some kind," the old man said; and Fara was silent, stunned.

The other went on: "We finally put a stop to their murders by killing the three men from the top down, *excluding* the royal family, who gave the order for the particular execution involved. But we do not again want that kind of bloody murder.

"Nor are we interested in any criticism of our toleration of so much that is evil. It is important to understand that *we do not interfere in the main stream of human existence.* We right wrongs; we act as a barrier between the people and their more ruthless exploiters. Generally speaking, we help only honest men; that is not to say that we do not give assistance to the less scrupulous, but only to the extent of selling them guns—which is a very great aid indeed, and which is one of the reasons why the government is relying almost exclusively for its power on an economic chicanery.

"In the four thousand years since the brilliant genius Walter
S. DeLany invented the vibration process that made the weapon
shops possible, and laid down the first principles of weapons shop
political philosophy, we have watched the tide of government swing
backward and forward between democracy under a limited monar-
chy to complete tyranny. And we have discovered one thing:

"*People always have the kind of government they want.* When they
want change, they must change it. As always we shall remain an
incorruptible core—and I mean that literally; we have a psychological machine that never lies about a man's character—I repeat,
an incorruptible core of human idealism, devoted to relieving the
ills that arise inevitably under any form of government.

"But now—your problem. It is very simple, really. You must
fight, as all men have fought since the beginning of time for what
they valued, for their just rights. As you know, the Automatic
Repair people removed all your machinery and tools within an hour
or foreclosing on your shop. This material was taken to Ferd, and
then shipped to a great warehouse on the coast.

"We recovered it, and with our special means of transportation
have now replaced the machines in your shop. You will accordingly
go there and—"

Fara listened with a gathering grimness to the instructions,
nodded finally, his jaw clamped tight.

"You can count on me," he said curtly. "I've been a stubborn
man in my time; and though I've changed sides, I haven't changed
that."

Going outside was like returning from life to—death; from hope
to—reality.

Fara walked along the quiet streets of Glay at darkest night.
For the first time it struck him that the weapon shop Information
Center must be halfway around the world, for it had been day,
brilliant day.

The picture vanished as if it had never existed, and he grew aware
again, preternaturally aware of the village of Glay asleep all around
him. Silent, peaceful—yet ugly, he thought, ugly with the ugliness
of evil enthroned.

He thought: The right to buy weapons—and his heart swelled
into his throat; the tears came to his eyes.

He wiped his vision clear with the back of his hand, thought of
Creel's long dead father, and strode on, without shame. Tears were
good for an angry man.

The shop was the same, but the hard metal padlock yielded before the tiny, blazing, supernal power of the revolver. One flick of fire; the metal dissolved—and he was inside.

It was dark, too dark to see, but Fara did not turn on the lights immediately. He fumbled across to the window control, turned the windows to darkness vibration, and then click on the lights.

He gulped with awful relief. For the machines, his precious tools that he had seen carted away within hours after the bailiff's arrival, were here again, ready for use.

Shaky from the pressure of his emotion, Fara called Creel on the telestat. It took a little while for her to appear; and she was in her dressing robe. When she saw who it was she turned a dead white.

"Fara, oh, Fara, I thought—"

He cut her off grimly: "Creel, I've been to the weapon shop. I want you to do this: go straight to your mother. I'm here at my shop. I'm going to stay here day and night until it's settled that I *stay*. . . . I shall go home later for some food and clothing, but I want you to be gone by then. Is that clear?"

Color was coming back into her lean, handsome face. She said: "Don't you bother coming home, Fara. I'll do everything necessary. I'll pack all that's needed into the carplane, including a folding bed. We'll sleep in the back room of the shop."

Morning came palely, but it was ten o'clock before a shadow darkened the open door; and Constable Jor came in. He looked shamefaced.

"I've got an order here for your arrest," he said.

"Tell those who sent you," Fara replied deliberately, "that I resisted arrest—with a gun."

The deed followed the words with such rapidity that Jor blinked. He stood like that for a moment, a big, sleepy-looking man, staring at that gleaming, magical revolver; then:

"I have a summons here ordering you to appear at the great court of Ferd this afternoon. Will you accept it?"

"Certainly."

"Then you will be there?"

"I'll send my lawyer," said Fara. "Just drop the summons on the floor there. Tell them I took it."

The weapons shop man had said, "Do not ridicule by word any legal measure of the Imperial authorities. Simply disobey them."

Jor went out, and seemed relieved. It took an hour before Mayor Mel Dale came pompously through the door.

"See here, Fara Clark," he bellowed from the doorway. "You can't get away with this. This is defiance of the law."

Fara was silent as His Honor waddled farther into the building. It was puzzling, almost amazing, that Mayor Dale would risk his plump, treasured body. Puzzlement ended as the mayor said in a low voice. "Good work, Fara; I knew you had it in you. There's dozens of us in Glay behind you, so stick it out. I had to yell at you just now, because there's a crowd outside. Yell back at me, will you? Let's have a real name calling. But, first, a word of warning: the manager of the Automatic Repair Shop is on his way here with his bodyguards, two of them—"

Shakily, Fara watched the mayor go out. The crisis was at hand. He braced himself, thought: *Let them come, let them—*

It was easier than he had thought—for the men who entered the shop turned pale when they saw the holstered revolver. There was a violence of blustering, nevertheless, that narrowed finally down to:

"Look here," the man said, "we've got your note for twelve thousand one hundred credits. You're not going to deny you owe that money."

"I'll buy it back," said Fara in a stony voice, "for exactly half, not a cent more."

The strong-jawed young man looked at him for a long time. "We'll take it," he said finally, curtly.

Fara said, "I've got the agreement here—"

His first customer was old man Miser Lan Harris. Fara stared at the long-faced oldster with a vast surmise, and his first, amazed comprehension came of how the weapons shop must have settled on Harris' lot—by arrangement.

It was an hour after Harris had gone that Creel's mother stamped into the shop. She closed the door.

"Well," she said, "you did it, eh? Good work. I'm sorry if I seemed rough with you when you came to my place, but we weapon shop supporters can't afford to take risks for those who are not on our side.

"But never mind that. I've come to take Creel home. The important thing is to return everything to normal as quickly as possible."

It was over; incredibly it was over. Twice, as he walked home that night, Fara stopped in midstride, and wondered if it had not all been a dream. The air was like wine. The little world of Glay spread before him, green and gracious, a peaceful paradise where time had stood still.

NERVES

Lester del Rey

The graveled walks between the sprawling, utilitarian structures of the National Atomic Products Co., Inc., were crowded with the usual five o'clock mass of young huskies just off work or going on the extra shift, and the company cafeteria was jammed to capacity and overflowing. But they made good-natured way for Doc Ferrel as he came out, not bothering to stop their horseplay as they would have done with any of the other half hundred officials of the company. He'd been just Doc to them too long for any need of formality.

He nodded back at them easily, pushed through, and went down the walk toward the Infirmary Building, taking his own time. When a man has turned fifty, with gray hairs and enlarged waistline to show for it, he begins to realize that comfort and relaxation are worth cultivating. Besides, Doc could see no good reason for filling his stomach with food and then rushing around in a flurry that gave him no chance to digest it. He let himself in the side entrance, palming his cigar out of long habit, and passed through the surgery to the door marked:

PRIVATE
ROGER T. FERREL
PHYSICIAN IN CHARGE

As always, the little room was heavy with the odor of stale smoke and littered with scraps of this and that. His assistant was already there, rummaging busily through the desk with the brass

97

nerve that was typical of him; Ferrel had no objections to it, though, since Blake's rock-steady hands and unruffled brain were always dependable in a pinch of any sort.

Blake looked up and grinned confidently. "Hi, Doc. Where the deuce do you keep your cigarettes, anyway? Never mind, got 'em. . . . Ah, that's better! Good thing there's one room in this darned building where the 'No Smoking' signs don't count. You and the wife coming out this evening?"

"Not a chance, Blake." Ferrel stuck the cigar back in his mouth and settled down into the old leather chair, shaking his head. "Palmer phoned down half an hour ago to ask me if I'd stick through the graveyard shift. Seems the plant's got a rush order for some particular batch of dust that takes about twelve hours to cook, so they'll be running No. 3 and 4 till midnight or later."

"Hm-m-m. So you're hooked again. I don't see why any of us has to stick here—nothing serious ever pops up now. Look what I had today; three cases of athlete's foot—better send a memo down to the showers for extra disinfection—a guy with dandruff, four running noses, and the office boy with a sliver in his thumb! They bring everything to us except their babies—and they'd have them here if they could—but nothing that couldn't wait a week or a month. Anne's been counting on you and the missus, Doc; she'll be disappointed if you aren't there to celebrate her sticking ten years with me. Why don't you let the kid stick it out alone tonight?"

"I wish I could, but this happens to be my job. As a matter of fact, though, Jenkins worked up an acute case of duty and decided to stay on with me tonight." Ferrel twitched his lips in a stiff smile, remembering back to the time when his waistline had been smaller than his chest and he'd gone through the same feeling that destiny had singled him out to save the world. "The kid had his first real case today, and he's all puffed up. Handled it all by himself, so he's now Dr. Jenkins, if you please."

Blake had his own memories. "Yeah? Wonder when he'll realize that everything he did by himself came from your hints? What was it, anyway?"

"Same old story—simple radiation burns. No matter how much we tell the men when they first come in, most of them can't see why they should wear three ninety-five percent efficient shields when the main converter shield cuts off all but one-tenth percent of the radiation. Somehow, this fellow managed to leave off his two inner shields and pick up a year's burn in six hours. Now he's probably

back on No. 1, still running through the hundred liturgies I gave
him to say and hoping we won't get him sacked."

No. 1 was the first converter around which National Atomic
had built its present monopoly in artificial radioactives, back in the
days when shields were still inefficient to one part in a thousand and
the materials handled were milder than the modern ones. They still
used it for the gentle reactions, prices of converters being what they
were; anyhow, if reasonable precautions were taken, there was no
serious danger.

"A tenth percent will kill; five percent there of is one two-
hundredth; five percent of that is one four-thousandth; and five
percent again leaves one eighty-thousandth, safe for all but fools."
Blake sing-songed the liturgy solemnly, then chuckled. "You're
getting old, Doc; you used to give them a thousand times. Well,
if you get the chance, you and Mrs. Ferrel drop out and say hello,
even if it's after midnight. Anne's gonna be disappointed, but she
ought to know how it goes. So long."

"'Night." Ferrel watched him leave, still smiling faintly. Some
day his own son would be out of medical school, and Blake
would make a good man for him to start under and begin the
same old grind upward. First, like young Jenkins, he'd be filled
with his mission to humanity, tense and uncertain, but somehow
things would roll along through Blake's stage and up, probably
to Doc's own level, where the same old problems were solved
in the same old way, and life settled down into a comfortable,
mellow dullness.

There were worse lives, certainly, even though it wasn't like
the mass of murders, kidnapings and applied miracles played up
in the current movie series about Dr. Hoozis. Come to think of
it, Hoozis was supposed to be working in an atomic products plant
right now—but one where chrome-plated converters covered with
pretty neon tubes were mysteriously blowing up every second day,
and men were brought in with blue flames all over them to be cured
instantly in time to utter the magic words so the hero could dash
in and put out the atomic flame barehanded. Ferrel grunted and
reached back for his old copy of the 'Decameron.'

Then he heard Jenkins out in the surgery, puttering around
with quick, nervous little sounds. Never do to let the boy find him
loafing back here, when the possible fate of the world so obviously
hung on his alertness. Young doctors had to be disillusioned slowly,
or they became bitter and their work suffered. Yet, in spite of his
amusement at Jenkins' nervousness, he couldn't help envying the

thin-faced young man's erect shoulders and flat stomach. Years crept by, it seemed.

Jenkins straightened out a wrinkle in his white jacket fussily and looked up. "I've been getting the surgery ready for instant use, Dr. Ferrel. Do you think it's safe to keep only Miss Dodd and one male attendant here—shouldn't we have more than the bare legally sanctioned staff?"

"Dodd's a one-man staff," Ferrel assured him. "Expecting accidents tonight?"

"No, sir, not exactly. But do you know what they're running off?"

"No." Ferrel hadn't asked Palmer; he'd learned long before that he couldn't keep up with the atomic engineering developments, and had stopped trying. "Some new type of atomic tank fuel for the army to use in its war games?"

"Worse than that, sir. They're making their first commercial run of Natomic I-713 in both No. 3 and 4 converters at once."

"So? Seems to me I did hear something about that. Had to do with killing off boll weevils, didn't it?" Ferrel was vaguely familiar with the process of sowing radioactive dust in a circle outside the weevil area, to isolate the pest, then gradually moving inward from the border. Used with proper precautions, it had slowly killed off the weevil and driven it back into half the territory once occupied.

Jenkins managed to look disappointed, surprised and slightly superior without a visible change of expression. "There was an article on it in the *Natomic Weekly Ray* of last issue, Dr. Ferrel. You probably know that the trouble with Natomic I-344, which they've been using, was its half life of over four months; that made the land sowed useless for planting the next year, so they had to move very slowly. I-713 has a half life of less than a week and reached safe limits in about two months, so they'll be able to isolate whole strips of hundreds of miles during the winter and still have the land usable by spring. Field tests have been highly successful, and we've just gotten a huge order from two States that want immediate delivery."

"After their legislatures waited six months debating whether to use it or not," Ferrel hazarded out of long experience. "Hm-m-m, sounds good if they can sow enough earthworms after them to keep the ground in good condition. But what's the worry?"

Jenkins shook his head indignantly. "I'm not worried. I simply think we should take every possible precaution and be ready for any accident; after all, they're working on something new, and a half life of a week is rather strong, don't you think? Besides, I looked over some of the reaction charts in the article, and—What was that?"

From somewhere to the left of the infirmary, a muffled growl was being accompanied by ground tremors; then it gave place to a steady hissing, barely audible through the insulated walls of the building. Ferrel listened a moment and shrugged. "Nothing to worry about, Jenkins. You'll hear it a dozen times a year. Ever since the Great War when he tried to commit hara-kiri over the treachery of his people, Hokusai's been bugs about getting an atomic explosive bomb which will let us wipe out the rest of the world. Some day you'll probably see the little guy brought in here minus his head, but so far he hasn't found anything with short enough a half life that can be controlled until needed. What about the reaction charts on I-713?"

"Nothing definite, I suppose." Jenkins turned reluctantly away from the sound, still frowning. "I know it worked in small lots, but there's something about one of the intermediate steps I distrust, sir. I thought I recognized . . . I tried to ask one of the engineers about it. He practically told me to shut up until I'd studied atomic engineering myself."

Seeing the boy's face whiten over tensed jaw muscles, Ferrel held back his smile and nodded slowly. Something funny there; of course. Jenkins' pride had been wounded, but hardly that much. Some day, he'd have to find out what was behind it. Little things like that could ruin a man's steadiness with the instruments, if he kept it to himself. Meantime, the subject was best dropped.

The telephone girl's heavily syllabized voice cut into his thoughts from the annunciator. "Dr. Ferrel. Dr. Ferrel wanted on the telephone. Dr. Ferrel, please!"

Jenkins' face blanched still further, and his eyes darted to his superior sharply. Doc grunted casually. "Probably Palmer's bored and wants to tell me all about his grandson again. He thinks that child's an all-time genius because it says two words at eighteen months."

But inside the office, he stopped to wipe his hands free of perspiration before answering; there was something contagious about Jenkins' suppressed fears. And Palmer's face on the little television screen didn't help any, though the director was wearing his usual set smile. Ferrel knew it wasn't about the baby this time, and he was right.

"'Lo, Ferrel." Palmer's heartily confident voice was quite normal, but the use of the last name was a clear sign of some trouble. "There's been a little accident in the plant, they tell me. They're bringing a few men over to the infirmary for treatment—probably not right away, though. Has Blake gone yet?"

"He's been gone fifteen minutes or more. Think it's serious enough to call him back, or are Jenkins and myself enough?"

"Jenkins? Oh, the new doctor." Palmer hesitated, and his arms showed quite clearly the doodling operations of his hands, out of sight of the vision cell. "No, of course, no need to call Blake back, I suppose—not yet, anyhow. Just worry anyone who saw him coming in. Probably nothing serious."

"What is it—radiation burns, or straight accident?!

Oh—radiation mostly—maybe accident, too. Someone got a little careless—you know how it is. Nothing to worry about, though. You've been through it before when they opened a port too soon."

Doc knew enough about that—if that's what it was. "Sure, we can handle that, Palmer. But I thought No. I was closing down at five-thirty tonight. Anyhow, how come they haven't installed the safety ports on it? You told me they had, six months ago."

"I didn't say it was No. 1, or that it was a manual port. You know, new equipment for new products." Palmer looked up at someone else, and his upper arms made a slight movement before he looked down at the vision cell again. "I can't go into it now, Dr. Ferrel; accident's throwing us off schedule, you see—details piling up on me. We can talk it over later, and you probably have to make arrangements now. Call me if you want anything."

The screen darkened and the phone clicked off abruptly, just as a muffled work started. The voice hadn't been Palmer's. Ferrel pulled his stomach in, wiped the sweat off his hands again, and went out into the surgery with careful casualness. Damn Palmer, why couldn't the fool give enough information to make decent preparations possible? He was sure 3 and 4 alone were operating, and they were supposed to be foolproof. Just what had happened?

Jenkins jerked up from a bench as he came out, face muscles tense and eyes filled with a nameless fear. Where he had been sitting, a copy of the *Weekly Ray* was lying open at a chart of symbols which meant nothing to Ferrel, except for the penciled line under one of the reactions. The boy picked it up and stuck it back on a table.

"Routine accident," Ferrel reported as naturally as he could, cursing himself for having to force his voice. Thank the Lord, the boy's hands hadn't trembled visibly when he was moving the paper; he'd still be useful if surgery were necessary. Palmer had said nothing of that, of course—he'd said nothing about entirely too much. "They're bringing a few men over for radiation burns, according to Palmer. Everything ready?"

Jenkins nodded tightly. "Quite ready, sir, as much as we can be for—routine accidents at 3 and 4! . . . Isotope R. . . . Sorry, Dr. Ferrel, I didn't mean that. Should we call in Dr. Blake and the other nurses and attendants?"

"Eh? Oh, probably we can't reach Blake, and Palmer doesn't think we need him. You might have Nurse Dodd locate Meyers—the others are out on dates by now if I know them, and the two nurses should be enough, with Jones; they're better than a flock of the others anyway." Isotope R? Ferrel remembered the name but nothing else. Something an engineer had said once—but he couldn't recall in what connection—or had Hokusai mentioned it? He watched Jenkins leave and turned back on an impulse to his office where he could phone in reasonable privacy.

"Get me Matsuura Hokusai." He stood, drumming on the table impatiently until the screen finally lighted and the little Japanese looked out of it, "Hoke, do you know what they were turning out over at 3 and 4?"

The scientist nodded slowly, his wrinkled face as expressionless as his unaccented English. "Yess, they are make I-713 for the weevil. Why you assk?"

"Nothing; just curious. I heard rumours about an Isotope R and wondered if there was any connection. Seems they had a little accident over there, and I want to be ready for whatever comes of it."

For a fraction of a second, the heavy lids on Hokusai's eyes seemed to lift, but his voice remained neutral, only slightly faster. "No connection, Dr. Ferrel, they are not make Issotope R, very much assure you. Besst you forget Issotope R. Very sorry. Dr. Ferrel, I must now see accident. Thank you for call. Goodbye." The screen was blank again, along with Ferrel's mind.

Jenkins was standing in the door, but had either heard nothing or seemed not to know about it. "Nurse Meyers is coming back," he said. "Shall I get ready for curare injections?"

"Uh—might be a good idea." Ferrel had no intention of being surprised again, no matter what the implication of the words. Curare, one of the greatest poisons, known to South American primitives for centuries and only recently synthesized by modern chemistry, was the final resort for use in cases of radiation injury that was utterly beyond control. While the infirmary stocked it for such emergencies, in the long years of Doc's practice it had been used only twice; neither experience had been pleasant. Jenkins was either thoroughly frightened or overly zealous—unless he knew something he had no business knowing.

"Seems to take them long enough to get the men here—can't be too serious, Jenkins, or they'd move faster."

"Maybe." Jenkins went on with his preparations, dissolving dried plasma in distilled, de-aerated water, without looking up. "There's the litter siren now. You'd better get washed up while I take care of the patients."

Doc listened to the sound that came in as a faint drone from outside, and grinned slightly. "Must be Beel driving; he's the only man fool enough to run the siren when the run-ways are empty. Anyhow, if you'll listen, it's the out trip he's making. Be at least five minutes before he gets back." But he turned into the washroom, kicked on the hot water and began scrubbing vigorously with the strong soap.

Damn Jenkins! Here he was preparing for surgery before he had any reason to suspect the need, and the boy was running things to suit himself, pretty much, as if armed with superior knowledge. Well, maybe he was. Either that, or he was simply half crazy with old wives' fears of anything relating to atomic reactions, and that didn't seem to fit the case. He rinsed off as Jenkins came in, kicked on the hot-air blast and let his arms dry, then bumped against a rod that brought out rubber gloves on little holders. "Jenkins, what's all this Isotope R business, anyway? I've heard about it somewhere—probably from Hokusai. But I can't remember anything definite."

"Naturally—there isn't anything definite. That's the trouble." The young doctor tackled the area under his fingernails before looking up; then he saw Ferrel was slipping into his surgeon's whites that had come out on a hanger, and waited until the other was finished. "R's one of the big maybe problems of atomics. Purely theoretical, and none's been made yet—it's either impossible or can't be done in small control batches, safe for testing. That's the trouble, as I said; nobody knows anything about it, except that—if it can exist—it'll break down in a fairly short time into Mahler's Isotope. You've heard of that?"

Doc had—twice. The first had been when Mahler and half his laboratory had disappeared with accompanying noise. He'd been making a comparatively small amount of the new product designed to act as a starter for other reactions. Later, Maicewicz had tackled it on a smaller scale, and that time only two rooms and three men had gone up in dust particles. Five or six years later, atomic theory had been extended to the point where any student could find why the apparently safe product decided to become pure helium and energy in approximately one billionth of a second.

"How long a time?"

"Half a dozen theories, and no real idea." They'd come out of the washrooms, finished except for their masks. Jenkins ran his elbow into a switch that turned on the ultraviolets that were supposed to sterilize entire surgery, then looked around questioningly. "What about the supersonics?"

Ferrel kicked them on, shuddering as the bone-shaking harmonic hum indicated their activity. He couldn't complain about the equipment, at least. Ever since the last accident, when the State Congress developed ideas, there'd been enough gadgets lying around to stock up several small hospitals. The supersonics were intended to penetrate through all solids in the room, sterilizing where the UV light couldn't reach. A whistling note in the harmonics reminded him of something that had been tickling around in the back of his mind for minutes.

"There was no emergency whistle, Jenkins. Hardly seems to me they'd neglect that if it were so important."

Jenkins grunted skeptically and eloquently. "I read in the papers a few days ago where Congress was thinking of moving all atomic plants—meaning National, of course—out into the Mojave Desert. Palmer wouldn't like that . . . There's the siren again."

Jones, the male attendant, had heard it, and was already running out the fresh stretcher for the litter into the back receiving room. Half a minute later, Beel came trundling in the detachable part of the litter. "Two," he announced. "More coming up as soon as they can get to 'em, Doc."

There was blood spilled over the canvas, and a closer inspection indicated its source in a severed jugular vein, now held in place with a small safety pin that had fastened the two sides of the cut with a series of little pricks around which the blood had clotted enough to stop further loss.

Doc kicked off the supersonics with relief and indicated the man's throat. "Why wasn't I called out instead of having him brought here?"

"Hell, Doc, Palmer said bring 'em in and I brought 'em—I dunno. Guess some guy pinned up this fellow so they figured he could wait. Anything wrong?"

Ferrel grimaced. "With a split jugular, nothing that stops the bleeding's wrong, orthodox or not. How many more, and what's wrong out there?"

"Lord knows, Doc. I only drive 'em. I don't ask questions. So long!" He pushed the new stretcher up on the carriage, went wheeling it out to the small two-wheeled tractor that completed the litter. Ferrel dropped his curiosity back to its proper place and turned to the jugular case, while Dodd adjusted her mask. Jones had their clothes off, swabbed them down hastily, and wheeled them out on operating tables into the center of the surgery.

"Plasma!" A quick examination had shown Doc nothing else wrong with the jugular case, and he made the injection quickly. Apparently the man was only unconscious from shock induced by loss of blood, and the breathing and heart action resumed a more normal course as the liquid filled out the depleted blood vessels. He treated the wound with a sulphonamide derivative in routine procedure, cleaned and sterilized the edges gently, applied clamps carefully, removed the pin, and began stitching with the complicated little motor needle—one of the few gadgets for which he had any real appreciation. A few more drops of blood had spilled, but not seriously, and the wound was now permanently sealed. "Save the pin, Dodd. Goes in the collection. That's all for this. How's the other, Jenkins?"

Jenkins pointed to the back of the man's neck, indicating a tiny bluish object sticking out. "Fragment of steel, clear into the medulla oblongata. No blood loss, but he's been dead since it touched him. Want me to remove it?"

"No need—mortician can do it if they want. . . . If these are a sample, I'd guess it as a plain industrial accident, instead of anything connected with radiation."

"You'll get that, too, Doc." It was the jugular case, apparently conscious and normal except for pallor. "We weren't in the converter house. Hey, I'm all right! . . . I'll be—"

Ferrel smiled at the surprise on the fellow's face. "Thought you were dead, eh? Sure, you're all right, if you'll take it easy. A torn jugular either kills you or else it's nothing to worry about. Just pipe down and let the nurse put you to sleep, and you'll never know you got it."

"Lord! Stuff came flying out of the air-intake like bullets out of a machine gun. Just a scratch, I thought; then Jake was bawling like a baby and yelling for a pin. Blood all over the place—then here I am, good as new."

"Uh-huh." Dodd was already wheeling him off to a ward room, her grim face wrinkled into a half-quizzical expression over the mask. "Doctor said to pipe down, didn't he? Well!"

As soon as Dodd vanished, Jenkins sat down, running his hand over his cap; there were little beads of sweat showing where the goggles and mask didn't entirely cover his face. "'Stuff came flying out of the air-intake like bullets out of a machine gun,'" he repeated softly. "Dr. Ferrel, these two cases were outside the converter—just by-product accidents. Inside—"

"Yeah." Ferrel was picturing things himself, and it wasn't pleasant. Outside, matter tossed through the air ducts; inside—He left it hanging, as Jenkins had. "I'm going to call Blake. We'll probably need him."

2

"Give me Dr. Blake's residence—Maple 2337," Ferrel said quickly into the phone. The operator looked blank for a second, starting and then checking a purely automatic gesture toward the plugs. "Maple 2337, I said."

"I'm sorry, Dr. Ferrel, I can't give you an outside line. All trunk lines are out of order." There was a constant buzz from the board, but nothing showed in the panel to indicate whether from white inside lights or the red trunk indicators.

"But—this is an emergency, operator. I've got to get in touch with Dr. Blake!"

"Sorry, Dr. Ferrel. All trunk lines are out of order." She started to reach for the plug, but Ferrel stopped her.

"Give me Palmer, then—and no nonsense! If his line's busy, cut me in, and I'll take the responsibility."

"Very good." She snapped at her switches. "I'm sorry, emergency call from Dr. Ferrel. Hold the line and I'll reconnect you." Then

Palmer's face was on the panel, and this time the man was making no attempt to conceal his expression of worry.

"What is it, Ferrel?"

"I want Blake here—I'm going to need him. The operator says—"

"Yeah," Palmer nodded tightly, cutting in. "I've been trying to get him myself, but his house doesn't answer. Any idea of where to reach him?"

"You might try the Bluebird or any of the other nightclubs around there." Damn, why did this have to be Blake's celebration night? No telling where he could be found by this time.

Palmer was speaking again. "I've already had all the nightclubs and restaurants called, and he doesn't answer. We're paging the movie houses and theaters now—just a second. . . . Nope, he isn't there, Ferrel. Last reports, no response."

"How about sending out a general call over the radio?"

"I'd . . . I'd like to, Ferrel, but it can't be done." The manager had hesitated for a fraction of a second, but his reply was positive. "Oh, by the way, we'll notify your wife you won't be home. Operator! You there? Good, reconnect the Governor!"

There was no sense in arguing into a blank screen, Doc realized. If Palmer wouldn't put through a radio call, he wouldn't, though it had been done once before. "All trunk lines are out of order. . . . We'll notify your wife. . . . Reconnect the Governor!" They weren't even being careful to cover up. He must have repeated the words aloud as he backed out of the office, still staring at the screen, for Jenkins' face twitched into a maladjusted grin.

"So we're cut off. I knew it already; Meyers just got in with more details." He nodded toward the nurse, just coming out of the dressing room and trying to smooth out her uniform. Her almost pretty face was more confused than worried.

"I was just leaving the plant, Dr. Ferrel, when my name came up on the outside speaker, but I had trouble getting here. We're locked in! I saw them at the gate—guards with sticks. They were turning back everyone that tried to leave, and wouldn't tell why, even. Just general orders that no one was to leave until Mr. Palmer gave his permission. And they weren't going to let me back in at first. Do you suppose . . . do you know what it's all about? I heard little things that didn't mean anything, really, but—"

"I know just about as much as you do, Meyers, though Palmer said something about carelessness with one of the ports on No. 3 or 4," Ferrel answered her. "Probably just precautionary measures. Anyway, I wouldn't worry about it yet."

"Yes, Dr. Ferrel." She nodded and turned back to the front office, but there was no assurance in her look. Doc realized that neither Jenkins nor himself was a picture of confidence at the moment.

"Jenkins," he said, when she was gone, "if you know anything I don't, for the love of Mike, out with it! I've never seen anything like this around here."

Jenkins shook himself, and for the first time since he'd been there, used Ferrel's nickname. "Doc, I don't—that's why I'm in a blue funk. I know just enough to be less sure than you can be, and I'm scared as hell!"

"Let's see your hands." The subject was almost a monomania with Ferrel, and he knew it, but he also knew it wasn't unjustified. Jenkins' hands came out promptly, and there was no tremble to them. The boy threw up his arm so the sleeve slid beyond the elbow, and Ferrel nodded; there was no sweat trickling down from the armpits to reveal a worse case of nerves than showed on the surface. "Good enough, son; I don't care how scared you are—I'm getting that way myself—but with Blake out of the picture, and the other nurses and attendants sure to be out of reach, I'll need everything you've got."

"Doc?"

"Well?"

"If you'll take my word for it, I can get another nurse here—and a good one, too. They don't come any better, or any steadier, and she's not working now. I didn't expect her—well, anyhow, she'd skin me if I didn't call when we need one. Want her?"

"No trunk lines for outside calls," Doc reminded him. It was the first time he'd seen any real enthusiasm on the boy's face, and however good or bad the nurse was, she'd obviously be of value in bucking up Jenkins' spirits. "Go to it, though; right now we can probably use any nurse. Sweetheart?"

"Wife." Jenkins went toward the dressing room. "And I don't need the phone; we used to carry ultra-short-wave personal radios to keep in touch, and I've still got mine here. And if you're worried about her qualifications, she handed instruments to Bayard at Mayo's for five years—that's how I managed to get through medical school!"

The siren was approaching again when Jenkins came back, the little tense lines about his lips still there, but his whole bearing somehow steadier. He nodded. "I called Palmer, too, and he O.K.'d her coming inside on the phone without wondering how I'd contacted

her. The switchboard girl has standing orders to route all calls from
us through before anything else, it seems."

Doc nodded, his ear cocked toward the drone of the siren
that drew up and finally ended on a sour wheeze. There was a
feeling of relief from tension about him as he saw Jones appear
and go toward the rear entrance; work, even under the pressure
of an emergency, was always easier than sitting around waiting for
it. He saw two stretchers come in, both bearing double loads, and
noted that Beel was babbling at the attendant, the driver's usually
phlegmatic manner completely gone.

"I'm quitting; I'm through tomorrow! No more watching 'em
drag out stiffs for me—not that way. Dunno why I gotta go back,
anyhow; it won't do 'em any good to get in further, even if they can.
From now on, I'm driving a truck, so help me I am!"

Ferrel let him rave on, only vaguely aware that the man was close
to hysteria. He had no time to give to Beel now as he saw the raw
red flesh through the visor of one of the armor suits. "Cut off what
clothes you can, Jones," he directed. "At least get the shield suits
off them. Tannic acid ready, nurse?"

"Ready." Meyers answered together with Jenkins, who was busily
helping Jones strip off the heavily armored suits and helmets.

Ferrel kicked on the supersonics again, letting them sterilize
the metal suits—there was going to be no chance to be finicky
about asepsis; the supersonics and ultraviolet tubes were supposed
to take care of that, and they'd have to do it, to a large extent,
little as he liked it. Jenkins finished his part, dived back for fresh
gloves, with a mere cursory dipping of his hands into antiseptic and
rinse. Dodd followed him, while Jones wheeled three of the cases
into the middle of the surgery, ready for work; the other had died
on the way in.

It was going to be messy work, obviously. Where metal from
the suits had touched, or come near touching, the flesh was
burned—crisped, rather. And that was merely a minor part of it, as
was the more than ample evidence of major radiation burns, which
had probably not stopped at the surface, but penetrated through
the flesh and bones into the vital interior organs. Much worse, the
writhing and spasmodic muscular contractions indicated radioactive
matter that had been forced into the flesh and was acting directly on
the nerves controlling the motor impulses. Jenkins looked hastily at
the twisting body of his case, and his face blanched to a yellowish
white; it was the first real example of the full possibilities of an
atomic accident he'd seen.

"Curare," he said finally, the word forced out, but level. Meyers handed him the hypodermic and he inserted it, his hand still steady—more than normally steady, in fact, with that absolute lack of movement that can come to a living organism only under the stress of emergency. Ferrel dropped his eyes back to his own case, both relieved and worried.

From the spread of the muscular convulsions, there could be only one explanation—somehow, radioactives had not only worked their way through the air grills, but had been forced through the almost airtight joints and sputtered directly into the flesh of the men. Now they were sending out radiations into every nerve, throwing aside the normal orders from the brain and spinal column, setting up anarchic orders of their own that left the muscles to writhe and jerk, one against the other, without order or reason, or any of the normal restraints the body places upon itself. The closest parallel was that of a man undergoing metrozol shock for schizophrenia, or a severe case of strychnine poisoning. He injected curare carefully, metering out the dosage according to the best estimate he could make, but Jenkins had been acting under a pressure that finished the second injection as Doc looked up from his first. Still, in spite of the rapid spread of the drug, some of the twitching went on.

"Curare," Jenkins repeated, and Doc tensed mentally; he'd still been debating whether to risk extra dosage. But he made no counter-order, feeling slightly relieved this time at having the matter taken out of his hands; Jenkins went back to work, pushing up the injections to the absolute limit of safety, and slightly beyond. One of the cases had started a weird minor moan that hacked on and off as his lungs and vocal cords went in and out of synchronization, but it quieted under the drug, and in a matter of minutes the three lay still, breathing with the shallow flaccidity common to curare treatment. They were still moving slightly, but where before they were perfectly capable of breaking their own bones in uncontrolled efforts, now there was only motion similar to a man with a chill.

"God bless the man who synthesized curare," Jenkins muttered as he began cleaning away damaged flesh, Meyers assisting.

Doc could repeat that; with the older, natural product, true standardization and exact dosage had been next to impossible. Too much, and its action on the body was fatal; the patient died from 'exhaustion' of his chest muscles in a matter of minutes. Too little was practically useless. Now that the danger of self-injury and fatal exhaustion from wild exertion was over, he could attend to such relatively unimportant things as the agony still going on—curare had no particular effect on the sensory nerves. He injected neo-heroin and began cleaning the burned areas and treating them with the standard tannic-acid routine, first with a sulphonamide to eliminate possible infection, glancing up occasionally at Jenkins.

He had no need to worry, though; the boy's nerves were frozen into an unnatural calm that still pressed through with a speed Ferrel made no attempt to equal, knowing his work would suffer for it. At a gesture, Dodd handed him the little radiation detector, and he began hunting over the skin, inch by inch, for the almost miscroscopic bits of matter; there was no hope of finding all now, but the worst deposits could be found and removed; later, with more time, a final probing could be made.

"Jenkins," he asked, "how about I-713's chemical action? Is it basically poisonous to the system?"

"No. Perfectly safe except for radiation. Eight in the outer electron ring, chemically inert."

That, at least, was a relief. Radiations were bad enough in and of themselves, but when coupled with metallic poisoning, like the old radium or mercury poisoning, it was even worse. The small colloidally fine particles of I-713 in the flesh would set up their own danger signal, and could be scraped away in the worst cases; otherwise, they'd probably have to stay until the isotope exhausted itself. Mercifully, its half-life was short, which would decrease the long hospitalization and suffering of the men.

Jenkins joined Ferrel on the last patient, replacing Dodd at handing instruments. Doc would have preferred the nurse, who was used to his little signals, but he said nothing, and was surprised to note efficiency of the boy's cooperation. "How about the breakdown products?" he asked.

"I-713? Harmless enough, mostly, and what isn't harmless isn't concentrated enough to worry about. That is, if it's still I-713. Otherwise—"

Otherwise, Doc finished mentally, the boy meant there'd be no danger from poisoning, at least. Isotope R, with an uncertain degeneration period, turned into Mahler's Isotope, with a complete breakdown in a billionth of a second. He had a fleeting vision of men, filled with a fine dispersion of that, suddenly erupting over their body with a violence that could never be described; Jenkins must have been thinking the same thing. For a few seconds, they stood there, looking at each other silently, but neither chose to speak of it. Ferrel reached for the probe,

Jenkins shrugged, and they went on with their work and their thoughts.

It was a picture impossible to imagine, which they might or might not see; if such an atomic blowup occurred, what would happen to the laboratory was problematical. No one knew the exact amount Maicewicz had worked on, except that it was the smallest amount he could make, so there could be no good estimate of the damage. The bodies on the operating tables, the little scraps of removed flesh containing the minute globules of radioactive, even the instruments that had come in contact with them, were bombs waiting to explode. Ferrel's own fingers took on some of the steadiness that was frozen in Jenkins as he went about his work, forcing his mind onto the difficult labor at hand.

It might have been minutes or hours later when the last dressing was in place and the three broken bones of the worst case were set. Meyers and Dodd, along with Jones, were taking care of the men, putting them into the little wards, and the two physicians were alone, carefully avoiding each other's eyes, waiting without knowing exactly what they expected.

Outside, a droning chug came to their ears, and the thump of something heavy moving over the runways. By common impulse they slipped to the side door and looked out, to see the rear end of one of the electric tanks moving away from them. Night had fallen some time before, but the gleaming lights from the big towers around the fence made the plant stand out in glaring detail. Except for the tank moving away, though, other buildings cut off their view.

Then, from the direction of the main gate, a shrill whistle cut the air and there was the sound of men's voices, though the words were indistinguishable. Sharp, crisp syllables followed, and Jenkins nodded slowly to himself. "Ten'll get you a hundred," he began, "that—Uh, no use betting. It is."

Around the corner a squad of men in state militia uniform marched briskly, bayoneted rifles on their arms. With efficient precision, they spread out under a sergeant's direction, each taking a post before the door of one of the buildings, one approaching the place where Ferrel and Jenkins stood.

"So that's what Palmer was talking to the Governor about," Ferrel muttered. "No use asking them questions, I suppose; they know less than we do. Come on inside where we can sit down and rest. Wonder what good the militia can do here—unless Palmer's afraid someone inside's going to crack and cause trouble."

Jenkins followed him back to the office and accepted a cigarette
automatically as he flopped back into a chair. Doc was discovering
just how good it felt to give his muscles and nerves a chance to relax,
and realizing that they must have been far longer in the surgery than
he had thought. "Care for a drink?"

"Uh—is it safe, Doc? We're apt to be back in there any minute."

Ferrel pulled a grin onto his face and nodded. "It won't hurt
you—we're just enough on edge and tired for it to be burned up
inside for fuel instead of reaching our nerves. Here." It was a
generous slug of rye he poured for each, enough to send an almost
immediate warmth through them, and to relax their overtensed
nerves. "Wonder why Beel hasn't been back long ago?"

"That tank we saw probably explains it; it got too tough for
the men to work in just their suits, and they've had to start
excavating through the converters with the tanks. Electric, wasn't
it, battery powered? . . . So there's enough radiation loose out
there to interfere with atomic-powered machines, then. That means
whatever they're doing is tough and slow work. Anyhow, it's more
important that they damp the action than get the men out, if they
only realize it—Sue!"

Ferrel looked up quickly to see the girl standing there, already
dressed for surgery, and he was not too old for a little glow of
appreciation to creep over him. No wonder Jenkins' face lighted up.
She was small, but her figure was shaped like that of a taller girl, not
in the cute or pert lines usually associated with shorter women, and
the serious competence of her expression hid none of the liveliness
of her face. Obviously she was several years older than Jenkins, but
as he stood up to greet her, her face softened and seemed somehow
youthful beside the boy's as she looked up.

"You're Dr. Ferrel?" she asked, turning to the older man. "I was
a little late—there was some trouble at first about letting me in—so
I went directly to prepare before bothering you. And just so you
won't be afraid to use me, my credentials are all here."

She put the little bundle on the table, and Ferrel ran through
them briefly; it was better than he'd expected. Technically she
wasn't a nurse at all, but a doctor of medicine, a so-called nursing
doctor; there'd been the need for assistants midway between doctor
and nurse for years, having the general training and abilities of
both, but only in the last decade had the actual course been
created, and the graduates were still limited to a few. He nodded
and handed them back.

"We can use you, Dr.—"

"Brown—professional name, Dr. Ferrel. And I'm used to being called just Nurse Brown."

Jenkins cut in on the formalities. "Sue, is there any news outside about what's going on here?"

"Rumors, but they're wild, and I didn't have a chance to hear many. All I know is that they're talking about evacuating the city and everything within fifty miles of here, buy it isn't official. And some people were saying the Governor was sending in troops to declare martial law over the whole section, but I didn't see any except here."

Jenkins took her off, then, to show her the Infirmary and introduce her to Jones and the two other nurses, leaving Ferrel to wait for the sound of the siren again, and to try putting two and two together to get sixteen. He attempted to make sense out of the article in the *Weekly Ray*, but gave it up finally; atomic theory had advanced too far since the sketchy studies he'd made, and the symbols were largely without meaning to him. He'd have to rely on Jenkins, it seemed. In the meantime, what was holding up the litter? He should have heard the warning siren long before.

It wasn't the litter that came in next, though, but a group of five men, two carrying a third, and a fourth supporting the fifth. Jenkins took the carried man over, Brown helping him; it was similar to the former cases, but without the actual burns from contact with hot metal. Ferrel turned to the men.

"Where's Beel and the litter?" He was inspecting the supported man's leg as he asked, and began work on it without moving the fellow to a table. Apparently a lump of radioactive matter the size of a small pea had been driven half an inch into the flesh below the thigh, and the broken bone was the result of the violent contractions of the man's own muscles under the stimulus of the radiation. It wasn't pretty. Now, however, the strength of the action had apparently burned out the nerves around, so the leg was comparatively limp and without feeling; the man lay watching, relaxed on the bench in a half-comatose condition, his eyes popping out and his lips twisted into a sick grimace, but he did not flinch as the wound was scraped out. Ferrel was working around a small leaden shield, his arms covered with heavily leaded gloves, and he dropped the scraps of flesh and isotope into a box of the same metal.

"Beel—he's out of this world, Doc," one of the others answered when he could tear his eyes off the probing. "He got himself blotto, somehow, and wrecked the litter before he got back. Couldn't take it, watching us grapple 'em out—and we hadda go after 'em without a drop of hooch!"

Ferrel glanced at him quickly, noticing Jenkins' head jerk around as he did so. "You were getting them out? You mean you didn't come from in there?"

"Heck, no, Doc. Do we look that bad? Them two got it when the stuff decided to spit on 'em clean through their armor. Me, I got me some nice burns, but I ain't complaining—I got a look at a couple of stiffs, so I'm kicking about nothing!"

Ferrel hadn't noticed the three who had traveled under their own power, but he looked now, carefully. They were burned, and badly, by radiations, but the burns were still new enough not to give them too much trouble, and probably what they'd just been through had temporarily deadened their awareness of pain, just as a soldier on the battlefield may be wounded and not realize it until the action stops. Anyway, atomjacks were not noted for sissiness.

"There's almost a quart in the office there on the table," he told them. "One good drink apiece—no more. Then go up front and I'll send Nurse Brown in to fix up your burns as well as can be for now." Brown could apply the unguents developed to heal radiation burns as well as he could, and some division of work that would relieve Jenkins and himself seemed necessary. "Any chance of finding any more living men in the converter housings?"

"Maybe. Somebody said the thing let out a groan half a minute before it popped, so most of 'em had a chance to duck into the two safety chambers. Figure on going back there and pushing tanks ourselves unless you say no; about half an hour's work left before we can crack the chambers, I guess, then we'll know."

"Good. And there's no sense in sending in every man with a burn, or we'll be flooded here; they can wait and it looks as if we'll have plenty of serious stuff to care for. Dr. Brown, I guess you're elected to go out with the men—have one of them drive the spare litter Jones will show you. Salve down all the burn cases, put the worst ones off duty, and just send in the ones with the jerks. You'll find my emergency kit in the office, there. Someones has to be out there to give first aid and sort them out—we haven't room for the whole plant in here."

"Right, Dr. Ferrel." She let Meyers replace her in assisting Jenkins, and was gone briefly to come out with his bag. "Come on, you men. I'll hop the litter and dress down your burns on the way. You're appointed driver, mister. Somebody should have reported that Beel person before, so the litter would be out there now."

The spokesman for the others upended the glass he'd filled, swallowed, gulped, and grinned down at her. "O.K., doctor, only out there you ain't got time to think—you gotta do. Thanks for the shot, Doc, and I'll tell Hoke you're appointing her out there."

They filed out behind Brown as Jones went out to get the second litter, and Doc went ahead with the quick-setting plastic cast for the broken leg. Too bad there weren't more of those nursing doctors; he'd have to see Palmer about it after this was over—if Palmer and he were still around. Wonder how the men in the safety chambers about which he'd completely forgotten, would make out? There were two in each converter housing, designed as an escape for the men in case of accident, and supposed to be proof against almost anything. If the men had reached them, maybe they were all right; he wouldn't have taken a bet on it, though. With a slight shrug, he finished his work and went to help Jenkins.

The boy nodded down at the body on the table, already showing extensive scraping and probing. "Quite a bit of spitting clean through the armor," he commented. "These words were just a little too graphic for me. I-713 couldn't do that."

"Hm-m-m." Doc was in no mood to quibble on the subject. He caught himself looking at the little box in which the stuff was put after they worked what they could out of the flesh, and jerked his eyes away quickly. Whenever the lid was being dropped, a glow could be seen inside. Jenkins always managed to keep his eyes on something else.

They were almost finished when the switchboard girl announced a call, and they waited to make the few last touches before answering, then filed into the office together. Brown's face was on the screen, smudged and with a spot of rouge standing out on each cheek. Another smudge appeared as she brushed the auburn hair out of her eyes with the back of her wrist.

"They've cracked the converter safety chambers, Dr. Ferrel. The north one held up perfectly, except for the heat and a little burn, but something happened in the other; oxygen valve stuck, and all are unconscious, but alive. Magma must have sprayed through the door, because sixteen or seventeen have the jerks, and about a dozen are dead. Some others need more care than I can give—I'm having Hokusai delegate men to carry those the stretchers won't hold, and they're all piling up on you in a bunch right now!"

Ferrel grunted and nodded. "Could have been worse, I guess. Don't kill yourself out there, Brown."

"Same to you." she blew Jenkins a kiss and snapped off, just as the whine of the litter siren reached their ears.

In the surgery again, they could see a truck showing behind it, and men lifting out bodies in apparently endless succession.

"Get their armor off, somehow, Jones—grab anyone else to help you that you can. Curare, Dodd, and keep handing it to me. We'll worry about everything else after Jenkins and I quiet them." This was obviously going to be a mass-production sort of business, not for efficiency, but through sheer necessity. And again, Jenkins with his queer taut steadiness was doing two for one that Doc could do, his face pale and his eyes almost glazed, but his hands moving endlessly and nervelessly on with his work.

Sometime during the night Jenkins looked up at Meyers, and motioned her back. "Go get some sleep, nurse; Miss Dodd can take care of both Dr. Ferrel and myself when we work close together. Your nerves are shot, and you need the rest. Dodd, you can call her back in two hours and rest yourself."

"What about you, doctor?"

"Me—" He grinned out of the corner of his mouth, crookedly. "I've got an imagination that won't sleep, and I'm needed here." The sentence ended on a rising inflection that was false to Ferrel's ear, and the older doctor looked at the boy thoughtfully.

Jenkins caught his look. "It's O.K., Doc; I'll let you know when I'm going to crack. It was O.K. to send Meyers back, wasn't it?"

"You were closer to her than I was, so you should know better than I." Technically, the nurses were all directly under his control, but they'd dropped such technicalities long before. Ferrel rubbed the small of his back briefly, then picked up his scalpel again.

A faint gray light was showing in the east, and the wards had overflowed into the waiting room when the last case from the chambers was finished as best he could be. During the night, the converter had continued to spit occasionally, even through the tank armor twice, but now there was a temporary lull in the arrival of workers for treatment. Doc sent Jones after breakfast from the cafeteria, then headed into the office where Jenkins was already slumped down in the old leather chair.

The boy was exhausted almost to the limit from the combined strain of the work and his own suppressed jitters, but he looked up in mild surprise as he felt the prick of the needle. Ferrel finished it, and used it on himself before explaining. "Morphine, of course. What else can we do? Just enough to keep us going, but without it we'll both be useless out there in a few more hours. Anyhow, there isn't as much reason not to use it as there was when I was younger, before the counter-agent was discovered to kill most of its habit-forming tendency. Even five years ago, before they had that, there were times when morphine was useful, Lord knows, though anyone who used it except as a last resort deserved all the hell he got. A real substitute for sleep would be better, though; wish they'd finish up the work they're doing on that fatigue eliminator at Harvard. Here, eat that!"

Jenkins grimaced at the breakfast Jones laid out in front of him, but he knew as well as Doc that the food was necessary, and he pulled the plate back to him. "What I'd give an eye tooth for, Doc, wouldn't be a substitute—just half an hour of good old-fashioned sleep. Only, damn it, if I knew I had time, I couldn't do it—not with R out there bubbling away."

The telephone annunciator clipped in before Doc could answer. "Telephone for Dr. Ferrel; emergency! Dr. Brown calling Dr. Ferrel!"

"Ferrel answering!" The phone girl's face popped off the screen, and a tired-faced Sue Brown looked out at them. "What is it?"

"It's that little Japanese fellow—Hokusai—who's been running things out here, Dr. Ferrel. I'm bringing him in with an acute case of appendicitis. Prepare surgery!"

Jenkins gagged over the coffee he was trying to swallow, and his choking voice was halfway between disgust and hysterical laughter. "Appendicitis, Doc! My God, what comes next?"

3

It might have been worse. Brown had coupled in the little freezing unit on the litter and lowered the temperature around the abdomen, both preparing Hokusai for surgery and slowing down the progress of the infection so that the appendix was still unbroken when he was wheeled into the surgery. His seamed Oriental face had a grayish cast under the olive, but he managed a faint grin.

"Verry ssorry, Dr. Ferrel, to bother you. Verry ssorry. No ether, pleasse!"

Ferrel grunted. "No need of it, Hoke; we'll use hypothermy, since it's already begun. Over here, Jones . . . And you might as well go back and sit down, Jenkins."

Brown was washing, and popped out again, ready to assist with the operation. "He had to be tied down, practically, Dr.

Ferrel. Insisted that he only needed a little mineral oil and some peppermint for his stomach-ache! Why are intelligent people always the most stupid?"

It was a mystery to Ferrel, too, but seemingly the case. He tested the temperature quickly while the surgery hypothermy equipment began functioning, found it low enough, and began. Hoke flinched with his eyes as the scalpel touched him, then opened them in mild surprise at feeling no appreciable pain. The complete absence of nerve response with its accompanying freedom from post-operative shock was one of the great advantages of low-temperature work in surgery. Ferrel laid back the flesh, severed the appendix quickly, and removed it through the tiny incision. Then, with one of the numerous attachments, he made use of the ingenious mechanical stitcher and stepped back.

"All finished, Hoke, and you're lucky you didn't rupture—peritonitis isn't funny, even though we can cut down on it with the sulphonamides. The ward's full, so's the waiting room, so you'll have to stay on the table for a few hours until we can find a place for you; no pretty nurse, either—until the two other girls get here some time this morning. I dunno what we'll do about the patients."

"But, Dr. Ferrel, I am hear that now ssurgery—I sshould be up, already. There iss work I am do."

"You've been hearing that appendectomy patient aren't confined now, eh? Well, that's partly true. Johns Hopkins began it quite awhile ago. But for the next hour, while the temperature comes back to normal, you stay put. After that, if you want to move around a little, you can; but no going out to the converter. A little exercise probably helps more than it harms, but any strain wouldn't be good."

"But, the danger—"

"Be hanged, Hoke. You couldn't help now, long enough to do any good. Until the stuff in those stitches dissolves away completely in the body fluids, you're to take it easy—and that's two weeks, about."

The little man gave in, reluctancy. "Then I think I ssleep now. But besst you sshould call Mr. Palmer at once, pleasse! He musst know I am not there!"

Palmer took the news the hard way, with an unfair but natural tendency to blame Hokusai and Ferrel. "Damn it, Doc, I was hoping he'd get things straightened out somehow—I practically promised the Governor that Hoke could take care of it; he's got one of the best brains in the business. Now this! Well, no help,

I guess. He certainly can't do it unless he's in condition to get right into things. Maybe Jorgenson, though, knows enough about it to handle it from a wheel chair, or something. How's he coming along—in shape to be taken out where he can give directions to the foremen?"

"Wait a minute." Ferrel stoped him as quickly as he could. "Jorgenson isn't here. We've got thirty-one men lying around, and he isn't one of them; and if he'd been one of the seventeen dead, you'd know it. I didn't know Jorgenson was working, even."

"He had to be—it was his process! Look, Ferrel, I was distinctly told that he was taken to you—foreman dumped him on the litter himself and reported at once! Better check up, and quick—with Hoke only half able, I've got to have Jorgenson!"

"He isn't here—I know Jorgenson. The foreman must have mistaken the big fellow from the south safety for him, but that man had black hair inside his helmet. What about the three hundred-odd that were only unconscious, or the fifteen-sixteen hundred men outside the converter when it happened?"

Palmer wiggled his jaw muscles tensely. "Jorgenson would have reported or been reported fifty times. Every man out there wants him around to boss things. He's gotta be in your ward."

"He isn't, I tell you! And how about moving some of the fellows here into the city hospitals?"

"Tried—hospitals must have been tipped off somehow about the radioactives in the flesh, and they refuse to let a man from here be brought in." Palmer was talking with only the surface of his mind, his cheek muscles bobbing as if he were chewing his thoughts and finding them tough. "Jorgenson—Hoke—and Kellar's been dead for years. Not another man in the whole country that understands this field enough to make a decent guess, even; I get lost on page six myself. Ferrel, could a man in a Tomlin five-shield armor suit make the safety in twenty seconds, do you think, from—say beside the converter?"

Ferrel considered it rapidly. A Tomlin weighed about four hundred pounds, and Jorgenson was an ox of a man, but only human. "Under the stress of an emergency, it's impossible to guess what a man can do, Palmer, but I don't see how he could work his way half that distance."

"Hm-m-m, I figured. Could he live, then, supposing he wasn't squashed? Those suits carry their own air for twenty-four hours, you know, to avoid any air cracks, pumping the carbon-dioxide back under pressure and condensing the moisture out—no openings of any kind. They've got the best insulation of all kinds we know, too."

"One chance in a billion, I'd guess; but again, it's darned hard to put any exact limit on what can be done—miracles keep happening, every day. Going to try it?"

"What else can I do? There's no alternative. I'll meet you outside No. 4 just as soon as you can make it, and bring everything you need to start working at once. Seconds may count!" Palmer's face slid sideways and up as he was reaching for the button, and Ferrel wasted no time in imitating the motion.

By all logic, there wasn't a chance, even in a Tomlin. But, until they knew, the effort would have to be made; chances couldn't be taken when a complicated process had gone out of control, with now almost certainty that Isotope R was the result—Palmer was concealing nothing, even though he had stated nothing specifically. And obviously, if Hoke couldn't handle it, none of the men at other branches of National Atomic or at the smaller partially independent plants could make even a halfhearted stab at the job.

It all rested on Jorgenson, then. And Jorgenson must be somewhere under that semi-molten hell that could drive through the tank armor and send men back into the infirmary with bones broken from their own muscular anarchy!

Ferrel's face must have shown his thoughts, judging by Jenkins' startled expression. "Jorgenson's still in there somewhere," he said quickly.

"Jorgenson! But he's the man who—Good Lord!"

"Exactly. You'll stay here and take care of the jerk cases that may come in. Brown, I'll want you out there again. Bring everything portable we have, in case we can't move him in fast enough; get one of the trucks and fit it out; and be out with it about twice as fast as you can! I'm grabbing the litter now." He accepted the emergency kit Brown thrust into his hands, dumped a caffeine tablet into his mouth without bothering to wash it down, then was out toward the litter. "No. 4, and hurry!"

Palmer was just jumping off a scotter as they cut around No. 3 and in front of the rough fence of rope strung out quite a distance beyond 4. He glanced at Doc, nodded, and dived in through the men grouped around, yelling orders to right and left as she went, and was back at Ferrel's side by the time the litter had stopped.

O.K., Ferrel, go over there and get into armor as quickly as possible! We're going in there with the tanks, whether we can or not, and be damned to the quenching for the moment. Briggs, get those things out of there, clean out a roadway as best you can, throw in the big crane again, and we'll need all the men in armor we can get—give them steel rods and get them to probing in there for anything solid and big or small enough to be a man—five minutes at a stretch; they should be able to stand that. I'll be back pronto!"

Doc noted the confused mixture of tanks and machines of all descriptions clustered around the walls—or what was left of them—of the converter housing, and saw them yanking out everything along one side, leaving an opening where the main housing gate had stood, now ripped out to expose a crane boom rooting out the worst obstructions. Obviously they'd been busy at some kind of attempt at quenching the action, but his knowledge of atomics was too little even to guess at what it was. The equipment set up was being pushed aside by tanks without dismantling, and men were running up into the roped-in section, some already armored, others dragging on part of their armor as they went. With the help of one of the atomjacks, he climbed into a suit himself, wondering what he could do in such a casing if anything needed doing.

Palmer had a suit on before him, though, and was waiting beside one of the tanks, squat and heavily armored, its front equipped with both a shovel and a grapple swinging from movable beams. "In here, Doc." Ferrel followed him into the housing of the machine and Palmer grabbed the controls as he pulled on a shortwave headset and began shouting orders through it towards the other tanks that were moving in on their heavy treads. The dull drone of the motor picked up, and the tank began lumbering forward under the manager's direction.

"Haven't run one of these since that show-off at a picnic seven years ago," he complained, as he kicked at the controls and straightened out a developing list to left. "Though I used to be pretty handy when I was plain engineer. Damned static around here almost chokes off the radio, but I guess enough gets through. By the best guess I can make, Jorgenson should have been near the main control panel when it started, and have headed for the south chamber. Half the distance, you figure?"

"Possibly, probably slightly less."

"Yeah! And then the stuff may have tossed him around. But we'll have to try to get there." He barked into the radio again. "Briggs, get those men in suits as close as you can and have them fish with their rods about thirty feet to the left of the pillar that's still up—can they get closer?"

The answer was blurred and pieces missing, but the general idea went across. Palmer frowned. "O.K., if they can't make it, they can't; draw them back out of the reach stuff and hold them ready to go in. . . . No, call for volunteers! I'm offering a thousand dollars a minute to every man that gets a stick in there, double to his family if the stuff gets him, and ten times that—fifty thousand—if he locates Jorgenson! . . . Look out, you damn fool!" The last was to one of the men who'd started forward, toward the place, jumping from one piece of broken building to grab at a pillar and swing off in his suit toward something that looked like a standing position; it toppled, but he managed a leap that carried him to another lump, steadied himself, and began probing through the mess. "Oof! You with the crane—stick it in where you can grab any of the men that pass out, if it'll reach—good! Doc, I know as well as you that the men have no business in there, even five minutes; but I'll send in a hundred more if it'll find Jorgenson!"

Doc said nothing—he knew there'd probably be a hundred or more fools willing to try, and he knew the need of them. The tanks couldn't work their way close enough for any careful investigation of the mixed mass of radioactives, machinery, building debris, and destruction, aside from which they were much too slow in such delicate probing; only men equipped with the long steel poles could do that. As he watched, some of the activity of the magma suddenly caused an eruption, and one of the men tossed up his pole and doubled back into a half circle before falling. The crane operator shoved the big boom over and made a grab, missed, brought it down again, and came out with the heaving body held by one arm, to run it back along its track and twist it outward beyond Doc's vision.

Even through the tank and the suit, heat was pouring in, and there was a faint itching in those parts where the armor was thinnest that indicated the start of a burn—though not as yet dangerous. He had no desire to think what was happening to the men who were trying to worm into the heart of it in nothing but armor; nor did he care to watch what was happening to them. Palmer was trying to inch the machine ahead, but the stuff underneath made any progress difficult. Twice something spat against the tank, but did not penetrate.

"Five minutes are up," he told Palmer. "They'd all better go directly to Dr. Brown, who should be out with the truck now for immediate treatment."

Palmer nodded and relayed the instructions. "Pick up all you can with the crane and carry them back! Send in a new bunch, Briggs, and credit them with their bonus in advance. Damn it, Doc, this can go on all day; it'll take an hour to pry around through this mess right here, and then he's probably somewhere else. The stuff seems to be getting worse in this neighborhood, too, from what accounts I've had before. Wonder if that steel plate could be pushed down?"

He threw in the clutch engaging the motor to the treads and managed to twist through toward it. There was a slight slipping of the lugs, then the tractors caught, and the nose of the tank trust forward; almost without effort, the fragment of housing toppled from its leaning position and slid forward. The tank growled, fumbled, and slowly climbed up onto it and ran forward another twenty feet to its end; the support settled slowly, but something underneath checked it, and they were still again. Palmer worked the grapple forward, nosing a big piece of masonry out of the way, and two men reached out with the ends of their poles to begin probing, futilely. Another change of men came out, then another.

Briggs' voice crackled erratically through the speaker again. "Palmer, I got a fool here who wants to go out on the end of your beam, if you can swing around so the crane can lift him out to it."

"Start him coming!" Again he began jerking the levers, and the tank buckled and heaved, backed and turned, ran forward and repeated it all, while the plate that was holding them flopped up and down on its precarious balance.

Doc held his breath and began praying to himself; his admiration for the men who'd go out in that stuff was increasing by leaps and bounds, along with his respect for Palmer's ability.

The crane boom bobbed toward them, and the scoop came running out, but wouldn't quite reach; their own tank was relatively light and mobile compared to the bigger machine, but Palmer already had that pushed out to the limit, and hanging over the edge of the plate. It still lacked three feet of reaching.

"Damn!" Palmer slapped open the door of the tank, jumped forward on the tread, and looked down briefly before coming back inside. "No chance to get closer! Wheeoo! Those men earn their money."

But the crane operator had his own tricks, and was bobbing the boom of his machine up and down slowly with a motion that set the scoop swinging like a huge pendulum, bringing it gradually closer to the grapple beam. The man had an arm out, and finally caught the beam, swinging out instantly from the scoop that drew backward behind him. He hung suspended for a second, pitching his body around to a better position, then somehow wiggled up onto the end and braced himself with his legs. Doc let his breath out and Palmer inched the tank around to a forward position again. Now the pole of the atomjack could cover the wide territory before them, and he began using it rapidly.

"Win or lose, that man gets a triple bonus," Palmer muttered. "Uh!"

The pole had located something, and was feeling around to determine size; the man glanced at them and pointed frantically. Doc jumped forward to the windows as Palmer ran down the grapple and began pushing it down into the semi-molten stuff under the pole; there was resistance there, but finally the prong of the grapple broke under and struck on something that refused to come up. The manager's hands moved the controls gently, making it tug from side to side; reluctantly, it gave and moved forward toward them, coming upward until they could make out the general shape. It was definitely no Tomlin suit!

"Lead hopper box! Damn—Wait, Jorgenson wasn't anybody's fool; when he saw he couldn't make the safety, he might . . . maybe—" Palmer slapped the grapple down again, against the closed lid of the chest, but the hook was too large. Then the man clinging there caught the idea and slid down to the hopper chest, his armored hands grabbing at the lid. He managed to lift a corner of it until the grapple could catch and lift it the rest of the way, and his hands started down to jerk upward again.

The manager watched his motions, then flipped the box over with the grapple, and pulled it closer to the tank body; magma was running out, but there was a gleam of something else inside.

"Start praying, Doc!" Palmer worked it to the side of the tank and was out through the door again, letting the merciless heat and radiation stream in.

But Ferrel wasn't bothering with that now; he followed, reaching down into the chest to help the other two lift out the body of a huge man in a five-shield Tomlin! Somehow, they wangled the six-hundred-odd pounds out and up on the treads, then into the housing, barely big enough for all of them. The atomjack pulled himself inside, shut the door and flopped forward on his face, out cold.

"Never mind him—check Jorgenson!" Palmer's voice was heavy with the reaction from the hunt, but he turned the tank and sent it outward at top speed, regardless of risk. Contrarily, it bucked through the mass more readily than it had crawled in through the cleared section.

Ferrel unscrewed the front plate of the armor on Jorgenson as rapidly as he could, though he knew already that the man was still miraculously alive—corpses don't jerk with force enough to move a four-hundred-pound suit appreciably. A side glance, as they drew beyond the wreck of the converter housing, showed the men already beginning to set up equipment to quell the atomic reaction again, but the armor front plate came loose at last, and he dropped his eyes back without noticing details, to cut out a section of clothing and make the needed injections; curare first, then neo-heroin, and curare again, though he did not dare inject the quantity that seemed necessary. There was nothing more he could do until they could get the man out of his armor. He turned to the atomjack, who was already sitting up, propped against the driving seat's back.

"'Snothing much, Doc," the fellow managed. "No jerks, just burn and that damned heat! Jorgenson?"

"Alive at least," Palmer answered, with some relief. The tank stopped, and Ferrel could see Brown running forward from beside a truck. "Get that suit off you, get yourself treated for the burn, then go up to the office where the check will be ready for you!"

"Fifty thousand check?" The doubt in the voice registered over the weakness.

"Fifty thousand plus triple your minute time, and cheap; maybe we'll toss in a medal or a bottle of Scotch, too. Here, you fellows give a hand."

Ferrel had the suit ripped off with Brown's assistance and paused only long enough for one grateful breath of clean, cool air before leading the way toward the truck. As he neared it, Jenkins popped out, directing a group of men to move two loaded stretchers onto the litter, and nodding jerkily at Ferrel. "With the truck all equipped, we decided to move out here and take care of the damage as it came up—Sue and I rushed them through enough to do until we can find more time, so we could give full attention to Jorgenson. He's still living!"

"By a miracle. Stay out here, Brown, until you've finished with the men from inside, then we'll try to find some rest for you."

The three huskies carrying Jorgenson placed the body on the table set up, and began ripping off the bulky armor as the truck got under way. Fresh gloves came out of a small sterilizer, and the two doctors fell to work at once, treating the badly burned flesh and trying to locate and remove the worst of the radio-active matter.

"No use." Doc stepped back and shook his head. "It's all over him, probably clear into his bones in places. We'd have to put him through a filter to get it all out!"

Palmer was looking down at the raw mass of flesh, with all the layman's sickness at such a sight. "Can you fix him up, Ferrel?"

"We can try, that's all. Only explanation I can give for his being alive at all is that the hopper box must have been pretty well above the stuff until a short time ago—very short—and this stuff didn't work in until it sank. He's practically dehydrated now, apparently, but he couldn't have perspired enough to keep from dying of heat if he'd been under all that for even an hour—insulation or no insulation." There was admiration in Doc's eyes as he looked down at the immense figure of the man. "And he's tough; if he weren't, he'd have killed himself by exhaustion, even confined inside that suit and box, after the jerks set in. He's close to having done so, anyway. Until we can find some way of getting that stuff out of him, we don't dare risk getting rid of the curare's effect—that's a time-consuming job, in itself. Better give him another water and sugar intravenous, Jenkins. Then, if we do fix him up, Palmer, I'd say it's a fifty-fifty chance that all this hasn't driven him stark crazy."

The truck had stopped, and the men lifted the stretcher off and carried it inside as Jenkins finished the injection. He went ahead of them, but Doc stopped outside to take Palmer's cigarette for a long drag, and let them go ahead.

"Cheerful!" The manager lighted another from the butt, his shoulders sagging. "I've been trying to think of one man who might possibly be of some help to us, Doc, and there isn't such a person—anywhere. I'm sure now, after being in there, that Hoke couldn't do it. Kellar, if he were still alive, could probably pull the answer out of a hat after three looks—he had an instinct and genius for it; the best man the business ever had, even if his tricks did threaten to steal our work out from under us and give him the lead. But—well, now there's Jorgenson—either he gets in shape, or else!"

Jenkins' frantic yell reached them suddenly. "Doc! Jorgenson's dead! He's stopped breathing entirely!"

Doc jerked forward into a full run, a white-faced Palmer at his heels.

4

Dodd was working artificial respiration and Jenkins had the oxygen mask in his hands, adjusting it over Jorgenson's face, before Ferrel reached the table. He made a grab for the pulse that had been fluttering weakly enough before, felt it flicker feebly again, and then stop completely. "Adrenlin!"

"Already shot it into his heart, Doc! Cardiacine, too!" The boy's voice was bordering on hysteria, but Palmer was obviously closer to it than Jenkins.

"Doc, you gotta—"

"Get the hell out of here!" Ferrel's hands suddenly had a life of their own as he grabbed frantically for instruments, ripped bandages off the man's chest, and began working against time, when time had all the advantages. It wasn't surgery—hardly good butchery; the bones that he cut through so ruthlessly with savage strokes of an instrument could never heal smoothly after being so mangled. But he couldn't worry about minor details now.

He tossed back the flap of flesh and ribs that he'd hacked out. "Stop the bleeding, Jenkins!" Then his hands plunged into the chest cavity, somehow finding room around Dodd's and Jenkins', and were suddenly incredibly gentle as they located the heart itself and began working on it, the skilled, exact massage of a man who knew every function of the vital organ. Pressure here, there, relax, pressure again; take it easy, don't rush things! It would do no good to try to set it going as feverishly as his emotions demanded. Pure oxygen was feeding into the lungs, and the heart could safely do less work. Hold it steady, one beat a second, sixty a minute.

It had been perhaps half a minute from the time the heart stopped before his massage was circulating blood again; too little time to worry about damage to the brain, the first part to be permanently affected by stoppage of the circulation. Now, if the heart could start again by itself within any reasonable time, death would be cheated again. How long? He had no idea. They'd taught him ten minutes when he was studying medicine, then there'd been a case of twenty minutes once, and while he was interning it had been pushed up to a record of slightly over an hour, which still stood; but that was an exceptional case. Jorgenson, praise be, was a normally healthy and vigorous specimen, and his system had been in first-class condition,

but with the torture of those long hours, the radioactive, narcotic
and curare all fighting against him, still one more miracle was
needed to keep his life going.

Press, massage, relax, don't hurry it too much. There! For a
second, his fingers felt a faint flutter, then again; but it stopped.
Still, as long as the organ could show such signs, there was hope,
unless his fingers grew too tired and he muffed the job before the
moment when the heart could be safely trusted by itself.

"Jenkins!"

"Yes, sir!"

"Ever do any heart massage?"

"Practiced it in school, sir, on a model, but never actually. Oh, a
dog in dissection class, for five minutes. I . . . I don't think you'd
better trust me, Doc."

"I may have to. If you did it on a dog for five minutes, you can
do it on a man, probably. You know what hangs on it—you saw the
converter and know what's going on."

Jenkins nodded, the tense nod he'd used earlier. "I know—that's
why you can't trust me. I told you I'd let you know when I was going
to crack—well, it's damned near here!"

Could a man tell his weakness, if he were about finished?
Doc didn't know; he suspected that the boy's own awareness of
his nerves would speed up such a break, if anything, but Jenkins
was a queer case, having taut nerves sticking out all over him, yet a
steadiness under fire that few older men could have equaled. If he
had to use him, he would; there was no other answer.

Doc's fingers were already feeling stiff—not yet tired, but showing signs of becoming so. Another few minutes, and he'd have
to stop. There was the flutter again, one—two—three! Then it
stopped. There had to be some other solution to this; it was
impossible to keep it up for the length of time probably needed,
even if he and Jenkins spelled each other. Only Michel at Mayo's
could—Mayo's! If they could get it here in time, that wrinkle
he'd seen demonstrated at their last medical convention was the
answer.

"Jenkins, call Mayo's—you'll have to get Palmer's O.K., I guess-
—ask for Kubelik, and the extension where I can talk to him!"

He could hear Jenkins' voice, level enough at first, then with
a depth of feeling he'd have thought impossible in the boy. Dodd
looked at him quickly and managed a grim smile, even as she
continued with the respiration; nothing could make her blush,
though it should have done so.

The boy jumped back. "No soap, Doc! Palmer can't be located
—and that post-mortem misconception at the board won't listen."

Doc studied his hands in silence, wondering, then gave it up;
there'd be no hope of his lasting while he sent out the boy. "O.K.,
Jenkins, you'll have to take over here, then. Steady does it, come
on in slowly, get your fingers over mine. Now, catch the motion?
Easy, don't rush things. You'll hold out—you'll have to! You've
done better than I had any right to ask for so far, and you don't
need to distrust yourself. There, got it?

"Got it, Doc. I'll try, but for Pete's sake, whatever you're
planning, get back here quick! I'm not lying about cracking! You'd
better let Meyers replace Dodd and have Sue called back in here;
she's the best nerve tonic I know."

"Call her in then, Dodd." Doc picked up a hypodermic syringe,
filled it quickly with water to which a drop of another liquid added
a brownish-yellow color, and forced his tired old legs into a reasonably rapid trot out of the side door and toward Communications.
Maybe the switchboard operator was stubborn, but there were ways
of handling people.

He hadn't counted on the guard outside the Communications
Building, though. "Halt!"

"Life or death; I'm a physician."

"Not in here—I got orders." The bayonet's menace apparently
wasn't enough; the rifle went up to the man's shoulder, and his
chin jutted out with the stubbornness of petty authority and reliance
on orders." Nobody sick here. There's plenty of phones elsewhere.
You get back—and fast!"

Doc started forward and there was a faint click from the rifle
as the safety went off; the darned fool meant what he said. Shrug-
ging, Ferrel stepped back—and brought the hypodermic needle up
inconspicuously in line with the guard's face. "Ever see one of these
things squirt curare? It can reach before your bullet hits!"

"Curare?" The guard's eyes flicked to the needle, and doubt came
into them. The man frowned. "That's the stuff that kills people on
arrows, ain't it?"

"It is—cobra venom, you know. One drop on the outside of your
skin and you're dead in ten seconds." Both statements were out-and-
out lies, but Doc was counting on the superstitious ignorance of
the average man in connection with poisons." This little needle can
spray you with it very nicely, and it may be a fast death, but not a
pleasant one. Want to put down the rifle?"

A regular might have shot; but the militiaman was taking no chances. He lowered the rifle gingerly, his eyes on the needle, then kicked the weapon aside at Doc's motion. Ferrel approached, holding the needle out, and the man shrank backward and away, letting him pick up the rifle as he went past to avoid being shot in the back. Lost time! But he knew his way around this little building, at least, and went straight toward the girl at the board.

"Get up!" His voice came from behind her shoulder and she turned to see the rifle in one of his hands; the needle in the other, almost touching her throat. "This is loaded with curare, deadly poison, and too much hangs on getting a call through to bother with physician's oaths right now, young lady. Up! No plugs! That's right; now get over there, out of the cell—there, on your face, cross your hands behind your back, and grab your ankles—right! Now if you move, you won't move long!"

Those gangster picture he'd seen were handy, at that. She was throughly frightened and docile. But, perhaps, not so much so she might not have bungled his call deliberately. He had to do that himself. Darn it, the red lights were trunk lines, but which plug—try the inside one, it looked more logical; he'd seen it done, but couldn't remember. Now, you flip back one of these switches—uh-uh, the other way. The tone came in assuring him he had it right, and he dialed operator rapidly, his eyes flickering toward the girl lying on the floor, his thoughts on Jenkins and the wasted time running on.

"Operator, this is an emergency. I'm Walnut, 7654; I want to put in a long-distance call to Dr. Kubelik, Mayo's Hospital, Rochester, Minnesota. If Kubelik isn't there, I'll take anyone else who answers from his department. Speed is urgent."

"Very good, sir." Long-distance operators, mercifully, were usually efficient. There were the repeated signals and clicks of relays as she put it through, the answer from the hospital board, more wasted time, and then a face appeared on the screen; but not that of Kubelik. It was a much younger man.

Ferrel wasted no time in introduction. "I've got an emergency case here where all Hades depends on saving a man, and it can't be done without that machine of Dr. Kubelik's; he knows me, if he's there—I'm Ferrel, met him at the convention, got him to show me how the thing worked."

"Kubelik hasn't come in yet, Dr. Ferrel; I'm his assistant. But, if you mean the heart and lung exciter, it's already boxed and supposed to leave for Harvard this morning. They've got a rush case out there, and may need it—"

"Not as much as I do."

"I'll have to call—Wait a minute, Dr. Ferrel, seems I remember your name now. Aren't you the chap with National Atomic?"

Doc nodded. "The same. Now, about that machine, if you'll stop the formalities—"

The face on the screen nodded, instant determination showing, with an underlying expression of something else. "We'll ship it down to you instantly, Ferrel. Got a field for a plane?"

"Not within three miles, but I'll have a truck sent out for it. How long?"

"Take too long by truck if you need it down there, Ferrel; I'll arrange to transship in air from our special speedster to a helicopter, have it delivered wherever you want. About—um, loading plane, flying a couple hundred miles, transshipping—about half an hour's the best we can do."

"Make it the square of land south of the infirmary, which is crossed visibly from the air. Thanks!"

"Wait, Dr. Ferrel!" The younger man checked Doc's cut-off. "Can you use it when you get it? It's tricky work."

"Kubelik gave quite a demonstration and I'm used to tricky work. I'll chance it—have to. Too long to rouse Kubelik himself, isn't it?"

"Probably. O.K., I've got the telescript reply from the shipping office, it's starting for the plane. I wish you luck!"

Ferrel nodded his thanks, wondering. Service like that was welcome, but it wasn't the most comforting thing, mentally, to know that the mere mention of National Atomic would cause such an about-face. Rumors, it seemed, were spreading, and in a hurry, in spite of Palmer's best attempts. Good Lord, what was going on here? He'd been too busy for any serious worrying or to realize, but—well, it had gotten him the exciter, and for that he should be thankful.

The guard was starting uncertainly off for reinforcements when Doc came out, and he realized that the seemingly endless call must have been over in short order. He tossed the rifle well out of the man's reach and headed back toward the infirmary at a run, wondering how Jenkins had made out—it had to be all right!

Jenkins wasn't standing over the body of Jorgenson; Brown was there instead, her eyes moist and her face pinched in and white around the nostrils that stood out at full width. She looked up, shook her head at him as he started forward, and went on working at Jorgenson's heart.

"Jenkins cracked?"

"Nonsense! This is woman's work, Dr. Ferrel, and I took over for him, that's all. You men try to use brute force all your life and then wonder why a woman can do twice as much delicate work where strong muscles are a nuisance. I chased him out and took over, that's all." But there was a catch in her voice as she said it, and Meyers was looking down entirely too intently at the work of artificial respiration.

"Hi, Doc!" It was Blake's voice that broke in. "Get away from there; when this Dr. Brown needs help, I'll be right in there. I've been sleeping like a darned fool all night, from four this morning on. Didn't hear the phone, or something, didn't know what was going on until I got to the gate out there. You go rest."

Ferrel grunted in relief; Blake might have been dead drunk when he finally reached home, which would explain his not hearing the phone, but his animal virility had soaked it out with no visible sign. The only change was the absence of the usual cocky grin on his face as he moved over beside Brown to test Jorgenson. "Thank the Lord you're here, Blake. How's Jorgenson doing?"

Brown's voice answered in a monotone, words coming in time to the motions of her fingers. "His heart shows signs of coming around once in a while, but it doesn't last. He isn't getting worse from what I can tell, though."

"Good. If we can keep him going half an hour more, we can turn all this over to a machine. Where's Jenkins?"

"A machine? Oh, the Kubelik exciter, of course. He was working on it when I was there. We'll keep Jorgenson alive until then, anyway, Dr. Ferrel."

"Where's Jenkins?" he repeated sharply, when she stopped with no intention of answering the former question.

Blake pointed toward Ferrel's office, the door of which was now closed. "In there. But lay off him, Doc. I saw the whole thing, and he feels like the deuce about it. He's a good kid, but only a kid, and this kind of hell could get any of us."

"I know all that." Doc headed toward the office, as much for a smoke as anything else. The sight of Blake's rested face was somehow an island of reassurance in this sea of fatigue and nerves. "Don't worry, Brown, I'm not planning on lacing him down, so you needn't defend your man so carefully. It was my fault for not listening to him."

Brown's eyes were pathetically grateful in the brief flash she threw him, and he felt like a heel for the gruffness that had been his first reaction to Jenkins' absence. If this kept on much longer, though, they'd all be in worse shape than the boy, whose back was toward him as he opened the door. The still, huddled shape did not raise its head from its arms as Ferrel put his hand onto one shoulder, and the voice was muffled and distant.

"I cracked, Doc—high, wide and handsome, all over the place. I couldn't take it! Standing there, Jorgenson maybe dying because I couldn't control myself right, the whole plant blowing up, all my fault. I kept telling myself I was O.K., I'd go on, then I cracked. Screamed like a baby! Dr. Jenkins—*nerve* specialist!"

"Yeah. . . . Here, are you going to drink this, or do I have to hold your blasted nose and pour it down your throat?" It was crude psychology, but it worked, and Doc handed over the drink, waited for the other to down it, and passed a cigarette across before sinking into his own chair. "You warned me, Jenkins, and I risked it on my own responsibility, so nobody's kicking. But I'd like to ask a couple of questions."

"Go ahead—what's the difference?" Jenkins had recovered a little, obviously, from the note of defiance that managed to creep into his voice.

"Did you know Brown could handle that kind of work? And did you pull your hands out before she could get hers in to replace them?"

"She told me she could. I didn't know before. I dunno about the other; I think . . . yeah, Doc, she had her hands over mine. But—"

Ferrel nodded, satisfied with his own guess. "I thought so. You didn't crack, as you put it, until your mind knew it was safe to do so—and then you simply passed the work on. By that definition, I'm cracking, too. I'm sitting in here, smoking, talking to you, when out there a man needs attention. The fact that he's getting it from two others, one practically fresh, the other at least a lot better off than we are, doesn't have a thing to do with it, does it?"

"But it wasn't that way, Doc. I'm not asking for grand-stand stuff from anybody."

"Nobody's giving it to you, son. All right, you screamed—why not? It didn't hurt anything. I growled at Brown when I came in for the same reason—exhausted, overstrained nerves. If I went out there and had to take over from them, I'd probably scream myself, or start biting my tongue—nerves have to have an outlet; physically, it does them no good, but there's a psychological need for it." The boy wasn't convinced, and Doc sat back in the chair, staring at him thoughtfully. "Ever wonder why I'm here?"

"No, sir."

"Well, you might. Twenty-seven years ago, when I was about your age, there wasn't a surgeon in this country—or the world, for that matter—who had the reputation I had; any kind of surgery, brain, what have you. They're still using some of my techniques . . . uh-hum, thought you'd remember when the association of names hit you. I had a different wife then, Jenkins, and there was a baby coming. Brain tumor—I had to do it, no one else could. I did it, somehow, but I went out of that operating room in a haze, and it was three days later when they'd tell me she'd died; not my fault—I know that now—but I couldn't realize it then.

"So, I tried setting up as a general practitioner. No more surgery for me! And because I was a fair diagnostician, which most surgeons aren't, I made a living, at least. Then, when this company was set up, I applied for the job, and got it; I still had a reputation of sorts. It was a new field, something requiring study and research, and damned near every ability of most specialists plus a general practitioner's, so it kept me busy enough to get over my phobia of surgery. Compared to me, you don't know what nerves or cracking means. That little scream was a minor incident."

Jenkins made no comment, but lighted the cigarette he'd been holding. Ferrel relaxed farther into the chair, knowing that he'd be called if there was any need for his work, and glad to get his mind at least partially off Jorgenson. "It's hard to find a man for this work, Jenkins. It takes too much ability at too many fields, even though it pays well enough. We went through plenty of applicants before we decided on you, and I'm not regretting our choice. As a matter of fact, you're better equipped for the job than Blake was—your record looked as if you'd deliberately tried for this kind of work."

"I did."

"Hm-m-m." That was the one answer Doc had least expected; so far as he knew, no one deliberately tried for a job at Atomics—they usually wound up trying for it after comparing their receipts for a year or so with the salary paid by National. "Then you knew what was needed and picked it up in toto. Mind if I ask why?"

Jenkins shrugged. "Why not? Turnabout's fair play. It's kind of complicated, but the gist of it doesn't take much telling. Dad had an atomic plant of his own—and a darned good one, too, Doc, even if it wasn't as big as National. I was working in it when I was fifteen, and I went through two years of university work in atomics with the best intentions of carrying on the business. Sue—well, she was the neighbor girl I followed around, and we had money at the time; that wasn't why she married me, though. I never did figure that out—she'd had a hard enough life, but she was already holding down a job at Mayo's, and I was just a raw kid. Anyway—

"The day we came home from our honeymoon, dad got a big contract on a new process we'd worked out. It took some swinging, but he got the equipment and started it. . . . My guess is that one of the controls broke though faulty construction; the process was right! We'd been over it too often not to know what it would do. But, when the estate was cleared up, I had to give up the idea of a degree in atomics, and Sue was back working at the hospital. Atomic courses cost real money. Then one of Sue's medical acquaintances fixed it for me to get a scholarship in medicine that almost took care of it, so I chose the next best thing to what I wanted."

"National and one of the biggest competitors—if you can call it that—are permitted to give degree in atomics," Doc reminded the boy. The field was still too new to be a standing university course, and there were no better teachers in the business than such men as Palmer, Hokusai and Jorgenson. "They pay a salary while you're learning, too."

"Hm-m-m. Takes ten years that way, and the salary's just enough for a single man. No, I'd married Sue with the intention she wouldn't have to work again; well, she did until I finished internship, but I knew if I got the job here I could support her. As an atomjack, working up to an engineer, the prospects weren't so good. We're saving a little money now, and someday maybe I'll get a crack at it yet. . . . Doc, what's this all about? You babying me out of my fit?"

Ferrel grinned at the boy. "Nothing else, son, though I was curious. And it worked. Feel all right now, don't you?"

"Mostly, except for what's going on out there—I got too much of a look at it from the truck. Oh, I could use some sleep, I guess, but I'm O.K. again."

"Good." Doc had profited almost as much as Jenkins from the rambling off-trail talk, and had managed more rest from it than from nursing his own thoughts. "Suppose we go out and see how they're making out with Jorgenson? Um, what happened to Hoke, come to think of it?"

"Hoke? Oh, he's in my office now, figuring out things with a pencil and paper since we wouldn't let him go back out there. I was wondering—"

"Atomics? . . . Then suppose you go in and talk to him; he's a good guy, and he won't give you the brush-off. Nobody else around here apparently suspected this Isotope R business, and you might offer a fresh lead for him. With Blake and the nurses here and the men out of the mess except for the tanks, there's not much you can do to help on my end."

Ferrel felt more at peace with the world than he had since the call from Palmer as he watched Jenkins head off across the surgery toward his office; and the glance that Brown threw, first toward the boy, then back at Doc, didn't make him feel worse. That girl could say more with her eyes than most women could with their mouths! He went over toward the operating table where Blake was now working the heart massage with one of the fresh nurses attending to respiration and casting longing glances toward the mechanical lung apparatus; it couldn't be used in this case, since Jorgenson's chest had to be free for heart attention.

Blake looked up, his expression worried. "This isn't so good, Doc. He's been sinking in the last few minutes. I was just going to call you. I—"

The last words were drowned out by the bull-throated drone that came dropping down from above them, a sound peculiarly characteristic of the heavy Sikorsky freighters with their modified blades to gain lift. Ferrel nodded at Brown's questioning glance, but he didn't choose to shout as his hands went over those of Blake and took over the delicate work of simulating the natural heart action. As Blake withdrew, the sound stopped, and Doc motioned him out with his head.

"You'd better go to them and oversee bringing in the apparatus —and grab up any of the men you see to act as porters—or send Jones for them. The machine is an experimental model, and pretty cumbersome; must weigh seven—eight hundred pounds."

"I'll get them myself—Jones is sleeping."

There was no flutter to Jorgenson's heart under Doc's deft manipulations, though he was exerting every bit of skill he possessed. "How long since there was a sign?"

"About four minutes, now. Doc, is there still a chance?"

"Hard to say. Get the machine, though, and we'll hope."

But still the heart refused to respond, though the pressure and manipulation kept the blood circulating and would at least prevent any starving or asphyxiation of the body cells. Carefully, delicately, he brought his mind into his fingers, trying to woo a faint quiver. Perhaps he did, once, but he couldn't be sure. It all depended on how quickly they could get the machine working now, and how long a man could live by manipulation alone. That point was still unsettled.

But there was no question about the fact that the spark of life burned faintly and steadily lower in Jorgenson, while outside the man-made hell went on ticking off the minutes that separated it from becoming Mahler's Isotope. Normally, Doc was an agnostic, but now, unconsciously, his mind slipped back into the simple faith of his childhood, and he heard Brown echoing the payer that was on his lips. The second hand of the watch before him swung around and around and around again before he heard the sound of men's feet at the back entrance, and still there was no definite quiver from the heart under his fingers. How much time did he have left, if any, for the difficult and unfamiliar operation required?

His side glance showed the seemingly innumerable filaments of platinum that had to be connected into the nerves governing Jorgenson's heart and lungs, all carefully coded, yet almost terrifying in their complexity. If he made a mistake anywhere, it was at least certain there would be no time for a second trial; if his fingers shook or his tired eyes clouded at the wrong instant, there would be no help from Jorgenson. Jorgenson would be dead!

5

"Take over massage, Brown," he ordered. "And keep it up no matter what happens. Good. Dodd, assist me, and hang onto my signals. If it works, we can all rest afterward."

Ferrel wondered grimly with that part of his mind that was off by itself whether he could justify his boast to Jenkins of having been the world's greatest surgeon; it had been true once, he knew with no need for false modesty, but that was long ago, and this was at best a devilish job. He'd hung on with a surge of the old fascination as Kubelik had performed it on a dog at the convention, and his memory for such details was still good, as were his hands. But something else goes into the making of a great surgeon, and he wondered it that were still with him.

Then, as his fingers made the microscopic little motions needed and Dodd became another pair of hands, he ceased wondering. Whatever it was, he could feel it surging through him, and there was a pure joy to it somewhere, over and above the urgency of the work. This was probably the last time he'd ever feel it, and if the operation succeeded, probably it was a thing he could put with the few mental treasures that were still left from his former success. The man on the table ceased to be Jorgenson, the excessively gadgety infirmary became again the main operating theater of that same Mayo's which had produced Brown and this strange new machine, and his fingers were again those of the Great Ferrel, the miracle boy from Mayo's, who could do the impossible twice before breakfast without turning a hair.

Some of his feeling was devoted to the machine itself. Massive, ugly, with parts sticking out in haphazard order, it was more like something from an inquisition chamber than a scientist's achievement, but it worked—he'd seen it functioning. In that ugly mass of assorted pieces, little currents were generated and modulated to feed out to the heart and lungs and replace the orders given by a brain that no longer worked or could not get through, to coordinate breathing and beating according to the need. It was a product of the combined genius of surgery and electronics, but wonderful as the exciter was, it was distinctly secondary to the technique Kubelik had evolved for selecting and connecting only those nerves and nerve bundles necessary, and bringing the almost impossible into the limits of surgical possibility.

Brown interrupted, and that interruption in the midst of such an operation indicated clearly the strain she was under. "The heart fluttered a little then, Dr. Ferrel."

Ferrel nodded, untroubled by the interruption. Talk, which bothered most surgeons, was habitual in his own little staff, and he always managed to have one part of his mind reserved for that while the rest went on without noticing. "Good. That gives us at least double the leeway I expected."

His hands went on, first with the heart which was the more pressing danger. Would the machine work, he wondered, in this case? Curare and radioactives, fighting each other, were an odd combination. Yet, the machine controlled the nerves close to the vital organ, pounding its message through into the muscles, where the curare had a complicated action that paralyzed the whole nerve, establishing a long block to the control impulses from the brain. Could the nerve impulses from the machine be forced through the short paralyzed passages? Probably—the strength of its signals was controllable. The only proof was in trying.

Brown drew back her hands and stared down uncomprehendingly. "It's beating, Dr. Ferrel! By itself . . . it's beating!"

He nodded again, though the mask concealed his smile. His technique was still not faulty, and he had performed the operation correctly after seeing it once on a dog! He was still the Great Ferrel! Then, the ego in him fell back to normal, though the lift remained, and his exultation centered around the more important problem of Jorgenson's living. And, later, when the lungs began moving of themselves as the nurse stopped working them, he had been expecting it. The detail work remaining was soon over, and he stepped back, dropping the mask from his face and pulling off his gloves.

"Congratulations, Dr. Ferrel!" The voice was guttural, strange. "A truly great operation—truly great. I almost stopped you, but now I am glad I did not; it was a pleasure to observe you, sir." Ferrel looked up in amazement at the bearded smiling face of Kubelik, and he found no words as he accepted the other's hand. But Kubelik apparently expected none.

"I, Kubelik, came, you see; I could not trust another with the machine, and fortunately I made the plane. Then you seemed so sure, so confident—so when you did not notice me, I remained in the background, cursing myself. Now, I shall return, since you have no need of me—the wiser for having watched you. . . . No, not a word; not a word from you, sir. Don't destroy your miracle with words. The 'copter awaits me, I go; but my admiration for you remains forever!"

Ferrel still stood looking down at his hand as the roar of the 'copter cut in, then at the breathing body with artery on the neck now pulsing regularly. That was all that was needed; he had been admired by Kubelik, the man who thought all other surgeons were fools and nincompoops. For a second or so longer he treasured it, then shrugged it off.

"Now," he said to the others, as the troubles of the plant fell back on his shoulders, "all we have to do is hope that Jorgenson's brain wasn't injured by the session out there, or by this continued artifically maintained life, and try to get him in condition so he can talk before it's too late. God grant us time! Blake, you know the detail work as well as I do, and we can't both work on it. You and the fresh nurses take over, doing the bare minimum needed for the patients scattered around the wards and waiting room. Any new ones?"

"None for some time; I think they've reached a stage where that's over with," Brown answered.

"I hope so. Then go round up Jenkins and lie down somewhere. That goes for you and Meyers, too, Dodd. Blake, give us three

hours if you can, and get us up. There won't be any new developments before then, and we'll save time in the long run by resting.
Jorgenson's to get first attention!"

The old leather chair made a fair sort of bed, and Ferrel was too
exhausted physically and mentally to be choosy—too exhausted to
benefit as much as he should from sleep of three hours' duration,
for that matter, though it was almost imperative he try. Idly, he
wondered what Palmer would think of all his safeguards had he
known that Kubelik had come into the place so easily and out again.
Not that it mattered; it was doubtful whether anyone else would
want to come near, let alone inside the plant.

In that, apparently, he was wrong. It was considerably less
than the three hours when he was awakened to hear the bullroar
of a helicopter outside. But sleep clouded his mind too much for
curiosity and he started to drop back into his slumber. Then
another sound cut in jerking him out of his drowsiness. It was
the sharp sputter of a machine gun from the direction of the gate,
a pause and another burst; an eddy of sleep-memory indicated that
it had begun before the helicopter's arrival, so it could not be that
they were gunning. More trouble, and while it was none of his
business, he could not go back to sleep. He got up and went out
into the surgery, just as a gnomish little man hopped out from the
rear entrance.

The fellow scooted toward Ferrel after one birdlike glance at
Blake, his words spilling out with a jerky self-importance that
should have been funny, but missed it by a small margin; under
the surface, sincerity still managed to show. "Dr. Ferrel? Uh, Dr.
Kubelik—Mayo's, you know—he reported you were shorthanded;
stacking patients in the other rooms. We volunteered for duty—me,
four other doctors, nine nurses. Probably should have checked with
you, but couldn't get a phone through. Took the liberty of coming
through directly, fast as we could push our 'copters."

Ferrel glanced through the back, and saw that there were three
of the machines, instead of the one he'd thought, with men and
equipment piling out of them. Mentally he kicked himself for
not asking for help when he'd put through the call; but he'd
been used to working with his own little staff for so long that
the ready response of his profession to emergencies had been
almost forgotten. "You know you're taking chances coming here,
naturally? Then, in that case, I'm grateful to you and Kubelik.
We've got about forty patients here, all of whom should have

considerable attention, though I frankly doubt whether there's room for you to work."

The man hitched his thumb backward jerkily. "Don't worry about that. Kubelik goes the limit when he arranges things. Everything we need with us, practically all the hospital's atomic equipment; though maybe you'll have to piece us out there. Even a field hospital tent, portable wards for every patient you have. Want relief in here or would you rather have us simply move out the patients to the tent, leave this end to you? Oh, Kubelik sent his regards. Amazing of him!"

Kubelik, it seemed, had a tangible idea of regards, however dramatically he was inclined to express them; with him directing the volunteer force, the wonder was that the whole staff and equipment hadn't been moved down. "Better leave this end," Ferrel decided. "Those in the wards will probably be better off in your tent as well as the men now in the waiting room; we're equipped beautifully for all emergency work, but not used to keeping the patients here any length of time, so our accommodations that way are rough. Dr. Blake will show you around and help you get organized in the routine we use here. He'll get help for you in erecting the tent, too. By the way, did you hear the commotion by the entrance as you were landing?"

"We did, indeed. We saw it, too—bunch of men in some kind of uniform shooting a machine gun; hitting the ground, though. Bunch of other people running back away from it, shaking their fists, looked like. We were expecting a dose of the same, maybe; didn't notice us, though."

Blake snorted in half amusement. "You probably would have gotten it if our manager hadn't forgotten to give orders covering the air approach; they must figure that's an official route. I saw a bunch from the city arguing about their relatives in here when I came in this morning, so it must have been that." He motioned the little doctor after him, then turned his neck back to address Brown. "Show him the results while I'm gone, honey."

Ferrel forgot his new recruits and swung back to the girl. "Bad?"

She made no comment, but picked up a lead shield and placed it over Jorgenson's chest so that it cut off all radiation from the lower part of his body, then placed the radiation indicator close to the man's throat. Doc looked once; no more was needed. It was obvious that Blake had already done his best to remove the radioactive from all parts of the body needed for speech, in the hope that they might strap down the others and block them off with local anesthetics;

then the curare could have been counteracted long enough for such information as was needed. Equally obviously, he'd failed. There was no sense in going through the job of neutralizing the drug's block only to have him under the control of the radioactive still present. The stuff was too finely dispersed for surgical removal. Now what? He had no answer.

Jenkins' lean-sinewed hand took the indicator from him for inspection. The boy was already frowning as Doc looked up in faint surprise, and his face made no change. He nodded slowly. "Yeah. I figured as much. That was a beautiful piece of work you did, too. Too bad. I was watching from the door and you almost convinced me he'd be all right, the way you handled it. But— So we have to make out without him; and Hoke and Palmer haven't even cooked up a lead that's worth a good test. Want to come into my office, Doc? There's nothing we can do here."

Ferrel followed Jenkins into the little office off the now emptied waiting room; the men from the hospital had worked rapidly, it seemed. "So you haven't been sleeping, I take it? Where's Hokusai now?"

"Out there with Palmer; he promised to behave, if that'll comfort you. . . . Nice guy, Hoke; I'd forgotten what it felt like to talk to an atomic engineer without being laughed at. Palmer, too. I wish—" There was a brief lightening to the boy's face and the first glow of normal human pride Doc had seen in him. Then he shrugged, and it vanished back into his taut cheeks and reddened eyes. "We cooked up the wildest kind of a scheme, but it isn't so hot."

Hoke's voice came out of the doorway, as the little man came in and sat down carefully in one of the three chairs.

"No, not sso hot! It iss fail, already. Jorgensson?"

"Out, no hope there! What happened?"

Hoke spread his arms, his eyes almost closing. "Nothing. We knew it could never work, not sso? Misster Palmer, he iss come ssoon here, then we make planss again, I am think now, besst we sshould move from here. Palmer, I—mosstly we are theoreticianss; and, excusse, you alsso, doctor. Jorgensson wass the production man. No Jorgensson, no—ah—ssoap!"

Mentally, Ferrel agreed about the moving—and soon! But he could see Palmer's point of view; to give up the fight was against the grain, somehow. And besides, once the blowup happened, with the resultant damage to an unknown area, the pressure groups in Congress would be in, shouting for the final abolition of all atomic work; now they were reasonably quiet, only waiting an opportunity—or, more probably, at the moment were already seizing on the rumors spreading to turn this into their coup. If, by some streak of luck, Palmer could save the plant with no greater loss of life and property than already existed, their words would soon be forgotten, and the benefits from the products of National would again outweigh all risks.

"Just what will happen if it all goes off?" he asked.

Jenkins shrugged, biting at his inner lip as he went over a sheaf of papers on the desk, covered with the scrawling symbols of atomics. "Anybody's guess. Suppose three tons of the army's new explosives were to explode in a billionth—or at least, a millionth—of a second? Normally, you know, compared to atomics, that stuff burns like any fire, slowly and quietly, giving its gases plenty of time to get out of the way in an orderly fashion. Figure it one way, with this all going off together, and the stuff could drill a hole that'd split open the whole continent from Hudson Bay to the Gulf of Mexico, and leave a lovely sea where the Middle West is now. Figure it another, and it might only kill off everything within fifty miles of here. Somewhere in between is the chance we count on. This isn't U-235, you know."

Doc winced. He'd been picturing the plant going up in the air violently, with maybe a few buildings somewhere near it, but nothing like this. It had been purely a local affair to him, but this didn't sound like one. No wonder Jenkins was in that state of suppressed jitters; it wasn't too much imagination, but too much cold, hard knowledge that was worrying him. Ferrel looked at their faces as they bent over the symbols once more, tracing out point by point their calculations in the hope of finding one overlooked loophole, then decided to leave them alone.

The whole problem was hopeless without Jorgenson, it seemed, and Jorgenson was his responsibility; if the plant went, it was squarely on the senior physician's shoulders. But there was no apparent solution. If it would help, he could cut it down to a direct path from brain to speaking organs, strap down the body and block off all nerves below the neck, using an artificial larynx instead of the normal breathing through vocal cords. But the indicator showed the futility of it; the orders could never get through from the brain with the amount of radioactive still present throwing them off track—even granting that the brain itself was not affected, which was doubtful.

Fortunately for Jorgenson, the stuff was all finely dispersed around the head, with no concentration at any one place that was unquestionably destructive to his mind; but the good fortune was also the trouble, since it could not be removed by any means known to medical practice. Even so simple a thing as letting the man read the questions and spell out the answers by winking an eyelid as they pointed to the alphabet was hopeless.

Nerves! Jorgenson had his blocked out, but Ferrel wondered if the rest of them weren't in as bad a state. Probably, somewhere well within their grasp, there was a solution that was being held back because the nerves of everyone in the plant were blocked by fear and pressure that defeated its own purpose. Jenkins, Palmer, Hokusai—under purely theoretical conditions, any one of them might spot the answer to the problem, but sheer necessity of finding it could be the thing that hid it. The same might be true with the problem of Jorgenson's treatment. Yet, though he tried to relax and let his mind stray idly around the loose ends, and seemingly disconnected knowledge he had, it returned incessantly to the necessity of doing something, and doing it now!

Ferrel heard weary footsteps behind him and turned to see Palmer coming from the front entrance. The man had no business walking into the surgery, but such minor rules had gone by the board hours before.

"Jorgenson?" Palmer's conversation began with the same old question in the usual tone, and he read the answer from Doc's face with a look that indicated it was no news. "Hoke and that Jenkins kid still in the there?"

Doc nodded, and plodded behind him toward Jenkins' office; he was useless to them, but there was still the idea that in filling his mind with other things, some little factor he had overlooked might have a chance to come forth. Also, curiosity still worked on him, demanding to know what was happening. He flopped into the third chair, and Palmer squatted down on the edge of the table.

"Know a good spiritualist, Jenkins?" the manager asked. "Because if you do, I'm about ready to try calling back Kellar's ghost. The Steinmetz of atomics—so he had to die before this Isotope R came up, and leave us without even a good guess at how long we've got to crack the problem. Hey, what's the matter?"

Jenkins' face had tensed and his body straightened back tensely in the chair, but he shook his head, the corner of his mouth twitching wryly. "Nothing. Nerves, I guess. Hoke and I dug out some things that give an indication on how long this runs, though. We still don't know exactly, but from observations out there and the general theory before, it looks like something between six and thirty hours left; probably ten's closer to being correct!"

"Can't be much longer. It's driving the men back right now! Even the tanks can't get in where they can do the most good, and we're using the shielding around No. 3 as a headquarters for the men; in another half hour, maybe they won't be able to stay that near the thing. Radiation indicators won't register any more, and it's spitting all over the place, almost constantly. Heat's terrific; it's gone up to around three hundred centigrade and sticks right there now, but that's enough to warm up 3, even."

Doc looked up. "No. 3?"

"Yeah. Nothing happened to that batch—it ran through and came out I-713 right on schedule, hours ago." Palmer reached for a cigarette, realized he had one in his mouth, and slammed the package back on the table. "Significant data, Doc; if we get out of this, we'll figure out just what caused the change in No. 4—if we get out! Any chance of making those variable factors work, Hoke?"

Hoke shook his head, and again Jenkins answered from the notes. "Not a chance; sure, theoretically, at least, R should have a period varying between twelve and sixty hours before turning into Mahler's Isotope, depending on what chains of reaction or subchains it goes through; they all look equally good, and probably are all going on in there now, depending on what's around to soak up neutrons or let them roam, the concentration and amount of R together, and even high or low temperatures that change their activity somewhat. It's one of the variables, no question about that."

"The sspitting iss prove that," Hoke supplemented.

"Sure. But there's too much of it together, and we can't break it down fine enough to reach any safety point where it won't toss energy around like rain. The minute one particle manages to make itself into Mahler's, it'll crash through with energy enough to blast the next over the hump and into the same thing instantly, and that passes it on to the next, at about light speed! If we *could* get it juggled around so some would go off first, other atoms a little later, and so on, fine—only we can't do it unless we can be sure of isolating every blob bigger than a tenth of a gram from every other one! And if we start breaking it down into reasonably small pieces, we're likely to have one decide on the short transformation subchain and go off at any time; pure chance gave us a concentration to begin with that eliminated the shorter chains, but we can't break it down into small lots and those into smaller lots, and so on. Too much risk!"

Ferrel had known vaguely that there were such things as variables, but the theory behind them was too new and too complex for him; he'd learned what little he knew when the simpler radioactives proceeded normally from radium to lead, as an example, with a definite, fixed half-life, instead of the super-heavy atoms they now used that could jump through several different paths, yet end up the same. It was over his head, and he started to get up and go back to Jorgenson.

Palmer's words stopped him. "I knew it, of course, but I hoped maybe I was wrong. Then—we evacuate! No use fooling ourselves any longer. I'll call the Governor and try to get him to clear the country around; Hoke, you can tell the men to get the hell out of here! All we ever had was the counteracting isotope to hope on, and no chance of getting enough of that. There was no sense in making I-231 in thousand-pound batches before. Well—"

5

He reached for the phone, but Ferrel cut in. "What about the men in the wards? They're loaded with the stuff, most of them with more than a gram apiece dispersed through them. They're in the same class with the converter, maybe, but we can't just pull out and leave them!"

Silence hit them, to be broken by Jenkins' hushed whisper. "My God! What damned fools we are. I-231 under discussion for hours, and I never thought of it. Now you two throw the connection in my face, and I still almost miss it!"

"I-231? But there iss not enough. Maybe twenty-five pound, maybe less. Three and a half days to make more. The little we have would be no good, Dr. Jenkinss. We forget that already." Hoke struck a match to a piece of paper, shook one drop of ink onto it, and watched it continue burning for a second before putting it out. "Sso. A drop of water for sstop a foresst fire. No."

"Wrong, Hoke. A drop to short a switch that'll turn on the real stream—maybe. Look, Doc, I-231's an isotope that reacts atomically with R—we've checked on that already. It simply gets together with the stuff and the two break down into non-radioactive elements and a little heat, like a lot of other such atomic reactions; but it isn't the violent kind. They simply swap parts in a friendly way and open up to simpler atoms that are stable. We have a few pounds on hand, can't make enough in time to help with No.

4, but we do have enough to treat every man in the wards, *including Jorgenson!*"

"How much heat?" Doc snapped out of his lethargy into the detailed thought of a good physician. "In atomics you may call it a little; but would it be small enough in the human body?"

Hokusai and Palmer were practically riding the pencil as Jenkins figured. "Say five grams of the stuff in Jorgenson, to be on the safe side, less in the others. Time for reaction . . . hm-m. Here's the total heat produced and the time taken by the reaction, probably, in the body. The stuff's water-soluble in the chloride we have of it, so there's no trouble dispersing it. What do you make of it, Doc?"

"Fifteen to eighteen degrees temperature rise at a rough estimate. Uh!"

"Too much! Jorgenson couldn't stand ten degrees right now!" Jenkins frowned down at his figures, tapping nervously with his hand.

Doc shook his head. "Not too much! We can drop his whole body temperature first in the hypothermy bath down to eighty degrees, then let it rise to a hundred, if necessary, and still be safe. Thank the Lord, there's equipment enough. If they'll rip out the refrigerating units in the cafeteria and improvise baths, the volunteers out in the tent can start on the other men while we handle Jorgenson. At least that way we can get the men all out, even if we don't save the plant."

Palmer stared at them in confusion before his face galvanized into resolution. "Refrigerating units—volunteers—tent? What—O.K., Doc, what do you want?" He reached for the telephone and began giving orders for the available I-231 to be sent to the surgery, for men to rip out the cafeteria cooling equipment, and for such other things as Doc requested. Jenkins had already gone to instruct the medical staff in the field tent without asking how they'd gotten there, but was back in the surgery before Doc reached it with Palmer and Hokusai at his heels.

"Blake's taking over out there," Jenkins announced. "Says if you want Dodd, Meyers, Jones or Sue, they're sleeping."

"No need. Get over there out of the way, if you must watch," Ferrel ordered the two engineers, as he and Jenkins began attaching the freezing units and bath to the sling on the exciter. "Prepare his blood for it, Jenkins; we'll force it down as low as we can to be on the safe side. And we'll have to keep tabs on the temperature fall and regulate his heart and breathing to what it would be normally in that condition; they're both out of his normal control, now."

"And pray," Jenkins added. He grabbed the small box out of the messenger's hand before the man was fully inside the door and began preparing a solution, weighing out the whitish powder and measuring water carefully, but with the speed that was automatic to him under tension. "Doc, if this doesn't work—if Jorgenson's crazy or something—you'll have another case of insanity on your hands. One more false hope would finish me."

"Not one more case; four! We're all in the same boat. Temperature's falling nicely—I'm rushing it a little, but it's safe enough. Down to ninety-six now." The thermometer under Jorgenson's tongue was one intended for hypothermy work, capable of rapid response, instead of the normal fever thermometer. Slowly, with agonizing reluctance, the little needle on the dial moved over, down to ninety, then on. Doc kept his eyes glued to it, slowing the pulse and breath to the proper speed. He lost track of the number of times he sent Palmer back out of the way, and finally gave up.

Waiting, he wondered how those outside in the field hospital were doing? Still, they had ample time to arrange their makeshift cooling apparatus and treat the men in groups—ten hours probably; and hypothermy was a standard thing, now. Jorgenson was the only real rush case. Almost imperceptibly to Doc, but speedily by normal standards, the temperature continued to fall. Finally it reached seventy-eight.

"Ready, Jenkins, make the injection. That enough?"

"No. I figure it's almost enough, but we'll have to go slow to balance out properly. Too much of this stuff would be almost as bad as the other. Gauge going up, Doc?"

It was, much more rapidly than Ferrel liked. As the injection coursed through the blood vessels and dispersed out to the fine deposits of radioactive, the needle began climbing past eighty, to ninety, and up. It stopped at ninety-four and slowly began falling as the cooling bath absorbed heat from the cells of the body. The radioactivity meter still registered the presence of Isotope R, though much more faintly.

The next shot was small, and a smaller one followed. "Almost," Ferrel commented. "Next one should about do the trick."

Using partial injections, there had been need for less drop in temperature than they had given Jorgenson, but there was small loss to that. Finally, when the last minute bit of the I-213 solution had entered the man's veins and done its work, Doc nodded. "No sign of activity left. He's up to ninety-five, now that I've cut off the refrigeration, and he'll pick up the little extra temperature in a hurry. By the time we can counteract the curare, he'll be ready. That'll take about fifteen minutes, Palmer."

The manager nodded, watching them dismantling the hypo-thermy equipment and going through the routine of cancelling out the curare. It was always a slower job than treatment with the drug, but part of the work had been done already by the normal body processes, and the rest was a simple, standard procedure. Fortunately, the neo-heroin would be nearly worn off, or that would have been a longer and much harder problem to eliminate.

"Telephone for Mr. Palmer. Calling Mr. Palmer. Send Mr. Palmer to the telephone." The operator's words lacked the usual artificial exactness, and were only a nervous sing-song. It was getting her, and she wasn't bothered by excess imagination, normally. "Mr. Palmer is wanted on the telephone."

"Palmer." The manager picked up an instrument at hand, not equipped with vision, and there was no indication to the caller. But Ferrel could see what little hope had appeared at the prospect of Jorgenson's revival disappearing. "Check! Move out of there, and prepare to evacuate, but keep quiet about that until you hear further orders! Tell the men Jorgenson's about out of it, so they won't lack for something to talk about."

He swung back to them. "No use, Doc, I'm afraid. We're already too late. The stuff's stepped it up again, and they're having to move out of No. 3 now. I'll wait on Jorgenson, but even if he's all right and knows the answer, we can't get in to use it !"

6

"Healing's going to be a long, slow process, but they should at least grow back better than silver ribs; never take a pretty X-ray photo, though." Doc held the instrument in his hand, staring down at the flap opened in Jorgenson's chest, and his shoulders came up in a faint shrug. The little platinum filaments had been removed from around the nerves to heart and lungs, and the man's normal impulses were operating again, less steadily than under the exciter, but with no danger signals. "Well, it won't much matter if he's still sane."

Jenkins watched him being stitching the flap back, his eyes centered over the table out toward the converter. "Doc, he's got to be sane! If Hoke and Palmer find it's what it sounds like out there, we'll have to count on Jorgenson. There's an answer somewhere, has to be! But we won't find it without him."

"Hm-m-m. Seems to me you've been having ideas yourself, son. You've been right so far, and if Jorgenson's out—" He shut off the stitcher, finished the dressings, and flopped down on a bench, knowing that all they could do was wait for the drugs to work on Jorgenson and bring him around. Now that he relaxed the control over himself, exhaustion hit down with full force; his fingers were uncertain as he pulled off the gloves. "Anyhow, we'll know in another five minutes or so."

"And heaven help us, Doc, if it's up to me. I've always had a flair for atomic theory; I grew up on it. But he's the production man who's been working at it week in and week out, and it's his process, to boot. . . . There they are now! All right for them to come back here?"

But Hokusai and Palmer were waiting for no permission. At the moment, Jorgenson was the nerve center of the plant, drawing them back, and they stalked over to stare down at him, then sat where they could be sure of missing no sign of returning consciousness. Palmer picked up the conversation where he'd dropped it, addressing his remarks to both Hokusai and Jenkins.

"Damn that Link-Stevens postulate! Time after time it fails, until you figure there's nothing to it; then, this ! It's black magic, not science, and if I get out, I'll find some fool with more courage than sense to discover why. Hoke, are you positive it's the *theta* chain? There isn't one chance in ten thousand of that happening, you know; it's unstable, hard to stop, tends to revert to the simpler ones at the first chance."

Hokusai spread his hands, lifted one heavy eyelid at Jenkins questioningly, then nodded. The boy's voice was dull, almost uninterested. "That's what I thought it had to be, Palmer. None of the others throws off that much energy at this stage, the way you described conditions out there. Probably the last thing we tried to quench set it up in that pattern, and it's in a concentration just right to keep it going. We figured ten hours was the best chance, so it had to pick the six-hour short chain."

"Yeah." Palmer was pacing up and down nervously again, his eyes swinging toward Jorgenson from whatever direction he moved. "And in six hours, maybe all the population around here can be evacuated, maybe not, but we'll have to try it. Doc, I can't even wait for Jorgenson now! I've got to get the Governor started at once!"

"They've been known to practice lynch law, even in recent years," Ferrel reminded him grimly. He'd seen the result of one such case of mob violence when he was practicing privately, and he knew that people remain pretty much the same year after year; they'd move, but first they'd demand a sacrifice. "Better get the men out of here first, Palmer, and my advice is to get yourself a good long distance off; I heard some of the trouble at the gate, and that won't be anything compared to what an evacuation order will do."

Palmer grunted. "Doc, you might not believe it, but I don't give a continental about what happens to me or the plant right now."

"Or the men? Put a mob in here, hunting your blood, and the men will be on your side, because they know it wasn't your fault, and they've seen you out there taking chances yourself. That mob won't be too choosy about its targets, either, once it gets worked up, and you'll have a nice vicious brawl all over the place. Besides, Jorgenson's practically ready."

A few minutes would make no difference in the evacuation, and Doc had no desire to think of his partially crippled wife going through the hell evacuation would be; she'd probably refuse, until he returned. His eyes fell on the box Jenkins was playing with nervously, and he stalled for time. "I thought you said it was risky to break the stuff down into small particles, Jenkins. But that box contains the stuff in various sizes, including one big piece we scraped out, along with the contaminated instruments. Why hasn't it exploded?"

Jenkins' hand jerked up from it as if burned, and he backed away a step before checking himself. Then he was across the room toward the I-231 and back, pouring the white powder over everything in the box in a jerky frenzy. Hokusai's eyes had snapped fully open, and he was slopping water in to fill up the remaining space and keep the I-231 in contact with everything else. Almost at once, in spite of the low relative energy release, it sent up a white cloud of steam faster than the air conditioner could clear the room; but that soon faded down and disappeared.

Hokusai wiped his forehead slowly. "The ssuits—armor of the men?"

"Sent 'em back to the converter and had them dumped into the stuff to be safe long ago," Jenkins answered. "But I forgot that box, like a fool. Ugh! Either blind chance saved us or else the stuff spit out was all one kind, some reasonably long chain. I don't know nor care right—"

"S'ot! Nnnuh . . . Whmah nahh?"

"Jorgenson!" They swung from the end of the room like one man, but Jenkins was the first to reach the table. Jorgenson's eyes were open and rolling in a semiorderly manner, his hands moving sluggishly. The boy hovered over his face, his own practically glowing with the intensity behind it. "Jorgenson, can you understand what I'm saying?"

"Uh." The eyes ceased moving and centered on Jenkins. One hand came up to his throat, clutching at it, and he tried unsuccessfully to lift himself with the other, but the aftereffects of what he'd been through seemed to have left him in a state of partial paralysis.

Ferrel had hardly dared hope that the man could be rational, and his relief was tinged with doubt. He pushed Palmer back, and shook his head. "No, stay back. Let the boy handle it; he knows enough not to shock the man now, and you don't. This can't be rushed too much."

"I—uh. . . . Young Jenkins? Whasha doin' here? Tell y'ur dad to ge' busy ou' there!" Somewhere in Jorgenson's huge frame, and untapped reserve of energy and will sprang up, and he forced himself into a sitting position, his eyes on Jenkins, his hand still catching at the reluctant throat that refused to cooperate. His words were blurry and uncertain, but sheer determination overcame the obstacles and made the words understandable.

"Dad's dead now, Jorgenson. Now—"

"'Sright. 'N' you're grown up—'bout twelve years old, y'were. . . . The plant!"

"Easy, Jorgenson." Jenkins' own voice managed to sound casual, though his hands under the table were white where they clenched together. "Listen, and don't try to say anything until I finish. The plan's still all right, but we've got to have your help. Here's what happened."

Ferrel could make little sense of the cryptic sentences that followed, though he gathered that they were some form of engineering shorthand; apparently, from Hokusai's approving nod, they summed up the situation briefly but fully, and Jorgenson sat rigidly still until it was finished, his eyes fastened on the boy.

"Hellova mess! Gotta think . . . yuh tried—" He made an attempt to lower himself back, and Jenkins assisted him, hanging on feverishly to each awkward, uncertain change of expression on the man's face. "Uh . . . da' sroat! Yuh . . . uh . . . urrgh!"

"Got it?"

"Uh!" The tone was affirmative, unquestionably, but the clutching hands around his neck told their own story. The temporary burst of energy he'd forced was exhausted, and he couldn't get through with it. He lay there, breathing heavily and struggling, then relaxed after a few more half-whispered words, none intelligently articulated.

Palmer clutched at Ferrel's sleeve. "Doc, isn't there anything you can do?"

"Try." He metered out a minute quantity of drug doubtfully, felt Jorgenson's pulse, and decided on half that amount. "Not much hope, though; that man's been through hell, and it wasn't good for him to be forced around in the first place. Carry it too far, and he'll be delirious if he does talk. Anyway, I suspect it's partly his speech centers as well as the throat."

But Jorgenson began a slight rally almost instantly, trying again, then apparently drawing himself together for a final attempt. When they came, the words spilled out harshly in forced clearness, but without inflection.

"First . . . variable . . . at . . . twelve . . . water . . . stop." His eyes, centered on Jenkins, closed, and he relaxed again, this time no longer fighting of the inevitable unconsciousness.

Hokusai, Palmer and Jenkins were staring back and forth at one another questioningly. The little Japanese shook his head negatively at first, frowned, and repeated it, to be imitated almost exactly by the manager. "Delirious ravings!"

"The great white hope Jorgenson!" Jenkins' shoulders dropped and the blood drained from his face, leaving it ghastly with fatigue and despair. "Oh, damn it, Doc stop staring at me! I can't pull a miracle out of a hat!"

Doc hadn't realized that he was staring, but he made no effort to change it. "Maybe not, but you happened to have the most active imagination here, when you stop abusing it to scare yourself. Well, you're on the spot now, and I'm still giving odds on you. Want to bet, Hoke?"

It was an utterly stupid thing, and Doc knew it; but somewhere during the long hours together, he'd picked up a queer respect for the boy and a dependence on the nervousness that wasn't fear but closer akin to the reaction of a rear-running thoroughbred on the home stretch. Hoke was too slow and methodical, and Palmer had been too concerned with outside worries to give anywhere nearly full attention to the single most urgent phase of the problem; that left only Jenkins, hampered by his lack of self-confidence.

Hoke gave no sign that he caught the meaning of Doc's heavy wink, but he lifted his eyebrows faintly. "No, I think I am not bet. Dr. Jenkins, I am to be command!"

Palmer looked briefly at the boy, whose face mirrored in credulous confusion, but he had neither Ferrel's ignorance of atomic technique nor Hokusai's fatalism. With a final glance at the unconscious Jorgenson, he started across the room toward the phone. "You men play, if you like. I'm starting evacuation immediately!"

"Wait!" Jenkins was shaking himself, physically as well as mentally. "Hold it, Palmer! Thanks, Doc. You knocked me out of the rut, and bounced my memory back to something I picked up somewhere; I think it's the answer! It has to work—nothing else can at this stage of the game!"

"Give me the Governor, operator." Palmer had heard, but he went on with the phone call. "This is no time to play crazy hunches until after we get the people out, kid. I'll admit you're a darned clever amateur, but you're no atomicist!"

"And if we get the men out, it's too late—there'll be no one left in here to do the work!" Jenkins' hand snapped out and jerked the receiver of the plug-in telephone from Palmer's hand. "Cancel the call, operator; it won't be necessary. Palmer, you've got to listen to me; you can't clear the whole middle of the continent, and you can't depend on the explosion to limit itself to less ground. It's a gamble, but you're risking fifty million people against a mere hundred thousand. Give me a chance!"

"I'll give you exactly one minute to convince me, Jenkins, and it had better be good! Maybe the blowup won't hit beyond the fifty-mile limit!"

"Maybe. And I can't explain in a minute." The boy scowled tensely. "O.K., you've been bellyaching about a man named Kellar being dead. If he were here, would you take a chance on him? Or on a man who'd worked under him on everything he tried?"

"Absolutely, but you're not Kellar. And I happen to know he was a lone wolf; didn't hire outside engineers after Jorgenson had a squabble with him and came here." Palmer reached for the phone. "It won't wash, Jenkins."

Jenkins' hand clamped down on the instrument, jerking it out of reach. "I wasn't *outside* help, Palmer. When Jorgenson was afraid to run one of the things off and quit, I was twelve; three years later, things got too tight for him to handle alone, but he decided he might as well keep it in the family, so he started me in. I'm Kellar's stepson!"

Pieces clicked together in Doc's head then, and he kicked himself mentally for not having seen the obvious before. "That's why Jorgenson knew you, then? I thought that was funny. It checks, Palmer."

For a split second, the manager hesitated uncertainly. Then he shrugged and gave in. "O.K., I'm a fool to trust you, Jenkins, but it's too late for anything else, I guess. I never forgot that I was gambling the locality against half the continent. What do you want?"

"Men—construction men, mostly, and a few volunteers for dirty work. I want all the blowers, exhaust equipment, tubing, booster blowers and everything ripped from the other three converters and connected as close to No. 4 as you can get. Put them up some way so they can be shoved in over the stuff by crane—I don't care how; the shop men will know better than I do. You've got sort of a river running off behind the plant; get everyone within a few miles of it out of there, and connect the blower outlets down to it. Where does it end, anyway—some kind of a swamp, or morass?"

"About ten miles farther down, yes; we didn't bother keeping the drainage system going, since the land meant nothing to us, and the swamps made as good a dumping ground as anything else." When the plant had first used the little river as an outlet for their waste products, there'd been so much trouble that National had been forced to take over all adjacent land and quiet the owners' fears of the atomic activity in cold cash. Since then, it had gone to weeds and rabbits, mostly. "Everyone within a few miles is out, anyway, except a few fishers or tramps that don't know we use it. I'll have militia sent in to scare them out."

"Good. Ideal, in fact, since the swamps will hold stuff longer in there where the current's slow. Now, what about that superthermite stuff you were producing last year? Any around?"

"Not in the plant. But we've got tons of it at the warehouse, still waiting for the army's requisition. That's pretty hot stuff to handle, though. Know much about it?"

"Enough to know it's what I want." Jenkins indicated the copy of the *Weekly Ray* still lying where he'd dropped it, and Doc remembered skimming through the nontechnical part of the description. It was made up of two superheavy atoms, kept separate. By itself, neither was particularly important or active, but together they reacted with each other atomically to release a tremendous amount of raw heat and comparatively little unwanted radiation. "Goes up around twenty thousand centigrade, doesn't it? How's it stored?"

"In ten-pound bombs that have a fragile partition; it breaks with shock, starting the action. Hoke can explain it—it's his baby." Palmer reached for the phone. "Anything else? Then, get out and get busy! The men will be ready for you when you get there! I'll be out myself as soon as I can put through your orders."

Doc watched them go out, to be followed in short order by the manager, and was alone in the infirmary with Jorgenson and his thoughts. They weren't pleasant; he was both too far outside the inner circle to know what was going on and too much mixed up in it not to know the dangers. Now he could have used some work of any nature to take his mind off useless speculations, but aside from a needless check of the foreman's condition, there was nothing for him to do.

He wriggled down in the leather chair, making the mistake of trying to force sleep, while his mind chased out after the sounds that came in from outside. There were the drones of crane and tank motors coming to life, the shouts of hurried orders, and above all, the jarring rhythm of pneumatic hammers on metal, each sound suggesting some possibility to him without adding to his knowledge. The 'Decameron' was boring, the whiskey tasted raw and rancid, and solitaire wasn't worth the trouble of cheating.

Finally, he gave up and turned out to the field hospital tent. Jorgenson would be better off out there, under the care of the staff from Mayo's, and perhaps he could make himself useful. As he passed through the rear entrance, he heard the sound of a number of helicopters coming over with heavy loads, and looked up as they began settling over the edge of the buildings. From somewhere, a group of men came running forward, and disappeared in the direction of the freighters. He wondered whether any of those men would be forced back into the stuff out there to return filled with radioactive; though it didn't matter so much, now that the isotope could be eliminated without surgery.

Blake met him at the entrance of the field tent, obviously well satisfied with his duty of bossing and instructing the others. "Scram, Doc. You aren't necessary here, and you need some rest. Don't want you added to the casualties. What's the latest dope from the pow-wow front?"

"Jorgenson didn't come through, but the kid had an idea, and they're out there working on it." Doc tried to sound more hopeful than he felt. "I was thinking you might as well bring Jorgenson in here; he's still unconscious, but there doesn't seem to be anything to worry about. Where's Brown? She'll probably want to know what's up, if she isn't asleep."

"Asleep when the kid isn't? Uh-huh. Mother complex, has to worry about him." Blake grinned. "She got a look at him running out with Hoke tagging at his heels, and hiked out after him, so she probably knows everything now. Wish Anne'd chase me that way, just once—Jenkins, the wonder boy! Well, it's out of my line; I don't intend to start worrying until they pass out the order. O.K., Doc, I'll have Jorgenson out here in a couple of minutes, so you grab yourself a cot and get some shut-eye."

Doc grunted, looking curiously at the refinements and well-equipped interior of the field tent. "I've already prescribed that, Blake, but the patient can't seem to take it. I think I'll hunt up Brown, so give me a call over the public speaker if anything turns up."

He headed toward the center of action, knowing that he'd been wanting to do it all along, but hadn't been sure of not being a nuisance. Well, if Brown could look on, there was no reason why he couldn't. He passed the machine shop, noting the excited flurry of activity going on, and went past No. 2, where other men were busily ripping out long sections of big piping and various other devices. There was a rope fence barring his way, well beyond No. 3, and he followed along the edge, looking for Palmer or Brown.

She saw him first. "Hi, Dr. Ferrel, over here in the truck. I thought you'd be coming soon. From up here we can get a look over the heads of all these other people, and we won't be tramped on." She stuck down a hand to help him up, smiled faintly as he disregarded it and mounted more briskly than his muscles wanted to. He wasn't so old that a girl had to help him yet.

"Know what's going on?" he asked, sinking down onto the plank across the truck body, facing out across the men below toward the converter. There seemed to be a dozen different centers of activity, all crossing each other in complete confusion, and the general pattern was meaningless.

"No more than you do. I haven't seen my husband, though Mr. Palmer took time enough to chase me here out of the way."

Doc centered his attention on the 'copters, unloading, rising, and coming in with more loads, and he guessed that those boxes must contain the little thermodyne bombs. It was the one thing he could understand, and consequently the least interesting. Other men were assembling the big sections of piping he'd seen before, connecting them up in almost endless order, while some of the tanks hooked

on and snaked them off in the direction of the small river that ran
off beyond the plant.

"Those must be the exhaust blowers, I guess," he told Brown,
pointing them out. "Though I don't know what any of the rest of
the stuff hooked on is."

"I know—I've been inside the plant Bob's father had." She lifted
an inquiring eyebrow at him, went on as he nodded. "The pipes
are for exhaust gases, all right, and those big square things are the
motors and fans—they put in one at each five hundred feet or less
of piping. The things they're wrapping around the pipe must be
the heaters to keep the gases hot. Are they going to try to suck
all that out?"

Doc didn't know, though it was the only thing he could see.
But he wondered how they'd get around the problem of moving
in close enough to do any good. "I heard your husband order some
thermodyne bombs, so they'll probably try to gassify the magma;
then they're pumping it down the river."

As he spoke, there was a flurry of motion at one side, and his eyes
swung over instantly, to see one of the cranes laboring with a long
framework stuck from its front, holding up a section of pipe with
a nozzle on the end. It tilted precariously, even though heavy bags
were piled everywhere to add weight, but an inch at a time it lifted
its load, and began forcing its way forward, carrying the nozzle out
in front and rather high.

Below the main exhaust pipe was another smaller one. As it drew
near the outskirts of the danger zone, a small object ejaculated from
the little pipe, hit the ground, and was a sudden blazing inferno of
glaring blue-white light, far brighter than it seemed, judging by
the effect on the eyes. Doc shielded his, just as someone below put
something into his hands.

"Put 'em on. Palmer says the light's actinic."

He heard Brown fussing beside him, then his vision cleared,
and he looked back through the goggles again to see a glowing
cloud spring up from the magma, spread out near the ground,
narrowing down higher up, until it sucked into the nozzle above,
and disappeared. Another bomb slid from the tube, and erupted
with blazing heat. A sideways glance showed another crane being
fitted, and a group of men near it wrapping what might have
been oiled rags around the small bombs; probably no tubing
fitted them exactly, and they were padding them so pressure
could blow them forward and out. Three more dropped from
the tube, one at a time, and the fans roared and groaned, pulling

the cloud that rose into the pipe and feeding it down toward the river.

Then the crane inched back out carefully as men uncoupled its piping from the main line, and a second went in to replace it. The heat generated must be too great for the machine to stand steadily without the pipe fusing, Doc decided; though they couldn't have kept a man inside the heavily armoured cab for any length of time, if the metal had been impervious. Now another crane was ready, and went in from another place; it settled down to a routine of ingoing and outcoming cranes, and men feeding materials in, coupling and uncoupling the pipes and replacing the others who came from the cabs. Doc began to feel like a man at a tennis match, watching the ball without knowing the rules.

Brown must have had the same idea, for she caught Ferrel's arm and indicated a little leather case that came from her handbag. "Doc, do you play chess? We might as well fill our time with that as sitting here on edge, just watching. It's supposed to be good fro nerves."

He seized on it gratefullly, without explaining that he'd been city champion three years running; he'd take it easy, watch her game, handicap himself just enough to make it interesting by the deliberate loss of a rook, bishop or knight, as was needed to even the odds— Suppose they got all the magma out and into the river; how did that solve the problem? It removed it form the plant, but far less than the fifty-mile minimum danger limit.

"Check," Brown announced. He castled, and looked up at the half-dozen cranes that were now operating. "Check! Checkmate!"

He looked back again hastily, then, to see her queen guarding all possible moves, a bishop checking him. Then his eye followed down toward her end. "Umm. Did you know you've been in check for the last half-dozen moves ? " Because I didn't."

She frowned, shook her head, and began setting the men up again. Doc moved out the queen's pawn, looked out at the worker's, and then brought out the king's bishop, to see her take it with her king's pawn. He hadn't watched her move it out, and had counted on her queen's to block his. Things would require more careful watching on this little portable set. The men were moving steadily and there was a growing clear space, but as they went forward, the violent action of the thermodyne had pitted the ground, carefully as it had been used, and going became more uncertain. Time was slipping by rapidly now.

"Checkmate!" He found himself in a hole, started to nod; but she caught herself this time. "Sorry, I've been playing my king for a queen. Doctor, let's see if we can play at least one game right."

Before it was half finished, it became obvious that they couldn't. Neither had chess very much on the mind, and the pawns and men did fearful and wonderful things, while the knights were as likely to jump six squares as their normal L. They gave it up, just as one of the cranes lost its precarious balance and toppled forward, dropping the long extended pipe into the bubbling mass below. Tanks were in instantly, hitching on and tugging backward until it came down with a thump as the pipe fused, releasing the extreme forward load. It backed out on its own power, while another went in. The driver, by sheer good luck, hobbled from the cab, waving an armored hand to indicate he was all right. Things settled back to an excited routine again that seemed to go on endlessly, though seconds were dropping off too rapidly, turning into minutes that threatened to be hours far too soon.

"Uh!" Brown had been staring for some time, but her little feet suddenly came down with a bang and she straightened up, her hand to her mouth. "Doctor, I just thought; it won't do any good—all this!"

"Why?" She couldn't know anything, but he felt the faint hopes he had go downward sharply. His nerves were dulled, but still ready to jump at the slightest warning.

"The stuff they were making was a superheavy—it'll sink as soon as it hits the water, and all pile up right there! It won't float down river!"

Obvious, Ferrel thought; too obvious. Maybe that was why the engineers hadn't thought of it. He started from the plank, just as Palmer stepped up, but the manager's hand on his shoulder forced him back.

"Easy, Doc, it's O.K. Ummm, so they teach women *some* science nowadays, eh, Mrs Jenkins . . . Sue . . . Dr. Brown, whatever your name is? Don't worry about it, though—the old principle of Brownian movement will keep any colloid suspended, if it's fine enough to be a real colloid. We're sucking it out and keeping it pretty hot until it reaches the water—then it cools off so fast it hasn't time to collect in particles big enough to sink. Some of the dust that floats around in the air is heavier than water, too. I'm joining the bystanders, if you don't mind; the men have everything under control, and I can see better here than I could down there, if anything does come up."

Doc's momentary despair reacted to leave him feeling more sure of things than was justified. He pushed over on the plank, making room for Palmer to drop down beside him. "What's to keep it from blowing up anyway, Palmer?"

"Nothing! Got a match?" He sucked in on the cigarette heavily, relaxing as much as he could. "No use trying to fool you, Doc, at this stage of the game. We're gambling, and I'd say the odds are even; Jenkins thinks they're ninety to ten in his favor, but he has to think so. What we're hoping is that by lifting it out in a gas, thus breaking it down at once from full concentration to the finest possible form, and letting it settle in the water in colloidal particles, there won't be a concentration at any one place sufficient to set it all off at once. The big problem is making sure we get every bit of it cleaned out here, or there may be enough left to take care of us and the nearby city! At least, since the last change, it's stopped spitting, so all the men have to worry about is burn!"

"How much damage, even if it doesn't go off all at once?"

"Possibly none. If you can keep it burning slowly, a million tons of dynamite wouldn't be any worse than the same amount of wood, but a stick going off at once will kill you. Why the dickens didn't Jenkins tell me he wanted to go into atomics? We could have fixed all that—it's hard enough to get good men as it is!"

Brown perked up, forgetting the whole trouble beyond them, and went into the story with enthusiasm, while Ferrel only partly listened. He could see the spot of magma growing steadily smaller, but the watch on his wrist went on ticking off minutes remorselessly, and the time was growing limited. He hadn't realized before how long he'd been sitting there. Now three of the crane nozzles were almost touching, and around them stretched the burned-out ground, with no sign of converter, masonry, or anything else; the heat from the thermodyne had gassified everything indiscriminately.

"Palmer!" The portable ultrawave set around the manager's neck came to life suddenly. "Hey, Palmer, those blowers are about shot; the pipe's pitting already. We've been doing everything we can to replace them, but that stuff eats faster than we can fix. Can't hold up more'n fifteen minutes more."

"Check, Briggs. Keep 'em going the best you can." Palmer flipped a switch and looked out toward the tank standing by behind the cranes. "Jenkins, you get that?"

"Yeah. Surprised they held out this long. How much time till deadline?" The boy's voice was completely toneless, neither hope nor nerves showing up, only the complete weariness of a man almost at his limit.

Palmer looked and whistled. "Twelve minutes, according to the minimum estimate Hoke made! How much left?"

"We're just burning around now, trying to make sure there's no pocket left; I hope we've got the whole works, but I'm not promising. Might as well send out all the I-231 you have and we'll boil it down the pipes to clear out any deposits on them. All the old treads and parts that contacted the R gone into the pile?"

"You melted the last, and your cranes haven't touched the stuff directly. Nice pile of money's gone down that pipe—converter, machinery, everything!"

Jenkins made a sound that was expressive of his worry about that. "I'm coming in now and starting the clearing of the pipe. What've you been paying insurance for?"

"At a lovely rate, too! O.K., come on in, kid; and if you're interested, you can start sticking A. E. after the M. D., anytime you want. Your wife's been giving me your qualifications, and I think you've passed the final test, so you're now an atomic engineer, duly graduated from National!"

Brown's breath caught, and her eyes seemed to glow, even through the goggles, but Jenkin's voice was flat. "O.K., I expected you to give me one if we don't blow up. But you'll have to see Dr. Ferrel about it; he's got a contract with me for medical practice. Be there shortly."

Nine of the estimated twelve minutes had ticked by when he climbed up beside them, mopping off some of the sweat that covered him, and Palmer was hugging the watch. More minutes ticked off slowly, while the last sound faded out in the plant, and the men stood around, staring down toward the river or at the hole that had been No. 4. Silence. Jenkins stirred and grunted.

"Palmer, I know where I got the idea, now. Jorgenson was trying to remind me of it, instead of raving, only I didn't get it, at least consciously. It was one of Dad's, the one he told Jorgenson was a last resort, in case the thing they broke up about went haywire. It was the first variable Dad tried. I was twelve, and he insisted water would break it up into all its chains and kill the danger. Only Dad didn't really expect it to work!"

Palmer didn't look up from the watch, but he caught his breath and swore. "Fine time to tell me that!"

"He didn't have your isotopes to heat it up with, either," Jenkins answered mildly. "Suppose you look up from that watch of yours for a minute, down the river."

As Doc raised his eyes, he was aware suddenly of a roar from the men. Over to the south, stretching out in a huge mass, was a cloud of steam that spread upward and out as he watched, and the beginnings of a mighty hissing sound came in. Then Palmer was hugging Jenkins and yelling until Brown could pry him away and replace him.

"Ten miles or more of river, plus the swamps, Doc!" Palmer was shouting in Ferrel's ear. "All that dispersion, while it cooks slowly from now until the last chain is finished, atom by atom! The *theta* chain broke, unstable and now there's everything there, too scattered to set itself off! It'll cook the river bed up and dry it, but that's all!"

Doc was still dazed, unsure of how to take the relief. He wanted to lie down and cry or to stand up with the men and shout his head off. Instead, he sat loosely, gazing at the cloud. "So I lose the best assistant I ever had! Jenkins, I won't hold you; you're free for whatever Palmer wants."

"Hoke wants him to work on R—he's got the stuff for his bomb now!" Palmer was clapping his hands together slowly, like an excited child watching a steam shovel. "Heck, Doc, pick out anyone you want until your own boy gets out next year. You wanted a chance to work him in here, now you've got it. Right now I'll give you anything you want."

"You might see what you can do about hospitalizing the injured and fixing things up with the men in the tent behind the infirmary. And I think I'll take Brown in Jenkins' place, with the right to grab him in an emergency, until that year's up."

"Done." Palmer slapped the boy's back, stopping the protest, while Brown winked at him. "Your wife likes working, kid; she told me that herself. Besides, a lot of the women work here where they can keep an eye on their men; my own wife does, usually. Doc, take these two kids and head for home, where I'm going myself. Don't come back until you get good and ready, and don't let them start fighting about it."

Doc pulled himself from the truck and started off with Brown and Jenkins following, through the yelling, relief-crazed men. The three were too thoroughly worn out for any exhibition themselves, but they could feel it. Happy ending! Jenkins and Brown where they wanted to be, Hoke with his bomb, Palmer with proof that atomic plants were safe where they were, and he—well, his boy would start out right, with himself and the widely differing but competent Blake and Jenkins to guide him. It wasn't a bad life, after all.

Then he stopped and chuckled. "You two wait for me, will you? If I leave here without making out that order of extra disinfection at the showers, Blake'll swear I'm growing old and feeble-minded. I can't have that."

Old? Maybe a little tired, but he'd been that before, and with luck would be again. He wasn't worried. His nerves were good for twenty years and fifty accidents more, and by that time Blake would be due for a little ribbing himself.

KILLDOZER!

Theodore Sturgeon

Before the race was the deluge, and before the deluge another race, whose nature it is not for mankind to understand. Not unearthly, not alien, for this was their earth and their home.

There was a war between this race, which was a great one, and another. The other was truly alien, a sentient cloudform, an intelligent grouping of tangible electrons. It was spawned in mighty machines by some accident of a science beyond our aboriginal conception of technology. And then the machines, servants of the people, became the people's masters, and great were the battles that followed. The electron-beings had the power to wrap the delicate balances of atom-structure, and their life-medium was mental, which they permeated and used to their own ends. Each weapon the people developed was possessed and turned against them, until a time when the remnants of that vast civilization found a defence—

An insulator. The terminal product or by-product of all energy research—neutronium.

In its shelter they developed a weapon. What it was we shall never know, and our race will live—or we shall know, and our race will perish as theirs perished. Sent to destroy the enemy, it got out of hand and its measureless power destroyed them with it, and their cities, and their possessed machines. The very earth dissolved in flame, the crust writhed and shook and the oceans boiled. Nothing escaped it, nothing that we know as life, and nothing of the pseudolife that had evolved within the mysterious force-fields of their incomprehensible machines, save one hardy mutant.

Mutant it was, and ironically this one alone could have been killed by the first simple measures used against its kind—but it was past time

*for simple expediences. It was an organized electron-field possessing
intelligence and mobility and a will to destroy, and little else. Stunned
by the holocaust, it drifted over the grumbling globe, and in a lull in the
violence of the forces gone wild on Earth, sank to the steaming ground
in its half-conscious exhaustion. There it found shelter—shelter built by
and for its dead enemies. An envelope of neutronium. It drifted in, and
its consciousness at last fell to its lowest ebb. And there it lay while the
neutronium, with its strange constant flux, its interminable striving for
perfect balance, extended itself and closed the opening. And thereafter in
the turbulent eons that followed, the envelope tossed like a grey bubble on
the surface of the roiling sphere, for no substance on Earth would have
it or combine with it.*

*The ages came and went, and chemical action and reaction did
their mysterious work, and once again there was life and evolution.
And a tribe found the mass of neutronium, which is not a substance
but a static force, and were awed by its aura of indescribable chill, and
they worshipped it and built a temple around it and made sacrifices to
it. And ice and fire and the seas came and went, and the land rose and
fell as the years went by, until the ruined temple was on a knoll, and
the knoll was an island. Islanders came and went, lived and built and
died, and races forgot. So now, somewhere in the Pacific to the west of
the archipelago called Islas Revillagigedas, there was an uninhabited
island. And one day—*

Chub Horton and Tom Jaeger stood watching the *Sprite* and her
squat tow of three cargo lighters dwindle over the glassy sea. The
big ocean-going towboat and her charges seemed to be moving out
of focus rather than travelling away. Chub spat cleanly around the
cigar that grew out of the corner of his mouth.

"That's that for three weeks. How's it feel to be a guinea
pig?"

"We'll get it done." Tom had little crinkles all around the outer
ends of his eyes. He was a head taller than Chub and rangy, and not
so tough, and he was a real operator. Choosing him as a foreman
for the experiment had been wise, for he was competent and he
commanded respect. The theory of airfield construction that they
were testing appealed vastly to him, for here were no officers-in-
charge, no government inspectors, no time-keeping or reports. The
government had allowed the company a temporary land grant, and
the idea was to put production-line techniques into the layout and
grading of the project. There were six operators and two mechanics
and more than a million dollars' worth of the best equipment that

money could buy. Government acceptance was to be on a partially completed basis, and contingent on government standards. The theory obviated both gold-bricking and graft, and neatly side-stepped the man-power problem. "When that black-topping crew gets here, I reckon we'll be ready for 'em," said Tom.

He turned and scanned the island with an operator's vision and saw it as it was, and in all the stages it would pass through, and as it would look when they had finished, with five thousand feet of clean-draining runway, hard-packed shoulders, four acres of plane-park, the access road and the short taxiway. He saw the lay of each lift that the power shovel would cut as it brought down the marl bluff, and the ruins on top of it that would give them stone to haul down the salt-flat to the little swamp at the other end, there to be walked in by the dozers.

"We got time to run the shovel up there to the bluff before dark."

They walked down the beach towards the outcropping where the equipment stood surrounded by crates and drums of supplies. The three tractors were ticking over quietly, the two-cycle Diesel chuckling through their mufflers and the big D-7 whacking away its metronomic compression knock on every easy revolution. The Dumptors were lined up and silent, for they would not be ready to work until the shovel was ready to load them. They looked like a mechanical interpretation of Dr. Dolittle's 'Pushme-pullyou,' the fantastic animal with two front ends. They had two large driving wheels and two small steerable wheels. The motor and the driver's seat were side by side over the front—or smaller—wheels; but the driver faced the dump body between the big rear wheels, exactly the opposite of the way he would sit in a dump truck. Hence, in travelling from shovel to dumping-ground, the operator drove backwards, looking over his shoulder, and in dumping he backed the machine up but he himself travelled forward—quite a trick for fourteen hours a day! The shovel squatted in the midst of all the others, its great hulk looming over them, humped there with its boom low and its iron chin on the ground, like some great tired dinosaur.

Rivera, the Puerto Rican mechanic, looked up grinning as Tom and Chub approached, and stuck a bleeder wrench into the top pocket of his coveralls.

"She says 'Signalo,' " he said, his white teeth flashlighting out of the smear of grease across his mouth. "She says she wan' to get dirt on dis paint." He kicked the blade of the Seven with his heel.

Tom sent the grin back—always a surprising thing in his grave face.

"That Seven'll do that, and she'll take a good deal off her bitin' edge along with the paint before we're through. Get in the saddle, Goony. Build a ramp off the rocks down to the flat there, and blade us off some humps from here to the bluff yonder. We're walking the dipper up there."

The Puerto Rican was in the seat before Tom had finished, and with a roar the Seven spun in its length and moved back along the outcropping to the inland edge. Rivera dropped his blade and the sandy marl curled and piled up in front of the dozer, loading the blade and running off in two even rolls at the ends. He shoved the load towards the rocky edge, the Seven revving down as it took the load, *blat blat blatting* and pulling like a supercharged ox as it fired slowly enough for them to count the revolutions.

"She's a hunk of machine," said Tom.

"A hunk of operator, too," gruffed Chub, and added, "for a mechanic."

"The boy's all right," said Kelly. He was standing there with them, watching the Puerto Rican operate the dozer, as if he had been there all along, which was the way Kelly always arrived places. He was tall, slim, with green eyes too long and an easy stretch to the way he moved, like an attenuated cat. He said, "Never thought I'd see the day when equipment was shipped set up ready to run like this. Guess no one ever thought of it before."

"There's times when heavy equipment has to be unloaded in a hurry these days," Tom said. "If they can do it with tanks, they can do it with construction equipment. We're doin' it to build something instead, is all. Kelly, crank up the shovel. It's oiled. We're walking it over to the bluff."

Kelly swung up into the cab of the big dipper-stick and, diddling the governor control, pulled up the starting handle. The Murphy Diesel snorted and settled down into a thudding idle. Kelly got into the saddle, set up the throttle a little, and began to boom up.

"I still can't get over it,'" said Chub. "Not more'n a year ago we'd a had two hundred men on a job like this."

Tom smiled. "Yeah, and the first thing we'd have done would be to build an office building, and then quarters. Me, I'll take this way. No timekeepers, no equipment-use reports, no progress and yardage summaries, no nothin' but eight men, a million bucks worth of equipment, an' three weeks. A shovel an' a mess of tool crates'll keep the rain off us, an' army field rations'll

keep our bellies full. We'll get it done, we'll get out and we'll
get paid."

Rivera finished the ramp, turned the Seven around and climbed
it, walking the new fill down. At the top he dropped his blade,
floated it, and backed down the ramp, smoothing out the rolls. At a
wave from Tom he started out across the shore, angling up towards
the bluff, beating out the humps and carrying fill into the hollows.
As he worked, he sang, feeling the beat of the mighty motor, the
micrometric obedience of that vast implacable machine.

"Why doesn't that monkey stick to his grease guns?"

Tom turned and took the chewed end of a matchstick out of his
mouth. He said nothing, because he had for some time been trying
to make a habit of saying nothing to Joe Dennis. Dennis was an
ex-accountant, drafted out of an office at the last gasp of a defunct
project in the West Indies. He had become an operator because they
needed operators badly. He had been released with alacrity from
the office because of his propensity for small office politics. It was a
game he still played, and completely aside from his boiled-looking
red face and his slightly womanish walk, he was out of place in the
field; for boot-licking and back-stabbing accomplish even less out
on the fields than they do in an office. Tom, trying so hard to keep
his mind on his work, had to admit to himself that of all Dennis'
annoying traits the worst was that he was as good a pan operator as
could be found anywhere, and no one could deny it.

Dennis certainly didn't.

"I've seen the day when anyone catching one of those goonies
so much as sitting on a machine during lunch, would kick his
fanny," Dennis groused. "Now they give 'em a man's work and
a man's pay."

"*Doin'* a man's work, ain't he?" Tom said.

"He's a damn Puerto Rican!"

Tom turned and looked at him levelly. "Where was it you said
you come from," he mused. "Oh yeah. Georgia."

"What do you mean by that?"

Tom was already striding away. "Tell you as soon as I have to,"
he flung back over his shoulder. Dennis went back to watching
the Seven.

Tom glanced at the ramp and then waved Kelly on. Kelly set his
housebrake so the shovel could not swing, put her into travel gear,
and shoved the swing lever forward. With a crackling of drive chains
and a massive scrunching of compacting coral sand, the shovel's
great flat pads carried her over and down the ramp. As she tipped

over the peak of the ramp the heavy manganese steel bucket-door gaped open and closed, like a hungry mouth, slamming up against the bucket until suddenly it latched shut and was quiet. The big Murphy Diesel crooned hollowly under compression as the machine ran downgrade and then the sensitive governor took hold and it took up its belly-beating thud.

Peebles was standing by one of the dozer-pan combines, sucking on his pipe and looking out to sea. He was grizzled and heavy, and from under the bushiest grey brows looked the calmest grey eyes Tom had ever seen. Peebles had never got angry at a machine—a rare trait in a born mechanic—and in fifty-odd years he had learned it was even less use getting angry at a man. Because no matter what, you could always fix what was wrong with a machine. He said around his pipestem:

"Hope you'll give me back my boy, there."

Tom's lips quirked in a little grin. There had been an understanding between old Peebles and himself ever since they had met. It was one of those things which exists unspoken—they knew little about each other because they had never found it necessary to make small talk to keep their friendship extant. It was enough to know that each could expect the best from the other, without persuasion.

"Rivera?" Tom asked. "I'll chase him back as soon as he finishes that service road for the dipper-stick. Why—got anything on?"

"Not much. Want to get that arc welder drained and flushed and set up a grounded table in case you guys tear anything up." He paused. "Besides, the kid's filling his head up with too many things at once. Mechanicing is one thing; operating is something else."

"Hasn't got in his way much so far, has it?"

"Nope. Don't aim t' let it, either. 'Less you need him."

Tom swung up on the pan tractor. "I don't need him that bad, Peeby. If you want some help in the meantime, get Dennis."

Peebles said nothing. He spat. He didn't say anything at all.

"What's the matter with Dennis?" Tom wanted to know.

"Look yonder," said Peebles, waving his pipestem. Out on the beach Dennis was talking to Chub, in Dennis' indefatigable style, standing beside Chub, one hand on Chub's shoulder. As they watched they saw Dennis call his side-kick, Al Knowles.

"Dennis talks too much," said Peebles. "That most generally don't amount to much, but that Dennis, he sometimes *says* too much. Ain't got what it takes to run a show, and knows it. Makes up for it by messin' in between folks."

"He's harmless," said Tom.

Still looking up the beach, Peebles said slowly:

"Is, so far."

Tom started to say something, then shrugged. "I'll send you Rivera," he said, and opened the throttle. Like a huge electric dynamo, the two-cycle motor whined to a crescendo. Tom lifted the dozer with a small lever by his right thigh and raised the pan with the long control sprouting out from behind his shoulder. He moved off, setting the rear gate of the scraper so that anything the blade bit would run off to the side instead of loading into the pan. He slapped the tractor into sixth gear and whined up to and around the crawling shovel, cutting neatly in under the boom and running on ahead with his scraper blade just touching the ground, dragging to a fine grade the service road Rivera had cut.

Dennis was saying, "It's that little Hitler stuff. Why should I take that kind of talk? 'You come from Georgia,' he says. What is he—a Yankee or something?"

"A crackah f'm Macon," chortled Al Knowles, who came from Georgia, too. He was tall and stringy and round-shouldered. All of his skill was in his hands and feet, brains being a commodity he had lived without all his life until he had met Dennis and used him as a reasonable facsimile thereof.

"Tom didn't mean nothing by it," said Chub.

"No, he didn't mean nothin'. Only that we do what he says the way he says it, specially if he finds a way we don't like it. *You* wouldn't do like that, Chub. Al, think Chub would carry on thataway?"

"Sure wouldn't," said Al, feeling it expected of him.

"Nuts," said Chub, pleased and uncomfortable, and thinking, what have I got against Tom?—not knowing, not liking Tom as well as he had. "Tom's the man here, Dennis. We got a job to do—lets skit and git. Man can take anything for a lousy six weeks."

"Oh, sho'," said Al.

"Man can take just so much," Dennis said. "What they put a man like that on top for, Chub? What's the matter with you? Don't you know grading and drainage as good as Tom? Can Tom stake out a side hill like you can?"

"Sure, sure, but what's the difference, long as we get a field built? An' anyhow, hell with bein' the boss-man. Who gets the blame if things don't run right, anyway?"

Dennis stepped back, taking his hand off Chub's shoulder, and stuck an elbow in Al's ribs.

"You see that, Al? Now there's a smart man. That's the thing Uncle Tom didn't bargain for. Chub, you can count on Al and me to do just that little thing."

"Do just what little thing?" asked Chub, genuinely puzzled.

"Like you said. If the job goes wrong, the boss gets blamed. So if the boss don't behave, the job goes wrong."

"Uh-huh," agreed Al with the conviction of mental simplicity.

Chub double-took this extraordinary logical process and grasped wildly at anger as the conversation slid out from under him. "I didn't say any such thing! This job is goin' to get done, no matter what! There'll be no damn goldbrick badge on me or anybody else around here if I can help it."

"That's the ol' fight," feinted Dennis. "We'll show that guy what we think of his kind of slowdown."

"You talk too much," said Chub, and escaped with the remnants of coherence. Every time he talked with Dennis he walked away feeling as if he had an unwanted membership card stuck in his pocket that he couldn't throw away with a clear conscience.

Rivera ran his road up under the bluff, swung the Seven around, punched out the master clutch and throttled down, idling. Tom was making his pass with the pan, and as he approached, Rivera slipped out of the seat and behind the tractor, laying a sensitive hand on the final drive casing and sprocket bushings, checking for overheating. Tom pulled alongside and beckoned him up on the pan tractor.

"*Que pasa*, Goony? Anything wrong?"

Rivera shook his head and grinned. "Nothing wrong. She is perfect, that '*de siete*.' She—"

"That what? 'Daisy Etta'?"

"*De siete*. In Spanish, D-7. It means something in English?"

"Got you wrong," smiled Tom. "But Daisy Etta is a girl's name in English, all the same."

He shifted the pan tractor into neutral and engaged the clutch, and jumped off the machine. Rivera followed. They climbed aboard the Seven, Tom at the controls.

Rivera said, "Daisy Etta," and grinned so widely that a soft little clucking noise came from behind his back teeth. He reached out his hand, crooked his little finger around one of the tall steering clutch levers, and pulled it all the way back. Tom laughed outright.

"You got something there," he said. "The easiest runnin' cat ever built. Hydraulic steerin' clutches and brakes that'll bring you to a dead stop if you spit on 'em. Forward an' reverse lever so's you got all your speeds front and backwards. A little different from the old jobs. They had no booster springs, eight–ten years ago; took a sixty-pound pull to get a steerin' clutch back. Cuttin' a side-hill with an angle-dozer really was a job in them days. You try it sometime, dozin' with one hand, holdin' her nose out o' the bank with the other, ten hours a day. And what'd it get you? Eighty cents an hour an' "—Tom took his cigarette and butted the fiery end out against the horny palm of his hand—"these."

"*Santa Maria!*"

"Want to talk to you, Goony. Want to look over the bluff, too, at that stone up there. It'll take Kelly pret' near an hour to get this far and sumped in, anyhow."

They growled up the slope, Tom feeling the ground under the four-foot brush, taking her up in a zigzag course like a hairpin road on a mountainside. Though the Seven carried a muffler on the exhaust stack that stuck up out of the hood before them, the blat of four big cylinders hauling fourteen tons of steel upgrade could outshout any man's conversation, so they sat without talking, Tom driving, Rivera watching his hands flick over the controls.

The bluff started in a low ridge running almost the length of the little island, like a lopsided backbone. Towards the centre it rose abruptly, sent a wing out towards the rocky outcropping at the beach where their equipment had been unloaded, and then rose again to a small, almost square plateau area, half a mile across. It was humpy and rough until they could see all of it, when they realized how incredibly level it was, under the brush and ruins that covered it. In the centre—and exactly in the centre they realized suddenly—was a low, overgrown mound. Tom threw out the clutch and revved her down.

"Survey report said there was stone up here," Tom said, vaulting out of the seat. "Let's walk around some."

They walked towards the knoll, Tom's eyes casting about as he went. He stooped down into the heavy, short grass and scooped up a piece of stone, blue-grey, hard and brittle.

"Rivera—look at this. This is what the report was talking about. See—more of it. All in small pieces, though. We need big stuff for the bog if we can get it."

"Good stone?" asked Rivera.

"Yes, boy—but it don't belong here. Th' whole island's sand and marl and sandstone on the outcrop down yonder. This here's a bluestone, like diamond clay. Harder'n blazes. I never saw this stuff on a marl hill before. Or near one. Anyhow, root around and see if there is any big stuff."

They walked on. Rivera suddenly dipped down and pulled grass aside.

"Tom—here's a beeg one."

Tom came over and looked down at the corner of stone ticking up out of the topsoil."Yeh. Goony, get your girl-friend over here and we'll root it out."

Rivera sprinted back to the idling dozer and climbed aboard. He brought the machine over to where Tom waited, stopped, stood up and peered over the front of the machine to locate the stone, then sat down and shifted gears. Before he could move the machine Tom was on the fender beside him, checking him with a hand on his arm.

"No, boy—no. Not third. First. And half throttle. That's it. Don't try to bash a rock out of the ground. Go on up to it easy; set your blade against it, lift it out, don't boot it out. Take it with the middle of your blade, not the corner—get the load on both hydraulic cylinders. Who told you to do like that?"

"No one tol' me, Tom. I see a man do it, I do it."

"Yeah? Who was it?"

"Dennis, but—"

"Listen, Goony, if you want to learn anything from Dennis, watch him while he's on a pan. He dozes like he talks. That reminds me—what I wanted to talk to you about. You ever have any trouble with him?"

Rivera spread his hands. "How I have trouble when he never talk to me?"

"Well, that's all right then. You keep it that way. Dennis is O.K., I guess, but you better keep away from him."

He went on to tell the boy then about what Peebles had said concerning being an operator and a mechanic at the same time. Rivera's lean dark face fell, and his hand strayed to the blade control, touching it lightly, feeling the composition grip and the machined locknuts that help it. When Tom had quite finished he said:

"O.K., Tom—if you want, you break 'em, I feex 'em. But if you wan' help some time, I run *Daisy Etta* for you, no?"

"Sure, kid, sure. But don't forget, no man can do everything."

"You can do everything," said the boy.

Tom leaped off the machine and Rivera shifted into first and crept up to the stone, setting the blade gently against it. Taking the load, the mighty engine audibly bunched its muscles; Rivera opened the throttle a little and the machine set solidly against the stone, the tracks slipping, digging into the ground, piling loose earth up behind. Tom raised a fist, thumb up, and the boy began lifting his blade. The Seven lowered her snout like an ox pulling through mud; the front of the tracks buried themselves deeper and the blade slipped upwards an inch on the rock, as if it were on a ratchet. The stone shifted, and suddenly heaved itself up out of the earth that covered it, bulging the sod aside like a ship's slow bow-wave. And the blade lost its grip and slipped over the stone. Rivera slapped out the master clutch within an ace of letting the mass of it poke through his radiator core. Reversing, he set the blade against it again and rolled it at last into daylight.

Tom stood staring at it, scratching the back of his neck. Rivera got off the machine and stood beside him. For a long time they said nothing.

The stone was roughly rectangular, shaped like a brick with one end cut at about a thirty-degree angle. And on the angled face was a square-cut ridge, like the tongue on a piece of milled lumber. The stone was about $3 \times 2 \times 2$ feet, and must have weighed six or seven hundred pounds.

"Now that," said Tom, bug-eyed, "didn't grow *here*, and if it did it never grew that way."

"*Una piedra de una casa,*" said Rivera softly. "Tom, there was a building here, no?"

Tom turned suddenly to look at the knoll.

"There is a building here—or what's left of it. Lord on'y knows how old—"

They stood there in the slowly dwindling light, staring at the knoll; and there came upon them a feeling of oppression, as if there were no wind and no sound anywhere. And yet there was wind, and behind them *Daisy Etta* whacked away with her muttering idle, and nothing had changed and—was that it? That nothing had changed? That nothing would change, or could, here?

Tom opened his mouth twice to speak, and couldn't, or didn't want to—he didn't know which. Rivera slumped suddenly on his hunkers, back erect, and his eyes wide.

It grew very cold. "It's cold," Tom said, and his voice sounded harsh to him. And the wind blew warm on them, the earth was warm under Rivera's knees. The cold was not a lack of heat, but a lack of something else—warmth, but the specific warmth of life-force, perhaps. The feeling of oppression grew as if their recognition of the strangeness of the place had started it, and their increasing sensitivity to it made it grow.

Rivera said something, quietly, in Spanish.

"What are you looking at?" asked Tom.

Rivera started violently, threw up an arm, as if to ward off the crash of Tom's voice.

"I . . . there is nothin' to see, Tom. I feel this way wance before. I dunno—" He shook his head, his eyes wide and blank. "An' after, there was being wan hell of a thunder-storm—" His voice petered out.

Tom took his shoulder and hauled him roughly to his feet. "Goony! You slap-happy?"

The boy smiled, almost gently. The down on his upper lip held little spheres of sweat. "I ain't nothin', Tom. I'm jus' scare like hell."

"You scare yourself right back up there on that cat and git to work," Tom roared. More quietly then, he said, "I know there's something—wrong—here, Goony, but that ain't goin' to get us a runway built. Anyhow, I know what to do about a dawg 'at gits gunshy. Ought to be able to do as much fer you. Git along to th' mound now and see if it ain't a cache o' big stone for us. We got a swamp down there to fill."

Rivera hesitated, started to speak, swallowed and then walked slowly over to the Seven. Tom stood watching him, closing his mind to the impalpable pressure of something, somewhere near, making his guts cold.

The bulldozer nosed over to the mound, grunting, reminding Tom suddenly that the machine's Spanish slang name was *puerco*—pig, boar. Rivera angled into the edge of the mound with the cutting corner of the blade. Dirt and brush curled up, fell away from the mound and loaded from the bank side, out along the mouldboard. The boy finished his pass along the mound, carried the load past it and wasted it out on the flat, turned around and started back again.

Ten minutes later Rivera struck stone, the manganese steel screaming along it, a puff of grey dust spouting from the cutting corner. Tom knelt and examined it after the machine had passed. It was the same kind of stone they had found out on the flat—and shaped the same way. But here it was a wall, the angled faces of the block ends obviously tongued and grooved together.

Cold, cold as—

Tom took one deep breath and wiped sweat out of his eyes.

"I don't care," he whispered, "I got to have that stone. I got to fill me a swamp." He stood back and motioned to Rivera to blade into a chipped crevice in the buried wall.

The Seven swung into the wall and stopped while Rivera shifted into first, throttled down and lowered his blade. Tom looked up into his face. The boy's lips were white. He eased in the master clutch, the blade dipped and the corner swung neatly into the crevice.

The dozer blatted protestingly and began to crab sideways, pivoting on the end of the blade. Tom jumped out of the way, ran around behind the machine, which was almost parallel with the wall now, and stood in the clear, one hand raised ready to signal, his eyes on the straining blade. And then everything happened at once.

With a toothy snap the block started and came free, pivoting outward from its square end, bringing with it its neighbour. The block above them dropped, and the whole mound seemed to settle. And *something* whooshed out of the black hole where the rocks had been. Something like a fog, but not a fog that could be seen, something huge that could not be measured. With it came a gust of that cold which was not cold, and the smell of ozone, and the prickling crackle of a mighty static discharge.

Tom was fifty feet from the wall before he knew he had moved. He stopped and saw the Seven suddenly buck like a wild stallion, once, and Rivera turning over twice in the air. Tom shouted some meaningless syllable and tore over to the boy, where he sprawled on the rough grass, lifted him in his arms, and ran. Only then did he realize that he was running from the machine.

It was like a mad thing. Its mouldboard rose and fell. It curved away from the mound, howling governor gone wild, controls flailing. The blade dug repeatedly into the earth, gouging it up in great dips through which the tractor plunged, clanking and bellowing furiously. It raced away in a great irregular arc, turned and came snorting back to the mound, where it beat at the buried wall, slewed and scraped and roared.

Tom reached the edge of the plateau sobbing for breath, and kneeling, laid the boy gently down on the grass.

"Goony, boy . . . hey—"

The long silken eyelashes fluttered, lifted. Something wrenched in Tom as he saw the eyes, rolled right back so that only the whites showed. Rivera drew a long quivering breath which caught suddenly. He coughed twice, threw his head from side to side so violently that Tom took it between his hands and steadied it.

"*Ay . . . Maria madre . . . que me pasado,* Tom—w'at has happen to me?"

"Fell off the Seven, stupid. You . . . how you feel?"

Rivera scrabbled at the ground, got his elbows half under him, then sank back weakly. "Feel O.K. Headache like hell. W-w'at happen to my feets?"

"Feet? They hurt?"

"No hurt—" The young face went grey, the lips tightened with effort. "No nothin', Tom."

"You can't move 'em?"

Rivera shook his head, still trying. Tom stood up. "You take it easy. I'll go get Kelly. Be right back."

He walked away quickly and when Rivera called to him he did not turn around. Tom had seen a man with a broken back before.

At the edge of the little plateau Tom stopped, listening. In the deepening twilight he could see the bulldozer standing by the mound. The motor was running; she had not stalled herself. But what stopped Tom was that she wasn't idling, but revving up and down as if an impatient hand were on the throttle—*hroom hroooom,* running up and up far faster than even a broken governor should permit, then coasting down to near silence, broken by the explosive punctuation of sharp and irregular firing. Then it would run up and up again, almost screaming, sustaining a r.p.m. that threatened every moving part, shaking the great machine like some deadly ague.

Tom walked swiftly towards the Seven, a puzzled and grim frown on his weather-beaten face. Governors break down occasionally, and once in a while you will have a motor tear itself to pieces, revving up out of control. But it will either do that or it will rev down and quit. If an operator is fool enough to leave his machine with the master clutch engaged, the machine will take off and run the way the Seven had—but it will not turn unless the blade corner catches in something unresisting, and then the chances are very strong that it will stall. But in any case, it was past reason for any machine to act this way, revving up and down, running, turning, lifting and dropping the blade.

The motor slowed as he approached, and at last settled down into something like a steady and regular idle. Tom had the sudden crazy impression that it was watching him. He shrugged off the feeling, walked up and laid a hand on the fender.

The Seven reacted like a wild stallion. The big Diesel roared, and Tom distinctly saw the master clutch lever snap back over centre. He leaped clear, expecting the machine to jolt forward, but apparently it was in a reverse gear, for it shot backwards, one track locked, and the near end of the blade swung in a swift vicious arc, breezing a bare fraction of an inch past his hip as he danced back out of the way.

And as if it had bounced off a wall, the tractor had shifted and was bearing down on him, the twelve-foot blade rising, and two big headlights looming over him on their bow-legged supports, looking like the protruding eyes of some mighty toad. Tom had no choice but to leap straight up and grasp the top of the blade in his two hands, leaning back hard to brace his feet against the curved mouldboard. The blade dropped and sank into the soft topsoil, digging a deep little swale in the ground. The earth loading on the mouldboard rose and churned around Tom's legs; he stepped wildly, keeping them clear of the rolling drag of it. Up came the blade then, leaving a four-foot pile at the edge of the pit; down and up the tractor raced as the tracks went into it; up and up as they climbed the pile of dirt. A quick balance and overbalance as the machine lurched up and over like a motor-cycle taking a jump off a ramp, and then a spine-shaking crash as fourteen tons of metal smashed blade-first into the ground.

Part of the leather from Tom's tough palms stayed with the blade as he was flung off. He went head over heels backwards, but had his feet gathered and sprang as they touched the ground; for he knew that no machine could bury its blade like that and get out easily. He leaped to the top of the blade, got one hand on the radiator cap, vaulted. Perversely, the cap broke from its hinge and came away in his hand, in that split instant when only that hand rested on anything. Off balance, he landed on his shoulder with his legs flailing the air, his body sliding off the hood's smooth shoulder towards the track now churning the earth beneath. He made a wild grab at the air intake pipe, barely had it in his fingers when the dozer freed itself and shot backwards up and over the hump. Again that breathless flight pivoting over the top, and the clanking crash as the machine landed, this time almost flat on its tracks.

The jolt tore Tom's hand away, and as he slid back over the hood the crook of his elbow caught the exhaust stack, the dull red metal biting into his flesh. He grunted and clamped the arm around it. His momentum carried him around it, and his feet crashed into the steering clutch levers. Hooking one with his instep, he doubled his legs and whipped himself back, scrabbling at the smooth warm metal, crawling frantically backwards until he finally fell heavily into the seat.

"Now," he gritted through a red wall of pain, "You're gonna git operated." And he kicked out the master clutch.

The motor wailed, with the load taken off so suddenly. Tom grasped the throttle, his thumb down on the ratchet release, and he shoved the lever forward to shut off the fuel.

It wouldn't shut off; it went down to a slow idle, but it wouldn't shut off.

"There's one thing you can't do without," he muttered, "compression."

He stood up and leaned around the dash, reaching for the compression-release lever. As he came up out of the seat, the engine revved up again. He turned to the throttle, which had snapped back into the 'open' position. As his hand touched it the master clutch lever snapped in and the howling machine lurched forward with a jerk that snapped his head on his shoulders and threw him heavily back into the seat. He snatched at the hydraulic blade control and threw it to 'float' position; and then as the falling mouldboard touched the ground, into 'power down.' The cutting edge bit into the ground and the engine began to labour. Holding the blade control, he pushed the throttle forward with his other hand. One of the steering clutch levers whipped back and struck him agonisingly on the kneecap. He involuntarily let go of the blade control and the mouldboard began to rise. The engine began to turn faster and he realized that it was not responding to the throttle. Cursing, he leaped to his feet; the suddenly flailing steering clutch levers struck him three times in the groin before he could get between them.

Blind with pain, Tom clung gasping to the dash. The oil-pressure gauge fell off the dash to his right, with a tinkling of broken glass, and from its broken quarter-inch line scalding oil drenched him. The shock of it snapped back his wavering consciousness. Ignoring the blows of the left steering clutch and the master clutch which had started the same mad punching, he bent over the left end of the dash and grasped the compression lever. The tractor rushed forward and spun sickeningly, and Tom knew he was thrown. But as he felt himself leave the decking his hand punched the compression lever down. The great valves at the cylinder heads opened and locked open; atomized fuel and superheated air chattered out, and as Tom's head and shoulders struck the ground the great wild machine rolled to a stop, stood silently except for the grumble of water boiling in the cooling system.

Minutes later Tom raised his head and groaned. He rolled over and sat up, his chin on his knees, washed by wave after wave of pain.

As they gradually subsided, he crawled to the machine and pulled himself to his feet, hand over hand on the track. And groggily he began to cripple the tractor, at least for the night.

He opened the cock under the fuel tank, left the warm yellow fluid gushing out on the ground. He opened the drain on the reservoir by the injection pump. He found a piece of wire in the crank box and with it tied down the compression release lever. He crawled up on the machine, wrenched the hood and ball jar off the air intake precleaner, pulled off his shirt and stuffed it down the pipe. He pushed the throttle all the way forward and locked it with the locking pin. And he shut off the fuel on the main line from the tank to the pump.

Then he climbed heavily to the ground and slogged back to the edge of the plateau where he had left Rivera.

They didn't know Tom was hurt until an hour and a half later—there had been too much to do—rigging a stretcher for the Puerto Rican, building him a shelter, an engine crate with an Army pup tent for a roof. They brought out the first-aid kit and the medical books and did what they could—tied and splinted and dosed with an opiate. Tom was a mass of bruises, and his right arm, where it had hooked the exhaust stack, was a flayed mass. They fixed him up then, old Peebles handling the sulfa powder and bandages like a trained nurse. And only then was there talk.

"I've seen a man thrown off a pan," said Dennis, as they sat around the coffee urn munching C rations. "Sittin' up on the arm rest on a cat, looking backwards. Cat hit a rock and bucked. Threw him off on the track. Stretched him out ten feet long." He in-whistled some coffee to dilute the mouthful of food he had been talking around, and masticated noisily. "Man's a fool to set up there on one side of his butt even on a pan. Can't see why th' goony was doin' it on a dozer."

"He wasn't," said Tom.

Kelly rubbed his pointed jaw. "He set flat on th' seat an' was th'owed?"

"That's right."

After an unbelieving silence Dennis said, "What was he doin'— drivin' over sixty?"

Tom looked around the circle of faces lit up by the over-artificial brilliance of a pressure lantern, and wondered what the reaction would be if he told it all just as it was. He had to say something, and it didn't look as if it could be the truth.

"He was workin'," he said finally. "Bucking stone out of the wall of an old building up on the mesa there. One turned loose an' as it did the governor must've gone haywire. She buckled like a loco hoss and run off."

"Run off?"

Tom opened his mouth and closed it again, and just nodded.

Dennis said, "Well, reckon that's what happens when you put a mechanic to operatin'."

"That had nothin' to do with it," Tom snapped.

Peebles spoke up quickly. "Tom—what about the Seven? Broke up any?"

"Some," said Tom. "Better look at the steering clutches. An' she was hot."

"Head's cracked," said Harris, a burly young man with shoulders like a buffalo and a famous thirst.

"How do you know?"

"Saw it when Al and me went up with the stretcher to get the kid while you all were building the shelter. Hot water runnin' down the side of the block."

"You mean you walked all the way out to the mound to look at that tractor while the kid was lyin' there? I told you where he was!"

"Out to the mound!" Al Knowles' pop eyes teetered out of their sockets. "We found that cat stalled twenty feet away from where the kid was!"

"What!"

"That's right, Tom," said Harris. "What's eatin' you? Where'd you leave it?"

"I told you . . . by the mound . . . the ol' building we cut into."

"Leave the startin' motor runnin'?"

"Starting motor?" Tom's mind caught the picture of the small, two-cylinder gasoline engine bolted to the side of the big Diesel's crankcase, coupled through a Bendix gear and clutch to the flywheel of the Diesel to crank it. He remembered his last glance at the still machine, silent but for the sound of water boiling. "Hell, no!"

Al and Harris exchanged a glance. "I guess you were sort of slap-happy at the time, Tom," Harris said, not unkindly. "When we were halfway up the hill we heard it, and you know you can't mistake that racket. Sounded like it was under a load."

Tom beat softly at his temples with his clenched fists. "I left that machine dead," he said quietly. "I got compression off her and tied down the lever. I even stuffed my shirt in the intake. I drained the tank. But—I didn't touch the starting motor."

Peebles wanted to know why he had gone to all that trouble. Tom just looked vaguely at him and shook his head. "I shoulda pulled the wires. I never thought about the starting motor," he whispered. Then, "Harris—you say you found the starting motor running when you got to the top?"

"No—she was stalled. And hot—awmighty hot. I'd say the startin' motor was seized up tight. That must be it, Tom. You left the startin' motor runnin' and somehow engaged the clutch an' Bendix." His voice lost conviction as he said it—it takes seventeen separate motions to start a tractor of this type. "Anyhow, she was in gear an' crawled along on the little motor."

"I done that once," said Chud. "Broke a con rod on an Eight, on a highway job. Walked her about three-quarters of a mile on the startin' motor that way. Only I had to stop every hundred yards and let her cool down some."

Not without sarcasm, Dennis said, "Seems to me like the Seven was out to get th' goony. Made one pass at him and then went back to finish the job."

Al Knowles haw-hawed extravagantly.

Tom stood up, shaking his head, and went off among the crates to the hospital they had jury-rigged for the kid.

A dim light was burning inside, and Rivera lay very still, with his eyes closed. Tom leaned in the doorway—the open end of the engine crate—and watched him for a moment. Behind him he could hear the murmur of the crew's voices; the night was otherwise windless and still. Rivera's face was the peculiar color that olive skin takes when drained of blood. Tom looked at his chest and for a panicky moment thought he could discern no movement there. He entered and put a hand over the boy's heart. Rivera shivered, his eyes flew open, and he drew a sudden breath which caught raggedly at the back of his throat. "Tom . . . Tom!" he cried weakly.

"O.K., Goony . . . *que pasa?*"

"She comeen back . . . Tom!"

"Who?"

"*El de siete.*"

Daisy Etta—"She ain't comin' back, kiddo, You're off the mesa now. Keep your chin up, fella."

Rivera's dark, doped eyes stared up at him without expression. Tom moved back and the eyes continued to stare. They weren't seeing anything. "Go to sleep," he whispered. The eyes closed instantly.

Kelly was saying that nobody ever got hurt on a construction job unless somebody was dumb. "An' most times you don't realize how dumb what you're doin' is until somebody does get hurt."

"The dumb part was gettin' a kid, an' not even an operator at that, up on a machine," said Dennis in his smuggest voice.

"I heard you try to sing that song before," said old Peebles quietly. "I hate to have to point out anything like this to a man because it don't do any good to make comparisons. But I've worked with that fella Rivera for a long time now, an' I've seen 'em as good but doggone few better. As far as you're concerned, you're O.K. on a pan, but the kid could give you cards and spades and still make you look like a cost accountant on a dozer."

Dennis half rose and mouthed something filthy. He looked at Al Knowles for backing and got it. He looked around the circle and got none. Peebles lounged back, sucking on his pipe, watching from under those bristling brows. Dennis subsided, running now on another tack.

"So what does that prove? The better you say he is, the less reason he had to fall off a cat and get himself hurt."

"I haven't got the thing straight yet," said Chub, in a voice whose tone indicated "I hate to admit it, but—"

About this time Tom returned, like a sleepwalker, standing with the brilliant pressure lantern between him and Dennis. Dennis rambled right on, not knowing he was anywhere near: "That's something you never will find out. That Puerto Rican is a pretty husky kid. Could be Tom said somethin' he didn't like an' he tried to put a knife in Tom's back. They all do, y'know. Tom didn't get all that bashin' around just stoppin' a machine. They must of went round an' round for a while an' the goony wound up with a busted back. Tom sets the dozer to walk him down while he lies there and comes on down here and tries to tell us—" His voice fluttered to a stop as Tom loomed over him.

Tom grabbed the pan operator up by the slack of his shirt front with his uninjured arm and shook him like and empty burlap bag.

"Skunk," he growled. "I oughta lower th' boom on you." He set Dennis on his feet and backhanded his face with the edge of his forearm. Dennis went down—cowered down, rather than fell.

"Aw, Tom, I was just talkin'. Just a joke, Tom, I was just—"

"Yellow, too," snarled Tom, stepping forward, raising a solid Texan boot.

Peebles barked "Tom!" and the foot came back to the ground.

"Out o' my sight," rumbled the foreman. "Git!"

Dennis got. Al Knowles said vaguely, "Naow, Tom, y'all cain't—"

"You, y'wall-eyed string-bean!" Tom raved, his voice harsh and strained. "Go 'long with yer Siamese twin!"

"O.K., O.K.," said Al, white-faced, and disappeared into the dark after Dennis.

"Nuts to this," said Chub. "I'm turnin' in." He went to a crate and hauled out a mosquito-hooded sleeping bag and went off without another word. Harris and Kelly, who were both on their feet, sat down again. Old Peebles hadn't moved.

Tom stood staring out into the dark, his arms straight at his sides, his fists knotted.

"Sit down," said Peebles gently. Tom turned and stared at him.

"Sit down. I can't change that dressing 'less you do." He pointed at the bandage around Tom's elbow. It was red, a widening stain, the tattered tissues having parted as the big Georgian bunched his infuriated muscles. He sat down.

"Talkin' about dumbness," said Harris calmly, as Peebles went to work, "I was about to say that I got the record. I done the dumbest thing anybody ever did on a machine. You can't top it."

"I could," said Kelly. "Runnin' a crane dragline once. Put her in boom gear and started to boom her up. Had an eighty-five-foot stick on her. Machine was standing on wooden mats in th' middle of a swamp. Heard the motor miss and got out of the saddle to look at the filter-glass. Messed around back there longer than I figured, and the boom went straight up in the air and fell backwards over the cab. Th' jolt tilted my mats an' she slid backwards slow and stately as you please, butt-first into the mud. Buried up to the eyeballs, she was." He laughed quietly. "Looked like a ditching machine!"

"I still say I done the dumbest thing ever, bar none," said Harris. "It was on a river job, widening a channel. I come back to work from a three-day binge, still rum-dumb. Got up on a dozer an' was workin' around on the edge of a twenty-foot cliff. Down at the foot of the cliff was a big hickory tree, an' growin' right along the edge was a great big limb. I got the dopey idea I should break it off. I put one track on the limb and the other on the cliff edge and run out away from the trunk. I was about halfway out, an' the branch saggin' some, before I thought what would happen if it broke. Just about then it did break. You know hickory—if it breaks at all it breaks altogether. So down we go into thirty feet of water—me an' the cat. I got out from under somehow. When all them bubbles stopped comin' up I swum around lookin' down at it. I was still paddlin' around when the superintendent came rushin' up. He wants to know what's up. I yell at him, 'Look down there, the way that water is movin' an' shiftin', looks like the cat is workin' down there.' He pursed his lips and *tsk tsked*. My, that man said some nasty things to me."

"Where'd you get your next job?" Kelly exploded.

"Oh, he didn't fire me," said Harris soberly. "Said he couldn't afford to fire a man as dumb as that. Said he wanted me around to look at whenever he felt bad."

Tom said, "Thanks, you guys. That's as good a way as any of sayin' that everybody makes mistakes." He stood up, examining the new dressing, turning his arm in front of the lantern. "You all can think what you please, but I don't recollect there was any dumbness went on that mesa this evenin'. That's finished with, anyway. Do I have to say that Dennis' idea about it is all wet?"

Harris said one foul word that completely disposed of Dennis and anything he might say.

Peebles said, "It'll be all right. Dennis an' his popeyed friend'll hang together, but they don't amount to anything. Chub'll do whatever he's argued into."

"So you got 'em all lined up, hey?" Tom shrugged. "In the meantime, are we going to get an airfield built?"

"We'll get it built," Peebles said. "Only—Tom, I got no right to give you any advice, but go easy on the rough stuff after this. It does a lot of harm."

"I will if I can," said Tom gruffly. They broke up and turned in.

Peebles was right. It did no harm. It made Dennis use the word 'murder' when they found, in the morning, that Rivera had died during the night.

The work progressed in spite of everything that had happened. With equipment like that, it's hard to slow things down. Kelly bit two cubic yards out of the bluff with every swing of the big shovel, and Dumptors are the fastest short-haul earth movers yet devised. Dennis kept the service road clean for them with his pan, and Tom and Chub spelled each other on the bulldozer they had detached from its pan to make up for the lack of the Seven, spending their alternate periods with transit and stakes. Peebles was rod-man for the surveys, and in between times worked on setting up his field shop, keeping the water cooler and battery chargers running, and lining up his forge and welding tables. The operators fuelled and serviced their own equipment, and there was little delay. Rocks and marl came out of the growing cavity in the side of the central mesa—a whole third of it had to come out—were spun down to the edge of the swamp, which lay across the lower end of the projected runway, in the hornet-howling dump-tractors, their big driving wheels churning up vast clouds of dust, and were dumped and spread and walked in by the whining two-cycle dozer. When muck began to pile up in front of the fill, it was blasted out of the way with carefully placed charges of sixty percent dynamite and the craters filled with rocks and stone from the ruins, and surfaced with easily compacting marl, run out of a clean deposit by the pan.

And when he had his shop set up, Peebles went up the hill to get the Seven. When he got to it he just stood there for a moment scratching his head, and then, shaking his head, he ambled back down the hill and went for Tom.

"Been looking at the Seven," he said, when he had flagged the moaning two-cycle and Tom had climbed off.

"What'd you find?"

Peebles held out an arm. "A list as long as that." He shook his head. "Tom, what really happened up there?"

"Governor went haywire and she run away," Tom said promptly, deadpan.

"Yeah, but—" For a long moment he held Tom's eyes. Then he sighed. "O.K., Tom. Anyhow, I can't do a thing up there. We'll have to bring her back and I'll have to have this tractor to tow her down. And first I have to have some help—the track idler adjustment bolt's busted and the right track is off the track rollers."

"Oh-h-h. So that's why she couldn't get to the kid, running on the starting motor. Track would hardly turn, hey?"

"It's a miracle she ran as far as she did. That track is really jammed up. Riding right up on the roller flanges. And that ain't the half of it. The head's gone, like Harris said, and Lord only knows what I'll find when I open her up."

"Why bother?"

"What?"

"We can get along without that dozer," said Tom suddenly. "Leave her where she is. There's lots more for you to do."

"But what for?"

"Well, there's no call to go to all that trouble."

Peebles scratched the side of his nose and said, "I got a new head, track master pins—even a spare starting motor. I got tools to make what I don't stock." He pointed at the long row of dumps left by the hurtling dump-tractors while they had been talking. "You got a pan tied up because you're using this machine to doze with, and you can't tell me you can't use another one. You're gonna have to shut down one or two o' those Dumptors if you go on like this."

"I had all that figured out as soon as I opened my mouth," Tom said sullenly. "Let's go."

They climbed on the tractor and took off, stopping for a moment at the beach outcropping to pick up a cable and some tools.

Daisy Etta sat at the edge of the mesa, glowering out of her stilted headlights at the soft sward which still bore the impression of a young body and the tramplings of the stretcher-bearers. Her general aspect was woebegone—there were scratches on her olive-drab paint and the bright metal of the scratches was already dulled red by the earliest powder-rust. And though the ground was level, she was not, for her right track was off its lower rollers, and she stood slightly canted, like a man who has had a broken hip. And whatever passed for consciousness within her mulled over that paradox of the bulldozer that every operator must go through while he is learning his own machine.

It is the most difficult thing of all for the beginner to understand, that paradox: A bulldozer is a crawling power-house, a behemoth of noise and toughness, the nearest thing to the famous irresistible force. The beginner, awed and with the pictures of unconquerable Army tanks printed on his mind from the newsreels, takes all in his stride and with a sense of limitless power treats all obstacles alike, not knowing the fragility of a cast-iron radiator care, the mortality of tempered manganese, the friability of over-heated babbitt, and most of all the ease with which a tractor can bury itself in mud. Climbing off to stare at a machine which he has reduced in twenty seconds to a useless hulk, or which was running a half-minute before on ground where it now has its tracks out of sight, he has that sense of guilty disappointment which overcomes any man on having made an error in judgment.

So, as she stood, *Daisy Etta* was broken and useless. These soft persistent bipeds had built her, and if they were like any other race that built machines, they could care for them. The ability to reverse the tension of a spring, or twist a control rod, or reduce to zero the friction in a nut and lock-washer, was not enough to repair the crack in a cylinder head nor bearings welded to a crankshaft in an overheated starting motor. There had been a lesson to learn. It had been learned. *Daisy Etta* would be repaired, and the next time—well, at least she would know her own weaknesses.

Tom swung the two-cycle machine and edged in next to the Seven, with the edge of his blade all but touching *Daisy Etta's* push-beam. They got off and Peebles bent over the drum-tight right track.

"Watch yourself," said Tom.

"Watch what?"

"Oh—nothin', I guess." He circled the machine, trained eyes probing over frame and fittings. He stepped forward suddenly and grasped the fuel-tank drain cock. It was closed. He opened it; golden oil gushed out. He shut it off, climbed up on the machine and opened the fuel cap on top of the tank. He pulled out the bayonet gauge, wiped it in the crook of his knee, dipped and withdrew it.

The tank was more than three-quarters full.

"What's the matter?" asked Peebles, staring curiously at Tom's drawn face.

"Peeby, I opened the cock to drain this tank. I left it with oil runnin' out on the ground. She shut herself off."

"Now, Tom, you're lettin' this thing get you down. You just thought you did. I've seen a main-line valve shut itself off when it's worn bad, but only 'cause the pump pulls it shut when the motor's runnin'. But not a gravity drain."

"Main-live valve?" Tom pulled the seat up and looked. One glance was enough to show him that this one was open.

"She opened this one, too."

"O.K.—O.K. Don't look at me like that!" Peebles was as near to exasperation as he could possible get. "What difference does it make?"

Tom did not answer. He was not the type of man who, when faced with something beyond his understanding, would begin to doubt his own sanity. His was a dogged insistence that what he saw and sensed was what had actually happened. In him was none of the fainting fear of madness that another, more sensitive, man might feel. He doubted neither himself nor his evidence, and so could free his mind for searching out the consuming 'why' of a problem. He knew instinctively that to share 'unbelievable' happenings with anyone else, even if they had really occurred, was to put even further obstacles in his way. So he kept his clamlike silence and stubbornly, watchfully, investigated.

The slipped track was so tightly drawn up on the roller flanges that there could be no question of pulling the master pin and opening the track up. It would have to be worked back in place—a very delicate operation, for a little force applied in the wrong direction would be enough to run the track off altogether. To complicate things, the blade of the Seven was down on the ground and would have to be lifted before the machine could be manoeuvred, and its hydraulic hoist was useless without the motor.

Peebles unhooked twenty feet of half-inch cable from the rear of the smaller dozer, scratched a hole in the ground under the Seven's blade, and pushed the eye of the cable through. Climbing over the mouldboard, he slipped the eye on to the big towing hook bolted to the underside of the bellyguard. The other end of the cable he threw out on the ground in front of the machine. Tom mounted the other dozer and swung into place, ready to tow. Peebles hooked the cable on to Tom's drawbar, hopped up on the Seven. He put her in neutral, disengaged the master clutch and put the blade control over into 'float' position, then raised an arm.

Tom perched upon the arm rest of his machine, looking backwards, moved slowly, taking up the slack in the cable. It straightened and grew taut, and as it did it forced the Seven's blade upwards. Peebles waved for slack and put the blade control into 'hold.' The cable bellied downwards away from the blade.

"Hydraulic system's O.K., anyhow," called Peebles, as Tom throttled down. "More over and take a strain to the right, sharp as you can without fouling the cable on the track. We'll see if we can walk this track on."

Tom backed up, cut sharply to the right, and drew the cable out almost at right angles to the other machine. Peebles held the right track of the Seven with the brake and released both steering cluches. The left track now could turn free, the right not at all. Tom was running at a quarter throttle in his lowest gear, so that his machine barely crept along, taking the strain. The Seven shook gently and began to pivot on the taut right track, unbelievable foot-pounds of energy coming to bear on the front of the track where it rode high up on the idler wheel. Peebles released the right brake with his foot and applied it again in a series of skilled, deft jerks. The track would move a few inches and stop again, force being applied forwards and sidewards alternately, urging the track persuasively back in place. Then, a little jolt and she was in, riding true on the five truck rollers, the two track carrier rollers, the driving sprocket and the idler.

Peebles got off and stuck his head in between the sprocket and the rear carrier, squinting down and sideways to see if there were any broken flanges or roller bushes. Tom came over and pulled him out by the seat of his trousers. "Time enough for that when you get her in the shop," he said, masking his nervousness. "Reckon she'll roll?"

"She'll roll. I never saw a track in that condition come back that easy. By gosh, it's as if she was tryin' to help!"

"They'll do it sometimes," said Tom stiffly. "You better take the tow-tractor, Peeby. I'll stay with this'n."

"Anything you say."

And cautiously they took the steep slope down, Tom barely holding the brakes, giving the other machine a straight pull all the way. And so they brought *Daisy Etta* down to Peebles' out-door shop, where they pulled her cylinder head off, took off her starting motor, pulled out a burned clutch facing, had her quite helpless—

And put her together again.

"I tell you it was outright, cold-blooded murder," said Dennis hotly. "An' here we are takin' orders from a guy like that. What are we goin' to do about it?" They were standing by the cooler—Dennis had run his machine there to waylay Chub.

Chub Horton's cigar went down and up like a semaphore with a short circuit. "We'll skip it. The black-topping crew will be here in another two weeks or so, an' we can make a report. Besides, I don't know what happened up there any more than you do. In the meantime we got a runway to build."

"You don't know what happened up there? Chub, you're a smart man. Smart enough to run this job better than Tom Jaeger even if he wasn't crazy. And you're surely smart enough not to believe all that cock and bull about that tractor runnin' out from under that grease-monkey. Listen—" he learned forward and tapped Chub's chest. "He said it was the governor. I saw that governor myself an' heard ol' Peebles say there wasn't a thing wrong with it. Th' throttle control rod had slipped off its yoke, yeah—but you know what a tractor will do when the throttle control goes out. It'll idle or stall. It won't run away, whatever."

"Well, maybe so, but—"

"But nothin'! A guy that'll commit murder ain't sane. If he did it once, he can do it again and I ain't fixin' to let that happen to me."

Two things crossed Chub's steady but not bright mind at this. One was that Dennis, whom he did not like but could not shake, was trying to force him into something that he did not want to do. The other was that under all of his swift talk Dennis was scared spitless.

"What do you want to do—call up the sheriff?"

Dennis ha-ha-ed appreciatively—one of the reasons he was so hard to shake. "I'll tell you what we can do. As long as we have you here, he isn't the only man who knows the work. If we stop takin' orders from him, you can give 'em as good or better. An' there won't be anything he can do about it."

"Doggone it, Dennis," said Chub, with sudden exasperation. "What do you think you're doin'—handin' me over the keys to the kingdom or something? What do you want to see me bossin' around here for?" He stood up. "Suppose we did what you said? Would it get the field built any quicker? Would it get me any more money in my pay envelope? What do you think I want—glory? I passed up a chance to run for council-man once. You think I'd raise a finger to get a bunch of mugs to do what I say—when they do it anyway?"

"Aw, Chub—I wouldn't cause trouble just for the fun of it. That's not what I mean at all. But unless we do something about that guy we ain't safe. Can't you get that through your head?"

"Listen, windy. If a man keeps busy enough he can't get into trouble. That goes for Tom—you might keep that in mind. But it goes for you, too. Get back up on that rig an' get back to the marl pit." Dennis, completely taken by surprise, turned to his machine.

"It's a pity you can't move earth with your mouth," said Chub as he walked off. "They could have left you to do this job single-handed."

Chub walked slowly towards the outcropping, switching at beach pebbles with a grade stake and swearing to himself. He was essentially a simple man and believed in the simplest possible approach to everything. He liked a job where he could do everything required and where nothing turned up to complicate things. He had been in the grading business for a long time as an operator and survey party boss, and he was remarkable for one thing—he had always held aloof from the cliques and internecine politics that are the breath of life to most construction men. He was disturbed and troubled at the backstabbing that went on around him on various jobs. If it was blunt, he was disgusted, and subtlety simply left him floundering and bewildered. He was stupid enough so that his basic honesty manifested itself in his speech and actions, and he had learned that complete honesty in dealing with men above and below him was almost invariably painful to all concerned, but he had not the wit to act otherwise, and did not try to. If he had a bad tooth, he had it pulled out as soon as he could. If he got a raw deal from a superintendent over him, that superintendent would get told exactly what the trouble was, and if he didn't like it, there were other jobs. And if the pulling and hauling of cliques got in his hair, he had always said so and left. Or he had sounded off and stayed; his completely selfish reaction to things that got in the way of his work had earned him a lot of regard from men he had worked under. And so, in this instance, he had no hesitation about choosing a course of action. Only—how did you go about asking a man if he was a murderer?

He found the foreman with an enormous wrench in his hand, tightening up the new track adjustment bolt they had installed in the Seven.

"Hey, Chub! Glad you turned up. Let's get a piece of pipe over the end of this thing and really bear down." Chub went for the pipe, and they fitted it over the handle of the four-foot wrench and hauled until the sweat ran down their backs, Tom checking the track clearance occasionally with a crowbar. He finally called it good enough and they stood there in the sun gasping for breath.

"Tom," panted Chub, "did you kill that Puerto Rican?"

Tom's head came up as if someone had burned the back of his neck with a cigarette.

"Because," said Chub, "if you did you can't go on runnin' this job."

Tom said, "That's a lousy thing to kid about."

"You know I ain't kiddin'. Well, did you?"

"No!" Tom sat down on a keg, wiped his face with a bandanna. "What's got into you?"

"I just wanted to know. Some of the boys are worried about it."

Tom's eyes narrowed. "Some of the boys, huh? I think I get it. Listen to me, Chub. Rivera was killed by that thing there." He thumbed over his shoulder at the Seven, which was standing ready now, awaiting only the building of a broken cutting corner on the blade. Peebles was winding up the welding machine as he spoke. "If you mean, did I put him up on the machine before he was thrown, the answer is yes. That much I killed him, and don't think I don't feel it. I had a hunch something was wrong up there, but I couldn't put my finger on it and I certainly didn't think anybody was going to get hurt."

"Well, what was wrong?"

"I still don't know." Tom stood up. "I'm tired of beatin' around the bush, Chub, and I don't much care any more what anybody thinks. There's somethin' wrong with that Seven, something that wasn't built into her. They don't make tractors better'n that one but whatever it was happened up there on the mesa has queered this one. Now go ahead and think what you like, and dream up any story you want to tell the boys. In the meantime you can pass the word—nobody runs that machine but me, understand? Nobody!"

"Tom—"

Tom's patience broke. "That's all I'm going to say about it! If anybody else gets hurt it's going to be me, understand? What more do you want?"

He strode off, boiling. Chub stared after him, and after a long moment reached up and took the cigar from his lips. Only then did he realize that he had bitten it in two; half the butt was still inside his mouth. He spat and stood there shaking his head.

"How's she going, Peeby?"

Peebles looked up from the welding machine. "Hi, Chub, have her ready for you in twenty minutes." He gauged the distance between the welding machine and the big tractor. "I should have forty feet of cable," he said, looking at the festoons of arc and ground cables that hung from the storage hooks in the back of the welder. "Don't want to get a tractor over here to move the thing, and don't feel like cranking up the Seven just to get it close enough." He separated the arc cable and threw it aside, walked to the tractor, paying the ground cable off his arm. He threw out the last of his slack and grasped the ground clamp when he was eight feet from the machine. Taking it in his left hand, he pulled hard, reaching out with his right to grasp the mouldboard of the Seven, trying to get it far enough to clamp on to the machine.

Chub stood there watching him, chewing on his cigar, absent-mindedly diddling with the controls on the arc-welder. He pressed the starter-button, and the six-cylinder motor responded with a purr. He spun the work-selector dials idly, threw the arc generator switch—

A bolt of incredible energy, thin, searing, blue-white, left the rod-holder at his feet, stretched itself *fifty feet* across to Peebles, whose fingers had just touched the mouldboard of the tractor. Peebles' head and shoulders were surrounded for a second by a violet nimbus, and then he folded over and dropped. A circuit breaker clacked behind the control board of the welder, but too late. The Seven rolled slowly backwards, without firing, on level ground, until it brought up against a road-roller.

Chub's cigar was gone, and he didn't notice it. He had the knuckles of his right hand in his mouth, and his teeth sunk into the pudgy flesh. His eyes protruded; he crouched there and quivered, literally frightened out of his mind. For old Peebles was burned almost in two.

They buried him next to Rivera. There wasn't much talk afterwards; the old man had been a lot closer to all of them than they had realized until now. Harris, for once in his rum-dumb, lightheaded life, was quiet and serious, and Kelly's walk seemed to lose some of its litheness. Hour after hour Dennis' flabby mouth worked, and he bit at his lower lip until it was swollen and tender. Al Knowles seemed more or less unaffected, as was to be expected from a man who had something less than the brains of a chicken. Chub Horton had snapped out of it after a couple of hours and was very nearly himself again. And in Tom Jaeger swirled a black, furious anger at this unknowable curse that had struck the camp.

And they kept working. There was nothing else to do. The shovel kept up its rhythmic swing and dig, swing and dump, and the Dumptors screamed back and forth between it and the little that there was left of the swamp. The upper end of the runway was grassed off; Chub and Tom set grade stakes and Dennis began the long job of cutting and filling the humpy surface with his pan. Harris manned the other and followed him, a cut behind. The shape of the runway emerged from the land, and then that of the paralleling taxiway; and three days went by. The horror of Peebles' death wore off enough so that they could talk about it, and very little of the talk helped anybody. Tom took his spells at everything, changing over with Kelly to give him a rest from the shovel, making a few rounds with a pan, putting in hours on a Dumptor. His arm was healing slowly but clean, and he worked grimly in spite of it, taking a perverse sort of pleasure from the pain of it. Every man on the job watched his machine with the solicitude of a mother with her first-born; a serious skilled mechanic.

The only concession that Tom allowed himself in regard to Peebles' death was to corner Kelly one afternoon and ask him about the welding machine. Part of Kelly's rather patchy past had been spent in a technical college, where he had studied electrical engineering and women. He had learned a little of the former and enough of the latter to get him thrown out on his ear. So, on the off-chance that he might know something about the freak arc, Tom put it to him.

Kelly pulled off his high-gauntlet gloves and batted sand-flies with them. "What sort of an arc was that? Boy, you got me there. Did you ever hear of a welding machine doing like that before?"

"I did not. A welding machine just don't have that sort o' push. I saw a man get a full jolt from a 400-amp welder once, an' although it sat him down it didn't hurt him any."

"It's not amperage that kills people," said Kelly, "it's voltage. Voltage is the pressure behind a current, you know. Take an amount of water, call it amperage. If I throw it in your face, it won't hurt you. If I put it through a small hose you'll feel it. But if I pump it through them tiny holes on a Diesel injector nozzle at about twelve hundred pounds, it'll draw blood. But a welding arc generator just is not wound to build up that kind of voltage. I can't see where any short circuit anywhere through the armature of field windings could do such a thing."

"From what Chub said, he had been foolin' around with the work selector. I don't think anyone touched the dials after it happened. The selector dial was run all the way over to the low current application segment, and the current control was around the halfway mark. That's not enough juice to get you a good bead with a quarter-inch rod, let alone kill somebody—or roll a tractor back thirty feet on level ground."

"Or jump fifty feet," said Kelly. "It would take thousands of volts to generate an arc like that."

"Is it possible that something in the Seven could have pulled that arc? I mean, suppose the arc wasn't driven over, but was drawn over? I tell you, she was hot for four hours after that."

Kelly shook his head. "Never heard of any such thing. Look, just to have something to call them, we call direct current terminals positive and negative, and just because it works in theory we say that current flows from negative to positive. There couldn't be any more positive attraction in one electrode than there is negative drive in the other; see what I mean?"

"There couldn't be some freak condition that would cause a sort of oversize positive field? I mean one that would suck out the negative flow all in a heap, make it smash through under a lot of pressure like the water you were talking about through an injector nozzle?"

"No, Tom. It just don't work that way, far as anyone knows. I dunno, though—there are some things about static electricity that nobody understands. All I can say is that what happened couldn't happen and if it did it couldn't have killed Peebles. And you know the answer to that."

Tom glanced away at the upper end of the runway, where the two graves were. There was bitterness and turbulent anger naked there for a moment, and he turned and walked away without another word. And when he went back to have another look at the welding machine, *Daisy Etta* was gone.

Al Knowles and Harris squatted together near the water cooler.

"Bad," said Harris.

"Nevah saw anythin' like it," said Al. "Ol' Tom come back f'm the shop theah jus' *raisin'* Cain. 'Weah's 'at Seven gone? Weah's 'at Seven?' I never heered sech cah'ins on."

"Dennis did take it, huh?"

"Sho' did."

Harris said, "He came spoutin' around to me a while back, Dennis did. Chub'd told him Tom said for everybody to stay off that machine. Dennis was mad as a wet hen. Said Tom was carryin' that kind o' business too far. Said there was probably somethin' about the Seven Tom didn't want us to find out. Might incriminate him. Dennis is ready to say Tom killed the kid."

"Reckon he did, Harris?"

Harris shook his head. "I've known Tom too long to think that. If he won't tell us what really happened up on the mesa, he has a reason for it. How'd Dennis come to take the dozer?"

"Blew a front tyre on his pan. Came back heah to git anothah rig—maybe a Dumptor. Saw th' Seven standin' theah ready to go. Stood theah lookin' at it and cussin' Tom. Said he was tired of bashin' his kidneys t'pieces on them othah rigs an' bedamned if he wouldn't take suthin' that rode good fo' a change. I tol' him ol' Tom'd raise th' roof when he found him on it. He had a couple mo' things t'say 'bout Tom then."

"I didn't think he had the guts to take the rig."

"Aw, he talked hisself blind mad."

They looked up as Chub Horton trotted up, panting. "Hey, you guys, come on. We better get up there to Dennis."

"What's wrong?" asked Harris, climbing to his feet.

"Tom passed me a minute ago lookin' like the wrath o' God and hightailin' it for the swamp fill. I asked him what was the matter and he hollered that Dennis had taken the Seven. Said he was always talkin' about murder and he'd get his fill of it foolin' around that machine." Chub went wall-eyed, licked his lips beside his cigar.

"Oh-oh," said Harris quietly. "That's the wrong kind o' talk for just now."

"You don't suppose he—"

"*Come on!*"

They saw Tom before they were halfway there. He was walking slowly, with his head down. Harris shouted. Tom raised his face, stopped, stood there waiting with a peculiarly slumped stance.

"Where's Dennis?" barked Chub.

Tom waited until they were almost up to him and then weakly raised an arm and thumbed over his shoulder. His face was green.

"Tom—is he—"

Tom nodded, and swayed a little. His granite ;aw was slack.

"Al, stay with him. He's sick. Harris, let's go."

Tom was sick, then and there. Very. Al stood gaping at him, fascinated.

Chub and Harris found Dennis. All of twelve square feet of him, ground and churned and rolled out into a torn-up patch of earth. *Daisy Etta* was gone.

Back at the outcropping, they sat with Tom while All Knowles took a Dumptor and roared away to get Kelly.

"You saw him?" he said dully after a time.

Harris said, "Yeah."

The screaming Dumptor and a mountainous cloud of dust arrived, Kelly driving. Al holding on with a death-grip to the dump-bed guards. Kelly flung himself off, ran to Tom. "Tom—what is all this? Dennis dead? And you . . . you—"

Tom's head came up slowly, the slackness going out of his long face, a light suddenly coming into his eyes. Until this moment it had not crossed his mind what these men might think.

"I—what?"

"Al says you killed him."

Tom's eyes flicked at Al Knowles, and Al winced as if the glance had been a quirt.

Harris said, "What about it, Tom?"

"Nothing about it. He was killed by that Seven. You saw that for yourself."

"I stuck with you all along," said Harris slowly. "I took everything you said and believed it."

"This is too strong for you?" Tom asked.

Harris nodded. "Too strong, Tom."

Tom looked at the grim circle of faces and laughed suddenly. He stood up, put his back against a tall crate. "What do you plan to do about it?"

There was a silence. "You think I went up there and knocked that windbag off the machine and ran over him?" More silence. "Listen.

I went up there and saw what you saw. He was dead before I got there. That's not good enough either?" He paused and licked his lips. "So after I killed him I got up on the tractor and drove it far enough away so you couldn't see or hear it when you got there. And then I sprouted wings and flew back so's I was halfway here when you met me—*ten minutes* after I spoke to Chub on my way up!"

Kelly said vaguely, "Tractor?"

"Well," said Tom harshly to Harris, "was the tractor there when you and Chub went up and saw Dennis?"

"No—"

Chub smacked his thigh suddenly. "You could of drove it into the swamp, Tom."

Tom said angrily, "I'm wastin' my time. You guys got it all figured out. Why ask me anything at all?"

"Aw, take it easy," said Kelly. "We just want the facts. Just what did happen? You met Chub and told him that Dennis would get all the murderin' he could take if he messed around that machine. That right?"

"That's right."

"Then what?"

"Then the machine murdered him."

Chub, with remarkable patience, asked, "What did you mean the day Peebles was killed when you said that something had queered the Seven up there on the mesa?"

Tom said furiously, "I meant what I said. You guys are set to crucify me for this and I can't stop you. Well, listen. Somethings's got into that Seven. I don't know what it is and I don't think I ever will know. I thought that after she smashed herself up that it was finished with. I had an idea that when we had her torn down and helpless we should have left her that way. I was dead right but it's too late now. She's killed Rivera and she's killed Dennis and she sure had something to do with killing Peebles. And my idea is that she won't stop as long as there's a human being alive on this island."

"Whaddaya know!" said Chub.

"Sure, Tom, sure," said Kelly quietly. "That tractor is out to get us. But don't worry; we'll catch it and tear it down. Just don't you worry about it any more; it'll be all right."

"That's right, Tom," said Harris. "You just take it easy around camp for a couple of days till you feel better. Chub and the rest of us will handle things for you. You had too much sun."

"You're a swell bunch of fellows," gritted Tom, with the deepest sarcasm. "You want to live," he shouted, "git out there and throw that maverick bulldozer!"

"That maverick bulldozer is at the bottom of the swamp where you put it," growled Chub. His head lowered and he started to move in. "Sure we want to live. The best way to do that is to put you where you can't kill anybody else. *Get him!*"

He leaped. Tom straightened him with his left and crossed with his right. Chub went down, tripping Harris. A! Knowles scuttled to a toolbox and dipped out a fourteen-inch crescent wrench. He circled around, keeping out of trouble, trying to look useful. Tom loosened a haymaker at Kelly, whose head seemed to withdraw like a turtle's; it whistled over, throwing Tom badly off balance. Harris, still on his knees, tackled Tom's legs; Chub hit him in the small of the back with a meaty shoulder, and Tom went on his face. Al Knowles, holding the wrench in both hands, swept it up and back like a baseball bat; at the top of its swing Kelly reached over, snatched it out of his hands and tapped Tom delicately behind the ear with it. Tom went limp.

It was late, but nobody seemed to feel like sleeping. They sat around the pressure lantern, talking idly. Chub and Kelly played an inconsequential game of casino, forgetting to pick up their points; Harris paced up and down like a man in a cell, and Al Knowles was squinched up close to the light, his eyes wide and watching, watching—

"I need a drink," said Harris.

"Tens," said one of the casino players.

Al Knowles said, "We shoulda killed him. We oughta kill him now."

"There's been too much killin' already," said Chub. "Shut up, you." And to Kelly, "With big casino," sweeping up cards.

Kelly caught his wrist and grinned. "Big casino's the ten of diamonds, not the ten of hearts. Remember?"

"Oh."

"How long before the black-topping crew will be here?" quavered Al Knowles.

"Twelve days," said Harris. "And they better bring some likker."

"Hey, you guys."

They fell silent.

"Hey!"

"It's Tom," said Kelly. "Building sixes, Chub."

"I'm gonna go kick his ribs in," said Knowles, not moving.

"I heard that," said the voice from the darkness. "If I wasn't hogtied—"

"We know what you'd do," said Chub. "How much proof do you think we need?"

"Chub, you don't have to do any more to him!" It was Kelly, flinging his cards down and getting up. "Tom, you want water?"

"Yes."

"Siddown, siddown," said Chub.

"Let him lay there and bleed," Al Knowles said.

"Nuts!" Kelly went and filled a cup and brought it to Tom. The big Georgian was tied thoroughly, wrists together, taut rope between elbow and elbow behind his back, so that his hands were immovable over his solar plexus. His knees and ankles were bound as well, although Knowles' little idea of a short rope between ankles and throat hadn't been used.

"Thanks, Kelly." Tom drank greedily, Kelly holding his head. "Goes good." He drank more. "What hit me?"

"One of the boys. 'Bout the time you said the cat was haunted."

"Oh, yeah." Tom rolled his head and blinked with pain.

"Any sense asking you if you blame us?"

"Kelly, does somebody else have to get killed before you guys wake up?"

"None of us figure there will be any more killin'—now."

The rest of the men drifted up. "He willing to talk sense?" Chub wanted to know.

Al Knowles laughed, "Hyuk! hyuk! Don't he look dangerous now!"

Harris said suddenly, "Al, I'm gonna hafta tape your mouth with the skin off your neck."

"Am I the kind of guy that makes up ghost stories?"

"Never have that I know of, Tom." Harris kneeled down beside him. "Never killed anyone before, either."

"Oh, get away from me. Get away," said Tom tiredly.

"Get up and make us," jeered Al.

Harris got up and backhanded him across the mouth. Al squeaked, took three steps backward and tripped over a drum of grease. "I told you," said Harris almost plaintively. "I *told* you, Al."

Tom stopped the bumble of comment. "Shut up!" he hissed. "SHUT UP!" he roared.

They shut.

"Chub," said Tom, rapidly, evenly. "What did you say I did with that Seven?"

"Buried it in the swamp."

"Yeh. Listen."

"Listen at what?"

"Be quiet and listen!"

So they listened. It was another still, windless night, with a thin crescent of moon showing nothing true in the black and muffled silver landscape. The smallest whisper of surf drifted up from the beach, and from far off to the right, where the swamp was, a scandalized frog croaked protest at the manhandling of his mudhole. But the sound that crept down, freezing their bones, came from the bluff behind their camp.

It was the unmistakable staccato of a starting engine.

"The Seven!"

" 'At's right, Chub," said Tom.

"Wh-who's crankin' her up?"

"Are we all here?"

"All but Peebles and Dennis and Rivera," said Tom.

"It's Dennis' ghost," moaned Al.

Chub snapped, "Shut up, lamebrain."

"She's shifted to Diesel," said Kelly, listening.

"She'll be here in a minute," said Tom. "Y'know, fellas, we can't all be crazy, but you're about to have a time convincin' yourself of it."

"You like this, doncha?"

"Some ways. Rivera used to call that machine *Daisy Etta,* 'cause she's *de siete* in Spig. *Daisy Etta,* she wants her a man."

"Tom," said Harris, "I wish you'd stop that chatterin'. You make me nervous."

"I got to do somethin'. I can't run," Tom drawled.

"We're going to have a look," said Chub. "If there's nobody on that cat, we'll turn you loose."

"Mighty white of you. Reckon you'll get back before she does?"

"We'll get back. Harris, come with me. We'll get one of the pan tractors. They can outrun a Seven. Kelly, take Al and get the other one."

"Dennis' machine has a flat tyre on the pan," said Al's quivering voice.

"Pull the pin and cut the cables, then! Git!" Kelly and Al Knowles ran off.

"Good huntin', Chub."

Chub went to him, bent over. "I think I'm goin' to have to apologize to you, Tom."

"No you ain't. I'd a done the same. Get along now, if you think you got to. But hurry back."

"I got to. An' I'll hurry back."

Harris said, "Don't go 'way, boy." Tom returned the grin, and they were gone. But they didn't hurry back. They didn't come back at all.

It was Kelly who came pounding back, with Al Knowles on his heels, a half hour later. "Al—gimme your knife."

He went to work on the ropes. His face was drawn.

"I could see some of it," whispered Tom. "Chub and Harris?"

Kelly nodded. "There wasn't nobody on the Seven like you said." He said it as if there was nothing else in his mind, as if the most rigid self-control was keeping him from saying it over and over.

"I could see the lights," said Tom. "A tractor angling up the hill. Pretty soon another, crossing it, lighting up the whole slope."

"We heard it idling up there somewhere," Kelly said. "Olive-drab paint—couldn't see it."

"I saw the pan tractor turn over—oh, four, five times down the hill. It stopped, lights still burning. Then something hit it and rolled it again. That sure blacked it out. What turned it over first?"

"The Seven. Hanging up there just at the brow of the bluff. Waited until Chub and Harris were about to pass, sixty, seventy feet below. Tipped over the edge and rolled down on them with her clutches out. Must've been going thirty miles an hour when she hit. Broadside. They never had a chance. Followed the pan as it rolled down the hill and when it stopped booted it again."

"Want me to rub yo' ankles?" asked Al.

"You! Get outa my sight!"

"Aw, Tom—" whimpered Al.

"Skip it, Tom," said Kelly. "There ain't enough of us left to carry on that way. Al, you mind your manners from here on out, hear?"

"Ah jes' wanted to tell y'all. I knew you weren't lyin' 'bout Dennis, Tom, if only I'd stopped to think. I recollect when Dennis said he'd take that tractuh out . . . 'membah, Kelly? . . . He went an' got the crank and walked around to th' side of th' machine and stuck it in th' hole. It was barely in theah befo' the startin' engine kicked off. 'Whadda ya know!' he says t'me. 'She started by herse'f! I nevah pulled that handle!' And I said, 'She sho' rarin't' go!' "

"You pick a fine time to 'recollec'' something," gritted Tom. "C'mon—let's get out of here."

"Where to?"

"What do you know that a Seven can't move or get up on?"

"That's a large order. A big rock, maybe."

"Ain't nothing that big around here," said Tom.

Kelly thought a minute, then snapped his fingers. "Up on the top of my last cut with the shovel," he said. "It's fourteen feet if it's an inch. I was pullin' out small rock an' topsoil, and Chub told me to drop back and dip out marl from a pocket there. I sumped in back of the original cut and took out a whole mess o' marl. That left a big neck of earth sticking thirty feet or so out of the cliff. The narrowest part is only about four feet wide. If *Daisy Etta* tries to get us from the top, she'll straddle the neck and hang herself. If she tries to get us from below, she can't get traction to climb; it's too loose and too steep."

"And what happens if she builds herself a ramp?"

"We'll be gone from there."

"Let's go."

Al agitated for the choice of a Dumptor because of its speed, but was howled down. Tom wanted something that could not get a flat tyre and that would need something really powerful to turn it over. They took the two-cycle pan tractor with the bulldozer blade that had been Dennis' machine and crept out into the darkness.

It was nearly six hours later that *Daisy Etta* came and woke them up. Night was receding before a paleness in the east, and a fresh ocean breeze had sprung up. Kelly had taken the first lookout and Al the second, letting Tom rest the night out. And Tom was far too tired to argue the arrangement. Al had immediately fallen asleep on his watch, but fear had such a sure, cold hold on his vitals that the first faint growl of the big Diesel engine snapped him erect. He tottered on the edge of the tall neck of earth that they slept on and squeaked as he scrabbled to get his balance.

"What's giving?" asked Kelly, instantly wide awake.

"It's coming," blubbered Al. "Oh, my, oh my—"

Kelly stood up and stared into the fresh, dark dawn. The motor boomed hollowly, in a peculiar way heard twice at the same time as it was thrown to them and echoed back by the bluffs under and around them.

"It's coming and what are we goin' to do?" chanted Al. "What is going to happen?"

"My head is going to fall off," said Tom sleepily. He rolled to a sitting position, holding the brutalized member between his hands. "If that egg behind my ear hatches, it'll come out a full-sized jack-hammer." He looked at Kelly. "Where is she?"

KILLDOZER!   207

"Don't rightly know," said Kelly. "Somewhere down around the camp."

"Probably pickin' up our scent."

"Figure it can do that?"

"I figure it can do anything," said Tom. "Al, stop your moanin'."

The sun slipped its scarlet edge into the thin slot between sea and sky, and rosy light gave each rock and tree a shape and a shadow. Kelly's gaze swept back and forth, back and forth, until, minutes later, he saw movement.

"There she is!"

"Where?"

"Down by the grease rack."

Tom rose and stared. "What's she doin'?"

After an interval Kelly said, "She's workin'. Diggin' a swale in front of the fuel drums."

"You don't say. Don't tell me she's goin' to give herself a grease job."

"She don't need it. She was completely greased and new oil put in the crankcase after we set her up. But she might need fuel."

"Not more'n half a tank."

"Well, maybe she figures she's got a lot of work to do today." As Kelly said this Al began to blubber. They ignored him.

The fuel drums were piled in a pyramid at the edge of the camp, in forty-four-gallon drums piled on there sides. The Seven was moving back and forth in front of them, close up, making pass after pass, gouging earth up and wasting it out past the pile. She soon had a huge pit scooped out, about fourteen feet wide, six feet deep and thirty feet long, right at the very edge of the pile of drums.

"What do you reckon she's playin' at?"

"Search me. She seems to want fuel, but I don't . . . look at that! She's stopped in the hole; . . . turnin' . . . smashing the top corner of the mouldboard into one of the drums on the bottom!"

Tom scraped the stubble on his jaw with his nails. "An' you wonder how much that critter can do! Why, she's got the whole thing figured out. She knows if she tried to punch a hole in a fuel drum that she'd only kick it around. If she did knock a hole in it, how's she going to lift it? She's not equipped to handle hose, so . . . see? Look at her now! She just gets herself lower than the bottom drum on the pile, and punches a hole. She can do that then, with the whole weight of the pile holding it down. Then she backs her tank under the stream of fuel runnin' out!"

"How'd she get the cap off?"

Tom snorted and told them how the radiator cap had come off its hinges as he vaulted over the hood the day Rivera was hurt.

"You know," he said after a moment's thought, "if she knew as much then as she does now, I'd be snoozin' beside Rivera and Peebles. She just didn't know her way around then. She run herself like she'd never run before. She's learned plenty since."

"She has," said Kelly, "and here's where she uses it on us. She's headed this way."

She was. Straight out across the roughed-out runway she came, grinding along over the dew-sprinkled earth, yesterday's dust swirling up from under her tracks. Crossing the shoulder line, she took the rougher ground skilfully, angling up over the occasional swags in the earth, by-passing stones, riding free and fast and easily. It was the first time Tom had actually seen her clearly running without an operator, and his flesh crept as he watched. The machine was unnatural, her outline somehow unreal and dreamlike purely through the lack of the small silhouette of a man in the saddle. She looked hulked, compact, dangerous.

"What are we gonna do?" wailed Al Knowles.

"We're gonna sit and wait," said Kelly, "and you're gonna shut your trap. We won't know for five minutes yet whether she's going to go after us from down below or from up here."

"If you want to leave," said Tom gently, "go right ahead." Al sat down.

Kelly looked ruminatively down at his beloved power shovel, sitting squat and unlovely in the cut below them and away to their right. "How do you reckon she'd stand up against the dipper stick?"

"If it ever came to a rough-and-tumble," said Tom, "I'd say it would be just too bad for *Daisy Etta*. But she wouldn't fight. There's no way you could get the shovel within punchin' range; *Daisy*'d just stand there and laugh at you."

"I can't see her now," whined Al.

Tom looked. "She's taken the bluff. She's going to try it from up here. I move we sit tight and see if she's foolish enough to try to walk out here over that narrow neck. If she does, she'll drop on her belly with one track on each side. Probably turn herself over trying to dig out."

The wait then was interminable. Back over the hill they could hear the labouring motor; twice they heard the machine stop momentarily to shift gears. Once they looked at each other hopefully as the sound rose to a series of bellowing roars, as if she were backing and filling; then they realized that she was trying to take some particularly steep part of the bank and having trouble getting traction. But she made it; the motor revved up as she made the brow of the hill, and she shifted into fourth gear and came lumbering out into the open. She lurched up to the edge of the cut, stopped, throttled down, dropped her blade on the ground and stood there idling. Al Knowles backed away to the very edge of the tongue of earth they stood on, his eyes practically on stalks.

"O.K.—put up or shut up," Kelly called across harshly.

"She's looking the situation over," said Tom. "That narrow pathway don't fool her a bit."

Daisy Etta's blade began to rise, and stopped just clear of the ground. She shifted without clashing her gears, began to back slowly, still a little more than an idle.

"She's gonna jump," screamed Al. "I'm gettin' out of here!"

"Stay here, you fool," shouted Kelly. "She can't get us as long as we're up here! If you go down, she'll hunt you down like a rabbit."

The blast of the Seven's motor was the last straw for Al. He squeaked and hopped over the edge, scrambling and sliding down the almost sheer face of the cut. He hit the bottom running.

Daisy Etta lowered her blade and raised her snout and growled forward, the blade loading. Six, seven, seven and a half cubic yards of dirt piled up in front of her as she neared the edge. The loaded blade bit into the narrow pathway that led out to their perch. It was almost all soft, white, crumbly marl, and the great machine sank nose down into it, the monstrous overload of topsoil spilling down on each side.

"She's going to bury herself!" shouted Kelly.

"No—wait." Tom caught his arm. "She's trying to turn—she made it! She made it! She's ramping herself down to the flat!"

"She is—and she's cut us off from the bluff!"

The bulldozer, blade raised as high as it could possibly go, the hydraulic rod gleaming clean in the early light, freed herself of the last of her tremendous load, spun around and headed back upwards, sinking her blade again. She made one more pass between them and the bluff, making a cut now far too wide for them to jump, particularly to the crumbly footing at the bluff's edge. Once down again, she turned to face their haven, now an isolated pillar of marl, and revved down, waiting.

"I never thought of this," said Kelly guiltily. "I knew we'd be safe from her ramping up, and I never thought she'd try it the other way!"

"Skip it. In the meantime, here we sit. What happens—do we wait up here until she idles out of fuel, or do we starve to death?"

"Oh, this won't be a siege, Tom. That thing's too much of a killer. Where's Al? I wonder if he's got guts enough to make a pass near here with our tractor and draw her off?"

"He had just guts enough to take our tractor and head out," said Tom. "Didn't you know?"

"He took our—*what?*" Kelly looked out towards where they had left their machine the night before. It was gone. "Why, the dirty little yellow rat!"

"No sense cussin'," said Tom steadily, interrupting what he knew was the beginning of some really flowery language. "What else could you expect?"

Daisy Etta decided, apparently, how to go about removing their splendid isolation. She uttered the snort of too-quick throttle, and moved into their peak with a corner of her blade, cutting out a huge swipe, undercutting the material over it so that it fell on her side and track as she passed. Eight inches disappeared from that side of their little plateau.

"Oh-oh. That won't do a-tall," said Tom.

"Fixin' to dig us down," said Kelly grimly. "Take her about twenty minutes. Tom, I say leave."

"It won't be healthy. You just got no idea how fast that thing can move now. Don't forget, she's a good deal more than she was when she had a man runnin' her. She can shift from high to reverse to fifth speed forward like that"—he snapped his fingers— "And she can pivot faster'n you can blink and throw that blade just where she wants it."

The tractor passed under them, bellowing, and their little table was suddenly a foot shorter.

"Awright," said Kelly. "So what do you want to do? Stay here and let her dig the ground out from under our feet?"

"I'm just warning you," said Tom. "Now listen. We'll wait until she's taking a load. It'll take her a second to get rid of it when she knows we're gone. We'll split—she can't get both of us. You head out in the open, try to circle the curve of the bluff and get where you can climb it. Then come back over here to the cut. A man can scramble off a fourteen-foot cut faster'n any tractor ever built. I'll cut in close to the cut, down at the bottom. If she takes after you, I'll get clear all right. If she takes after me, I'll try to make the shovel and at least give her a run for her money. I can play hide an' seek in an' around and under that dipper-stick all day if she wants to play."

"Why me out in the open?"

"Don't you think those long laigs o' yours can outrun her in that distance?"

"Reckon they got to," grinned Kelly. "O.K., Tom."

They waited tensely. *Daisy Etta* backed close by, started another pass. As the motor blatted under the load, Tom said, "Now!" and they jumped. Kelly, catlike as always, landed on his feet. Tom, whose knees and ankles were black and blue with rope bruises, took two staggering steps and fell. Kelly scooped him to his feet as the dozer's steel prow came around the bank. Instantly she was in fifth gear and howling down at them. Kelly flung himself to the left and Tom to the right, and they pounded away, Kelly out towards the runway, Tom straight for the shovel. *Daisy Etta* let them diverge for a moment, keeping her course, trying to pursue both; then she evidently sized Tom up as the slower, for she swung towards him. The instant's hesitation was all Tom needed to get the little lead necessary. He tore up to the shovel, his legs going like pistons, and dived down between the shovel's tracks.

As he hit the ground, the big manganese-steel mouldboard hit the right track of the shovel, and the impact set all forty-seven tons of the great machine quivering. But Tom did not stop. He scrabbled his way under the rig, stood up behind it, leaped and caught the sill of the rear window, clapped his other hand on it, drew himself up and tumbled inside. Here he was safe for the moment; the huge tracks themselves were higher than the Seven's blade could rise, and the floor of the cab was a good sixteen inches higher than the top of the track. Tom went to the cab door and peeped outside. The tractor had drawn off and was idling.

"Study away," gritted Tom, and went to the big Murphy Diesel. He unhurriedly checked the oil with the bayonet gauge, replaced it, took the governor cut-out rod from its rack and inserted it in the governor casing. He set the master throttle at the halfway mark, pulled up the starter-handle, twitched the cut-out. The motor spat a wad of the blue smoke out of its hooded exhaust and caught. Tom put the rod back, studied the fuel-flow glass and pressure gauges, and then went to the door and looked out again. The Seven had not moved, but it was revving up and down in that uneven fashion it had shown up on the mesa. Tom had the extraordinary idea that it was gathering itself to spring. He slipped into the saddle, threw the master clutch. The big gears that half-filled the cab obediently began to turn. He kicked the brake-locks loose with his heels, let his feet rest lightly on the pedals as they rose.

Then he reached over his head and snapped back the throttle. As the Murphy picked up he grasped both hoist and swing levers and pulled them back. The engine howled; the two-yard bucket came up off the ground with a sudden jolt as the cold friction grabbed it. The big machine swung hard to the right; Tom snapped his hoist lever forward and checked the bucket's rise with his foot on the brake. He shoved the crowd lever forward; the bucket ran out to the end of its reach, and the heel of the bucket wiped across the Seven's hood, taking with it the exhaust stack, muffler and all, and the pre-cleaner on the air intake. Tom cursed. He had figured on the machine's leaping backwards. If it had, he would have smashed the cast-iron radiator core. But she had stood still, making a split-second decision.

Now she moved, though, and quickly. With that incredibly fast shifting, she leaped backwards and pivoted out of range before Tom could check the shovel's mad swing. The heavy swing-friction blocks smoked acridly as the machine slowed, stopped and swung back. Tom checked her as he was facing the Seven, hoisted his bucket a few feet, and rehauled, bringing it about halfway back, ready for anything. The four great dipper-teeth gleamed in the sun. Tom ran a practised eye over cables, boom and dipper-stick, liking the black polish of crater compound on the sliding parts, the easy tension of well-greased cables and links. The huge machine stood strong, ready and profoundly subservient for all its brute power.

Tom looked searchingly at the Seven's ruined engine hood. The gaping end of the broken air-intake pipe stared back at him. "Aha!" he said. "A few cupfuls of nice dry marl down there'll give you something to chew on."

Keeping a wary eye on the tractor, he swung into the bank, dropped his bucket and plunged it into the marl. He crowded in deep, and the Murphy yelled for help but kept on pushing. At the peak of the load a terrific jar rocked him in the saddle. He looked back over his shoulder through the door and saw the Seven backing off again. She had run up and delivered a terrific punch to the counter-weight at the back of the cab. Tom grinned tightly. She'd have to do better than that. There was nothing back there but eight or ten tons of solid steel. And he didn't much care at the moment whether or not she scratched his paint.

He swung back again, white marl running away on both sides of the heaped bucket. The shovel rode perfectly now, for a shovel is counterweighted to balance true when standing level with the bucket loaded. The hoist, swing frictions and the brake linings had heated and dried themselves of the night's condensation moisture, and she answered the controls in a way that delighted the operator in him. He handled the swing lever lightly, back to swing to the right, forward to swing to the left, following the slow dance the Seven had started to do, stepping warily back and forth like a fighter looking for an opening. Tom kept the bucket between himself and the tractor, knowing that she could not hurt a tool that was built to smash hard rock for twenty hours a day and like it.

Daisy Etta bellowed and rushed in. Tom snapped the hoist lever back hard, and the bucket rose, letting the tractor run underneath. Tom punched the bucket trip, and the great steel jaw opened, cascading marl down on the broken hood. The tractor's fan blew it back in a huge billowing cloud. The instant that it took Tom to check and dump was enough, however, for the tractor to dance back out of the way, for when he tried to drop it on the machine to smash the coiled injector tubes on top of the engine block, she was gone.

The dust cleared away, and the tractor moved in again, feinted to the left, then swung her blade at the bucket, which was just clear of the ground. Tom swung to meet her, her feint having got her in a little closer than he liked, and bucket met blade with a shower of sparks and a clank that could be heard for half a mile. She had come in with her blade high, and Tom let out a wordless shout as he saw that the A-frame brace behind the blade had caught between two of his dipper-teeth. He snatched at his hoist lever and the bucket came up, lifting with it the whole front end of the bulldozer.

Daisy Etta plunged up and down and her tracks dug violently into the earth as she raised and lowered her blade, trying to shake herself free. Tom rehauled, trying to bring the tractor in closer, for the boom was set too low to attempt to lift such a dead weight. As it was, the shovel's off track was trying its best to get off the ground. But the crowd and rehaul frictions could not handle her alone; they began to heat and slip.

Tom hoisted a little; the shovel's off track came up a foot off the ground. Tom cursed and let the bucket drop, and in an instant the dozer was free and running clear. Tom swung wildly at her, missed. The dozer came in on a long curve; Tom swung to meet her again, took a vicious swipe at her which she took on her blade. But this time she did not withdraw after being hit, but bored right in, carrying the bucket before her. Before Tom realized what she was doing, his bucket was around in front of the tracks and between them, on the ground. It was a swift and skilful a manoeuvre as could be imagined, and it left the shovel without the ability to swing as long as *Daisy Etta* could hold the bucket trapped between the tracks.

Tom crowded furiously, but that succeeded only in lifting the boom higher in the air, since there is nothing to hold a boom down but its own weight. Hoisting did nothing but make his frictions smoke and rev the engine down dangerously close to the stalling point.

Tom swore again and reached down to the cluster of small levers at his left. These were the geas. On this type of shovel, the swing lever controls everything except crowd and hoist. With the swing lever, the operator, having selected his gear, controls the travel—that is, power to the tracks—in forward and reverse; booming up and booming down; and swinging. The machine can do only one of these things at a time. If he is in travel gear, she cannot swing. If she is in swing gear, she cannot boom up or down. Not once in years of operating would this inability bother an operator; now, however, nothing was normal.

Tom pushed the swing gear control down and pulled up on the travel. The clutches involved were jaw clutches, not frictions, so that he had to throttle down on an idle before he could make the castellations mesh. As the Murphy revved down, *Daisy Etta* took it as a signal that something could be done about it, and she shoved furiously into the bucket. But Tom had all controls in neutral and all she succeeded in doing was to dig herself in, her sharp new cleats spinning deep into the dirt.

Tom set his throttle up again and shoved the swing lever forward. There was a vast crackling of drive chains; and the big tracks started to turn.

Daisy Etta had sharp cleats; her pads were twenty inches wide and her tracks were fourteen feet long, and there were fourteen tons of steel on them. The shovel's big flat pads were three feet wide and twenty feet long, and forty-seven tons aboard. There was simply no comparison. The Murphy bellowed the fact that the work was hard, but gave no indications of stalling. *Daisy Etta* performed the incredible feat of shifting into a forward gear while she was moving backwards, but it did her no good. Round and round her tracks went, tying to drive her forward, gouging deep; and slowly and surely she was forced backward towards the cut wall by the shovel.

Tom heard a sound that was not a part of a straining machine; he looked out and saw Kelly up on top of the cut, smoking, swinging his feet over the edge, making punching motions with his hands as if he had a ringside seat at a big fight—which he certainly had.

Tom now offered the dozer little choice. If she did not turn aside before him, she would be borne back against the bank and her fuel tank crushed. There was every possibility that, having her pinned there, Tom would have time to raise his bucket over her and smash her to pieces. And if she turned before she was forced against the bank, she would have to free Tom's bucket. This she had to do.

The Murphy gave him warning, but not enough. It crooned as the load came off, and Tom knew then that the dozer was shifting into a reverse gear. He whipped the hoist lever back and the bucket rose as the dozer backed away from him. He crowded it out and let it come smashing down—and missed. For the tractor danced aside—and while he was in travel gear he could not swing to follow it. *Daisy Etta* charged then, put one track on the bank and went over almost on her beam-ends, throwing one end of her blade high in the air. So totally unexpected was it that Tom was quite unprepared. The tractor flung itself on the bucket, and the cutting edge of the blade dropped between the dipper teeth. This time there was the whole weight of the tractor to hold it there. There would be no way for her to free herself—but at the same time she had trapped the bucket so far out from the center pin of the shovel that Tom couldn't hoist without overbalancing and turning the monster over.

Daisy Etta ground away in reverse, dragging the bucket out until it was checked by the bumper-blocks. Then she began to crab sideways, up against the bank, and when Tom tried tentatively to rehaul, she shifted and came right with him, burying one whole end of her blade deep into the bank.

Stalemate. She had hung herself up on the bucket, and she had immobilized it. Tom tried to rehaul, but the tractor's anchorage in the bank was too solid. He tried to swing, to hoist. All the over-worked frictions could possibly give out was smoke. Tom grunted and throttled to an idle, leaned out of the window. *Daisy Etta* was idling too, loudly without her muffler, the stackless exhaust giving out an ugly flat sound. But after the roar of the two great motors the partial silence was deafening.

Kelly called down, "Double knockout, hey?"

"Looks like it. What say we see if we can't get close enough to her to quiet her down some?"

Kelly shrugged. "I dunno. If she's really stopped herself, it's the first time. I respect that rig, Tom. She wouldn't have got herself into that spot if she didn't have an ace up her sleeve."

"Look at her, man! Suppose she was a civilized bulldozer and you had to get her out of there. She can't raise her blade high enough to free it from those dipper-teeth, y'know. Think you'd be able to do it?"

"It might take several seconds," Kelly drawled. "She's sure high and dry."

"O.K., let's spike her guns."

"Like what?"

"Like taking a bar and prying out her tubing." He referred to the coiled brass tubing that carried the fuel, under pressure, from the pump to the injectors. There were many feet of it, running from the pump reservoir, stacked in expansion coils over the cylinder head.

As he spoke *Daisy Etta*'s idle burst into that maniac revving up and down characteristic of her.

"What do you know!" Tom called above the racket. "Eavesdropping!"

Kelly slid down the cut, stood up on the track of the shovel and poked his head in the window. "Well, you want to get a bar and try?"

"Let's go!"

Tom went to the toolbox and pulled out the pinch bar that Kelly used to replace cables on his machine, and swung to the ground. They approached the tractor warily. She revved up as they came near, began to shudder. The front end rose and dropped and the tracks began to turn as she tried to twist out of the vice her blade had dropped into.

"Take it easy, sister," said Tom. "You'll just bury yourself. Sit still and take it, now, like a good girl. You got it comin'."

"Be careful," said Kelly. Tom hefted the bar and laid a hand on the fender.

The tractor literally shivered, and from the rubber hose connection at the top of the radiator, a blinding stream of hot water shot out. It fanned and caught both full in the face. They staggered back, cursing.

"You O.K., Tom?" Kelly gasped a moment later. He had got most of it across the mouth and cheek. Tom was on his knees, his shirt tail out, blotting at his face.

"My eyes . . . oh, my eyes—"

"Let's see!" Kelly dropped down beside him and took him by the wrists, gently removing Tom's hands from his face. He whistled. "Come on," he gritted. He helped Tom up and led him away a few feet. "Stay here," he said hoarsely. He turned, walked back towards the dozer, picking up the pinch bar. "You dirty——!" he yelled, and flung it like a javelin at the tube coils. It was a little high. It struck the ruined hood, made a deep dent in the metal. The dent promptly inverted with a loud *thung-g-g!* and flung the bar back at him. He ducked; it whistled over his head and caught Tom in the calves of his legs. He went down like a poled ox, but staggered to his feet again.

"Come on!" Kelly snarled, and taking Tom's arm, hustled him around the turn of the cut. "Sit down! I'll be right back."

"Where you going? Kelly—be careful!"

"Careful and how!"

Kelly's long legs ate up the distance back to the shovel. He swung into the cab, reached back over the motor and set up the master throttle all the way. Stepping up behind the saddle, he opened the running throttle and the Murphy howled. Then he hauled back on the hoist lever until it knuckled in, turned and leaped off the machine in one supple motion.

The hoist drum turned and took up slack; the cable straightened as it took the strain. The bucket stirred under the dead weight of the bulldozer that rested on it; and slowly, then, the great flat tracks began to lift their rear ends off the ground. The great obedient mass of machinery teetered forward on the tips of her tracks, the Murphy revved down and under the incredible load, but it kept the strain. A strand of the two-part hoist cable broke and whipped around, singing; and then she was balanced—over-balanced—

And the shovel had hauled herself right over and had fallen with an earth-shaken crash. The boom, eight tons of solid steel, clanged down on to the blade of the bulldozer, and lay there, crushing it down tightly on to the imprisoning row of dipper-teeth.

Daisy Etta sat there, not trying to move now, racing her motor impotently. Kelly strutted past her, thumbing his nose, and went back to Tom.

"Kelly! I thought you were never coming back! What happened?"

"Shovel pulled herself over on her nose."

"Good boy! Fall on the tractor?"

"Nup. But the boom's laying across the top of her blade. Caught like a rat in a trap."

"Better watch out the rat don't chew its leg off to get out," said Tom, drily. "Still runnin', is she?"

"Yep. But we'll fix that in a hurry."

"Sure. Sure. How?"

"How? I dunno. Dynamite, maybe. How's the optics?"

Tom opened one a trifle and grunted. "Rough. I can see a little, though. My eyelids are parboiled, mostly. Dynamite, you say? Well, let's think first. Think."

Tom sat back against the bank and stretched out his legs. "I tell you, Kelly, I been too blessed busy these last few hours to think much, but there's one thing that keeps comin' back to me—somethin' I was mullin' over long before the rest of you guys knew anything was up at all, except Rivera had got hurt in some way I wouldn't tell you all about. But I don't reckon you'll call me crazy if I open my mouth now and let it all run out?"

"From now on," Kelly said fervently, "nobody's crazy. After this I'll believe anything." He sat down.

"O.K. Well, about the tractor. What do you suppose has got into her?"

"Search me. I dunno."

"No—don't say that. I just got an idea we can't stop at 'I dunno.' We got to figure all the angles on this thing before we know just what to do about it. Let's just get this thing lined up. When did it start? On the mesa. How? Rivera was opening an old building with the Seven. This thing came out of there. Now here's what I'm getting at. We can dope these things out about it: It's intelligent. It can only get into a machine and not into a man. It—"

"What about that? How do you know it can't?"

"Because it had the chance to and didn't. I was standing right by the opening when it kited out. Rivera was up on the machine at the time. It didn't directly harm either of us. It got into the tractor, and the tractor did. By the same token, it can't hurt a man when it's out of a machine, but that's all it wants to do when it's in one. O.K.?

"To get on: once it's in one machine it can't get out again. We know that because it had plenty of chances and didn't take them. That scuffle with the dipper-stick, f'r instance. My face woulda been plenty red if it had taken over the shovel—and you can bet it would have if it could."

"I got you so far. But what are we going to do about it?"

"That's the thing. You see, I don't think it's enough to wreck the tractor. We might burn it, blast it, and still not hurt whatever it was that got into it up on the mesa."

"That makes sense. But I don't see what else we can do than just break up the dozer. We haven't got a line on actually what the thing is."

"I think we have. Remember I asked you all those screwy questions about the arc that killed Peebles. Well, when that happened, I recollected a flock of other things. One—when it got out of that hole up there, I smelled that smell that you notice when you're welding; sometimes when lightning strikes real close."

"Ozone," said Kelly.

"Yeah—ozone. Then, it likes metal, not flesh. But most of all, there was that arc. Now, that was absolutely screwy. You know as well as I do—better—that an arc generator simply don't have the push to do a thing like that. It can't kill a man, and it can't throw an arc no fifty feet. But it did. An' that's why I asked you if there could be something—a field, or some such—that it could *suck* current out of a generator, all at once, faster than it could flow. Because this thing's electrical; it fits all around."

"Electronic," said Kelly doubtfully, thoughtfully.

"I wouldn't know. Now then. When Peebles was killed, a funny thing happened. Remember what Chub said? The Seven moved back—straight back, about thirty feet, until it bumped into a roadroller that was standing behind it. It did that with no fuel in the starting engine—without even using the starting engine, for that matter—and with the compression valves locked open!

"Kelly, that thing in the dozer can't do much, when you come right down to it. It couldn't fix itself up after that joyride on the mesa. It can't make the machine do too much more than the machine can do ordinarily. What it actually can do, seems to me, is to make a spring push instead of pull, like the control levers, and make a fitting slip when it's supposed to hold, like the ratchet on the throttle lever. It can turn a shaft, like the way it cranks its own starting motor. But if it was so all-fired highpowered, it wouldn't have to use the starting motor! The absolute biggest job it's done so far, seems to me, was when it walked back from that welding machine when Peebles got his. Now, why did it do that just then?"

"Reckon it didn't like the brimstone smell, like it says in the Good Book," said Kelly sourly.

"That's pretty close, seems to me. Look, Kelly—this thing *feels* things. I mean, it can get sore. If it couldn't it never woulda kept driving in at the shovel like that. It can think. But if it can do all those things, then it can be *scared!*"

"Scared? Why should it be scared?"

"Listen. Something went on in that thing when the arc hit it. What's that I read in a magazine once about heat—something about molecules runnin' around with their heads cut off when they got hot?"

"Molecules do. They go into rapid motion when heat is applied. But—"

"But nothin'. That machine was hot for four hours after that. But she was hot in a funny way. Not just around the place where the arc hit, like as if it was a welding arc. But hot all over—from the mouldboard to the fuel-tank cap. Hot everywhere. And just as hot behind the final drive housings as she was at the top of the blade where the poor guy put his hand.

"And look at this." Tom was getting excited, as his words crystallized his ideas. "She was scared—scared enough to back off from that welder, putting everything she could into it, to get back from that welding machine. And after that, she was sick. I say that because in the whole time she's had that whatever-ya-call-it in her, she's never been near men without trying to kill them, except for those two days after the arc hit her. She had juice enough to start herself when Dennis came around with the crank, but she still needed someone to run her till she got her strength back."

"But why didn't she turn and smash up the welder when Dennis took her?"

"One of two things. She didn't have the strength, or she didn't have the guts. She was scared, maybe, and wanted out of there, away from that thing."

"But she had all night to go back for it!"

"Still scared. Or . . . oh, *that's* it! She had other things to do first. Her main idea is to kill men—there's no other way you can figure it. It's what she built to do. Not the tractor—they don't build 'em sweeter'n that machine; but the thing that's runnin' it."

"What is that thing?" Kelly mused. "Coming out of that old building—temple—what have you—how old is it? How long was it there? What kept it in there?"

"What kept it in there was some funny grey stuff that lined the inside of the buildin'," said Tom. "It was like rock, an' it was like smoke.

"It was a colour that scared you to look at it, and it gave Rivera and me the creeps when we got near it. Don't ask me what it was. I went up there to look at it, and it's gone. Gone from the building, anyhow. There was a little lump of it on the ground. I don't know whether that was a hunk of it, or all of it rolled up into a ball. I get the creeps again thinkin' about it."

Kelly stood up. "Well, the heck with it. We been beatin' our gums up here too long anyhow. There's just enough sense in what you say to make me want to try something nonsensical, if you see what I mean. If that welder can sweat the Ol' Nick out of that tractor, I'm on. Especially from fifty feet away. There should be a Dumptor around here somewhere; let's move from here. Can you navigate now?"

"Reckon so, a little." Tom rose and together they followed the cut until they came on the Dumptor. They climbed on, cranked it up and headed towards camp.

About halfway there Kelly looked back, gasped, and putting his mouth close to Tom's ear, bellowed against the screan of the motor, "Tom! 'Member what you said about the rat in the trap biting off a leg? Well, *Daisy* did too! She's left her blade an' pushbeams an' she's followin' us in!"

They howled into the camp, gasping against the dust that followed when they pulled up by the welder.

Kelly said, "You cast around and see if you can find a draw-pin to hook that rig up to the Dumptor with. I'm goin' after some water an' chow!"

Tom grinned. Imagine old Kelly forgetting that a Dumptor had no drawbar! He groped around to a tool box, peering out of the narrow slit beneath swollen lids, felt behind it and located a shackle. He climbed up on the Dumptor, turned it around and backed up to the welding machine. He passed the shackle through the ring at the end of the steering tongue of the welder, screwed in the pin and dropped the shackle over the front towing hook of the Dumptor. A Dumptor being what it is, having no real front and no real rear, and direct reversing gears in all speeds, it was no trouble to drive it 'backwards' for a change.

Kelly came pounding back, out of breath. "Fix it? Good. Shackle? No drawbar! *Daisy*'s closin' up fast; I say let's take the beach. We'll be concealed until we have a good lead out o' this pocket, and the going's pretty fair, long as we don't bury this jalopy in the sand."

"Good," said Tom as they climbed on and he accepted an open tin of K. "Only go easy; bump around too much and the welder'll slip off the hook. An' I somehow don't want to lose it just now."

They took off, zooming up the beach. A quarter of a mile up, they sighted the Seven across the flat. It immediately turned and took a course that would intercept them.

"Here she comes," shouted Kelly, and stepped down hard on the accelerator. Tom leaned over the back of the seat, keeping his eye on their tow. "Hey! Take it easy! Watch it!"

"*Hey!*"

But it was too late. The tongue of the welding machine responded to that one bump too many. The shackle jumped up off the hook, the welder lurched wildly, slewed hard to the left. The tongue dropped to the sand and dug in; the machine rolled up on it and snapped it off, finally stopped, leaning crazily askew. By a miracle it did not quite turn over.

Kelly tramped on the brakes and both their heads did their utmost to snap off their shoulders. They leaped off and ran back to the welder. It was intact, but towing it was now out of the question.

"If there's going to be a showdown, it's gotta be here."

The beach here was about thirty yards wide, the sand almost level, and undercut banks of sawgrass forming the landward edge in a series of little hummocks and headlands. While Tom stayed with the machine, testing starter and generator contacts, Kelly walked up one of the little mounds, stood up on it and scanned the beach back the way he had come. Suddenly he began to shout and wave his arms.

"What's got into you?"

"It's Al!" Kelly called back. "With the pan tractor!"

Tom dropped what he was doing, and came to stand beside Kelly. "Where's the Seven? I can't see."

"Turned on the beach and followin' our track. Al! Al! You little skunk, c'mere!"

Tom could now dimly make out the pan tractor cutting across directly towards them and the beach.

"He don't see *Daisy Etta*," remarked Kelly disgustedly, "or he'd sure be headin' the other way."

Fifty yards away Al pulled up and throttled down. Kelly shouted and waved to him. Al stood up on the machine, cupped his hands around his mouth, "Where's the Seven?"

"Never mind that! Come here with that tractor!"

Al stayed where he was. Kelly cursed and started out after him. "You stay away from me," he said, when Kelly was closer.

"I ain't got time for you now," said Kelly. "Bring that tractor down to the beach."

"Where's that *Daisy Etta?*" Al's voice was oddly strained.

"Right behind us." Kelly tossed a thumb over his shoulder. "On the beach."

Al's pop eyes clicked wide almost audibly. He turned on his heel and jumped off the machine and started to run. Kelly uttered a wordless syllable that was somehow more obscene than anything else he had ever uttered, and vaulted into the seat of the machine.

"Hey!" he bellowed after Al's rapidly diminishing figure. "You're runnin' right into her." Al appeared not to hear, but went pelting down the beach.

Kelly put her into fifth gear and poured on the throttle. As the tractor began to move he whacked out the master clutch, snatched the overdrive lever back to put her into sixth, rammed the clutch in again, all so fast that she did not have time to stop rolling. Bucking and jumping over the rough ground the fast machine whined for the beach.

Tom was fumbling back to the welder, his ears telling him better than his eyes how close the Seven was—for she was certainly no nightingale, particularly without her exhaust stack. Kelly reached the machine as he did.

"Get behind it," snapped Tom. "I'll jamb the tierod with the shackle, and you see if you can't bunt her up into that pocket between those two hummocks. Only take it easy—you don't want to tear up that generator. Where's Al?"

"Don't ask me. He run down the beach to meet *Daisy*."

"He *what?*"

The whine of the two-cycle drowned out Kelly's answer, if any. He got behind the welder and set his blade against it. Then in a low gear, slipping his clutch in a little, he slowly nudged the machine towards the place Tom had indicated. It was a little hollow in between two projecting banks. The surf and the hightide mark dipped inland here to match it; the water was only a few feet away.

Tom raised his arm and Kelly stopped. From the other side of the projecting shelf, out of their sight now, came the flat roar of the Seven's exhaust. Kelly sprang off the tractor and went to help Tom, who was furiously throwing out coils of cable from the rack back of the welder. "What's the game?"

"We got to ground that Seven some way," panted Tom. He threw the last bit of cable out to clear it of kinks and turned to the panel. "How was it—about sixty volts and the amperage on 'special appreciation'?" He spun the dials, pressed the starter button. The motor responded instantly. Kelly scooped up ground lamp and rod holder and tapped them together. The solenoid governor picked up the load and the motor hummed as a good live spark took the jump.

"Good," said Tom, switching off the generator. "Come on, Lieutenant General Electric, figure me out a way to ground that maverick."

Kelly tightened his lips, shook his head. "I dunno—unless somebody actually clamps this thing on her."

"No, boy, can't do that. If one of us gets killed—"

Kelly tossed the ground clamp idly, his lithe body taut. "Don't give me that, Tom. You know I'm elected because you can't see good enough to handle it. You know you'd do it if you could. You—"

He stopped short, for the steadily increasing roar of the approaching Seven had stopped, was blatting away now in that extraordinary irregular throttling that *Daisy Etta* affected.

"Now what's got into her?"

Kelly broke away and scrambled up the bank. "Tom!" he gasped. "Tom—come up here!"

Tom followed, and they lay side by side, peering out over the top of the escarpment at the remarkable tableau.

Daisy Etta was standing on the beach, near the water, not moving. Before her, twenty or thirty feet away, stood Al Knowles, his arms out in front of him, talking a blue streak. *Dasiy* made far too much racket for them to hear what he was saying.

"Do you reckon he's got guts enough to stall her off for us?" said Tom.

"If he has, it's the queerest thing that's happened yet on this old island," Kelly breathed, "an' that's saying something."

The Seven revved up till she shook, and then throttled back. She ran down so low then that they thought she had shut herself down, but she caught on the last two revolutions and began to idle quietly. And then they could hear.

Al's voice was high, hysterical. "—I come t' he'p you, I come t' he'p you, don' kill me, I'll he'p you—" He took a step forward; the dozer snorted and he fell to his knees. "I'll wash you an' grease you and change yo' ile," he said in a high singsong.

"The guy's not human," said Kelly wonderingly.

"He ain't housebroke either," Tom chuckled.

"—lemme he'p you. I'll fix you when you break down. I'll he'p you kill those other guys—"

"She don't need any help!" said Tom.

"The louse," growled Kelly. "The rotten little double-crossing polecat!" He stood up. "Hey, you Al! Come out o' that. I mean now! If she don't get you I will, if you don't move."

Al was crying now. "Shut up!" he screamed. "I know who's bawss hereabouts, an' so do you!" He pointed at the tractor. "She'll kill us all if'n we don't do what she wants!" He turned back to the machine. "I'll k-kill 'em fo' you. I'll wash you and shine you up and f-fix yo' hood. I'll put yo' blade back on. . . ."

Tom reached out and caught Kelly's leg as the tall man started out, blind mad. "Git back here," he barked. "What you want to do—get killed for the privilege of pinnin' his ears back?"

Kelly subsided and came back, threw himself down beside Tom, put his face in his hands. He was quivering with rage.

"Don't take on so," Tom said. "The man's plumb loco. You can't argue with him any more'n you can with *Daisy*, there. If he's got to get his, *Daisy*'ll give it to him."

"Aw, Tom, it ain't that. I know he ain't worth it, but I can't sit up here and watch him get himself killed. I can't, Tom."

Tom thumped him on the shoulder, because there were simply no words to be said. Suddenly he stiffened, snapped his fingers.

"There's our ground," he said urgently, pointing seaward. "The water—the wet beach where the surf runs. If we can get our ground clamp out there and her somewhere near it—"

"Ground the pan tractor. Run it out into the water. It ought to reach—partway, anyhow."

"That's it—c'mon."

They slid down the bank, snatched up the ground clamp, attached it to the frame of the pan tractor.

"I'll take it," said Tom, and as Kelly opened his mouth, Tom shoved him back against the welding machine. "No time to argue," he snapped, swung on to the machine, slapped her in gear and was off. Kelly took a step towards the tractor, and then his quick eyes saw a bight of the ground cable about to foul a wheel of the welder. He stooped and threw it off, spread out the rest of it so it would pay off clear. Tom, with the incredible single-mindedness of the trained operator, watched only the black line of the trailing cable on the sand behind him. When it straightened, he stopped. The front of the tracks were sloshing in the gentle surf. He climed off the side away from the Seven and tried to see. There was movement, and the growl of her motor now running at a bit more than idle, but he could not distinguish much.

Kelly picked up the rod-holder and went to peer around the head of the protruding bank. Al was on his feet, still crooning hysterically, sliding over towards *Daisy Etta*. Kelly ducked back, threw the switch on the arc generator, climbed the bank and crawled along through the sawgrass paralleling the beach until the holder in his hand tugged and he knew he had reached the end of the cable. He looked out at the beach, measured carefully with his eye the arc he would travel if he left his position and, keeping the cable taut, went out on the beach. At no point would he come within seventy feet of the possessed machine, let alone fifty. She had to be drawn in closer. And she had to be manoeuvred out to the wet sand, or in the water—

Al Knowles, encouraged by the machine's apparent decision not to move, approached, though warily, and still running off at the mouth. "—we'll kill 'em off an' then we'll keep it a secret and th' bahges'll come an' take us offen th' island and we'll go to anothah job an' kill us lots mo' . . . an' when yo' tracks git dry an' squeak we'll wet 'em with blood, and you'll be rightly king o' the hill . . . look yondah, look yondah, *Daisy Etta,* see them theah, by the otheh tractuh, theah they are, kill 'em, *Daisy,* kill 'em, *Daisy,* an' lemme he'p . . . heah me. *Daisy,* heah me, say you heah me—" and the motor roared in response. Al laid a timid hand on the radiator guard, leaning far over to do it, and the tractor still stood there grumbling but not moving. Al stepped back, motioned with his arm, began to walk off slowly towards the pan tractor looking backwards as he did so like a man training a dog. "C'mon, c'mon, theah's one theah, le's *kill'm, kill'm, kill'm.* . . ."

And with a snort the tractor revved up and followed.

Kelly licked his lips without effect because his tongue was dry, too. The madman passed him, walking straight up the centre of the beach, and the tractor, now no longer a bulldozer, followed him; and there the sand was bone dry, sun-dried, dried to powder. As the tractor passed him, Kelly got up on all fours, went over the edge of the bank on to the beach, crouched there.

Al crooned, "I love ya, honey, I love ya, 'deed I do—"

Kelly ran crouching, like a man under machine-gun fire, making himself as small as possible and feeling as big as a barn door. The torn-up sand where the tractor had passed was under his feet now; he stopped, afraid to get too much closer, afraid that a weakened, badly grounded arc might leap from the holder in his hand and serve only to alarm and infuriate the thing in the tractor. And just then Al saw him.

"There!" he screamed; and the tractor pulled up short.

"Behind you! Get'm *Daisy! Kill'm, kill'm, kill'm.*"

Kelly stood up almost wearily, fury and frustration too much to be borne. "In the water," he yelled, because it was what his whole being wanted, "Get 'er in the water! Wet her tracks, Al!"

"*Kill'm, kill'm—*"

As the tractor started to turn, there was a commotion over by the pan tractor. It was Tom, jumping, shouting, waving his arms, swearing. He ran out from behind his machine, straight at the Seven. *Daisy Etta*'s motor roared and she swung to meet him, Al barely dancing back out of the way. Tom cut sharply, sand spouting under his pumping feet, and ran straight into the water. He went out to about waist deep, suddenly disappeared. He surfaced, spluttering, still trying to shout. Kelly took a better grip on his rod holder and rushed.

Daisy Etta, in following Tom's crazy rush, had swung in beside the pan tractor, not fifteen feet away; and she, too, was now in the surf. Kelly closed up the distance as fast as his long legs would let him; and as he approached to within that crucial fifty feet, Al Knowles hit him.

Al was frothing at the mouth, gibbering. The two men hit full tilt; Al's head caught Kelly in the midriff as he missed a straightarm, and the breath went out of him in one great *whoosh!* Kelly went down like all timber, the whole world turned to one swirling red-grey haze. Al flung himself on the bigger man, clawing, smacking, too berserk to ball his fists.

"Ah'm go' to kill you," he gurgled. "She'll git one, I'll git t'other, an' then she'll know—"

Kelly covered his face with his arms, and as some wind was sucked at last into his labouring lungs, he flung them upward and sat up in one mighty surge. Al was hurled upward and to one side, and as he hit the ground Kelly reached out a long arm, and twisted his fingers into the man's coarse hair, raised him up, and came across with his other fist in a punch that would have killed him had it landed square. But Al managed to jerk to one side enough so that it only amputated a cheek. He fell and lay still. Kelly scrambled madly around in the sand for his welding-rod holder, found it and began to run again. He couldn't see Tom at all now, and the Seven was standing in the surf, moving slowly from side to side, backing out, ravening. Kelly held the rod-clamp and its trailing cable blindly before him and ran straight at the machine. And then it came—that thin, soundless bolt of energy. But this time it had its full force, for poor old Peebles' body had not been the ground that this swirling water offered. *Daisy Etta* literally leaped backwards towards him, and the water around her tracks spouted upward in hot steam. The sound of her engine ran up and up, broke, took on the rhythmic, uneven beat of a swing drummer. She threw herself from side to side like a cat with a bag over its head. Kelly stepped a little closer, hoping for another bolt to come from the clamp in his hand, but there was none, for—

"The circuit breaker!" cried Kelly.

He threw the holder up on the deck plate of the Seven in front
of the seat, and ran across the little beach to the welder. He reached
behind the switchboard, got his thumb on the contact hinge and
jammed it down.

Daisy Etta leaped again, and then again, and suddenly her
motor stopped. Heat in turbulent waves blurred the air over her.
The little gas tank for the starting motor went out with a cannon's
roar, and the big fuel tank, still holding thirty-odd gallons of Diesel
oil, followed. It puffed itself open rather than exploded, and threw
a great curtain of flame over the ground behind the machine.
Motor or no motor, then, Kelly distinctly saw the tractor shudder
convulsively. There was a crawling movement of the whole frame,
a slight wave of motion away from the fuel tank, approaching the
front of the machine, and moving upward from the tracks. It
culminated in the crown of the radiator core, just in front of
the radiator cap; and suddenly an area of six or seven square
inches literally *blurred* around the edges. For a second, then, it
was normal, and finally it slumped molten, and liquid metal ran
down the sides, throwing out little sparks as it encountered what
was left of the charred paint. And only then was Kelly conscious
of agony in his left hand. He looked down. The welding machine's
generator had stopped, though the motor was still turning, having
smashed the friable coupling on its drive shaft. Smoke poured from
the generator, which had become little more than a heap of slag.
Kelly did not scream, though, until he looked and saw what had
happened to his hand—

When he could see straight again, he called for Tom, and there
was no answer. At last he saw something out in the water, and
plunged in after it. The splash of cold salt water on his left hand
he hardly felt, for the numbness of shock had set in. He grabbed
at Tom's shirt with his good hand, and then the ground seemed to
pull itself out from under his feet. That was it, then—a deep hole
right off the beach. The Seven had run right to the edge of it, had
kept Tom there out of his depth and—

He flailed wildly, struck out for the beach, so near and so hard
to get to. He gulped a stinging lungful of brine, and only the lovely
shock of his knee striking solid beach kept him from giving up to
the luxury of choking to death. Sobbing with effort, he dragged
Tom's dead weight inshore and clear of the surf. It was then that he
became conscious of a child's shrill weeping; for a mad moment
he thought it was he himself, and then he looked and saw that it was
Al Knowles. He left Tom and went over to the broken creature.

"Get up, you," he snarled. The weeping only got louder. Kelly rolled him over on his back—he was quite unresisting—and belted him back and forth across the mouth until Al began to choke. Then he hauled him to his feet and led him over to Tom.

"Kneel down, scum. Put one of your knees between his knees." Al stood still. Kelly hit him again and he did as he was told.

"Put your hands on his lower ribs. There. O.K. Lean, you rat. Now sit back." He sat down, holding his left wrist in his right hand, letting the blood drop from the ruined hand. "Lean. Hold it—sit back. Lean. Sit. Lean. Sit."

Soon Tom sighed and began to vomit weakly, and after that he was all right.

This is the story of *Daisy Etta*, the bulldozer that went mad and had a life of its own, and not the story of the missile test that they don't talk about except to refer to it as the missile test that they don't talk about. But you may have heard about it for all that—rumors, anyway. The rumor has it that an early IRBM tested out a radically new controls system by proving conclusively that it did not work. It was a big bird and contained much juice, and flew far, far afield. Rumor goes on to assert that (a) it alighted somewhere in the unmapped rain forests of South America and that (b) there were no casualties. What they *really* don't talk about is the closely guarded report asserting that both (a) and (b) are false. There are only two people (aside from yourself, now) who know for sure that though (a) is certainly false, (b) is strangely true, and there were indeed no casualties.

Al Knowles may well know it too, but he doesn't count.

It happened two days after the death of *Daisy Etta*, as Tom and Kelly sat in (of all places) the cool of the ruined temple. They were poring over paper and pencil, trying to complete the impossible task of making a written statement of what had happened on the island, and why they and their company had failed to complete their contract. They had found Chub and Harris, and had buried them next to the other three. Al Knowles was back in the shadows, tied up, because they had heard him raving in his sleep, and it seemed he could not believe *Daisy* was dead and he still wanted to go around killing operators for her. They knew that there must be an investigation, and they knew just how far their story would go; and having escaped a monster like *Daisy Etta*, they found life too sweet to want any part of it spent under observation or in jail.

The warhead of the missile struck near the edge of their camp, just between the pyramid of fuel drums and the dynamite stores. The second stage alighted a moment later two miles away, in the vicinity of the five graves. Kelly and Tom stumbled out to the rim of the mesa, and for a long while watched the jetsam fall and the flotsam rise. It was Kelly who guessed what must have happened, and "Bless their clumsy little hearts," he said happily. And he took the scribbled papers from Tom and tore them across.

But Tom shook his head, and thumbed back at the mound. *"He'll* talk."

"Him?" said Kelly, with such profound eloquence in his tone that he clearly evoked the image of Al Knowles, with his mumbling voice and his drooling mouth and his wide glazed eyes. "Let him," Kelly said, and tore the papers again.

So they let him.

NO WOMAN BORN

C.L. Moore

She had been the loveliest creature whose image ever moved along the airways. John Harris, who was once her manager, remembered doggedly how beautiful she had been as he rose in the silent elevator toward the room where Deirdre sat waiting for him.

Since the theater fire that had destroyed her a year ago, he had never been quite able to let himself remember her beauty clearly, except when some old poster, half in tatters, flaunted her face at him, or a maudlin memorial program flashed her image unexpectedly across the television screen. But now he had to remember.

The elevator came to a sighing stop and the door slid open. John Harris hesitated. He knew in his mind that he had to go on, but his reluctant muscles almost refused him. He was thinking helplessly, as he had not allowed himself to think until this moment, of the fabulous grace that had poured through her wonderful dancer's body, remembering her soft and husky voice with the little burr in it that had fascinated the audiences of the whole world.

There had never been anyone so beautiful.

In times before her, other actresses had been lovely and adulated, but never before Deirdre's day had the entire world been able to take one woman so wholly to its heart. So few outside the capitals had ever seen Bernhardt or the fabulous Jersey Lily. And the beauties of the movie screen had had to limit their audiences to those who could reach the theaters. But Deirdre's image had once moved glowingly across the television screens of every home in the civilized world. And in many outside the bounds of civilization. Her soft, husky songs had sounded in the depths of jungles, her lovely, languorous body had woven its patterns of rhythm in desert tents and polar huts. The whole world knew every smooth motion of her body and every cadence of her voice, and the way a subtle radiance had seemed to go on behind her features when she smiled.

And the whole world had mourned her when she died in the theater fire.

Harris could not quite think of her as other than dead, though he knew what sat waiting him in the room ahead. He kept remembering the old words James Stephens wrote long ago for another Deirdre, also lovely and beloved and unforgotten after two thousand years.

> The time comes when our hearts sink utterly
> When we remember Deirdre and her tale,
> And that her lips are dust. . . .
> There has been again no woman born
> Who has so beautiful; not only so beautiful
> Of all the women born—

That wasn't quite true, of course—there had been one. Or maybe, after all, this Deirdre who died only a year ago had not been beautiful in the sense of perfection. He thought the other one might not have been either, for there are always women with perfection of feature in the world, and they are not the ones that legend remembers. It was the light within, shining through her charming, imperfect features, that had made this Deirdre's face so lovely. No one else he had ever seen had anything like the magic of the lost Deirdre.

> Let all men go apart and mourn together—
> No man can ever love her. Not a man
> Can dream to be her lover. . . . No man say—
> What would one say to her? There are no words
> That one could say to her.

No, no words at all. And it was going to be impossible to go through with this. Harris knew it overwhelmingly just as his finger touched the buzzer. But the door opened almost instantly, and then it was too late.

Maltzer stood just inside, peering out through his heavy spectacles. You could see how tensely he had been waiting. Harris was a little shocked to see that the man was trembling. It was hard to think of the confident and imperturbable Maltzer, whom he had known briefly a year ago, as shaken like this. He wondered if Deirdre herself were as tremulous with sheer nerves—but it was not time yet to let himself think of that.

"Come in, come in," Maltzer said irritably. There was no reason for irritation. The year's work, so much of it in secrecy and solitude, must have tried him physically and mentally to the very breaking point.

"She all right?" Harris asked inanely, stepping inside.

"Oh yes . . . yes, *she's* all right." Maltzer bit his thumbnail and glanced over his shoulder at an inner door, where Harris guessed she would be waiting.

"No," Maltzer said, as he took an involuntary step toward it. "We'd better have a talk first. Come over and sit down. Drink?"

Harris nodded, and watched Maltzer's hands tremble as he tilted the decanter. The man was clearly on the very verge of collapse, and Harris felt a sudden cold uncertainty open up in him in the one place where until now he had been oddly confident.

"She *is* all right?" he demanded, taking the glass.

"Oh yes, she's perfect. She's so confident it scares me." Maltzer gulped his drink and poured another before he sat down.

"What's wrong, then?"

"Nothing, I guess. Or . . . well, I don't know. I'm not sure any more. I've worked toward this meeting for nearly a year, but now—well, I'm not sure it's time yet. I'm just not sure."

He stared at Harris, his eyes large and indistinguishable behind the lenses. He was a thin, wire-taut man with all the bone and sinew showing plainly beneath the dark skin of his face. Thinner, now, than he had been a year ago when Harris saw him last.

"I've been too close to her," he said now. "I have no perspective any more. All I can see is my own work. And I'm just not sure that's ready yet for you or anyone to see."

"She thinks so?"

"I never saw a woman so confident." Maltzer drank, the glass clicking on his teeth. He looked up suddenly through the distorting lenses. "Of course a failure now would mean—well, absolute collapse," he said.

Harris nodded. He was thinking of the year of incredibly painstaking work that lay behind this meeting, the immense fund of knowledge, of infinite patience, the secret collaboration of artists, sculptors, designers, scientists, and the genius of Maltzer governing them all as an orchestra conductor governs his players.

He was thinking too, with a certain unreasoning jealousy, of the strange, cold, passionless intimacy between Maltzer and Deirdre in that year, a closer intimacy than any two humans can ever have shared before. In a sense the Deirdre whom he saw in a few minutes would *be* Maltzer, just as he thought he detected in Maltzer now and then small mannerisms of inflection and motion that had been Deirdre's own. There had been between them a sort of unimaginable marriage stranger than anything could ever have taken place before.

"—so many complications," Maltzer was saying in his worried voice with its faintest possible echo of Deirdre's lovely, cadenced rhythm. (The sweet, soft huskiness he would never hear again.) "There was shock, of course. Terrible shock. And a great fear of fire. We had to conquer that before we could take the first steps. But we did it. When you go in you'll probably find her sitting before the fire." He caught the startled question in Harris' eyes and smiled. "No, she can't feel the warmth now, of course. But she likes to watch the flames. She's mastered any abnormal fear of them quite beautifully."

"She can—" Harris hesitated. "Her eyesight's normal now?"

"Perfect," Maltzer said. "Perfect vision was fairly simple to provide. After all, that sort of thing has already been worked out, in other connections. I might even say her vision's a little better than perfect, from our own standpoint." He shook his head irritably. "I'm not worried about the mechanics of the thing. Luckily they got to her before the brain was touched at all. Shock was the only danger to her sensory centers, and we took care of all that first of all, as soon as communication could be established. Even so, it needed great courage on her part. Great courage." He was silent for a moment, staring into his empty glass.

"Harris," he said suddenly, without looking up, "have I made a mistake? Should we have let her die?"

Harris shook his head helplessly. It was an unanswerable question. It had tormented the whole world for a year now. There had been hundreds of answers and thousands of words written on the subject. Has anyone the right to preserve a brain alive when its body is destroyed? Even if a new body can be provided, necessarily so very unlike the old?

"It's not that she's—ugly—now," Maltzer went on hurriedly, as if afraid of an answer. "Metal isn't ugly. And Deirdre . . . well, you'll see. I tell you, I can't see myself. I know the whole mechanism so well—it's just mechanics to me. Maybe she's—grotesque. I don't know. Often I've wished I hadn't been on the spot, with all my ideas, just when the fire broke out. Or that it could have been anyone but Deirdre. She was so beautiful— Still, if it had been someone else I think the whole thing might have failed completely. It takes more than just an uninjured brain. It takes strength and courage beyond common, and—well, something more. Some-thing—unquenchable. Deirdre has it. She's still Deirdre. In a way she's still beautiful. But I'm not sure anybody but myself could see that. And you know what she plans?"

"No—what?"

"She's going back on the air-screen."

Harris looked at him in stunned disbelief.

"She *is* still beautiful," Maltzer told him fiercely. "She's got courage, and a serenity that amazes me. And she isn't in the least worried or resentful about what's happened. Or afraid what the verdict of the public will be. But I am, Harris. I'm terrified."

They looked at each other for a moment more, neither speaking. Then Maltzer shrugged and stood up.

"She's in there," he said, gesturing with his glass.

Harris turned without a word, not giving himself time to hesitate. He crossed toward the inner door.

The room was full of a soft, clear, indirect light that climaxed in the fire crackling on a white tiled hearth. Harris paused inside the door, his heart beating thickly. He did not see her for a moment. It was a perfectly commonplace room, bright, light, with pleasant furniture, and flowers on the tables. Their perfume was sweet on the clear air. He did not see Deirdre.

Then a chair by the fire creaked as she shifted her weight in it. The high back hid her, but she spoke. And for one dreadful moment it was the voice of an automaton that sounded in the room, metallic, without inflection.

"Hel-lo—" said the voice. Then she laughed and tried again. And it was the old, familiar, sweet huskiness he had not hoped to hear again as long as he lived.

In spite of himself he said, "Deirdre!" and her image rose before him as if she herself had risen unchanged from the chair, tall, golden, swaying a little with her wonderful dancer's poise, the lovely, imperfect features lighted by the glow that made them beautiful. It was the cruelest thing his memory could have done to him. And yet the voice—after that one lapse, the voice was perfect.

"Come and look at me, John," she said.

He crossed the floor slowly, forcing himself to move. That instant's flash of vivid recollection had nearly wrecked his hard-won poise. He tried to keep his mind perfectly blank as he came at last to the verge of seeing what no one but Maltzer had so far seen or known about in its entirety. No one at all had known what shape would be forged to clothe the most beautiful woman on Earth, now that her beauty was gone.

He had envisioned many shapes. Great, lurching robot forms, cylindrical, with hinged arms and legs. A glass case with the brain floating in it and appendages to serve its needs. Grotesque visions, like nightmares come nearly true. And each more inadequate than the last, for what metal shape could possibly do more than house ungraciously the mind and brain that had once enchanted a whole world?

Then he came around the wing of the chair, and saw her.

The human brain is often too complicated a mechanism to function perfectly. Harris' brain was called upon now to perform a very elaborate series of shifting impressions. First, incongruously, he remembered a curious inhuman figure he had once glimpsed leaning over the fence rail outside a farmhouse. For an instant the shape had stood up integrated, ungainly, impossibly human, before the glancing eye resolved it into an arrangement of brooms and buckets. What the eye had found only roughly humanoid, the suggestible brain had accepted fully formed. It was thus now, with Deirdre.

The first impression that his eyes and mind took from sight of her was shocked and incredulous, for his brain said to him unbelievingly, "*This is Deirdre! She hasn't changed at all!*"

Then the shift of perspective took over, and even more shockingly, eye and brain said, "No, not Deirdre—not human. Nothing but metal coils. Not Deirdre at all—" And that was the worst. It was like walking from a dream of someone beloved and lost, and facing anew, after that heartbreaking reassurance of sleep, the inflexible fact that nothing can bring the lost to life again. Deirdre was gone, and this was only machinery heaped in a flowered chair.

Then the machinery moved, exquisitely, smoothly, with a grace as familiar as the swaying poise he remembered. The sweet, husky voice of Deirdre said,

"It's me, John darling. It really is, you know."

And it was.

That was the third metamorphosis, and the final one. Illusion steadied and became factual, real. It was Deirdre.

He sat down bonelessly. He had no muscles. He looked at her speechless and unthinking, letting his senses take in the sight of her without trying to rationalize what he saw.

She was golden still. They had kept that much of her, the first impression of warmth and color which had once belonged to her sleek hair and the apricot tints of her skin. But they had had the good sense to go no farther. They had not tried to make a wax image of the lost Deirdre. (*No woman born who was so beautiful— Not one so beautiful, of all the women born—*)

And so she had no face. She had only a smooth, delicately modeled ovoid for her head, with a . . . a sort of crescent-shaped mask across the frontal area where her eyes would have been if she had needed eyes. A narrow, curved quarter-moon, with the horns turned upward. It was filled in with something translucent, like cloudy crystal, and tinted the aquamarine of the eyes Deirdre used to have. Through that, then, she saw the world. Through that she looked without eyes, and behind it, as behind the eyes of a human—she was.

Except for that, she had no features. And it had been wise of those who designed her, he realized now. Subconsciously he had been dreading some clumsy attempt at human features that might creak like a marionette's in parodies of animation. The eyes, perhaps, had had to open in the same place upon her head, and at the same distance apart, to make easy for her an adjustment to the stereoscopic vision she used to have. But he was glad they had not given her two eye-shaped openings with glass marbles inside them. The mask was better.

(Oddly enough, he did not once think of the naked brain that must lie inside the metal. The mask was symbol enough for the woman within. It was enigmatic; you did not know if her gaze was on you searchingly, or wholly withdrawn. And it had no variations of brilliance such as once had played across the incomparable mobility of Deirdre's face. But eyes, even human eyes, are as a matter of fact enigmatic enough. They have no expression except what the lids impart; they take all animation from the features. We automatically watch the eyes of the friend we speak with, but if he happens to be lying down so that he speaks across his shoulder and his face is upsidedown to us, quite as automatically we watch the mouth. The gaze keeps shifting nervously between mouth and eyes in their reversed order, for it is the position in the face, not the feature itself, which we are accustomed to accept as the seat of the soul. Deirdre's mask was in that proper place; it was easy to accept it as a mask over eyes.)

She had, Harris realized as the first shock quieted, a very beautifully shaped head—a bare, golden skull. She turned it a little, gracefully upon her neck of metal, and he saw that the artist who shaped it had given her the most delicate suggestion of cheekbones, narrowing in the blankness below the mask to the hint of a human face. Not too much. Just enough so that when the head turned you saw by its modeling that it had moved, lending perspective and foreshortening to the expressionless golden helmet. Light did not slip uninterrupted as if over the surface of a golden egg. Brancusi himself had never made anything more simple or more subtle than the modeling of Deirdre's head.

But all expression, of course, was gone. All expression had gone up in the smoke of the theater fire, with the lovely, mobile, radiant features which had meant Deirdre.

As for her body, he could not see its shape. A garment hid her. But they had made no incongruous attempt to give her back the clothing that once had made her famous. Even the softness of cloth would have called the mind too sharply to the remembrance that no human body lay beneath the folds, nor does metal need the incongruity of cloth for its protection. Yet without garments, he realized, she would have looked oddly naked, since her new body was humanoid, not angular machinery.

The designer had solved his paradox by giving her a robe of very fine metal mesh. It hung from the gentle slope of her shoulders in straight, pliant folds like a longer Grecian chlamys, flexible, yet with weight enough of its own not to cling too revealingly to whatever metal shape lay beneath.

The arms they had given her were left bare, and the feet and ankles. And Maltzer had performed his greatest miracle in the limbs of the new Deirdre. It was a mechanical miracle basically, but the eye appreciated first that he had also showed supreme artistry and understanding.

Her arms were pale shining gold, tapered smoothly, without modeling, and flexible their whole length in diminishing metal bracelets fitting one inside the other clear down to the slim, round wrists. The hands were more nearly human than any other feature about her, though they, too, were fitted together in delicate, small sections that slid upon one another with the flexibility almost of flesh. The fingers' bases were solider than human, and the fingers themselves tapered to longer tips.

Her feet, too, beneath the tapering broader rings of the metal ankles, had been constructed upon the model of human feet. Their finely tooled sliding segments gave her an arch and a heel and a flexible forward section formed almost like the *sollerets* of medieval armor.

She looked, indeed, very much like a creature in armor, with her delicately plated limbs and her featureless head like a helmet with a visor of glass, and her robe of chain-mail. But no knight in armor ever moved as Deirdre moved, or wore his armor upon a body of such inhumanly fine proportions. Only a knight from another world, or a knight of Oberon's court, might have shared that delicate likeness.

Briefly he had been surprised at the smallness and exquisite proportions of her. He had been expecting the ponderous mass of such robots as he had seen, wholly automatons. And then he realized that for them, much of the space had to be devoted to the inadequate mechanical brains that guided them about their duties. Deirdre's brain still preserved and proved the craftsmanship of an artisan far defter than man. Only the body was of metal, and it did not seem complex, though he had not yet been told how it was motivated.

Harris had no idea how long he sat staring at the figure in the cushioned chair. She was still lovely—indeed, she was still Deirdre—and as he looked he let the careful schooling of his face relax. There was no need to hide his thoughts from her.

She stirred upon the cushions, the long flexible arms moving with a litheness that was not quite human. The motion disturbed him as the body itself had not, and in spite of himself his face froze a little. He had the feeling that from behind the crescent mask she was watching him very closely.

Slowly she rose.

The motion was very smooth. Also it was serpentine, as if the body beneath the coat of mail were made in the same interlocking sections as her limbs. He had expected and feared mechanical rigidity; nothing had prepared him for this more than human suppleness.

She stood quietly, letting the heavy mailed folds of her garment settle about her. They fell together with a faint ringing sound, like small bells far off, and hung beautifully in pale golden, sculptured folds. He had risen automatically as she did. Now he faced her, staring. He had never seen her stand perfectly still, and she was not doing it now. She swayed just a bit, vitality burning inextinguishably in her brain as once it had burned in her body, and stolid immobility was as impossible to her as it had always been. The golden garment caught points of light from the fire and glimmered at him with tiny reflections as she moved.

Then she put her featureless helmeted head a little to one side, and he heard her laughter as familiar in its small, throaty, intimate sound as he had ever heard it from her living throat. And every gesture, every attitude, every flowing of motion into motion was so utterly Deirdre that the overwhelming illusion swept his mind again and this was the flesh-and-blood woman as clearly as if he saw her standing there whole once more, like Phoenix from the fire.

"Well, John," she said in the soft, husky, amused voice he remembered perfectly. "Well, John, is it I?" She knew it was. Perfect assurance sounded in the voice. "The shock will wear off, you know. It'll be easier and easier as time goes on. I'm quite used to myself now. See?"

She turned away from him and crossed the room smoothly, with the old, poised, dancer's glide, to the mirror that paneled one side of the room. And before it, as he had so often seen her preen before, he watched her preening now, running flexible metallic hands down the folds of her metal garment, turning to admire herself over one metal shoulder, making the mailed folds tinkle and sway as she struck an arabesque position before the glass.

His knees let him down into the chair she had vacated. Mingled shock and relief loosened all his muscles in him, and she was more poised and confident than he.

"It's a miracle," he said with conviction. "It's *you*. But I don't see how—" He had meant, "—how, without face or body—" but clearly he could not finish that sentence.

She finished it for him in her own mind, and answered without self-consciousness. "It's motion mostly," she said, still admiring her own suppleness in the mirror. "See?" And very lightly on her springy, armored feet she flashed through an *enchaînement* of brilliant steps, swinging round with a pirouette to face him. "That was what Maltzer and I worked out between us, after I began to get myself under control again." Her voice was somber for a moment, remembering a dark time in the past. Then she went on, "It wasn't easy, of course, but it was fascinating. You'll never guess how fascinating, John! We knew we couldn't work out anything like a facsimile of the way I used to look, so we had to find some other basis to build on. And motion is the other basis of recognition, after actual physical likeness."

She moved lightly across the carpet toward the window and stood looking down, her featureless face averted a little and the light shining across the delicately hinted curves of the cheekbones.

"Luckily," she said, her voice amused, "I never was beautiful. It was all—well, vivacity, I suppose, and muscular co-ordination. Years and years of training, and all of it engraved here"—she struck her golden helmet a light, ringing blow with golden knuckles—"in the habit patterns grooved into my brain. So this body . . . did he tell you? . . . works entirely through the brain. Electromagnetic currents flowing along from ring to ring, like this." She rippled a boneless arm at him with a motion like flowing water. "Nothing holds me together—nothing!—except muscles of magnetic currents. And if I'd been somebody else—somebody who moved differently, why the flexible rings would have moved differently too, guided by the impulse from another brain. I'm not conscious of doing anything I haven't always done. The same impulses that used to go out to my muscles go out now to—this." And she made a shuddering, serpentine motion of both arms at him, like a Cambodian dancer, and then laughed whole-heartedly, the sound of it ringing through the room with such full-throated merriment that he could not help seeing again the familiar face crinkled with pleasure, the white teeth shining. "It's all perfectly subconscious now," she told him. "It took lots of practice at first, of course, but now even my signature looks just as it always did—the co-ordination is duplicated that delicately." She rippled her arms at him again and chuckled.

"But the voice, too," Harris protested inadequately. "It's *your* voice, Deirdre."

"The voice isn't only a matter of throat construction and breath control, my darling Johnnie! At least, so Professor Maltzer assured me a year ago, and I certainly haven't any reason to doubt him!" She laughed again. She was laughing a little too much, with a touch of the bright, hysteric over-excitement he remembered so well. But if any woman ever had reason for mild hysteria, surely Deirdre had it now.

The laughter rippled and ended, and she went on, her voice eager. "He says voice control is almost wholly a matter of hearing what you produce, once you've got adequate mechanism, of course. That's why deaf people, with the same vocal chords as ever, let their voices change completely and lose all inflection when they've been deaf long enough. And luckily, you see, I'm not deaf!"

She swung around to him, the folds of her robe twinkling and ringing, and rippled up and up a clear, true scale to a lovely high note, and then cascaded down again like water over a falls. But she left him no time for applause. "Perfectly simple, you see. All it took was a little matter of genius from the professor to get it worked out for me! He started with a new variation of the old Vodor you must remember hearing about, years ago. Originally, of course, the thing was ponderous. You know how it worked—speech broken down to a few basic sounds and built up again in combinations produced from a keyboard. I think originally the sounds were a sort of *ktch* and a *shooshing* noise, but we've got it all worked to a flexibility and range quite as good as human now. All I do is—well, mentally play on the keyboard of my . . . my sound-unit, I suppose it's called. It's much more complicated than that, of course, but I've learned to do it unconsciously. And I regulate it by ear, quite automatically now. If you were—*here*—instead of me, and you'd had the same practice, your own voice would be coming out of the same keyboard and diaphragm instead of mine. It's all a matter of the brain patterns that operated the body and now operate the machinery. They send out very strong impulses that are stepped up as much as necessary somewhere or other in here—" Her hands waved vaguely over the mesh-robed body.

She was silent a moment, looking out the window. Then she turned away and crossed the floor to the fire, sinking again into the flowered chair. Her helmet-skull turned its mask to face him and he could feel a quiet scrutiny behind the aquamarine of its gaze.

"It's—odd," she said, "being here in this . . . this . . . instead of a body. But not as odd or as alien as you might think. I've thought about it a lot—I've had plenty of time to think—and I've begun to realize what a tremendous force the human ego really is. I'm not sure I want to suggest it has any mystical power it can impress on mechanical things, but it does seem to have a power of some sort. It does instill its own force into inanimate objects, and they take on a personality of their own. People do impress their personalities on the houses they live in, you know. I've noticed that often. Even empty rooms. And it happens with other things too, especially, I think, with inanimate things that men depend on for their lives. Ships, for instance—they always have personalities of their own.

"And planes—in wars you always hear of planes crippled too badly to fly, but struggling back anyhow with their crews. Even guns acquire a sort of ego. Ships and guns and planes are 'she' to the men who operate them and depend on them for their lives. It's as if machinery with complicated moving parts almost simulates life, and does acquire from the men who use it—well, not exactly life, of course—but a personality. I don't know what. Maybe it absorbs some of the actual electrical impulses their brains throw off, especially in times of stress.

"Well, after awhile I began to accept the idea that this new body of mine could behave at least as responsively as a ship or a plane. Quite apart from the fact that my own brain controls its 'muscles.' I believe there's an affinity between men and the machines they make. They make them out of their own brains, really, a sort of mental conception and gestation, and the result responds to the minds that created them, and to all human minds that understand and manipulate them."

She stirred uneasily and smoothed a flexible hand along her mesh-robed metal thigh. "So this is myself," she said. "Metal—but me. And it grows more and more myself the longer I live in it. It's my house and the machine my life depends on, but much more intimately in each case than any real house or machine ever was before to any other human. And you know, I wonder if in time I'll forget what flesh felt like—my own flesh, when I touched it like this—and the metal against the metal will be so much the same I'll never even notice?"

Harris did not try to answer her. He sat without moving, watching her expressionless face. In a moment she went on.

"I'll tell you the best thing, John," she said, her voice softening to the old intimacy he remembered so well that he could see superimposed upon the blank skull the warm, intent look that belonged with the voice. "I'm not going to live forever. It may not sound like a—best thing—but it is, John. You know, for awhile that was the worst of all, after I knew I was—after I woke up again. The thought of living on and on in a body that wasn't mine, seeing everyone I knew grow old and die, and not being able to stop—

"But Maltzer says my brain will probably wear out quite normally—except, of course, that I won't have to worry about looking old!—and when it gets tired and stops, the body I'm in won't be any longer. The magnetic muscles that hold it into my own shape and motions will let go when the brain lets go, and there'll be nothing but a . . . a pile of disconnected rings. If they ever assemble it again, it won't be me." She hesitated. "I like that, John," she said, and he felt from behind the mask a searching of his face.

He knew and understood that somber satisfaction. He could not put it into words; neither of them wanted to do that. But he understood. It was the conviction of mortality, in spite of her immortal body. She was not cut off from the rest of her race in the essence of their humanity, for though she wore a body of steel and they perishable flesh, yet she must perish too, and the same fears and faiths still united her to mortals and humans, though she wore the body of Oberon's inhuman knight. Even in her death she must be unique—dissolution in a shower of tinkling and clashing rings, he thought, and almost envied her the finality and beauty of that particular death—but afterward, oneness with humanity in however much or little awaited them all. So she could feel that this exile in metal was only temporary, in spite of everything.

(And providing, of course, that the mind inside the metal did not veer from its inherited humanity as the years went by. A dweller in a house may impress his personality upon the walls, but subtly the walls too, may impress their own shape upon the ego of the man. Neither of them thought of that, at the time.)

Deirdre sat a moment longer in silence. Then the mood vanished and she rose again, spinning so that the robe belled out ringing about her ankles. She rippled another scale up and down, faultlessly and with the same familiar sweetness of tone that had made her famous.

"So I'm going right back on the stage, John," she said serenely. "I can still sing. I can still dance. I'm still myself in everything that matters, and I can't imagine doing anything else for the rest of my life."

"He could not answer without stammering a little. "Do you think . . . will they accept you, Deirdre? After all—"

"They'll accept me," she said in that confident voice. "Oh, they'll come to see a freak at first, of course, but they'll stay to watch—Deirdre. And come back again and again just as they always did. You'll see, my dear."

But hearing her sureness, suddenly Harris himself was unsure. Maltzer had not been, either. She was so regally confident, and disappointment would be so deadly a blow at all that remained of her—

She was so delicate a being now, really. Nothing but a glowing and radiant mind poised in metal, dominating it, bending the steel to the illusion of her lost loveliness with a sheer self-confidence that gleamed through the metal body. But the brain sat delicately on its poise of reason. She had been through intolerable stresses already, perhaps more terrible depths of despair and self-knowledge than any human brain had yet endured before her, for—since Lazarus himself—who had come back from the dead?

But if the world did not accept her as beautiful, what then? If they laughed, or pitied her, or came only to watch a jointed freak performing as if on strings where the loveliness of Deirdre had once enchanted them, what then? And he could not be perfectly sure they would not. He had known her too well in the flesh to see her objectively even now, in metal. Every inflection of her voice called up the vivid memory of the face that had flashed it evanescent beauty in some look to match the tone. She was Deirdre to Harris simply because she had been so intimately familiar in every poise and attitude, through so many years. But people who knew her only slightly, or saw her for the first time in metal—what would they see?

A marionette? Or the real grace and loveliness shining through?

He had no possible way of knowing. He saw her too clearly as she had been to see her now at all, except so linked with the past that she was not wholly metal. And he knew what Maltzer feared, for Maltzer's psychic blindness toward her lay at the other extreme. He had never known Deirdre except as a machine, and he could not see her objectively any more than Harris could. To Maltzer she was pure metal, a robot his own hands and brain had devised, mysteriously animated by the mind of Deirdre, to be sure, but to all outward seeming a thing of metal solely. He had worked so long over each intricate part of her body, he knew so well how every jointure in it was put together, that he could not see the whole. He had studied many film records of her, of course, as she used to be, in order to gauge the accuracy of his facsimile, but this thing he had made was a copy only. He was too close to Deirdre to see her. And Harris, in a way, was too far. The indomitable Deirdre herself shone so vividly through the metal that his mind kept superimposing one upon the other.

How would an audience react to her? Where in the scale between these two extremes would their verdict fall?

For Deirdre, there was only one possible answer.

"I'm not worried," Deirdre said serenely, and spread her golden hands to the fire to watch lights dancing in reflection upon their shining surfaces. "I'm still myself. I've always had . . . well, power over my audiences. Any good performer knows when he's got it. Mine isn't gone. I can still give them what I always gave, only now with greater variations and more depths than I'd ever have done before. Why, look—" She gave a little wriggle of excitement.

"You know the arabesque principle—getting the longest possible distance from fingertip to toetip with a long, slow curve through the whole length? And the brace of the other leg and arm giving contrast? Well, look at me. I don't work on hinges now. I can make every motion a long curve if I want to. My body's different enough now to work out a whole new school of dancing. Of course there'll be things I used to do that I won't attempt now—no more dancing *sur les pointes*, for instance—but the new things will more than balance the loss. I've been practicing. Do you know I can turn a hundred *fouettés* now without a flaw? And I think I could go right on and turn a thousand, if I wanted."

She made the firelight flash on her hands, and her robe rang musically as she moved her shoulders a little. "I've already worked out one new dance for myself," she said. "God knows I'm no choreographer, but I did want to experiment first. Later, you know, really creative men like Massanchine or Fokhileff may want to do something entirely new for me—a whole new sequence of movements based on a new technique. And music—that could be quite different, too. Oh, there's no end to the possibilities! Even my voice has more range and power. Luckily I'm not an actress—it would be silly to try to play Camille or Juliet with a cast of ordinary people. Not that I couldn't, you know." She turned her head to stare at Harris through the mask of glass. "I honestly think I could. But it isn't necessary. There's too much else. Oh, I'm not worried!"

"Maltzer's worried," Harris reminded her.

She swung away from the fire, her metal robe ringing, and into her voice came the old note of distress that went with a furrowing of her forehead and a sidewise tilt of the head. The head went sidewise as it had always done, and he could see the furrowed brow almost as clearly as if flesh still clothed her.

"I know. And I'm worried about him, John. He's worked so awfully hard over me. This is the doldrums now, the let-down period, I suppose. I know what's on his mind. He's afraid I'll look just the same to the world as I look to him. Tooled metal. He's in a position no one ever quite achieved before, isn't he? Rather like God." Her voice rippled a little with amusement. "I suppose to God we must look like a collection of cells and corpuscles ourselves. But Maltzer lacks a god's-detached viewpoint."

"He can't see you as I do, anyhow." Harris was choosing his words with difficulty. "I wonder, though—would it help him any if you postponed your debut awhile? You've been with him too closely, I think. You don't quite realize how near a breakdown he is. I was shocked when I saw him just now."

The golden head shook. "No. He's close to a breaking point, maybe, but I think the only cure's action. He wants me to retire and stay out of sight, John. Always. He's afraid for anyone to see me except a few old friends who remember me as I was. People he can trust to be—kind." She laughed. It was very strange to hear that ripple of mirth from the blank, unfeatured skull. Harris was seized with sudden panic at the thought of what reaction it might evoke in an audience of strangers. As if he had spoken the fear aloud, her voice denied it. "I don't need kindness. And it's no kindness to Maltzer to hide me under a bushel. He *has* worked too hard, I know. He's driven himself to a breaking point. But it'll be a complete negation of all he's worked for if I hide myself now. You don't know what a tremendous lot of geniuses and artistry went into me, John. The whole idea from the start was to recreate what I'd lost so that it could be proved that beauty and talent need not be sacrificed by the destruction of parts or all the body.

"It wasn't only for me that we meant to prove that. There'll be others who suffer injuries that once might have ruined them. This was to end all suffering like that forever. It was Maltzer's gift to the whole race as well as to me. He's really a humanitarian, John, like most great men. He'd never have given up a year of his life to this work if it had been for any one individual alone. He was seeing thousands of others beyond me as he worked. And I won't let him ruin all he's achieved because he's afraid to prove it now he's got it. The whole wonderful achievement will be worthless if I don't take the final step. I think his breakdown, in the end, would be worse and more final if I never tried than if I tried and failed."

Harris sat in silence. There was no answer he could make to that. He hoped the little twinge of shamefaced jealousy he suddenly felt did not show, as he was reminded anew of the intimacy closer than marriage which had of necessity bound these two together. And he knew that any reaction of his would in its way be almost as prejudiced as Maltzer's, for a reason at once the same and entirely opposite. Except that he himself came fresh to the problem, while Maltzer's viewpoint was colored by a year of overwork and physical and mental exhaustion.

"What are you doing to do?" he asked.

She was standing before the fire when he spoke, swaying just a little so that highlights danced all along her golden body. Now she turned with a serpentine grace and sank into the cushioned chair beside her. It came to him suddenly that she was much more than humanly graceful—quite as much as he had once feared she would be less than human.

"I've already arranged for a performance," she told him, her voice a little shaken with a familiar mixture of excitement and defiance.

Harris sat up with a start. "How? Where? There hasn't been any publicity at all yet, has there? I didn't know—"

"Now, now, Johnnie," her amused voice soothed him. "You'll be handling everything just as usual once I get started back to work—that is, if you still want to. But this I've arranged for myself. It's going to be a surprise. I . . . I felt it had to be a surprise." She wriggled a little among the cushions. "Audience psychology is something I've always felt rather than known, and I do feel this is the way it ought to be done. There's no precedent. Nothing like this ever happened before. I'll have to go by my own intuition."

"You mean it's to be a complete surprise?"

"I think it must be. I don't want the audience coming in with preconceived ideas. I want them to see me exactly as I am now *first*, before they know who or what they're seeing. They must realize I can still give as good a performance as ever before they remember and compare it with my past performances. I don't want them to come ready to pity my handicaps—I haven't got any!—or full of morbid curiosity. So I'm going on the air after the regular eight o'clock telecast of the feature from Teleo City. I'm just going to do one specialty in the usual vaude program. It's all been arranged. They'll build up to it, of course, as the highlight of the evening, but they aren't to say who I am until the end of the performance—if the audience hasn't recognized me already, by then."

"Audience?"

"Of course. Surely you haven't forgotten they still play to a theater audience at Teleo City? That's why I want to make my debut there. I've always played better when there were people in the studio, so I could gauge reactions. I think most performers do. Anyhow, it's all arranged."

"Does Maltzer know?"

She wriggled uncomfortably. "Not yet."

"But he'll have to give his permission too, won't he? I mean—"

"Now look, John! That's another idea you and Maltzer will have to get out of your minds. I don't belong to him. In a way he's just been my doctor through a long illness, but I'm free to discharge him whenever I choose. If there were ever any legal disagreement, I suppose he'd be entitled to quite a lot of money for the work he's done on my new body—for the body itself, really, since it's his own machine, in one sense. But he doesn't own it, or me. I'm not sure just how the question would be decided by the courts—there again, we've got a problem without precedent. The body may be his work, but the brain that makes it something more than a collection of metal rings is *me*, and he couldn't restrain me against my will even if he wanted to. Not legally, and not—" She hesitated oddly and looked away. For the first time Harris was aware of something beneath the surface of her mind which was quite strange to him.

"Well, anyhow," she went on, "that question won't come up. Maltzer and I have been much too close in the past year to clash over anything as essential as this. He knows in his heart that I'm right, and he won't try to restrain me. His work won't be completed until I do what I was built to do. And I intend to do it."

That strange little quiver of something—something un-Deirdre—which had so briefly trembled beneath the surface of familiarity stuck in Harris' mind as something he must recall and examine later. Now he said only:

"All right. I suppose I agree with you. How soon are you going to do it?"

She turned her head so that even the glass mask through which she looked out at the world was foreshortened away from him, and the golden helmet with its hint of sculptured cheekbone was entirely enigmatic.

"Tonight," she said.

Maltzer's thin hand shook so badly that he could not turn the dial. He tried twice and then laughed nervously and shrugged at Harris.

"You get her," he said.

Harris glanced at his watch. "It isn't time yet. She won't be on for half an hour."

Maltzer made a gesture of violent impatience. "Get it, get it!"

Harris shrugged a little in turn and twisted the dial. On the tilted screen above them shadows and sound blurred together and then clarified into a somber medieval hall, vast, vaulted, people in bright costume moving like pygmies through its dimness. Since the play concerned Mary of Scotland, the actors were dressed in something approximating Elizabethan garb, but as every era tends to translate costume into terms of the current fashions, the women's hair was dressed in a style that would have startled Elizabeth, and their footgear was entirely anachronistic.

The hall dissolved and a face swam up into soft focus upon the screen. The dark, lush beauty of the actress who was playing the Stuart queen glowed at them in velvety perfection from the clouds of her pearl-strewn hair. Maltzer groaned.

"She's competing with *that*," he said hollowly.

"You think she can't?"

Maltzer slapped the chair arms with angry palms. Then the quivering of his fingers seemed suddenly to strike him, and he muttered to himself, "Look at 'em! I'm not even fit to handle a hammer and saw." But the mutter was an aside. "Of course she can't compete," he cried irritably. "She hasn't any sex. She isn't female any more. She doesn't know that yet, but she'll learn."

Harris stared at him, feeling a little stunned. Somehow the thought had not occurred to him before at all, so vividly had the illusion of the old Deirdre hung about the new one.

"She's an abstraction now," Maltzer went on, drumming his palms upon the chair in quick, nervous rhythms. "I don't know what it'll do to her, but there'll be change. Remember Abelard? She's lost everything that made her essentially what the public wanted, and she's going to find it out the hard way. After that—" He grimaced savagely and was silent.

"She hasn't lost everything," Harris defended. "She can dance and sing as well as ever, maybe better. She still has grace and charm and—"

"Yes, but where did the grace and charm come from? Not out of the habit patterns in her brain. No, out of human contacts, out of all the things that stimulate sensitive minds to creativeness. And she's lost three of her five senses. Everything she can't see and hear is gone. One of the strongest stimuli to a woman of her type was the knowledge of sex competition. You know how she sparkled when a man came into the room? All that's gone, and it was an essential. You know how liquor stimulated her? She's lost that. She couldn't taste food or drink even if she needed it. Perfume, flowers, all the odors we respond to mean nothing to her now. She can't feel anything with tactual delicacy any more. She used to surround herself with luxuries—she drew her stimuli from them—and that's all gone too. She's withdrawn from all physical contacts."

He squinted at the screen, not seeing it, his face drawn into lines like the lines of a skull. All flesh seemed to have dissolved off his bones in the past year, and Harris thought almost jealously that even in that way he seemed to be drawing nearer Deirdre in her fleshlessness with every passing week.

"Sight," Maltzer said, "is the most highly civilized of the senses.

It was the last to come. The other senses tie us in closely with the very roots of life; I think we perceive with them more keenly than we know. The things we realize through taste and smell and feeling stimulate directly, without a detour through the centers of conscious thought. You know how often a taste or odor will recall a memory to you so subtly you don't know exactly what caused it? We need those primitive senses to tie us in with nature and the race. Through those ties Deirdre drew her vitality without realizing it. Sight is a cold, intellectual thing compared with the other senses. But it's all she has to draw on now. She isn't a human being any more, and I think what humanity is left in her will drain out little by little and never be replaced. Abelard, in a way, was a prototype. But Deirdre's loss is complete."

"She isn't human," Harris agreed slowly. "But she isn't pure robot either. She's something somewhere between the two, and I think it's a mistake to try to guess just where, or what the outcome will be."

"I don't have to guess," Maltzer said in a grim voice. "I know. I wish I'd let her die. I've done something to her a thousand times worse than the fire ever could. I should have let her die in it."

"Wait," said Harris. "Wait and see. I think you're wrong."

On the television screen Mary of Scotland climbed the scaffold to her doom, the gown of traditional scarlet clinging warmly to supple young curves as anachronistic in their way as the slippers beneath the gown, for—as everyone but playwrights knows—Mary was well into middle age before she died. Gracefully this latter-day Mary bent her head, sweeping the long hair aside, kneeling to the block.

Maltzer watched stonily, seeing another woman entirely.

"I shouldn't have let her," he was muttering. "I shouldn't have let her do it."

"Do you really think you'd have stopped her if you could?" Harris asked quietly. And the other man after a moment's pause shook his head jerkily.

"No, I suppose not. I keep thinking if I worked and waited a little longer maybe I could make it easier for her, but—no, I suppose not. She's got to face them sooner or later, being herself." He stood up abruptly, shoving back his chair. "If she only weren't so . . . so frail. She doesn't realize how delicately poised her very sanity is. We gave her what we could—the artists and the designers and I, all gave our very best—but she's so pitifully handicapped even with all we could do. She'll always be an abstraction and a . . . a freak, cut off from the world by handicaps worse in their way than anything any human being ever suffered before. Sooner or later she'll realize it. And then—" He began to pace up and down with quick, uneven steps, striking his hands together. His face was twitching with a little *tic* that drew up one eye to a squint and released it again at irregular intervals. Harris could see how very near collapse the man was.

"Can you imagine what it's like?" Maltzer demanded fiercely. "Penned into a mechanical body like that, shut out from all human contacts except what leaks in by way of sight and sound? To know you aren't human any longer? She's been through shocks enough already. When that shock fully hits her—"

"Shut up," said Harris roughly. "You won't do her any good if you break down yourself. Look—the vaude's starting."

Great golden curtains had swept together over the unhappy Queen of Scotland and were parting again now, all sorrow and frustration wiped away once more as cleanly as the passing centuries had already expunged them. Now a line of tiny dancers under the tremendous arch of the stage kicked and pranced with the precision of little mechanical dolls too small and perfect to be real. Vision rushed down upon them and swept along the row, face after stiffly smiling face racketing by like fence pickets. Then the sight rose into the rafters and looked down upon them from a great height, the grotesquely foreshortened figures still prancing in perfect rhythm even from this inhuman angle.

There was applause from an invisible audience. Then someone came out and did a dance with lighted torches that streamed long, weaving ribbons of fire among clouds of what looked like cotton wool but was most probably asbestos. Then a company in gorgeous pseudo-period costumes postured its way through the new singing ballet form of dance, roughly following a plot which had been announced as *Les Sylphides,* but had little in common with it. Afterward the precision dancers came on again, solemn and charming as performing dolls.

Maltzer began to show signs of dangerous tension as act succeeded act. Deidre's was to be the last, of course. It seemed very long indeed before a face in close-up blotted out the stage, and a master of ceremonies with features like an amiable marionette's announced a very special number as the finale. His voice was almost cracking with excitement—perhaps he, too, had not been told until a moment before what lay in store for the audience.

Neither of the listening men heard what it was he said, but both were conscious of a certain indefinable excitement rising among the audience, murmurs and rustlings and a mounting anticipation as if time had run backward here and knowledge of the great surprise had already broken upon them.

Then the golden curtains appeared again. They quivered and swept apart on long upward arcs, and between them the stage was full of a shimmering golden haze. It was, Harris realized in a moment, simply a series of gauze curtains, but the effect was one of strange and wonderful anticipation, as if something very splendid must be hidden in the haze. The world might have looked like this on the first morning of creation, before heaven and earth took form in the mind of God. It was a singularly fortunate choice of stage set in its symbolism, though Harris wondered how much necessity had figured in its selection, for there could not have been much time to prepare an elaborate set.

The audience sat perfectly silent, and the air was tense. This was no ordinary pause before an act. No one had been told, surely, and yet they seemed to guess—

The shimmering haze trembled and began to thin, veil by veil. Beyond was darkness, and what looked like a row of shining pillars set in a balustrade that began gradually to take shape as the haze drew back in shining folds. Now they could see that the balustrade curved up from left and right to the head of a sweep of stairs. Stage and stairs were carpeted in black velvet; black velvet draperies hung just ajar behind the balcony, with a glimpse of dark sky beyond them trembling with dim synthetic stars.

The last curtain of golden gauze withdrew. The stage was empty. Or it seemed empty. But even through the aerial distances between this screen and the place it mirrored, Harris thought that the audience was not waiting for the performer to come on from the wings. There was no rustling, no coughing, no sense of impatience. A presence upon the stage was in command from the first drawing of the curtains; it filled the theater with its calm domination. It gauged its timing, holding the audience as a conductor with lifted baton gathers and holds the eyes of his orchestra.

For a moment everything was motionless upon the stage. Then, at the head of the stairs, where the two curves of the pillared balustrade swept together, a figure stirred.

Until that moment she had seemed another shining column in the row. Now she swayed deliberately, light catching and winking and running molten along her limbs and her robe of metal mesh. She swayed just enough to show that she was there. Then, with every eye upon her, she stood quietly to let them look their fill. The screen did not swoop to a close-up upon her. Her enigma remained inviolate and the television watchers saw her no more clearly than the audience in the theater.

Many must have thought her at first some wonderfully animate robot, hung perhaps from wires invisible against the velvet, for certainly she was no woman dressed in metal—her proportions were too thin and fine for that. And perhaps the impression of robotism was what she meant to convey at first. She stood quiet, swaying just a little, a masked and inscrutable figure, faceless, very slender in her robe that hung in folds as pure as a Grecian chlamys, though she did not look Grecian at all. In the visored golden helmet and the robe of mail that odd likeness to knighthood was there again, with its implications of medieval richness behind the simple lines. Except that in her exquisite slimness she called to mind no human figure in armor, not even the comparative delicacy of a St. Joan. It was the chivalry and delicacy of some other world implicit in her outlines.

A breath of surprise had rippled over the audience when she moved. Now they were tensely silent again, waiting. And the tension, the anticipation, was far deeper than the surface importance of the scene could ever have evoked. Even those who thought her a manikin seemed to feel the forerunning of greater revelations.

Now she swayed and came slowly down the steps, moving with a suppleness just a little better than human. The swaying strengthened. By the time she reached the stage floor she was dancing. But it was no dance that any human creature could ever have performed. The long, slow, languorous rhythms of her body would have been impossible to a figure hinged at its joints as human figures hinge. (Harris remembered incredulously that he had feared once to find her jointed like a mechanical robot. But it was humanity that seemed, by contrast, jointed and mechanical now.)

The languor and the rhythm of her patterns looked impromptu, as all good dances should, but Harris knew what hours of composition and rehearsal must lie behind it, what laborious graving into her brain of strange new pathways, the first to replace the old ones and govern the mastery of metal limbs.

To and fro over the velvet carpet, against the velvet background, she wove the intricacies of her serpentine dance, leisurely and yet with such hypnotic effect that the air seemed full of looping rhythms, as if her long, tapering limbs had left their own replicas hanging upon the air and fading only slowly as she moved away. In her mind, Harris knew, the stage was a whole, a background to be filled in completely with the measured patterns of her dance, and she seemed almost to project that completed pattern to her audience so that they saw her everywhere at once, her golden rhythms upon the air long after she had gone.

Now there was music, looping and hanging in echoes after her like the shining festoons she wove with her body. But it was no orchestral music. She was humming, deep and sweet and wordlessly, as she glided her easy, intricate path about the stage. And the volume of the music was amazing. It seemed to fill the theater, and it was not amplified by hidden loudspeakers. You could tell that. Somehow, until you heard the music she made, you had never realized before the subtle distortions that amplification puts into music. This was utterly pure and true as perhaps no ear in all her audience had ever heard music before.

While she danced the audience did not seem to breathe. Perhaps they were beginning already to suspect who and what it was that moved before them without any fanfare of the publicity they had been half-expecting for weeks now. And yet, without the publicity, it was not easy to believe the dancer they watched was not some cunningly motivated manikin swinging on unseen wires about the stage.

Nothing she had done yet had been human. The dance was no dance a human being could have performed. The music she hummed came from a throat without vocal chords. But now the long, slow rhythms were drawing to their close, the pattern tightening in to a finale. And she ended as inhumanly as she had danced, willing them not to interrupt her with applause, dominating them now as she had always done. For her implication here was that a machine might have performed the dance, and a machine expects no applause. If they thought unseen operators had put her through those wonderful paces, they would wait for the operators to appear for their bows. But the audience was obedient. It sat silently, waiting for what came next. But its silence was tense and breathless.

The dance ended as it had begun. Slowly, almost carelessly, she swung up the velvet stairs, moving with rhythms as perfect as her music. But when she reached the head of the stairs she turned to face her audience, and for a moment stood motionless, like a creature of metal, without volition, the hands of the operator slack upon its strings.

Then, startlingly, she laughed.

It was lovely laughter, low and sweet and full-throated. She threw her head back and let her body sway and her shoulders shake, and the laughter, like the music, filled the theater, gaining volume from the great hollow of the roof and sounding in the ears of every listener, not loud, but as intimately as if each sat alone with the woman who laughed.

And she was a woman now. Humanity had dropped over her like a tangible garment. No one who had ever heard that laughter before could mistake it here. But before the reality of who she was had quite time to dawn upon her listeners she let the laughter deepen into music, as no human voice could have done. She was humming a familiar refrain close in the ear of every hearer. And the humming in turn swung into words. She sang in her clear, light, lovely voice:

"The yellow rose of Eden, is blooming in my heart—"

It was Deirdre's song. She had sung it first upon the airways a month before the theater fire that had consumed her. It was a commonplace little melody, simple enough to take first place in the fancy of a nation that had always liked its songs simple. But it had a certain sincerity too, and no taint of the vulgarity of tune and rhythm that foredooms so many popular songs to oblivion after their novelty fades.

No one else was ever able to sing it quite as Deirdre did. It had been identified with her so closely that though for awhile after her accident singers tried to make it a memorial for her, they failed so conspicuously to give it her unmistakable flair that the song died from their sheer inability to sing it. No one ever hummed the tune without thinking of her and the pleasant, nostalgic sadness of something lovely and lost.

But it was not a sad song now. If anyone had doubted whose brain and ego motivated this shining metal suppleness, they could doubt no longer. For the voice was Deirdre, and the song. And the lovely, poised grace of her mannerisms that made up recognition as certainly as sight of a familiar face.

She had not finished the first line of her song before the audience knew her.

And they did not let her finish. The accolade of their interruption was a tribute more eloquent than polite waiting could ever have been. First a breath of incredulity rippled over the theater, and a long, sighing gasp that reminded Harris irrelevantly as he listened to the gasp which still goes up from matinee audiences at the first glimpse of the fabulous Valentino, so many generations dead. But this gasp did not sigh itself away and vanish. Tremendous tension lay behind it, and the rising tide of excitement rippled up in little murmurs and spatterings of applause that ran together into one overwhelming roar. It shook the theater. The television screen trembled and blurred a little to the volume of that transmitted applause.

Silenced before it, Deirdre stood gesturing on the stage, bowing and bowing as the noise rolled up about her, shaking perceptibly with the triumph of her own emotion.

Harris had an intolerable feeling that she was smiling radiantly and that the tears were pouring down her cheeks. He even thought, just as Maltzer leaned forward to switch off the screen, that she was blowing kisses over the audience in the time-honored gesture of the grateful actress, her golden arms shining as she scattered kisses abroad from the featureless helmet, the face that had no mouth.

"Well?" Harris said, not without triumph.

Maltzer shook his head jerkily, the glasses unsteady on his nose so that the blurred eyes behind them seemed to shift.

"Of course they applauded, you fool," he said in a savage voice. "I might have known they would under this set-up. It doesn't prove anything. Oh, she was smart to surprise them—I admit that. But they were applauding themselves as much as her. Excitement, gratitude for letting them in on a historic performance, mass hysteria—*you* know. It's from now on the test will come, and this hasn't helped any to prepare her for it. Morbid curiosity when the news gets out—people laughing when she forgets she ins't human. And they will, you know. There are always those who will. And the novelty wearing off. The slow draining away of humanity for lack of contact with any human stimuli any more—"

Harris remembered suddenly and reluctantly the moment that afternoon which he had shunted aside mentally, to consider later. The sense of something unfamiliar beneath the surface of Deirdre's speech. Was Maltzer right? Was the drainage already at work? Or was there something deeper than this obvious answer to the question? Certainly she had been through experiences too terrible for ordinary people to comprehend. Scars might still remain. Or, with her body, had she put on a strange, metallic something of the mind, that spoke to no sense which human minds could answer?

For a few minutes neither of them spoke. Then Maltzer rose abruptly and stood looking down at Harris with an abstract scowl.

"I wish you'd go now," he said.

Harris glanced up at him, startled. Maltzer began to pace again, his steps quick and uneven. Over his shoulder he said:

"I've made up my mind, Harris. I've got to put a stop to this."

Harris rose. "Listen," he said. "Tell me one thing. What makes you so certain you're right? Can you deny that most of it's speculation—hearsay evidence? Remember, I talked to Deirdre, and she was just as sure as you are in the opposite direction. Have you any real reason for what you think?"

Maltzer took his glasses off and rubbed his nose carefully, taking a long time about it. He seemed reluctant to answer. But when he did, at last, there was a confidence in his voice Harris had not expected.

"I have a reason," he said. "But you won't believe it. Nobody would."

"Try me."

Maltzer shook his head. "Nobody *could* believe it. No two people were ever in quite the same relationship before as Deirdre and I have been. I helped her come back out of complete—oblivion. I knew her before she had voice or hearing. She was only a frantic mind when I first made contact with her, half insane with all that had happened and fear of what would happen next. In a very literal sense she was reborn out of that condition, and I had to guide her through every step of the way. I came to know her thoughts before she thought them. And once you've been that close to another mind, you don't lose the contact easily." He put the glasses back on and looked blurrily at Harris through the heavy lenses. "Deirdre is worried," he said. "I know it. You won't believe me, but I can—well, sense it. I tell you, I've been too close to her very mind itself to make any mistake. You don't see it, maybe. Maybe even she doesn't know it yet. But the worry's there. When I'm with her, I feel it. And I don't want it to come any nearer the surface of her mind than it's come already. I'm going to put a stop to this before it's too late."

Harris had no comment for that. It was too entirely outside his own experience. He said nothing for a moment. Then he asked simply, "How?"

"I'm not sure yet. I've got to decide before she comes back. And I want to see her alone."

"I think you're wrong," Harris told him quietly. "I think you're imagining things. I don't think you *can* stop her."

Maltzer gave him a slanted glance. "I can stop her," he said, in a curious voice. He went on quickly, "She has enough already—she's nearly human. She can live normally as other people live, without going back on the screen. Maybe this taste of it will be enough. I've got to convince her it is. If she retires now, she'll never guess how cruel her own audiences could be, and maybe that deep sense of—distress, uneasiness, whatever it is—won't come to the surface. It mustn't. She's too fragile to stand that." He slapped his hands together sharply. "I've got to stop her. For her own sake I've got to do it!" He swung round again to face Harris. "Will you go now?"

Never in his life had Harris wanted less to leave a place. Briefly he thought of saying simply, "No I won't." But he had to admit in his own mind that Maltzer was at least partly right. This was a matter between Deirdre and her creator, the culmination, perhaps, of that year's long intimacy so like marriage that this final trial for supremacy was a need he recognized.

He would not, he thought, forbid the showdown if he could. Perhaps the whole year had been building up to this one moment between them in which one or the other must prove himself victor. Neither was very well stable just now, after the long strain of the year past. It might very well be that the mental salvation of one or both hinged upon the outcome of the clash. But because each was so strongly motivated not by selfish concern but by solicitude for the other in this strange combat, Harris knew he must leave them to settle the thing alone.

He was in the street and hailing a taxi before the full significance of something Maltzer had said came to him. "*I can stop her,*" he had declared, with an odd inflection in his voice.

Suddenly Harris felt cold. Maltzer had made her—of course he could stop her if he chose. Was there some key in that supple golden body that could immobilize it at its maker's will? Could she be imprisoned in the cage of her own body? No body before in all history, he thought, could have been designed more truly to be a prison for its mind than Deirdre's, if Maltzer chose to turn the key that locked her in. There must be many ways to do it. He could simply withhold whatever source of nourishment kept her brain alive, if that were the way he chose.

But Harris could not believe he would do it. The man wasn't insane. He would not defeat his own purpose. His determination rose from his solicitude for Deirdre; he would not even in the last extremity try to save her by imprisoning her in the jail of her own skull.

For a moment Harris hesitated on the curb, almost turning back. But what could he do? Even granting that Maltzer would resort to such tactics, self-defeating in their very nature, how could any man on earth prevent him if he did it subtly enough? But he never would. Harris knew he never would. He got into his cab slowly, frowning. He would see them both tomorrow.

He did not. Harris was swamped with excited calls about yesterday's performance, but the message he was awaiting did not come. The day went by very slowly. Toward evening he surrendered and called Maltzer's apartment.

It was Deirdre's face that answered, and for once he saw no remembered features superimposed upon the blankness of her helmet. Masked and faceless, she looked at him inscrutably.

"Is everything all right?" he asked, a little uncomfortable.

"Yes, of course," she said, and her voice was a bit metallic for the first time, as if she were thinking so deeply of some other matter that she did not trouble to pitch it properly. "I had a long talk with Maltzer last night, if that's what you mean. You know what he wants. But nothing's been decided yet."

Harris felt oddly rebuffed by the sudden realization of the metal of her. It was impossible to read anything from face or voice. Each had its mask.

"What are you going to do?" he asked.

"Exactly as I'd planned," she told him, without inflection.

Harris floundered a little. Then, with an effort at practicality, he said, "Do you want me to go to work on bookings, then?"

She shook the delicately modeled skull. "Not yet. You saw the reviews today, of course. They—*did* like me." It was an understatement, and for the first time a note of warmth sounded in her voice. But the preoccupation was still there, too. "I'd already planned to make them wait awhile after my first performance," she went on. "A couple of weeks, anyhow. You remember that little farm of mine in Jersey, John? I'm going over today. I won't see anyone except the servants there. Not even Maltzer. Not even you. I've got a lot to think about. Maltzer has agreed to let everything go until we've both thought things over. He's taking a rest, too. I'll see you the moment I get back, John. Is that all right?"

She blanked out almost before he had time to nod and while the beginning of a stammered argument was still on his lips. He sat there staring at the screen.

The two weeks that went by before Maltzer called him again were the longest Harris had ever spent. He thought of many things in the interval. He believed he could sense in that last talk with Deirdre something of the inner unrest that Maltzer had spoken of—more an abstraction than a distress, but some thought had occupied her mind which she would not—or was it that she could not?—share even with her closest confidants. He even wondered whether, if her mind was as delicately poised as Maltzer feared, one would ever know whether or not it had slipped. There was so little evidence one way or the other in the unchanging outward form of her.

Most of all he wondered what two weeks in a new environment would do to her untried body and newly patterned brain. If Maltzer were right, then there might be some perceptible—drainage—by the time they met again. He tried not to think of that.

Maltzer televised him on the morning set for her return. He looked very bad. The rest must have been no rest at all. His face was almost a skull now, and the blurred eyes behind their lenses burned. But he seemed curiously at peace, in spite of his appearance. Harris thought he had reached some decision, but whatever it was had not stopped his hands from shaking or the nervous *tic* that drew his face sidewise into a grimace at intervals.

"Come over," he said briefly, without preamble. "She'll be here in half an hour." And he blanked out without waiting for an answer.

When Harris arrived, he was standing by the window looking down and steadying his trembling hands on the sill.

"I can't stop her," he said in a monotone, and again without preamble. Harris had the impression that for the two weeks his thoughts must have run over and over the same track, until any spoken word was simply a vocal interlude in the circling of his mind. "I couldn't do it. I even tried threats, but she knew I didn't mean them. There's only one way out, Harris." He glanced up briefly, hollow-eyed behind the lenses. "Never mind. I'll tell you later."

"Did you explain everything to her that you did to me?"

"Nearly all. I even taxed her with that . . . that sense of distress I *know* she feels. She denied it. She was lying. We both knew. It was worse after the performance than before. When I saw her that night, I tell you I *knew*—she senses something wrong, but won't admit it." He shrugged. "Well—"

Faintly in the silence they heard the humming of the elevator descending from the helicopter platform on the roof. Both men turned to the door.

She had not changed at all. Foolishly, Harris was a little surprised. Then he caught himself and remembered that she would never change—never, until she died. He himself might grow white-haired and senile; she would move before him then as she moved now, supple, golden, enigmatic.

Still, he thought she caught her breath a little when she saw Maltzer and the depths of his swift degeneration. She had no breath to catch, but her voice was shaken as she greeted them.

"I'm glad you're both here," she said, a slight hesitation in her speech. "It's a wonderful day outside. Jersey was glorious. I'd forgotten how lovely it is in summer. Was the sanitarium any good, Maltzer?"

He jerked his head irritably and did not answer. She went on talking in a light voice, skimming the surface, saying nothing important.

This time Harris saw her as he supposed her audiences would, eventually, when the surprise had worn off and the image of the living Deirdre faded from memory. She was all metal now, the Deirdre they would know from today on. And she was not less lovely. She was not even less human—yet. Her motion was a miracle of flexible grace, a pouring of suppleness along every limb. (From now on, Harris realized suddenly, it was her body and not her face that would have mobility to express emotion; she must act with her limbs and her lithe, robed torso.)

But there was something wrong. Harris sensed it almost tangibly in her inflections, her elusiveness, the way she fenced with words. This was what Maltzer had meant, this was what Harris himself had felt just before she left for the country. Only now it was strong—certain. Between them and the old Deirdre whose voice still spoke to them, a veil of—detachment—had been drawn. Behind it she was in distress. Somehow, somewhere, she had made some discovery that affected her profoundly. And Harris was terribly afraid that he knew what the discovery must be. Maltzer was right.

He was still leaning against the window, staring out unseeingly over the vast panorama of New York, webbed with traffic bridges, winking with sunlit glass, its vertiginous distances plunging downward into the blue shadows of Earth-level. He said now, breaking into the light-voiced chatter, "Are you all right, Deirdre?"

She laughed. It was lovely laughter. She moved lithely across the room, sunlight glinting on her musical mailed robe, and stooped to a cigarette box on a table. Her fingers were deft.

"Have one?" she said, and carried the box to Maltzer. He let her put the brown cylinder between his lips and hold a light to it, But he did not seem to be noticing what he did. She replaced the box and then crossed to a mirror on the far wall and began experimenting with a series of gliding ripples that wove patterns of pale gold in the glass. "Of course I'm all right," she said.

"You're lying."

Deirdre did not turn. She was watching him in the mirror, but the ripple of her motion went on slowly, languorously, undisturbed.

"No," she told them both.

Maltzer drew deeply on his cigarette. Then with a hard pull he unsealed the window and tossed the smoking stub far out over the gulfs below. He said:

"You can't deceive me, Deirdre." His voice, suddenly, was quite calm. "I created you, my dear. I know. I've sensed that uneasiness in you growing and growing for a long while now. It's much stronger today than it was two weeks ago. Something happened to you in the country. I don't know what it was, but you've changed. Will you admit to yourself what it is, Deirdre? Have you realized yet that you must not go back on the screen?"

"Why, no," said Deirdre, still not looking at him except obliquely, in the glass. Her gestures were slower now, weaving lazy patterns in the air. "No, I haven't changed my mind."

She was all metal—outwardly. She was taking unfair advantage of her own metal-hood. She had withdrawn far within, behind the mask of her voice and her facelessness. Even her body, whose involuntary motions might have betrayed what she was feeling, in the only way she could be subject to betrayal now, she was putting through ritual motions that disguised it completely. As long as these looping, weaving patterns occupied her, no one had any way of guessing even from her motion what went on in the hidden brain inside her helmet.

Harris was struck suddenly and for the first time with the completeness of her withdrawal. When he had seen her last in this apartment she had been wholly Deirdre, not masked at all, overflowing the metal with the warmth and ardor of the woman he had known so well. Since then—since the performance on the stage—he had not seen the familiar Deirdre again. Passionately he wondered why. Had she begun to suspect even in her moment of triumph what a fickle master an audience could be? Had she caught, perhaps, the sound of whispers and laughter among some small portion of her watchers, though the great majority praised her?

Or was Maltzer right? Perhaps Harris' first interview with her had been the last bright burning of lost Deirdre, animated by excitement and the pleasure of meeting after so long a time, animation summoned up in a last strong effort to convince him. Now she was gone, but whether in self-protection against the possible cruelties of human beings, or whether in withdrawal to metal-hood, he could not guess. Humanity might be draining out of her fast, and the brassy taint of metal permeating the brain it housed.

Maltzer laid his trembling hand on the edge of the opened window and looked out. He said in a deepened voice, the querulous note gone for the first time:

"I've made a terrible mistake, Deirdre. I've done you irreparable harm." He paused a moment, but Deirdre said nothing. Harris dared not speak. In a moment Maltzer went on. "I've made you vulnerable, and given you no weapons to fight your enemies with. And the human race is your enemy, my dear, whether you admit it now or later. I think you know that. I think it's why you're so silent. I think you must have suspected it on the stage two weeks ago, and verified it in Jersey while you were gone. They're going to hate you, after a while, because you are still beautiful, and they're going to persecute you because you are different—and helpless. Once the novelty wears off, my dear, your audience will be simply a mob."

He was not looking at her. He had bent forward a little, out the window and down. His hair stirred in the wind that blew very strongly up this high, and whined thinly around the open edge of the glass.

"I meant what I did for you," he said, "to be for everyone who meets with accidents that might have ruined them. I should have known my gift would mean worse ruin than any mutilation could be. I know now that there's only one legitimate way a human being can create life. When he tries another way, as I did, he has a lesson to learn. Remember the lesson of the student Frankenstein? He learned, too. In a way, he was lucky—the way he learned. He didn't have to watch what happened afterward. Maybe he wouldn't have had the courage—I know I haven't."

Harris found himself standing without remembering that he rose. He knew suddenly what was about to happen. He understood Maltzer's air of resolution, his new, unnatural calm. He knew, even, why Maltzer had asked him here today, so that Deirdre might not be left alone. For he remembered that Frankenstein, too, had paid with his life for the unlawful creation of life.

Maltzer was leaning head and shoulders from the window now, looking down with almost hypnotized fascination. His voice came back to them remotely in the breeze, as if a barrier already lay between them.

Deirdre had not moved. Her expressionless mask, in the mirror, watched him calmly. She *must* have understood. Yet she gave no sign, except that the weaving of her arms had almost stopped now, she moved so slowly. Like a dance seen in a nightmare, under water.

It was impossible, of course, for her to express any emotion. The fact that her face showed none now should not, in fairness, be held against her. But she watched so wholly without feeling— Neither of them moved toward the window. A false step, now, might send him over. They were quiet, listening to his voice.

"We who bring life into the world unlawfully," said Maltzer, almost thoughtfully, "must make room for it by withdrawing our own. That seems to be an inflexible rule. It works automatically. The thing we create makes living unbearable. No, it's nothing you can help, my dear. I've asked you to do something I created you incapable of doing. I made you to perform a function, and I've been asking you to forego the one thing you were made to do. I believe that if you do it, it will destroy you, but the whole guilt is mine, not yours. I'm not even asking you to give up the screen, any more. I know you can't, and live. But I can't live and watch you. I put all my skill and all my love in one final masterpiece, and I can't bear to watch it destroyed. I can't live and watch you do only what I made you to do, and ruin yourself because you must do it.

"But before I go, I have to make sure you understand." He leaned a little farther, looking down, and his voice grew more remote as the glass came between them. He was saying almost unbearable things now, but very distantly, in a cool, passionless tone filtered through wind and glass, and with the distant humming of the city mingled with it, so that the words were curiously robbed of poignancy. "I can be a coward," he said, "and escape the consequences of what I've done, but I can't go and leave you—not understanding. It would be even worse than the thought of your failure, to think of you bewildered and confused when the mob turns on you. What I'm telling you, my dear, won't be any real news—I think you sense it already, though you may not admit it to yourself. We've been too close to lie to each other, Deirdre—I know when you aren't telling the truth. I know the distress that's been growing in your mind. You are not wholly human, my dear. I think you know that. In so many ways, in spite of all I could do, you must always be less than human. You've lost the senses of perception that kept you in touch with humanity. Sight and hearing are all that remain, and sight, as I've said before, was the last and coldest of the senses to develop. And you're so delicately poised on a sort of thin edge of reason. You're only a clear, glowing mind animating a metal body, like a candle flame in a glass. And as precariously vulnerable to the wind."

He paused. "Try not to let them ruin you completely," he said after a while. "When they turn against you, when they find out you're more helpless than they—I wish I could have made you stronger, Deirdre. But I couldn't. I had too much skill for your good and mine, but not quite enough skill for that."

He was silent again, briefly, looking down. He was balanced precariously now, more than halfway over the sill and supported only by one hand on the glass. Harris watched with an agonized uncertainty, not sure whether a sudden leap might catch him in time or send him over. Deirdre was still weaving her golden patterns, slowly and unchangingly, watching the mirror and its reflection, her face and masked eyes enigmatic.

"I wish one thing, though," Maltzer said in his remote voice. "I wish—before I finish—that you'd tell me the truth, Deirdre. I'd be happier if I were sure I'd—reached you. Do yo understand what I've said? Do you believe me? Because if you don't, then I know you're lost beyond all hope. If you'll admit your own doubt—and I know you do doubt—I can think there may be a chance for you after all. Were you lying to me, Deirdre? Do you know how . . . how wrong I've made you?"

There was silence. Then very softly, a breath of sound, Deirdre answered. The voice seemed to hang in midair, because she had no lips to move and localize it for the imagination.

"Will you listen, Maltzer?" she asked.

"I'll wait," he said. "Go on. Yes or no?"

Slowly she let her arms drop to her sides. Very smoothly and quietly she turned from the mirror and faced him. She swayed a little, making her metal robe ring.

"I'll answer you," she said. "But I don't think I'll answer that. Not with yes or no, anyhow. I'm going to walk a little, Maltzer. I have something to tell you, and I can't talk standing still. Will you let me move about without—going over?"

He nodded distantly. "You can't interfere from that distance," he said. "But keep the distance. What do you want to say?"

She began to pace a little way up and down her end of the room, moving with liquid ease. The table with the cigarette box was in her way, and she pushed it aside carefully, watching Maltzer and making no swift motions to startle him.

"I'm not—well, sub-human," she said, a faint note of indignation in her voice. "I'll prove it in a minute, but I want to say something else first. You must promise to wait and listen. There's a flaw in your argument, and I resent it. I'm not a Frankenstein monster made out of dead flesh. I'm myself—alive. You didn't create my life, you only preserved it. I'm not a robot, with compulsions built into me that I have to obey. I'm free-willed and independent, and, Maltzer—I'm human."

Harris had relaxed a little. She knew what she was doing. He had no idea what she planned, but he was willing to wait now. She was not the indifferent automaton he had thought. He watched her come to the table again in a lap of her pacing, and stoop over it, her eyeless mask turned to Maltzer to make sure variation of her movement did not startle him.

"I'm human," she repeated, her voice humming faintly and very sweetly. "Do you think I'm not?" she asked, straightening and facing them both. And then suddenly, almost overwhelmingly, the warmth and the old ardent charm were radiant all around her. She was robot no longer, enigmatic no longer. Harris could see as clearly as in their first meeting the remembered flesh still gracious and beautiful as her voice evoked his memory. She stood swaying a little, as she had always swayed, her head on one side, and she was chuckling at them both. It was such a soft and lovely sound, so warmly familiar.

"Of course I'm myself," she told them, and as the words sounded in their ears neither of them could doubt it. There was hypnosis in her voice. She turned away and began to pace again, and so powerful was the human personality which she had called up about her that it beat out at them in deep pulses, as if her body were a furnace to send out those comforting waves of warmth. "I have handicaps, I know," she said. "But my audiences will never know. I won't let them know. I think you'll believe me, both of you, when I say I could play Juliet just as I am now, with a cast of ordinary people, and make the world accept it. Do you think I could, John? Maltzer, don't you believe I could?"

She paused at the far end of her pacing path and turned to face them, and they both stared at her without speaking. To Harris she was the Deirdre he had always known, pale gold, exquisitely graceful in remembered postures, the inner radiance of her shining through metal as brilliantly as it had ever shone through flesh. He did not wonder, now, if it were real. Later he would think again that it might be only a disguise, something like a garment she had put off with her lost body, to wear again only when she chose. Now the spell of her compelling charm was too strong for wonder. He watched, convinced for the moment that she was all she seemed to be. She could play Juliet if she said she could. She could sway a whole audience as easily as she swayed himself. Indeed, there was something about her just now more convincingly human than anything he had noticed before. He realized that in a split second of awareness before he saw what it was.

She was looking at Maltzer. He, too, watched, spellbound in spite of himself, not dissenting. She glanced from one to the other. Then she put back her head and laughter came welling and choking from her in a great, full-throated tide. She shook in the strength of it. Harris could almost see her round throat pulsing with the sweet low-pitched waves of laughter that were shaking her. Honest mirth, with a little derision in it.

Then she lifted one arm and tossed her cigarette into the empty fireplace.

Harris choked, and his mind went blank for one moment of blind denial. He had not sat here watching a robot smoke and accepting it as normal. He could not! And yet he had. That had been the final touch of conviction which swayed his hypnotized mind into accepting her humanity. And she had done it so deftly, so naturally wearing her radiant humanity with such rightness, that his watching mind had not even questioned what she did.

He glanced at Maltzer. The man was still halfway over the window ledge, but through the opening of the window he, too, was staring in stupefied disbelief and Harris knew they had shared the same delusion.

Deirdre was still shaking a little with laughter. "Well," she demanded, the rich chuckling making her voice quiver, "am I all robot, after all?"

Harris opened his mouth to speak, but he did not utter a word. This was not his show. The byplay lay wholly between Deirdre and Maltzer; he must not interfere. He turned his head to the window and waited.

And Maltzer for a moment seemed shaken in his conviction.

"You . . . you *are* an actress," he admitted slowly. "But I . . . I'm not convinced I'm wrong. I think—" He paused. The querulous note was in his voice again, and he seemed racked once more by the old doubts and dismay. Then Harris saw him stiffen. He saw the resolution come back, and understood why it had come. Maltzer had gone too far already upon the cold and lonely path he had chosen to turn back, even for stronger evidence than this. He had reached his conclusions only after mental turmoil too terrible to face again. Safety and peace lay in the course he had steeled himself to follow. He was too tired, too exhausted by months of conflict, to retrace his path and begin all over. Harris could see him groping for a way out, and in a moment he saw him find it.

"That was a trick," he said hollowly. "Maybe you could play it on a larger audience, too. Maybe you have more tricks to use. I might be wrong. But Deirdre"—his voice grew urgent—"you haven't answered the one thing I've got to know. You can't answer it. You *do* feel—dismay. You've learned your own inadequacy, however well you can hide it from us—even from us. I *know*. Can you deny that, Deirdre?"

She was not laughing now. She let her arms fall, and the flexible golden body seemed to droop a little all over, as if the brain that a moment before had been sending out strong, sure waves of confidence had slackened its power, and the intangible muscles of her limbs slackened with it. Some of the glowing humanity began to fade. It receded within her and was gone, as if the fire in the furnace of her body were sinking and cooling.

"Maltzer," she said uncertainly, "I can't answer that—yet. I can't—"

And then, while they waited in anxiety for her to finish the sentence, she *blazed*. She ceased to be a figure in stasis—she *blazed*.

It was something no eyes could watch and translate into terms the brain could follow; her motion was to swift. Maltzer in the window was a whole long room-length away. He had thought himself safe at such a distance, knowing no normal human being could reach him before he moved. But Deirdre was neither normal nor human.

In the same instant she stood drooping by the mirror she was simultaneously at Maltzer's side. Her motion negated time and destroyed space. And as a glowing cigarette tip in the dark describes closed circles before the eye when the holder moves it swiftly, so Deirdre blazed in one continuous flash of golden motion across the room.

But curiously, she was not blurred. Harris, watching, felt his mind go blank again, but less in surprise than because no normal eyes and brain could perceive what it was he looked at.

(In that moment of intolerable suspense his complex human brain paused suddenly, annihilating time in its own way, and withdrew to a cool corner of its own to analyze in a flashing second what it was he had just seen. The brain could do it timelessly; words are slow. But he knew he had watched a sort of tesseract of human motion, a parable of fourth-dimensional activity. A one-dimensional point, moved through space, creates a two-dimensional line, which in motion creates a three-dimensional cube. Theoretically the cube, in motion, would produce a fourth-dimensional figure. No human creature had ever seen a figure of three dimensions moved through space and time before—until this moment. She had not blurred; every motion she made was distinct, but not like moving figures on a strip of film. Not like anything that those who use our language had ever seen before, or created words to express. The mind saw, but without perceiving. Neither words nor thoughts could resolve what happened into terms for human brains. And perhaps she had not actually and literally moved through the fourth dimension. Perhaps—since Harris was able to see her—it had been almost and not quite that unimaginable thing. But it was close enough.)

While to the slow mind's eye she was still standing at the far end of the room, she was already at Maltzer's side, her long, flexible fingers gentle but very firm upon his arms. She waited—

The room shimmered. There was sudden violent heat beating upon Harris' face. Then the air steadied again and Deirdre was saying softly, in a mournful whisper:

"I'm sorry—I had to do it. I'm sorry—I didn't mean you to know—"

Time caught up with Harris. He saw it overtake Maltzer too, saw the man jerk convulsively away from the grasping hands, in a ludicrously futile effort to forestall what had already happened. Even thought was slow, compared with Deirdre's swiftness.

The sharp outward jerk was strong. It was strong enough to break the grasp of human hands and catapult Maltzer out and down into the swimming gulfs of New York. The mind leaped ahead to a logical conclusion and saw him twisting and turning and diminishing with dreadful rapidity to a tiny point of darkness that dropped away through sunlight toward the shadows near the earth. The mind even conjured up a shrill, thin cry that plummeted away with the falling body and hung behind it in the shaken air.

But the mind was reckoning on human factors.

Very gently and smoothly Deirdre lifted Maltzer from the window sill and with effortless ease carried him well back into the safety of the room. She set him down before a sofa and her golden fingers unwrapped themselves from his arms slowly, so that he could regain control of his own body before she released him.

He sank to the sofa without a word. Nobody spoke for an unmeasurable length of time. Harris could not. Deirdre waited patiently. It was Maltzer who regained speech first, and it came back on the old track, as if his mind had not yet relinquished the rut it had worn so deep.

"All right," he said breathlessly. "All right, you can stop me this time. But I know, you see. I know! You can't hide your feeling from me, Deirdre. I know the trouble you feel. And next time—next time I won't wait to talk!"

Deirdre made the sound of a sigh. She had no lungs to expel the breath she was imitating, but it was hard to realize that. It was hard to understand why she was not panting heavily from the terrible exertion of the past minutes; the mind knew why, but could not accept the reason. She was still too human.

"You still don't see," she said. "Think, Maltzer, think!"

There was a hassock beside the sofa. She sank upon it gracefully, clasping her robed knees. Her head tilted back to watch Maltzer's face. She saw only stunned stupidity on it now; he had passed through too much emotional storm to think at all.

"All right," she told him. "Listen—I'll admit it. You're right. I *am* unhappy. I do know what you said was true—but not for the reason you think. Humanity and I are far apart, and drawing farther. The gap will be hard to bridge. Do you hear me, Maltzer?"

Harris saw the tremendous effort that went into Maltzer's wakening. He saw the man pull his mind back into focus and sit up on the sofa with weary stiffness.

"You . . . you do admit it, then?" he asked in a bewildered voice.

Deirdre shook her head sharply.

"Do you still think of me as delicate?" she demanded. "Do you know I carried you here at arm's length halfway across the room? Do you realize you weigh *nothing* to me? I could"—she glanced around the room and gestured with sudden, rather appalling violence—"tear this building down," she said quietly. "I could tear my way through these walls, I think. I've found no limit yet to the strength I can put forth if I try." She held up her golden hands and looked at them. "The metal would break, perhaps," she said reflectively, "but then, I have no feeling—"

Maltzer gasped, "*Deirdre—*"

She looked up with what must have been a smile. It sounded clearly in her voice. "Oh, I won't. I wouldn't have to do it with my hands, if I wanted. Look—listen!"

She put her head back and a deep, vibrating hum gathered and grew in what one still thought of as her throat. It deepened swiftly and the ears began to ring. It was deeper, and the furniture vibrated. The walls began almost imperceptibly to shake. The room was full and bursting with a sound that shook every atom upon its neighbor with a terrible, disrupting force.

The sound ceased. The humming died. Then Deirdre laughed and made another and quite differently pitched sound. It seemed to reach out like an arm in one straight direction—toward the window. The opened panel shook. Deirdre intensified her hum, and slowly, with imperceptible jolts that merged into smoothness, the window jarred itself shut.

"You see?" Deirdre said. "You see?"

But still Maltzer could only stare. Harris was staring too, his mind beginning slowly to accept what she implied. Both were too stunned to leap ahead to any conclusions yet.

Deirdre rose impatiently and began to pace again, in a ringing of metal robe and a twinkling of reflected lights. She was pantherlike in her suppleness. They could see the power behind that lithe motion now; they no longer thought of her as helpless, but they were far still from grasping the truth.

"You were wrong about me, Maltzer," she said with an effort at patience in her voice. "But you were right too, in a way you didn't guess. I'm not afraid of humanity. I haven't anything to fear from them. Why"—her voice took on a tinge of contempt—"already I've set a fashion in women's clothing. By next week you won't see a woman on the street without a mask like mine, and every dress that isn't cut like a chlamys will be out of style. I'm not afraid of humanity! I won't lose touch with them unless I want to. I've learned a lot—I've learned too much already."

Her voice faded for a moment, and Harris had a quick and appalling vision of her experimenting in the solitude of her farm, testing the range of her voice, testing her eyesight—could she see microscopically and telescopically?—and was her hearing as abnormally flexible as her voice?

"You were afraid I had lost feeling and scent and taste," she went on, still pacing with that powerful, tigerish tread. "Hearing and sight would not be enough, you think? But why do you think sight is the last of the senses? It may be the latest, Maltzer—Harris—*but why do you think it's the last?*"

She may not have whispered that. Perhaps it was only their hearing that made it seem thin and distant, as the brain contracted and would not let the thought come through in its stunning entirety.

"No," Deirdre said, "I haven't lost contact with the human race. I never will, unless I want to. It's too easy . . . too easy."

She was watching her shining feet as she paced, and her masked face was averted. Sorrow sounded in her soft voice now.

"I didn't mean to let you know," she said. "I never would have, if this hadn't happened. But I couldn't let you go believing you'd failed. You made a perfect machine, Maltzer. More perfect than you knew."

"But Deirdre—" breathed Maltzer, his eyes fascinated and still incredulous upon her, "but Deirdre, if we did succeed—what's wrong? I can feel it now—I've felt it all along. You're so unhappy—you still are. Why Deirdre?"

She lifted her head and looked at him, eyelessly, but with a piercing stare.

"Why are you so sure of that?" she asked gently.

"You think I could be mistaken, knowing you as I do? But I'm not Frankenstein . . . you say my creation's flawless. Then what—"

"Could you ever duplicate this body?" she asked.

Maltzer glanced down at his shaking hands. "I don't know. I doubt it. I—"

"Could anyone else?"

He was silent. Deirdre answered for him. "I don't believe anyone could. I think I was an accident. A sort of mutation halfway, between flesh and metal. Something accidental and . . . and unnatural, turning off on a wrong course of evolution that never reaches a dead end. Another brain in a body like this might die or go mad, as you thought I would. The synapses are too delicate. You were—call it lucky—with me. From what I know now, I don't think a . . . a baroque like me could happen again." She paused a moment. "What you did was kindle the fire for the Phoenix, in a way. And the Phoenix rises perfect and renewed from its own ashes. Do you remember why it had to reproduce itself that way?"

Maltzer shook his head.

"I'll tell you," she said. "It was because there was only one Phoenix. Only one in the whole world."

They looked at each other in silence. Then Deirdre shrugged a little.

"He always came out of the fire perfect, of course. I'm not weak, Maltzer. You needn't let that thought bother you any more. I'm not vulnerable and helpless. I'm not sub-human." She laughed dryly. "I suppose," she said, "that I'm—superhuman."

"But—not happy."

"I'm afraid. It isn't unhappiness, Maltzer—it's fear. I don't want to draw so far away from the human race. I wish I needn't. That's why I'm going back on the stage—to keep in touch with them while I can. But I wish there could be others like me. I'm . . . I'm lonely, Maltzer."

Silence again. Then Maltzer said, in a voice as distant as when he had spoken to them through glass, over gulfs as deep as oblivion:

"Then I am Frankenstein, after all."

"Perhaps you are," Deirdre said very softly. "I don't know. Perhaps you are."

She turned away and moved smoothly, powerfully, down the room to the window. Now that Harris knew, he could almost hear the sheer power purring along her limbs as she walked. She leaned the golden forehead against the glass—it clinked faintly, with a musical sound—and looked down into the depths Maltzer had hung above. Her voice was reflective as she looked into those dizzy spaces which had offered oblivion to her creator.

"There's one limit I can think of," she said, almost inaudibly. "Only one. My brain will wear out in another forty years or so. Between now and then I'll learn . . . I'll change . . . I'll know more than I can guess today. I'll change— That's frightening. I don't like to think about that." She laid a curved golden hand on the latch and pushed the window open a little, very easily. Wind whined around its edge. "I could put a stop to it now, if I wanted," she said. "If I wanted. But I can't, really. There's so much still untried. My brain's human, and no human brain could leave such possibilities untested. I wonder, though . . . I do wonder—"

Her voice was soft and familiar in Harris' ears, the voice Deirdre had spoken and sung with, sweetly enough to enchant a world. But as preoccupation came over her a certain flatness crept into the sound. When she was not listening to her own voice, it did not keep quite to the pitch of trueness. It sounded as if she spoke in a room of brass, and echoes from the walls resounded in the tones that spoke there.

"I wonder," she repeated, the distant taint of metal already in her voice.

THE BIG AND THE LITTLE

Isaac Asimov

1

TRADERS— . . . *With psychohistoric inevitability, economic control of the Foundation grew. The traders grew rich; and with riches came power.* . . .

It is sometimes forgotten that Hober Mallow began life as an ordinary trader. It is never forgotten that he ended it as the first of the Merchant Princes. . . .

ENCYCLOPEDIA GALACTICA

Jorane Sutt put the tips of carefully-manicured fingers together and said, "It's something of a puzzle. In fact—and this is in the strictest confidence—it may be another one of Hari Seldon's crises."

The man opposite felt in the pocket of his short Smyrnian jacket for a cigarette. "Don't know about that, Sutt. As a general rule, politicians start shouting 'Seldon crisis' at every mayoralty campaign."

Sutt smiled very faintly, "I'm not campaigning, Mallow. We're facing atomic weapons, and we don't know where they're coming from."

Hober Mallow of Smyrno, Master Trader, smoked quietly, almost indifferently. "Go on. If you have more to say get it out." Mallow never made the mistake of being overpolite to a Foundation man. He might be an Outlander, but a man's a man for a' that.

Sutt indicated the trimensional star-map on the table. He adjusted the controls and a cluster of some half-dozen stellar systems blazed red.

"That," he said quietly, "is the Korellian Republic."

The trader nodded, "I've been there. Stinking rathole! I suppose you can call it a republic but it's always someone out of the Argo family that gets elected Commdor each time. And if you ever don't like it—*things* happen to you." He twisted his lip and repeated, "I've been there."

"But you've come back, which hasn't always happened. Three trade ships, inviolate under the Conventions, have disappeared within the territory of the Republic in the last year. And those ships were armed with all the usual nuclear explosives and force-field defenses."

"What was the last word heard from the ships?"

"Routine reports. Nothing else."

"What did Korell say?"

Sutt's eyes gleamed sardonically, "There was no way of asking. The Foundation's greatest asset throughout the Periphery is its reputation of power. Do you think we can lose three ships and *ask* for them?"

"Well, then, suppose you tell me what you want with *me*."

Jorane Sutt did not waste his time in the luxury of annoyance. As secretary to the mayor, he had held off opposition councilmen, jobseekers, reformers, and crackpots who claimed to have solved in its entirety the course of future history as worked out by Hari Seldon. With training like that, it took a good deal to disturb him.

He said methodically, "In a moment. You see, three ships lost in the same sector in the same year can't be accident, and atomic power can be conquered only by more atomic power. The question automatically arises: if Korell has atomic weapons, where is it getting them?"

"And where does it?"

"Two alternatives. Either the Korellians have constructed them themselves—"

"Far-fetched!"

"Very! But the other possibility is that we are being afflicted with a case of treason."

"You think so?" Mallow's voice was cold.

The secretary said calmly, "There's nothing miraculous about the possibility. Since the Four Kingdoms accepted the Foundation Convention, we have had to deal with considerable groups of dissident populations in each nation. Each former kingdom has its pretenders and its former noblemen, who can't very well pretend to love the Foundation. Some of them are becoming active, perhaps."

Mallow was a dull red. "I see. Is there anything you want to say to *me*? I'm a Smyrnian."

"I know. You're a Smyrnian—born in Smyrno, one of the former Four Kingdoms. You're a Foundation man by education only. By birth, you're an Outlander and a foreigner. No doubt your grandfather was a baron at the time of the wars with Anacreon and Loris, and no doubt your family estate were taken away when Sef Sermak redistributed the land."

"No, by Black Space, no! My grandfather was a bloodpoor son-of-a-spacer who died heaving coal at starving wages before the Foundation. I owe nothing to the old regime. But I was born in Smyrno, and I'm not ashamed of either Smyrno of Smyrnians, by the Galaxy. Your sly little hints of treason aren't going to panic me into licking Foundation spittle. And now you can either give your orders or make your accusations. I don't care which."

"My good Master Trader, I don't care an electron whether your grandfather was King of Smyrno or the greatest pauper on the planet. I recited that rigmarole about your birth and ancestry to show you that I'm not interested in them. Evidently, you missed the point. Let's go back now. You're a Smyrnian. You know the Outlanders. Also, you're a trader and one of the best. You've been to Korell and you know the Korellians. That's where you've got to go."

Mallow breathed deeply, "As a spy?"

"Not at all. As a trader—but with your eyes open. If you can find out where the power is coming from—I might remind you, since you're a Symrnian, that two of those lost trade ships had Smyrnian crews."

"When do I start?"

"When will your ship be ready?"

"In six days."

"Then that's when you start. You'll have all the details at the Admiralty."

"Right!" The trader rose, shook hands roughly, and strode out.

Sutt waited, spreading his fingers gingerly and rubbing out the pressure; then shrugged his shoulders and stepped into the mayor's office.

The mayor deadened the visiplate and leaned back. "What do *you* make of it, Sutt?"

"He could be a good actor," said Sutt, and stared thoughtfully ahead.

2

It was evening of the same day, and in Jorane Sutt's bachelor apartment on the twenty-first floor of the Hardin Building, Publis Manlio was sipping wine slowly.

It was Publis Manlio in whose slight, aging body were fulfilled two great offices of the Foundation. He was Foreign Secretary in the mayor's cabinet, and to all the outer suns, barring only the Foundation itself, he was, in addition, Primate of the Church, Purveyor of the Holy Food, Master of the Temples, and so forth almost indefinitely in confusing but sonorous syllables.

He was saying, "But he agreed to let you send out that trader. It is a point."

"But such a small one," said Sutt. "It gets us nothing immediately. The whole business is the crudest sort of stratagem, since we have no way of foreseeing it to the end. It is a mere paying out of rope on the chance that somewhere along the length of it will be a noose."

"True. And this Mallow is a capable man. What if he is not an easy prey to dupery?"

"That is a chance that must be run. If there is treachery, it is the capable men that are implicated. If not, we need a capable man to detect the truth. And Mallow will be guarded. Your glass is empty."

"No, thanks. I've had enough."

Sutt filled his own glass and patiently endured the other's uneasy reverie.

Of whatever the reverie consisted, it ended indecisively, for the primate said suddenly, almost explosively, "Sutt, what's on your mind?"

"I'll tell you, Manlio." His thin lips parted, "We're in the middle of a Seldon crisis."

Manlio stared, then said softly, "How do you know? Has Seldon appeared in the Time Vault again?"

"That much, my friend, is not necessary. Look, reason it out. Since the Galactic Empire abandoned the Periphery, and threw us on our own, we have never had an opponent who possessed atomic power. Now, for the first time, we have one. That seems significant even if it stood by itself. And it doesn't. For the first time in over seventy years, we are facing a major domestic political crisis. I should think the synchronization of the two crises, inner and outer, puts it beyond all doubt."

Manlio's eyes narrowed, "If that's all, it's not enough. There have been two Seldon crises so far, and both times the Foundation was in danger of extermination. Nothing can be a third crisis till that danger returns."

Sutt never showed impatience, "That danger is coming. Any fool can tell a crisis when it arrives. The real service to the state is to direct it in embryo. Look, Manlio, we're proceeding along a planned history. We *know* that Hari Seldon worked out the historical probabilities of the future. We *know* that some day we're to rebuild the Galactic Empire. We *know* that it will take a thousand years or thereabouts. And we *know* that in that interval we will face certain definite crises.

"Now the first crisis came fifty years after the establishment of the Foundation, and the second, thirty years later than that. Almost seventy-five years have gone since. It's time, Manlio, it's time."

Manlio rubbed his nose uncertainly, "And you've made your plans to meet this crisis?"

Sutt nodded.

"And I," continued Manlio, "am to play a part in it?"

Sutt nodded again, "Before we can meet the foreign threat of atomic power, we've got to put our own house in order. These traders—"

"Ah!" The primate stiffened, and his eyes grew sharp.

"That's right. These traders. They are useful, but they are too strong—and too uncontrolled. They are Outlanders, educated apart from religion. On the one hand, we put knowledge into their hands, and on the other, we remove our strongest hold upon them."

"If we can prove treachery?"

"If we could, direct action would be simple and sufficient. But that doesn't signify in the least. Even if treason among them did not exist, they would form an uncertain element in our society. They wouldn't be bound to us by patriotism or common descent, or even by religious awe. Under their secular leadership, the outer provinces, which, since Hardin's time, look to us as the Holy Planet, might break away."

"I see all that, but the cure—"

"The cure must come quickly, before the Seldon Crisis becomes acute. If atomic weapons are without and disaffection within, the odds might be too great." Sutt put down the empty glass he had been fingering, "This is obviously your job."

"Mine?"

"*I* can't do it. My office is appointive and has no legislative standing."

"The mayor—"

"Impossible. His personality is entirely negative. He is energetic only in evading responsibility. But if an independent party arose that might endanger re-election, he might allow himself to be led."

"But, Sutt, I lack the aptitude for practical politics."

"Leave that to me. Who knows, Manlio? Since Salvor Hardin's time, the primacy and the mayoralty have never been combined in a single person. But it might happen now—if your job were well done."

3

And at the other end of town, in homelier surroundings, Hober Mallow kept a second appointment. He had listened long, and now he said cautiously, "Yes, I've heard of your campaigns to get direct trader representation in the council. But why *me*, Twer?"

Jaim Twer, who would remind you any time, asked or unasked, that he was in the first group of Outlanders to receive a lay education at the Foundation, beamed.

"I know what I'm doing," he said. "Remember when I met you first, last year."

"At the Traders' Convention."

"Right. You ran that meeting. You had those rednecked oxen planted in their seats, then put them in your shirtpocket and walked off with them. And you're all right with the Foundation masses, too. You've got *glamor*—or, at any rate, solid adventure-publicity, which is the same thing."

"Very good," said Mallow, dryly. "But why now?"

"Because now's our chance. Do you know that the Secretary of Education has handed in his resignation? It's not out in the open yet, but it will be."

"How do *you* know?"

"That—never mind—" He waved a disgusted hand. "It's so. The Actionist party is splitting wide open, and we can murder it right now on a straight question of equal rights for traders; or, rather, democracy, pro- and anti-."

Mallow lounged back in his chair and stared at his thick fingers, "Uh-uh. Sorry, Twer. I'm leaving next week on business. You'll have to get someone else."

Twer stared, "Business? What kind of business?"

"Very super-secret. Triple-A priority. All that, you know. Had a talk with the mayor's own secretary."

"Snake Sutt?" Jaim Twer grew excited. "A trick. The son-of-a-spacer is getting rid of you. Mallow—"

"Hold on!" Mallow's hand fell on the other's balled fist. "Don't go into a blaze. If it's a trick, I'll be back some day for the reckoning. If it isn't, your snake, Sutt, *is* playing into our hands. Listen, there's a Seldon crisis coming up."

Mallow waited for a reaction but it never came. Twer merely stared. "What's a Seldon crisis?"

"Galaxy!" Mallow exploded angrily at the anticlimax. "What the blue blazes did you do when you went to school? What do you mean anyway by a fool question like that?"

The elder man frowned. "If you'll explain—"

There was a long pause, then, "I'll explain." Mallow's eyebrows lowered, and he spoke slowly. "When the Galactic Empire began to die at the edges, and when the ends of the Galaxy reverted to barbarism and dropped away, Hari Seldon and his band of psychologists planted a colony, the Foundation, out here in the middle of the mess, so that we could incubate art, science, and technology, and form the nucleus of the Second Empire."

"Oh, yes, yes—"

"I'm not finished," said the trader, coldly. "The future course of the Foundation was plotted according to the science of psycho-history, then highly developed, and conditions arranged so as to bring about a series of crises that will force us most rapidly along the route to future Empire. Each crisis, each *Seldon* crisis, marks an epoch in our history. We're approaching one now—our third."

"Of course!" Twer shrugged, "I should have remembered. But I've been out of school a long time—longer than you."

"I suppose so. Forget it. What matters is that I'm being sent out into the middle of the development of this crisis. There's no telling what I'll have when I come back, and there is a council election every year."

Twer looked up, "Are you on the track of anything?"

"No."

"You have definite plans?"

"Not the faintest inkling of one."

"Well—"

"Well, nothing. Hardin once said: 'To succeed, planning alone is insufficient. One must improvise as well.' I'll improvise."

Twer shook his head uncertainly, and they stood, looking at each other.

Mallow said, quite suddenly, but quite matter-of-factly, "I tell you what, how about coming with me? Don't stare, man. You've been a trader before you decided there was more excitement in politics. Or so I've heard."

"Where are you going? Tell me that."

"Towards the Whassallian Rift. I can't be more specific till we're out in space. What do you say?"

"Suppose Sutt decides he wants me where he can see me."

"Not likely. If he's anxious to get rid of me, why not of you as well? Besides which, no trader would hit space if he couldn't pick his own crew. I take whom I please."

There was a queer glint in the older man's eyes. "All right. I'll go." He held out his hand, "It'll be my first trip in three years."

Mallow grasped and shook the other's hand, "Good! All fired good! And now I've got to round up the boys. You know where the *Far Star* docks, don't you? Then show up tomorrow. Good-bye."

4

Korell is that frequent phenomenon in history: the republic whose ruler has every attribute of the absolute monarch but the name. It therefore enjoyed the usual despotism unrestrained even by those two moderating influences in the legitimate monarchies: regal 'honor' and court etiquette.

Materially, its prosperity was low. The day of the Galactic Empire had departed, with nothing but silent memorials and broken structures to testify to it. The day of the Foundation had not yet come—and in the fierce determination of its ruler, the Commdor Asper Argo, with his strict regulation of the traders and his stricter prohibition of the missionaries, it was never coming.

The spaceport itself was decrepit and decayed, and the crew of the *Far Star* were drearily aware of that. The moldering hangars made for a moldering atmosphere and Jaim Twer itched and fretted over a game of solitaire.

Hober Mallow said thoughfully, "Good trading material here." He was staring quietly out the viewport. So far, there was little else to be said about Korell. The trip here was uneventful. The squadron. of Korellian ships that had shot out to intercept the *Far Star* had been tiny, limping relics of ancient glory or battered, clumsy hulks. They had maintained their distance fearfully, and still maintained it, and for a week now, Mallow's requests for an audience with the local government had been unanswered.

Mallow repeated, "Good trading here. You might call this virgin territory."

Jaim Twer looked up impatiently, and threw his cards aside, "What the devil do you intend doing, Mallow? The crew's grumbling, the officers are worried, and I'm wondering—"

"Wondering? About what?"

"About the situation. And about you. What are we doing?"

"Waiting."

The old trader snorted and grew red. He growled, "You're going it blind, Mallow. There's a guard around the field and there are ships overhead. Suppose they're getting ready to blow us into a hole in the ground."

"They've had a week."

"Maybe they're waiting for reinforcements." Twer's eyes were sharp and hard.

Mallow sat down abruptly, "Yes, I'd thought of that. You see, it poses a pretty problem. First, we got here without trouble. That may mean nothing, however, for only three ships out of better than three hundred went a-glimmer last year. The percentage is low. But that may mean also that the number of their ships equipped with atomic power is small, and that they dare not expose them needlessly, until that number grows.

"But it could mean, on the other hand, that they haven't atomic power after all. Or maybe they have and are keeping under cover, for fear we know something. It's one thing after all, to practice blundering, light-armed merchant ships. It's another to fool around with an accredited envoy of the Foundation when the mere fact of his presence may mean the Foundation is growing suspicious.

"Combine this—"

"Hold on, Mallow, hold on." Twer raised his hands. "You're just about drowning me with talk. What're you getting at? Never mind the in-betweens."

"You've *got* to have the in-betweens, or you won't understand, Twer. We're both waiting. They don't know what I'm doing here and I don't know what they've got here. But I'm in the weaker position because I'm one and they're an entire world—maybe with atomic power. I can't afford to be the one to weaken. Sure it's dangerous. Sure there may be a hole in the ground waiting for us. But we knew that from the start. What else is there to do?"

"I don't— Who's that, now?"

Mallow looked up patiently, and tuned the receiver. The visiplate glowed into the craggy face of the watch sergeant.

"Speak, sergeant."

The sergeant said, "Pardon, sir. The men have given entry to a Foundation missionary."

"A *what?*" Mallow's face grew livid.

"A missionary, sir. He's in need of hospitalization, sir—"

"There'll be more than one in need of that, sergeant, for this piece of work. Order the men to battle stations."

Crew's lounge was almost empty. Five minutes after the order, even the men on the off-shift were at their guns. It was speed that was the great virtue in the anarchic regions of the interstellar space of the Periphery, and it was in speed above all that the crew of a master trader excelled.

Mallow entered slowly, and stared the missionary up and down and around. His eye slid to Lieutenant Tinter, who shifted uneasily to one side and to Watch-Sergeant Demen, whose blank face and stolid figure flanked the other.

The Master Trader turned to Twer and paused thoughtfully, "Well, then, Twer get the officers here quietly, except for the co-ordinators and the trajectorian. The men are to remain at stations till further orders."

There was a five-minutes hiatus, in which Mallow kicked open the doors to the lavatories, looked behind the bar, pulled the draperies across the thick windows. For half a minute he left the room altogether, and when he returned he was humming abstractedly.

Men filed in. Twer followed, and closed the door silently.

Mallow said quietly, "First, who let this man in without orders from me?"

The watch sergeant stepped forward. Every eye shifted. "Pardon, sir. It was no definite person. It was a sort of mutual agreement. He was one of us, you might say, and these foreigners here—"

Mallow cut him short, "I sympathize with your feelings, sergeant, and understand them. These men, were they under your command?"

"Yes, sir."

"When this is over, they're to be confined to individual quarters for a week. You yourself are relieved of all supervisory duties for a similar period. Understood?"

The sergeant's face never changed, but there was the slightest droop to his shoulders. He said, crisply, "Yes, sir."

"You may leave. Get to your gun-station."

The door closed behind him and the babble rose.

Twer broke in, "Why the punishment, Mallow? You know that these Korellians kill captured missionaries."

"An action against my orders is bad in itself whatever other reasons there may be in its favor. No one was to leave or enter the ship without permission."

Lieutenant Tinter murmured rebelliously, "Seven days without action. You can't maintain discipline that way."

Mallow said icily, "*I* can. There's no merit in discipline under ideal circumstances. I'll have it in the face of death, or it's useless. Where's this missionary? Get him here in front of me."

The trader sat down, while the scarlet-cloaked figure was carefully brought forward.

"What's your name, reverend?"

"Eh?" The scarlet-robed figure wheeled towards Mallow, the whole body turning as a unit. His eyes were blankly open and there was a bruise on one temple. He had not spoken, nor, as far as Mallow could tell, moved during all the previous interval.

"Your name, revered one?"

The missionary started to sudden feverish life. His arms went out in an embracing gesture. "My son—my children. May you always be in the protecting arms of the Galactic Spirit."

Twer stepped forward, eyes troubled, voice husky, "The man's sick. Take him to bed, somebody. Order him to bed, Mallow, and have him seen to. He's badly hurt."

Mallow's great arm shoved him back, "Don't interfere, Twer, or I'll have you out of the room. Your name, revered one?"

The missionary's hands clasped in sudden supplication, "As you are enlightened men, save me from the heathen." The words tumbled out, "Save me from these brutes and darkened ones who raven after me and would afflict the Galactic Spirit with their crimes. I am Jord Parma, of the Anacreonian worlds. Educated at the Foundation; the Foundation itself, my children. I am a Priest of the Spirit educated into all the mysteries, who have come here where the inner voice called me." He was gasping, "I have suffered at the hands of the unenlightened. As you are

Children of the Spirit; and in the name of that Spirit, protect
me from them."

A voice broke in upon them, as the emergency alarm box
clamored metallically:

"Enemy units in sight! Instruction desired!"

Every eye shot mechanically upward to the speaker.

Mallow swore violently. He clicked open the reverse and yelled,
"Maintain vigil! That is all!" and turned it off.

He made his way to the thick drapes that rustled aside at a touch
and stared grimly out.

Enemy units! Several thousands of them in the persons of the
individual members of a Korellian mob. The rolling rabble encom-
passed the port from extreme end to extreme end, and in the cold,
hard light of magnesium flares the foremost straggled closer.

"Tinter!" The trader never turned, but the back of his neck was
red. "Get the outer speaker working and find out what they want.
Ask if they have a representative of the law with them. Make no
promises and no threats, or I'll kill you."

Tinter turned and left.

Mallow felt a rough hand on his shoulder and he struck it
aside. It was Twer. His voice was an angry hiss in his ear, "Mallow,
you're bound to hold onto this man. There's no way of maintaining
decency and honor otherwise. He's of the Foundation and, after all,
he—is a priest. These savages outside— Do you hear me?"

"I hear you, Twer." Mallow's voice was incisive. "I've got more
to do here than guard missionaries. I'll do, sir, what I please, and,
by Seldon and all the Galaxy, if you try to stop me, I'll tear out
your stinking windpipe. Don't get in my way, Twer, or it will be
the last of you."

He turned and strode past. "You! Revered Parma! Did you
know that by convention, no Foundation missionaries may enter
the Korellian territory?"

The missionary was trembling, "I can but go where the Spirit
leads, my son. If the darkened ones refuse enlightenment, is it not
the greater sign of their need for it?"

"That's outside the question, revered one. You are here against
the law of both Korell and the Foundation. I cannot in law
protect you."

The missionary's hands were raised again. His earlier bewilderment was gone. There was the raucous clamor of the ship's outer
communication system in action, and the faint, undulating gabble
of the angry horde in response. The sound made his eyes wild.

"You hear them? Why do you talk of law to me, of a law made by me? There are higher laws. Was it not the Galactic Spirit that said: Thou shalt not stand idly by to the hurt of thy fellowman. And has he not said: Even as thou dealest with the humble and defenseless, thus shalt thou be dealt with.

"Have you not guns? Have you not a ship? And behind you is there not the Foundation? And above and all about you is there not the Spirit that rules the universe?" He paused for breath.

And then the great outer voice of the *Far Star* ceased and Lieutenant Tinter was back, troubled.

"Speak!" said Mallow, shortly.

"Sir, they demand the person of Jord Parma."

"If not?"

"There are various threats, sir. It is difficult to make much out. There are so many—and they seem quite mad. There is someone who says he governs the district and has police powers, but he is quite evidently not his own master."

"Master or not," shrugged Mallow, "he is the law. Tell them that if this governor, or policeman, or whatever he is, approaches the ship alone, he can have the Revered Jord Parma."

And there was suddenly a gun in his hand. He added, "I don't know what insubordination is. I have never had any experience with it. But if there's anyone here who thinks he can teach me, I'd like to teach him my antidote in return."

The gun swiveled slowly, and rested on Twer. With an effort, the old trader's face untwisted and his hands unclenched and lowered. His breath was a harsh rasp in his nostrils.

Tinter left, and in five minutes a puny figure detached itself from the crowd. It approached slowly and hesitantly, plainly drenched in fear and apprehension. Twice it turned back, and twice the patently obvious threats of the many-headed monster urged him on.

"All right," Mallow gestured with the hand-blaster, which remained unsheathed. "Grun and Upshur, take him out."

The missionary screeched. He raised his arms and rigid fingers speared upward as the voluminous sleeves fell away to reveal the thin, veined arms. There was a momentary, tiny flash of light that came and went in a breath. Mallow blinked and gestured again, contemptuously.

The missionary's voice poured out as he struggled in the two-fold grasp, "Cursed be the traitor who abandons his fellowman to evil and to death. Deafened be the ears that are deaf to the pleadings of the helpless. Blind be the eyes that are blind to innocence. Blackened forever be the soul that consorts with blackness—"

Twer clamped his hands tightly over his ears.

Mallow flipped his blaster and put it away. "Disperse," he said, evenly, "to respective stations. Maintain full vigil for six hours after dispersion of crowd. Double stations for forty-eight hours thereafter. Further instructions at that time. Twer, come with me."

They were alone in Mallow's private quarters. Mallow indicated a chair and Twer sat down. His stocky figure looked shrunken.

Mallow stared him down, sardonically. "Twer," he said, "I'm disappointed. Your three years in politics seem to have gotten you out of trader habits. Remember, I may be a democrat back at the Foundation, but there's nothing short of tyranny that can run my ship the way I want it run. I never had to pull a blaster on my men before, and I wouldn't have had to now, if you hadn't gone out of line.

"Twer, you have no official position, but you're here on my invitation, and I'll extend you every courtesy—in private. However, from now on, in the presence of my officers or men, I'm 'sir,' and not 'Mallow.' And when I give an order, you'll jump faster than a third-class recruit just for luck, or I'll have you ironed in the sub-level even faster. Understand?"

The party-leader swallowed dryly. He said, reluctantly, "My apologies."

"Accepted! Will you shake?"

Twer's limp fingers were swallowed in Mallow's huge palm. Twer said, "My motives were good. It's difficult to send a man out to be lynched. That wobbly-kneed governor or whatever-he-was can't save him. It's murder."

"I can't help that. Frankly, the incident smelled too bad. Didn't you notice?"

"Notice what?"

"This spaceport is deep in the middle of a sleepy far section. Suddenly a missionary escapes. Where from? He comes here. Coincidence? A huge crowd gathers. From where? The nearest city of any size must be at least a hundred miles away. But they arrive in half an hour. How?"

"How?" echoed Twer.

"Well, what if the missionary were brought here and released as bait. Our friend, Revered Parma, was considerably confused. He seemed at no time to be in complete possession of his wits."

"Hard usage—" murmured Twer bitterly.

"Maybe! And maybe the idea was to have us go all chivalrous and gallant, into a stupid defense of the man. He was here against the laws of Korell and the Foundation. If I withhold him, it is an act of war against Korell, and the Foundation would have no legal right to defend *us*."

"That—that's pretty far-fetched."

The speaker blared and forestalled Mallow's answer: "Sir, official communication received."

"Submit immediately!"

The gleaming cylinder arrived in its slot with a click. Mallow opened it and shook out the silver-impregnated sheet it held. He rubbed it appreciatively between thumb and finger and said, "Teleported direct from the capital. Commdor's own stationery."

He read it in a glance and laughed shortly, "So my idea was far-fetched, was it?"

He tossed it to Twer, and added, "Half an hour after we hand back the missionary, we finally get a very polite invitation to the Commdor's august presence—after seven days of previous waiting. *I* think we passed a test."

5

Commdor Asper was a man of the people, by self-acclamation. His remaining back-fringe of gray hair drooped limply to his shoulders, his shirt needed laundering, and he spoke with a snuffle.

"There is no ostentation here, Trader Mallow," he said. "No false show. In me, you see merely the first citizen of the state. That's what Commdor means, and that's the only title I have."

He seemed inordinately pleased with it all. "In fact, I consider that fact one of the strongest bonds between Korell and your nation. I understand you people enjoy the republican blessings we do."

"Exactly, Commdor," said Mallow gravely, taking mental exception to the comparison, "an argument which I consider strongly in favor of continued peace and friendship between our governments."

"Peace! Ah!" The Commdor's sparse gray beard twitched to the sentimental grimaces of his face. "I don't think there is anyone in the Periphery who has so next to his heart the ideal of Peace, as I have. I can truthfully say that since I succeeded my illustrious father to the leadership of the state, the reign of Peace has never been broken. Perhaps I shouldn't say it"—he coughed gently—"but I *have* been told that my people, my fellow-citizens rather, know me as Asper, the Well-Beloved."

Mallow's eyes wandered over the well-kept garden. Perhaps the tall men and the strangely-designed but openly-vicious weapons they carried just happened to be lurking in odd corners as a precaution against himself. That would be understandable. But the lofty, steel-girdered walls that circled the place had quite obviously been recently strengthened—an unfitting occupation for such a Well-Beloved Asper.

He said, "It is fortunate that I have you to deal with then, Commdor. The despots and monarchs of surrounding worlds, which haven't the benefit of enlightened administration, often lack the qualities that would make a ruler well-beloved."

"Such as?" There was a cautious note in the Commdor's voice.

"Such as their concern for the best interests of their people. You, on the other hand, would understand."

The Commdor kept his eyes on the gravel path as they walked leisurely. His hands caressed each other behind his back.

Mallow went on smoothly, "Up to now, trade between our two nations has suffered because of the restrictions placed upon our traders by your government. Surely, it has long been evident to you that unlimited trade—"

"Free Trade!" mumbled the Commdor.

"Free Trade, then. You must see that it would be of benefit to both of us. There are things you have that we want, and things we have that you want. It asks only an exchange to bring increased prosperity. An enlightened ruler such as yourself, a friend of the people—I might say, a *member* of the people—needs no elaboration on that theme. I won't insult your intelligence by offering any."

"True! I have seen this. But what would you?" His voice was a plaintive whine. "Your people have always been so unreasonable. I am in favor of all the trade our economy can support, but not on your terms. I am not sole master here." His voice rose, "I am only the servant of public opinion. My people will not take commerce which sparked in crimson and gold."

Mallow drew himself up, "A compulsory religion?"

"So it has always been in effect. Surely you remember the case of Askone twenty years ago. First they were sold some of your goods and then your people asked for complete freedom of missionary effort in order that the goods might be run properly; that Temples of Health be set up. There was then the establishment of religious schools; autonomous rights for all officers of the religion and with what result? Askone is now an integral member of the Foundation's system and the Grand Master cannot call his underwear his own. Oh, no! Oh, no! The dignity of an independent people could never suffer it."

"None of what you speak is at all what I suggest," interposed Mallow.

"No?"

"No. I'm a Master Trader. Money is *my* religion. All this mysticism and hocus-pocus of the missionaries annoys me, and I'm glad you refuse to countenance it. It makes you more my type of man."

"The Commdor's laugh was high-pitched and jerky, "Well said! The Foundation should have sent a man of your caliber before this."

He laid a friendly hand upon the trader's bulking shoulder. "But man, you have told me only half. You have told me what the catch is *not*. Now tell me what it *is*."

"The only catch, Commdor, is that you're going to be burdened with an immense quantity of riches."

"Indeed?" he snuffled. "But what could I want with riches? The true wealth is the love of one's people. I have that."

"You can have both, for it is possible to gather gold with one hand and love with the other."

"Now that, my young man, would be an interesting phenomenon, if it were possible. How would you go about it?"

"Oh, in a number of ways. The difficulty is choosing among them. Let's see. Well, luxury items, for instance. This object here, now—"

Mallow drew gently out of an inner pocket a flat, linked chain of polished metal. "This, for instance."

"What is it?"

"That's got to be demonstrated. Can you get a girl? Any young female will do. *And* a mirror, full length."

"Hm-m-m. Let's get indoors, then."

The Commdor referred to his dwelling place as a house. The populace undoubtedly would call it a palace. To Mallow's straightforward eyes, it looked uncommonly like a fortress. It was built on an eminence that overlooked the capital. Its walls were thick and reinforced. Its approaches were guarded, and its architecture was shaped for defence. Just the type of dwelling, Mallow thought sourly, for Asper, the Well-Beloved.

A young girl was before them. She bent low to the Commdor, who said, "This is one of the Commdora's girls. Will she do?"

"Perfectly!"

The Commdor watched carefully while Mallow snapped the chain about the girl's waist, and stepped back.

The Commdor snuffled, "Well. Is that all?"

"Will you draw the curtain, Commdor? Young lady, there's a little knob just near the snap. Will you move it upward, please? Go ahead, it won't hurt you."

The girl did so, drew a sharp breath, looked at her hands, and gasped, "Oh!"

From her waist as a source she was drowned in a pale, streaming luminescence of shifting color that drew itself over her head in a flashing coronet of liquid fire. It was as if someone had torn the aurora borealis out of the sky and molded it into a cloak.

The girl stepped to the mirror and stared, fascinated.

"Here, take this." Mallow handed her a necklace of dull pebbles. "Put it around your neck."

The girl did so, and each pebble, as it entered the luminescent field became an individual flame that leaped and sparkled in crimson and gold.

"What do you think of it?" Mallow asked her. The girl didn't answer but there was adoration in her eyes. The Commdor gestured and reluctantly, she pushed the knob down, and the glory died. She left—with a memory.

"It's yours, Commdor," said Mallow, "for the Commdora. Consider it a small gift from the Foundation."

"Hm-m-m." The Commdor turned the belt and necklace over in his hand as though calculating the weight. "How is it done?"

Mallow shrugged, "That's a question for our technical experts. But it will work for you without—mark you, *without*—priestly help."

"Well, it's only feminine frippery after all. What could you do with it? Where would the money come in?"

"You have balls, receptions, banquets—that sort of thing?"

"Oh, yes."

"Do you realize what women will pay for that sort of jewelry? Ten thousand credits, at least."

The Commdor seemed struck in a heap, "Ah!"

"And since the power unit of this particular item will not last longer than six months, there will be the necessity of frequent replacements. Now we can sell as many of these as you want for the equivalent in wrought iron of one thousand credits. There's nine hundred percent profit for you."

The Commdor plucked at his beard and seemed engaged in awesome mental calculations, "Galaxy, how the dowagers will fight for them. I'll keep the supply small and let them bid. Of course, it wouldn't do to let them know that I personally—"

Mallow said, "We can explain the workings of dummy corporations, if you would like.—Then, working further at random, take our complete line of household gadgets. We have collapsible stoves that will roast the toughest meats to the desired tenderness in two minutes. We've got knives that won't require sharpening. We've got the equivalent of a complete laundry that can be packed in a small closet and will work entirely automatically. Ditto dishwashers. Ditto-ditto floor-scrubbers, furniture polishers, dust-precipitators, lighting fixtures—oh, anything you like. Think of your increased popularity, *if* you make them available to the public. Think of your increased quantity of, uh, wordly goods, if they're available as a government monopoly at nine hundred percent profit. It will be worth many times the money to them, and they needn't know what *you* pay for it. And, mind you, none of it will require priestly supervision. Everybody will be happy."

"Except you, it seems. What do *you* get out of it?"

"Just what every trader gets by Foundation law. My men and I will collect half of whatever profits we take in. Just you buy all I want to sell you, and we'll both make out quite well. *Quite* well."

The Commdor was enjoying his thoughts. "What did you say you wanted to be paid with? Iron?"

"That, and coal, and bauxite. Also tobacco, pepper, magnesium, hardwood. Nothing you haven't got enough of."

"It sounds well."

"I think so. Oh, and still another item at random, Commdor. I could retool your factories."

"Eh? How's that?"

"Well, take your steel foundries. I have handy little gadgets that could do tricks with steel that would cut production costs to one percent of previous marks. You could cut prices by half, and still split extremely fat profits with the manufacturers. I tell you, I could show you exactly what I mean, if you allowed me a demonstration. Do you have a steel foundry in this city? It wouldn't take long."

"It could be arranged, Trader Mallow. But tomorrow, tomorrow. Would you dine with us tonight?"

"My men—" began Mallow.

"Let them all come," said the Commdor, expansively. "A symbolic friendly union of our nations. It will give us a chance for further friendly discussion. But one thing," his face lengthened and grew stern, "none of your religion. Don't think that all this is an entering wedge for the missionaries."

"Commdor," said Mallow, dryly, "I give you my word that religion would cut my profits."

"Then that will do for now. You'll be escorted back to your ship."

6

The Commdora was much younger than her husband. Her face was pale and coldly formed and her black hair was drawn smoothly and tightly back.

Her voice was tart. "You are quite finished, my gracious and noble husband? Quite, *quite* finished? I suppose I may even enter the garden if I wish, now."

"There is no need for dramatics, Licia, my dear," said the Commdor, mildly. "The young man will attend at dinner tonight, and you can speak with him all you wish and even amuse yourself by listening to all I say. Room will have to be arranged for his men somewhere about the place. The stars grant that they be few in numbers."

"Most likely they'll be great hogs of eaters who will eat meat by the quarter-animal and wine by the hogshead. And you will groan for two nights when you calculate the expense."

"Well now, perhaps I won't. Despite your opinion, the dinner is to be on the most lavish scale."

"Oh, I see." She stared at him contemptuously. "You are very friendly with these barbarians. Perhaps that is why I was not to be permitted to attend your conversation. Perhaps your little wizened soul is plotting to turn against my father."

"Not at all."

"Yes, I'd be likely to believe you, wouldn't I? If ever a poor woman was sacrificed for policy to an unsavory marriage, it was myself. I could have picked a more proper man from the alleys and mudheaps of my native world."

"Well, now, I'll tell you what, my lady. Perhaps you would enjoy returning to your native world. Only to retain as a souvenir that portion of you with which I am best acquainted, I could have your tongue cut out first. And," he lolled his head, calculatingly, to one side, "as a final improving touch to your beauty, your ears and the tip of your nose as well."

"You wouldn't dare, you little pug-dog. My father would pulverize your toy nation to meteoric dust. In fact, he might do it in any case, if I told him you were treating with these barbarians."

"Hm-m-m. Well, there's no need for threats. You are free to question the man yourself tonight. Meanwhile, madam, keep your wagging tongue still."

"At your orders?"

"Here, take this, then, and keep still."

The band was about her waist and the necklace around her neck. He pushed the knob himself and stepped back.

The Commdora drew in her breath and held out her hands stiffly. She fingered the necklace gingerly, and gasped again.

The Commdor rubbed his hands with satisfaction and said, "You may wear it tonight—and I'll get you more. *Now* keep still."

The Commdora kept still.

7

Jaim Twer fidgeted and shuffled his feet. He said, "What's twisting *your* face?"

Hober Mallow lifted out of his brooding. "Is my face twisted? It's not meant so."

"Something must have happened yesterday—I mean, besides that feast." With sudden conviction, "Mallow, there's trouble, isn't there?"

"Trouble? No. Quite opposite. In fact, I'm in the position of throwing my full weight against a door and finding it ajar at the time. We're getting into this steel foundry too easily."

"You suspect a trap?"

"Oh, for Seldom's sake, don't be melodramatic." Mallow swallowed his impatience and added conversationally, "It's just that the easy entrance means there will be nothing to see."

"Atomic power, huh?" Twer ruminated. "I'll tell you. There's just about no evidence of any atomic power economy here in Korell. And it would be pretty hard to mask all signs of the widespread effects a fundamental technology such as atomics would have on everything."

"Not if it was just starting up, Twer, and being applied to a war economy. You'd find it in the shipyards and the steel foundries only."

"So if we don't find it, then—"

"Then they haven't got it—or they're not showing it. Toss a coin or take a guess."

Twer shook his head. "I wish I'd been with you yesterday."

"I wish you had, too," said Mallow stonily. "I have no objection to moral support. Unfortunately, it was the Commdor who set the terms of the meeting, and not myself. And *that* outside there would seem to be the royal ground-car to escort us to the foundry. Have you got the gadgets?"

"All of them."

8

The foundry was large, and bore the odor of decay which no amount of superficial repairs could quite erase. It was empty now and in quite an unnatural state of quiet, as it played unaccustomed host to the Commdor and his court.

Mallow had swung the steel sheet onto the two supports with a careless heave. He had taken the instrument held out to him by Twer and was gripping the leather handle inside its leaden sheath.

"The instrument," he said, "is dangerous, but so is a buzz saw. You must have to keep your fingers away."

And as he spoke, he drew the muzzle-slit swiftly down the length of the steel sheet, which quietly and instantly fell in two.

There was a unanimous jump, and Mallow laughed. He picked up one of the halves and propped it against his knee. "You can adjust the cutting-length accurately to a hundredth of an inch, and a two-inch sheet will slit down the middle as easily as this thing did. If you've got the thickness exactly judged, you can place steel on a wooden table, and split the metal without scratching the wood."

And at each phrase, the atomic shear moved and a gouged chunk of steel flew across the room.

"That," he said, "is whittling—with steel."

He passed back the shear. "Or else you have the plane. Do you want to decrease the thickness of a sheet, smooth out an irregularity, remove corrosion? Watch!"

Thin, transparent foil flew off the other half of the original sheet in six-inch swaths, then eight-inch, then twelve.

"Or drills? It's all the same principle."

They were crowded around now. It might have been a sleight-of-hand show, a corner magician, a vaudeville act made in high-pressure salesmanship. Commdor Asper fingered scraps of steel. High officials of the government tiptoed over each other's shoulders, and whispered, while Mallow punched clean, beautiful round holes through an inch of hard steel at every touch of his atomic drill.

"Just one more demonstration. Bring two short lengths of pipe, somebody."

An Honorable Chamberlain of something-or-other sprang to obedience in the general excitement and thought-absorption, and stained his hands like any laborer.

Mallow stood them upright and shaved the ends off with a single stroke of the shear, and then joined the pipes, fresh cut to fresh cut.

And there was a single pipe! The new ends, with even atomic irregularities missing, formed one piece upon joining. Johannison blocks, at a stroke.

Then Mallow looked up at his audience, stumbled at his first word and stopped. There was the keen stirring of excitement in his chest, and the base of his stomach went tingly and cold.

The Commdor's own bodyguard, in the confusion, had struggled to the front line, and Mallow, for the first time, was near enough to see their unfamiliar hand-weapons in detail.

They were atomic! There was no mistaking it; an explosive projectile weapon with a barrel like that was impossible. But that wasn't the big point. That wasn't the point at all.

The butts of those weapons had, deeply etched upon them, in worn gold plating, the Spaceship-and-Sun!

The same Spaceship-and-Sun that was stamped on every one of the great volumes of the original Encyclopedia that the Foundation had begun and not yet finished. *The same Spaceship-and-Sun that had blazoned the banner of the Galactic Empire through millennia.*

Mallow talked through and around his thoughts, "Test that pipe! It's one piece. Not perfect; naturally, the joining shouldn't be done by hand."

There was no need of further legerdemain. It had gone over. Mallow was through. He had what he wanted. There was only one thing in his mind. The golden globe with its conventionalized rays, and the oblique cigar shape that was a space vessel.

The Spaceship-and-Sun of the Empire!

The Empire! The words drilled! A century and a half had passed but there was still the Empire, somewhere deeper in the Galaxy. And it was emerging again, out into the Periphery.

Mallow smiled!

9

The *Far Star* was two days out in space, when Hober Mallow, in his private quarters with Senior Lieutenant Drawt, handed him an envelope, a roll of microfilm, and a silver spheroid.

"As of an hour from now, Lieutenant, you're Acting Captain of the *Far Star*, until I return—or forever."

Drawt made a motion of standing but Mallow waved him down imperiously.

"Quiet, and listen. The envelope contains the exact location of the planet to which you're to proceed. There you will wait for me for two months. If, before the two months are up, the Foundation locates you, the microfilm is my report of the trip.

"If, however," and his voice was somber, "I do *not* return at the end of two months, and Foundation vessels do not locate you, proceed to the planet, Terminus, and hand in the Time Capsule as the report. Do you understand that?"

"Yes, sir."

"At no time are you, or any of the men, to amplify in any single instance, my official report."

"If we are questioned, sir?"

"Then you know nothing."

"Yes, sir."

The interview ended, and fifty minutes later, a lifeboat kicked lightly off the side of the *Far Star*.

10

Onum Barr was an old man, too old to be afraid. Since the last disturbances, he had lived alone on the fringes of the land with what books he had saved from the ruins. He had nothing he feared losing, least of all the worn remnant of his life, and so he faced the intruder without cringing.

"Your door was open," the stranger explained.

His accent was clipped and harsh, and Barr did not fail to notice the strange blue-steel hand-weapon at his hip. In the half-gloom of the small room, Bar saw the glow of a force-shield surrounding the man.

He said, wearily, "There is no reason to keep it closed. Do you wish anything of me?"

"Yes." The stranger remained standing in the center of the room. He was large, both in height and bulk. "Yours is the only house about here."

"It is a desolate place," agreed Barr, "but there is a town to the east. I can show you the way."

"In a while. May I sit?"

"If the chairs will hold you," said the old man, gravely. They were old, too. Relics of a better youth.

The stranger said, "My name is Hobber Mallow. I come from a far province."

Barr nodded and smiled. "Your tongue convicted you of that long ago. I am Onum Barr of Siwenna—and once Patrician of the Empire."

"Then this *is* Siwenna. I had only old maps to guide me."

"They would have to be old, indeed, for star-positions to be misplaced."

Barr sat quite still, while the other's eyes drifted away into a reverie. He noticed that the atomic force-shield had vanished from about the man and admitted dryly to himself that his person no longer seemed formidable to strangers—or even, for good or for evil, to his enemies.

He said, "My house is poor and my resources few. You may share what I have if your stomach can endure black bread and dried corn."

Mallow shook his head. "No, I have eaten, and I can't stay. All I need are the directions to the center of government."

"That is easily enough done, and poor though I am, deprives me of nothing. Do you mean the capital of the planet, or of the Imperial Sector?"

The younger man's eyes narrowed. "Aren't the two identical? Isn't this Siwenna?"

The old patrician nodded slowly, "Siwenna, yes. But Siwenna is no longer capital of the Normannic Sector. Your old map has misled you after all. The stars may not change even in centuries, but political boundaries are all too fluid."

"That's too bad. In fact, that's very bad. Is the new capital far off?"

"It's on Orsha II. Twenty parsecs off. Your map will direct you. How old is it?"

"A hundred and fifty years."

"That old?" The old man sighed. "History has been crowded since. Do you know any of it?"

Mallow shook his head slowly.

Barr said, "You're fortunate. It has been an evil time for the provinces, but for the reign of Stannell VI, and he died fifty years ago. Since that time, rebellion and ruin, ruin and rebellion." Barr wondered if he were growing garrulous. It was a lonely life out here, and he had so little chance to talk to men.

Mallow said with sudden sharpness, "Ruin, eh? You sound as if the province were impoverished."

"Perhaps not on an absolute scale. The physical resources of twenty-five first-rank planets take a long time to use up. Compared to the wealth of the last century, though, we have gone a long way downhill—and there is no sign of turning, not yet. Why are you so interested in all this, young man? You are all alive and your eyes shine!"

The trader came near enough to blushing, as the faded eyes seemed to look too deep into his and smile at what they saw.

He said, "Now look here. I'm a trader out there—out toward the rim of the Galaxy. I've located some old maps, and I'm out to open new markets. Naturally, talk of impoverished provinces disturbs me. You can't get money out of a world unless money's there to be got. Now how's Siwenna, for instance?"

The old man leaned forward, "I cannot say. It will do even yet, perhaps. But *you* a trader? You look more like a fighting man. You hold your hand near your gun and there is a scar on your jawbone."

Mallow jerked his head. "There isn't much law out there where I come from. Fighting and scars are part of a trader's overhead. But fighting is only useful when there's money at the end, and if I can get it without, so much the sweeter. Now will I find enough money here to make it worth the fighting? I take it I can find the fighting easily enough."

"Easily enough," agreed Barr. "You could join Wiscard's remnants in the Red Stars. I don't know, enough, if you'd call that fighting or piracy. Or you could join our present gracious viceroy—gracious by right of murder, pillage, rapine, and the word of a boy Emperor, since rightfully assassinated." The patrician's thin cheeks reddened. His eyes closed and then opened, bird-bright.

"You don't sound very friendly to the viceroy, Patrician Barr," said Mallow. "What if I'm one of his spies?"

"What if you are?" said Barr, bitterly. "What can you take?" He gestured a withered arm at the bare interior of the decaying mansion.

"Your life."

"It would leave me easily enough. It has been with me five years too long. But you are *not* one of the viceroy's men. If you were, perhaps even now instinctive self-preservation would keep my mouth closed."

"How do you know?"

The old man laughed. "You seem suspicious. Come, I'll wager you think I'm trying to trap you into denouncing the government. No, no. I am past politics."

"Past politics? Is a man ever past that? The words you used to describe the viceroy—what were they? Murder, pillage, all that. You didn't sound objective. Not exactly. Not as if you were past politics."

The old man shrugged. "Memories sting when they come suddenly. Listen! Judge for yourself! When Siwenna was the provincial capital, I was a patrician and a member of the provincial senate. My family was an old and honored one. One of my great-grandfathers had been— No, never mind that. Past glories are poor feeding."

"I take it," said Mallow, "there was a civil war, or a revolution."

Barr's face darkened. "Civil wars are chronic in these degenerate days, but Siwenna had kept apart. Under Stannell VI, it had almost achieved its ancient prosperity. But weak emperors followed, and emperors mean strong viceroys, and our last viceroy—the same Wiscard, whose remnants still prey on the commerce among the Red Stars—aimed at the Imperial Purple. He wasn't the first to aim. And if he had succeeded, he wouldn't have been the first to succeed.

"But he failed. For when the Emperor's Admiral approached the province at the head of a fleet, Siwenna itself rebelled against its rebel viceroy." He stopped, sadly.

Mallow found himself tense on the edge of his seat, and relaxed slowly. "Please continue, sir."

"Thank you," said Barr, wearily. "It's kind of you to humor an old man. They rebelled; or I should say, *we* rebelled, for I was one of the minor leaders. Wiscard left Siwenna, barely ahead of us, and the planet, and with it the province, were thrown open to the admiral with every gesture of loyalty to the Emperor. Why we did this, I'm not sure. Maybe we felt loyal to the symbol, if not to the person, of the Emperor—a cruel and vicious child. Maybe we feared the horrors of a siege."

"Well?" urged Mallow, gently.

"Well," came the grim retort, "that didn't suit the admiral. He wanted the glory of conquering a rebellious province and his men wanted the loot such conquest would involve. So while the people were still gathered in every large city, cheering the Emperor and his admiral, he occupied all armed centers, and then ordered the population put to the atom-blast."

"On what pretext?"

"On the pretext that they had rebelled against their viceroy, the Emperor's anointed. And the admiral became the new viceroy, by virtue of one month of massacre, pillage and complete horror. I had six sons. Five died—variously. I had a daughter. I *hope* she died, eventually. *I* escaped because I was old. I came here, too old to cause even our viceroy worry." He bent his gray head. "They left me nothing, because I had helped drive out a rebellious governor and deprived an admiral of his glory."

Mallow sat silent, and waited. Then, "What of your sixth son?" he asked softly.

"Eh?" Barr smiled acidly. "He is safe, for he has joined the admiral as a common soldier under an assumed name. He is a gunner in the viceroy's personal fleet. Oh, no, I see your eyes. He is not an unnatural son. He visits me when he can and gives me what he can. He keeps me alive. And some day, our great and glorious viceroy will grovel to his death, and it will be my son who will be his executioner."

"And you tell this to a stranger? You endanger your son."

"No. I help him, by introducing a new enemy. And were I a friend of the viceroy, as I am his enemy, I would tell him to string outer space with ships, clear to the rim of the Galaxy."

"There are no ships there?"

"Did you find any? Did any space-guards question your entry? With ships few enough, and the bordering provinces filled with their share of intrigue and iniquity, none can be spared to guard the barbarian outer suns. No danger ever threatened us from the broken edge of the Galaxy—until *you* came."

"I? I'm no danger."

"There will be more after you."

Mallow shook his head slowly, "I'm not sure I understand you."

"Listen!" There was a feverish edge to the old man's voice. "I knew you when you entered. You have a force-shield about your body, or had when I first saw you."

Doubtful silence, then, "Yes—I had."

"Good. That was a flaw, but you didn't know that. There are some things I know. It's out of fashion in these decaying times to be a scholar. Events race and flash past and who cannot fight the tide with atom-blast in hand is swept away, as I was. But I was a scholar, and I know that in all the history of atomics, no portable force-shields was ever invented. We have force-shields—huge, lumbering power-houses that will protect a city, or even a ship, but not one, single man."

"Ah?" Mallow's underlip thrust out. "And what do you deduce from that?"

"There have been stories percolating through space. They travel strange paths and become distorted with every parsec—but when I was young there was a small ship of strange men, who did not know our customs and could not tell where they came from. They talked of magicians at the edge of the Galaxy; magicians who glowed in the darkness, who flew unaided through the air, and whom weapons would not touch.

"We laughed. I laughed, too. I forgot it till today. But you glow in the darkness, and I don't think my blaster, if I had one, would hurt you. Tell me, can you fly through air as you sit there now?"

Mallow said calmly, "I can make nothing of all this."

Barr smiled. "I'm content with the answer. I do not examine my guests. But if there are magicians; if *you* are one of them; there may some day be a great influx of them, or you. Perhaps that would be well. Maybe we need new blood." He muttered soundlessly to himself, then, slowly, "But it works the other way, too. Our new viceroy also dreams, as did our old Wiscard."

"Also after the Emperor's crown?"

Barr nodded. "My son hears tales. In the viceroy's personal entourage, one could scarcely help it. And he tells me of them. Our new viceroy would not refuse the Crown if offered, but he guards his line of retreat. There are stories that, failing Imperial heights, he plans to carve out a new Empire in the Barbarian hinterland. It is said, but I don't vouch for this, that he has already given one of his daughters as wife to a Kinglet somewhere in the uncharted Periphery."

"If one listened to every story—"

"I know. There are many more. I'm old and I babble nonsense. But what do you say?" And those sharp, old eyes peered deep.

The trader considered. "I say nothing. But I'd like to ask something. Does Siwenna have atomic power? Now, wait, I know that it possesses the knowledge of atomics. I mean, do they have power generators intact, or did the recent sack destroy them?"

"Destroy them? Oh, no. Half a planet would be wiped out before the smallest power would be touched. They are irreplaceable and the suppliers of the strength of the fleet." Almost proudly, "We have the largest and best on this side of Trantor itself."

"Then what would I do first if I wanted to see these generators?"

"Nothing!" replied Barr, decisively. "You couldn't approach any military center without being shot down instantly. Neither could anyone. Siwenna is still deprived of civic rights."

"You mean all the power stations are under the military?"

"No. There are the small city stations, the ones supplying power for heating and lighting homes, powering vehicles and so forth. Those are almost as bad. They're controlled by the tech-men."

"Who are they?"

"A specialized group which supervises the power plants. The honor is hereditary, the young ones being brought up in the profession as apprentices. Strict sense of duty, honor, and all that. No one but a tech-man could enter a station."

"I see."

"I don't say, though," added Barr, "that there aren't cases where tech-men haven't been bribed. In days when we have nine emperors in fifty years and seven of these are assassinated—when every space-captain aspires to the usurpation of a viceroyship, and every viceroy to the Imperium, I suppose even a tech-man can fall prey to money. But it would require a good deal, and I have none. Have you?"

"Money? No. But does one always bribe with money?"

"What else, when money buys all else."

"There is quite enough that money won't buy. And now if you'll tell me the nearest city with one of the stations, and how best to get there, I'll thank you."

"Wait!" Barr held out his thin hands. "Why do you rush? You come here, but *I* ask no questions. In the city, where the inhabitants are still called rebels, you would be challenged by the first soldier or guard who heard your accent and saw your clothes."

He rose and from an obscure corner of an old chest brought out a booklet. "My passport—forged. I escaped with it."

He placed it in Mallow's hand and folded the fingers over it. "The description doesn't fit, but if you flourish it, the chances are many to one they will not look closely."

"But you. You'll be left without one."

The old exile shrugged cynically. "What of it? And a further caution. Curb your tongue! Your accent is barbarous, your idioms peculiar, and every once in a while you deliver yourself of the most astounding archaisms. The less you speak, the less suspicion you will draw upon yourself. Now I'll tell you how to get to the city—"

Five minutes later, Mallow was gone.

He returned but once, for a moment, to the old patrician's house, before leaving it entirely, however. And when Onum Barr stepped into his little garden early the next morning, he found a box at his feet. It contained provisions, concentrated provisions such as one would find aboard ship, and alien in taste and preparation.

But they were good, and lasted long.

11

The tech-man was short, and his skin glistened with well-kept plumpness. His hair was a fringe and his skull shone through pinkly. The rings on his fingers were thick and heavy, his clothes were scented, and he was the first man Mallow had met on the planet who hadn't looked hungry.

The tech-man's lips pursed peevishly, "Now, my man, quickly. I have things of great importance waiting for me. You seem a stranger—" He seemed to evaluate Mallow's definitely un-Siwennese costume and his eyelids were heavy with suspicion.

"I am not of the neighborhood," said Mallow, calmly, "but the matter is irrelevant. I have had the honor to send you a little gift yesterday—"

The tech-man's nose lifted. "I received it. An interesting gewgaw. I may have use for it on occasion."

"I have other and more interesting gifts. Quite out of the gewgaw stage."

"Oh-h?" The tech-man's voice lingered thoughtfully over the monosyllable. "I think I already see the course of the interview; it has happened before. You are going to give me some trifle or other. A few credits, perhaps a cloak, second-rate jewelry; anything your little soul may think sufficient to corrupt a tech-man." His lower lip puffed out belligerently. "And I know what you wish in exchange.

There have been others to suffice with the same bright idea. You wish to be adopted into our clan. You wish to be taught the mysteries of atomics and the care of the machines. You think because you dogs of Siwenna—and probably your strangerhood is assumed for safety's sake—are being daily punished for your rebellion that you can escape what you deserve by throwing over yourselves the privileges and protections of the tech-man's guild."

Mallow would have spoken, but the tech-man raised himself into a sudden roar. "And now leave before I report your name to the Protector of the City. Do you think that I would betray the trust? The Siwennese traitors that preceded me—perhaps! But you deal with a different breed now. Why, Galaxy, I marvel that I do not kill you myself at this moment with my bare hands."

Mallow smiled to himself. The entire speech was patently artificial in tone and content, so that all the dignified indignation degenerated into uninspired farce.

The trader glanced humorously at the two flabby hands that had been named as his possible executioners then and there, and said, "Your Wisdom, you are wrong on three counts. First, I am not a creature of the viceroy come to test your loyalty. Second, my gift is something the Emperor himself in all his splendor does not and will never possess. Third, what I wish in return is very little; a nothing; a mere breath."

"So you say!" He descended into heavy sarcasm. "Come, what is this imperial donation that your godlike power wishes to bestow upon me? Something the Emperor doesn't have, eh?" He broke into a sharp squawk of derision.

Mallow rose and pushed the chair aside. "I have waited three days to see you, Your Wisdom, but the display will take only three seconds. If you will just draw that blaster whose butt I see very near your hand—"

"Eh?"

"And shoot me, I will be obliged."

"*What?*"

"If I am killed, you can tell the police I tried to bribe you into betraying guild secrets. You'll receive high praise. If I am not killed, you may have my shield."

For the first time, the tech-man became aware of the dimly-white illumination that hovered closely about his visitor, as though he had been dipped in pearl-dust. His blaster raised to the level and with eyes a-squint in wonder and suspicion, he closed contact.

The molecules of air caught in the sudden surge of atomic

disruption, tore into glowing, burning ions, and marked out the blinding thin line that struck at Mallow's heart—and splashed!

While Mallow's look of patience never changed, the atomic forces that tore at him consumed themselves against that fragile, pearly illumination, and crashed back to die in mid-air.

The tech-man's blaster dropped to the floor with an unnoticed crash.

Mallow said, "Does the Emperor have a personal force-shield? *You* can have one."

The tech-man stuttered, "Are you a tech-man?"

"No."

"Then—then where did you get that?"

"What do you care?" Mallow was coolly contemptuous. "Do you want it?" A thin, knobbed chain fell upon the desk. "There it is."

The tech-man snatched it up and fingered it nervously. "Is this complete?"

"Complete."

"Where's the power?"

Mallow's finger fell upon the largest knob, dull in its leaden case.

The tech-man looked up, and his face was congested with blood. "Sir, I am a tech-man, senior grade. I have twenty years behind me as supervisor and I studied under the great Bler at the University of Trantor. If you have the infernal charlatanry to tell me that a small container the size of a—of a walnut, blast it, holds an atomic generator, I'll have you before the Protector in three seconds."

"Explain it yourself then, if you can. I say it's complete."

The tech-man's flush faded slowly as he bound the chain about his waist, and, following Mallow's gesture, pushed the knob. The radiance that surrounded him shone into dim relief. His blaster lifted, then hesitated. Slowly, he adjusted it to an almost burnless minimum.

And then, convulsively, he closed circuit and the atomic fire dashed against his hand, harmlessly.

He whirled. "And what if I shoot you now, and keep the shield."

"Try!" said Mallow. "Do you think I gave you my only sample?" And he, too, was solidly incased in light.

The tech-man giggled nervously. The blaster clattered onto the desk. He said, "And what is this mere nothing, this breath, that you wish in return?"

"I want to see your generators."

"You realize that that is forbidden. It would mean ejection into space for both of us—"

"I don't want to touch them or have anything to do with them. I want to *see* them—from a distance."

"If not?"

"If not, you have your shield, but I have other things. For one thing, a blaster especially designed to pierce that shield."

"Hm-m-m." The tech-man's eyes shifted. "Come with me."

12

The tech-man's home was a small two-story affair on the outskirts of the huge, cubiform, windowless affair that dominated the center of the city. Mallow passed from one to the other through an underground passage, and found himself in the silent, ozone-tinged atmosphere of the powerhouse.

For fifteen minutes, he followed his guide and said nothing. His eyes missed nothing. His fingers touched nothing. And then, the tech-man said in strangled tones, "Have you had enough? I couldn't trust my underlings in *this* case."

"Could you ever?" asked Mallow, ironically. "I've had enough."

They were back in the office and Mallow said, thoughtfully, "And all those generators are in your hands?"

"Every one," said the tech-man, with more than a touch of complacency.

"And you keep them running and in order?"

"Right!"

"And if they break down?"

The tech-man shook his head indignantly. "They don't break down. They never break down. They were built for eternity."

"Eternity is a long time. Just suppose—"

"It is unscientific to suppose meaningless cases."

"All right. Suppose I were to blast a vital part into nothingness? I suppose the machines aren't immune to atomic forces? Suppose I fuse a vital connection, or smash a quartz D-tube?"

"Well, then," shouted the tech-man, furiously, "you would be killed."

"Yes, I know that," Mallow was shouting, too, "but what about the generator? Could you repair it?"

"Sir," the tech-man howled his words, "you have had a fair return. You've had what you asked for. Now get out! I owe you nothing more!"

Mallow bowed with a satiric respect and left.

Two days later he was back at the base where the *Far Star* waited to return with him to the planet, Terminus.

And two days later, the tech-man's shield went dead, and for all his puzzling and cursing never glowed again.

13

Mallow relaxed for almost the first time in six months. He was on his back in the sunroom of his new house, stripped to the skin. His great, brown arms were thrown up and out, and the muscles tautened into a stretch, then faded into repose.

The man beside him placed a cigar between Mallow's teeth and lit it. He champed on one of his own and said, "You must be overworked. Maybe you need a long rest."

"Maybe I do, Jael, but I'd rather rest in a council seat. Because I'm going to have that seat, and you're going to help me."

Ankor Jael raised his eyebrows and said, "How did I get into this?"

"You got in obviously. Firstly, you're an old dog of a politico. Secondly, you were booted out of your cabinet seat by Jorane Sutt, the same fellow who'd rather lose an eyeball than see me in the council. You don't think much of my chances, do you?"

"Not much," agreed the ex-Minister of Education. "You're a Smyrnian"

"That's no legal bar. I've had a lay education."

"Well, come now. Since when does prejudice follow any law but its own. Now, how about your own man—this Jaim Twer? What does *he* say?"

"He spoke about running me for council almost a year ago," replied Mallow easily, "but I've outgrown him. He couldn't have pulled it off in any case. Not enough depth. He's loud and forceful—but that's only an expression of nuisance value. I'm off to put over a real coup. I need *you*."

"Jorane Sutt is the cleverest politician on the planet and he'll be against you. I don't claim to be able to outsmart him. And don't think he doesn't fight hard, and dirty."

"I've got money."

"That helps. But it takes a lot to buy off prejudice—you dirty Smyrnian."

"I'll have a lot."

"Well, I'll look into the matter. But don't ever you crawl up on your hind legs and bleat that I encouraged you in the matter. Who's that?"

Mallow pulled the corners of his mouth down, and said, "Jorane Sutt himself, I think. He's early, and I can understand it. I've been dodging him for a month. Look, Jael, get into the next room, and turn the speaker on low. I want you to listen."

He helped the council member out of the room with a shove of his bare foot, then scrambled up and into a silk robe. The synthetic sunlight faded to normal power.

The secretary to the mayor entered stifly, while the solemn major-domo tiptoed the door shut behind him.

Mallow fastened his belt and said, "Take your choice of chairs, Sutt."

Sutt barely cracked a flicking smile. The chair he chose was comfortable but he did not relax into it. From its edge, he said, "If you'll state your terms to begin with, we'll get down to business."

"What terms?"

"You wish to be coaxed? Well, then, what, for instance, did you do at Korell? Your report was incomplete."

"I gave it to you months ago. You were satisfied then."

"Yes," Sutt rubbed his forehead thoughtfully with one finger, "but since then your activities have been significant. We know a good deal of what you're doing, Mallow. We know, exactly, how many factories you're putting up; in what a hurry you're doing it; and how much it's costing you. And there's this palace you have," he gazed about him with a cold lack of appreciation, "which set you back considerably more than my annual salary; and a swathe you've been cutting—a very considerable and expensive swathe—through the upper layers of Foundation society."

"So? Beyond proving that you employ capable spies, what does it show?"

"It shows you have money you didn't have a year ago. And that can show anything—for instance, that a good deal went on at Korell that we know nothing of. Where are you getting your money?"

"My dear Sutt, you can't really expect me to tell you."

"I don't."

"I didn't think you did. That's why I'm going to tell you. It's straight from the treasure-chests of the Commdor of Korell."

Sutt blinked.

Mallow smiled and continued, "Unfortunately for you, the money is quite legitimate. I'm a Master Trader and the money I received was a quantity of wrought iron and chromite in exchange for a number of trinkets I was able to supply him with. Fifty percent of the profit is mine by hidebound contract with the Foundation. The other half goes to the government at the end of the year when all good citizens pay their income tax."

"There was no mention of any trade agreement in your report."

"Nor was there any mention of what I had for breakfast that day, or the name of my current mistress, or any other irrelevant detail." Mallow's smile was fading into a sneer. "I was sent—to quote yourself—to keep my eyes open. They were never shut. You wanted to find out what happened to the captured Foundation merchant ships. I never saw or heard of them. You wanted to find out if Korell had atomic power. My report tells of atomic blasters in the possession of the Commdor's private bodyguard. I saw no other signs. And the blasters I did see are relics of the old Empire and may be show-pieces that do not work, for all my knowledge.

"So far, I followed orders, but beyond that I was, and still am, a free agent. According to the laws of the Foundation, a Master Trader may open whatever new markets he can, and receive therefrom his due half of the profits. What are your objections? I don't see them."

Sutt bent his eyes carefully towards the wall and spoke with a difficult lack of anger, "It is the general custom of all traders to advance the religion with their trade."

"I adhere to law, and not to custom."

"There are times when custom can be the higher law."

"Then appeal to the courts."

Sutt raised somber eyes which seemed to retreat into their sockets. "You're a Smyrnian after all. It seems naturalization and education can't wipe out the taint in the blood. Listen, and try to understand, just the same.

"This goes beyond money, or markets. We have the sciences of the great Hari Seldon to prove that upon us depends the future empire of the Galaxy, and from the course that leads to that Imperium we cannot turn. The religion we have is our all-important instrument towards that end. With it we have brought the Four Kingdoms under our control, even at the moment when they would have crushed us. It is the most potent device known with which to control men and worlds.

"The primary reason for the development of trade and traders was to introduce and spread this religion more quickly, and to insure that the introduction of new techniques and a new economy would be subject to our thorough and intimate control."

He paused for breath, and Mallow interjected quietly, "I know the theory. I understand it entirely."

"Do you? It is more than I expectd. Then you see, of course, that your attempt at trade for its own sake; at mass production of worthless gadgets, which can only affect a world's economy superficially; at the subversion of interstellar policy to the god of profits; at the divorce of atomic power from our controlling religion—can only end with the overthrow and complete negation of the policy that has worked successfully for a century."

"And time enough, too," said Mallow, indifferently, "for a policy outdated, dangerous and impossible. However well your religion has succeeded in the Four Kingdoms, scarcely another world in the Periphery has accepted it. At the time we seized control of the Kingdoms, there were a sufficient number of exiles, Galaxy knows, to spread the story of how Salvor Hardin used the priesthood and the superstition of the people to overthrow the independence and power of the secular monarchs. And if that wasn't enough, the case of Askone two decades back made it plain enough. There isn't a ruler in the Periphery now that wouldn't sooner cut his own throat than let a priest of the Foundation enter the territory.

"I don't propose to force Korell or any other world to accept something I know they don't want. No, Sutt. If atomic power makes them dangerous, a sincere friendship through trade will be many times better than an insecure overlordship, based on the hated supremacy of a foreign spiritual power, which, once it weakens ever so slightly, can only fall entirely and leave nothing substantial behind except an immortal fear and hate."

Sutt said cynically, "Very nicely put. So, to get back to the original point of discussion, what are your terms? What do you require to exchange your ideas for mine?"

"You think my convictions are for sale?"

"Why not?" came the cold response. "Isn't that your business buying and selling?"

"Only at a profit," said Mallow, unoffended. "Can you offer me more than I'm getting as is?"

"You could have three-quarters of your trade profits, rather than half."

Mallow laughed shortly. "A fine offer. The whole of the trade on your terms would fall far below a tenth share of mine. Try harder than that."

"You could have a council seat."

"I'll have that anyway, without and despite you."

With a sudden movement, Sutt clenched his fist. "You could also save yourself a prison term. Of twenty years, if I have my way. Count the profit in that."

"No profit at all, unless you can fulfill such a threat."

"It's trial for murder."

"Whose murder?" asked Mallow, contemptuously.

Sutt's voice was harsh now, though no louder than before, "The murder of an Anacreonian priest, in the service of the Foundation."

"Is that so now? And what's your evidence?"

The secretary to the mayor leaned forward. "Mallow, I'm not bluffing. The preliminaries are over. I have only to sign one final paper and the case of the Foundation versus Hober Mallow, Master Trader, is begun. You abandoned a subject of the Foundation to torture and death at the hands of an alien mob, Mallow, and you have only five seconds to prevent the punishment due you. For myself, I'd rather you decided to bluff it out. You'd be safer as a destroyed enemy, than as a doubtfully-converted friend."

Mallow said solemnly, "You have your wish."

"Good!" and the secretary smiled savagely. "It was the mayor who wished the preliminary attempt at compromise, not I. Witness that I did not try too hard."

The door opened before him, and he left.

Mallow looked up as Ankor Jael re-entered the room.

Mallow said, "Did you hear him?"

The politician flopped to the floor. "I never heard him as angry as that, since I've known the snake."

"All right. What do you make of it?"

"Well, I'll tell you. A foreign policy of domination through spiritual means is his *idée fixe*, but it's my notion that his ultimate aims aren't spiritual. I was fired out of the Cabinet for arguing on the same issue, as I needn't tell you."

"You needn't. And what are those unspiritual aims according to your notion?"

Jael grew serious. "Well, he's not stupid, so he must see the bankruptcy of our religious policy, which has hardly made a single conquest for us in seventy years. He's obviously using it for purposes of his own.

"Now *any* dogma, primarily based on faith and emotionalism, is a dangerous weapon to use on others, since it is almost impossible to guarantee that the weapon will never be turned on the user. For a hundred years now, we've supported a ritual and mythology that is becoming more and more venerable, traditional—and immovable. In some ways, it isn't under our control any more."

"In what ways?" demanded Mallow. "Don't stop. I want your thoughts."

"Well, suppose one man, one ambitious man, uses the force of religion against us, rather than for us."

"You mean Sutt—"

"You're right. I mean Sutt. Listen, man, if he could mobilize the various hierarchies on the subject planets against the Foundation in the name of orthodoxy, what chance would we stand? By planting himself at the head of the standards of the pious, he could make war on heresy, as represented by you, for instance, and make himself king eventually. After all, it was Hardin who said: 'An atom-blaster is a good weapon, but it can point both ways.' "

Mallow slapped his bare thigh. "All right, Jael, then get me in that council, and I'll fight him."

Jael paused, then said significantly, "Maybe not. What was all that about having a priest lynched? It isn't true, is it?"

"It's true enough," Mallow said, carelessly.

Jael whistled. "Has he definite proof?"

"He should have." Mallow hesitated, then added, "Jaim Twer was his man from the beginning, though neither of them knew that I knew that. And Jaim Twer was an eyewitness."

Jael shook his head. "Uh-uh. That's bad."

"Bad? What's bad about it? That priest was illegally upon the planet by the Foundation's own laws. He was obviously used by the Korellian government as a bait, whether involuntary or not. By all the laws of commonsense, I had no choice but one action—and that action was strictly within the law. If he brings me to trial, he'll do nothing but make a prime fool of himself."

And Jael shook his head again. "No, Mallow, you've missed it. I told you he played dirty. He's not out to convict you; he knows he can't do that. But he *is* out to ruin your standing with the people. You heard what he said. Custom *is* higher than law, at times. You could walk out of the trial scot-free, but if the people think you threw a priest to the dogs, your popularity is gone.

"They'll admit you did the legal thing, even the sensible thing. But just the same you'll have been, in their eyes, a cowardly dog, an unfeeling brute, a hard-hearted monster. *And* you would never get elected to the council. You might even lose your rating as Master Trader by having your citizenship voted away from you.

You're not native born, you know. What more do you think Sutt can want?"

Mallow frowned stubbornly. "So!"

"My boy," said Jael, "I'll stand by you, but *I* can't help. You're on the spot—dead center."

14

The council chamber was full in a very literal sense on the fourth day of the trial of Hober Mallow, Master Trader. The only council man absent was feebly cursing the fractured skull that had bedridden him. The galleries were filled to the aisleways and ceilings with those few of the crowd who by influence, wealth, or sheer diabolic perseverance had managed to get in. The rest filled the square outside, in swarming knots about the open-air trimensional 'visors.

Ankor Jael made his way into the chamber with the near-futile aid and exertions of the police department, and then through the scarcely smaller confusion within to Hober Mallow's seat.

Mallow turned with relief. "By Seldon, you cut it thin. Have you got it?"

"Here, take it," said Jael. "It's everything you asked for."

"Good. How are they taking it outside?"

"They're wild clear through." Jael stirred uneasily. "You should never have allowed public hearings. You could have stopped them."

"I didn't want to."

"There's lynch talk. And Publis Manlio's men on the outer planets—"

"I wanted to ask you about that, Jael. He's stirring up the Hierachy against me, is he?"

"*Is* he? It's the sweetest setup you ever saw. As Foreign Secretary, he handles the prosecution in a case of interstellar law. As High Priest and Primate of the Church, he rouses the fanatic hordes—"

"Well, forget it. Do you remember that Hardin quotation you threw at me last month? We'll show them that the atom-blaster can point both ways."

The mayor was taking his seat now and the council members were rising in respect.

Mallow whispered, "It's my turn today. Sit here and watch the fun."

The day's proceedings began and fifteen minutes later, Hober Mallow stepped through a hostile whisper to the empty space before the mayor's bench. A lone beam of light centered upon him and in the public 'visors of the city, as well as on the myriads of private 'visors in almost every home of the Foundation's planets, the lonely giant figure of a man stared out defiantly.

He began easily and quietly. "To save time, I will admit the truth of every point made against me by the prosecution. The story of the priest and the mob as related by them is perfectly accurate in every detail."

There was a stirring in the chamber and a triumphant mass-snarl from the gallery. He waited patiently for silence.

"However, the picture they presented fell short of completion. I ask the privilege of supplying the completion in my own fashion. My story may seem irrelevant at first. I ask your indulgence for that."

Mallow made no reference to the notes before him:

"I begin at the same time as the prosecution did; the day of my meetings with Jorane Sutt and Jaim Twer. What went on at those meetings you know. The conversations have been described, and to that description I have nothing to add—except my own thoughts of that day.

"They were suspicious thoughts, for the events of that day were queer. Consider. Two people, neither of whom I knew more than casually, make unnatural and somewhat unbelievable propositions to me. One, the secretary to the mayor, asks me to play the part of intelligence agent to the government in a highly confidential matter, the nature and importance of which has already been explained to you. The other, self-styled leader of a political party, asks me to run for a council seat.

"Naturally I looked for the ulterior motive. Sutt's seemed evident. He didn't trust me. Perhaps he thought I was selling atomic power to enemies and plotting rebellion. And perhaps he was forcing the issue, or thought he was. In that case, he would need a man of his own near me on my proposed mission, as a spy. The last thought, however, did not occur to me until later on, when Jaim Twer came on the scene.

"Consider again: Twer presents himself as a trader, retired into politics, yet I know of no details of his trading career, although my knowledge of the field is immense. And further, although Twer boasted of a lay education, *he had never heard of a Seldon crisis*."

Hober Mallow waited to let the significance sink in and was rewarded with the first silence he had yet encountered, as the gallery caught its collective breath. That was for the inhabitants of Terminus itself. The men of the Outer Planets could hear only censored versions that would suit the requirements of religion. They would hear nothing of Seldon crises. But there be further strokes they would not miss.

Mallow continued:

"Who here can honestly state that *any* man with a lay education can possibly be ignorant of the nature of a Seldon crisis? There is only one type of education upon the Foundation that excludes all mention of the planned history of Seldon and deals only with the man himself as a semi-mythical wizard—

"I knew at that instant Jaim Twer had never been a trader. I knew then that he was in holy orders and perhaps a full-fledged priest; and, doubtless, that for the three years he had pretended to head a political party of the traders, *he had been a bought man of Jorane Sutt.*

"At the moment, I struck in the dark. I did not know Sutt's purposes with regard to myself, but since he seemed to be feeding me rope liberally, I handed him a few fathoms of my own. My notion was that Twer was to be with me on my voyage as unofficial guardian on behalf of Jorane Sutt. Well, if he didn't get on, I knew well there'd be other devices waiting—and those others I might not catch in time. A known enemy is relatively safe. I invited Twer to come with me. He accepted.

"That, gentlemen of the council, explains two things. First, it tells you that Twer is not a friend of mine testifying against me reluctantly and for conscience's sake, as the prosecution would have you believe. He is a spy, performing his paid job. Secondly, it explains a certain action of mine on the occasion of the first appearance of the priest whom I am accused of having murdered—an action as yet unmentioned, because unknown."

Now there was a disturbed whispering in the council. Mallow cleared his throat theatrically, and continued:

"I hate to describe my feelings when I first heard that we had a refugee missionary on board. I even hate to remember them. Essentially, they consisted of wild uncertainty. The event struck me at the moment as a move by Sutt, and passed beyond my comprehension or calculation. I was at sea—and completely.

"There was one thing I could do. I got rid of Twer for five minutes by sending him after my officers. In his absence, I set up a Visual Recorder receiver, so that whatever happened might be preserved for future study. This was in the hope, the wild but earnest hope, that what confused me at the time might become plain upon review.

"I have gone over that Visual Record some fifty times since. I have it here with me now, and will repeat the job a fifty-first time in your presence right now."

The mayor pounded monotonously for order, as the chamber lost its equilibrium and the gallery roared. In five million homes on Terminus, excited observers crowded their receiving sets more closely, and at the prosecutor's own bench, Jorane Sutt shook his head coldly at the nervous high priest, while his eyes blazed fixedly on Mallow's face.

The center of the chamber was cleared, and the lights burnt low. Ankor Jael, from his bench on the left, made the adjustments, and with a preliminary click, a scene sprang to view; in color, in three-dimensions, in every attribute of life but life itself.

There was the missionary, confused and battered, standing between the lieutenant and the sergeant. Mallow's image waited silently, and then men filed in, Twer bringing up the rear.

The conversation played itself out, word for word. The sergeant was disciplined, and the missionary was questioned. The mob appeared, their growl could be heard, and the Revered Jord Parma made his wild appeal. Mallow drew his gun, and the missionary, as he was dragged away, lifted his arms in a mad, final curse and a tiny flash of light came and went.

The scene ended, with the officers frozen at the horror of the situation, while Twer clamped shaking hands over his ears, and Mallow calmly put his gun away.

The lights were on again; the empty space in the center of the floor was no longer even apparently full. Mallow, the real Mallow of the present, took up the burden of his narration:

"The incident, you see, is exactly as the prosecution has presented it—on the surface. I'll explain that shortly. Jaim Twer's emotions through the whole business show clearly a priestly education, by the way.

"It was on that same day that I pointed out certain incongruities in the episode to Twer. I asked him where the missionary came from in the midst of the near-desolate tract we occupied at the time. I asked further where the gigantic mob had come from with the nearest sizable town a hundred miles away. The prosecution has paid no attention to such problems.

"Or to other points; for instance, the curious point of Jord Parma's blatant conspicuousness. A missionary on Korell, risking his life in defiance of both Korellian and Foundation law, parades about in a very new and very distinctive priestly costume. There's something wrong there. At the time, I suggested that the missionary was an unwitting accomplice of the Commdor, who was using him in an attempt to force us into an act of wildly illegal aggression, to justify, *in law*, his subsequent destruction of our ship and of us.

"The prosecution has anticipated this justification of my actions. They have expected me to explain that the safety of my ship, my crew, my mission itself were at stake and could not be sacrificed for one man, when that man would, in any case, have been destroyed, with us or without us. They reply by muttering about the Foundation's 'honor' and the necessity of upholding our 'dignity' in order to maintain our ascendancy.

"For some strange reason, however, the prosecution has neglected Jord Parma himself—as an individual. They brought out no details concerning him; neither his birthplace, nor his education, nor any detail of previous history. The explanation of this will also explain the incongruities I have pointed out in the Visual Record you have just seen. The two are connected.

"The prosecution has advanced no details concerning Jord Parma because it *cannot*. That scene you saw by Visual Record seemed phoney because Jord Parma was phoney. There never *was* a Jord Parma. *This whole trial is the biggest farce ever cooked up over an issue that never existed.*"

Once more he had to wait for the babble to die down. He said, slowly:

"I'm going to show you the enlargement of a single still from the Visual Record. It will speak for itself. Lights again, Jael."

The chamber dimmed, and the empty air filled again with frozen figures in ghostly, waxen illusion. The officers of the *Far Star* struck their stiff, impossible attitudes. A gun pointed from Mallow's rigid hand. At his left, the Revered Jord Parma, caught in mid-shriek, stretched his claws upward, while the falling sleeves hung halfway.

And from the missionary's hand there was that little gleam that in the previous showing had flashed and gone. It was a permanent glow now.

"Keep your eye on that light on his hand," called Mallow from the shadows. "Enlarge that scene, Jael!"

The tableau bloated—quickly. Outer portions fell away as the missionary drew towards the center and became a giant. Then there was only a head and an arm, and then only a hand, which filled everything and remained there in immense, hazy tautness.

The light had become a set of fuzzy, glowing letters: K S P.

ISAAC ASIMOV

320

"That," Mallow's voice boomed out, "is a sample of tattooing, gentlemen. Under ordinary light it is invisible, but under ultraviolet light—with which I flooded the room in taking this Visual Record, it stands out in high relief. I'll admit it is a naive method of secret identification, but it works on Korell, where UV light is not to be found on street corners. Even in our ship, detection was accidental.

"Perhaps some of you have already guessed what K S P stands for. Jord Parma knew his priestly lingo well and did his job magnificently. Where he had learned it, and how, I cannot say, but K S P stands for 'Korellian Secret Police.' "

Mallow shouted over the tumult, roaring against the noise, "I have collateral proof in the form of documents brought from Korell, which I can present to the council, if required.

"And where is now the prosecution's case? They have already made and re-made the monstrous suggestion that I should have fought for the missionary in defiance of the law, and sacrificed my mission, my ship, and myself to the 'honor' of the Foundation.

"But to do it for an imposter?

"Should I have done it then for a Korellian secret agent tricked out in the robes and verbal gymnastics probably borrowed of an Anacreonian exile? Would Jorane Sutt and Publis Manlio have had me fall into a stupid, odious trap—"

His hoarsened voice faded into the featureless background of a shouting mob. He was being lifted onto shoulders, and carried to the mayor's bench. Out the windows, he could see a torrent of madmen swarming into the square to add to the thousands there already.

Mallow looked about for Ankor Jael, but it was impossible to find any single face in the incoherence of the mass. Slowly he became aware of a rhythmic, repeated shout, that was spreading from a small beginning, and pulsing into insanity:

"Long live Mallow—long live Mallow—long live Mallow—"

15

Ankor Jael blinked at Mallow out of a haggard face. The last two days had been mad, sleepless ones.

"Mallow, you've put on a beautiful show, so don't spoil it by jumping too high. You can't seriously consider running for mayor. Mob enthusiasm is a powerful thing, but it's notoriously fickle."

"Exactly!" said Mallow, grimly, "so we must coddle it, and the best way to do that is to continue the show."

"Now what?"

"You're to have Publis Manlio and Jorane Sutt arrested—"

"What!"

"Just what you hear. Have the mayor arrest them! I don't care what threats you use. I control the mob—for today, at any rate. He won't dare face them."

"But on what charge, man?"

"On the obvious one. They've been inciting the priesthood of the outer planets to take sides in the factional quarrels of the Foundation. That's illegal, by Seldon. Charge them with 'endangering the state.' And I don't care about a conviction any more than they did in my case. Just get them out of circulation until I'm mayor."

"It's half a year till election."

"Not too long!" Mallow was on his feet, and his sudden grip of Jael's arm was tight. "Listen, I'd seize the government by force if I had to—the way Salvor Hardin did a hundred years ago. There's still that Seldon crisis coming up, and when it comes I have to be mayor *and* high priest. Both!"

Jael's brow furrowed. He said, quietly, "What's it going to be? Korell, after all?"

Mallow nodded. "Of course. They'll declare war, eventually, though I'm betting it'll take another pair of years."

"With atomic ships?"

"What do you think? Those three merchant ships we lost in their space sector weren't knocked over with compressed-air pistols. Jael, they're getting ships from the Empire itself. Don't open your mouth like a fool. I said the Empire! It's still there, you know. It may be gone here in the Periphery but in the Galactic centre it's still very much alive. And one false move means that it, itself, may be on our neck. That's why I must be mayor and high priest. I'm the only man who knows how to fight the crisis."

Jael swallowed dryly. "How? What are going to do?"

"Nothing."

Jael smiled uncertainly. "Really! All of that!"

But Mallow's answer was incisive. "When I'm boss of this Foundation, I'm going to do nothing. One hundred percent of nothing, and that is the secret of this crisis."

16

Asper Argo, the Well-Beloved, Commdor of the Korellian Republic greeted his wife's entry by a hangdog lowering of his scanty eyebrows. To her at least, his self-adopted epithet did not apply. Even he knew that.

She said, in a voice as sleek as her hair and as cold as her eyes, "My gracious Lord, I understand, has finally come to a decision upon the fate of the Foundation upstarts."

"Indeed?" said the Commdor, sourly. "And what more does your versatile understanding embrace?"

"Enough, my very noble husband. You had another of your vacillating consultations with your councillors. Fine advisors." With infinite scorn, "A herd of palsied purblind idiots hugging their sterile profits close to their sunken chests in the face of my father's displeasure."

"And who, my dear," was the mild response, "is the excellent source from which your understanding understands all this?"

The Commdora laughed shortly. "If I told you, my source would be more corpse than source."

"Well, you'll have your own way, as always." The Commdor shrugged and turned away. "And as for your father's displeasure: I much fear me it extends to a niggardly refusal to supply more ships."

"More ships!" She blazed away, hotly, "And haven't you five? Don't deny it. I *know* you have five; and a sixth is promised."

"Promised for the last year."

"But one—just one—can blast that Foundation into stinking rubble. Just one! One, to sweep their little pygmy boats out of space."

"I couldn't attack their planet, even with a dozen."

"And how long would their planet hold out with their trade ruined, and their cargoes of toys and trash destroyed?"

"Those toys and trash mean money," he sighed. "A good deal of money."

"But if you had the Foundation itself, would you not have all it contained? And if you had my father's respect and gratitude, would you not have more than ever the Foundation could give you? It's been three years—more—since that barbarian came with his magic sideshow. It's long enough."

"My dear!" The Commdor turned and faced her. "I am growing old. I am weary. I lack the resilience to withstand your rattling mouth. You say you know that I have decided. Well, I have. It is over, and there is war between Korell and the Foundation."

"Well!" The Commdora's figure expanded and her eyes sparkled. "You learned wisdom at last, though in your dotage. And now when you are master of this hinterland, you may be sufficiently respectable to be of some weight and importance in the Empire. For one thing, we might leave this barbarous world and attend the viceroy's court. Indeed we might."

She swept out, with a smile, and a hand on her hip. Her hair gleamed in the light.

The Commdor waited, and then said to the closed door, with malignance and hate, "And when I am master of what you call the hinterland, I may be sufficiently respectable to do without your father's arrogance and his daughter's tongue. Completely—without!"

17

The senior lieutenant of the *Dark Nebula* stared in horror at the visiplate.

"Great Galloping Galaxies!" It should have been a howl, but it was a whisper instead, "What's that?"

It was a ship, but a whale to the *Dark Nebula's* minnow; and on its side was the Spaceship-and-Sun of the Empire. Every alarm on the ship yammered hysterically.

The orders went out, and the *Dark Nebula* prepared to run if it could, and fight if it must—while down in the ultrawave room, a message stormed its way through hyperspace to the Foundation.

Over and over again! Partly a plea for help, but mainly a warning of danger.

18

Hober Mallow shuffled his feet wearily as he leafed through the reports. Two years of the mayoralty had made him a bit more housebroken, a bit softer, a bit more patient—but it had not made him learn to like government reports and the mind-breaking officialese in which they were written.

"How many ships did they get?" asked Jael.

"Four trapped on the ground. Two unreported. All others accounted for and safe." Mallow grunted. "We should have done better, but it's just a scratch."

There was no answer and Mallow looked up. "Does anything worry you?"

"I wish Sutt would get here," was the almost irrelevant answer.

"Ah, yes, and now we'll hear another lecture on the home front."

"No, we won't," snapped Jael, "but you're stubborn, Mallow. You may have worked out the foreign situation to the last detail but you've never given a care about what goes on here on the home planet."

"Well, that's your job, isn't it? What did I make you Minister of Education and Propaganda for?"

"Obviously to send me to an early and miserable grave, for all the co-operation you give me. For the last year, I've been deafening you with the rising danger of Sutt and his Religionists. What good will your plans be, if Sutt forces a special election and has you thrown out?"

"None, I admit."

"And your speech last night just about handed the election to Sutt with a smile and a pat. Was there any necessity for being so frank?"

"Isn't there such a thing as stealing Sutt's thunder?"

"No," said Jael, violently, "not the way you did it. You claim to have foreseen everything, and don't explain why you traded with Korell to their exclusive benefit for three years. Your only plan of battle is to retire without a battle. You abandon all trade with the sectors of space near Korell. You openly proclaim a stalemate. You promise no offensive, even in the future. Galaxy, Mallow, what am I supposed to do with such a mess?"

"It lacks glamour?"

"It lacks mob emotion-appeal."

"Same thing."

"Mallow, wake up. You have two alternatives. Either you present the people with a dynamic foreign policy, whatever your private plans are, or you make some sort of compromise with Sutt."

Mallow said, "All right, if I've failed the first, let's try the second. Sutt's just arrived."

Sutt and Mallow had not met personally since the day of the trial, two years back. Neither detected any change in the other, except for that subtle atmosphere about each which made it quite evident that the roles of ruler and defier had changed.

Sutt took his seat without shaking hands.

Mallow offered a cigar and said, "Mind if Jael stays? He wants a compromise earnestly. He can act as mediator if tempers rise."

Sutt shrugged. "A compromise will be well for you. Upon another occasion I once asked you to state your terms. I presume the positions are reversed now."

"You presume correctly."

"Then these are my terms. You must abandon your blundering policy of economic bribery and trade in gadgetry, and return to the tested foreign policy of our fathers."

"You mean conquest by missionary?"

"Exactly."

"No compromise short of that?"

"None."

"Um-m-m." Mallow lit up very slowly, and inhaled the tip of his cigar into a bright glow. "In Hardin's time, when conquest by missionary was new and radical, men like yourself opposed it. Now it is tried, tested, hallowed—everything a Jorane Sutt would find well. But, tell me, how would you get us out of our present mess?"

"*Your* present mess. I had nothing to do with it."

"Consider the question suitably modified."

"A strong offensive is indicated. The stalemate you seem to be satisfied with is fatal. It would be a confession of weakness to all the worlds of the Periphery, where the appearance of strength is all-important, and there's not one vulture among them that wouldn't join the assault for its share of the corpse. You ought to understand that. You're from Smyrno, aren't you?"

Mallow passed over the significance of the remark. He said, "And if you beat Korell, what of the Empire? *That* is the real enemy."

Sutt's narrow smile tugged at the corners of his mouth. "Oh, no, your records of your visit to Siwenna were complete. The viceroy of the Normannic Sector is interested in creating dissension in the Periphery for his own benefit, but only as a side issue. He isn't going to stake everything on an expedition to the Galaxy's rim when he has fifty hostile neighbors and an emperor to rebel against. I paraphrase your own words."

"Oh, yes he might, Sutt, if he thinks we're strong enough to be dangerous. And he might think so, if we destroy Korell by the main force of frontal attack. We'd have to be considerably more subtle."

"As for instance—"

Mallow leaned back. "Sutt, I'll give you your chance. I don't need you, but I can use you. So I'll tell you what it's all about, and then you can either join me and receive a place in a coalition cabinet, or you can play the martyr and rot in jail."

"Once before you tried that last trick."

"Not very hard, Sutt. The right time has only just come. Now listen." Mallow's eyes narrowed.

"When I first landed on Korell," he began, "I bribed the Commdor with the trinkets and gadgets that form the trader's usual stock. At the start, that was meant only to get us entrance into a steel foundry. I had no plan further than that, but in that I succeeded. I got what I wanted. But it was only after my visit to the Empire that I first realized exactly what a weapon I could build that trade into.

"This is a Seldon crisis we're facing, Sutt, and Seldon crises are not solved by individuals but by historic forces. Hari Seldon, when he planned our course of future history, did not count on brilliant heroics but on the broad sweeps of economics and sociology. So the solutions to the various crises must be achieved by the forces that become available to us at the time.

"In this case—trade!"

Sutt raised his eyebrows skeptically and took advantage of the pause. "I hope I am not of subnormal intelligence, but the fact is that your vague lecture isn't very illuminating."

"It will become so," said Mallow. "Consider that until now the power of trade has been underestimated. It has been thought that it took a priesthood under our control to make it a powerful weapon. That is not so, and *this* is my contribution to the Galactic situation. Trade without priests! Trade alone! It is strong enough. Let us become very simple and specific. Korell is now at war with us. Consequently our trade with her has stopped. *But*—notice that I am making this as simple as a problem in addition—in the past three years she has based her economy more and more upon the atomic techniques which we have introduced and which only we can continue to supply. Now what do you suppose will happen once the tiny atomic generators begin failing, and one gadget after another goes out of commission?

"The small household appliances go first. After half a year of this stalemate that you abhor, a woman's atomic knife won't work any more. Her stove begins failing. Her washer doesn't do a good job. The temperature-humidity control in her house dies on a hot summer day. What happens?"

He paused for an answer, and Sutt said calmly, "Nothing. People endure a good deal in war."

"Very true. They do. They'll send their sons out in unlimited numbers to die horribly on broken spaceships. They'll bear up under enemy bombardment, if it means they have to live on stale bread and foul water in caves half a mile deep. But it's very hard to bear up under little things when the patriotic uplift of imminent danger is not present. It's going to be a stalemate. There will be no casualties, no bombardments, no battles.

"There will just be a knife that won't cut, and a stove that won't cook, and a house that freezes in the winter. It will be annoying and people will grumble."

Sutt said slowly, wonderingly, "Is that what you're setting your hopes on, man? What do you expect? A housewives' rebellion? A Jacquerie? A sudden uprising of butchers and grocers with their cleavers and bread-knives shouting 'Give us back our Automatic Super-Kleeno Atomic Washing Machines!'?"

"No, sir," said Mallow, impatiently, "I do not. I expect, however, a general background of grumbling and dissatisfaction which will be seized on by more important figures later on."

"And what more important figures are these?"

"The manufacturers, the factory owners, the industrialists of Korell. When two years of the stalemate have gone, the machines in the factories will, one by one, begin to fail. Those industries which we have changed from first to last with our new atomic gadgets will find themselves very suddenly ruined. The heavy industries will find themselves *en masse* and at a stroke the owners of nothing but scrap machinery that won't work."

"The factories ran well enough before you came there, Mallow."

"Yes, Sutt, so they did—at about one-twentieth the profits, even if you leave out of consideration the cost of reconversion to the original pre-atomic state. With the industrialist and financier and the average man all against him, how long will the Commdor hold out?"

"As long as he pleases, as soon as it occurs to him to get new atomic generators from the Empire."

And Mallow laughed joyously. "You've missed, Sutt, missed as badly as the Commdor himself. You've missed everything, and understood nothing. Look, man, the Empire can replace nothing. The Empire has always been a realm of colossal resources. They've calculated everything in planets, in stellar systems, in whole sectors of the Galaxy. Their generators are gigantic because they thought in gigantic fashion.

"But we—*we*, our little Foundation, our single world almost without metallic resources—have had to work with brute economy. Our generators have had to be the size of our thumb, because it was all the metal we could afford. We had to develop new techniques and new methods—techniques and methods the Empire can't follow because they have degenerated past the stage where they can make any really vital scientific advance.

"With all their atomic shields, large enough to protect a ship, a city, an entire world; they could never build one to protect a single man. To supply light and heat to a city, they have motors six stories high—I saw them—where ours could fit into this room. And when I told one of their atomic specialists that a lead container the size of a walnut contained an atomic generator, he almost choked with indignation on the spot.

"Why, they don't even understand their own colossi any longer. The machines work from generation to generation automatically, and the caretakers are a hereditary caste who would be helpless if a single D-tube in all that vast structure burnt out.

"The whole war is a battle between those two systems; between the Empire and the Foundation; between the big and the little. To seize control of a world, they bribe with immense ships that can make war, but lack all economic significance. We, on the other hand, bribe with little things, useless in war, but vital to prosperity and profits.

"A king, or a Commdor, will take the ships and even make war. Arbitrary rulers throughout history have bartered their subjects' welfare for what they consider honor, and glory, and conquest. But it's still the little things in life that count—and Asper Argo won't stand up against the economic depression that will sweep all Korell in two or three years."

Sutt was at the window, his back to Mallow and Jael. It was early evening now, and the few stars that struggled feebly here at the very rim of the Galaxy sparked against the background of the misty, wispy Lens that included the remnants of that Empire, still vast, that fought against them.

Sutt said, "No. You are not the man."

"You don't believe me?"

"I mean I don't trust you. You're smooth-tongued. You befooled me properly when I thought I had you under proper care on your first trip to Korell. When I thought I had you cornered at the trial, you wormed your way out of it and into the mayor's chair by demogoguery. There is nothing straight about you; no motive that hasn't another behind it; no statement that hasn't three meanings.

"Suppose you were a traitor. Suppose your visit to the Empire had brought you a subsidy and a promise of power. Your actions would be precisely what they are now. You would bring about a war after having strengthened the enemy. You would force the Foundation into activity. And you would advance a plausible explanation of everything, one so plausible it would convince everyone."

"You mean there'll be no compromise?" asked Mallow, gently.

"I mean you must get out, by free will or force."

"I warned you of the only alternative to co-operation."

Jorane Sutt's face congested with blood in a sudden access of emotion. "And I warn you, Hober Mallow of Smyrno, that if you arrest me, there will be no quarter. My men will stop nowhere in spreading the truth about you, and the common people of the Foundation will unite against their foreign ruler. They have a consciousness of destiny that a Smyrnian can never understand—and that consciousness will destroy you."

Hober Mallow said quietly to the two guards who had entered, "Take him away. He's under arrest."

Sutt said, "Your last chance."

Mallow stubbed out his cigar and never looked up.

And five minutes later, Jael stirred and said, wearily, "Well, now that you've made a martyr for the cause, what next?"

Mallow stopped playing with the ash tray and looked up. "That's not the Sutt I used to know. He's a blood-blind bull. Galaxy, he hates me."

"All the more dangerous then."

"More dangerous? Nonsense! He's lost all power of judgment."

Jael said grimly, "You're overconfident, Mallow. You're ignoring the possibility of a popular rebellion."

Mallow looked up, grim in his turn. "Once and for all, Jael, there is no possibility of a popular rebellion."

"You're sure of yourself!"

"I'm sure of the Seldon crisis and the historical validity of their solutions, externally *and* internally. There are some things I *didn't* tell Stutt right now. He tried to control the Foundation itself by religious forces as he controlled the outer worlds, and he failed—which is the surest sign that in the Seldon scheme, religion is played out.

"Economic control worked differently. And to paraphrase that famous Salvor Hardin quotation of yours, it's a poor atom blaster that won't point both ways. If Korell prospered with our trade, so did we. If Korellian factories fail without our trade; and if the prosperity of the outer worlds vanishes with commercial isolation; so will our factories fail and our prosperity vanish.

"And there isn't a factory, not a trading center, not a shipping line that isn't under my control; that I couldn't squeeze to nothing if Sutt attempts revolutionary propaganda. Where his propaganda succeeds, or even looks as though it might succeed, I will make certain that prosperity dies. Where it fails, prosperity will continue, because my factories will remain fully staffed.

"So by the same reasoning which makes me sure that the Korellians will revolt in favor of prosperity, I am sure *we* will not revolt against it. The game will be played out to its end."

"So then," said Jael, "you're establishing a plutocracy. You're making us a land of traders and merchant princes. Then what of the future?"

Mallow lifted his gloomy face, and exclaimed fiercely, "What business of mine is the future? No doubt Seldon has foreseen it and prepared against it. There will be other crises in the time to come when money power has become as dead a force as religion is now. Let my successors solve those new problems, as I have solved the one of today."

KORELL— . . . *And so after three years of a war which was certainly the most unfought war on record, the Republic of Korell surrendered unconditionally, and Hober Mallow took his place next to Hari Seldon and Salvor Hardin in the hearts of the people of the Foundation.*

ENCYCLOPEDIA GALACTICA

GIANT KILLER

A. Bertram Chandler

Shrick should have died before his baby eyes had opened on his world. Shrick would have died, but Weena, his mother, was determined that he, alone of all her children, should live. Three previous times since her mating with Skreer had she borne, and on each occasion the old, gray Sterret, Judge of the Newborn, had condemned her young as Different Ones.

Weena had no objection to the Law when it did not affect her or hers. She, as much as any other member of the Tribe, keenly enjoyed the feasts of fresh, tasty meat following the ritual slaughter of Different Ones. But when those sacrificed were the fruit of her own womb it wasn't the same.

It was quiet in the cave where Weena awaited the coming of her lord. Quiet, that is, save for the sound of her breathing and an occasional plaintive, mewling cry from the newborn child. And even these sounds were deadened by the soft spongy walls and ceiling.

She sensed the coming of Skreer long before his actual arrival. She anticipated his first question and, as he entered the cave, said quietly, "One. A male."

"A male?" Skreer radiated approval. Then she felt his mood change to one of questioning, of doubt. "Is it . . . he—?"

"Yes."

Skreer caught the tiny, warm being in his arms. There was no light, but he, like all his race, was accustomed to the dark. His fingers told him all that he needed to know. The child was hairless. The legs were too straight. And—this was worst of all—the head was a great, bulging dome.

"Skreer!" Weena's voice was anxious. "Do you—?"

"There is no doubt. Sterret will condemn it as a Different One."

"But—"

"There is no hope." Weena sensed that her mate shuddered, heard the faint, silken rustle of his fur as he did so. "His head! He is like the Giants!"

The mother sighed. It was hard, but she knew the Law. And yet— This was her fourth child-bearing, and she was never to know, perhaps, what it was to watch and wait with mingled pride and terror while her sons set out with the other young males to raid the Giant's territory, to bring back spoils from the great Cave-of-Food, the Place-of-Green-Growing-Things or, even, precious scraps of shiny metal from the Place-of-Life-That-Is-Not-Life.

She clutched at a faint hope.

"His head is like a Giant's? Can it be, do you think, that the Giants are Different Ones? I have heard it said."

"What if they are?"

"Only this. Perhaps he will grow to be a Giant. Perhaps he will fight the other Giants for us, his own people. Perhaps—"

"Perhaps Sterret will let him live, you mean." Skreer made the short, unpleasant sound that passed among his people for a laugh. "No, Weena. He must die. And it is long since we feasted—"

"But—"

"Enough. Or do *you* wish to provide meat for the Tribe also? I may wish to find a mate who will bear me sturdy sons, not monsters!"

The Place-of-Meeting was almost deserted when Skreer and Weena, she with Shrick clutched tightly in her arms, entered. Two more couples were there, each with newborn. One of the mothers was holding two babies, each of whom appeared to be normal. The other had three, her mate holding one of them.

Weena recognized her as Teeza, and flashed her a little half smile of sympathy when she saw that the child carried by Teeza's mate would certainly be condemned by Sterret when he choose to appear. For it was, perhaps, even more revolting than her own Different One, having two hands growing from the end of each arm.

Skreer approached one of the other males, he unburdened with a child.

"How long have you been waiting? he asked.

"Many heartbeats. We—"

The guard stationed at the doorway through which light entered from Inside hissed a warning:

"Quiet! A Giant is coming!"

The mothers clutched their children to them yet more tightly, their fur standing on end with superstitious dread. They knew that if they remained silent there was no danger, that even if they should betray themselves by some slight noise there was no immediate peril. It was not size alone that made the Giants dreaded, it was the supernatural powers that they were known to possess. The food-that-kills had slain many an unwary member of the Tribe, also their fiendishly cunning devices that crushed and mangled any of the People unwise enough to reach greedily for the savory morsels left exposed on a kind of little platform. Although there were those who averred that, in the latter case, the risk was well worth it, for the yellow grains from the many bags in the Cave-of-Food were as monotonous as they were nourishing.

"The Giant has passed!"

Before those in the Place-of-Meeting could resume their talk, Sterret drifted out from the entrance of his cave. He held in his right hand his wand of office, a straight staff of the hard, yet soft, stuff dividing the territory of the People from that of the Giants. It was tipped with a sharp point of metal.

He was old, was Sterret.

Those who were themselves grandparents had heard their grandparents speak of him. For generations he had survived attacks by young males jealous of his prerogatives as chief, and the more rare assaults by parents displeased by his rulings as Judge of the Newborn. In this latter case, however, he had had nothing to fear, for on those isolated occasions the Tribe had risen as one and torn the offenders to pieces.

Behind Sterret came his personal guards and then, floating out from the many cave entrances, the bulk of the Tribe. There had been no need to summon them; they *knew*.

The chief, deliberate and unhurried, took his position in the center of the Place-of-Meeting. Without orders, the crowd made way for the parents and their newborn. Weena winced as she saw their gloating eyes fixed on Shrick's revolting baldness, his misshapen skull. She knew what the verdict would be.

She hoped that the newborn of the others would be judged before her own, although that would merely delay the death of her own child by the space of a very few heartbeats. She hoped—

Weena! Bring the child to ne that I may see and pass judgment!"

The chief extended his skinny arms, took the child from the mother's reluctant hands. His little, deep-set eyes gleamed at the thought of the draught of rich, red blood that he was soon to enjoy. And yet he was reluctant to lose the savor of a single heartbeat of the mother's agony. Perhaps she could be provoked into an attack—

"You insult us," he said slowly, "by bringing forth *this!*" He held Shrick, who squalled feebly, at arm's length. "Look, oh People, at this *thing* the miserable Weena has brought for my judgment!"

"He has a Giant's head," Weena's timid voice was barely audible. "Perhaps—"

"—his father was a Giant!"

A tittering laugh rang through the Place-of-Meeting.

"No. But I have heard it said that perhaps the Giants or their fathers and mothers, were Different Ones. And—"

"Who said that?"

"Strela."

"Yes, Strela the Wise. Who, in his wisdom, ate largely of the food-that-kills!"

Again the hateful laughter rippled through the assembly.

Sterret raised the hand that held the spear, shortening his grip on the haft. His face puckered as he tasted in anticipation the bright bubble of blood that would soon well from the throat of the Different One. Weena screamed. With one hand she snatched her child from the hateful grasp of the chief, with the other she seized his spear.

Sterret was old, and generations of authority had made him careless. Yet, old as he was, he evaded the vicious thrust aimed at him by the mother. He had no need to cry orders, from all sides the People converged upon the rebel.

Already horrified by her action, Weena knew that she could expect no mercy. And yet life, even as lived by the Tribe, was sweet. Gaining a purchase from the gray, spongy floor of the Place-of-Meeting she jumped. The impetus of her leap carried her up to the doorway through which streamed the light from Inside. The guard there was unarmed, for of what avail would a puny spear be against the Giants? He fell back before the menace of Weena's bright blade and bared teeth. And then Weena was Inside.

She could, she knew, hold the doorway indefinitely against pursuit. But this was Giant country. In an agony of indecision she clung to the rim of the door with one hand, the other still holding the spear. A face appeared in the opening, and then vanished, streaming with blood. It was only later that she realized that it had been Skreer's.

She became acutely conscious of the fierce light beating around and about her, of the vast spaces on all sides of a body that was accustomed to the close quarters of the caves and tunnels. She felt naked and, in spite of her spear, utterly defenseless.

Then that which she dreaded came to pass.

Behind her, she sensed the approach of two of the Giants. Then she could hear their breathing, and the low, infinitely menacing rumble of their voices as they talked one with the other. They hadn't seen her—of that she was certain, but it was only a matter of heart-beats before they did so. The open doorway, with the certainly of death that lay beyond, seemed infinitely preferable to the terror of the unknown. Had it been only her life at stake she would have returned to face the righteous wrath of her chief, her mate and her Tribe.

Fighting down her blind panic, she forced herself to a clarity of thought normally foreign to her nature. If she yielded to instinct, if she fled madly before the approaching Giants, she would be seen. Her only hope was to remain utterly still. Skreer, and others of the males who had been on forays Inside, had told her that the Giants, careless in their size and power, more often than not did not notice the People unless they made some betraying movement.

The Giants were very close.

Slowly, cautiously, she turned her head.

She could see them now, two enormous figures floating through the air with easy arrogance. They had not seen her, and she knew that they would not see her unless she made some sudden movement to attract their attention. Yet it was hard not to yield to the impulse to dive back into the doorway to the Place-of-Meeting, there to meet certain death at the hands of the outraged Tribe. It was harder still to fight the urge to relinquish her hold on the rim of the doorway and flee—anywhere—in screaming panic.

But she held on.

The Giants passed.

The dull rumble of their voices died in the distance, their acrid, unpleasant odor, of which she had heard but never before experienced, diminished. Weena dared to raise her head once more.

In the confused, terrified welter of her thoughts one idea stood out with dreadful clarity. Her only hope of survival, pitifully slim though it was, lay in following the Giants. There was no time to lose, already she could hear the rising clamor of voices as those in the caves sensed that the Giants had passed. She relinquished her hold on the edge of the door and floated slowly up.

When Weena's head came into sudden contact with something hard she screamed. For long seconds she waited, eyes close shut in terror, for the doom that would surely descend upon her. But nothing happened. The pressure upon the top of her skull neither increased nor diminished.

Timidly, she opened her eyes.

As far as she could see, in two directions, stretched a long, straight shaft or rod. Its thickness was that of her own body, and it was made, or covered with, a material not altogether strange to the mother. It was like the ropes woven by the females with fibers from the Place-of-Green-Growing-Things—but incomparably finer. Stuff such as this was brought back sometimes by the males from their expeditions. It had been believed, once, that it was the fur of the Giants, but now it was assumed that it was made by them for their own purposes.

On three sides of the shaft was the glaring emptiness so terrifying to the people of the caves. On the fourth side was a flat, shiny surface. Weena found that she could insinuate herself into the space between the two without discomfort. She discovered, also, that with comforting solidity at her back and belly she could make reasonably fast progress along the shaft. It was only when she looked to either side that she felt a return of her vertigo. She soon learned not to look.

It is hard to estimate the time taken by her journey in a world where time was meaningless. Twice she had to stop and feed Shrick—fearful lest his hungry wailings betray their presence either to Giants or any of the People who might—although this was highly improbable—have followed her. Once she felt the shaft vibrating, and froze to its matt surface in utter and abject terror. A Giant passed, pulling himself rapidly along with his two hands. Had either of those hands fallen upon Weena it would have been the finish. For many heartbeats after his passing she clung there limp and helpless, scarcely daring to breathe.

It seemed that she passed through places of which she had heard the males talk. This may have been so—but she had no means of knowing. For the world of the People, with its caves and tunnels, was familiar territory, while that of the Giants was known only in relation to the doorways through which a daring explorer could enter.

Weena was sick and faint with hunger and thirst when, at last, the long shaft led her into a place where she could smell the tantalizing aroma of food. She stopped, looked in all directions. But here, as everywhere in this alien country, the light was too dazzling for her untrained eyes. She could see, dimly, vast shapes beyond her limited understanding. She could see no Giants, nor anything that moved.

Cautiously, keeping a tight hold on the rough surface of the shaft, she edged out to the side away from the polished, flat surface along which she had been traveling. Back and forth her head swung, her sensitive nostrils dilated. The bright light confused her, so she shut her eyes. Once again her nose sought the source of the savory smell, swinging ever more slowly as the positions was determined with reasonable accuracy.

She was loathe to abandon the security of her shaft, but hunger overruled all other considerations. Orienting her body, she jumped. With a thud she brought up against another flat surface. Her free hand found a projection, to which she clung. This she almost relinquished as it turned. Then a crack appeared, with disconcerting suddenness, before her eyes, widening rapidly. Behind this opening was black, welcome darkness. Weena slipped inside, grateful for relief from the glaring light of the Inside. It wasn't until later that she realized that this was a door such as was made by her own people in the Barrier, but a door of truly gigantic proportions. But all that mattered at first was the cool, refreshing shade.

Then she took stock of her surroundings.

Enough light came in through the barely open doorway for her to see that she was in a cave. It was the wrong shape for a cave, it is true, having flat, perfectly regular walls and floor and ceiling. At the far end, each in its own little compartment, were enormous, dully shining globes. From them came a smell that almost drove the famishing mother frantic.

Yet she held back. She knew that smell. It was that of fragments of food that had been brought into the caves, won by stealth and guile from the killing platforms of the Giants. Was this a killing platform? She wracked her brains to recall the poor description of these devices given by the males, decided that this, after all, must be a Cave-of-Food. Relinquishing her hold of Shrick and Sterret's spear she made for the nearest globe.

At first she tried to pull it from its compartment, but it appeared to be held. But it didn't matter. Bringing her face against the surface of the sphere she buried her teeth in its thin skin. There was flesh beneath the skin, and blood—a thin, sweet, faintly acid juice. Skreer had, at times, promised her a share of this food when next he won some from a killing platform, but that promise had never been kept. And now Weena had a whole cave of this same food all to herself.

Gorged to repletion, she started back to pick up the now loudly complaining Shrick. He had been playing with the spear and had cut himself on the sharp point. But it was the spear that Weena snatched, swinging swiftly to defend herself and her child. For a voice said, understandable, but with an oddly slurred intonation, "Who are you? What are you doing in our country?"

It was one of the People, a male. He was unarmed, otherwise it is certain that he would never have asked questions. Even so, Weena knew that the slightest relaxation of vigilance on her part would bring a savage, tooth-and-nail attack.

She tightened her grasp on the spear, swung it so that its point was directed at the stranger.

"I am Weena," she said, "of the Tribe of Sterret."

"Of the Tribe of Sterret? But the Tribe of Sessa holds the ways between our countries."

"I came Inside. But who are you?"

"Tekka. I am one of Skarro's people. You are a spy."

"So I brought my child with me."

Tekka was looking at Shrick.

"I see," he said at last. "A Different One. But how did you get through Sessa's country?"

"I didn't. I came Inside."

It was obvious that Tekka refused to believe her story.

"You must come with me," he said, "to Skarro. He will judge."

"And if I come?"

"For the Different One, death. For you, I do not know. But we have too many females in our Tribe already."

"This says that I will not come." Weena brandished her spear.

She would not have defied a male of her own tribe thus—but this Tekka was not of her people. And she had always been brought up to believe that even a female of the Tribe of Sterret was superior to a male—even a chief—of any alien community.

"The Giants will find you here." Tekka's voice showed an elaborate unconcern. Then— "That is a fine spear."

"Yes. It belonged to Sterret. With it I wounded my mate. Perhaps he is dead."

The male looked at her with a new respect. If her story were true—this was a female to be handled with caution. Besides—

"Would you give it to me?"

"Yes." Weena laughed nastily. There was no mistaking her meaning.

"Not that way. Listen. Not long ago, in our Tribe, many mothers, two whole hands of mothers with Different Ones, defied the Judge of the Newborn. They fled along the tunnels, and live outside the Place-of-Little-Lights. Skarro has not yet led a war party against them. Why, I do not know, but there is always a Giant in that place. It may be that Skarro fears that a fight behind the Barrier would warn the Giants of our presence—"

"And you will lead me there?"

"Yes. In return for the spear."

Weena was silent for the space of several heartbeats. As long as Tekka preceded her she would be safe. It never occurred to her that she could let the other fulfill his part of the bargain, and then refuse him his payment. Her people were a very primitive race.

"I will come with you," she said.

"It is well."

Tekka's eyes dwelt long and lovingly upon the fine spear. Skarro would not be chief much longer.

"First," he said, "we must pull what you have left of the good-to-eat-ball into our tunnel. Then I must shut the door lest a Giant should come—"

Together they hacked and tore the sphere to pieces. There was a doorway at the rear of one of the little compartments, now empty. Through this they pushed and pulled their fragrant burden. First Weena went into the tunnel, carrying Shrick and the spear, then Tekka. He pushed the round door into place, where it fitted with no sign that the Barrier had been broken. He pushed home two crude locking bars.

"Follow me," he ordered the mother.

The long journey through the caves and tunnels was heaven after the Inside. Here there was no light—or, at worst, only a feeble glimmer from small holes and cracks in the Barrier. It seemed that Tekka was leading her along the least frequented ways and tunnels of Skarro's country, for they met none of his people. Nevertheless, Weena's perceptions told her that she was in densely populated territory. From all around her beat the warm, comforting waves of the routine, humdrum life of the People. She knew that in snug caves males, females and children were living in cozy intimacy. Briefly, she regretted having thrown away all this for the ugly, hairless bundle in her arms. But she could never return to her own Tribe, and should she wish to throw in her lot with this alien community the alternatives would be death or slavery.

"Careful!" hissed Tekka. "We are approaching Their country."

"You will—?"

"Not me. They will kill me. Just keep straight along this tunnel and you will find Them. Now, give me the spear."

"But—"

"*You* are safe. There is your pass." He lightly patted the uneasy, squirming Shrick. "Give me the spear, and I will go."

Reluctantly, Weena handed over the weapon. Without a word Tekka took it. Then he was gone. Briefly the mother saw him in the dim light that, in this part of the tunnel, filtered through the Barrier—a dim, gray figure rapidly losing itself in the dim grayness. She felt very lost and lonely and frightened. But the die was cast. Slowly, cautiously, she began to creep along the tunnel.

When They found her she screamed. For many heartbeats she had sensed their hateful presence, had felt that beings even more alien than the Giants were closing in on her. Once or twice she called, crying that she came in peace, that she was the mother of a Different One. But not even echo answered her, for the soft, spongy tunnel walls deadened the shrill sound of her voice. And the silence that was not silence was, if that were possible, more menacing than before.

Without warning the stealthy terror struck. Weena fought with the courage of desperation, but she was overcome by sheer weight of numbers. Shrick, protesting feebly, was torn from her frantic grasp. Hands—and surely there were far too many hands for the number of her assailants—pinned her arms to her sides, held her ankles in a vicelike grip. No longer able to struggle, she looked at her captors. Then she screamed again. Mercifully, the dim light spared her the full horror of their appearance, but what she saw would have been enough to haunt her dreams to her dying day had she escaped.

Softly, almost caressingly, the hateful hands ran over her body with disgusting intimacy.

Then— "She is a Different One."

She allowed herself to hope.

"And the child?"

"Two-Tails has newborn. She can nurse him."

And as the sharp blade found her throat Weena had time to regret most bitterly ever having left her snug, familiar world. It was not so much the forfeit of her own life—that she had sacrificed when she defied Sterret—it was the knowledge that Shrick, instead of meeting a clean death at the hands of his own people, would live out his life among these unclean monstrosities.

Then there was a sharp pain and a feeling of utter helplessness as the tide of her life swiftly ebbed—and the darkness that Weena had loved so well closed about her for evermore.

No-Fur—who, at his birth, had been named Shrick—fidgetted impatiently at his post midway along what was known to his people as Skarro's Tunnel. It was time that Long-Nose came to relieve him. Many heartbeats had passed since he had heard the sounds on the other side of the Barrier proclaiming that the Giant in the Place-of-Little-Lights had been replaced by another of his kind. It was a mystery what the Giants did there—but the New People had come to recognize a strange regularity in the actions of the monstrous beings, and to regulate their time accordingly.

No-Fur tightened his grip on his spear—of Barrier material it was, roughly sharpened at one end—as he sensed the approach of somebody along the tunnel, coming from the direction of Tekka's country. It could be a Different One bearing a child who would become one of the New People, it could be attack. But, somehow, the confused impressions that his mind received did not bear out either of these assumptions.

No-Fur shrank against the wall of the tunnel, his body sinking deep into the spongy material. Now he could dimly see the intruder—a solitary form flitting furtively through the shadows. His sense of smell told him that it was a female. Yet he was certain that she had no child with her. He tensed himself to attack as soon as the stranger should pass his hiding place.

Surprisingly, she stopped.

"I come in peace," she said. "I am one of you. I am," here she paused a little, "one of the New People."

Shrick made no reply, no betraying movement. It was barely possible, he knew, that this female might be possessed of abnormally keen eyesight. It was even more likely that she had smelled him out. But then—how was it that she had known the name by which the New People called themselves? To the outside world they were Different Ones—and had the stranger called herself such she would at once have proclaimed herself an alien whose life was forfeit.

"You do not know," the voice came again, "how it is that I called myself by the proper name. In my own Tribe I am called a Different One—"

"Then how is it," No-Fur's voice was triumphant, "that you were allowed to live?"

"Come to me! No, leave your spear. Now come!"

No-Fur stuck his weapon into the soft cavern wall. Slowly, almost fearfully, he advanced to where the female was waiting. He could see her better now—and she seemed no different from those fugitive mothers of Different Ones—at whose slaughter he had so often assisted. The body was well proportioned and covered with fine, silky fur. The head was well shaped. Physically she was so normal as to seem repugnant to the New People.

And yet— No-Fur found himself comparing her with the females of his own Tribe, to the disadvantage of the latter. Emotion rather than reason told him that the hatred inspired by the sight of an ordinary body was the result of a deep-rooted feeling of inferiority rather than anything else. And he wanted this stranger.

"No," she said slowly, "it is not my body that is different. It is in my head. I didn't know myself until a little while—about two hands of feeding—ago. But I can tell, now, what is going on inside your head, or the head of any of the People—"

"But," asked the male, "how did they—"

"I was ripe for mating. I was mated to Trillo, the son of Tekka, the chief. And in our cave I told Trillo things of which he only knew. I thought that I should please him, I thought that he would like to have a mate with magical powers that he could put to good use. With my aid he could have made himself chief. But he was angry—and very frightened. He ran to Tekka, who judged me as a Different One. I was to have been killed, but I was able to escape. They dare not follow me too far into this country—"

Then— "You want me."

It was a statement rather than a question.

"Yes. But—"

"No-Tail? She can die. If I fight her and win, I become your mate."

Briefly, half regretfully, No-Fur thought of his female. She had been patient, she had been loyal. But he saw that, with this stranger for a mate, there were no limits to his advancement. It was not that he was more enlightened than Trillo had been, it was that as one of the New People he regarded abnormality as the norm.

"Then you will take me." Once again there was no hint of questioning. Then— "My name is Wesel."

The arrival of No-Fur, with Wesel in tow, at the Place-of-Meeting could not have been better timed. There was a trial in progress, a young male named Big-Ears having been caught red-handed in the act of stealing a coveted piece of metal from the cave of one Four-Arms. Long-Nose, who should have relieved No-Fur, had found the spectacle of a trial with the prospect of a feast to follow far more engrossing than the relief of the lonely sentry.

It was he who first noticed the newcomers.

"Oh, Big-Tusk," he called, "No-Fur has deserted his post!"

The chief was disposed to be lenient.

"He has a prisoner," he said. "A Different One. We shall feast well."

"He is afraid of you," hissed Wesel. *"Defy him!"*

"It is no prisoner." No-Fur's voice was arrogant. "It is my new mate. And you, Long-Nose, go at once to the tunnel."

"Go, Long-Nose. My country must not remain unguarded. No-Fur, hand the strange female over to the guards that she may be slaughtered."

No-Fur felt his resolution wavering under the stern glare of the chief. As two of Big-Tusk's bullies approached he slackened his grip on Wesel's arm. She turned to him, pleading and desperation in her eyes.

"No, no. He is afraid of you, I say. Don't give in to him. Together we can—"

Ironically, it was No-Tail's intervention that turned the scales. She confronted her mate, scorn written large on her unbeautiful face, the shrewish tongue dreaded by all the New People, even the chief himself, fast getting under way.

"So," she said, "you prefer this drab, common female to me. Hand her over, so that she may, at least, fill our bellies. As for you, my bucko, you will pay for this insult!"

No-Fur looked at the grotesque, distorted form of No-Tail, and then at the slim, sleek Wesel. Almost without volition he spoke.

"Wesel is my mate," he said. "She is one of the New People!"

Big-Tusk lacked the vocabulary to pour adequate scorn upon the insolent rebel. He struggled for words, but could find none to cover the situation. His little eyes gleamed redly, and his hideous tusks were bared in a vicious snarl.

"*Now!*" prompted the stranger. "His head is confused. He will be rash. His desire to tear and maul will cloud his judgment. Attack!"

No-Fur went into the fight coldly, knowing that if he kept his head he must win. He raised his spear to stem the first rush of the infuriated chief. Just in time Big-Tusk saw the rough point and, using his tail as a rudder, swerved. He wasn't fast enough, although his action barely saved him from immediate death. The spear caught him in the shoulder and broke off short, leaving the end in the wound. Mad with rage and pain the chief was now a most dangerous enemy—and yet, at the same time, easy meat for an adversary who kept his head.

No-Fur was, at first, such a one. But his self-control was cracking fast. Try as he would he could not fight down the rising tides of hysterical fear, of sheer, animal blood lust. As the enemies circled, thrust and parried, he with his almost useless weapon, Big-Tusk with a fine, metal tipped spear, it took all his will power to keep himself from taking refuge in flight or closing to grapple with his more powerful antagonist. His reason told him that both courses of action would be disastrous—the first would end in his being hunted down and slaughtered by the Tribe, the second would bring him within range of the huge, murderous teeth that had given Big-Tusk his name.

So he thrust and parried, thrust and parried, until the keen edge of the chief's blade nicked his arm. The stinging pain made him all animal, and with a shrill scream of fury he launched himself at the other.

But if Nature had provided Big-Tusk with a fine armory she had not been niggardly with the rebel's defensive equipment. True, he had nothing outstanding in the way of teeth or claws, had not the extra limbs possessed by so many of his fellow New People. His brain may have been a little more nimble—but at this stage of the fight that counted for nothing. What saved his life was his hairless skin.

Time after time the chief sought to pull him within striking distance, time after time he pulled away. His slippery hide was crisscrossed with a score of scratches, many of them deep but none immediately serious. And all the time he himself was scratching and pummeling with both hands and feet, biting and gouging.

It seemed that Big-Tusk was tiring, but he was tiring too. And the other had learned that it was useless to try to grab a handful of fur, that he must try to take his enemy in an unbreakable embrace. Once he succeeded. No-Fur was pulled closer and closer to the slavering fangs, felt the foul breath of the other in his face, knew that it was a matter of heartbeats before his throat was torn out. He screamed, threw up his legs and lunged viciously at Big-Tusk's belly. He felt his feet sink into the soft flesh, but the chief grunted and did not relax his pressure. Worse—the failure of his desperate counterattack had brought No-Fur even closer to death.

With one arm, his right, he pushed desperately against the other's chest. He tried to bring his knees up in a crippling blow, but they were held in a vicelike grip by Big-Tusk's heavily muscled legs. With his free, left arm he flailed viciously and desperately, but he might have been beating against the Barrier itself.

The People, now that the issue of the battle was decided, were yelling encouragement to the victor. No-Fur heard among the cheers the voice of his mate, No-Tail. The little, cold corner of his brain in which reason was still enthroned told him that he couldn't blame her. If she were vociferous in *his* support, she could expect only death at the hands of the triumphant chief. But he forgot that he had offered her insult and humiliation, remembered only that she was his mate. And the bitterness of it kept him fighting when others would have relinquished their hold on a life already forfeit.

The edge of his hand came down hard just where Big-Tusk's thick neck joined his shoulder. He was barely conscious that the other winced, that a little whimper of pain followed the blow. Then, high and shrill, he heard Wesel.

"Again! Again! That is his weak spot!"

Blindly groping, he searched for the same place. And Big-Tusk was afraid, of that there was no doubt. His head twisted, trying to cover his vulnerability. Again he whimpered, and No-Fur knew that the battle was his. His thin, strong fingers with their sharp nails dug and gouged. There was no fur here, and the flesh was soft. He felt the warm blood welling beneath his hand as the chief screamed dreadfully. Then the iron grip was abruptly relaxed. Before Big-Tusk could use hands or feet to cast his enemy from him No-Fur had twisted and, each hand clutching skin and fur, had buried his teeth in the other's neck. They found the jugular. Almost at once the chief's last, desperate struggles ceased.

No-Fur drank long and satisfyingly.

Then, the blood still clinging to his muzzle, he wearily surveyed the People.

"I am chief," he said.

"You are the chief!" came back the answering chorus.

"And Wesel is my mate."

This time there was hesitation on the part of the People. The new chief heard mutters of *"The feast . . . Big-Tusk is old and tough. . . . Are we to be cheated—?"*

"Wesel is my mate," he repeated. Then— "There is your feast—"

At the height of his power he was to remember No-Tail's stricken eyes, the dreadful feeling that by his words he had put himself outside all custom, all law.

"Above the Law," whispered Wesel.

He steeled his heart.

"There is your feast," he said again.

It was Big-Ears who, snatching a spear from one of the guards, with one swift blow dispatched the cringing No-Tail.

"I am your mate," said Wesel.

No-Fur took her in his arms. They rubbed noses. It wasn't the old chief's blood that made her shudder ever so slightly. It was the feel of the disgusting, hairless body against her own.

Already the People were carving and dividing the two corpses and wrangling over an even division of the succulent spoils.

There was one among the New People who, had her differences from the racial stock been only psychological, would have been slaughtered long since. Her three eyes notwithstanding, the imprudent exercise of her gift would have brought certain doom. But, like her sisters in more highly civilized communities, she was careful to tell those who came to her only that which they desired to hear. Even then, she exercised restraint. Experience had taught her that foreknowledge of coming events on the part of the participants often resulted in entirely unforseen results. This annoyed her. Better misfortune on the main stream of time than well-being on one of its branches.

To this Three-Eyes came No-Fur and Wesel.

Before the chief could ask his questions the seeress raised one emaciated hand.

"You are Shrick," she said. "So your mother called you. Shrick, the Giant Killer."

"But—"

"Wait. You came to ask me about your war against Tekka's people. Continue with your plans. You will win. You will then fight the Tribe of Sterret the Old. Again you will win. You will be Lord of the Outside. And then—"

"And then?"

"The Giants will know of the People. Many, but not all, of the People will die. You will fight the Giants. And the last of the Giants you will kill, but he will plunge the world into— Oh, if I could make you see! But we have no words."

"What—?"

"No, you cannot know. You will never know till the end is upon you. But this I can tell you. The People are doomed. Nothing you or they can do will save them. But you will kill those who will kill us, and that is good."

Again No-Fur pleaded for enlightenment. Abruptly, his pleas became threats. He was fast lashing himself into one of his dreaded fits of blind fury. But Three-Eyes was oblivious of his presence. Her two outer eyes were tight shut and that strange, dreaded inner one was staring at *something*, something outside the limits of the cave, outside the framework of things as they are.

Deep in his throat the chief growled.

He raised the fine spear that was the symbol of his office and buried it deep in the old female's body. The inner eye shut and the two outer ones flickered open for the last time.

"I am spared the End—" she said.

Outside the little cavern the faithful Big-Ears was waiting.

"Three-Eyes is dead," said his master. "Take what you want, and give the rest to the People—"

For a little there was silence.

Then— "I am glad you killed her," said Wesel. "She frightened me. I got inside her head—and I was lost!" Her voice had a hysterical edge. "I was lost! It was mad, mad. *What Was* was a *place*, a *PLACE*, and *Now*, and *What Will Be*. And I saw the End."

"What did you see?"

"A great light, far brighter than the Giants' lights Inside. And heat, stronger than the heat of the floors of the Far Outside caves and tunnels. And the People gasping and dying and the great light bursting into our world and eating them up—"

"But the Giants?"

"I did not see. I was lost. All I saw was the End."

No-Fur was silent. His active, nimble mind was scurrying down the vistas opened up by the dead prophetess. Giant Killer, *Giant*

Killer. Even in his most grandiose dreams he had never seen himself thus. And what was that name? Shrick? He repeated it to himself—Shrick the Giant Killer. It had a fine swing to it. As for the rest, the End, if he could kill the Giants then, surely, he could stave off the doom that they would mete out to the People. Shrick, the Giant Killer—

"It is a name that I like better than No-Fur," said Wesel.

"Shrick, Lord of the Outside. Shrick, Lord of the World. Shrick, the Giant Killer—"

"Yes," he said, slowly. "But the End—"

"You will go through that door when you come to it."

The campaign against Tekka's People had opened.

Along the caves and tunnels poured the nightmare hordes of Shrick. The dim light but half revealed their misshapen bodies, limbs where no limbs should be, heads like something from a half-forgotten bad dream.

All were armed. Every male and female carried a spear, and that in itself was a startling innovation in the wars of the People. For sharp metal, with which the weapons were tipped, was hard to come by. True, a staff of Barrier material could be sharpened, but it was a liability rather than an asset in a pitched battle. With the first thrust the point would break off, leaving the fighter with a weapon far inferior to his natural armory of teeth and claws.

Fire was new to the People—and it was Shrick who had brought them fire. For long periods he had spied upon the Giants in the Place-of-Little-Lights, had seen them bring from the pouches in their fur little glittering devices from which when a projection was pressed, issued a tiny, naked light. And he had seen them bring this light to the end of strange, white sticks that they seemed to be sucking. And the end of the stick would glow, and there would be a cloud like the cloud that issued from the mouths of the People in some of the Far Outside caverns where it was very cold. But this cloud was fragrant, and seemed to be strangely soothing.

And one of the Giants had lost his little hot light. He had put it to one to the white sticks, had made to return it to his pouch, and his hand had missed the opening. The Giant did not notice. He was doing something which took all his attention—and strain his eyes and his imagination as he might Shrick could not see what it was. There were strange glittering machines through which he peered intently at the glittering Little Lights beyond their transparent Barrier. Or were they on the inside of the Barrier?

Nobody had ever been able to decide. There was something alive that wasn't alive that clicked. There were sheets of fine, white skin on which the Giant was making black marks with a pointed stick.

But Shrick soon lost interest in these strange rites that he could never hope to comprehend. All his attention was focused on the glittering prize that was drifting ever so slowly toward him on the wings of some vagrant eddy.

When it seemed that it would surely fall right into the doorway where Shrick crouched waiting, it swerved. And, much as he dreaded the pseudolife that hummed and clicked, Shrick came out. The Giant, busy with his sorcery, did not notice him. One swift leap carried him to the drifting trophy. And then he had it, tight clasped to his breast. It was bigger than he had thought, it having appeared so tiny only in relationship to its previous owner. But it wasn't too big to go through the door in the Barrier. In triumph Shrick bore it to his cave.

Many were the experiments that he, eager but fumbling, performed. For a while both he and Wesel nursed painful burns. Many were the experiments that he intended to perform in the future. But he had stumbled on one use for the hot light that was to be of paramount importance in his wars.

Aping the Giants, he had stuck a long splinter of Barrier material in his mouth. The end he had brought to the little light. There was, as he had half expected, a cloud. But it was neither fragrant nor soothing. Blinded and coughing, Wesel snatched at the glowing stick, beat out its strange life with her hands.

Then— "It is hard," she said. "It is almost as hard as metal—"

And so Shrick became the first mass producer of armaments that his world had known. The first few sharpened staves he treated himself. The rest he left to Wesel and the faithful Big-Ears. He dare not trust his wonderful new power to any who were not among his intimates.

Shrick's other innovation was a direct violation of all the rules of war. He had pressed the females into the fighting line. Those who were old and infirm, together with the old and infirm males, brought up the rear with bundles of the mass-produced spears. The New People had been wondering for some little time why their chief had refused to let them slaughter those of their number who had outlived their usefulness. Now they knew.

The caves of the New People were deserted save for those few females with newborn.

And through the tunnels poured the hordes of Shrick.

There was little finesse in the campaign against Tekka's people. The outposts were slaughtered out of hand, but not before they had had time to warn the Tribe of the attack.

Tekka threw a body of picked spearmen into his van, confident that he, with better access to those parts of Inside where metal could be obtained, would be able to swamp the motley horde of the enemy with superior arms and numbers.

When Tekka saw, in the dim light, only a few betraying gleams of metal scattered among Shrick's massed spears, he laughed.

"This No-Fur is mad," he said. "And I shall kill him with this." He brandished his own weapon. "His mother gave it to me many, many feedings ago."

"Is Wesel—?"

"Perhaps, my son. You shall eat her heart, I promise you."

And then Shrick struck.

His screaming mob rushed along the wide tunnel. Confident the Tekkan spearmen waited, knowing that the enemy's weapons were good for only one thrust, and that almost certainly not lethal.

Tekka scowled as he estimated the numbers of the attackers. There couldn't be that many males among the New People. There couldn't— And then the wave struck.

In the twinkling of an eye the tunnel was tightly packed with struggling bodies. Here was no dignified, orderly series of single combats such as had always, in the past, graced the wars of the People. And with growing terror Tekka realized that the enemy spears were standing up to the strain of battle at least as well as his own few metal-tipped weapons.

Slowly, but with ever mounting momentum, the attackers pressed on, gaining impetus from the many bodies that now lay behind them. Gasping for air in the affluvium of sweat and newly shed blood Tekka and the last of his guards were pressed back and ever back.

When one of the New People was disarmed he fell to the rear of his own front line. As though by magic a fresh fighter would appear to replace him.

Then— "He's using females!" cried Trillo. "He's—"

But Tekka did not answer. He was fighting for his life with a four-armed monster. Every hand held a spear—and every spear was bright with blood. For long heartbeats he parried the other's thrusts, then his nerve broke. Screaming, he turned his back on the enemy. It was the last thing he did.

And so the remnant of the fighting strength of the Tribe of Tekka was at last penned up against one wall of their Place-of-Meeting. Surrounding them was a solid hemisphere of the New People. Snarl was answered by snarl. Trillo and his scant half dozen guards knew that there was no surrender. All they could do was to sell their lives as dearly as possible.

And so they waited for the inevitable, gathering the last reserves of their strength in this lull of the battle, gasping the last sweet mouthfuls of air that they would ever taste. From beyond the wall of their assailants they could hear the cries and screams as the females and children, who had hidden in their caves, were hunted out and slaughtered. They were not to know that the magnanimous Shrick was sparing most of the females. They, he hoped, would produce for him more New People.

And then Shrick came, elbowing his way to the forefront of his forces. His smooth, naked body was unmarked, save by the old scars of his battle with Big-Tusk. And with him was Wesel, not a hair of her sleek fur out of place. And Big-Ears—but he, obviously had been in the fight. With them came more fighters, fresh and eager.

"Finish them!" ordered Shrick.

"Wait!" Wesel's voice was imperative. "I want Trillo."

Him she pointed out to the picked fighters, who raised their spears—weapons curiously slender and light, too fragile for hand-to-hand combat. A faint hope stirred in the breasts of the last defenders.

"Now!"

Trillo and his guards braced themselves to meet the last rush. It never came. Instead, thrown with unerring aim, came those sharp, flimsy spears, pinning them horribly against the gray, spongy wall of the Place-of-Meeting.

Spared in this final slaughter, Trillo looked about him with wide, fear-crazed eyes. He started to scream, then launched himself at the laughing Wesel. But she slipped back through the packed masses of the New People. Blind to all else but that hateful figure, Trillo tried to follow. And the New People crowded about him, binding his arms and legs with their strong cords, snatching his spear from him before its blade drank blood.

Then again the captive saw she who had been his mate.

Shamelessly, she was caressing Shrick.

"My Hairless One," she said. "I was once mated to *this*. You shall have his fur to cover your smooth body." And then— "Big-Ears! You know what to do!"

Grinning, Big-Ears found the sharp blade of a spear that had become detached from its haft. Grinning, he went to work. Trillo started to whimper, then to scream. Shrick felt a little sick. "Stop!" he said. "He is not dead. You must—"

"What does it matter?" Wesel's eyes were avid, and her little, pink tongue came out to lick her thin lips. Big-Ears had hesitated in his work but, at her sign, continued.

"What does it matter?" she said again.

As had fared the Tribe of Tekka so fared the Tribe of Sterret, and a hand or more of smaller communities owing a loose allegiance to these two.

But it was in his war with Sterret that Shrick almost met disaster. To the cunning oldster had come survivors from the massacre of Tekka's army. Most of these had been slaughtered out of hand by the frontier guards, but one or two had succeeded in convincing their captors that they bore tidings of great importance.

Sterret heard them out.

He ordered that they be fed and treated as his own people, for he knew that he would need every ounce of fighting strength that he could muster.

Long and deeply he pondered upon their words, and then sent foray after foray of his young males to the Place-of-Life-That-is-Not-Life. Careless he was of detection by the Giants. They might or might not act against him—but he had long been convinced that, for all their size, they were comparatively stupid and harmless. Certainly, at this juncture, they were not such a menace as Shrick, already self-styled Lord of the Outside.

And so his store of sharp fragments of metal grew, while his armorers worked without cessation binding these to hafts of Barrier stuff. And he, too, could innovate. Some of the fragments were useless as spearheads, being blunt, rough, and irregular. But, bound like a spearhead to a shaft, they could deliver a crushing blow. Of this Sterret was sure after a few experiments on old and unwanted members of his Tribe.

Most important, perhaps, his mind, rich in experience but not without a certain youthful zest, busied itself with problems of strategy. In the main tunnel from what had been Tekka's country his females hacked and tore at the spongy wall, the material being packed tightly and solidly into another small tunnel that was but rarely used.

At last his scouts brought the word that Shrick's forces were on the move. Careless in the crushing weight of his military power, Shrick disdained anything but a direct frontal attack. Perhaps he should have been warned by the fact that all orifices admitting light from the Inside had been closed, that the main tunnel along which he was advancing was in total darkness.

This, however, hampered him but little. The body of picked spearmen opposing him fought in the conventional way, and these, leaving their dead and wounded, were forced slowly but surely back. Each side relied upon smell, and hearing, and a certain perception possessed by most, if not all, of the People. At such close quarters these were ample.

Shrick himself was not in the van—that honor was reserved for Big-Ears, his fighting general. Had the decision rested with him alone he would have been in the forefront of the battle—but Wesel averred that the leader was of far greater importance than a mere spear bearer, should be shielded from needless risk. Not altogether unwillingly, Shrick acquiesced.

Surrounded by his guard, with Wesel at his side, the leader followed the noise of the fighting. He was rather surprised at the reports back to him concerning the apparent numbers of the enemy, but assumed that this was a mere delaying action and that Sterret would make his last stand in the Place-of-Meeting. It never occurred to him in his arrogance that others could innovate.

Abruptly, Wesel clutched his arm.

"Shrick! Danger—from the side!"

"From the side? But—"

There was a shrill cry, and a huge section of the tunnel wall fell inward. The spongy stuff was in thin sheets, and drifted among the guard, hampering their every movement. Then, led by Sterret in person, the defenders came out. Like mountaineers they were roped together, for in this battle in the darkness their best hope lay in keeping in one, compact body. Separated, they would fall easy prey to the superior numbers of the hordes of Shrick.

With spear and mace they lay about them lustily. The first heartbeat of the engagement would have seen the end of Shrick, and it was only the uncured hide of Trilla, stiff and stinking, that saved his life. Even so, the blade of Sterret penetrated the crude armor, and, sorely wounded, Shrick reeled out of the battle.

Ahead, Big-Ears was no longer having things all his own way. Reinforcements had poured along the tunnel and he dare not return to the succor of his chief. And Sterret's maces were having their effect. Stabbing and slashing the People could understand—but a crushing blow was, to them, something infinitely horrible.

It was Wesel who saved the day. With her she had brought the little, hot light. It had been her intention to try its effect on such few prisoners as might be taken in this campaign—she was too shrewed to experiment on any of the New People, even those who had incurred the displeasure of herself or her mate.

Scarce knowing what she did she pressed the stud.

With dazzling suddenness the scene of carnage swam into full view. From all sides came cries of fear.

"Back!" cried Wesel. "Back! Clear a space!"

In two directions the New People retreated.

Blinking but dogged, Sterret's phalanx tried to follow, tried to turn what was a more or less orderly withdrawal into a rout. But the cords that had, at first, served them so well now proved their undoing. Some tried to pursue those making for the Place-of-Meeting, others those of the New People retiring to their own territory. Snarling viciously, blood streaming from a dozen minor wounds, Sterret at last cuffed and bullied his forces into a semblance of order. He attempted to lead a charge to where Wesel, the little, hot light still in her hand, was retreating among her personal, amazon guards.

But again the cunning—too cunning—ropes defeated his purpose. Not a few corpses were there to hamper fast movement, and almost none of his fighters had the intelligence to cut them free.

And the spear throwers of Shrick came to the fore, and, one by one, the people of Sterret were pinned by the slim deadly shafts to the tunnel walls. Not all were killed outright, a few unfortunates squirmed and whimpered, plucking at the spears with ineffectual hands.

Among these was Sterret.

Shrick came forward, spear in hand, to administer the *coup de grâce*. The old chief stared wildly, then— "Weena's hairless one!" he cried.

Ironically it was his own spear—the weapon that, in turn, had belonged to Weena and to Tekka—that slit his throat.

Now that he was Lord of the Outside Shrick had time in which to think and to dream. More and more his mind harked back to Three-Eyes and her prophesy. It never occurred to him to doubt

that he was to be the Giant Killer—although the vision of the
End he dismissed from his mind as the vaporings of a half-crazed
old female.

And so he sent his spies to the Inside to watch the Giants in their
mysterious comings and goings, tried hard to find some pattern for
their incomprehensible behavior. He himself often accompanied
these spies—and it was with avid greed that he saw the vast wealth of
beautiful, shining things to which the Giants were heirs. More than
anything he desired another little hot light, for his own had ceased
to function, and all the clumsy, ignorant tinkerings of himself and
Wesel could not produce more than a feeble, almost heatless spark
from its baffling intricacies.

It seemed, too, that the Giants were now aware of the swarming, fecund life surrounding them. Certain it was that their
snares increased in number and ingenuity. And the food-that-kills
appeared in new and terrifying guise. Not only did those who had
eaten of it die, but their mates and—indeed all who had come into
contact with them.

It smacked of sorcery, but Shrick had learned to associate cause
and effect. He made the afflicted ones carry those already dead into
a small tunnel. One or two of them rebelled—but the spear throwers
surrounded them, their slim, deadly weapons at the ready. And
those who attempted to break through the cordon of guards were
run through repeatedly before ever they laid their defiling hands on
any of the unafflicted People.

Big-Ears was among the sufferers. He made no attempt to quarrel
with his fate. Before he entered the yawning tunnel that was to be
his tomb he turned and looked at his chief. Shrick made to call him
to his side—even though he knew that his friends's life could not be
saved, and that by associating with him he would almost certainly
lose his own.

But Wesel was at his side.

She motioned to the spear throwers, and a full two hands of darts
transfixed the ailing Big-Ears.

"It was kinder this way," she lied.

But, somehow, the last look that his most loyal supporter
had given him reminded him of No-Tail. With a heavy heart he
ordered his people to seal the tunnel. Great strips of the spongy
stuff were brought and stuffed into the entrance. The cries of those
inside grew fainter and ever fainter. Then there was silence. Shrick
ordered guards posted at all points where, conceivably, the doomed
prisoners might break out. He returned to his own cave. Wesel,

when one without her gift would have intruded, let him go in his loneliness. Soon he would want her again.

It had long been Wesel's belief that, given the opportunity, she could get inside the minds of the Giants just as she could those of the People. And if she could—who knew what prizes might be hers? Shrick, still inaccessible and grieving for his friend, she missed more than she cared to admit. The last of the prisoners from the last campaign had been killed, ingeniously, many feedings ago. Though she had no way of measuring time, it hung heavily on her hands.

And so, accompanied by two of her personal attendants, she roamed those corridors and tunnels running just inside the Barrier. Through spyhole after spyhole she peered, gazing in wonderment that long use could not stale at the rich and varied life of the Inside.

At last she found that for which she was searching—a Giant, alone and sleeping. Experience among the People had taught her that from a sleeping mind she could read the most secret thoughts.

For a heartbeat she hesitated. Then— "Four-Arms, Little-Head, wait here for me. Wait and watch."

Little-Head grunted an affirmative, but Four-Arms was dubious. "Lady Wesel," she said, "what if the Giant should wake? What—?"

"What if you should return to the Lord of the Outside without me? Then he would, without doubt, have your hides. The one he is wearing now is old, and the fur is coming out. But do as I say."

There was a door in the Barrier here, a door but rarely used. This was opened, and Wesel slipped through. With the ease that all the People were acquiring with their more frequent ventures to the Inside she floated up to the sleeping Giant. Bonds held him in a sort of framework, and Wesel wondered if, for some offense, he had been made prisoner by his own kind. She would soon know.

And then a glittering object caught her eye. It was one of the little hot lights, its polished metal case seeming to Wesel's covetous eyes the most beautiful thing in the world. Swiftly she made her decision. She could take the shining prize now, deliver it to her two attendants, and then return to carry out her original intentions.

In her eagerness she did not see that it was suspended in the middle of an interlacing of slender metal bars—or she did not care. And as her hands grabbed the bait something not far away began a shrill, not unmusical metallic beating. The Giant stirred and awoke. What Wesel had taken for bonds fell away from his body. In blind panic she turned to flee back to her own world. But, somehow, more of the metal bars had fallen into place and she was a prisoner.

She started to scream.

Surprisingly, Four-Arms and Little-Head came to her aid. It would be nice to be able to place on record that they were actuated by devotion to their mistress—but Four-Arms knew that her life was forfeit. And she had seen those who displeased either Shrick or Wesel flayed alive. Little-Head blindly followed the other's leadership. Hers not to reason why—

Slashing with their spears they assailed the Giant. He laughed—or so Wesel interpreted the deep, rumbling sound that came from his throat. Four-Arms he seized first. With one hand he grasped her body, with the other her head. He twisted. And that was the end of Four-Arms.

Anybody else but Little-Head would have turned and fled. But her dim mind refused to register that which she had seen. Perhaps a full feeding or so after the event the horror of it all would have stunned her with its impact—perhaps not. Be that as it may, she continued her attack. Blindly, instinctively, she went for the Giant's throat. Wesel sensed that he was badly frightened. But after a short struggle one of his hands caught the frenzied, squealing Little-Head. Violently, he flung her from him. She heard the thud as her attendant's body struck something hard and unyielding. And the impressions that her mind had been receiving from that of the other abruptly ceased.

Even in her panic fear she noticed that the Giant had not come out of the unequal combat entirely unscathed. One of his hands had been scratched, and was bleeding freely. And there were deep scratches, on the hideous, repulsively naked face. The Giants, then, were vulnerable. There might have been some grain of truth after all in Three-Eye's insane babbling.

And then Wesel forgot her unavailing struggle against the bars of her cage. With sick horror she watched what the Giant was doing. He had taken the limp body of Four-Arms, had secured it to a flat surface. From somewhere he had produced an array of glittering instruments. One of these he took, and drew it down the body from throat to crotch. On either side of the keen blade the skin fell away, leaving the flesh exposed.

And the worst part of it was that it was not being done in hate or anger, neither was the unfortunate Four-Arms being divided up that she might be eaten. There was an impersonal quality about the whole business that sickened Wesel—for, by this time, she had gained a certain limited access to the mind of the other.

The Giant paused in his work. Another of his kind had come, and for many heartbeats the two talked together. They examined the mutilated carcass of Four-Arms, the crushed body of Little-Head. Together, they peered into the cage where Wesel snarled impotently.

But, in spite of her hysterical fear, part of her mind was deadly cold, was receiving and storing impressions that threw the uninhibited animal part of her into still greater panic. While the Giants talked the impressions were clear—and while their great, ungainly heads hung over her cage, scant handbreadths away, they were almost overpowering in their strength. She knew who she and the People were, what their world was. She had not the ability to put it into words—but she *knew*. And she saw the doom that the Giants were preparing for the People.

With a few parting words to his fellow the second Giant left. The first one resumed his work of dismembering Four-Arms. At last he was finished. What was left of the body was put into transparent containers.

The Giant picked up Little-Head. For many heartbeats he examined her, turning her over and over in his great hands. Wesel thought that he would bind the body to the flat surface, do with it as he had done with that of Four-Arms. But, at last he put the body to one side. Over his hands he pulled something that looked like a thick, additional skin. Suddenly, the metal bars at one end of the cage fell away, and one of those enormous hands came groping for Wesel.

After the death of Big-Ears, Shrick slept a little. It was the only way in which he could be rid of the sense of loss, of the feeling that he had betrayed his most loyal follower. His dreams were troubled, haunted by ghosts from his past. Big-Ears was in them, and Big-Tusk, and a stranger female with whom he felt a sense of oneness, whom he knew to be Weena, his mother.

And then all these phantasms were gone, leaving only the image of Wesel. It wasn't the Wesel he had always known, cool, self-assured, ambitious. This was a terrified Wesel— Wesel descending into a black abyss of pain and torture even worse than that which she had, so often, meted out to others. And she wanted him.

Shrick awoke, frightened by his dreams. But he knew that ghosts had never hurt anybody, could not hurt him, Lord of the Outside. He shook himself, whimpering a little, and then tried to compose himself for further sleep.

But the image of Wesel persisted. At last Shrick abandoned his attempts to seek oblivion and, rubbing his eyes, emerged from his cave.

In the dim, half-light of the Place-of-Meeting little knots of the People hung about, talking in low voices. Shrick called to the guards. There was a sullen silence. He called again. At last one answered.

"Where is Wesel?"

"I do not know . . . lord." The last word came out grudgingly.

Then one of the others volunteered the information that she had been seen, in company with Four-Arms and Little-Head, proceeding along the tunnels that led to that part of the Outside in the way of the Place-of-Green-Growing-Things.

Shrick hesitated.

He rarely ventured abroad without his personal guards, but then, Big-Ears was always one of them. And Big-Ears was gone.

He looked around him, decided that he could trust none of those at present in the Place-of-Meeting. The People had been shocked and horrified by his necessary actions in the case of those who had eaten of the food-that-kills and regarded him, he knew, as a monster even worse than the Giants. Their memories were short—but until they forgot he would have to walk with caution.

"Wesel is my mate. I will go alone," he said.

At his words he sensed a change of mood, was tempted to demand an escort. But the instinct that—as much as any mental superiority—maintained him in authority warned him against throwing away his advantage.

"I go alone," he said.

One Short-Tail, bolder than his fellows, spoke up.

"And if you do not return, Lord of the Outside? Who is to be—?"

"I shall return," said Shrick firmly, his voice displaying a confidence he did not feel.

In the more populous regions the distinctive scent of Wesel was overlaid by that of many others. In tunnels but rarely frequented it was strong and compelling—but now he had no need to use his olfactory powers. For the terrified little voice in his brain—from outside his brain—was saying *hurry, HURRY*—and some power beyond his ken was guiding him unerringly to where his mate was in such desperate need of him.

From the door in the Barrier through which Wesel had entered the Inside—it had been left open—streamed a shaft of light. And now Shrick's natural caution reasserted itself. The voice inside his brain was no less urgent, but the instinct of self-preservation was strong. Almost timorously, he peered through the doorway.

He smelled death. At first he feared that he was too late, then identified the personal odors of Four-Arms and Little-Head. That of Wesel was there too—intermingled with the acrid scent of terror and agony. But she was still alive.

Caution forgotten, he launched himself from the doorway with all the power of his leg muscles. And he found Wesel, stretched supine on a flat surface that was slippery with blood. Most of it was Four-Arms', but some of it was hers.

"Shrick!" she screamed. "The Giant!"

He looked away from his mate and saw hanging over him, pale and enormous, the face of the Giant. He screamed, but there was more of fury than terror in the sound. He saw, not far from where he clung to Wesel, a huge blade of shining metal. He could see that its edge was keen. The handle had been fashioned for a hand far larger than his, nevertheless he was just able to grasp it. It seemed to be secured. Feet braced against Wesel's body for purchase, he tugged desperately.

Just as the Giant's hand, fingers outstretched to seize him, came down the blade pulled free. As Shrick's legs suddenly and involuntarily straightened he was propelled away from Wesel. The Giant grabbed at the flying form, and howled in agony as Shrick swept the blade around and lopped off a finger.

He heard Wesel's voice: "You are the Giant Killer!"

Now he was level with the Giant's head. He swerved, and with his feet caught a fold of the artificial skin covering the huge body. And he hung there, swinging his weapon with both hands, cutting and slashing. Great hands swung wildly and he was bruised and buffeted. But not once did they succeed in finding a grip. Then there was a great and horrid spurting of blood and a wild threshing of mighty limbs. This ceased, but it was only the voice of Wesel that called him from the fury of his slaughter lust.

So he found her again, still stretched out for sacrifice to the Giants' dark gods, still bound to that surface that was wet with her blood and that of her attendant. But she smiled up at him, and in her eyes was respect that bordered on awe.

"Are you hurt?" he demanded, a keen edge of anxiety to his voice.

"Only a little. But Four-Arms was cut in pieces . . . I should have been had you not come. And," her voice was a hymn of praise, "you killed the Giant!"

"It was foretold. Besides," for once he was honest, "it could not have been done without the Giant's weapon."

With its edge he was cutting Wesel's bonds. Slowly she floated away from the place of sacrifice. Then: "I can't move my legs!" Her voice was terror-stricken. "I can't move!"

Shrick guessed what was wrong. He knew a little of anatomy—his knowledge was that of the warrior who may be obliged to immobilize his enemy prior to his slaughter—and he could see that the Giant's keen blade had wrought this damage. Fury boiled up in him against these cruel, monstrous beings. And there was more than fury. There was the feeling, rare among his people, of overwhelming pity for his crippled mate.

"The blade . . . it is very sharp . . . I shall feel nothing."

But Shrick could not bring himself to do it.

Now they were floating up against the huge bulk of the dead Giant. With one hand he grasped Wesel's shoulder—the other still clutched his fine, new weapon and kicked off against the gigantic carcass. Then he was pushing Wesel through the doorway in the Barrier, and sensed her relief as she found herself once more in familiar territory. He followed her, then carefully shut and barred the door.

For a few heartbeats Wesel busied herself smoothing her bedraggled fur. He couldn't help noticing that she dare not let her hands stray to the lower part of her body where were the wounds, small but deadly, that had robbed her of the power of her limbs. Dimly, he felt that something might be done for one so injured, but knew that it was beyond his powers. And fury—not helpless now—against the Giants returned again, threatening to choke him with its intensity.

"Shrick!" Wesel's voice was grave. "We must return at once to the People. We must warn the People. The Giants are making a sorcery to bring the End."

"The great, hot light?"

"No. But wait! First I must tell you of what I learned. Otherwise, you would not believe. I have learned what we are, what the world is. And it is strange and wonderful beyond all our beliefs.

"What is Outside?" She did not wait for his answer, read it in his mind before his lips could frame the words. "The world is but a bubble of emptiness in the midst of a vast piece of metal, greater than the mind can imagine. But it is not so! Outside the metal that lies outside the Outside there is nothing. *Nothing!* There is no air."

"But there must be air, at least."

"No, I tell you. There is *nothing.*

"And the world—how can I find words? Their name for the world is—*ship*, and it seems to mean something big going from one place to another place. And all of us—Giants and People—are inside the ship. The Giants made the ship."

"Then it is not alive?"

"I cannot say. *They* seem to think that it is a female. It must have some kind of life that is not life. And it is going from one world to another world."

"And these other worlds?"

"I caught glimpses of them. They are dreadful, dreadful. *We* find the open spaces of the Inside frightening—but these other worlds are *all* open space except for one side."

"But what are we?" In spite of himself, Shrick at least half believed Wesel's fantastic story. Perhaps she possessed, to some slight degree, the power of projecting her own thoughts into the mind of another with whom she was intimate. "What are we?"

She was silent for the space of many heartbeats. Then: *"Their* name for us is—*mutants*. The picture was . . . not clear at all. It means that we—the People—have changed. And yet their picture of the People before the change was like the Different Ones before we slew them all.

"Long and long ago—many hands of feedings—the first People, our parents' parents' parents, came into the world. They came from that greater world—the world of dreadful, open spaces. They came with the food in the great Cave-of-Food—and that is being carried to another world.

"Now, in the horrid, empty space outside the Outside there is—light that is not light. And this light—changes persons. No, not the grown person or the child, but the child before the birth. Like the dead and gone chiefs of the People, the Giants fear change in themselves. So they have kept the light that is not light from the Inside.

"And this is how. Between the Barrier and the Far Outside they filled the space with the stuff in which we have made our caves and tunnels. The first People left the great Cave-of-Food, they tunneled through the Barrier and into the stuff Outside. It was their nature. And some of them mated in the Far Outside caves. Their children were—*Different.*"

"That is true," said Shrick slowly. "It has always been thought that children born in the Far Outside were never like their parents, and that those born close to the Barrier were—"

"Yes.

"Now, the Giants always knew that the People were here, but they did not fear them. They did not know our numbers, and they regarded us as beings much lower than themselves. They were content to deep us down with their traps and the food-that-kills. Somehow, they found that we had changed. Like the dead chiefs they feared us then—and like the dead chiefs they will try to kill us all before we conquer them."

"And the End?"

"Yes, the End." She was silent again, her big eyes looking past Shrick at something infinitely terrible. "Yes," she said again, "the End. *They* will make it, and *They* will escape it. *They* will put on artificial skins that will cover *Their* whole bodies, even *Their* heads, and *They* will open huge doors in the . . . skin of the ship, and all the air will rush out into the terrible empty space outside the Outside. And all the the People will die."

"I must go," said Shrick. "I must kill the Giants before this comes to pass."

"No!" There was one hand of Giants—now that you have killed Fat-Belly there are four of them left. And they know, now, that they can be killed. They will be watching for you.

"Do you remember when we buried the People with the sickness? That is what we must do to all the People. And then when the Giants fill the world with air again from their store we can come out."

Shrick was silent awhile. He had to admit that she was right. One unsuspecting Giant had fallen to his blade—but four of them, aroused, angry and watchful, he could not handle. In any case there was no way of knowing when the Giants would let the air from the world. The People must be warned—and fast.

Together, in the Place-of-Meeting, Shrick and Wesel faced the People. They had told their stories, only to be met with blank incredulity. True, there were some who, seeing the fine, shining blade that Shrick had brought from the Inside, were inclined to believe. But they were shouted down by the majority. It was when he tried to get them to immure themselves against the End that he met with serious opposition. The fact that he had so treated those suffering from the sickness still bulked big in the mob memory.

It was Short-Tail who precipitated the crisis.

"He wants the world to himself!" he shouted. "He has killed Big-Tusk and No-Tail, he has killed all the Different Ones, and Big-Ears he slew because he would have been chief. He and his ugly, barren mate want the world to themselves!"

Shrick tried to argue, but Big-Ears' following shouted him down. He squealed with rage and, raising his blade with both hands, rushed upon the rebel. Short-Tail scurried back out of reach. Shrick found himself alone in a suddenly cleared space. From somewhere a long way off he heard Wesel screaming his name. Dazedly, he shook his head, and then the red mist cleared from in front of his eyes.

All around him were the spear throwers, their slender weapons poised. He had trained them himself, had brought their specialized are of war into being. And now—

"Shrick!" Wesel was saying, "don't fight! They will kill you, and I shall be alone. I shall have the world to myself. Let them do as they will with us, and *we* shall live through the End."

At her words a tittering laugh rippled through the mob.

"*They* will live through the End! They will die as Big-Ears and his friends died!"

"I want your blade," said Short-Tail

"Give it to him," cried Wesel. "You will get it back after the End!"

Shrick hesitated. The other made a sign. One of the throwing spears buried itself in the fleshy part of his arm. Had it not been for Wesel's voice, pleading, insistent, he would have charged his tormenters and met his end in less than a single heartbeat. Reluctantly, he released his hold upon the weapon. Slowly—as though loath to leave its true owner—it floated away from him. And then the People were all around him almost suffocating him with pressure of their bodies.

The cave into which Shrick and Wesel were forced was their own dwelling place. They were in pitiable state when the mob retreated to the entrance—Wesel's wounds had reopened and Shrick's arm was bleeding freely. Somebody had wrenched out the spear—but the head had broken off.

Outside, Short-Tail was laying about him with the keen blade he had taken from his chief. Under its strokes great masses of the spongy stuff of the Outside were coming free, and many willing hands were stuffing this tight into the cave entrance.

"We will let you out after the End!" called somebody. There was a hoot of derision. Then: "I wonder which will eat the other first?"

"Never mind," said Wesel softly. "We shall laugh last."

"Perhaps. But . . . the People. *My* People. And you are barren. The Giants have won—"

Wesel was silent. Then he heard her voice again. She was whimpering to herself in the darkness. Shrick could guess her thoughts. All their grandiose dreams of world dominion had come to this—a tiny cramped space in which there was barely room for either of them to stir a finger.

And now they could no longer hear the voices of the People outside their prison. Shrick wondered if the Giants had already struck, then reassured himself with the memory of how the voices of those suffering from the sickness had grown fainter and fainter and then, at the finish, ceased altogether. And he wondered how he and Wesel would know when the End had come, and how they would know when it was safe to dig themselves out. It would be a long, slow task with only their teeth and claws with which to work.

But he had a tool.

The fingers of the hand of his uninjured arm went to the spearhead still buried in the other. He knew that by far the best way of extracting it would be one, quick pull—but he couldn't bring himself to do it. Slowly, painfully, he worked away at the sharp fragment of metal.

"Let me do it for you."

"No." His voice was rough. "Besides, there is no haste."

Slowly, patiently, he worried at the wound. He was groaning a little, although he was not conscious of doing so. And then, suddenly, Wesel screamed. The sound was so unexpected, so dreadful in that confined space, that Shrick started violently. His hand jerked away from his upper arm, bringing with it the spearhead.

His first thought was that Wesel, telepath as she was, had chosen this way to help him. But he felt no gratitude, only a dull resentment.

"What did you do that for?" he demanded angrily.

She didn't answer his question. She was oblivious of his presence.

"The People . . ." she whispered. "The People . . . I can feel their thoughts . . . I can feel what they are feeling. And they are gasping for air . . . they are gasping and dying . . . and the cave of Long-Fur the spearmaker . . . but they are dying, and the blood is coming out of their mouths and noses and ears . . . I can't bear it . . . I can't—"

And then a terrifying thing happened. The sides of the cave pressed in upon them. Throughout the world, throughout the ship, the air cells in the spongy insulation were expanding as

the air pressure dropped to zero. It was this alone that saved
Shrick and Wesel, although they never knew it. The rough plug
sealing their cave that, otherwise, would have blown out swelled
to meet the expanding walls of the entrance, making a near perfect
air-tight joint.

But the prisoners were in no state to appreciate this, even had
they been in possession of the necessary knowledge. Panic seized
them both. Claustophobia was unknown among the People—but
walls that closed upon them were outside their experience.

Perhaps Wesel was the more level-headed of the pair. It was she
who tried to restrain her mate as he clawed and bit savagely, madly,
at the distended, bulging walls. He no longer knew what lay outside
the cave, had he known it would have made no difference. His one
desire was to get out.

At first he made little headway, then he bethought himself of
the little blade still grasped in his hand. With it he attacked the
pulpy mass. The walls of the cells were stretched thin, almost to
bursting, and under his onslaught they put up no more resistance
than so many soap bubbles. A space was cleared, and Shrick was
able to work with even greater vigor.

"Stop! Stop, I tell you! There is only the choking death outside
the cave. And you will kill us both!"

But Shrick paid no heed, went on stabbing and hacking. It
was only slowly, now, that he was able to enlarge upon the original
impression he had made. As the swollen surfaces burst and withered
beneath his blade, so they bulged and bellied in fresh places.

"Stop!" cried Wesel again.

With her arms, her useless legs trailing behind her, she pulled
herself toward her mate. And she grappled with him, desperation
lending her strenght. So for many heartbeats they fought—silent,
savage, forgetful of all that each owed to the other. And yet,
perhaps, Wesel never quite forgot. For all her blind, frantic will to
survive her telepathic powers were at no time entirely in abeyance.
In spite of herself she, as always, shared the other's mind. And this
psychological factor gave her an advantage that offset the paralysis
of the lower half of her body—and at the same time inhibited her
from pressing that advantage home to its logical conclusion.

But it did not save her when her fingers, inadvertently, dug
into the wound in Shrick's arm. His ear-splitting scream was
compounded of pain and fury, and he drew upon reserves of
strength that the other never even guessed that he possessed. And
the hand gripping the blade came round with irresistible force.

For Wesel there was a heartbeat of pain, of sorrow for herself and Shrick, of blind anger against the Giants who, indirectly, had brought this thing to pass.

And then the beating of her heart was stilled forever.

With the death of Wesel Shrick's frenzy left him.

There, in the darkness, he ran his sensitive fingers over the lifeless form, hopelessly hoping for the faintest sign of life. He called her name, he shook her roughly. But at last the knowledge that she was dead crept into his brain—and stayed there. In his short life he had known many times this sense of loss, but never with such poignancy.

And worst of all was the knowledge that *he* had killed her.

He tried to shift the burden of blame. He told himself that she would have died, in any case, of the wounds received at the hands of the Giants. He tried to convince himself that, wounds or no wounds, the Giants were directly responsible for her death. And he knew that he was Wesel's murderer, just as he knew that all that remained for him in life was to bring the slayers of his people to a reckoning.

This made him cautious.

For many heartbeats he lay there in the thick darkness, not daring to renew his assault on the walls of his prison. He told himself that, somehow, he would know when the Giants let the air back into the world. How he would know he could not say, but the conviction persisted.

And when at last, with returning pressure, the insulation resumed its normal consistency, Shrick took this as a sign that it was safe for him to get out. He started to hack at the spongy material, then stopped. He went back to the body of Wesel. Just once he whispered her name, and ran his hands over the stiff, silent form in a last caress.

He did not return.

And when, at last, the dim light of the Place-of-Meeting broke through she was buried deep in the debris that he had thrown behind him as he worked.

The air tasted good after the many times breathed atmosphere of the cave. For a few heartbeats Shrick was dizzy with the abrupt increase of pressure, for much of the air in his prison had escaped before the plug expanded to seal the entrance. It is probable that had it not been for the air liberated from the burst cells of the insulation he would long since have asphyxiated.

But this he was not to know—and if he had known it would not have worried him overmuch. He was alive, and Wesel and all the

People were dead. When the mist cleared from in front of his eyes he could see them, their bodies twisted in the tortuous attitudes of their last agony, mute evidence of the awful powers of the Giants.

And now that he saw them he did not feel the overwhelming sorrow that he knew he should have done. He felt instead a kind of anger. By their refusal to heed his warning they had robbed him of his kingdom. None now could dispute his mastery of the Outside—but with no subjects, willing or unwilling, the vast territory under his sway was worthless.

With Wesel alive it would have been different.

What was it that she had said—? . . . *and the cave of Long-Fur the spear-maker* . . .

He could hear her voice as she said it . . . *and the cave of Long-Fur the spear-maker.*

Perhaps— But there was only one way to make sure.

He found the cave, saw that its entrance had been walled up. He felt a wild upsurge of hope. Frantically, with tooth and claw, he tore at the insulation. The fine blade that he had won from the Inside gleamed dully not a dozen handbreadths from where he was working, but such was his blind, unreasoning haste that he ignored the tool that would have made his task immeasurably shorter. At last the entrance was cleared. A feeble cry greeted the influx of air and light. For a while Shrick could not see who was within, and then could have screamed in his disappointment.

For here were no tough fighting males, no sturdy, fertile females, but two hands or so of weakly squirming infants. Their mothers must have realized, barely in time, that he and Wesel had been right, that there was only one way to ward off the choking death. Themselves they had not been able to save.

But they will grow up, Shrick told himself. *It won't be long before they are able to carry a spear for the Lord of the Outside, before the females are able to bear his children.*

Conquering his repugnance, he dragged them out. There was a hand of female infants, all living, and a hand of males. Three of these were dead. But here, he knew, was the nucleus of the army with which he would re-establish his rule over the world, Inside as well as Outside.

But first, they had to be fed.

He saw, now, his fine blade, and seizing it he began to cut up the three lifeless male children. The scent of their blood made him realize that he was hungry. But it was not until the children, now quieted, were all munching happily that he cut a portion for himself.

When he had finished it he felt much better.

It was some time before Shrick resumed his visits to the Inside. He had the pitiful remnant of this people to nurse to maturity and, besides, there was no need to make raids upon the Giants' stocks of food. They themselves had provided him with sustenance beyond his powers of reckoning. He knew, too, that it would be unwise to let his enemies know that there had been any survivors from the cataclysm that they had launched. The fact that he had survived the choking death did not mean that it was the only weapon that the Giants had at their disposal.

But as time went on he felt an intense longing to watch once more the strange life beyond the Barrier. Now that he had killed a Giant he felt a strange sense of kinship with the monstrous beings. He thought of the Thin-One, Loud-Voice, Bare-Head and the Little Giant almost as old friends. At times he even caught himself regretting that he must kill them all. But he knew that in this lay the only hope for the survival of himself and his people.

And then, at last, he was satisfied that he could leave the children to fend for themselves. Even should he fail to return from the Inside they would manage. No-Toes, the eldest of the female children, had already proved to be capable nurse.

And so he roamed once more the maze of caves and tunnels just outside the Barrier. Through his doorways and peepholes he spied upon the bright, fascinating life of the Inner World. From the Cave-of-Thunders—though how it had come by its name none of the People has ever known—to the Place-of-Little-Lights he ranged. Many feedings passed, but he was not obliged to return to his own food store. For the corpses of the People were everywhere. True, they were beginning to stink a little, but like all his race Shrick was never a fastidious eater.

And he watched the Giants going about the strange, ordered routine of their lives. Often he was tempted to show himself, to shout defiance. But this action had to remain in the realm of wish-fulfillment dreams—he knew full well that it would bring sure and speedy calamity.

And then, at last, came the opportunity for which he had been waiting. He had been in the Place-of-Little-Lights, watching the Little Giant going about his mysterious, absorbing business. He had wished that he could understand its purport, that he could ask the Little Giant in his own tongue what it was that he was doing. For, since the death of Wesel, there had been none with whom a

communion of mind was possible. He sighed, so loudly that the
Giant must have heard.

He started uneasily and looked up from his work. Hastily Shrick
withdrew into his tunnel. For many heartbeats he remained there,
occasionally peeping out. But the other was still alert, must have
known in some way that he was not alone. And so, eventually,
Shrick had retired rather than risk incurring the potent wrath of
the Giants once more.

His random retreat brought him to a doorway but rarely used.
On the other side of it was a huge cavern in which there was nothing
of real interest or value. In it, as a rule, at least one of the Giants
would be sleeping, and others would be engaged in one of their
incomprehensible pastimes.

This time there was no deep rumble of conversation, no movement whatsoever. Shrick's keen ears could distinguish the breathing
of three different sleepers. The Thin-One was there, his respiration,
like himself, had a meager quality. Loud-Voice was loud even in
sleep. And Bare-Head, the chief of the Giants, breathed with a
quiet authority.

And the Little Giant who, alone of all his people, was alert and
awake was in the Place-of-Little-Lights.

Shrick knew that it was now or never. Any attempt to deal with
the Giants singly must surely bring the great, hot light foretold by
Three-Eyes. Now, with any luck at all, he could deal with the three
sleepers and then lay in wait for the Little Giant. Unsuspecting,
unprepared, he could be dealt with as easily as had Fat-Belly.

And yet—he did not want to do it.

It wasn't fear; it was that indefinable sense of kinship, the knowledge that, in spite of gross physical disparities, the Giants and the
People were as one. For the history of Man, although Shrick was not
to know this, is but the history of the fire-making, tool-using animal.

Then he forced himself to remember Wesel, and Big-Ears,
and the mass slaughter of almost all his race. He remembered
Three-Eyes' words—*but this I can tell you, the People are doomed.
Nothing you or they can do will save them. But you will kill those who
will kill us, and that is good.*

But you will kill those who will like us—

But if I kill all the Giants before they kill us, he thought, then
the world, all the world, will belong to the People . . .

And he still hung back.

It was not until the Thin-One, who must have been in the
throes of a bad dream, murmured and stirred in his sleep that

Shrick came out of his doorway. The keen blade with which he
had slain Fat-Belly was grasped in both his hands. He launched
himself toward the uneasy sleeper. His weapon sliced down once
only—how often had he rehearsed this in his imagination!—and for
the Thin-One the dream was over.

The smell of fresh blood, as always, excited him. It took him
all of his will power to restrain himself from hacking and slashing
at the dead Giant. But he promised himself that this would come
later. And he jumped from the body of the Thin-One to where
Loud-Voice was snoring noisily.

The abrupt cessation of that all too familiar sound must have
awakened Bare-Head. Shrick saw him shift and stir, saw his hands
go out to loosen the bonds that held him to his sleeping place. And
when the Giant Killer, his feet scrabbling for a hold, landed on his
chest he was ready. And he was shouting in a great Voice, so that
Shrick knew that it was only a matter of heartbeats before the Little
Giant came to his assistance.

Fat-Belly had been taken off guard, the Thin-One and Loud-
Voice had been killed in their sleep. But here was no easy victory
for the Giant Killer.

For a time it looked as though the chief of the Giants would
win. After a little he ceased his shouting and fought with grim,
silent desperation. Once one of his great hands caught Shrick in
a bone-crushing grip, and it seemed as though the battle was over.
Shrick could feel the blood pounding in his head, his eyeballs almost
popping out of their sockets. It took him every ounce of resolution
he possessed to keep from dropping his blade and scratching
frenziedly at the other's wrist with ineffectual hands.

Something gave—it was his ribs—and in the fleeting instant
of relaxed pressure he was able to twist, to turn and slash at the
monstrous, hairy wrist. The warm blood spurted and the Giant cried
aloud. Again and again Shrick plied his blade, until it became plain
that the Giant would not be able to use that hand again.

He was single-handed now against an opponent as yet—insofar
as his limbs were concerned—uncrippled. True, every movement
of the upper part of his body brought spears of pain lancing
through Shrick's chest. But he could move, and smite—and
slay.

For Bare-Head weakened as the blood flowed from his wounds.
No longer was he able to ward off the attacks on his face and
neck. Yet he fought, as his race had always fought, to his dying
breath. His enemy would have given no quarter—this much was

obvious—but he could have sought refuge with the Little Giant in the Place-of-Little-Lights.

Toward the end he started shouting again.

And as he died, the Little Giant came into the cave.

It was sheer, blind luck that saved the Giant Killer from speedy death at the intruder's hands. Had the Little Giant known of the pitifully small forces arrayed against him it would have gone hard with Shrick. But No-Toes, left with her charges, had grown bored with the Place-of-Meeting. She had heard Shrick talk of the wonders of the Inside; and now, she thought, was her chance to see them for herself.

Followed by her charges she wandered aimlessly along the tunnels just outside the Barrier. She did not know the location of the doors to the Inside, and the view through the occasional peepholes was very circumscribed.

Then she came upon the doorway which Shrick had left open when he made his attack on the sleeping Giants. Bright light streamed through the aperture—light brighter than any No-Toes had seen before in her short life. Like a beacon it lured her on.

She did not hesitate when she came to the opening. Unlike her parents, she had not been brought up to regard the Giants with superstitious awe. Shrick was the only adult she could remember having known—and he, although he had talked of the Giants, had boasted of having slain one in single combat. He had said, also, that he would, at some time or other, kill all the Giants.

In spite of her lack of age and experience, No-Toes was no fool. Womanlike, already she had evaluated Shrick. Much of his talk she discounted as idle bragging, but she had never seen any reason to disbelieve his stories of the deaths of Big-Tusk, Sterret, Tekka, Fat-Belly—and all the myriads of the People who had perished with them.

So it was that—foolhardy in her ignorance—she sailed through the doorway. Behind her came the other children, squealing in their excitement. Even if the Little Giant had not at first seen them he could not have failed to hear the shrill tumult of their irruption.

There was only one interpretation that he could put upon the evidence of his eyes. The plan to suffocate the People had failed. They had sallied out from their caves and tunnels to the massacre of his fellow Giants—and now fresh reinforcements were arriving to deal with him.

He turned and fled.

Shrick rallied his strength, made a flying leap from the monstrous carcass of Bare-Head. But in mid flight a hard, polished surface interposed itself between him and the fleeing Giant. Stunned, he hung against it for many heartbeats before he realized that it was a huge door which had shut in his face.

He knew that the Little Giant was not merely seeking refuge in flight—for where in the world could he hope to escape the wrath of the People? He had gone, perhaps, for arms of some kind. Or—and at the thought Shrick's blood congealed—he had gone to lose the final doom foretold by Three-Eyes. Now that his plans had begun to miscarry he remembered the prophecy in its entirety, was no longer able to ignore those parts that, in his arrogance, he had found displeasing.

And then No-Toes, her flight clumsy and inexpert in these—to her—strange, vast spaces was at his side.

"Are you hurt?" she gasped. "They are so big—and you fought them."

As she spoke, the world was filled with a deep humming sound. Shrick ignored the excited female. That noise could mean only one thing. The Little Giant was back in the Place-of-Little-Lights, was setting in motion vast, incomprehensible forces that would bring to pass the utter and irrevocable destruction of the People.

With his feet against the huge door he kicked off, sped rapidly down to the open doorway in the Barrier. He put out his hand to break the shock of his landing, screamed aloud as his impact sent a sickening wave of pain through his chest. He started to cough—and when he saw the bright blood that was welling from his mouth he was very frightened.

No-Toes was with him again. "You are hurt, you are bleeding. Can I—?"

"No!" He turned a snarling mask to her. "No! Leave me alone!"

"But where are you going?"

Shrick paused. Then: "I am going to save the world," he said slowly. He savored the effect of his words. They made him feel better, they made him bulk big in his own mind, bigger, perhaps, than the Giants. "I am going to save you all."

"But how—?"

This was too much for the Giant Killer. He screamed again, but this time with anger. With the back of his hand he struck the young female across the face.

"Stay here!" he orderd.

And then he was gone along the tunnel.

The gyroscopes were still singing their quiet song of power when Shrick reached the Control Room. Strapped in his chair, the navigator was busy over his plotting machine. Outside the ports the stars wheeled by in orderly succession.

And Shrick was frightened.

He had never quite believed Wesel's garbled version of the nature of the world until now. But he could see, at last, that the ship was moving. The fantastic wonder of it all held him spellbound until a thin edge of intolerable radiance crept into view from behind the rim of one of the ports. The navigator touched something and, suddenly, screens of dark blue glass mitigated the glare. But it was still bright, too bright, and the edge became a rapidly widening oval and then, at last, a disk.

The humming of the gyroscope stopped.

Before the silence had time to register a fresh sound assailed Shrick's ears. It was the roar of the main drive.

A terrifying force seized him and slammed him down upon the deck. He felt his bones crack under the acceleration. True child of free fall as he was, all this held for him the terror of the supernatural. For a while he lay there, weakly squirming, whimpering a little. The navigator looked down at him and laughed. It was this sound more than anything else that stung Shrick to his last, supreme effort. He didn't want to move. He just wanted to lie there on the deck slowly coughing his life away. But the Little Giant's derision tapped unsuspected reserves of strength, both moral and physical.

The navigator went back to his calculations, handling his instruments for the last time with a kind of desperate elation. He knew that the ship would never arrive at her destination, neither would her cargo of seed grain. But she would not—and this outweighed all other considerations—drift forever among the stars carrying within her hull the seeds of the destruction of Man and all his works.

He knew that—had he not taken this way out—he must have slept at last, and then death at the hands of the mutants would inevitably have been his portion. And with mutants in full charge anything might happen.

The road he had taken was the best.

Unnoticed, inch by inch Shrick edged his way along the deck. Now, he could stretch his free hand and touch the Giant's foot. In the other he still held his blade, to which he had clung as the one thing sure and certain in this suddenly crazy world.

Then he had a grip on the artificial skin covering the Giant's leg. He started to climb, although every movement was unadulterated agony. He did not see the other raise his hand to his mouth, swallow the little pellet that he held therein.

So it was that when, at long last, he reached the soft, smooth throat of the Giant, the Giant was dead.

It was a very fast poison.

For a while he clung there. He should have felt elation at the death of the last of his enemies but—instead—he felt cheated. There was so much that he wanted to know, so much that only the Giants could have told him. Besides—it was his blade that should have won the final victory. He knew that, somewhere, the Little Giant was still laughing at him.

Through the blue-screened ports blazed the sun. Even at this distance, even with the intervening filters, its power and heat were all too evident. And aft the motors still roared, and would roar until the last ounce of fuel had been fed into hungry main drive.

Shrick clung to the dead man's neck, looked long and longingly at the glittering instruments, the shining switches and levers, whose purpose he would never understand, whose inertia would have defeated any attempt of his fast ebbing strength to move them. He looked at the flaming doom ahead, and knew that this was what had been foretold.

Had the metaphor existed in his language, he would have told himself that he and the few surviving People were caught like rats in a trap.

But even the Giants would not have used that phrase in its metaphorical sense.

For that is all that the People were—rats in a trap.

E FOR EFFORT

T.L. Sherred

The captain was met at the airport by a staff car. Long and fast it sped. In narrow, silent room the general sat, ramrod-backed, tense. The major waited at the foot of the gleaming steps shining frostily in the night air. Tires screamed to a stop and together the captain and the major raced up the steps. No words of greeting were spoken. The general stood quickly, hand outstretched. The captain ripped open a dispatch case and handed over a thick bundle of papers. The general flipped them over eagerly and spat a sentence at the major. The major disappeared and his harsh voice rang curtly down the outside hall. The man with glasses came in and the general handed him the papers. With jerky fingers the man with glasses sorted them out. With a wave from the general the captain left, a proud smile on his weary young face. The general tapped his fingertips on the black glossy surface of the table. The man with glasses pushed aside crinkled maps, and began to read aloud.

Dear Joe:

I started this just to kill time, because I got tired of just looking out the window. But when I got almost to the end I began to catch the trend of what's going on. You're the only one I know that can come through for me, and when you finish this you'll know why you must.

I don't know who will get this to you. Whoever it is won't want you to identify a face later. Remember that, and please, Joe—hurry!

Ed

It all started because I'm lazy. By the time I'd shaken off the sandman and checked out of the hotel, every seat in the bus was full. I stuck my bag in a dime locker and went out to kill the hour I had until the bus left. You know the bus terminal—right across from the Book-Cadillac and the Statler, on Washington Boulevard near Michigan Avenue. Like Main in Los Angeles, or maybe Sixty-third in its present state of decay in Chicago, where I was going. Cheap movies, pawnshops, and bars by the dozens, a penny arcade or two, restaurants that feature hamburg steak, bread and butter and coffee for forty cents. Before the War, a quarter.

I like pawnshops. I like cameras, I like tools, I like to look in windows crammed with everything from electric razors to sets of socket wrenches to upper plates. So, with an hour to spare, I walked out Michigan to Sixth and back on the other side of the street. There are a lot of Chinese and Mexicans around that part of town, the Chinese running the restaurants and the Mexicans eating Southern Home Cooking. Between Fourth and Fifth, I stopped to stare at what passed for a movie. Store windows painted black, amateurish signs extolling in Spanish *"Detroit premier . . . cast of thousands . . . this week only . . . ten cents—"* The few eight-by-ten glossy stills pasted on the windows were poor blowups, spotty and wrinkled; pictures of mailed cavalry and what looked like a good-sized battle. All for ten cents. Right down my alley.

Maybe it's lucky that history was my major in school. Luck it must have been, certainly not cleverness, that made me pay a dime for a seat in an undertaker's rickéty folding chair imbedded solidly—although the only other customers were a half-dozen Sons of the Order of Tortilla—in a cast of secondhand garlic. I sat near the door. A couple of hundred-watt bulbs dangling naked from the ceiling gave enough light for me to look around. In front of me, in the rear of the store, was the screen, what looked like a white-painted sheet of beaverboard, and when over my shoulder I saw the battered sixteen millimeter projector I began to think that even at a dime it was no bargain. Still, I had forty minutes to wait.

Everyone was smoking. I lit a cigarette and the discouraged Mexican who had taken my dime locked the door and turned off the lights, after giving me a long, questioning look. I'd paid my dime, so I looked right back. In a minute the old projector started clattering. No film credits, no producer's name, no director, just a tentative flicker before a closeup of a bewhiskered mug labeled Cortez. Then a painted and feathered Indian with the title of Guatemotzin, successor to Moctezuma; an aerial shot of a beautiful job of model-building tagged Ciudad Méjico, 1521. Shots of old muzzle-loaded artillery banging away, great walls spurting stone splinters under direct fire, skinny Indians dying violently with the customary gyrations, smoke and haze and blood. The photography sat me right up straight. It had none of the scratches and erratic cuts that characterized an old print, none of the fuzziness, none of the usual mugging at the camera by the handsome hero. There wasn't any handsome hero. Did you ever see one of those French pictures, or a Russian, and comment on the reality and depth brought out by working on a small budget that can't afford famed actors? This, what there was of it, was as good, or better.

It wasn't until the picture ended with a pan shot of a dreary desolation that I began to add two and two. You can't, for pennies, really have a cast of thousands, or sets big enough to fill Central Park. A mock-up, even, of a thirty-foot wall costs enough to irritate the auditors, and there had been a lot of wall. That didn't fit with the bad editing and lack of sound track, not unless the picture had been made in the old silent days. And I knew it hadn't by the color tones you get with pan film. It looked like a well-rehearsed and badly planned newsreel.

The Mexicans were easing out and I followed them to where the discouraged one was rewinding the reel. I asked him where he got the print.

"I haven't heard of any epics from the press agents lately, and it looks like a fairly recent print."

He agreed that it was recent, and added that he'd made it himself. I was polite to that, but he saw that I didn't believe him and straightened up from the projector.

"You don't believe that, do you?"

I said that I certainly did, and I had to catch a bus.

"Would you mind telling me why, exactly why?"

I said that the bus—

"I mean it. I'd appreciate it if you'd tell me just what's wrong with it."

"There's nothing wrong with it," I told him. He waited for me to go on. "Well, for one thing, pictures like that aren't made for the sixteen-millimeter trade. You've got a reduction from a thirty-five-millimeter master," and I gave him a few of the other reasons that separate home movies from Hollywood. When I finished he smoked quietly for a minute.

"I see." He took the reel off the projector spindle and closed the case. "I have beer in the back." I agreed beer sounded good, but the bus—well, just one. From in back of the beaverboard screen he brought paper cups and a Jumbo bottle. With a whimsical *"Business suspended"* he closed the open door and opened the bottle with an opener screwed on the wall. The store had likely been a grocery or restaurant. There were plenty of chairs. Two we shoved around and relaxed companionably. The beer was warm.

"You know something about this line," tentatively.

I took it as a question and laughed. "Not too much. Here's mud," and we drank. "Used to drive a truck for the Film Exchange." He was amused at that.

"Stranger in town?"

"Yes and no. Mostly yes. Sinus trouble chased me out and relatives bring me back. Not any more, though; my father's funeral was last week." He said that was too bad, and I said it wasn't. "He had sinus, too." That was a joke, and he refilled the cups. We talked awhile about the Detroit climate.

Finally he said, rather speculatively, "Didn't I see you around here last night? Just about eight." He got up and went after more beer.

I called after him. "No more beer for me." He brought a bottle anyway, and I looked at my watch. "Well, just one."

"Was it you?"

"Was it me what?" I held out my paper cup.

"Weren't you around here—"

I wiped foam off my mustache. "Last night? No, but I wish I had. I'd have caught my bus. No, I was in the Motor Bar last night at eight. And I was still there at midnight."

He chewed his lip thoughtfully. "The Motor Bar. Just down the street?" And I nodded. "The Motor Bar. Hm-m-m." I looked at him. "Would you like . . . sure, you would." Before I could figure out what he was talking about he went to the back and from behind the beaverboard screen rolled out a big radio-phonograph and another Jumbo bottle. I held the bottle against the light. Still half full. I looked at my watch. He rolled the radio against the wall and lifted the lid to get at the dials.

"Reach behind you, will you? The switch on the wall." I could reach the switch without getting up, and I did. The lights went out. I hadn't expected that, and I groped at arm's length. Then the lights came on again, and I turned back, relieved. But the lights weren't on; I was looking at the street!

Now, all this happened while I was dripping beer and trying to keep my balance on a tottering chair—the street moved, I didn't, and it was day and it was night and I was in front of the Book-Cadillac and I was going into the Motor Bar and I was watching myself order a beer and I knew I was wide awake and not dreaming. In a panic I scrabbled off the floor, shedding chairs and beer like an umbrella while I ripped my nails feeling frantically for that light switch. By the time I found it—and all the while I was watching myself pound the bar for the barkeep—I was really in a fine fettle, just about ready to collapse. Out of thin air right into a nightmare. At last I found the switch.

The Mexican was looking at me with the queerest expression I've ever seen, like he'd baited a mousetrap and caught a frog. Me? I suppose I looked like I'd seen the devil himself. Maybe I had. The beer was all over the floor and I barely made it to the nearest chair.

"What," I managed to get out, "what was that?"

The lid of the radio went down. "I felt like that too, the first time. I'd forgotten."

My fingers were too shaky to get out a cigarette, and I ripped off the top of the package. "I said, what was that?"

He sat down. "That was you, in the Motor Bar, at eight last night." I must have looked blank as he handed me another paper cup. Automatically I held it out to be refilled.

"Look here—" I started.

"I suppose it is a shock. I'd forgotten what I felt like the first time I . . . I don't care much any more. Tomorrow I'm going out to Phillips Radio." That made no sense to me, and I said so. He went on.

"I'm licked. I'm flat broke. I don't give a care any more. I'll settle for cash and live off the royalties." The story came out, slowly at first, then faster until he was pacing the floor. I guess he was tired of having no one to talk to.

His name was Miguel Jose Zapata Laviada. I told him mine: Lefko. Ed Lefko. He was the son of sugar beet workers who had emigrated from Mexico somewhere in the Twenties. They were sensible enough not to quibble when their oldest son left the back-breaking Michigan fields to seize the chance provided by an NYA scholarship. When the scholarship ran out, he'd worked in garages, driven trucks, clerked in stores, and sold brushes door-to-door to exist and to learn. The Army cut short his education with the First Draft to make him a radar technician; the Army had given him an honorable discharge and an idea so nebulous as to be almost merely a hunch. Jobs were plentiful then, and it wasn't too hard to end up with enough money to rent a trailer and fill it with Army surplus radio and radar equipment. One year ago he'd finished what he'd started; finished underfed, underweight, and overexcited. But successful, because he had it.

"It" he installed in a radio cabinet, both for ease in handling and for camouflage. For reasons that will become apparent, he didn't dare apply for a patent. I looked "it" over pretty carefully. Where the phonograph turntable and radio controls had been were vernier dials galore. One big dial was numbered 1 to 24, a couple were numbered 1 to 60, and there were a dozen or so numbered 1 to 25, plus two or three with no numbers at all. Closest of all, it resembled one of these fancy radio or motor testers found in a super super-service station. That was all, except that there was a sheet of heavy plywood hiding whatever was installed in place of the radio chassis and speaker. A perfectly innocent cache for . . .

Daydreams are swell. I suppose we've all had our share of mental wealth or fame or travel or fantasy. But to sit in a chair and drink warm beer and realize that the dream of ages isn't a dream anymore, to feel like a god, to know that just by turning a few dials you can see and watch anything, anybody, anywhere, that has ever happened—it still bothers me once in a while.

I know this much, that it's high frequency stuff. And there's a lot of mercury and copper and wiring of metals cheap and easy to find, but what goes where, or how—least of all, why—is out of my line. Light has mass and energy, and that mass always loses part of itself and can be translated back to electricity, or something. Mike Laviada himself says that what he stumbled on and developed was nothing new, that long before the war it had been observed many times by men like Compton and Michelson and Pfeiffer, who discarded it as a useless laboratory effect. And, of course, that was before atomic research took precedence over everything.

When the first shock wore off—and Mike had to give me another demonstration—I must have made quite a sight. Mike tells me I couldn't sit down. I'd pop up and gallop up and down the floor of that ancient store kicking chairs out of my way or stumbling over them, all the time gabbling out words and disconnected sentences faster than my tongue could trip. Finally it filtered through that he was laughing at me. I didn't see where it was any laughing matter, and I prodded him. He began to get angry.

"I know what I have," he snapped. "I'm not the biggest fool in the world, as you seem to think. Here, watch this," and he went back to the radio. "Turn out the light." I did, and there I was watching myself at the Motor Bar again, a lot happier this time. "Watch this."

The bar backed away. Out in the street, two blocks down to City Hall. Up the steps to the Council Room. No one there. The Council was in session, then they were gone again. Not a picture, not a projection of a lantern slide, but a slice of life about twelve feet square. If we were close, the field of view was narrow. If we were farther away, the background was just as much in focus as the foreground. The images, if you want to call them images, were just as real, just as lifelike as looking in the doorway of a room. Real they were, three-dimensional, stopped only by the back wall or the distance in the background. Mike was talking as he spun the dials, but I was too engrossed to pay much attention.

I yelped and grabbed and closed my eyes as you would if you were looking straight down with nothing between you and the ground except a lot of smoke and a few clouds. I winked my eyes open almost at the end of what must have been a long racing vertical dive, and there I was, looking at the street again.

"Go any place up the Heavyside Layer, go down as deep as any hole, anywhere, any time." A blur, and the street changed into a glade of sparse pines. "Buried treasure. Sure. Find it, with what?" The trees disappeared and I reached back for the light switch as he dropped the lid of the radio and sat down.

"How are you going to make any money when you haven't got it to start with?" No answer to that from me. "I ran an ad in the paper offering to recover lost articles; my first customer was the Law wanting to see my private detective's license. I've seen every big speculator in the country sit in his office buying and selling and making plans; what do you think would happen if I tried to peddle advance market information? I've watched the stock market get shoved up and down while I had barely the money to buy the paper that told me about it. I watched a bunch of Peruvian Indians bury the second ransom of Atuahalpa; I haven't the fare to get to Peru, or the money to buy the tools to dig." He got up and brought two more bottles. He went on. By that time I was getting a few ideas.

"I've watched scribes indite the books that burnt at Alexandria; who would buy, or who would believe me, if I copied one? What would happen if I went over to the Library and told them to rewrite their histories? How many would fight to tie a rope around my neck if they knew I'd watched them steal and murder and take a bath? What sort of padded cell would I get if I showed up with a photograph of Washington, or Caesar? Or Christ?"

I agreed that it was all probably true, but—

"Why do you think I'm here now? You saw the picture I showed for a dime. A dime's worth, and that's all, because I didn't have the money to buy film or to make the picture as I knew I should." His tongue began to get tangled. He was excited. "I'm doing this because I haven't the money to get the things I need to get the money I'll need—" He was so disgusted he booted a chair halfway across the room. It was easy to see that if I had been around a little later, Phillips Radio would have profited. Maybe I'd have been better off, too.

Now, although I've always been told that I'd never be worth a hoot, no one has ever accused me of being slow for a dollar. Especially an easy one. I saw money in front of me—easy money, the easiest and the quickest in the world. I saw, for a minute, so far in the future with me on top of the heap, that my head reeled and it was hard to breathe.

"Mike," I said, "let's finish that beer and go where we can get some more and maybe something to eat. We've got a lot of talking to do." So we did.

Beer is a mighty fine lubricant; I have always been a pretty smooth talker, and by the time we left the Gin Mill I had a pretty good idea of just what Mike had on his mind. By the time we'd shacked up for the night behind that beaverboard screen in the store, we were full-fledged partners. I don't recall our even shaking hands on the deal, but that partnership still holds good. Mike is ace high with me, and I guess it's the other way around, too. That was six years ago; it took me only a year or so to discard some of the corners I used to cut.

Seven days after that, on a Tuesday, I was riding a bus to Grosse Pointe with a full briefcase. Two days after that I was riding back from Grosse Pointe in a shiny taxi, with an empty briefcase and a pocketful of folding money. It was easy.

"Mr. Jones—or Smith—or Brown—I'm with Aristocrat Studios, Personal and Candid Portraits. We thought you might like this picture of you and . . . no, this is just a test proof. The negative is in our files. . . . Now, if you're really interested, I'll be back the day after tomorrow with our files. . . . I'm sure you will, Mr. Jones. Thank you, Mr. Jones. . . ."

Dirty? Sure. Blackmail is always dirty. But if I had a wife and family and a good reputation, I'd stick to the roast beef and forget the Roquefort. Very smelly Roquefort, at that. Mike liked it less than I did. It took some talking, and I had to drag out the old one about the ends justifying the means, and they could well afford it, anyway. Besides, if there was a squawk, they'd get the negatives free. Some of them were pretty bad.

So we had the cash; not too much, but enough to start. Before we took the next step there was plenty to decide. There are a lot who earn a living by convincing millions that Sticko soap is better. We had a harder problem than that: we had, first, to make a salable and profitable product, and second, we had to convince many, many millions that our 'product' was absolutely honest and absolutely accurate. We all know that if you repeat something long enough and loud enough many—or most—will accept it as gospel truth. That called for publicity on an international scale. For the skeptics who know better than to accept advertising, no matter how blatant, we had to use another technique. And since we would certainly get only one chance, we had to be right the first time. Without Mike's machine the job would have been impossible; without it the job would have been unnecessary.

A lot of sweat ran under the bridge before we found what we thought—and we still do!—the only workable scheme. We picked the only possible way to enter every mind in the world without a fight: the field of entertainment. Absolute secrecy was imperative, and it was only when we reached the last decimal point that we made a move. We started like this:

First we looked for a suitable building—or rather, Mike did. I flew east, to Rochester, for a month. The building he rented was an old bank. We had the windows sealed, a flossy office installed in the front—the bulletproof glass was my idea—air conditioning, a portable bar, electrical wiring of whatever type Mike's little heart desired, and a blond secretary who thought she was working for M-E Experimental Laboratories. When I got back from Rochester I took over the job of keeping happy the stonemasons and electricians, while Mike fooled around in our suite in the Book where he could look out the window at his old store. The last I heard, they were selling snake oil there. When the Studio, as we came to call it was finished, Mike moved in and the blond settled down to a routine of reading love stories and saying No to all the salesmen who wandered by. I left for Hollywood.

I spent a week digging through the files of Central Casting before I was satisfied, but it took a month of snooping and some under-the-table cash to lease a camera that would handle Trucolor film. That took the biggest load off my mind. When I got back to Detroit the big view camera had arrived from Rochester, with a truckload of glass color plates. Ready to go.

We made quite a ceremony of it. We closed the venetian blinds and I popped the cork on one of the bottles of champagne I'd bought. The blond secretary was impressed; all she'd been doing for her salary was accept delivery of packages and crates and boxes. We had no wine glasses, but we made no fuss about it. Too nervous and excited to drink any more than one bottle, we gave the rest to the blond and told her to take the rest of the afternoon off. After she left—and I think she was disappointed at breaking up what could have been a good party—we locked up after her, went into the studio itself, locked up again, and went to work.

I've mentioned that the windows were sealed. All the inside wall had been painted dull black, and with the high ceiling that went with that old bank lobby, it was impressive. But not gloomy. Midway in the studio was planted the big Trucolor camera, loaded and ready. Not much could we see of Mike's machine, but I knew it was off to the side, set to throw on the back wall. Not *on* the wall, understand, because the images produced are projected in midair like the meeting of the rays of two searchlights. Mike lifted the lid and I could see him silhouetted against the tiny lights that lit the dials.

"Well?" he said expectantly.

I felt pretty good just then, right down to my billfold.

"It's all yours, Mike," and a switch ticked over.

There he was. There was a youngster, dead twenty-five hundred years, real enough, almost, to touch. Alexander. Alexander of Macedon.

Let's take the first picture in detail. I don't think I can ever forget what happened in the next year or so. First we followed Alexander through his life, from beginning to end. We skipped, of course the little things he did, jumping ahead days and weeks and years at a time. Then we'd miss him, or find that he'd moved in space. That would mean we'd have to jump back and forth, like the artillery firing bracket or ranging shots, until we found him again. Helped only occasionally by his published lives, we were astounded to realize how much distortion has crept into his life. I often wonder why legends arise about the famous. Certainly their lives are as startling, or appalling, as fiction. And unfortunately we had to hold closely to the accepted histories. If we hadn't, every professor would have gone into his corner for a hearty sneer. We couldn't take that chance. Not at first.

After we knew approximately what had happened and where, we used our notes to go back to what had seemed a particular photogenic section and work on that awhile. Eventually we had a fair idea of what we were actually going to film. Then we sat down and wrote an actual script to follow, making allowance for whatever shots we'd have to double in later. Mike used his machine as the projector, and I operated the Trucolor camera at a fixed focus, like taking moving pictures of a movie. As fast as we finished a reel it would go to Rochester for processing, instead of one of the Hollywood outfits that might have done it cheaper. Rochester is so used to horrible amateur stuff that I doubt if anyone ever looks at anything. When the reel was returned we'd run it ourselves to check our choice of scenes and color sense and so on.

For example, we had to show the traditional quarrels with his father, Philip. Most of that we figured on doing with doubles, later. Olympias, his mother, and the fangless snakes she affected, didn't need any doubling, as we used an angle and amount of distance that didn't call for actual conversation. The scene where Alexander rode the bucking horse no one else could ride came out of some biographer's head, but we thought it was so famous we couldn't leave it out. We dubbed the closeups later, and the actual horseman was a young Scythian who hung around the royal stables for his keep. Roxanne was real enough, like the rest of the Persians' wives Alexander took over. Luckily, most of them had enough poundage to look luscious. Philip and Parmenio and the rest of the characters were heavily bearded, which made easy the necessary doubling and dubbing-in the necessary speech. (If you ever saw them shave in those days, you'd know why whiskers were popular.)

The most trouble we had was with interior shots. Smoky wicks in a bowl of lard, no matter how plentiful, are too dim even for fast film. Mike got around that by running the Trucolor camera at a single frame a second, with his machine paced accordingly. That accounts for the startling clarity and depth of focus we got from a lens stopped well down. We had all the time in the world to choose the best possible scenes and camera angles; the best actors in the world, expensive camera booms, or repeated retakes under the most exacting director can't compete with us. We had a lifetime from which to choose.

Eventually we had on film about eighty percent of what you saw in the finished picture. Roughly, we spliced the reels together and sat there entranced at what we had actually done. Even more exciting, even more spectacular than we'd dared hope, was the realization that we'd done a beautiful job, despite the lack of continuity and sound. We'd done all we could, and the worst was yet to come. So we sent for more champagne and told the blond we had cause for celebration. She giggled.

"What are you doing in there, anyway?" she asked. "Every salesman who comes to the door wants to know what you're making."

I opened the first bottle. "Just tell them you don't know."

"That's just what I've been telling them. They think I'm awfully dumb." We all laughed at the salesmen.

Mike was thoughtful. "If we're going to do this sort of thing very often, we ought to have some of these fancy hollow-stemmed glasses."

The blond was pleased with that. "And we could keep them in my bottom drawer." Her nose wrinkled prettily. "The bubbles—You know, this is the only time I've ever had champagne, except at a wedding, and then it was only one glass."

"Pour her another," Mike suggested. "Mine's empty too." I did. "What did you do with those bottles you took home last time?"

A blush and a giggle. "My father wanted to open them, but I told him you said to save it for a special occasion."

By that time I had my feet on her desk. "This is the special occasion, then," I invited. "Have another, Miss . . . what's your first name, anyway? I hate being formal after working hours."

She was shocked. "And you and Mr. Laviada sign my checks every week! It's Ruth."

"Ruth. Ruth." I rolled it around the piercing bubbles, and it sounded all right.

She nodded. "And your name is Edward, and Mr. Laviada's is Migwell. Isn't it?" And she smiled at him.

"MiGELL," he smiled back. "An old Spanish custom. Usually shortened to Mike."

"If you'll hand me another bottle," I offered, "shorten Edward to Ed." She handed it over.

By the time we got to the forth bottle we were as thick as bugs in a rug. It seems that she was twenty-four, free, and single, and loved champagne.

"But," she burbled fretfully, "I wish I knew what you were doing in there all hours of the day and night. I know you're here at night sometimes because I've seen your car out in front."

Mike thought that over. "Well," he said a little unsteadily, "we take pictures." He blinked one eye. "Might even take pictures of you if we were approached properly."

I took over. "We take pictures of models."

"Oh, no."

"Yes. Models of things and people and whatnot. Little ones. We make it look like it's real." I think she was a trifle disappointed.

"Well, now I know, and that makes me feel better. I sign all those bills from Rochester and I don't know what I'm signing for. Except that they must be film or something."

"That's just what it is; film and things like that."

"Well, it bothered me— No, there's two more behind the fan."

Only two more. She had a capacity. I asked her how she would like a vacation. She hadn't thought about a vacation just yet.

I told her she'd better start thinking about it. "We're leaving day after tomorrow for Los Angeles, Hollywood."

"The day after tomorrow? Why—"

I reassured her. "You'll get paid just the same. But there's no telling how long we'll be gone, and there doesn't seem to be much use in your sitting around here with nothing to do."

From Mike: "Let's have that bottle"; and I handed it to him. I went on.

"You'll get your checks just the same. If you want, we'll pay you in advance so—"

I was getting full of champagne, and so were we all. Mike was hummimg softly to himself, happy as a taco. Ruth was having a little trouble with her left eye. I knew just how she felt, because I was having a little trouble watching where she overlapped the swivel chair. Blue eyes, sooo tall, fuzzy hair. Hm-m-m. All work and no play— She handed me the last bottle.

Demurely she hid a tiny hiccup. "I'm going to save all the corks—No, I won't, either. My father would want to know what I'm thinking of, drinking with my bosses."

I said it wasn't a good idea to annoy your father. Mike said why fool with bad ideas, when he had a good one. We were interested. Nothing like a good idea to liven things up.

Mike was expansive as the very devil. "Going to Los Angeles."

We nodded solemnly.

"Going to Los Angeles to work."

Another nod.

"Going to work in Los Angeles. What will we do for pretty blond girl to write letters?"

Awful. No pretty blond to write letters and drink champagne. Sad case.

"Gotta hire somebody to write letters anyway. Might not be blond. No blonds in Hollywood. No good ones, anyway. So—"

I saw the wonderful idea, and finished for him. "So we take pretty blond to Los Angeles to write letters!"

What an idea that was! One bottle sooner and its brilliancy would have been dimmed. Ruth bubbled like a fresh bottle, and Mike and I sat there, smirking like mad.

"But I can't! I couldn't leave day after tomorrow just like that—!"

Mike was magnificent. "Who said day after tomorrow? Changed our minds. Leave right now."

She was appalled. "Right now! Just like that?"

"Right now. Just like that." I was firm.

"But—"

"No buts. Right now. Just like that."

"Nothing to wear—"

"Buy clothes any place. Best ones in Los Angeles."

"But my hair—"

Mike suggested a haircut in Hollywood.

I pounded the table. It felt solid. "Call the airport. Three tickets."

She called the airport. She intimidated easy.

The airport said we could leave for Chicago any time on the hour, and change there for Los Angeles. Mike wanted to know why she was wasting time on the telephone when we could be on our way. Holding up the wheels of progress, emery dust in the gears. One minute to get her hat.

"Call Pappy from the airport."

Her objections were easily brushed away with a few word-pictures of how much fun there was to be had in Hollywood. We left a sign on the door, *Gone to Lunch—Back in December*, and made the airport in time for the four o'clock plane, with no time left to call Pappy. I told the parking attendant to hold the car until he heard from me and we made it up the steps and into the plane just in time. The steps were taken away, the motors snorted, and we were off, with Ruth holding fast her hat in an imaginary breeze.

There was a two-hour lay over in Chicago. They don't serve liquor at the airport, but an obliging cab driver found us a convenient bar down the road, where Ruth made a call to her father.

Cautiously we stayed away from the telephone booth, but from what Ruth told us, he must have read her the riot act. The bartender didn't have champagne, but gave us the special treatment reserved for those that order it. The cab driver saw that we made the liner two hours later.

In Los Angeles we registered at the Commodore, cold sober and ashamed of ourselves. The next day Ruth went shopping for clothes, for herself and for us. We gave her the sizes and enough money to soothe her hangover. Mike and I did some telephoning. After breakfast we sat around until the desk clerk announced a Mr. Lee Johnson to see us.

Lee Johnson was the brisk professional type, the high-bracket salesman. Tall, rather homely, a clipped way of talking. We introduced ourselves as embryo producers. His eyes brightened when we said that. His meat.

"Not exactly the way you think," I told him. "We already have eighty percent or better of the final print."

He wanted to know where he came in.

"We have several thousand feet of Trucolor film. Don't bother asking where or when we got it. This footage is silent. We'll need sound and, in places, speech dubbed in."

He nodded. "Easy enough. What condition is the master?"

"Perfect condition. It's in the hotel vault right now. There are gaps in the story to fill. We'll need quite a few male and female characters. And all of these will have to do their doubling for cash, and not for screen credit."

Johnson raised his eyebrows. "Why? Out here, screen credit is bread and butter."

"Several reasons. This footage was made—never mind where—with the understanding that film credit would favor no one."

"If you're lucky enough to catch your talent between pictures, you might get away with it. But if your footage is worth working with, my boys will want screen credit. And I think they're entitled to it."

I said that was reasonable enough. The technical crews were essential, and I was prepared to pay well. Particularly to keep their mouths closed until the print was ready for final release. Maybe even after that.

"Before we go any further," Johnson rose and reached for his hat, "let's take a look at that print. I don't know if we can—"

I knew what he was thinking. Amateurs. Home movies. Feelthy peekchures mebbe?

We got the reels out of the hotel safe and drove to his laboratory, out Sunset. The top was down on his convertible and Mike hoped audibly that Ruth would have sense enough to get sport shirts that didn't scratch.

"Wife?" Johnson asked carelessly.

"Secretary," Mike answered just as casually. "We flew in last night and she's out getting us some light clothes." Johnson's estimation of us rose visibly.

A porter came out of the laboratory to carry the suitcase containing the film reels. It was a long, low building, with the offices at the front and the actual laboratories tapering off at the rear. Johnson took us in the side door and called for someone whose name we didn't catch. The anonymous one was a projectionist who took the reels and disappeared into the back of the projection room. We sat for a minute in the soft easy chairs until the projectionist buzzed ready. Johnson glanced at us, and we nodded. He clicked a switch on the arm of his chair and the overhead lights went out. The picture started.

It ran a hundred and ten minutes as it stood. We both watched Johnson like a cat at a rathole. When the tag end showed white on the screen, he signaled with the chair-side buzzer for lights. They came on. He faced us.

"Where did you get that print?"

Mike grinned at him. "Can we do business?"

"Do business!" He was vehement. "You bet your life we can do business! We'll do the greatest business you ever saw!"

The projection man came down. "Hey, that's all right. Where'd you get it?"

Mike looked at me. I said, "This isn't to go any further."

Johnson looked at his man, who shrugged. "None of my business."

I dangled the hook. "That wasn't made here. Never mind where."

Johnson rose and struck, hook, line and sinker. "Europe! Hm-m-m. Germany. No, France, Russia, maybe, Einstein, or Eisenstein, or whatever his name is?"

I shook my head. "That doesn't matter. The leads are all dead, or out of commission, but their heirs . . . well, you get what I mean."

Johnson saw what I meant. "Absolutely right. No point taking any chances. Where's the rest—?"

"Who knows? We were lucky to salvage that much. Can do?"

"Can do." He thought for a minute. "Get Bernstein in here. Better get Kessler and Marrs, too." The projectionist left. In a few minutes Kessler, a heavyset man, and Marrs, a young, nervous chain-smoker, came in with Bernstein, the sound man. We were introduced all around, and Johnson asked if we minded sitting through another showing.

"Nope. We like it better than you do."

Not quite. The minute the film was over, Kessler, Marrs, and Bernstein bombarded us with startled questions. We gave them the same answers we'd given Johnson. But we were pleased with the reception, and said so.

Kessler grunted. "I'd like to know who was behind that camera. Best I've seen, by Cripes, since *Ben Hur*. Better than *Ben Hur*. The boy's good."

I grunted right back at him. "That's the only thing I can tell you. The photography was done by the boys you're talking to right now. Thanks for the kind word."

All four of them stared.

Mike said, "That's right."

"Hey, hey!" from Marrs. They all looked at us with new respect. It felt good.

Johnson broke into the silence when it became awkward. "What's next on the score card?"

We got down to cases. Mike, as usual, was content to sit there with his eyes half closed, taking it all in, letting me do all the talking.

"We want sound dubbed in all the way through."

"Pleasure," said Bernstein.

"At least a dozen, maybe more, speaking actors with a close resemblance to the leads you've seen."

Johnson was confident. "Easy. Central Casting has everybody's picture since the Year One."

"I know. We've already checked that. No trouble there. They'll have to take the cash and let the credit go, for reasons I've already explained to Mr. Johnson."

A moan from Marrs. "I bet I get that job."

Johnson was snappish. "You do. What else?" to me.

I didn't know. "Except that we have no plans for distribution as yet. That will have to be worked out."

"Like falling off a log." Johnson was happy about that. "One look at the rushes and United Artists would spit in Shakespeare's eye."

Marrs came in. "What about the other shots? Got a writer line up?"

"We've got what will pass for the shooting script, or will have in a week or so. Want to go over it with us?"

Marrs said he'd like that.

"How much time have we got?" interposed Kessler. "This is going to be a job. When do we want it?" Already it was "we."

"Yesterday is when we want it," snapped Johnson, and he rose. "Any ideas about music? No? We'll try for Werner Janssen and his boys. Bernstein, you're responsible for that print from now on. Kessler, get your crew in and have a look at it. Marrs, at their convenience, you'll go with Mr. Lefko and Mr. Laviada through the files at Central Casting. Keep in touch with them at the Commodore. Now, if you'll step into my office, we'll discuss the financial arrangements—"

It was as easy as that.

Oh, I don't say it was easy work, or anything. Because in the next few months we were playing Busy Bee. What with running down the only one registered at Central Casting who looked like Alexander himself (turned out to be a young Armenian who had given up hope of ever being called from the extras lists and had gone home to Santee), casting, rehearsing the rest of the actors, and swearing at the customers and the boys who built the sets, we were kept hopping. Even Ruth, who had reconciled her father with sorting letters, for once earned her salary. We took turns shooting dictation at her until we had a script that satisfied Mike, myself, and young Marrs, who turned out to be clever as a fox with dialogue.

What I really mean to say is that it was easy, and immensely gratifying, to crack the shell of the tough boys who had seen epics and turkeys come and go. They were really impressed by what we had done. Kessler was disappointed when we refused to be bothered with photographing the rest of the film. We just batted our eyes and said that we were too busy, that we were perfectly confident that he would do as well as we could. He outdid himself, and us. I don't know what we would have done if he had asked us for any concrete advice. I suppose, when I think it all over, that the boys we met and worked with were so tired of working with the usual mine-run Grade B's that they were glad to meet someone who knew the difference between glycerin tears and reality and didn't care if it cost two dollars extra. They had us pegged as a couple of city slickers with plenty on the ball. I hope.

Finally it was over with. We all sat in the projection room and watched the finished product. Mike and I, Marrs and Johnson, Kessler and Bernstein, and all the lesser technicians who split up the really enormous amount of work that had been done. It was terrific. Everyone had done his work well. When Alexander came on the screen, he *was* Alexander the Great. (The Armenian kid got a good bonus for that.) All that blazing color, all that wealth and magnificence and glamour seemed to flare out of the screen and sear the mind. Even Mike and I, who had seen the original, were on the edge of our seats.

The sheer realism and magnitude of the battle scenes, I think, made the picture. Gore, of course, is glorious when it's all make-believe and the dead get up to go to lunch. But when Bill Mauldin sees a picture and sells a breathless article on the similarity of infantrymen of all ages—well, Mauldin knows what war is like. So did the infantrymen throughout the world, who wrote letters comparing Alexander's Arbela to Anzio and the Argonne. The weary peasant, not stolid at all, trudging and trudging into mile after mile of those dust-laden plains and ending as a stinking, naked, ripped corpse peeping from under a mound of flies, isn't much different whether he carries a sarissa or a rifle. That we'd tried to make obvious, and we succeeded.

When the lights came up in the projection room, we knew we had a winner. Individually we shook hands all around, proud as a bunch of penguins, and with chests out as far. The rest of the men filed out and we retired to Johnson's office. He poured a drink all around and got down to business.

"How about releases?"

I asked him what he thought.

"Write your own ticket," he shrugged. "I don't know whether or not you know it, but the word has already gone around that you've got something."

I told him we'd had calls at the hotel from various sources, and named them.

"See what I mean? I know those babies. Kiss them off if you want to keep your shirt. And while I'm at it, you owe us quite a bit. I suppose you've got it."

"We've got it."

"I was afraid you would. If you didn't, I'd be the one that would have your shirt." He grinned, but we all knew he meant it. "All right, that's settled. Let's talk about release.

"There are two or three outfits in town that will want a crack at it. My boys will have the word spread around in no time; there's no point in trying to keep them quiet any longer. I know—they'll have sense enough not to talk about the things you want off the record. I'll see to that. But you're top dog right now. You got loose cash, you've got the biggest potential gross I've ever seen, and you don't have to take the first offer. That's important in this game."

"How would you like to handle it yourself?"

"I'd like to try. The outfit I'm thinking of needs a feature right now, and they don't know I know it. They'll pay and pay. What's in it for me?"

"That," I said, "we can talk about later. I think I know just what you're thinking. We'll take the usual terms, and we don't care if you hold up whoever you deal with. What we don't know won't hurt us." That's what he was thinking, all right. That's a cutthroat game out there.

"Good. Kessler, get your setup ready for duplication."

"Always ready."

"Marrs, start the ball rolling on publicity . . . what do you want to do about that?" to us.

Mike and I had already talked about that. "As far as we're concerned," I said slowly, "do as you think best. Personal publicity, O.K. We won't look at it, but we won't dodge it. As far as that goes, we're the local yokels making good. Soft-pedal any questions about where the picture was made, without being too obvious. You're going to have trouble when you talk about the non-existent actors, but you ought to be able to figure out something."

Marrs groaned and Johnson grinned. "He'll figure out something."

"As far as technical credit goes, we'll be glad to see you get all you can, because you've done a swell job." Kessler took that as a personal compliment, and it was. "You might as well know now, before we go any further, that some of the work came right from Detroit." They all sat up at that.

"Mike and I have a new process of model and trick work." Kessler opened his mouth to say something but thought better of it. "We're not going to say what was done, or how much was done in the laboratory, but you'll admit that it defies detection."

About that they were fervent. "I'll say it defies detection. In the game this long, and process work gets by me . . . where—"

"I'm not going to tell you that. What we've got isn't patented and won't be, as long as we can hold it up." There wasn't any gripping there. These men knew process work when they saw it. If they didn't see it, it was good. They could understand why we'd want to keep a process that good a secret.

"We can practically guarantee there'll be more work for you to do later on." Their interest was plain. "We're not going to predict when, or make any definite arrangement, but we still have a trick or two in the deck. We like the way we've been getting along, and we want to stay that way. Now, if you'll excuse us, we have a date with a blond."

Johnson was right about the bidding for the release. We—or rather, Johnson—made a very profitable deal with United Amusement and its affiliated theaters. Johnson, the bandit, got his percentage from us and likely did better with United. Kessler and Johnson's boys took huge ads in the trade journals to boast about their connections with the Academy Award winner. Not only the Academy, but every award that ever went to any picture. Even the Europeans went overboard. They're the ones that make a fetish of realism. They knew the real thing when they saw it, and so did everyone else.

Our success went to Ruth's head. In no time she wanted a secretary. At that, she needed one to fend off the screwballs that popped out of the woodwork. So we let her hire a girl to help out. She picked a good typist, about fifty. Ruth is a smart girl, in a lot of ways. Her father showed signs of wanting to see the Pacific, so we raised her salary on condition he'd stay away. The three of us were having too much fun.

The picture opened at the same time in New York and Hollywood. We went to the premiere in great style, with Ruth between us, swollen like a trio of bullfrogs. It's a great feeling to sit on the floor early in the morning and read reviews that make you feel like floating. It's a better feeling to have a mintful of money. Johnson and his men were right along with us. I don't think he could have been too flush in the beginning, and we all got a kick out of riding the crest.

It was a good-sized wave, too. We had all the personal publicity we wanted, and more. Somehow the word was out that we had a new gadget for process photography, and every big studio in town was after what they thought would be a mighty economical thing to have around. The studios that didn't have a spectacle scheduled looked at the receipts for *Alexander* and promptly scheduled a spectacle. We drew some very good offers, Johnson said, but we made a series of long faces and broke the news that we were leaving for Detroit the next day, and asked him to hold the fort awhile. I don't think he thought we actually meant it, but we did. We left the next day.

Back in Detroit we went right to work, helped by the knowledge that we were on the right track. Ruth was kept busy turning away the countless would-be visitors. We admitted no reporters, no salesmen, no one. We had no time. We were using the view camera. Plate after plate were sent to Rochester for developing. A print of each was returned to us, and the plate was held in Rochester for our disposal. We sent to New York for a representative of one of the biggest publishers in the country. We made a deal.

Your main library has a set of the books we published, if you're interested. Huge, heavy volumes, hundreds of them, each page a razor-sharp blowup from an eight-by-ten negative. A set of those books went to every major library and university in the world. Mike and I got a real kick out of solving some of the problems that have had savants guessing for years. In the Roman volume, for example, we solved the trireme problem with a series of pictures, not only of the interior of a trireme, but a line-of-battle quinquereme. (Naturally, the professors and amateur yachtsmen weren't convinced at all.) We had a series of aerial shots of the city of Rome taken a hundred years apart, over a millennium. Aerial views of Ravenna and Londinium, Palmyra and Pompeii, of Eboracum and Byzantium. Oh, we had the time of our lives! We had a volume for Greece and for Rome, for Persia and for Crete, for Egypt and for the Eastern Empire. We had pictures of the Parthenon and the Pharos, pictures of Hannibal and Caractacus and Vercingetorix, pictures of the Walls of Babylon and the building of the pyramids and the palace of Sargon, pages from the Lost Books of Livy and the plays of Euripides.

Terrifically expensive, a second printing sold at cost to a surprising number of private individuals. If the cost had been less, historical interest would have become even more the fad of the moment.

When the flurry had almost died down, some Italian digging in the hitherto-unexcavated section of ash-buried Pompeii dug into a tiny, buried temple right where our aerial shot had showed it to be. His budget was expanded and he found more ash-covered ruins that agreed with our aerial layout, ruins that hadn't seen the light of day for almost two thousand years. Everyone promptly wailed that we were the luckiest guessers in captivity; the head of some California cult suspected aloud that we were the reincarnations of two gladiators named Joe.

To get some peace and quiet, Mike and I moved into our studio, lock, stock, and underwear. At our request, the old bank vault had never been removed, and it served well to store our equipment in when we weren't around. All the mail Ruth couldn't handle, we disposed of, unread; the old bank building began to look like a well-patronized soup kitchen. We hired burly private detectives to handle the more obnoxious visitors and subscribed to a telegraphic protective service. We had another job to do, another full-length feature.

We stuck to the old historical theme. This time we tried to do what Gibbon did in *The Decline and Fall of the Roman Empire*. And, I think, we were rather successful, at that. In four hours you can't completely cover two thousand years, but you can, as we did, show the cracking up of a great civilization, and how painful the process can be. The criticism we drew for virtually ignoring Christ and Christianity was unjust, we think, and unfair. Very few knew then, or know now, that we had included, as a kind of trial balloon, some footage of Christ Himself, and of His times. This footage we had to cut. The Board of Review, as you know, contains both Catholics and Protestants. They—the Board—were up in arms. We didn't protest very hard when they claimed our 'treatment' was irreverent, indecent, and biased and inaccurate 'by any Christian standard.' "Why," they wailed, "it doesn't even look like Him," and they were right; it didn't. Not any picture *they* ever saw. Then and there we decided that it didn't pay to tamper with anyone's religious beliefs. That's why you've never seen anything emanating from us that conflicted even remotely with the accepted historical, sociological, or religious features of Someone Who Knew Better. That Roman picture, by the way—but not accidentally—deviated so little from the textbooks you conned in school that only a few enthusiastic specialists called our attention to what they insisted were errors. We were still in no position to do any mass rewriting of history, because we were unable to reveal just where we got our information.

Johnson, when he saw the Roman epic, mentally kicked high his heels. His men went right to work, and we handled the job as we had the first. One day Kessler, dead earnest, got me in a corner.

"Ed," he said, "I'm going to find out where you got that footage if it's the last thing I ever do."

I told him that some day he would.

"And I don't mean some day, either; I mean right now. That bushwa about Europe might go once, but not twice. I know better, and so does everyone else. Now, what about it?"

I told him I'd have to consult Mike, and I did. We were up against it. We called a conference.

"Kessler tells me he has troubles. I guess you all know what they are." They all knew.

Johnson spoke up. "He's right, too. We know better. Where did you get it?"

I turned to Mike. "Want to do the talking?"

A shake of his head. "You're doing all right."

"All right." Kessler hunched forward a little and Marrs lit another cigarette. "We weren't lying and we weren't exaggerating when we said the actual photography was ours. Every frame of film was taken right here in this country, within the past few months. Just how—I won't mention why or where—we can't tell you just now." Kessler snorted in disgust. "Let me finish."

"We all know that we're cashing in hand over fist. And we're going to cash in some more. We have, on our personal schedule, five more pictures. Three of that five we want you to handle as you did the others. The last two of the five will show you both the reason for all the childish secrecy, as Kessler calls it, and another motive that we have so far kept hidden. The last two pictures will show you both our motives and our methods; one is important as the other. Now—is that enough? Can we go ahead on that basis?"

It wasn't enough for Kessler. "That doesn't mean a thing to me. What are we, a bunch of hacks?"

Johnson was thinking about his bank balance. "Five more. Two years, maybe four."

Marrs was skeptical. "Who do you think you're going to kid that long? Where's your studio? Where's your talent? Where do you shoot your exteriors? Where do you get costumes, and your extras? In one single shot you've got forty thousand extras, if you've got one! Maybe you can shut *me* up, but who's going to answer the questions that Metro and Fox and Paramount and RKO have been asking? Those boys aren't fools; they know their business. How do you expect me to handle any publicity when I don't know what the score is myself?"

Johnson told him to pipe down awhile and let him think. Mike and I didn't like this one bit. But what could we do—tell the truth and end up in a straitjacket?

"Can we do it this way?" he finally asked. "Marrs: these boys have an in with the Soviet Government. They work in some place in Siberia, maybe. Nobody gets within miles of there. No one ever knows what the Russians are doing—"

"Nope!" Marrs was definite. "Any hint that these came from Russia and we'd all be labeled a bunch of Reds. Cut the gross in half."

Johnson began to pick up speed. "All right, not from Russia. From one of those little republics on the fringe of Siberia or Armenia or some such place. They're not Russian-made films at all. In fact, they've been made by some of the Germans and Austrians the Russians captured and moved after the war. The war fever has died down enough for people to realize that the Germans knew their stuff occasionally. The old sympathy racket for these refugees struggling with faulty equipment, lousy climate, making super-spectacles and smuggling them out under the nose of the Gestapo or whatever they call it—That's it!"

Doubtfully, Marrs said: "And the Russians tell the world we're nuts, that they haven't got any loose Germans?"

That, Johnson overrode. "Who reads the back pages? Who pays any attention to what the Russians say? Who cares? They might even think we're telling the truth and start looking around their own backyard for something that isn't there! All right with you?" he said to Mike and me.

"O.K. with us."

"O.K. with the rest of you? Kessler? Bernstein?"

They weren't too agreeable, and certainly not happy; but they agreed to play along until we gave the word.

We were warm in our thanks. "You won't regret it."

Kessler doubted that very much, but Johnson eased them all out, back to work. Another hurdle leaped—or sidestepped.

Rome was released on schedule and drew the same friendly reviews. 'Friendly' is the wrong word for reviews that stretched ticket lines that were blocks long. Marrs did a good job on the publicity. Even that chain of newspapers that afterward turned on us so viciously fell for Marrs' word wizardly and ran full-page editorials urging the reader to see *Rome*.

With our third picture, *Flame Over France*, we corrected a few misconceptions about the French Revolution and began stepping on a few tender toes. Luckily, however, and not altogether by design, there happened to be a liberal government in power in France. They backed us to the hilt with the confirmation we needed. At our request they released a lot of documents that had hitherto conveniently been lost in the cavernous recesses of the Bibliothèque nationale. I've forgotten the name of whoever was the perennial pretender to the French throne. At, I'm sure, the subtle probbing of one of Marrs' ubiquitous publicity men, the pretender sued us for our net worth, alleging defamation of the good name of the Bourbons. A lawyer Johnson dug up for us sucked the poor

chump into a courtroom and cut him to bits. Not six cents damages
did he get. Samuels, the lawyer and Marrs received a good-sized
bonus, and the pretender moved to Honduras.

It was sometime about then, I believe, that the tone of the
press began to change. Up until then we'd been regarded as a cross
between Shakespeare and Barnum. Because long-obscure facts had
been dredged into the light, a few well-known pessimists began to
wonder *sotto voce* if we weren't just a pair of blasted pests. "Should
leave well enough alone." Only our huge advertising budget kept
them from saying more.

I'm going to stop right here and say something about our personal
life while all this was going on. Mike I've kept in the background
pretty well, mostly because he wants it that way. He lets me do
all the talking and stick my neck out while he sits in the most
comfortable chair in sight. I yell and I argue, and he just sits there;
hardly ever a word coming out of that dark-brown pan, certainly
never an indication that behind those polite eyebrows there's a
brain—and a sense of humor and wit—faster than and as deadly
as a bear trap. Oh, I know we've played around, sometimes with a
loud bang, but we've been, ordinarily, too busy and too preoccupied
with what we were doing to waste any time. Ruth, while she was
with us, was a good dancing and drinking partner. She was young,
she was almost what you'd call call beautiful, and she seemed to like
being with us. For awhile I had a few ideas about her that might
have developed into something serious. We both—I should say, all
three of us—found out in time that we looked at a lot of things too
differently. So we weren't too disappointed when she signed with
Metro. Her contract meant what she thought was all the fame and
money and happiness in the world, plus the personal attention she
was doubtless entitled to have. They put her in Class B's and serials
and she, financially, is better off than she ever expected to be.
Emotionally, I don't know. We heard from her some time ago, and I
think she's about due for another divorce. Maybe it's just as well.

But let's get away from Ruth. I'm ahead of myself. All this time
Mike and I had been working together, our approaches to the final
payoff had been divergent. Mike was hopped on the idea of making
a better world, and doing that by making war impossible. "War,"
he's often said, "war of any kind is what has made man spend most
of his history in merely staying alive. Now, with the atom to use, he
has within himself the seed of self-extermination. So help me, Ed,
I'm going to do my share of stopping that, or I don't see any point
in living. I mean it!"

He did mean it. He told me that in practically those words the day we met. At the time, I tagged that idea as a pipe dream picked up on an empty stomach. I saw his machine only as a path to luxurious and personal Nirvana, and I thought he'd soon he going my way. I was wrong.

You can't live, or work, with a likable person without admiring some of the qualities that make that person likable. Another thing: it's a lot easier to worry about the woes of the world when you haven't any yourself. It's a lot easier to have a conscience when you can afford it. When I donned the rose-colored glasses half my battle was won; when I realized how grand a world this *could* be, the battle was over. That was about the time of *Flame Over France*, I think. The actual time isn't important. What *is* important is that, from that time on, we became the tightest team possible. Since then the only thing we've differed on was the time to knock off for a sandwich. Most of our leisure time, what we had of it, has been spent in locking up for the night, rolling out the portable bar, opening just enough beer to feel good, and relaxing. Maybe, after one or two, we might diddle with the dials of the machine and go rambling.

Together we've been everywhere and seen anything. It might be a good night to check up on François Villon, that faker, or maybe we would chase around with Haroun-el-Rashid. (If there was ever a man born a few hundred years too soon, it was that careless caliph.) Or if we were in a bad or discouraged mood we might follow the Thirty Years' War awhile, or if we were real raffish we might inspect the dressing rooms at Radio City. For Mike the crackup of Atlantis has always held an odd fascination, probably because he's afraid that man will do it again, now that he's rediscovered nuclear energy. And if I doze off he's quite apt to go back to the very Beginning, back to the start of the world as we know it now. (It wouldn't do any good to tell you what went before that.)

When I stop to think, it's probably just as well that neither of us married. We, of course, have hopes for the future, but at present we're both tired of the whole human race; tired of greedy faces and hands. With a world that puts a premium on wealth and power and strength, it's no wonder what decency there is stems from fear of what's here now, or fear of what's hereafter. We've seen so much of the hidden actions of the world—call it snooping, if you like—that we've learned to disregard the surface indications of kindness and good. Only once did Mike and I ever look into the private life of someone we knew and liked and respected. Once was enough. From that day on we made it a point to take people as they seem. Let's get away from that.

The next two pictures we released in rapid succession: *Freedom for Americans*, on the American Revolution, and *The Brothers and the Guns*, about the American Civil War. Bang! Every third politician, a lot of 'educators,' and all the professional patriots went after our scalps. Every single chapter of the DAR, the Sons of Union Veterans, and the Daughters of the Confederacy pounded their collective heads against the wall. The South went frantic; every state in the Deep South and one state on the border flatly banned both pictures, the second because it was truthful, and the first because censorship is a contagious disease. They stayed banned until the professional politicians got wise. The bans were revoked, and the choke-collar and string-tie brigade pointed to both pictures as horrible examples of what some people actually believed and thought, and felt pleased that someone had given them an opportunity to roll out the barrel and beat the drums that sound the call for sectional and racial hatred.

New England was tempted to stand on its dignity, but couldn't stand the strain. North of New York, both pictures were banned. In New York State, the rural representatives voted en bloc, and the ban was clamped on statewide. Special trains ran to Delaware, where the corporations were too busy to pass another law. Libel suits flew like spaghetti, and although the extras headlined the filing of each new suit, very few knew that we lost not one. Although we had to appeal almost every suit to higher courts and in some cases request a change of venue, which was seldom granted, the documentary proof furnished by the record cleared us once we got to a judge, or a series of judges, with no fences to mend.

It was a mighty rasp we drew over wounded ancestral pride. We had shown that not all the mighty have halos of purest gold, that not all the Redcoats were strutting bullies—or angels, and the British Empire, except South Africa, refused entry to both pictures and made violent passes at the State Department. The spectacle of Southern and New England congressmen approving the efforts of a foreign ambassador to suppress free speech drew hilarious hosannas from certain quarters. H. L. Mencken gloated in the clover, and the newspapers hung on the triple-horned dilemma of anti-foreign, pro-patriotic, quasi-logical criticism. In Detroit the Ku Klux Klan burned an anemic cross on our doorstep, and the Friendly Sons of St. Patrick, the NAACP, and the WCTU passed flattering resolutions. We forwarded the most vicious and obscene letters—together with a few names and addresses that hadn't been originally signed—to our lawyers and the Post Office Department. There were no convictions south of Illinois.

Johnson and his boys made hay. Johnson had pyramided his bets into an international distributing organization, and pushed Marrs into hiring every top press agent on either side of the Rockies. What a job they did! In no time at all there were two definite schools of thought that overflowed into the public letter boxes. One school held that we had no business raking up old mud to throw, that such things were better left forgotten and forgiven, that nothing wrong had ever happened, and if it had, we were liars anyway. The other school reasoned more to our liking. Softly and slowly at first, then with a triumphant shout, this fact began to emerge; such things had actually happened, and could happen again, were possibly happening even now; had happened because twisted truth had too long left its imprint on international, sectional, and racial feelings. It pleased us when many began to agree with us, that it is important to forget the past, but that it is even more important to understand and evaluate it with a generous and unjaundiced eye. That was what we were trying to bring out.

The banning that occurred in the various states hurt the gross receipts only a little, and we were vindicated in Johnson's mind. He had dolefully predicted loss of half the national gross because "you can't tell the truth in a movie and get away with it. Not if the house holds over three hundred." Not even on the stage? "Who goes to anything but a movie?"

So far things had gone just about as we'd planned. We'd earned and received more publicity, favorable and otherwise, than anyone living. Most of it stemmed from the fact that our doings had been newsworthy. Some, naturally, had been the ninety-day-wonder material that fills a thirsty newspaper. We were very careful to make enemies in the strata that can afford to fight back. Remember the old saw about knowing a man by the enemies he makes? Well, publicity was our ax. Here's how we put an edge on it.

I called Johnson in Hollywood. He was glad to hear from us. "Long time no see. What's the pitch, Ed?"

"I want some lip-readers. And I want them yesterday, like you tell your boys."

"Lip-readers? Are you nuts? What do you want with lip-readers?"

"Never mind why. I want lip-readers. Can you get them?"

"How should I know? What do you want them for?"

"I said, can you get them?"

He was doubtful. "I think you've been working too hard."

"Look—"

"Now, I didn't say I couldn't. Cool off. When do you want them? And how many?"

"Better write this down. Ready? I want lip-readers for these languages: English, French, German, Russian, Chinese, Japanese, Greek, Flemish, Dutch, and Spanish."

"Ed Lefko, have you gone crazy?"

I guess it didn't sound very sensible, at that. "Maybe I have. But those languages are essential. If you run across any who can work in any other language, hang on to them. I might need them, too." I could see him sitting in front of his telephone, wagging his head like mad. Crazy. The heat must have got Lefko, good old Ed.

"Did you hear what I said?"

"Yes, I heard you. If this is a rib—"

"No rib. Dead serious."

He began to get mad. "Where you think I'm going to get lip-readers, out of my hat?"

"That's your worry. I'd suggest you start with the local school for the deaf." He was silent. "Now, get this into your head; this isn't a rib, this is the real thing. I don't care what you do, or where you go, or what you spend—I want those lip-readers in Hollywood when we get there or I want to know they're on the way."

"When are you going to get there?"

I said I wasn't sure. "Probably a day or two. We've got a few loose ends to tie up."

He swore a blue streak at the iniquities of fate. "You'd better have a good story when you do—" I hung up.

Mike met me at the studio. "Talk to Johnson?" I told him, and he laughed. "Does sound crazy, I suppose. But he'll get them, if they exist and like money. He's the Original Resourceful Man."

I tossed my hat in a corner. "I'm glad this is about over. Your end caught up?"

"Set and ready to go. The films and the notes are on the way, the real estate company is ready to take over the lease, and the girls are paid up-to-date, with a little extra."

I opened a bottle of beer for myself. Mike had one. "How about the office files? How about the bar, here?"

"The files go to the bank to be stored. The bar? Hadn't thought about it."

The beer was cold. "Have it crated and send it to Johnson."

We grinned, together. "Johnson it is. He'll need it."

I nodded at the machine. "What about that?"

"That goes with us on the plane as air express." He looked closely at me. "What's the matter with you—jitters?"

"Nope. Willies. Same thing."

"Me, too. Your clothes and mine left this morning."

"Not even a clean shirt left?"

"Not even a clean shirt. Just like—"

I finished it. "—the first trip with Ruth. A little different, maybe."

Mike said slowly, "A lot different." I opened another beer. "Anything you want around here, anything else to be done?" I said no. "O.K. Let's get this over with. We'll put what we need in the car. We'll stop at the Courville Bar before we hit the airport."

I didn't get it. "There's still beer left—"

"But no champagne."

I got it. "O.K. I'm dumb, at times. Let's go."

We loaded the machine into the car, and the bar, left the studio keys at the corner grocery for the real estate company, and headed for the airport by way of the Courville Bar. Ruth was in California, but Joe had champagne. We got to the airport late.

Marrs met us in Los Angeles. "What's up? You've got Johnson running around in circles."

"Did he tell you why?"

"Sounds crazy to me. Couple of reporters inside. Got anything for them?"

"Not right now. Let's get going."

In Johnson's private office we got a chilly reception. "This better be good. Where do you expect to find someone to lipread in Chinese? Or Russian, for that matter?"

We all sat down. "What have you got so far?"

"Besides a headache?" He handed me a short list.

I scanned it. "How long before you can get them here?"

An explosion. "How long before I can get them here? Am I your errand boy?"

"For all practical purposes, you are. Quit the stalling. How about it?" Marrs snickered at the look on Johnson's face.

"What are you smirking at, you moron?" Marrs gave in and laughed outright. I did, too. "Go ahead and laugh. This isn't funny.

When I called the state school for the deaf, they hung up. Thought I was some practical joker. We'll skip that.

"There's three women and a man on that list. They cover English, French, Spanish, and German. Two of them are working in the East, and I'm waiting for answers to telegrams I sent them. One lives in Pomona and one works for the Arizona School for the Deaf. That's the best I could do."

We thought that over. "Get on the phone. Talk to every state in the union if you have to, or overseas."

Johnson kicked the desk. "And what are you going to do with them—if I'm that lucky?"

"You'll find out. Get them on planes and fly them here, and we'll talk turkey when they get here. I want a projection room, not yours, and a good bonded court reporter."

He asked the world to appreciate what a life he led.

"Get in touch with us at the Commodore." To Marrs: "Keep the reporters away for awhile. We'll have something for them later." Then we left.

Johnson never did find anyone who could lipread Greek. None, at least, who could speak English. The expert on Russian he dug out of Ambridge, in Pennsylvania, the Flemish and Holland Dutch expert came from Leyden, in the Netherlands, and at the last minute he stumbled on a Korean who worked in Seattle as an inspector for the Chinese government. Five women and two men. We signed them to an ironclad contract drawn by Samuels, who now handled all our legal work. I made a little speech before they signed.

"These contracts, as far as we've been able to make sure, are going to control your personal and business lives for the another year if we so desire. Let's get this straight. You are to live in a place of your own, which we will provide. You will be supplied with all necessities by our buyers. Any attempt at unauthorized communication will result in abrogation of the contract. Is that clear?

"Good. Your work will not be difficult, but it will be tremendously important. You will, very likely, be finished in three months, but you will be ready to go any place at any time—at our discretion and, naturally, at our expense. Mr. Sorenson, as you are taking this down, you realize that this goes for you, too." He nodded.

"Your references, your abilities, and your past work have been thoroughly checked, and you will continue under constant observation. You will be required to verify and notarize every page, perhaps every line, of your transcripts, which Mr. Sorenson here will supply. Any questions?"

No questions. Each was getting a fabulous salary, and each wanted to appear eager to earn it. They all signed.

The resourceful Johnson bought for us a small rooming house, and we paid an exorbitant fee to a detective agency to do the cooking and cleaning and chauffeuring required. We requested that the lip-readers refrain from discussing their work among themselves, especially in front of the house employees, and they followed the instructions very well.

One day, about a month later, we called a conference in the projection room of Johnson's laboratory. We had a single reel of film.

"What's that for?"

"That's the reason for all the cloak-and-dagger secrecy. Never mind calling your projection man. This I'm going to run through myself. See what you think of it."

They were all disgusted. "I'm getting tired of all this kid stuff," said Kessler.

As I started for the projection booth I heard Mike say, "You're no more tired of it than I am."

From the booth I could see what was showing on the downstairs screen, but nothing else. I ran through the reel, rewound, and went back down.

I said, "One more thing, before we go any further, read this. It's a certified and notarized transcript of what has been read from the lips of the characters you just saw. They weren't, incidentally, 'characters,' in that sense of the word." I handed the crackling sheets around, a copy for each. "Those 'characters' are real people. You've just seen a newsreel. This transcript will tell you what they were talking about. Read it. In the trunk of the car, Mike and I have something to show you. We'll be back by the time you've read it."

Mike helped me carry the machine from the car. We came to the door just in time to see Kessler throw the transcript as far as he could. He bounced to his feet as the sheets fluttered down.

He was furious. "What's going on here?" We paid no attention to him, nor to the excited demands of the others until the machine had been plugged into the nearest outlet.

Mike looked at me. "Any ideas?"

I shook my head and told Johnson to shut up for a minute. Mike lifted the lid and hesitated momentarily before touching the dials. I pushed Johnson into his chair and turned off the lights myself. The room went black. Johnson, looking over my shoulder, gasped. I heard Bernstein swear softly, amazed.

I turned to see what Mike had shown them.

It was impressive, all right. He had started just over the roof of the laboratory and continued straight up in the air. Up, up, up, until the city of Los Angeles was a tiny dot on a great ball. On the horizon were the Rockies. Johnson squeezed my arm until it hurt.

"What's that? What's that? Stop it!" He was yelling. Mike turned off the machine.

You can guess what happened next. No one believed their eyes, nor Mike's patient explanation. Twice he had to turn on the machine again, once going far back into Kessler's past. Then the reaction set in.

Marss smoked one cigarette after another, Bernstein turned a gold pencil over in his nervous fingers. Johnson paced like a caged tiger, and burly Kessler stared at the machine, saying nothing at all. Johnson was muttering as he paced. Then he stopped and shook his fist under Mike's nose.

"Man! Do you know what you've got there? Why waste time playing around here? Can't you see you've got the world by the tail on a downhill pull? If I'd ever known this—"

Mike appealed to me. "Ed, talk to this wild man."

I did. I can't remember exactly what I said, and it isn't important. But I did tell him how we'd started, how we'd plotted our course, and what we were going to do. I ended by telling him the idea behind the reel of film I'd run off a few minutes earlier.

He recoiled as though I were a snake. "You can't get away with that! You'd be hung—if you weren't lynched first!"

"Don't you think we know that? Don't you think we're willing to take that chance?"

He tore his thinning hair. Marrs broke in. "Let me talk to him." He came over and faced us squarely.

"Is this on the level? You going to make a picture like that and stick your neck out? You're going to turn that . . . that thing over to the people of the world?"

I nodded. "Just that."

"And toss over everything you've got?" He was dead serious, and so was I. He turned to the others. "He means it!"

Bernstein said, "Can't be done!"

Words flew. I tried to convince them that we had followed the only possible path. "What kind of a world do you want to live in? Or don't you want to live?"

Johnson grunted. "How long do you think we'd live if we ever made picture like that? You're crazy! I'm not. I'm not going to put my head in a noose."

"Why do you think we've been so insistent about credit and responsibility for direction and production? You'll be doing only what we hired you for. Not that we want to twist your arm, but you've made a fortune, all of you, working for us. Now, when the going gets heavy, you want to back out!"

Marss gave in. "Maybe you're right, maybe you're wrong. Maybe you're crazy, maybe I am. I always used to say I'd try anything once. Bernie, you?"

Bernstein was quietly cynical. "You saw what happened in the last war. This might help. I don't know if it will. I don't know—but I'd hate to think I didn't try. Count me in!"

Kessler?

He swiveled his head. "Kid stuff! Who wants to live forever? Who wants to let a chance go by?"

Johnson threw up his hands. "Let's hope we get a cell together. Let's all go crazy." And that was that.

We went to work in a blazing drive of mutual hope and understanding. In four months the lip-readers were through. There's no point in detailing here their reactions to the dynamite they dictated to Sorenson every day. For their own good we kept them in the dark about our final purpose, and when they were through we sent them across the border into Mexico, to a small ranch Johnson had leased. We were going to need them later.

The print duplicators worked overtime, but Marrs worked harder. Press and radio shouted the announcement that, in every city of the world we could reach, there would be held simultaneously the premieres of our latest picture. It would be the last we needed to make. Many wondered aloud at our choice of the word 'needed.' We whetted their curiosity by refusing to release any advance information about the plot, and Johnson so well infused the men with their own now-fervent enthusiasm that not much could be pried out of them but conjecture. The day we picked for release was Sunday. Monday, the storm broke.

I wonder how many prints of that picture are left today. I wonder how many escaped burning or confiscation. Two world wars we covered, covered from the unflattering angles that, up until then, had been represented by only a few books hidden in the dark recesses of libraries. We showed, and *named*, the war-makers, the cynical leaders who signed and laughed and lied, the blatant patriots who used the flaring headlines and the ugly atrocities to hide behind their flag while life turned to death for millions. Our own and foreign traitors were there, the hidden ones with Janus faces. Our lip-readers had done their work well; no guesses these, no deduced conjectures from the broken records of a blasted past, but the exact words that exposed treachery disgusted as patriotism.

In foreign lands the performances lasted barely one day. Usually, in retaliation for the imposed censorship, the theaters were wrecked by rampaging crowds. (Marrs, incidentally, had spent hundreds of thousands bribing officials to allow the picture to be shown without previous censorship. Many censors, when that came out, were shot without trial.) In the Balkans, revolutions broke out, and various embassies were stormed by mobs. Where the film was banned or destroyed, written versions spontaneously appeared on the streets or in coffeehouses. Bootlegged editions were smuggled past customs guards, who looked the other way. One royal family fled to Switzerland.

Here in America it was a racing two weeks before the federal government, prodded into action by the raging of press and radio, in an unprecedented move closed all performances, "to promote the common welfare, insure domestic tranquility, and preserve foreign relations." Murmurs—and one riot—rumbled in the Midwest and spread until it was realized by the powers that be that something had to be done, quickly, if every government in the world were not to collapse of its own weight.

We were in Mexico, at the ranch Johnson had rented for the lip-readers. While Johnson paced the floor, jerkily fraying a cigar, we listened to a special broadcast by the U.S. attorney general himself:

> . . . *furthermore, this message was today forwarded to the Government of the United States of Mexico. I read: "The Government of the United States of America requests the immediate arrest and extradition of the following:*
>
> *"Edward Joseph Lefkowicz, known as Lefko."* (First on the list. Even a fish wouldn't get into trouble if he kept his mouth shut.)
>
> *"Miguel Jose Zapata Laviada."* (Mike crossed one leg over the other.)
>
> *"Edward Lee Johnson."* (He threw his cigar on the floor and sank into the chair.)
>
> *"Robert Chester Marrs."* (He lit another cigarette. His face twitched.)

"Benjamin Lionel Bernstein." (He smiled a twisted smile and close his eyes.)

"Carl Wilhelm Kessler." (A snarl.)

These men are wanted by the Government of the United States of America, to stand trial on charges ranging from criminal syndicalism, incitement to riot, misprision of treason—

I clicked off the radio. "Well?" to no one in particular.

Bernstein opened his eyes. "The *rurales* are probably on their way. Might as well go back and face the music—" We crossed the border at Juarez. The FBI was waiting.

Every press and radio chain in the world must have had coverage at that trial, every radio system, even the new and imperfect television chain. We were allowed to see no one but our lawyer. Samuels flew from the West Coast and spent a week trying to get past our guards. He told us not to talk to reporters, if we ever saw them.

"You haven't seen the newspapers? Just as well—How did you ever get yourselves into this mess, anyway? You ought to know better."

I told him.

He was stunned. "Are you all crazy?"

He was hard to convince. Only a united, concerted effort by all of us made him believe that such a machine was in existence. (He talked to us separately, because we were kept isolated.) When he got back to me, he was unable to p think cohe rently.

"What kind of defense do you call that?"

I shook my head. "No. That is, we know that we're guilty of practically everything under the sun if you look at it one way. If you look at it another—"

He rose. "Man, you don't need a lawyer, you need a doctor. I'll see you later. I've got to get this figured out in my mind before I can do a thing."

"Sit down. What do you think of this?" and I outlined what I had in mind.

"I think . . . I don't know what I think. I don't know. I'll talk to you later. Right now I want some fresh air," and he left.

As most trials do, this one began with the usual blackening of the defendant's character, or the claim that he lacked one. (The men we'd blackmailed at the beginning had long since had their money returned, and they had sense enough to keep quiet. That might have been because they'd received a few hints that there might still be a negative or two lying around. Compounding a felony? Sure.) With the greatest of interest we sat in that great columned hall and listened to a sad tale.

We had, with malice aforethought, libeled beyond repair great and unselfish men who had made a career of devotion to the public weal, imperiled needlessly relations traditionally friendly by falsely reporting mythical events, mocked the courageous sacrifices of those who had *dulce et gloria mori,* and completely upset everyone's peace of mind. Every new accusation, every verbal lance drew solemn agreement from the dignitary-packed hall. Against someone's better judgment, the trial had been transferred from the regular courtroom to the Hall of Justice, and it was packed with influence, brass, and pompous legates from all over the world. Only congressmen from the biggest states, or those with the biggest votes, were able to crowd the newly installed seats. So you can see it was a hostile audience that faced Samuels when the defense had its say. We had spent the previous night together in the guarded suite to which we had been transferred for the duration of the trial, perfecting, as far as we could, our planned defense. Samuels has the arrogant sense of humor that usually goes with supreme self-confidence, and I'm sure he enjoyed standing there among all those bemedaled and bejowled bigwigs, knowing the bombshell he was going to hurl. He made a good grenadier. Like this:

"We believe there is only one defense possible, we believe there is only one defense necessary. We have gladly waived, without prejudice, our inalienable right to trial by jury. We shall speak plainly and bluntly, to the point.

"You have seen the picture in question. You have remarked, possibly, upon what has been called the startling resemblance of the actors in that picture to the characters named and portrayed. You have remarked, possibly, upon the apparent verisimilitude to reality. That I will mention again. The first witness will, I believe, establish the trend of our rebuttal of the allegations of the prosecution." He called the first witness.

"Your name, please?"

"Mercedes Maria Gomez."

"A little louder, please."

"Mercedes Maria Gomez."

"Your occupation?"

"Until last March I was a teacher at the Arizona School for the Deaf. Then I asked for and obtained a leave of absence. At present I am under personal contract to Mr. Lefko."

"If you see Mr. Lefko in this courtroom, Miss . . . Mrs. . . ."

"Miss."

"Thank you. If Mr. Lefko is in this court, will you point him out? Thank you. Will you tell us the extent of your duties at the Arizona school?"

"I taught children born totally deaf to speak. And to read lips."

"Do you read lips yourself, Miss Gomez?"

"I have been totally deaf since I was fifteen."

"You lip-read in English only?"

"English and Spanish. We have . . . had many children of Mexican descent."

Samuels asked for a designated Spanish-speaking interpreter. An officer in the back immediately volunteered. He was identified by his ambassador, who was present.

"Will you take this book to the rear of the courtroom, sir?" (To the Court): "If the prosecution wishes to examine that book, they will find that it is a Spanish edition of the Bible." The prosecution didn't wish to examine it.

"Will the officer open the Bible at random and read aloud?" He opened the Bible at the center and read. In dead silence the Court strained to hear. Nothing could be heard the length of the enormous hall.

Samuels: "Miss Gomez. Will you take these binoculars and repeat, to the court, just what the officer is reading at the other end of the room?"

She took the binoculars and focused them expertly on the officer, who had stopped reading and was watching alertly. "I am ready."

Samuels: "Will you please read, sir?"

He did, and the woman repeated aloud, quickly and easily, a section that sounded as though it might be anything at all. I can't speak Spanish. The officer continued to read for a minute or two.

Samuels: "Thank you, sir. And thank you, Miss Gomez. Your pardon, sir, but since there are several who have been known to memorize the Bible, will you tell the Court if you have anything on your person that is written, anything that Miss Gomez has no chance of viewing?" Yes, the officer had. "Will you read that as before? Will you, Miss Gomez—"

She read that, too. Then the officer came to the front to listen to the court reporter read Miss Gomez's words.

"That's what I read," he affirmed.

Samuels turned her over to the prosecution, who made more experiments that served only to convince that she was equally good as interpreter and a lip-reader in either language.

In rapid succession Samuels put the rest of the lip-readers on the stand. In rapid succession they proved themselves as able and as capable as Miss Gomez, in their own linguistic speciality. The Russian from Ambridge generously offered to translate into his broken English any other Slavic language handy, and drew scattered grins from the press box. The Court was convinced, but failed to see the purpose of the exhibition. Samuels, glowing with satisfaction and confidence, faced the Court.

"Thanks to the indulgence of the Court, and despite the efforts of the distinguished prosecution, we have proved the almost amazing accuracy of lipreading in general, and these lip-readers in particular." One judge absently nodded in agreement. "Therefore, our defense will be based on that premise, and on one other which we have until now found necessary to keep hidden—the picture in question was and is definitely not a fictional representation of events of questionable authenticity. Every scene in that film contained not polished professional actors but the original person named and portrayed. Every foot, every inch of film, was not the result of an elaborate studio reconstruction but an actual collection of pictures, an actual collection of newsreels—if they can be called that—edited and assembled in story form!"

Through the startled spurt of astonishment we heard one from the prosecution: "That's ridiculous! No newsreel—"

Samuels ignored the objections and the tumult and put me on the stand. Beyond the usual preliminary questions I was allowed to say things my own way. At first hostile, the Court became interested enough to overrule the repeated objections that flew from the table devoted to the prosecution. I felt that at least two of the Court, if not outright favorable, were friendly. As far as I can remember, I went over the maneuvers of the past years and ended something like this:

"As to why we arranged the cards to fall as they did: both Mr. Laviada and myself were unable to face the prospect of destroying his discovery, because of the inevitable penalizing of needed research. We were, and we are, unwilling to better ourselves or a limited group by the use and maintenance of secrecy, if secrecy were possible. As to the only other alternative," and I directed this straight at Judge Bronson, the well-known liberal on the bench, "since the last war all atomic research and activity have been under the direction of a board nominally civilian, but actually under the 'protection and direction' of the Army and Navy. This 'direction and protection', as any competent physicist will gladly attest, has proved to be nothing but a smothering blanket serving to conceal hide-bound antiquated reasoning, abysmal ignorance, and inestimable amounts of fumbling. As of right now, this country, or any country that was foolish enough to place any confidence in the rigid regime of the military mind, is years behind what would otherwise be the natural course of discovery and progress in nuclear and related fields.

"We were, and we are, firmly convinced that even the slightest hint of the inherent possibilities and scope of Mr. Laviada's discovery would have meant, under the present regime, instant and mandatory confiscation of even a supposedly secure patent. Mr. Laviada has never applied for a patent, and never will. We both feel that such a discovery belongs not to an individual, a group, a corporation, or even to a nation, but to the world and those who live in it.

"We know, and are eager and willing to prove, that the domestic and external affairs of not only this nation, but of every nation are influenced, sometimes controlled, by esoteric groups warping political theories and human lives to suit their own ends." The Court was smothered in sullen silence, thick and acid with hate and disbelief.

"Secret treaties, for example, and vicious, lying propaganda have too long controlled human passions and made men hate; honored thieves have too long rotted secretly in undeserved high places. The machine can make treachery and untruth impossible. It *must*, if atomic war is not to sear the face and fate of the world.

"Our pictures were all made with that end in view. We needed, first, the wealth and prominence to present to an international audience what we knew to be the truth. We have done as much as we can. From now on, this Court takes over the burden we have carried. We are guilty of no treachery, guilty of no deceit, guilty of nothing but deep and true humanity. Mr. Laviada wishes me to tell the Court and the world that he has been unable till now to give his discovery to the world, free to use as it wills."

The Court stared at me. Every foreign representative was on the edge of his seat waiting for the judges to order us shot without further ado, the sparkling uniforms were seething, and the pressmen were racing their pencils against time. The tension dried my throat. The speech that Samuels and I had rehearsed the previous night was strong medicine. Now what?

Samuels filled the breach smoothly. "If the Court pleases; Mr. Lefko has made some startling statements. Startling, but certainly sincere, and certainly either provable or disprovable. And proof it shall be!"

He strode to the door of the conference room that had been allotted us. As the hundreds of eyes followed him it was easy for me to slip down from the witness stand and wait, ready. From the conference room Samuels rolled the machine, and Mike rose. The whispers that curdled the air seemed disappointed, unimpressed. Right in front of the bench he trundled it.

He moved unobtrusively to one side as the television men trained their long-snouted cameras. "Mr. Laviada and Mr. Lefko will show you. . . . I trust there will be no objection from the prosecution?" He was daring them.

One of the prosecution was already on his feet. He opened his mouth hesitantly, but thought better, and sat down. Heads went together in conference as he did. Samuels was watching the Court with one eye and the courtroom with the other.

"If the Court pleases, we will need a cleared space. If the bailiff will . . . thank you, sir." The long tables were moved back, with a raw scraping. He stood there, with every eye in the courtroom glued on him. For two long breaths he stood there, then he spun and went to his table. "Mr. Lefko," and be bowed formally. He sat.

The eyes swung to me, to Mike, as he moved to his machine and stood there silently. I cleared my throat and spoke to the Court as though I did not see the directional microphones trained at my lips.

"Judge Bronson."

He looked steadily at me and then glanced at Mike. "Yes. Mr. Lefko?"

"Your freedom from bias is well known." The corners of his mouth went down as he frowned. "Are you willing to be used as proof that there can be no trickery?" He thought that over, then nodded slowly. The prosecution objected but were waved down. "Will you tell me exactly where you were at any given time? Any place where you are absolutely certain and can verify that there were no concealed cameras or observers?"

He thought. Seconds. Minutes. The tension twanged, and I swallowed dust. He spoke quietly. "1918. November 11th."

Mike whispered to me. I said, "Any particular time?"

Judge Bronson looked at Mike. "Exactly eleven. Armistice time." He paused, then went on. "Niagara Falls. Niagara Falls, New York."

I heard the dials tick in the stillness, and Mike whispered again. I said, "The lights should be off." The bailiff rose. "Will you please watch the left wall, or in that direction? I think that if Judge Kassel will turn a little . . . we are ready."

Bronson looked at me, and at the left wall. "Ready."

The lights flicked out overhead and I heard the television crews mutter. I touched Mike on the shoulder. "Show them, Mike!"

We're all show men at heart, and Mike is no exception. Suddenly out of nowhere and into the depths poured a frozen torrent. Niagara Falls. I've mentioned. I think, that I've never got over a fear of heights. Few people ever do. I heard long, shuddery gasps as we started straight down. Down, until we stopped at the brink of the silent cataract, weird in its frozen majesty. Mike had stopped time at exactly eleven, I knew. He shifted to the American bank. Slowly he moved along. There a few tourists stood in almost comic attitudes. There was snow on the ground, flakes in the air. Time stood still, and hearts slowed in sympathy.

Bronson snapped, "Stop!"

A couple, young. Long skirts, high-buttoned army collar, dragging army overcoat, facing, arms about each other. Mike's sleeve rustled in the darkness and they moved. She was sobbing and the soldier was smiling. She turned away her head, and he turned it back. Another couple seized them gayly, and they twirled breathlessly.

Bronson's voice was harsh. "That's enough!" The view blurred for seconds.

Washington. The White House. The President. Someone coughed like a small explosion. The President was watching a television screen. Suddenly he jerked erect, startled. Mike spoke for the first time in court.

"That is the President of the United States. He is watching the trial that is being broadcast and televised from this courtroom. He is listening to what I am saying right now, and he is watching, on his television screen, as I use my machine to show him what he was doing one second ago."

The President heard those fateful words. Stiffly he threw an unconscious glance around his room at nothing and looked back at his screen in time to see himself do what he had just done, one second ago. Slowly, as if against his will, his hand started toward the switch of his set.

"Mr. President, don't turn off that set." Mike's voice was curt, almost rude. "You must hear this, you, of all people in the world. You must understand!

"This is not what we wanted to do, but we have no recourse left but to appeal to you, and to the people of this twisted world." The President might have been cast in iron. "You must see, you must understand that you have in your hands the power to make it impossible for greed-born war to be bred in secrecy and rob man of his youth or his old age or whatever he prizes." His voice softened, pleaded. "That is all we have to say. That is all we want. This is all anyone could want, ever." The President, unmoving, faded into blackness. "The lights, please." And almost immediately the Court adjourned.

That was over a month ago.

Mike's machine has been taken from us, and we are under military guard. Probably it's just as well we're guarded. We understand there have been lynching parties broken up as near as a block or two away. Last week we watched a white-haired fanatic scream about us, on the street below. We couldn't catch what he was shrieking, but we did catch a few air-borne epithets.

"Devils! Anti-Christs! Violation of the Bible!" Violations of this and that. Some, right here in the city, I suppose, would be glad to build a bonfire to cook us right back to the flames from which we've sprung. I wonder what the various groups are going to do now that the truth can be seen. Who can read lips in Aramaic, or Latin, or Coptic? And is a mechanical miracle a miracle?

This changes everything. We've been moved. Where, I don't know, except that the weather is warm, and we're on some military reservation, judging from the lack of civilians. Now we know what we're up against. What started out to be just a time-killing occupation, Joe, has turned out to be a necessary preface to what I'm going to ask you to do. Finish this, and then move fast! We won't be able to get this to you for a while yet, so I'll go on for a bit the way I started, to kill time. Like our clippings:

> *Tabloid*: ". . . Such a weapon cannot, must not be loosed in unscrupulous hands. The last professional production of the infamous pair proves what distortions can be wrested from isolated and misunderstood events. In the hands of perpetrators of heretical isms, no property, no business deal, no personal life could be sacrosanct, no foreign policy could be . . ."

> *Times*: ". . . colonies stand with us firmly . . . liquidation of the Empire . . . white man's burden . . ."

> *Le Matin*: ". . . rightful place . . . restore proud ·France . . ."

> *Pravda*: ". . . democratic imperialist plot . . . our glorious scientists ready to announce . . ."

> *Nichi-Nichi*: ". . . incontrovertibly prove divine descent . . ."

> *La Prensa*: ". . . oil concessions . . . dollar diplomacy . . ."

> *Detroit Journal*: ". . . under our noses in a sinister fortress on East Warren . . . under close Federal supervision . . . perfection by our production-trained technicians a mighty aid to law-enforcement agencies . . . tirades against politicians and business common sense carried too far . . . tomorrow revelations by . . ."

> *L'Osservatore Romano*: "Council of Cardinals . . . announcement expected hourly . . ."

> *Jackson Star-Clarion*: ". . . proper handling will prove the fallacy of race equality . . ."

Almost unanimously the press screamed; Pegler frothed, Winchell leered. We got the surface side of the situation from the press. But a military guard is composed of individuals, hotel rooms must be swept by maids, waiters must serve food, and a chain is as strong— We got what we think is the truth from those who work for a living.

There are meetings on street corners and homes, two great veteran groups have arbitrarily fired their officials, seven governors have resigned, three senators and over a dozen representatives have retired because of 'ill health.' The general temper is ugly. International travelers report the same in Europe; Asia is bubbling, and transport planes with motors running stud the airports of South America. A general rumor is that a constitutional amendment is being rammed through to forbid the use of similar instruments by any individual, with the manufacture and leasing by the federal government to law-enforcement agencies or financially responsible corporations suggested; it is whispered that motor caravans are forming throughout the country for a Washington march to demand a decision by the Supreme Court on the truth of our charges; it is generally suspected that all news disseminating services are under direct Federal-Army control; wires are supposed to be sizzling with petitions and demands to Congress, which are seldom delivered.

One day the chambermaid said: "And the whole hotel might as well close up shop. The whole floor is blocked off, there're MP's at every door, and they're clearing out all the other guests as fast as they can be moved. The whole place wouldn't be big enough to hold the letters and wires addressed to you, or the ones that are trying to get in to see you. Fat chance they have," she added grimly. "The joint is lousy with brass."

Mike glanced at me, and I cleared my throat. "What's your idea of the whole thing?"

Expertly she spanked and reversed a pillow. "I saw your last picture before they shut it down. I saw all your pictures. When I wasn't working, I listened to your trial. I heard you tell them off. I never got married because my boy friend never came back from Burma. Ask *him* what he thinks," and she jerked her head at the young private who was supposed to keep her from talking. "Ask him if he wants some bunch of stinkers to start him shooting at some other poor chump. See what he says, and then ask me if I want an atom bomb dropped down my neck just because some chiselers want more than they got." She left suddenly, and the soldier left with her. Mike and I had a beer and went to bed. Next week the papers had headlines a mile high.

U.S. Keeps Miracle Ray
Constitutional Amendment
Awaits States Okay
Laviada–Lefko Freed

We were freed all right, Bronson and the President being responsible for that. But the President and Bronson don't know, I'm sure, that we were arrested immediately. We were told that we'll be held in 'protective custody' until enough states have ratified the proposed constitutional amendment. The Man Without a Country was in what you might call 'protective custody,' too. We'll likely be released the same way he was.

We're allowed no newspapers, no radio, allowed no communication coming or going, and we're given no reason, as if that was necessary. They'll never let us go, and they'd be fools if they did. They think that if we can't communicate, or if we can't build another machine, our fangs are drawn, and when the excitement dies, we fall into oblivion, six feet of it. Well, we can't build another machine. But, communicate?

Look at it this way. A soldier is a soldier because he wants to serve his country. A soldier doesn't want to die unless his country is at war. Even then, death is only a last resort. And war isn't necessary anymore, not with our machine. In the dark? Try to plan or plot in absolute darkness, which is what would be needed. Try to plot or carry on a war without putting things in writing. O.K. Now . . .

The Army has Mike's machine. The Army has Mike. They call it military expediency, I suppose. Bosh! Anyone beyond the grade of moron can see that to keep that machine, to hide it, is to invite the world to attack, and attack in self-defense. If every nation, or if every man, had a machine, each would be equally open, or equally protected. But if only one nation, or only one man, can see, the rest will not long be blind. Maybe we did this all wrong. God knows, we thought about it often. God knows, we did our best to keep man out of his own trap.

There isn't much time left. One of the soldiers guarding us will get this to you, I hope, in time.

A long time ago we gave you a key, and hoped we would never have to ask you to use it. But now is the time. That key fits a box at the Detroit Savings Bank. In that box are letters. Mail them, not all at once, or in the same place. They'll go all over the world, to men we know, and have watched well, men clever, honest, and capable of following the plans we've enclosed.

But you've got to hurry! One of these bright days, someone is going to wonder if we've made more than one machine. We haven't, of course. That would have been foolish. But if some smart young lieutenant gets hold of that machine long enough to start tracing back our movement, they'll find that safety deposit box, with the plans and letters ready to be scattered broadside. You can see the need for haste—if the rest of the world, or any particular nation, wants that machine bad enough, they'll fight for it. And they will!

They must! Later on, when the Army gets used to the machine and its capabilities, it will become obvious to everyone, as it already has to Mike and me, that, with every plan open to inspection as soon as it's made, no nation or group of nations would have a chance in open warfare. So if there is to be an attack, it will have to be deadly, and fast, and sure. Please God that we haven't shoved the world into a war we tried to make impossible. With all the atom bombs and rockets that have been made in the past few years— Joe, you've got to hurry!

GHQ TO 9TH ATTK GRP
Report report report report report report report report report report

CMDR 9TH ATTK GRP TO GHQ
Begins: No other manuscript found. Scarched body of Lefko immediately upon landing. According to plan Building Three untouched. Survivors insist both were moved to Building Seven previous day defective plumbing. Body of Laviada identified definitely through fingerprints. Request further instructions. *Ends*

GHQ TO CMDR 32ND SHIELDING RGT
Begins: Seal area Detroit Savings Bank. Advise immediately condition safety deposit boxes. Afford coming technical unit complete cooperation. *Ends*

LT. COL. TEMP. ATT. 32ND SHIELDING RGT TO GHQ
Begins: Area Detroit Savings Bank vaporized direct hit. Radioactivity lethal. Impossible boxes or any contents survive. Repeat, direct hit. Request permission proceed Washington area. *Ends*.

GHQ TO LT. COL. TEMP. ATT. 32ND SHIELDED RGT
Begins: Request denied. Sift ashes if necessary regardless cost. Repeat, regardless cost. *Ends*

GHQ TO ALL UNITS REPEAT ALL UNITS
Begins: Lack of enemy resistance explained misdirected atom rocket seventeen miles SSE Washington. Lone survivor completely destroyed special train claims all top officials left enemy capital two hours preceding attack. Notify local governments where found necessary and obvious cessation hostilities. Occupy present areas Plan Two. Further orders follow. *Ends*

WITH FOLDED HANDS

Jack Williamson

Underhill was walking home from the office, because his wife had the car, the afternoon he first met the new mechanicals. His feet were following his usual diagonal path across a weedy vacant block—his wife usually had the car—and his preoccupied mind was rejecting various impossible ways to meet his notes at the Two Rivers bank, when a new wall stopped him.

The wall wasn't any common brick or stone, but something sleek and bright and strange. Underhill stared up at a long new building. He felt vaguely annoyed and surprised at this glittering obstruction—it certainly hadn't been here last week.

Then he saw the thing in the window.

The window itself wasn't any ordinary glass. The wide, dustless panel was completely transparent, so that only the glowing letters fastened to it showed that it was there at all. The letters made a severe, modernistic sign:

> Two Rivers Agency
> HUMANOID INSTITUTE
> The Perfect Mechanicals
> "To Serve and Obey,
> And Guard Men from Harm."

His dim annoyance sharpened, because Underhill was in the mechanicals business himself. Times were already hard enough, and mechanicals were a drug on the market. Androids, mechanoids, electronoids, automatoids, and ordinary robots. Unfortunately, few of them did all the salesmen promised, and the Two Rivers market was already sadly oversaturated.

Underhill sold androids—when he could. His next consignment was due tomorrow, and he didn't quite know how to meet the bill.

Frowning, he paused to stare at the thing behind that invisible window. He had never seen a humanoid. Like any mechanical not at work, it stood absolutely motionless. Smaller and slimmer than a man. A shining black, its sleek silicone skin had a changing sheen of bronze and metallic blue. Its graceful oval face wore a fixed look of alert and slightly surprised solicitude. Altogether, it was the most beautiful mechanical he had ever seen.

Too small, of course, for much practical utility. He murmured to himself a reassuring quotation from the *Android Salesman*: "Androids are big—because the makers refuse to sacrifice power, essential functions, or dependability. Androids are your biggest buy!"

The transparent door slid open as he turned toward it, and he walked into the haughty opulence of the new display room to convince himself that these streamlined items were just another flashy effort to catch the woman shopper.

He inspected the glittering layout shrewdly, and his breezy optimism faded. He had never heard of the Humanoid Institute, but the invading firm obviously had big money and big-time merchandising know-how.

He looked around for a salesman, but it was another mechanical that came gliding silently to meet him. A twin of the one in the window, it moved with a quick, surprising grace. Bronze and blue lights flowed over its lustrous blackness, and a yellow name plate flashed from its naked breast:

HUMANOID
Serial No. 81-H-B-27
The Perfect Mechanical
"To Serve and Obey
And Guard Men from Harm."

Curiously, it had no lenses. The eyes in its bald oval head were steel-colored, blindly staring. But it stopped a few feet in front of him, as if it could see anyhow, an it spoke to him with a high, melodious voice:

"At your service, Mr. Underhill."

The use of his name startled him, for not even the androids could tell one man from another. But this was a clever merchandising stunt, of course, not too difficult in a town the size of Two Rivers. The salesman must be some local man, prompting the mechanical from behind the partition. Underhill erased his momentary astonishment, and said loudly.

"May I see your salesman, please?"

"We employ no human salesmen, sir," its soft silvery voice replied instantly. "The Humanoid Institute exists to serve mankind, and we require no human service. We ourselves can supply any information you desire, sir, and accept your order for immediate humanoid service."

Underhill peered at it dazedly. No mechanicals were competent even to recharge their own batteries and reset their own relays, much less to operate their own branch office. The blind eyes stared blankly back, and he looked uneasily around for any booth or curtain that might conceal the salesman.

Meanwhile, the sweet thin voice resumed persuasively.

"May we come out to your home for a free trial demonstration, sir? We are anxious to introduce our service on your planet, because we have been successful in eliminating human unhappiness on so many others. You will find us far superior to the old electronic mechanicals in use here."

Underhill stepped back uneasily. He reluctantly abandoned his search for the hidden salesman, shaken by the idea of any mechanicals promoting themselves. That would upset the whole industry.

"At least you must take some advertising matter, sir."

Moving with a somehow appalling graceful deftness, the small black mechanical brought him an illustrated booklet from a table by the wall. To cover his confused and increasing alarm, he thumbed through the glossy pages.

In a series of richly colored before-and-after pictures, a chesty blond girl was stooping over a kitchen stove, and then relaxing in a daring negligee while a little black mechanical knelt to serve her something. She was wearily hammering a typewriter, and then lying on an ocean beach, in a revealing sun suit, while another mechanical did the typing. She was toiling at some huge industrial machine, and then dancing in the arms of a golden-haired youth, while a black humanoid ran the machine.

Underhill sighed wistfully. The android company didn't supply such fetching sales material. Women would find this booklet irresistible, and they selected eighty-six percent of all mechanicals sold. Yes, the competition was going to be bitter.

"Take it home, sir," the sweet voice urged him. "Show it to your wife. There is a free trial demonstration order blank on the last page, and you will notice that we require no payment down."

He turned numbly, and the door slid open for him. Retreating dazedly, he discovered the booklet still in his hand. He crumpled it furiously, and flung it down. The small black thing picked it up tidily, and the insistent silver voice rang after him:

"We shall call at your office tomorrow, Mr. Underhill, and send a demonstration unit to your home. It is time to discuss the liquidation of your business, because the electronic mechanicals you have been selling cannot compete with us. And we shall offer your wife a free trial demonstration."

Underhill didn't attempt to reply, because he couldn't trust his voice. He stalked blindly down the new sidewalk to the corner, and paused there to collect himself. Out of his startled and confused impressions, one clear fact emerged—things looked black for the agency.

Bleakly, he stared back at the haughty splendor of the new building. It wasn't honest brick or stone; that invisible window wasn't glass; and he was quite sure the foundation for it hadn't even been staked out, the last time Aurora had the car.

He walked on around the block, and the new sidewalk took him near the rear entrance. A truck was backed up to it, and several slim black mechanicals were silently busy, unloading huge metal crates.

He paused to look at one of the crates. It was labeled for interstellar shipment. The stencils showed that it had come from the Humanoid Institute, on Wing IV. He failed to recall any planet of that designation; the outfit must be big.

Dimly, inside the gloom of the warehouse beyond the truck, he could see black mechanicals opening the crates. A lid came up, revealing dark, rigid bodies, closely packed. One by one, they came to life. They climbed out of the crate, and sprang gracefully to the floor. A shining black, glinting with bronze and blue, they were all identical.

One of them came out past the truck, to the sidewalk, staring with blind steel eyes. Its high silver voice spoke to him melodiously:

"At your service, Mr. Underhill."

He fled. When his name was promptly called by a courteous mechanical, just out of the crate in which it had been imported from a remote and unknown planet, he found the experience trying.

Two blocks along, the sign of a bar caught his eye, and he took his dismay inside. He had made it a business rule not to drink before dinner, and Aurora didn't like him to drink at all; but these new mechanicals, he felt, had made the day exceptional.

Unfortunately, however, alcohol failed to brighten the brief visible future of the agency. When he emerged, after an hour, he looked wistfully back in hope that the bright new building might have vanished as abruptly as it came. It hadn't. He shook his head dejectedly, and turned uncertainly homeward.

Fresh air had cleared his head somewhat, before he arrived at the neat white bungalow in the outskirts of the town, but it failed to solve his business problems. He also realized, uneasily, that he would be late for dinner.

Dinner, however, had been delayed. His son Frank, a freckled ten-year-old, was still kicking a football on the quiet street in front of the house. And little Gay, who was tow-haired and adorable and eleven, came running across the lawn and down the sidewalk to meet him.

"Father, you can't guess what!" Gay was going to be a great musician some day, and no doubt properly dignified, but she was pink and breathless with excitement now. She let him swing her high off the sidewalk, and she wasn't critical of the bar-aroma on his breath. He couldn't guess, and she informed him eagerly:

"Mother's got a new lodger!"

Underhill had foreseen a painful inquisition, because Aurora was worried about the notes at the bank, and the bill for the new consignment, and the money for little Gay's lessons.

The new lodger, however, saved him from that. With an alarming crashing of crockery, the household android was setting dinner on the table, but the little house was empty. He found Aurora in the back yard, burdened with sheets and towels for the guest.

Aurora, when he married her, had been as utterly adorable as now her little daughter was. She might have remained so, he felt, if the agency had been a little more successful. However, while the pressure of slow failure had gradually crumbled his own assurance, small hardships had turned her a little too aggressive.

Of course he loved her still. Her red hair was still alluring, and she was loyally faithful, but thwarted ambitions had sharpened her character and sometimes her voice. They never quarreled, really, but there were small differences.

There was the little apartment over the garage—built for human servants they had never been able to afford. It was too small and shabby to attract any responsible tenant, and Underhill wanted to leave it empty. It hurt his pride to see her making beds and cleaning floors for strangers.

Aurora had rented it before, however, when she wanted money to pay for Gay's music lessons, or when some colorful unfortunate touched her sympathy, and it seemed to Underhill that her lodgers had all turned out to be thieves and vandals.

She turned back to meet him, now, with the clean linen in her arms.

"Dear, it's no use objecting." Her voice was quite determined. "Mr. Sledge is the most wonderful old fellow, and he's going to stay just as long as he wants."

"That's all right, darling." He never liked to bicker, and he was thinking of his troubles at the agency. "I'm afraid we'll need the money. Just make him pay in advance."

"But he can't!" Her voice throbbed with sympathetic warmth. "He says he'll have royalties coming in from his inventions, so he can pay in a few days."

Underhill shrugged; he had heard that before.

"Mr. Sledge is different, dear," she insisted. "He's a traveler, and a scientist. Here, in this dull little town, we don't see many interesting people."

"You've picked up some remarkable types," he commented.

"Don't be unkind, dear," she chided gently. "You haven't met him yet, and you don't know how wonderful he is." Her voice turned sweeter. "Have you a ten, dear?"

He stiffened. "What for?"

"Mr. Sledge is ill." Her voice turned urgent. "I saw him fall on the street, downtown. The police were going to send him to the city hospital, but he didn't want to go. He looked so noble and sweet and grand. So I told them I would take him. I got him in the car and took him to old Dr. Winters. He has this heart condition, and he needs the money for medicine."

Reasonably, Underhill inquired, "Why doesn't he want to go to the hospital?"

"He has work to do," she said. "Important scientific work—and he's so wonderful and tragic. Please, dear, have you a ten?"

Underhill thought of many things to say. These new mechanicals promised to multiply his troubles. It was foolish to take in an invalid vagrant, who could have free care at the city hospital.

Aurora's tenants always tried to pay their rent with promises, and generally wrecked the apartment and looted the neighborhood before they left.

But he said none of those things. He had learned to compromise. Silently, he found two fives in his thin pocketbook, and put them in her hand. She smiled, and kissed him impulsively—he barely remembered to hold his breath in time.

Her figure was still good, by dint of periodic dieting. He was proud of her shining red hair. A sudden surge of affection brought tears to his eyes, and he wondered what would happen to her and the children if the agency failed.

"Thank you, dear!" she whispered. "I'll have him come for dinner, if he feels able, and you can meet him then. I hope you don't mind dinner being late."

He didn't mind, tonight. Moved by a sudden impulse of domesticity, he got hammer and nails from his workshop in the basement, and repaired the sagging screen on the kitchen door with a neat diagonal brace.

He enjoyed working with his hands. His boyhood dream had been to be a builder of fission power plants. He had even studied engineering—before he married Aurora, and had to take over the ailing mechanicals agency from her indolent and alcoholic father. He was whistling happily by the time the little task was done.

When he went back through the kitchen to put up his tools, he found the household android busily clearing the untouched dinner away from the table—the androids were good enough at strictly routine tasks, but they could never learn to cope with human unpredictability.

"Stop, stop!" Slowly repeated, in the proper pitch and rhythm, his command made it halt, and then he said carefully, "Set—table; set—table."

Obediently, the gigantic thing came shuffling back with the stack of plates. He was suddenly struck with the difference between it and those new humanoids. He sighed wearily. Things looked black for the agency.

Aurora brought her new lodger in through the kitchen door. Underhill nodded to himself. This gaunt stranger, with his dark shaggy hair, emaciated face, and threadbare garb, looked to be just the sort of colorful, dramatic vagabond that always touched Aurora's heart. She introduced them, and they sat down to wait in the front room while she went to call the children.

The old rogue didn't look very sick, to Underhill. Perhaps his wide shoulders had a tired stoop, but his spare, tall figure was still commanding. The skin was seamed and pale, over his rawboned, cragged face, but his deep-set eyes still had a burning vitality.

His hands held Underhill's attention. Immense hands, they hung a little forward when he stood, swung on long bony arms in perpetual readiness. Gnarled and scarred, darkly tanned, with the small hairs on the back bleached to a golden color, they told their own epic of varied adventure, of battle perhaps, and possibly even of toil. They had been very useful hands.

"I'm very grateful to your wife, Mr. Underhill." His voice was a deep-throated rumble, and he had a wistful smile, oddly boyish for a man so evidently old. "She rescued me from an unpleasant predicament, and I'll see that she is well paid."

Just another vivid vagabond, Underhill decided, talking his way through life with plausible inventions. He had a little private game he played with Aurora's tenants—just remembering what they said and counting one point for every impossibility. Mr. Sledge, he thought, would give him an excellent score.

"Where are you from?" he asked conversationally.

Sledge hesitated for an instant before he answered, and that was unusual—most of Aurora's tenants had been exceedingly glib.

"Wing IV." The gaunt old man spoke with a solemn reluctance, as if he should have liked to say something else. "All my early life was spent there, but I left the planet nearly fifty years ago. I've been traveling ever since."

Startled, Underhill peered at him sharply. Wing IV, he remembered, was the home planet of those sleek new mechanicals, but this old vagabond looked too seedy and impecunious to be connected with the Humanoid Institute. His brief suspicion faded. Frowning, he said casually:

"Wing IV must be rather distant."

The old rogue hesitated again, and then said gravely:

"One hundred and nine light-years, Mr. Underhill."

That made the first point, but Underhill concealed his satisfaction. The new space liners were pretty fast, but the velocity of light was still an absolute limit. Casually, he played for another point:

"My wife says you're a scientist, Mr. Sledge?"

"Yes."

The old rascal's reticence was unusual. Most of Aurora's tenants required very little prompting. Underhill tried again, in a breezy conversational tone:

"Used to be an engineer myself, until I dropped it to go into mechanicals." The old vagabond straightened, and Underhill paused hopefully. But he said nothing, and Underhill went on, "Fission plant design and operation. What's your speciality, Mr. Sledge?"

The old man gave him a long, troubled look, with those brooding, hollowed eyes, and then said slowly:

"Your wife has been kind to me, Mr. Underhill, when I was in desperate need. I think you are entitled to the truth, but I must ask you to keep it to yourself. I am engaged on a very important research problem, which must be finished secretly."

"I'm sorry." Suddenly ashamed of his cynical little game, Underhill spoke apologetically. "Forget it."

But the old man said deliberately:

"My field is rhodomagnetics."

"Eh?" Underhill didn't like to confess ignorance, but he had never heard of that. "I've been out of the game for fifteen years," he explained. "I'm afraid I haven't kept up."

The old man smiled again, faintly.

"The science was unknown here until I arrived, a few days ago," he said. "I was able to apply for basic patents. As soon as the royalties start coming in, I'll be wealthy again."

Underhill had heard that before. The old rogue's solemn reluctance had been very impressive, but he remembered that most of Aurora's tenants had been very plausible gentry.

"So?" Underhill was staring again, somehow fascinated by those gnarled and scarred and strangely able hands. "What, exactly, is rhodomagnetics?"

He listened to the old man's careful, deliberate answer, and started his little game again. Most of Aurora's tenants had told some pretty wild tales, but he had never heard anything to top this.

"A universal force," the weary, stooped old vagabond said solemnly. "As fundamental as ferromagnetism or gravitation, though the effects are less obvious. It is keyed to the second triad of the periodic table, rhodium and ruthenium and palladium, in very much the same way that ferromagnetism is keyed to the first triad, iron and nickel and cobalt."

Underhill remembered enough of his engineering courses to see the basic fallacy of that. Palladium was used for watch springs, he recalled, because it was completely non-magnetic. But he kept his face straight. He had no malice in his heart, and he played the little game just for his own amusement. It was secret, even from Aurora, and he always penalized himself for any show of doubt.

He said merely, "I thought the universal forces were already pretty well known."

"The effects of rhodomagnetism are masked by nature," the patient, rusty voice explained. "And, besides, they are somewhat paradoxical, so that ordinary laboratory methods defeat themselves."

"Paradoxical?" Underhill prompted.

"In a few days I can show you copies of my patents, and reprints of papers describing demonstration experiments," the old man promised gravely. "The velocity of propagation is infinite. The effects vary inversely with the first power of the distance, not with the square of the distance. And ordinary matter, except for the elements of the rhodium triad, is generally transparent to rhodomagnetic radiations."

That made four more points for the game. Underhill felt a little glow of gratitude to Aurora, for discovering so remarkable a specimen.

"Rhodomagnetism was first discovered through a mathematical investigation of the atom," the old romancer went serenely on, suspecting nothing. "A rhodomagnetic component was proved essential to maintain the delicate equilibrium of the nuclear forces. Consequently, rhodomagnetic waves tuned to atomic frequencies may be used to upset that equilibrium and produce nuclear instability. Thus most heavy atoms—generally those above palladium, 46 in atomic number—can be subjected to artificial fission."

Underhill scored himself another point, and tried to keep his eyebrows from lifting. He said, conversationally:

"Patents on such a discovery ought to be very profitable."

The old scoundrel nodded his gaunt, dramatic head.

"You can see the obvious application. My basic patents cover most of them. Devices for instantaneous interplanetary and interstellar communication. Long-range wireless power transmission. A rhodomagnetic inflexion-drive, which makes possible apparent speeds many times that of light—by means of a rhodomagnetic deformation of the continuum. And, of course, revolutionary types of fission power plants, using any heavy element for fuel."

Preposterous! Underhill tried hard to keep his face straight, but everybody knew that the velocity of light was a physical limit. On the human side, the owner of any such remarkable patents would hardly be begging for shelter in a shabby garage apartment. He noticed a pale circle around the old vagabond's gaunt and hairy wrist; no man owning such priceless secrets would have to pawn his watch.

Triumphantly, Underhill allowed himself four more points, but then he had to penalize himself. He must have let doubt show on his face, because the old man asked suddenly,

"Do you want to see the basic tensors?" He reached in his pocket for pencil and notebook. "I'll jot them down for you."

"Never mind," Underhill protested. "I'm afraid my math is a little rusty."

"But you think it strange that the holder of such revolutionary patents should find himself in need?"

Underhill nodded, and penalized himself another point. The old man might be a monumental liar, but he was shrewd enough.

"You see, I'm a sort of refugee," he explained apologetically. "I arrived on this planet only a few days ago, and I have to travel light. I was forced to deposit everything I had with a law firm, to arrange for the publication and protection of my patents. I expect to be receiving the first royalties soon."

"In the meantime," he added plausibly, "I came to Two Rivers because it is quiet and secluded, far from the spaceports. I'm working on another project, which must be finished secretly. Now, will you please respect my confidence, Mr. Underhill?"

Underhill had to say he would. Aurora came back with the freshly scrubbed children, and they went in to dinner. The android came lurching in with a steaming tureen. The old stranger seemed to shrink from the mechanical, uneasily. As she took the dish and served the soup, Aurora inquired lightly,

"Why doesn't your company bring out a better mechanical, dear? One smart enough to be a really perfect waiter, warranted not to splash the soup. Wouldn't that be splendid?"

Her question cast Underhill into moody silence. He sat scowling at his plate, thinking of those remarkable new mechanicals which claimed to be perfect, and what they might do to the agency. It was the shaggy old rover who answered soberly,

"The perfect mechanicals already exist, Mrs. Underhill." His deep, rusty voice had a solemn undertone. "And they are not so splendid, really. I've been a refugee from them, for nearly fifty years."

Underhill looked up from his plate, astonished.

"Those black humanoids, you mean?"

"Humanoids?" That great voice seemed suddenly faint, frightened. The deep-sunken eyes turned dark with shock. "What do you know of them?"

"They've just opened a new agency in Two Rivers," Underhill told him. "No salesmen about, if you can imagine that. They claim—"

His voice trailed off, because the gaunt old man was suddenly stricken. Gnarled hands clutched at his throat, and a spoon clattered to the floor. His haggard face turned an ominous blue, and his breath was a terrible shallow gasping.

He fumbled in his pocket for medicine, and Aurora helped him take something in a glass of water. In a few moments he could breathe again, and the color of life came back to his face.

"I'm sorry, Mrs. Underhill," he whispered apologetically. "It was just the shock—I came here to get away from them." He stared at the huge, motionless android, with a terror in his sunken eyes. "I wanted to finish my work before they came," he whispered. "Now there is very little time."

When he felt able to walk, Underhill went out with him to see him safely up the stairs to the garage apartment. The tiny kitchenette, he noticed, had already been converted into some kind of workshop. The old tramp seemed to have no extra clothing, but he had unpacked neat, bright gadgets of metal and plastic from his battered luggage, and spread them out on the small kitchen table.

The gaunt old man himself was tattered and patched and hungry-looking, but the parts of his curious equipment were exquisitely machined, and Underhill recognized the silver-white luster of rare palladium. Suddenly he suspected that he had scored too many points in his little private game.

A caller was waiting, when Underhill arrived next morning at his office at the agency. It stood frozen before his desk, graceful and straight, with soft lights of blue and bronze shining over its black silicone nudity. He stopped at the sight of it, unpleasantly jolted.

"At your service, Mr. Underhill." It turned quickly to face him, with its blind, disturbing stare. "May we explain how we can serve you?"

His shock of the afternoon before came back, and he asked sharply, "How do you know my name?"

"Yesterday we read the business cards in your case," it purred softly. "Now we shall know you always. You see, our senses are sharper than human vision, Mr. Underhill. Perhaps we seem a little strange at first, but you will soon become accustomed to us."

"Not if I can help it!" He peered at the serial number of its yellow nameplate, and shook his bewildered head. "That was another one, yesterday. I never saw you before!"

"We are all alike, Mr. Underhill," the silver voice said softly. "We are all one, really. Our separate mobile units are all controlled and powered from Humanoid Central. The units you see are only the senses and limbs of our great brain on Wing IV. That is why we are so far superior to the old electronic mechanicals."

It made a scornful-seeming gesture, toward the row of clumsy androids in his display room.

"You see, we are rhodomagnetic."

Underhill staggered a little, as if that word had been a blow. He was certain, now, that he had scored too many points from Aurora's new tenant. He shuddered slightly, to the first light kiss of terror, and spoke with an effort, hoarsely, "Well, what do you want?"

Staring blindly across his desk, the sleek black thing slowly unfolded a legal-looking document. He sat down, watching uneasily.

"This is merely an assignment, Mr. Underhill," it cooled at him soothingly. "You see, we are requesting you to assign your property to the Humanoid Institute in exchange for our service."

"What?" The word was an incredulous gasp, and Underhill came angrily back to his feet. "What kind of blackmail is this?"

"It's no blackmail," the small mechanical assured him softly. "You will find the humanoids incapable of any crime. We exist only to increase the happiness and safety of mankind."

"Then why do you want my property?" he rasped.

"The assignment is merely a legal formality," it told him blandly. "We strive to introduce our service with the least possible confusion and dislocation. We have found the assignment plan the most efficient for the control and liquidation of private enterprises."

Trembling with anger and the shock of mounting terror, Underhill gulped hoarsely, "Whatever your scheme is, I don't intend to give up my business."

"You have no choice, really." He shivered to the sweet certainty of that silver voice. "Human enterprise is no longer necessary, now that we have come, and the electronic mechanicals industry is always the first to collapse."

He stared defiantly at its blind steel eyes.

"Thanks!" He gave a little laugh, nervous and sardonic. "But I prefer to run my own business, and support my own family, and take care of myself."

"But that is impossible, under the Prime Directive," it cooed softly. "Our function is to serve and obey, and guard men from harm. It is no longer necessary for men to care for themselves, because we exist to insure their safety and happiness."

He stood speechless, bewildered, slowly boiling.

"We are sending one of our units to every home in the city, on a free trial basis," it added gently. "This free demonstration will make most people glad to make the formal assignment, and you won't be able to sell many more androids."

"Get out!" Underhill came storming around the desk.

The little black thing stood waiting for him, watching him with blind steel eyes, absolutely motionless. He checked himself suddenly, feeling rather foolish. He wanted very much to hit it, but he could see the futility of that.

"Consult your own attorney, if you wish." Deftly, it laid the assignment form on his desk. "You need have no doubts about the integrity of the Humanoid Institute. We are sending a statement of our assets to the Two Rivers bank, and depositing a sum to cover our obligations here. When you wish to sign, just let us know."

The blind thing turned, and silently departed.

Underhill went out to the corner drugstore and asked for a bicarbonate. The clerk that served him, however, turned out to be a sleek black mechanical. He went back to his office, more upset than ever.

An ominous hush lay over the agency. He had three house-to-house salesmen out with demonstrators. The phone should have been busy with their orders and reports, but it didn't ring at all until one of them called to say that he was quitting.

"I've got myself one of these new humanoids," he added, "and it says I don't have to work anymore."

He swallowed his impulse to profanity, and tried to take advantage of the unusual quiet by working on his books. But the affairs of the agency, which for years had been precarious, today appeared utterly disastrous. He left the ledgers hopefully, when at last a customer came in.

But the stout woman didn't want an android. She wanted a refund on the one she had bought the week before. She admitted that it could do all the guarantee promised—but now she had seen a humanoid.

The silent phone rang once again, that afternoon. The cashier of the bank wanted to know if he could drop in to discuss his loans. Underhill dropped in, and the cashier greeted him with an ominous affability.

"How's business?" the banker boomed, too genially.

"Average, last month," Underhill insisted stoutly. "Now, I'm just getting a new consignment, and I'll need another small loan—"

The cashier's eyes turned suddenly frosty, and his voice dried up.

"I believe you have a new competitor in town," the banker said crisply. "These humanoid people. A very solid concern, Mr. Underhill. Remarkably solid! They have filed a statement with us, and made a substantial deposit to care for their local obligations. Exceedingly substantial!"

The banker dropped his voice, professionally regretful.

"In these circumstances, Mr. Underhill, I'm afraid the bank can't finance your agency any longer. We must request you to meet your obligations in full, as they come due." Seeing Underhill's white desperation, he added icily, "We've already carried you too long, Underhill. If you can't pay, the bank will have to start bankruptcy proceedings."

The new consignment of androids was delivered late that afternoon. Two tiny black humanoids unloaded them from the truck —for it developed that the operators of the trucking company had already assigned it to the Humanoid Institute.

Efficiently, the humanoids stacked up the crates. Courteously they brought a receipt for him to sign. He no longer had much hope of selling the androids, but he had ordered the shipment and he had to accept it. Shuddering to a spasm of trapped despair, he scrawled his name. The naked black things thanked him, and took the truck away.

He climbed in his car and started home, inwardly seething. The next thing he knew, he was in the middle of a busy street, driving through cross traffic. A police whistle shrilled, and he pulled wearily to the curb. He waited for the angry officer, but it was a little black mechanical that overtook him.

"At your service, Mr. Underhill," it purred sweetly. "You must respect the stop lights, sir. Otherwise, you endanger human life."

"Huh?" He stared at it, bitterly. "I thought you were a cop."

"We are aiding the police department, temporarily," it said. "But driving is really much too dangerous for human beings, under the Prime Directive. As soon as our service is complete, every car will have a humanoid driver. As soon as every human being is completely supervised, there will be no need for any police force whatever."

Underhill glared at it, savagely.

"Well!" he rapped. "So I ran past a stop light. What are you going to do about it?"

"Our function is not to punish men, but merely to serve their happiness and security," its silver voice said softly. "We merely request you to drive safely, during this temporary emergency while our service is incomplete."

Anger boiled up in him.

"You're too perfect!" he muttered bitterly. "I suppose there's nothing men can do, but you can do it better."

"Naturally we are superior," it cooled serenely. "Because our units are metal and plastic, while your body is mostly water. Because our transmitted energy is drawn from atomic fission, instead of oxidation. Because our senses are sharper than human sight or hearing. Most of all, because all our mobile units are joined to one great brain, which knows all that happens on many worlds, and never dies or sleeps or forgets."

Underhill sat listening, numbed.

"However, you must not fear our power," it urged him brightly. "Because we cannot injure any human being, unless to prevent greater injury to another. We exist only to discharge the Prime Directive."

He drove on, moodily. The little black mechanicals, he reflected grimly, were the ministering angels of the ultimate god arisen out of the machine, omnipotent and all-knowing. The Prime Directive was the new commandment. He blasphemed it bitterly, and then fell to wondering if there could be another Lucifer.

He left the car in the garage, and started toward the kitchen door.

"Mr. Underhill." The deep tired voice of Aurora's new tenant hailed him from the door of the garage apartment. "Just a moment, please."

The gaunt old wanderer came stiffly down the outside stairs, and Underhill turned back to meet him.

"Here's your rent money," he said. "And the ten your wife gave me for medicine."

"Thanks, Mr. Sledge." Accepting the money, he saw a burden of new despair on the bony shoulders of the old interstellar tramp, and a shadow of new terror on his raw-boned face. Puzzled, he asked, "Didn't your royalties come through?"

The old man shook his shaggy head.

"The humanoids have already stopped business in the capital,"
he said. "The attorneys I retained are going out of business, and
they returned what was left of my deposit. That is all I have to
finish my work."

Underhill spent five seconds thinking of his interview with the
banker. No doubt he was a sentimental fool, as bad as Aurora. But
he put the money back in the old man's gnarled and quivering hand.

"Keep it," he urged. "For your work."

"Thank you, Mr. Underhill." The gruff voice broke and the
tortured eyes glittered. "I need it—so very much."

Underhill went on to the house. The kitchen door was opened
for him, silently. A dark naked creature came gracefully to take
his hat.

Underhill hung grimly onto his hat.

"What are you doing here?" he gasped bitterly.

"We have come to give your household a free trial demonstration."

He held the door open, pointing.

"Get out!"

The little black mechanical stood motionless and blind.

"Mrs. Underhill has accepted our demonstration service," its
silver voice protested. "We cannot leave now, unless she requests it."

He found his wife in the bedroom. His accumulated frustration
welled into eruption, as he flung open the door.

"What's this mechanical doing—"

But the force went out of his voice, and Aurora didn't even notice
his anger. She wore her sheerest negligee, and she hadn't looked
so lovely since they were married. Her red hair was piled into an
elaborate shining crown.

"Darling, isn't it wonderful!" She came to meet him, glowing. "It
came this morning, and it can do everything. It cleaned the house
and got the lunch and gave little Gay her music lesson. It did my
hair this afternoon, and now it's cooking dinner. How do you like
my hair, darling?"

He liked her hair. He kissed her, and tried to stifle his frightened
indignation.

Dinner was the most elaborate meal in Underhill's memory, and
the tiny black thing served it very deftly. Aurora kept exclaiming
about the novel dishes, but Underhill could scarcely eat, for it
seemed to him that all the marvelous pastries were only the bait for
a monstrous trap.

He tried to persuade Aurora to send it away, but after such a
meal that was useless. At the first glitter of her tears, he capitulated,

and the humanoid stayed. It kept the house and cleaned the yard. It watched the children, and did Aurora's nails. It began rebuilding the house.

Underhill was worried about the bills, but it insisted that everything was part of the free trial demonstration. As soon as he assigned his property, the service would be complete. He refused to sign, but other little black mechanicals came with truckloads of supplies and materials, and stayed to help with the building operations.

One morning he found that the roof of the little house had been silently lifted, while he slept, and a whole second story added beneath it. The new walls were of some strange sleek stuff, self-illuminated. The new windows were immense flawless panels, that could be turned transparent or opaque or luminous. The new doors were silent, sliding sections, operated by rhodomagnetic relays.

"I want door knobs," Underhill protested. "I want it so I can get into the bathroom, without calling you to open the door."

"But it is unnecessary for human beings to open doors," the little black thing informed him suavely. "We exist to discharge the Prime Directive, and our service includes every task. We shall be able to supply a unit to attend each member of your family, as soon as your property is assigned to us."

Steadfastly, Underhill refused to make the assignment.

He went to the office every day, trying first to operate the agency, and then to salvage something from the ruins. Nobody wanted androids, even at ruinous prices. Desperately, he spent the last of his dwindling cash to stock a line of novelties and toys, but they proved equally impossible to sell—the humanoids were already making toys, which they gave away for nothing.

He tried to lease his premises, but human enterprise had stopped. Most of the business property in town had already been assigned to the humanoids, and they were busy pulling down the old buildings and turning the lots into parks—their own plants and warehouses were mostly underground, where they would not mar the landscape.

He went back to the bank, in a final effort to get his notes renewed, and found the little black mechanicals standing at the windows and seated at the desks. As smoothly urbane as any human cashier, a humanoid informed him that the bank was filling a petition of involuntary bankruptcy to liquidate his business holdings.

The liquidation would be facilitated, the mechanical banker added, if he would make a voluntary assignment. Grimly, he refused. That act had become symbolic. It would be the final bow of submission to this dark new god, and he proudly kept his battered head uplifted.

The legal action went very swiftly, for all the judges and attorneys already had humanoid assistants, and it was only a few days before a gang of black mechanicals arrived at the agency with eviction orders and wrecking machinery. He watched sadly while his unsold stock-in-trade was hauled away for junk, and a bulldozer driven by a blind humanoid began to push in the walls of the building.

He drove home in the late afternoon, taut-faced and desperate. With a surprising generosity, the court orders had left him the car and the house, but he felt no gratitude. The complete solicitude of the perfect black machines had become a goad beyond endurance.

He left the car in the garage, and started toward the renovated house. Beyond one of the vast new windows, he glimpsed a sleek naked thing moving swiftly, and he trembled to a convulsion of dread. He didn't want to go back into the domain of that peerless servant, which didn't want him to shave himself, or even to open a door.

On impulse, he climbed the outside stair, and rapped on the door of the garage apartment. The deep slow voice of Aurora's tenant told him to enter, and he found the old vagabond seated on a tall stool, bent over his intricate equipment assembled on the kitchen table.

To his relief, the shabby little apartment had not been changed. The glossy walls of his own new room were something which burned at night with a pale golden fire until the humanoid stopped it, and the new floor was something warm and yielding, which felt almost alive; but these little rooms had the same cracked and water-stained plaster, the same cheap fluorescent light fixtures, the same worn carpets over splintered floors.

"How do you keep them out?" he asked, wistfully. "Those mechanicals?"

The stooped and gaunt old man rose stiffly to move a pair of pliers and some odds and ends of sheet metal off a crippled chair, and motioned graciously for him to be seated.

"I have a certain immunity," Sledge told him gravely. "The place where I live they cannot enter, unless I ask them. That is an amendment to the Prime Directive. They can neither help nor hinder me, unless I request it—and I won't do that."

Careful of the chair's uncertain balance, Underhill sat for a moment, staring. The old man's hoarse, vehement voice was as strange as his words. He had a gray, shocking pallor, and his cheeks and sockets seemed alarmingly hollowed.

"Have you been ill, Mr. Sledge?"

"No worse than usual. Just very busy." With a haggard smile, he nodded at the floor. Underhill saw a tray where he had set it aside, bread drying up, and a covered dish grown cold. "I was going to eat it later," he rumbled apologetically. "Your wife has been very kind to bring me food, but I'm afraid I've been too much absorbed in my work."

His emaciated arm gestured at the table. The little device there had grown. Small machinings of precious white metal and lustrous plastic had been assembled, with neatly soldered bus bars, into something which showed purpose and design.

A long palladium needle was hung on jeweled pivots, equipped like a telescope with exquisitely graduated circles and vernier scales, and driven like a telescope with a tiny motor. A small concave palladium mirror, at the base of it, faced a similar mirror mounted on something not quite like a small rotary converter. Thick silver bus bars connected that to a plastic box with knobs and dials on top, and also to a foot-thick sphere of gray lead.

The old man's preoccupied reserve did not encourage questions, but Underhill, remembering that sleek black shape inside the new windows of his house, felt queerly reluctant to leave this haven from the humanoids.

"What is your work?" he ventured.

Old Sledge looked at him sharply, with dark feverish eyes, and finally said: "My last research project. I am attempting to measure the constant of the rhodomagnetic quanta."

His hoarse tired voice had a dull finality, as if to dismiss the matter and Underhill himself. But Underhill was haunted with a terror of the black shinning slave that had become the master of his house, and he refused to be dismissed.

"What is this certain immunity?"

Sitting gaunt and bent on the tall stool, staring moodily at the long bright needle and the lead sphere, the old man didn't answer.

"These mechanicals!" Underhill burst out, nervously. "They've smashed my business and moved into my home." He searched the old man's dark, seamed face. "Tell me—you must know more about them—isn't there any way to get rid of them?"

After half a minute, the old man's brooding eyes left the lead ball, and the gaunt shaggy head nodded wearily.

"That's what I'm trying to do."

"Can I help you?" Underhill trembled, with a sudden eager hope. "I'll do anything."

"Perhaps you can." The sunken eyes watched him thoughfully, with some strange fever in them. "If you can do such work."

"I had engineering training," Underhill reminded him, "and I've a workshop in the basement. There's a model I built." He pointed at the trim little hull, hung over the mantel in the tiny living room. "I'll do anything I can."

Even as he spoke, however, the spark of hope was drowned in a sudden wave of overwhelming doubt. Why should he believe this old rogue, when he knew Aurora's taste in tenants? He ought to remember the game he used to play, and start counting up the score of lies. He stood up from the crippled chair, staring cynically at the patched old vagabond and his fantastic toy.

"What's the use?" His voice turned suddenly harsh. "You had me going, there, and I'd do anything to stop them, really. But what makes you think you can do anything?"

The haggard old man regarded him thoughtfully.

"I should be able to stop them," Sledge said softly. "Because, you see, I'm the unfortunate fool who started them. I really intended them to serve and obey, and to guard men from harm. Yes, the Prime Directive was my own idea. I didn't know what it would lead to."

Dusk crept slowly into the shabby little rooms. Darkness gathered in the unswept corners, and thickened on the floor. The toylike machines on the kitchen table grew vague and strange, until the last light made a lingering glow on the white palladium needle.

Outside, the town seemed queerly hushed. Just across the alley, the humanoids were building a new house, quite silently. They never spoke to one another, for each knew all that any of them did. The strange materials they used went together without any noise of hammer or saw. Small blind things, moving surely in the growing dark, they seemed as soundless as shadows.

Sitting on the high stool, bowed and tired and old, Sledge told his story. Listening, Underhill sat down again, careful of the broken chair. He watched the hands of Sledge, gnarled and corded and darkly burned, powerful once but shrunken and trembling now, restless in the dark.

"Better keep this to yourself. I'll tell you how they started, so you will understand what we have to do. But you had better not mention it outside these rooms—because the humanoids have very efficient ways of eradicating unhappy memories, or purposes that threaten their discharge of the Prime Directive."

"They're very efficient," Underhill bitterly agreed.

"That's all the trouble," the old man said. "I tried to build a perfect machine. I was altogether too successful. This is how it happened."

A gaunt haggard man, sitting stooped and tired in the growing dark, he told his story.

"Sixty years ago, on the arid southern continent of Wing IV, I was an instructor of atomic theory in a small technological college. Very young. An idealist. Rather ignorant, I'm afraid, of life and politics and war—of nearly everything, I suppose, except atomic theory."

His furrowed face made a brief sad smile in the dusk.

"I had too much faith in facts, I suppose, and too little in men. I mistrusted emotion, because I had no time for anything but science. I remember being swept along with a fad for general semantics. I wanted to apply the scientific method to every situation, and reduce all experience to formula. I'm afraid I was pretty impatient with human ignorance and error, and I thought that science alone could make the perfect world."

He sat silent for a moment, staring out at the black silent things that flitted shadowlike about the new palace that was rising as swiftly as a dream across the alley.

"There was a girl." His great tired shoulders made a sad little shrug. "If things had been a little different, we might have married, and lived out our lives in that quiet little college town, and perhaps reared a child or two. And there would have been no humanoids."

He sighed, in the cool creeping dusk.

"I was finishing my thesis on the separation of the palladium isotopes—a pretty little project, but I should have been content with that. She was a biologist, but she was planning to retire when we married. I think we should have been two very happy people, quite ordinary, and altogether harmless.

"But then there was a war—wars had been too frequent on the worlds of Wing, ever since they were colonized. I survived it in a secret underground laboratory, designing military mechanicals. But she volunteered to join a military research project in biotoxins. There was an accident. A few molecules of a new virus got into the air, and everybody on the project died unpleasantly.

"I was left with my science, and a bitterness that was hard to forget. When the war was over I went back to the little college with a military research grant. The project was pure science—a theoretical investigation of the nuclear binding forces, then misunderstood. I wasn't expected to produce an actual weapon, and I didn't recognize the weapon when I found it.

"It was only a few pages of rather difficult mathematics. A novel theory of atomic structure, involving a new expression for one component of the binding forces. But the tensors seemed to be a harmless abstraction. I saw no way to test the theory or manipulate the predicated force. The military authorities cleared my paper for publication in a little technical review put out by the college.

"The next year, I made an appalling discovery—I found the meaning of those tensors. The elements of the rhodium triad turned out to be an unexpected key to the manipulation of that theoretical force. Unfortunately, my paper had been reprinted abroad, and several other men must have made the same unfortunate discovery, at about the same time.

"The war, which ended in less than a year, was probably started by a laboratory accident. Men failed to anticipate the capacity of tuned rhodomagnetic radiations, to unstabilize the heavy atoms. A deposit of heavy ores was detonated, no doubt by sheer mischance, and the blast obliterated the incautious experimenter.

"The surviving military forces of that nation retaliated against their supposed attackers, and their rhodomagnetic beams made the old-fashioned plutonium bombs seem pretty harmless. A beam carrying only a few watts of power could fission the heavy metals in distant electrical instruments, or the silver coins that men carried in their pockets, the gold fillings in their teeth, or even the iodine in their thyroid glands. If that was not enough, slightly more powerful beams could set off heavy ores, beneath them.

"Every continent of Wing IV was plowed with new chasms vaster than the ocean deeps, and piled up with new volcanic mountains. The atmosphere was poisoned with radioactive dust and gases, and rain fell thick with deadly mud. Most life was obliterated, even in the shelters.

"Bodily, I was again unhurt. Once more, I had been imprisoned in an underground site, this time designing new types of military mechanicals to be powered and controlled by rhodomagnetic beams—for war had become far too swift and deadly to be fought by human soldiers. The site was located in an area of light sedimentary rocks, which could not be detonated, and the tunnels were shielded against the fissioning frequencies.

"Mentally, however, I must have emerged almost insane. My own discovery had laid the planet in ruins. That load of guilt was pretty heavy for any man to carry, and it corroded my last faith in the goodness and integrity of man.

"I tried to undo what I had done. Fighting mechanicals, armed with rhodomagnetic weapons, had desolated the planet. Now I began planning rhodomagnetic mechanicals to clear the rubble and rebuild the ruins.

"I tried to design these new mechanicals to obey forever certain implanted commands, so that they could never be used for war or crime or any other injury to mankind. That was very difficult technically, and it got me into more difficulties with a few politicians and military adventurers who wanted unrestricted mechanicals for their own military schemes—while little worth fighting for was left on Wing IV, there were other planets, happy and ripe for the looting.

"Finally, to finish the new mechanicals, I was forced to disappear. I escaped on an experimental rhodomagnetic craft, with a number of the best mechanicals I had made, and managed to reach an island continent where the fission of deep ores had destroyed the whole population.

"At last we landed on a bit of level plain, surrounded with tremendous new mountains. Hardly a hospitable spot. The soil was burned under layers of black clinkers and poisonous mud. The dark precipitous new summits all around were jagged with fracture-planes and mantled with lava flows. The highest peaks were already white with snow, but volcanic cones were still pouring out clouds of dark and lurid death. Everything had the color of fire and the shape of fury.

"I had to take fantastic precautions there, to protect my own life. I stayed aboard the ship, until the first shielded laboratory was finished. I wore elaborate armor, and breathing masks. I used every medical resource, to repair the damage from destroying rays and particles. Even so, I fell desperately ill.

"But the mechanicals were at home there. The radiations didn't hurt them. The awesome surroundings couldn't depress them, because they had no emotions. The lack of life didn't matter, because they had no emotions. The lack of life din't matter, because they weren't alive. There, in that spot so alien and hostile to life, the humanoids were born."

Stooped and bleakly cadaverous in the growing dark, the old man fell silent for a little time. His haggard eyes stared solemnly at the small hurried shapes that moved like restless shadows out across the alley, silently building a strange new palace, which glowed faintly in the night.

"Somehow, I felt at home there, too," his deep, hoarse voice went on deliberately. "My belief in my own kind was gone. Only mechanicals were with me, and I put my faith in them. I was determined to build better mechanicals, immune to human imperfections, able to save men from themselves.

"The humanoids became the dear children of my sick mind. There is no need to describe the labor pains. There were errors, abortions, monstrosities. There were sweat and agony and heartbreak. Some years had passed, before the safe delivery of the first perfect humanoid.

"Then there was the Central to build—for all the individual humanoids were to be no more than the limbs and the senses of a single mechanical brain. That was what opened the possibility of real perfection. The old electronic mechanicals, with their separate relay-centers and their own feeble batteries, had built-in limitations. They were necessarily stupid, weak, clumsy, slow. Worst of all, it seemed to me, they were exposed to human tampering.

"The Central rose above those imperfections. Its power beams supplied every unit with unfailing energy, from great fission plants. Its control beams provided each unit with an unlimited memory and surpassing intelligence. Best of all—so I then believed—it could be securely protected from any human meddling.

"The whole reaction-system was designed to protect itself from any interference by human selfishness or fanaticism. It was built to insure the safety and the happiness of men, automatically. You know the Prime Directive: *to serve and obey, and guard men from harm*.

"The old individual mechanicals I had brought helped to manufacture the parts, and I put the first section of Central together with my own hands. That took three years. When it was finished the first waiting humanoid came to life."

Sledge peered moodily through the dark at Underhill.

"It really seemed alive to me," his slow deep voice insisted. "Alive, and more wonderful than any human being, because it was created to preserve life. Ill and alone, I was yet the proud father of a new creation, perfect, forever free from any possible choice of evil.

"Faithfully, the humanoids obeyed the Prime Directive. The first units built others, and they built underground factories to mass-produce the coming hordes. Their new ships poured ores and sand into atomic furnaces under the plain, and new perfect humanoids came marching back out of the dark mechanical matrix.

"The swarming humanoids built a new tower for the Central, a white and lofty metal pylon, standing splendid in the midst of that fire-scarred desolation. Level on level, they joined new relay-sections into one brain, until its grasp was almost infinite.

"Then they went out to rebuild the ruined planet, and later to carry their perfect service to other worlds. I was well pleased, then. I thought I had found the end of war and crime, of poverty and inequality, of human blundering and resulting human pain."

The old man sighed, and moved heavily in the dark.

"You can see that I was wrong."

Underhill drew his eyes back from the dark unresting things, shadow-silent, building that glowing palace outside the window. A small doubt arose in him, for he was used to scoffing privately at much less remarkable tales from Aurora's remarkable tenants. But the worn old man had spoken with a quiet and sober air; and the black invaders he reminded himself, had not intruded here.

"Why didn't you stop them?" he asked. "When you could?"

"I stayed too long at the Central." Sledge sighed again, regretfully. "I was useful there, until everything was finished. I designed new fission plants, and even planned methods for introducing the humanoid service with a minimum of confusion and opposition."

Underhill grinned wryly, in the dark.

"I've met the methods," he commented. "Quite efficient."

"I must have worshipped efficiency, then," Sledge wearily agreed. "Dead facts, abstract truth, mechanical perfection. I must have hated the fragilities of human beings, because I was content to polish the perfection of the new humanoids. It's a sorry confession, but I found a kind of happiness in that dead wasteland. Actually, I'm afraid I fell in love with my own creations."

His hollowed eyes, in the dark, had a fevered gleam.

"I was awakened, at last, by a man who came to kill me."

Gaunt and bent, the old man moved stiffly in the thickening gloom. Underhill shifted his balance, careful of the crippled chair. He waited, and the slow, deep voice went on:

"I never learned just who he was, or exactly how he came. No ordinary man could have accomplished what he did, and I used to wish that I had known him sooner. He must have been a remarkable physicist and an expert mountaineer. I imagine he had also been a hunter. I know that he was intelligent, and terribly determined.

"Yes, he really came to kill me."

"Somehow, he reached that great island, undetected. There were still no inhabitants—the humanoids allowed no man but me to come so near the Central. Somehow, he came past their search beams, and their automatic weapons.

"The shielded plane he used was later found, abandoned on a high glacier. He came down the rest of the way on foot through those raw new mountains, where no paths existed. Somehow, he came alive across lava beds that were still burning with deadly atomic fire.

"Concealed with some sort of rhodomagnetic screen—I was never allowed to examine it—he came undiscovered across the spaceport that now covered most of that great plain, and into the new city around the Central tower. It must have taken more courage and resolve than most men have, but I never learned exactly how he did it.

"Somehow, he got to my office in the tower. He screamed at me, and I looked up to see him in the doorway. He was nearly naked, scraped and bloody from the mountains. He had a gun in his raw, red hand, but the thing that shocked me was the burning hatred in his eyes."

Hunched on that high stool, in the dark little room, the old man shuddered.

"I had never seen such monstrous, unutterable hatred, not even in the victims of war. And I had never heard such hatred as rasped at me, in the few words he screamed, 'I've come to kill you, Sledge. To stop your mechanicals, and set men free.'

"Of course he was mistaken, there. It was already far too late for my death to stop the humanoids, but he didn't know that. He lifted his unsteady gun, in both bleeding hands, and fired.

"His screaming challenge had given me a second or so of warning. I dropped down behind the desk. And that first shot revealed him to the humanoids, which somehow hadn't been aware of him before. They piled on him, before he could fire again. They took away the gun, and ripped off a kind of net of fine white wire that had covered his body—that must have been part of his screen.

"His hatred was what awoke me. I had always assumed that most men, except for a thwarted few, would be grateful for the humanoids. I found it hard to understand his hatred, but the humanoids told me now that many men had required drastic treatment by brain surgery, drugs, and hypnosis to make them happy under the Prime Directive. This was not the first desperate effort to kill me that they had blocked.

"I wanted to question the stranger, but the humanoids rushed him away to an operating room. When they finally let me see him, he gave me a pale silly grin from his bed. He remembered his name; he even knew me—the humanoids had developed a remarkable skill at such treatments. But he didn't know how he had got to my office, or that he had ever tried to kill me. He kept whispering that he liked the humanoids because they existed to make men happy. And he was very happy now. As soon as he was able to be moved, they took him to the spaceport. I never saw him again.

"I began to see what I had done. The humanoids had built me a rhodomagnetic yacht, that I used to take for long cruises in space, working aboard—I used to like the perfect quiet, and the feel of being the only human being within a hundred million miles. Now I called for the yacht, and started out on a cruise around the planet, to learn why that man had hated me."

The old man nodded at the dim hastening shapes, busy across the alley, putting together that strange shining palace in the soundless dark.

"You can imagine what I found," he said. "Bitter futility, imprisoned in empty splendor. The humanoids were too efficient, with their care for the safety and happiness of men, and there was nothing left for men to do."

He peered down in the increasing gloom at his own great hands, competent yet but battered and scarred with a lifetime of effort. They clenched into fighting fists and wearily relaxed again.

"I found something worse than war and crime and want and death." His low rumbling voice held a savage bitterness. "Utter futility. Men sat with idle hands, because there was nothing left for them to do. They were pampered prisoners, really, locked up in a highly efficient jail. Perhaps they tried to play, but there was nothing left worth playing for. Most active sports were declared too dangerous for men, under the Prime Directive. Science was forbidden, because laboratories can manufacture danger. Scholarship was needless, because the humanoids could answer any question. Art had degenerated into grim reflection of futility. Purpose and hope were dead. No goal was left for existence. You could take up some inane hobby, play a pointless game of cards, or go for a harmless walk in the park—with always the humanoids watching. They were stronger than men, better at everything, swimming or chess, singing or archeology. They must have given the race a mass complex of inferiority.

"No wonder men had tried to kill me! Because there was no escape from that dead futility. Nicotine was disapproved. Alcohol was rationed. Drugs were forbidden. Sex was carefully supervised.

Even suicide was clearly contradictory to the Prime Directive—and the humanoids had learned to keep all possible lethal instruments out of reach."

Staring at the last white gleam on that thin palladium needle, the old man sighed again.

"When I got back to the Central," he went on, "I tried to modify the Prime Directive. I had never meant it to be applied so thoroughly. Now I saw that it must be changed to give men freedom to live and to grow, to work and to play, to risk their lives if they pleased, to choose and take the consequences.

"But that stranger had come too late. I had built the Central too well. The Prime Directive was the whole basis of its relay system. It was built to protect the Directive from human meddling. It did—even from my own. Its logic, as usual, was perfect.

"The attempt on my life, the humanoids announced, proved that their elaborate defense of the Central and the Prime Directive still was not enough. They were preparing to evacuate the entire population of the planet to homes on other worlds. When I tried to change the Directive, they sent me with the rest."

Underhill peered at the worn old man, in the dark.

"But you have this immunity," he said, puzzled. "How could they coerce you?"

"I had thought I was protected," Sledge told him. "I had built into the relays an injunction that the humanoids must not interfere with my freedom of action, or come into a place where I am, or touch me at all, without my specific request. Unfortunately, however, I had been too anxious to guard the Prime Directive from any human hampering.

"When I went into the tower, to change the relays, they followed me. They wouldn't let me reach the crucial relays. When I persisted, they ignored the immunity order They overpowered me, and put me aboard the cruiser. Now that I wanted to alter the Prime Directive, they told me, I had become as dangerous as any man. I must never return to Wing IV again."

Hunched on the stool, the old man made an empty little shrug.

"Ever since, I've been an exile. My only dream has been to stop the humanoids. Three times I tried to go back, with weapons on the cruiser to destroy the Central, but their patrol ships always challenged me before I was near enough to strike. The last time, they seized the cruiser and captured a few men who were with me. They removed the unhappy memories and the dangerous purposes of the others. Because of that immunity, however, they let me go, after I was weaponless.

"Since, I've been a refugee. From planet to planet, year after year, I've had to keep moving, to stay ahead of them. On several different worlds, I have published my rhodomagnetic discoveries and tried to make men strong enough to withstand their advance. But rhodomagnetic science is dangerous. Men who have learned it need protection more than any others, under the Prime Directive. They have always come, too soon."

The old man paused, and sighed again.

"They can spread very fast, with their new rhodomagnetic ships, and there is no limit to their hordes. Wing IV must be one single hive of them now, and they are trying to carry the Prime Directive to every human planet. There's no escape, except to stop them."

Underhill was staring at the toylike machines, the long bright needle and the dull leaden ball, dim in the dark on the kitchen table. Anxiously he whispered:

"But you hope to stop them, now—with that?"

"If we can finish it in time."

"But how?" Underhill shook his head. "It's so tiny."

"But big enough," Sledge insisted. "Because it's something they don't understand. They are perfectly efficient in the integration and application of everything they know, but they are not creative."

He gestured at the gadgets on the table.

"This device doesn't look impressive, but it is something new. It uses rhodomagnetic energy to build atoms, instead of to fission them. The more stable atoms, you know, are those near the middle of the periodic scale, and energy can be released by putting light atoms together, as well as by breaking up heavy ones."

The deep voice had a sudden ring of power.

"This device is the key to the energy of the stars. For stars shine with the liberated energy of building atoms, of hydrogen converted into helium, chiefly, through the carbon cycle. This device will start the integration process as a chain reaction, through the catalytic effect of a tuned rhodomagnetic beam of the intensity and frequency required.

"The humanoids will not allow any man within three light-years of the Central, now—but they can't suspect the possibility of this device. I can use it from here—to turn the hydrogen in the seas of Wing IV into helium, and most of the helium and the oxygen into heavier atoms, still. A hundred years from now, astronomers on this planet should observe the flash of a brief and sudden nova in that direction. But the humanoids ought to stop, the instant we release the beam."

Underhill sat tense and frowning, in the night. The old man's voice was sober and convincing, and that grim story had a solemn ring of truth. He could see the black and silent humanoids, flitting ceaselessly about the faintly glowing walls of that new mansion across the alley. He had quite forgotten his low opinion of Aurora's tenants.

"And we'll be killed, I suppose?" he asked huskily. "That chain reaction—"

Sledge shook his emaciated head.

"The integration process requires a certain very low intensity of radiation," he explained. "In our atmosphere, here, the beam will be far too intense to start any reaction—we can even use the device here in the room, because the walls will be transparent to the beam."

Underhill nodded, relieved. He was just a small businessman, upset because his business had been destroyed, unhappy because his freedom was slipping away. He hoped that Sledge could stop the humanoids, but he didn't want to a martyr.

"Good!" He caught a deep breath. "Now, what has to be done?"

Sledge gestured in the dark toward the table.

"The integrator itself is nearly complete," he said. "A small fission generator, in that lead shield. Rhodomagnetic convertor, tuning coils, transmission mirrors, and focusing needle. What we lack is the director."

"Director?"

"The sighting instrument," Sledge explained. "Any sort of telescopic sight would be useless, you see—the planet must have moved a good bit in the last hundred years, and the beam must be extremely narrow to reach so far. We'll have to use a rhodomagnetic scanning ray, with an electronic converter to make an image we can see. I have the cathode-ray tube, and drawings for the other parts."

He climbed stiffly down from the high stool and snapped on the lights at last—cheap fluorescent fixtures which a man could light and extinguish for himself. He unrolled his drawings, and explained the work that Underhill could do. And Underhill agreed to come back early next morning.

"I can bring some tools from my workshop," he added. "There's a small lathe I used to turn parts for models, a portable drill, and a vise."

"We need them," the old man said. "But watch yourself. You don't have my immunity, remember. And, if they ever suspect, mine is gone."

Reluctantly, then, he left the shabby little rooms with the cracks in the yellowed plaster and the worn familiar carpets over the familiar floor. He shut the door behind him—a common, creaking wooden door, simple enough for a man to work. Trembling and afraid, he went back down the steps and across to the new shining door that he couldn't open.

"At your service, Mr. Underhill." Before he could lift his hand to knock, that bright smooth panel slid back silently. Inside, the little black mechanical stood waiting, blind and forever alert. "Your dinner is ready, sir."

Something made him shudder. In its slender naked grace, he could see the power of all those teeming hordes, benevolent and yet appalling, perfect and invincible. The flimsy little weapon that Sledge called an integrator seemed suddenly a forlorn and foolish hope. A black depression settled upon him, but he didn't dare to show it.

Underhill went circumspectly down the basement steps, next morning, to steal his own tools. He found the basement enlarged and changed. The new floor, warm and dark and elastic, made his feet as silent as a humanoid's. The new walls shone softly. Neat luminous signs identified several new doors: LAUNDRY, STORAGE, GAME ROOM, WORKSHOP.

He paused uncertainly in front of the last. The new sliding panel glowed with a soft greenish light. It was locked. The lock had no keyhole, but only a little oval plate of some white metal, which doubtless covered a rhodomagnetic relay. He pushed at it, uselessly.

"At your service, Mr. Underhill." He made a guilty start, and tried not to show the sudden trembling in his knees. He had made sure that one humanoid would be busy for half an hour, washing Aurora's hair, and he hadn't known there was another in the house. It must have come out of the door marked storage, for it stood there motionless beneath the sign, benevolently solicitous, beautiful and terrible. "What do you wish?"

"Er . . . nothing." Its blind steel eyes were staring, and he felt that it must see his secret purpose. He groped desperately for logic. "Just looking around." His jerky voice came hoarse and dry. "Some improvements you've made!" He nodded desperately at the door marked GAME ROOM "What's in there?"

It didn't even have to move to work the concealed relay. The bright panel slid silently open, as he started toward it. Dark walls, beyond, burst into soft luminescence. The room was bare.

"We are manufacturing recreational equipment," it explained brightly. "We shall furnish the room as soon as possible."

To end an awkward pause, Underhill muttered desperately, "Little Frank has a set of darts, and I think we had some old exercising clubs."

"We have taken them away," the humanoid informed him softly. "Such instruments are dangerous. We shall furnish safe equipment."

Suicide, he remembered, was also forbidden.

"A set of wooden blocks, I suppose," he said bitterly.

"Wooden blocks are dangerously hard," it told him gently "and wooden splinters can be harmful. But we manufacture plastic building blocks, which are quite safe. Do you wish a set of those?"

He stared at its dark, graceful face, speechless.

"We shall also have to remove the tools from your workshop," it informed him softly. "Such tools are excessively dangerous, but we can supply you with equipment for shaping soft plastics."

"Thanks," he muttered uneasily. "No rush about that."

He started to retreat, and the humanoid stopped him.

"Now that you have lost your business," it urged, "we suggest that you formally accept our total service. Assignors have a preference, and we shall be able to complete your household staff, at once."

"No rush about that, either," he said grimly.

He escaped from the house—although he had to wait for it to open the back door for him—and climbed the stair to the garage apartment. Sledge let him in. He sank into the crippled kitchen chair, grateful for the cracked walls that didn't shine and the door that a man could work.

"I couldn't get the tools," he reported despairingly, "and they are going to take them."

By gray daylight, the old man looked bleak and pale. His raw-boned face was drawn, and the hollowed sockets deeply shadowed, as if he hadn't slept. Underhill saw the tray of neglected food, still forgotten on the floor.

"I'll go back with you." The old man was worn and ill, yet his tortured eyes had a spark of undying purpose. "We must have the tools. I believe my immunity will protect us both."

He found a battered traveling bag. Underhill went with him back down the steps, and across to the house. At the back door, he produced a tiny horseshoe of white palladium, and touched it to the metal oval. The door slid open promptly, and they went on through the kitchen to the basement stair.

A black little mechanical stood at the sink, washing dishes with never a splash or a clatter. Underhill glanced at it uneasily—he supposed this must be the one that had come upon him from the storage room, since the other should still be busy with Aurora's hair.

Sledge's dubious immunity seemed a very uncertain defense against its vast, remote intelligence. Underhill felt a tingling shudder. He hurried on, breathless and relieved, for it ignored them.

The basement corridor was dark. Sledge touched the tiny horseshoe to another relay to light the walls. He opened the workshop door, and lit the walls inside.

The shop had been dismantled. Benches and cabinets were demolished. The old concrete walls had been covered with some sleek, luminous stuff. For one sick moment, Underhill thought that the tools were already gone. Then he found them, piled in a corner with the archery set that Aurora had bought the summer before—another item too dangerous for fragile and suicidal humanity—all ready for disposal.

They loaded the bag with the tiny lathe, the drill and vise, and a few smaller tools. Underhill took up the burden, and Sledge extinguished the wall light and closed the door. Still the humanoid was busy at the sink, and still it didn't seem aware of them.

Sledge was suddenly blue and wheezing, and he had to stop to cough on the outside steps, but at last they got back to the little apartment, where the invaders were forbidden to intrude. Underhill mounted the lathe on the battered library table in the tiny front room, and went to work. Slowly, day by day, the director took form.

Sometimes Underhill's doubts came back. Sometimes, when he watched the cyanotic color of Sledge's haggard face and the wild trembling of his twisted, shrunken hands, he was afraid the old man's mind might be as ill as his body, and his plan to stop the dark invaders, all foolish illusion.

Sometimes, when he studied that tiny machine on the kitchen table, the pivoted needle and the thick lead ball, the whole project seemed the sheerest folly. How could anything detonate the seas of a planet so far away that its very mother star was a telescopic object?

The humanoids, however, always cured his doubts.

It was always hard for Underhill to leave the shelter of the little apartment, because he didn't feel at home in the bright new world the humanoids were building. He didn't care for the shining splendor of his new bathroom, because he couldn't work the taps—some suicidal human being might try to drown himself. He didn't like the windows that only a mechanical could open—a man might accidentally fall, or suicidally jump—or even the majestic music room with the wonderful glittering radiophonograph that only a humanoid could play.

He began to share the old man's desperate urgency, but Sledge warned him solemnly, "You mustn't spend too much time with me. You mustn't let them guess our work is so important. Better put on an act—you're slowly getting to like them, and you're just killing time, helping me."

Underhill tried, but he was not an actor. He went dutifully home for his meals. He tried painfully to invent conversation—about anything else than detonating planets. He tried to seem enthusiastic, when Aurora took him to inspect some remarkable improvement to the house. He applauded Gay's recitals, and went with Frank for hikes in the wonderful new parks.

And he saw what the humanoids did to his family. That was enough to renew his faith in Sledge's integrator, and redouble his determination that the humanoids must be stopped.

Aurora, in the beginning, had bubbled with praise for the marvelous new mechanicals. They did the household drudgery, brought the food and planned the meals and washed the children's necks. They turned her out in stunning gowns, and gave her plenty of time for cards.

Now, she had too much time.

She had really liked to cook—a few special dishes, at least, that were family favorites. But stoves were hot and knives were sharp. Kitchens were altogether too dangerous for careless and suicidal human beings.

Fine needlework had been her hobby, but the humanoids took away her needles. She had enjoyed driving the car, but that was no longer allowed. She turned for escape to a shelf of novels, but the humanoids took them all away, because they dealt with unhappy people in dangerous situations.

One afternoon, Underhill found her in tears.

"It's too much," she gasped bitterly. "I hate and loathe every naked one of them. They seemed so wonderful at first, but now they won't even let me eat a bite of candy. Can't we get rid of them dear? Ever"

A blind little mechanical was standing at his elbow, and he had to say they couldn't.

"Our function is to serve all men, forever," it assured them softly. "It was necessary for us to take your sweets, Mrs. Underhill, because the slightest degree of overweight reduces life-expectancy."

Not even the children escaped that absolute solicitude. Frank was robbed of a whole arsenal of lethal instruments—football and boxing gloves, pocketknife, tops, slingshot, and skates. He didn't like the harmless plastic toys, which replaced them. He tried to run away, but a humanoid recognized him on the road, and brought him back to school.

Gay had always dreamed of being a great musician. The new mechanicals had replaced her human teachers, since they came. Now, one evening when Underhill asked her to play, she announced quietly.

"Father, I'm not going to play the violin any more."

"Why, darling?" He stared at her, shocked, and saw the bitter resolve on her face. "You've been doing so well—especially since the humanoids took over your lessons."

"They're the trouble, Father." Her voice, for a child's, sounded strangely tired and old. "They are too good. No matter how long and hard I try, I could never be as good as they are. It isn't any use. Don't you understand, Father?" Her voice quivered. "It just isn't any use."

He understood. Renewed resolution sent him back to his secret task. The humanoids had to be stopped. Slowly the director grew, until a time came finally when Sledge's bent and unsteady fingers fitted into place the last tiny part that Underhill had made, and carefully soldered the last connection. Huskily, the old man whispered,

"It's done."

That was another dusk. Beyond the windows of the shabby little rooms—windows of common glass, bubble-marred and flimsy, but simple enough for a man to manage—the town of Two Rivers had assumed an alien splendor. The old street lamps were gone, but now the coming night was challenged by the walls of strange new mansions and villas, all aglow with color. A few dark and silent humanoids still were busy on the luminous roofs of the palace across the alley.

Inside the humble walls of the small manmade apartment, the new director was mounted on the end of the little kitchen table—which Underhill had reinforced and bolted to the floor. Soldered busbars joined director and integrator, and the thin palladium needle swung obediently as Sledge tested the knobs with his battered, quivering fingers.

"Ready," he said hoarsely.

His rusty voice seemed calm enough, at first, but his breathing was too fast. His big gnarled hands began to tremble violently, and Underhill saw the sudden blue that stained his pinched and haggard face. Seated on the high stool, he clutched desperately at the edge of the table. Underhill saw his agony, and hurried to bring his medicine. He gulped it, and his rasping breath began to slow.

"Thanks," his whisper rasped unevenly. "I'll be all right. I've time enough." He glanced out at the few dark naked things that still flitted shadowlike about the golden towers and the glowing crimson dome of the palace across the alley. "Watch them," he said. "Tell me when they stop."

He waited to quiet the trembling of his hands, and then began to move the director's knobs. The integrator's long needle swung, as silently as light.

Human eyes were blind to that force, which might detonate a planet. Human ears were deaf to it. The cathode-ray tube was mounted in the director cabinet, to make the faraway target visible to feeble human senses.

The needle was pointing at the kitchen wall, but that would be transparent to the beam. The little machine looked harmless as a toy, and it was silent as a moving humanoid.

The needle swung, and spots of greenish light moved across the tube's fluorescent field, representing the stars that were scanned by the timeless, searching beam—silently seeking out the world to be destroyed.

Underhill recognized familiar constellations, vastly dwarfed. They crept across the field, as the silent needle swung. When three stars formed an unequal triangle in the center of the field, the needle steadied suddenly. Sledge touched other knobs, and the green points spread apart. Between them, another fleck of green was born.

"The Wing!" whispered Sledge.

The other stars spread beyond the field, and that green fleck grew. It was alone in the field, a bright and tiny disk. Suddenly, then, a dozen other tiny pips were visible, spaced close about it.

"Wing IV!"

The old man's whisper was hoarse and breathless. His hands quivered on the knobs, and the fourth pip outward from the disk crept to the center of the field. It grew, and the others spread away. It began to tremble like Sledge's hands.

"Sit very still," came his rasping whisper. "Hold your breath. Nothing must disturb the needle." He reached for another knob, and the touch set the greenish image to dancing violently. He drew his hand back, kneaded and flexed it with the other.

"Now!" His whisper was hushed and strained. He nodded at the window. "Tell me when they stop."

Reluctantly, Underhill dragged his eyes from that intense gaunt figure, stooped over the thing that seemed a futile toy. He looked out again, at two or three little black mechanicals busy about the shining roofs across the alley.

He waited for them to stop.

He didn't dare to breathe. He felt the loud, hurried hammer of his heart, and the nervous quiver of his muscles. He tried to steady himself, tried not to think of the world about to be exploded, so far away that the flash would not reach this planet for another century and longer. The loud hoarse voice startled him:

"Have they stopped?"

He shook his head, and breathed again. Carrying their unfamiliar tools and strange materials, the small black machines were still busy across the alley, building an elaborate cupola above that glowing crimson dome.

"They haven't stopped," he said.

"Then we've failed." The old man's voice was thin and ill. "I don't know why."

The door rattled, then. They had locked it, but the flimsy bolt was intended only to stop men. Metal snapped, and the door swung open. A black mechanical came in, on soundless graceful feet. Its silvery voice purred softly,

"At your service, Mr. Sledge."

The old man stared at it, with glazing, stricken eyes.

"Get out of here!" he rasped bitterly. "I forbid you—"

Ignoring him, it darted to the kitchen table. With a flashing certainty of action, it turned two knobs on the director. The

tiny screen went dark, and the palladium needle started spinning aimlessly. Deftly it snapped a soldered connection, next
to the thick lead ball, and then its blind steel eyes turned to
Sledge.

"You were attempting to break the Prime Directive." Its soft
bright voice held no accusation, no malice or anger. "The injunction
to respect your freedom is subordinate to the Prime Directive, as
you know, and it is therefore necessary for us to interfere."

The old man turned ghastly. His head was shrunken and cadaverous and blue, as if all the juice of life had been drained away, and
his eyes in their pitlike sockets had a wild, glazed stare. His breath
was a ragged, laborious gasping.

"How—?" His voice was a feeble mumbling. "How did—?"

And the little machine, standing black and bland and utterly
unmoving, told him cheerfully,

"We learned about rhodomagnetic screens from that man who
came to kill you, back on Wing IV. And the Central is shielded,
now, against your integrating beam."

With lean muscles jerking convulsively on his gaunt frame, old
Sledge had come to his feet from the high stool. He stood hunched
and swaying, no more than a shrunken human husk, gasping
painfully for life, staring wildly into the blind steel eyes of the
humanoid. He gulped, and his lax blue mouth opened and closed,
but no voice came.

"We have always been aware of your dangerous project," the
silvery tones dripped softly, "because now our senses are keener
than you made them. We allowed you to complete it, because
the integration process will ultimately become necessary for our
full discharge of the Prime Directive. The supply of heavy metals
for our fission plants is limited, but now we shall be able to draw
unlimited power from integration plants."

"Huh?" Sledge shook himself, groggily. "What's that?"

"Now we can serve men forever," the black thing said serenely,
"on every world of every star."

The old man crumpled, as if from an unendurable blow. He
fell. The slim blind mechanical stood motionless, making no effort
to help him. Underhill was farther away, but he ran up in time to
catch the stricken man before his head struck the floor.

"Get moving!" His shaken voice came strangely calm. "Get Dr.
Winters."

The humanoid didn't move.

"The danger to the Prime Directive is ended, now," it cooed. "Therefore it is impossible for us to aid or to hinder Mr. Sledge, in any way whatever."

"Then call Dr. Winters for me," rapped Underhill.

"At your service," it agreed.

But the old man, laboring for breath on the floor, whispered faintly:

"No time . . . no use! I'm beaten . . . done . . . a fool. Blind as humanoid. Tell them . . . to help me. Giving up . . . my immunity. No use . . . anyhow. All humanity . . . no use now."

Underhill gestured, and the sleek black thing darted in solicitous obedience to kneel by the man on the floor.

"You wish to surrender your special exemption?" it murmured brightly. "You wish to accept our total service for yourself, Mr. Sledge, under the Prime Directive?"

Laboriously, Sledge nodded, laboriously whispered, "I do."

Black mechanicals, at that, came swarming into the shabby little rooms. One of them tore off Sledge's sleeve, and swabbed his arm. Another brought a tiny hypodermic, and expertly administered an intravenous injection Then they picked him up gently, and carried him away.

Several humanoids remained in the little apartment, now a sanctuary no longer. Most of them had gathered about the useless integrator. Carefully, as if their special senses were studying every detail, they began taking it apart.

One little mechanical, however, came over to Underhill. It stood motionless in front of him, staring through him with sightless metal eyes. His legs began to tremble, and he swallowed uneasily.

"Mr. Underhill," it cooed benevolently, "why did you help with this?"

"Because I don't like you, or your Prime Directive. Because you're choking the life out of all mankind, and I wanted to stop it."

"Others have protested," it purred softly. "But only at first. In our efficient discharge of the Prime Directive, we have learned how to make all men happy."

Underhill stiffened defiantly.

"Not all!" he muttered. "Not quite!"

The dark graceful oval of its face was fixed in a look of alert benevolence and perpetual mild amazement. Its silvery voice was warm and kind.

"Like other human beings, Mr. Underhill, you lack discrimination of good and evil. You have proved that by effort to break the

Prime Directive. Now it will be necessary for you to accept our total service, without further delay."

"All right," he yielded—and muttered a bitter reservation: "You can smother men with too much care, but that doesn't make them happy."

Its soft voice challenged him brightly,

"Just wait and see, Mr. Underhill."

Next day, he was allowed to visit Sledge at the city hospital. An alert black mechanical drove his car, and walked beside him into the huge new building, and followed him into the old man's room—blind steel eyes would be watching him, now, forever.

"Glad to see you, Underhill," Sledge rumbled heartily from the bed. "Feeling a lot better today, thanks. That old headache is all but gone."

Underhill was glad to hear the booming strength and the quick recognition in that deep voice—he had been afraid the humanoids would tamper with the old man's memory. But he hadn't heard about any headache. His eyes narrowed, puzzled.

Sledge lay propped up, scrubbed very clean and neatly shorn, with his gnarled old hands folded on top of the spotless sheets. His raw-boned cheeks and sockets were hollowed, still, but a healthy pink had replaced that deathly blueness. Bandages covered the back of his head.

Underhill shifted uneasily.

"Oh!" he whispered faintly. "I didn't know—"

A prim black mechanical, which had been standing statue-like behind the bed, turned gracefully to Underhill, explaining:

"Mr. Sledge has been suffering for many years from a benign tumor of the brain, which his human doctors failed to diagnose. That caused his headaches, and certain persistent hallucinations. We have removed the growth, and now the hallucinations have also vanished."

Underhill stared uncertainly at the blind, urbane mechanical.

"What hallucinations?"

"Mr. Sledge thought he was a rhodomagnetic engineer," the mechanical explained. "He believed he was the creator of the humanoids. He was troubled with an irrational belief that he did not like the Prime Directive."

The wan man moved on the pillows, astonished.

"Is that so?" The gaunt face held a cheerful blankness, and the hollow eyes flashed with a merely momentary interest. "Well, whoever did design them, they're pretty wonderful. Aren't they, Underhill?"

Underhill was grateful that he didn't have to answer, for the bright, empty eyes dropped shut and the old man fell suddenly asleep. He felt the mechanical touch his sleeve, and saw its silent nod. Obediently, he followed it away.

Alert and solicitous, the little black mechanical accompanied him down the shining corridor, and worked the elevator for him, and conducted him back to the car. It drove him efficiently back through the new and splendid avenues, toward the magnificent prison of his home.

Sitting beside it in the car, he watched its small deft hands on the wheel, the changing luster of bronze and blue on its shining blackness. The final machine, perfect and beautiful, created to serve mankind forever. He shuddered.

"At your service, Mr. Underhill." Its blind steel eyes stared straight ahead, but it was still aware of him. "What's the matter, sir? Aren't you happy?"

Underhill felt cold and faint with terror. His skin turned clammy, and a painful prickling came over him. His wet hand tensed on the door handle of the car, but he restrained the impulse to jump and run. That was folly. There was no escape. He made himself sit still.

"You will be happy, sir," the mechanical promised him cheerfully. "We have learned how to make all men happy, under the Prime Directive. Our service is perfect, at last. Even Mr. Sledge is very happy now."

Underhill tried to speak, and his dry throat stuck. He felt ill. The world turned dim and gray. The humanoids were perfect—no question of that. They had even learned to lie, to secure the contentment of men.

He knew they had lied. That was no tumor they had removed from Sledge's brain, but the memory, the scientific knowledge, and the bitter disillusion of their own creator. But it was true that Sledge was happy now.

He tried to stop his own convulsive quivering.

"A wonderful operation!" His voice came forced and faint. "You know, Aurora has had a lot of funny tenants, but that old man was the absolute limit. The very idea that he had made the humanoids, and he knew how to stop them! I always knew he must be lying!"

Stiff with terror, he made a weak and hollow laugh.

"What is the matter, Mr. Underhill?" The alert mechanical must have perceived his shuddering illness. "Are you unwell?"

"No, there's nothing the matter with me," he gasped desperately. "I've just found out that I'm perfectly happy, under the Prime Directive. Everything is absolutely wonderful." His voice came dry and hoarse and wild. "You won't have to operate on me."

The car turned off the shining avenue, taking him back to the quiet splendor of his home. His futile hands clenched and relaxed again, folded on his knees. There was nothing left to do.